Street Song

'Alley balley balley bee
sitting on your mammy's knee,
greeting for a wee bawbee
tae buy some coulther's candy . . .'

Glasgow street song (Trad.)

EMMA BLAIR
OMNIBUS

Street Song

●

The Princess of Poor Street

LITTLE, BROWN AND COMPANY

A Little, Brown Book
This edition first published in Great Britain by Little, Brown in 2001
The Emma Blair Omnibus Copyright © Emma Blair 2001

Previously published separately:
Street Song first published in Great Britain by Sphere Books 1986
Published by Warner Books 1993
Copyright © Emma Blair 1986
The Princess of Poor Street first published in Great Britain by Michael Joseph 1986
Published by Sphere Books Ltd 1987
Published by Warner Books 1993
Copyright © Emma Blair 1986

A CIP catalogue record for this book
is available from the British Library.

ISBN 0 316 85888 9

Printed and bound in Italy

Little, Brown and Company (UK)
Brettenham House
Lancaster Place
London WC2E 7EN

Street Song

●

*The Princess
of Poor Street*

SUSAN

Susan's eyes were wide with fear and apprehension as she stepped through the door into Miss Buchan's school. She was flanked on either side by her parents.

'Captain and Mrs Gibb, how nice to see you again,' Miss Buchan said, stepping forward to shake their hands. 'And how are you today, Susan?'

Susan stared at Miss Buchan, not attempting to reply.

'Are you looking forward to your stay with us? We're certainly looking forward to having you here.'

Susan's gaze left Miss Buchan to travel round the wood-panelled entrance hall. She might have been a small animal plucked rudely from its nest.

'Answer Miss Buchan,' Jean, her mother, prompted.

But still Susan said nothing.

'Quite understandable in the circumstances,' Miss Buchan smiled. 'She'll soon come round though. She does know why she's here, doesn't she?'

'Oh yes,' Jean replied. 'It's all been explained to her quite thoroughly. Hasn't it, my angel?'

Susan moved closer to Jean, reaching out to clutch her mother's coat.

'Would you like to help her settle into the dormitory or do you think it best to leave right away?' Miss Buchan asked.

Jean looked at her husband Keith for an answer.

Keith was hating this, feeling guilty as hell. Ever since learning the regiment was to be posted abroad, and deciding to leave Susan behind, he'd been trying to convince himself he'd

3

have arrived at the same decision if she'd been a boy.

'I think we should leave right away,' he said.

Trembling, Jean reached down to kiss Susan on the cheek. 'Mummy and Daddy will write to you every week and Miss Buchan or one of her staff will read the letters to you. Now be a good girl and do as you're told and we'll see you again when we come home on leave.'

Keith opened his wallet and extracted a fiver which he pressed into Susan's hand. 'Pocket money,' he said, 'which I think Miss Buchan better look after in the meantime.'

'I'll see she gets it as she needs it,' Miss Buchan said, taking the fiver from Susan.

'Well, that's it then, I think,' Keith said. Swinging Susan into his arms he pecked her on the cheek. Having deposited her back on the ground again he cleared his throat.

'Jenny!' Miss Buchan called out to a hovering girl. 'You take Susan's case up to dormitory C. Bed fourteen will be hers.'

'Yes, Miss Buchan,' Jenny said obediently. Lifting Susan's small case she walked with it towards the staircase at the rear of the entrance hall.

'Charming girl,' Miss Buchan said. 'Parents died tragically so now we look after her.'

Jean clucked sympathy.

''Bye 'bye, angel,' Jean said, her eyes brimming over with tears.

Susan stared up at her mother, a profound betrayal written clearly across her face.

Keith reached down and shook his daughter's hand. This was even more difficult than he'd anticipated. Taking Jean by the arm he turned her round and marched her to the door. Miss Buchan put her hand on Susan's shoulder in case she tried to bolt after her parents. But she didn't. Jean had one last look over her shoulder at the door. Then it closed behind her and Susan was cut off from sight.

'You and I are going to get on just fine,' Miss Buchan said. 'You have my word on that. Now, how about a nice cup of tea and a cake? And while we're having it you can tell me all about yourself. What you like and dislike, that sort of thing.'

As though in a trance, Susan followed Miss Buchan to her study, where she was told to sit on a chair in front of a cheery fire.

With the cake there were scones, pancakes and crumpets. But Susan ate nothing, mumbling she wasn't hungry.

Miss Buchan did her best to draw and distract Susan, to no avail. Susan sat staring into the fire as though seeing strange sights in its depths.

That night Miss Buchan personally saw to Susan getting ready for bed.

When all the girls in the dormitory were ready, Miss Buchan led them in prayers, shortly after which the lights were turned out. Susan lay in the darkness listening to the breathing all around her. After a while she pulled the blankets over her head and there, securely muffled in her womb-like cocoon, she broke down and quietly cried her eyes out.

It was a day she'd remember for the rest of her life.

The first holidays to come up were the Christmas ones. The girls, with the exception of seven, either went home or to friends and relatives whom they'd spend the break with.

Susan was one of the seven.

Miss Buchan did her best by those with nowhere else to go. She bought them individual presents and there was a goose and crackers. After Christmas dinner they all sat round in a circle drinking lemonade and singing carols. Then they played charades and blind man's bluff.

By far and away the youngest of the seven, Susan received extra special attention from Miss Buchan. Several of the older girls made a fuss of her and generally mothered her.

Susan said little, as was her wont, her large doe eyes drinking everything in.

Before coming to the school she'd been a happy, vivacious, extroverted child. Now she was withdrawn and painfully shy, forever trying to blend into the background as though she didn't want anyone to notice she was there. Naturally, neither

Miss Buchan nor any of the staff knew there'd been such a big change in her as they hadn't known what she was like beforehand.

When the small party had subsided somewhat Miss Buchan took Susan to one side.

'Would you like me to read the letter that came with your Christmas card now?' she asked.

Susan's eyes lit up. The letter readings were the highlight of her week, Jean having kept her word and written regularly. Susan sat with her hands cupping her chin as she avidly listened to her mother's words.

Mummy and Daddy were missing her. Daddy was frightfully busy while there never seemed enough hours in the day for all the things Mummy had to do. The letter ended with the promise, as it always did, that Mummy and Daddy would see her during the summer when they'd be returning home on leave.

When she fell asleep that night Susan dreamed the same dream she'd been having regularly since arriving at the school. Mummy and Daddy were arriving home – home being the house they'd all lived in before Mummy and Daddy went abroad – and Mummy was saying they were never ever going to leave their daughter again and when Mummy and Daddy went overseas at the end of Daddy's leave they'd be taking their darling Susan with them.

Miss Buchan laid the letter down and sighed. There were times she hated running a school and this was one of them.

She passed a hand wearily over her face. Well, she thought, she may as well get this over and done with. That was always the easiest way in the long run, she'd learned. She opened the door to her study and hailed a passing girl.

'Find Susan Gibb and bring her to me right away,' she said.

'Yes, Miss Buchan,' the girl replied and scuttled off.

She settled herself back behind her desk again and folded her hands in front of her. She was still in that position when there was a timid knock on the door.

'Come in!' she called out.

Susan entered, closing the door behind her as she'd been taught to do.

'You wanted to see me, Miss Buchan?'

'Sit down, child. There's another letter from your parents which is addressed to me as well as yourself.'

'Has Daddy been hurt?' Susan asked quickly.

'No. Nothing like that.'

Miss Buchan spread the letter in front of her and smoothed it with her hand.

Susan sat expectant, waiting.

Slowly Miss Buchan said, 'Due to circumstances beyond their control your parents won't be coming home to Scotland this summer, after all.'

To Susan it was the end of the world. Since entering the school her entire life had become geared to the forthcoming summer and the reappearance of her parents from abroad.

Miss Buchan lifted up two white fivers which she showed Susan. 'The Captain has sent this as pocket money. I, of course, shall be looking after it for you. Would you like some now?'

Susan shook her head.

Miss Buchan came round from behind her desk to kneel beside Susan. 'I'm awfully sorry,' she said. 'We all know how much you were looking forward to their coming back.'

Biting back tears, Susan came to her feet. 'May I go now, Miss, please?' she asked.

'Wouldn't you like me to read the letter to you?'

Susan shook her head. At the door she paused. 'Did they say when they'll be coming home?' she asked.

'No, they didn't.'

Susan closed the door quietly behind her.

Miss Buchan stood at her study window gazing out into the garden. She was watching Susan who was standing by a tree apart from the other girls.

What a sad and lonely little creature, Miss Buchan thought.

7

There were times when she wanted to take Susan in her arms and hug her, but of course she couldn't do that. That would have been showing favouritism, which she strictly disciplined herself against.

She watched Susan pick up the wild hedgehog that often came to that part of the garden and which Susan had made friends with. The girl stroked the hedgehog and whispered endearments to it, talking to it as though it was a person rather than an animal.

So much love to give, Miss Buchan thought. So much love.

'I saw Blackie yesterday,' Susan said to the hedgehog, whom she had christened Spike. 'He came and sat in the tree and sang to me. He told me his wife has had three little blackbirds and when they're old enough he's going to bring them over and show them to us. Isn't that marvellous?'

Spike's little brown eyes gazed up at Susan. She was the only girl in the school whom he uncurled for.

Susan gently stroked his snout. If Spike had been a cat he would have purred.

'When are you going to meet a nice lady hedgehog and have a family, Spike? I think it's high time, don't you? And when you have your family will you bring them to show to me just like Blackie has promised to do? We could sit round in a circle and have a pretend tea party, which I think would be ever so much fun. Perhaps squirrel would come if we asked him nicely. You like squirrel, don't you? Yes, of course you do, even if he is a bit crotchety at times.'

The squirrel referred to was an old red one who often came to the tree in the garden. All the other girls were scared of the squirrel because of its sharp teeth, but not Susan, who on a number of occasions had actually hand-fed the rodent.

The idea that Blackie had a family, far less that he was going to bring them to show to her, was pure fiction on her part. When it came to animals Susan had an extremely vivid imagination.

One of the teachers, called Miss Cairncross, came out of the

8

school and rang the handbell to announce the resumption of classes.

'I'll have to go now, Spike,' Susan said. 'I'd much rather stay and talk to you but I'm afraid I have to go and do my lessons. Will you be here tomorrow? Well I'll be here looking for you hoping you've been able to make it. Goodbye now and make sure you look after yourself.'

She stroked the hedgehog's snout one last time before very carefully setting him back on the ground.

''Bye Spike. Be a good boy now!' Actually she didn't know for certain that Spike was a male. She just assumed he was.

She retreated a few steps before turning and breaking into a run. She felt happy as she always did when she'd been with her friends the animals.

'Yes, Susan?' Miss Buchan asked. Susan was in her study having requested an interview.

'Please, Miss. The money my Daddy sent me.'

'Yes?'

'Could I use some of it to buy a pet with? A dog or a cat? I'd look after it all by myself so it would be no trouble to anyone else.' Susan looked expectantly at Miss Buchan, her face radiant with hope.

Miss Buchan knew her reply was going to hurt Susan but for the moment she couldn't see how she could do otherwise.

'I'm afraid a personal pet is out of the question,' she said. Susan's face dropped.

Her heart went out to the little girl. She continued softly, 'You see if I allow one personal pet in the school then lots of the girls might want one. And then where would we be? We'd be a menagerie instead of a school. If I could make an exception I would, Susan, but you must understand there can never be exceptions. It just isn't fair on the others.'

Susan's lower lip trembled.

'I appreciate only too well what a pet would mean to you but you must see my position. I'm sorry Susan.'

9

Susan nodded, not trusting herself to speak. The animals in the garden were all very well but her time with them was extremely limited. Depending on when she could get into the garden and when they would put in an appearance. Sometimes a whole week could go by without her seeing Spike or Blackie or squirrel.

A pet of her own would have been totally different, however. She would have been able to be with it every evening and all weekend when there were no lessons.

After Susan had gone Miss Buchan twiddled her pencil, which she finally threw on to the desk in front of her.

'Damn!'

She was a woman who rarely swore.

Miss Buchan marched into the assembly room with a box under her arm and the assembly room fell silent.

She placed the box on the table at the end of the room and then turned to face the girls.

'A mouse was seen last week and another yesterday!' she said.

Some of the girls gasped while others giggled.

'I will not have mice in my school!' Miss Buchan said sternly. 'They are unhygienic. What are they, girls?'

'Unhygienic!' the girls chorused in unison.

'What does that mean, Agnes McDonald?'

'Unclean, Miss.'

'Quite correct. Unclean. And I will have nothing in my school which is that. So ... we have a problem: mice. What's the solution to the problem?'

Several hands shot in the air.

'Mary Geddes?'

'Traps, Miss. Baited with cheese.'

'Very good, Mary. But I think we might do even better than that.'

Her gaze swept over the room. 'Helen Moyes?'

'A cat, Miss.'

'The solution I favour myself, Helen. A good mouser.'

Turning to the table she lifted the top off the box and reached inside.

'Oh!' the girls said, when they saw the kitten Miss Buchan held.

'Now Mr Samson, the janitor, says he hasn't time to look after a cat, which leaves it up to us. I myself would undertake the task of maintaining this kitten but unfortunately I spend so much time looking after you girls I have absolutely none left over for the training of an animal. This being the case I'm hoping one of you will volunteer to look after and train our little friend here. Someone who is good with animals and knows how to handle them. Now, any volunteers?'

Several dozen hands were lifted.

'Hmm ...' said Miss Buchan, pretending to consider each eager face in turn.

Finally she gestured at Susan. 'Stand up, Susan Gibb.'

Susan stood, a tiny figure almost lost amongst some of the taller girls.

'Do you think you'd be able to train this kitten, Susan?'

'Oh yes, Miss!'

'You'd have to spend a great deal of time with him you understand?'

Susan's eyes shone. 'Yes, Miss.'

'And he's to be a working cat. Not a pet.'

'Yes, Miss.'

Miss Buchan pursed her lips and furrowed her brow as though deep in cogitation. Finally she said, 'Members of the staff have noticed how good you are with the animals out in the garden, Susan, so I think you might well be the right person to look after the school cat.'

There was a pause and then she went on, 'Well, come along girl, don't just stand there gawping. Come and collect the beast.'

Later, when she was back in the privacy of her study, Miss Buchan smiled. She hummed gaily as she set about marking some papers.

*

11

That night, Susan installed Tiddles, as she'd decided to call the kitten, in a cardboard box by the side of her bed.

'Goodnight, Tiddles,' she said, kissing the kitten on the head. 'Sleep tight and don't let the bugs bite.'

'He'd better not have bugs,' the girl in the next bed said. Several other girls tittered. Susan patted Tiddles, soothing him to lie still. The kitten mewed contentedly.

Susan slipped into bed feeling the happiest she'd been since her parents had gone abroad. She wasn't alone any more. She had something to care for which would care for her in return. Something to help fill the huge aching hole her parents' departure had created in her.

Keith and Jean Gibb did manage to take leave in Scotland the second summer after they'd enrolled Susan as a boarder in Miss Buchan's School for Young Ladies.

As they were home for four weeks, and rather than stay in a hotel, Keith rented a house, which came complete with servants.

Susan hated the house on sight, thinking it dark and gloomy. A cheerless, friendless place with echoing corridors and high vaulted ceilings which often as not were hidden in shadow.

However, that didn't really matter. All that did was that her Mummy and Daddy were home and the three of them were together again.

She was so excited that for the first few days she hardly stopped talking and followed Jean nearly everywhere she went. To begin with, Jean found this charming but after a little while it began to grate on her nerves. It seemed to her she could hardly turn round without falling over Susan, who was continually under her feet.

Keith too became irritated with Susan. Her constant questions seemed to go on without end.

'What was it like there, Daddy? Why did you do this, Daddy? Why did you do that? How does this work, Daddy? How does that ...?'

'For God's sake, stop bothering me!' he exclaimed angrily one night as she'd innocently asked him yet another question while he was in the middle of knotting his black tie.

Tears sprang into Susan's eyes as she backed away a little from him.

'Can't you see I'm busy?' he said irritably.

'Sorry, Daddy.'

'And don't snivel. I can't stand children who snivel!'

'Sorry, Daddy.'

'And do stop saying sorry Daddy.'

'Sor . . . yes, Daddy.' Head bowed, she left the room.

With a sigh of exasperation Keith left his tie. His concentration was broken, he'd never do it now. He'd get Jean to knot it for him when she came through. She always made a better job of it than he did, anyway.

A little later, when Jean appeared, he told her what had happened.

Jean pulled a face. 'I think we've just become unused to having a child around,' she said. 'One of the drawbacks of having her at boarding school.'

'And another thing,' Keith went on, 'she's forever wanting to be picked up and cuddled. It's positively unnatural.'

'It's no such thing! If anything, it's the contrary. She hasn't seen us for two years, after all!'

'Well, I still don't like it,' he grumbled. 'It doesn't feel right.'

'Stop being such an army stuffed shirt! It's a little girl of six we're talking about, not some hulking lad of sixteen or seventeen.'

'I am not a stuffed shirt!' he exclaimed.

'You are sometimes. And pompous with it.'

Keith spluttered with indignation, his deep tan turning pink in places.

Jean laughed and kissed him which mollified him somewhat. 'You don't mind *me* cuddling you,' she teased.

'That's different. You're a woman. My wife.'

'And she's your daughter.'

He looked thoughtful and his eyes took on a faraway look as he poured them both sherries.

'I'm sorry she wasn't the boy you really wanted,' Jean said softly. 'But if a boy wasn't to be, then he wasn't to be.'

'I know that,' Keith replied, staring into the deep brown of his drink. 'Let's just be thankful we've been blessed with a child at all.'

'If only she wouldn't ask so many questions and keep pestering me all the time.'

'I'll speak to her about it,' Jean said.

Jean knew then she was right. They had become totally unused to having a child around. Not only that, they'd become set and selfish in their ways.

'What!' exclaimed Gerald, Keith's older brother. 'You mean the child's been in Glasgow all this time without us knowing about it? What were you thinking of, man?'

Keith knew fine well what he'd been thinking of. Drat Susan for coming out with the fact she'd been spending all her holidays at school.

'I don't see why you should be inconvenienced. After all,' and Keith relished saying this bit, 'you're both getting on a bit now. Hardly up to active young children, I wouldn't have thought.'

'We might be old but we're hardly decrepit yet,' Emmaline, Gerald's wife, retorted.

Keith put the hint of a knowing smile on his face calculated to convey to his sister-in-law that he thought otherwise. He knew it would infuriate her. Like many once beautiful people he knew, Emmaline hated the thought of the ravages of time.

Susan sat very still, aware she'd somehow angered her father - although for the life of her she couldn't think how.

'Next Christmas Susan must come and stay with us,' Emmaline said firmly. 'And I won't hear otherwise.'

'That's not fair on you,' Keith said.

'Nonsense!' Gerald replied. 'We'd love to have her. Would do us both the world of good to have someone young around

14

the house again. She'd be the one doing *us* a favour, I can tell you.'

'Would you like to come and stay with us at Christmas, Susan?' Emmaline asked.

Susan hung her head and nodded.

'Imagine her spending Christmas at school! How ridiculous!' Gerald said.

Keith remembered then the stories he'd heard from the dead Michael and James about what a good father Gerald had been. Both his boys had positively doted on him. His own guilt at being irritable and snappy with Susan rose up in him. And this guilt he somehow transformed in his mind into being Gerald's fault. He glowered at his brother, all the old feelings of inadequacy and being second best coming crowding back.

Everything Gerald touched or was connected with turned to gold. Women, business, conversation. Whereas he ... 'We'll sort something out before Jean and I go back abroad,' he said, thinking, like hell he would! They hadn't found out the name of Susan's school yet and that's the way he'd try and keep it.

'What beautiful pearls those are,' he said, changing the subject. 'They caught my eye the moment I saw them.'

'They were a present from Gerald,' Emmaline replied smugly.

The topic of Susan and Christmas was gradually forgotten.

Susan was playing with Tiddles in the garden when one of the girls came rushing up to say she was wanted right away in Miss Buchan's study.

'Come in!' Miss Buchan's voice called out when she knocked on the door.

For a moment she failed to recognise the figure sitting across from Miss Buchan. Then the penny dropped.

'Mummy!' she squealed and rushed into her mother's arms. It was only the second time her mother had been home during the five years she'd been at school.

'My, how tall you've grown!' Jean said, a catch in her voice. 'Here, let me have a look at you.'

She held Susan at arm's length and shook her head wonderingly. 'I wouldn't have known you. You're a young lady now, not a child any more.'

'Is Daddy with you?' Susan asked excitedly.

'He's had to stay on in London for a few days. Army work. I've come on ahead as we felt one of us should be at Aunt Emmaline's funeral. She died unexpectedly a few days ago.'

'Oh!' said Susan, not knowing what else to say. She'd thought of her Aunt Em and Uncle Gerald several times in the intervening years, having been expecting them to contact her as they'd promised they would, but they never had.

'How long are you and Daddy home for this time?' she asked.

A worried frown settled on Jean's deeply tanned face, a face that had begun to wither from too much exposure to tropical sun.

'Times being what they are, Daddy thinks it best I stay on in Glasgow for a while, at least until we see what's what.'

'Very sensible in the circumstances,' Miss Buchan said.

Jean turned to Miss Buchan. 'That man Hitler, you understand. The Army are extremely worried about him and what he might do.'

'I think we all are,' Miss Buchan said.

'So,' Jean said turning her attention back to Susan. 'That means I'll be renting a house for six months at least. Now what do you want to do? You can either live with me and attend here during the day or else remain on as a boarder, coming home at weekends. The choice is up to you.'

Susan thought that an odd question to ask. How could there be any doubt but that she'd want to live with her mother? Anything other would have been unthinkable. Didn't her mother understand that?

'I'll stay with you, Mummy,' she said excitedly. 'Starting tonight if you like.'

Jean laughed. 'Hey, hold on a minute! Let me find a house to rent first.'

Susan suddenly thought of Tiddles and her face fell.

16

Officially Tiddles was the school cat which would mean she'd have to leave him behind.

'What's wrong?' Jean asked.

In a rush of words Susan explained about the cat.

'Hmm!' said Miss Buchan.

'I'm sure we can buy you another cat,' Jean said, thinking that would resolve the problem. But it didn't.

'It wouldn't be the same, Mummy. Tiddles is Tiddles.'

'I think I have the solution,' Miss Buchan said. 'Tiddles hasn't been a great success as a mouser despite your valiant efforts to teach him, Susan. So I think it best I retire him and we'll buy another school cat.'

Susan beamed. 'Oh thank you, Miss Buchan!'

'We'll gave to find a good home for him of course. Any suggestions?'

Susan whirled on Jean. 'Please Mummy?'

'You bring Tiddles with you when you come home.'

Susan's day was complete.

'I'm sorry about Em,' Keith said to Gerald. 'I did my best to make the funeral but it was just impossible.'

Gerald nodded. He looked gaunt and haggard and there were dark circles under his eyes. He'd taken the loss of his wife badly.

'At least it was quick,' he said. 'That was a blessing.'

Keith tried to look sympathetic. In reality Emmaline's death meant nothing at all to him.

Gerald poured two very large whiskies. He'd been drinking heavily since his wife's death. As he and Keith drank his eyes misted over in introspection. He was thinking about his two sons, Michael and James, who'd been killed at Ypres. He'd been thinking a lot about them lately.

'Is there going to be another war?' he asked abruptly.

'Some people in the Army think so but I personally don't believe it'll come about. It would be insanity on Herr Hitler's part.'

'There are a lot of people say he is insane.'

17

Keith snorted. 'About as insane as you or I. Cunning is the word I'd use. And devious.'

'And yet you're insisting Jean stays home for a while?'

'There's no harm being on the safe side. Just in case I'm wrong.'

'You were always the cautious one,' Gerald said smiling. 'Even as a little boy.'

They drank for a little while in silence and then Gerald said, 'You know what Em's death means, don't you?'

'No?'

'When I go everything will come to you. My half of the brewery, our house, my entire estate. All yours, Keith.'

Keith couldn't meet his brother's steady gaze. 'Let's hope it's a long time before it comes to that,' he said.

'What'll you do with the brewery? Sell?'

Keith pondered that. It wasn't something he'd given a lot of thought to. 'I don't know,' he replied eventually.

'It's not as easy to run as you once thought. I hope you realise that.'

Keith bridled. 'Are you saying I couldn't do it?'

'I'm saying no such thing. All I'm doing is warning you that if you do decide to take over my seat, do so with your eyes wide open.'

Keith made up his mind there and then. When the time came he would take over the brewery and what's more he'd make an even better job of running it than Gerald had!

Gerald smiled inwardly. He could see from the expression on Keith's face that he'd succeeded. He'd grown very fond of the brewery over the years. It was only right and proper it stay on in the family for as long as that was possible.

Three months later Hitler invaded Poland.

Susan hated the house her parents had rented. If anything, it was even gloomier than the previous one.

She clutched Tiddles to her as she stared in dismay at what was to be her bedroom. It was small and pokey and there was a funny smell in the air which she later identified as damp.

'Oh, Tiddles!' she said, clutching the cat to her. 'This place is horrid.'

Tiddles mewed his agreement.

The one bright spot was the garden, which was an overgrown jungle perfect for keeping pets in. She wondered if her parents would allow her to keep rabbits and a tortoise. That thought cheered her a little.

At the beginning of the war, Keith was seconded from his regiment and posted on to the General Staff in London. He was promoted to the rank of Major and given a desk. He was back in admin again. Nothing more than a bloody glorified filing clerk, was how he described himself.

He and Jean debated whether or not she should join him in London. But for various reasons, including the fact he steadily maintained it would be a short conflict, it was decided best for her to remain in Glasgow with Susan.

He came up to Scotland when he could and occasionally she journeyed down to spend the weekend with him. When Jean went south Susan was looked after by the old housekeeper Jean had employed, a Mrs Sinclair.

It was during one of her infrequent visits to London that Jean brought Keith the news of Gerald's death from cancer.

Keith's eyes gleamed when he heard this. If it hadn't been for the war he would have resigned his commission instantly and gone straight back to Glasgow to take over the brewery. But as things were, that would have to wait.

Susan lay on her bed with Tiddles curled up beside her. Her eyes were wide as she read an American film magazine Mrs Sinclair the housekeeper had managed to get hold of for her. The magazine was pre-war and concerned mainly with the films of Clark Gable, whom she adored.

Susan loved films and went as often as she was able – which was frequently – as much as three or four times a week. She went on her own and sometimes with Mrs Sinclair who was as nearly as big a film fan as she was. She would have liked to go with her mother but Jean was always busy with either socialising or voluntary war work. It was a rare week when Jean spent an evening at home.

The truth was, Susan was exceptionally lonely outside school hours. She had one or two friends locally whom she visited and played with and occasionally even stayed the night with. Those nights were treasured in her memory and she often wistfully wished there were more of them. There could have been, as her friends' Mummies liked her and said she could stay as often as she liked but Jean had objected, saying she mustn't make a pest of herself.

The best times of all were when Daddy came up from London and they were all together again. But sadly these times were few and far between, becoming even fewer as the war dragged on and on.

Then there were her friends in the garden, whom she adored and lavished a great deal of time on. There was Soppy, the long-eared rabbit, who had a bad leg and an adorable expression. And the frogs she'd reared from tadpoles, who lived in the culvert at the very end of the garden. And Caw-caw the rook, who had fierce glinting eyes and a vicious way of stabbing with his beak.

Susan sighed and laid down her magazine. Lying back she closed her eyes. Someday, she told herself, her Prince Charming would come along. He'd look just like Clark Gable and be ever so romantic. He would open doors for her and always see that she walked on the inside of the pavement. He would gaze long and steadily into her eyes and his kisses would burn like fire. His name would be Clark or Tyrone, and he would be the most handsome, dashing man there had ever been. He would be madly in love with her and as a result never leave her side. And when he came along she'd never ever be lonely again.

At twelve years of age she was in the throes of puberty.

Keith smiled jubilantly to himself as his car swept through the front gates of Black Lion Brewery. With the war over and his commission resigned he was now ready to take over where Gerald had left off.

He'd arranged for a board to look after the brewery in the interim and his first job now would be to get rid of them. Their usefulness was over. He no longer needed them.

He parked his car and then sat to savour the moment. He'd been looking forward to this ever since Gerald had died. At long, long last he was now coming into his own.

He thought grimly of his Army career and especially the last war years. He'd never really got on in the Army. In his estimation, events had conspired against him. To begin with, he'd lost out by being kept in India during the first war, and then during the second he'd been anchored to a desk.

Still, if nothing else, he'd learned a great deal about admin and running things, which would stand him in good stead now.

A member of staff materialised to open his car door for him. 'Good morning, Mr Gibb,' the man said. 'And a pleasant one it is too.'

Keith got out of the car and straightened himself to his full height. Turning to the man he said in a cold, steely voice, '*Major* Gibb.' He intended starting as he meant to go on.

Keith sucked on his pipe contentedly. He'd had a hard day at work but only because everything at the brewery was going so well.

He glanced across to where Susan sat reading one of the trashy magazines she forever seemed to have her nose buried in. At seventeen she was a fully developed young woman who would soon be leaving school and going to college. She wanted to be a vet, which pleased him fine. There were a lot worse professions for a young woman to take up than that.

Not that he expected her to be a vet for long. Surely some eligible young man would come along and snap her up? And what sort of young man would that be? he wondered.

21

He remembered then he'd seen a notice displayed at the Conservative club the other night, saying there was to be a dance this coming weekend. It might be an idea for him to encourage her to attend not only that dance but other functions the Conservative club held for its young folk. For there he could be more or less assured she would meet the right sort of young man from the correct sort of background.

His heart warmed to the idea of her marrying someone rich and influential, and, what was more important, one day having a son who would inherit from both sides of the family.

A son! His grandson! A wee lad who could restore his family to the wealth and position they'd once enjoyed and which his father had gambled away and lost by bad speculation.

If he could live to see that, he'd die a happy man.

'Would you like to dance?'

Susan turned round to face a young man a little older than herself. He was good-looking but not excessively so.

'Thank you,' she replied.

They walked on to the dance floor and he put his arms round her. The dance was a waltz.

'I haven't seen you here before,' he said.

'I've been a few times.'

'It's nice to see a new face. Especially a pretty one.'

She liked that as she did all flattery.

'Isn't it exciting?' she said.

'What?'

'Princess Elizabeth getting married.'

'Oh *that*!'

The dance was being held in honour of the occasion.

'I think *he's* ever so attractive. Real yummy.'

The young man laughed. 'I'm sure he'd love to hear himself described as yummy.'

'You say that as though you know him.'

'I do. Sort of. We've met on a number of occasions.'

Susan's eyes opened wide. 'Really?'

'I play in London from time to time and as he's very keen on sport he sometimes comes to watch. When he isn't at sea, that is.'

'What do you play?'

'Squash. Have you ever seen a game?'

She shook her head.

'Very fast. Very exciting. And definitely not for girls.'

'When are you playing again?'

'Next week at a little club I go to called the Hillhead and Kelvinbridge Sports Club. Know it?'

She shook her head again.

On a sudden impulse he said, 'Would you like to come and watch the game? I could pick you up in my car and we could have a coffee or a drink afterwards?'

She laughed at the suddenness of his proposal. 'I don't even know your name!' she said.

'It's Nigel. What's yours?'

'Susan.'

'All right Susan. Is it a date?'

'Which night is it?'

'Friday.'

She was free Friday night and didn't think her parents would object. 'You'll pick me up?' she said.

They made the arrangements after which they danced together for the rest of the night.

'Have a nice time then!' Keith said, he and Jean having escorted Susan and Nigel to the door, which he now shut behind the young couple.

'Nigel McBeth!' he said delightedly to Jean. 'Son of Geoffrey McBeth, head of McBeth shipping line. Which only happens to be one of the largest shipping lines in the country. Why, the man must be a millionaire many times over.' He paused to chuckle before adding, 'I'll say this for Susan. When she picks them she *certainly* picks them.'

'Very nice boy, I thought,' Jean said, nodding her approval.

'I wonder if he's an only child?' Keith mused.

He escorted Jean back to the room where they'd been

23

entertaining Nigel while Susan got ready and poured them both drinks. He couldn't remember when he'd been so excited.

'We'll have to do everything to encourage the pair of them,' he said.

'Isn't it a bit early for that?'

'Perhaps. But a little encouragement certainly won't do any harm.'

'Give it a week or two and I could invite him for tea,' Jean said.

'Or better still, his parents as well!'

Jean looked thoughtful. 'We must be careful not to appear too pushy. That would do far more harm than good.'

'Hmm!' replied Keith.

'Anyway,' Jean said practically. 'This might be so much conjecture on our part. It's their first time out together, after all. They might well discover they don't like one another or don't particularly get on.'

Keith made up his mind to have a word with Susan the next day. She must be made to see what an advantageous match this would be. If she and Nigel did start going out regularly she must do everything in her power to develop and deepen the relationship. And if everything went well and they did decide to get married perhaps he could persuade them to add Susan's family name to that of Nigel's.

McBeth-Gibb, he thought. Yes, it had a ring to it.

A smile crept over his face. If they agreed to the joining of the names it would go a long way to help make up for the disappointment of Susan's being born a girl and, despite every effort on his and Jean's part, an only child to boot.

Combined with McBeth, the Gibb name would go on bigger and more glorious than ever. And that would be a far greater achievement than anything Gerald had managed.

He prayed to God in His Heaven everything went well tonight. A good start would be most important.

*

24

Susan and Nigel had been going out for six months when he decided to show her over his father's private yacht, which was at that time lying anchored in the Gare Loch.

They motored down on a sunny Saturday morning with the intention of picnicking aboard before travelling back sometime round about late afternoon or early evening.

Susan loved the run to the coast insisting the car windows be wide open so she could drink in the fresh tangy air that became progressively saltier the closer they got to the sea.

The yacht was a sixty-footer, painted sparkling white from stern to bow and flying the McBeth shipping pennant.

'She's beautiful,' Susan said as they clambered aboard.

'Shall we take her out?'

'Could we?'

Nigel smiled, 'Of course. There's a resident crew of three and that's what they're paid for.'

He left her standing by the wheel while he went below to issue orders.

Within five minutes they were under way.

'Want to steer?' Nigel asked as they rounded Kilcreggan Point heading for the Clyde.

'I wouldn't know how.'

'I'll show you.'

He stood behind her, his hands over hers as she took the wheel.

'It's awful heavy and it keeps trying to drag to the left,' she said, a frown of concentration on her face.

He eased the yacht back on course. 'You must control it. Not it you,' he said.

Flying spume lashed her face, making her feel tremendously exhilarated. Her feet tingled to the reverberations of the engine, while overhead gulls screamed and squawked having mistaken them for a fishing vessel.

'I could get to like this,' she said.

'Our whole family love boats and ships,' Nigel said. 'Always have, which is no doubt how we originally got into the business.'

25

Susan already knew he had an unmarried sister and that there had been an older brother killed at sea during the war, drowned in the south Atlantic after his ship had been torpedoed. But she didn't know anything about the rest of his family.

'Lots of aunts, uncles and cousins,' Nigel replied when she asked him. 'Some of them in the family business, others doing all sorts of things. I've even got an uncle who has a factory which makes lamps and lampshades. Does quite well out of it, too.'

'I envy you your large family circle,' she replied wistfully. 'I had two cousins an awful lot older than me but they were killed in the first war. Daddy had a married brother but I never saw them much. They asked me to go to their place for Christmas once when I was quite young but somehow that never materialised. Uncle Gerald and his wife, Aunt Em, are both dead now, as are all Mummy's family.'

'It's a shame you never had a brother or sister.'

'Daddy desperately wanted a boy. I don't think he's ever forgiven me for being a girl.'

'That's an exaggeration surely?'

Susan shook her head.

'Poor Susan,' he said, and kissed her neck.

She shivered, suddenly aware of their closeness.

'Shall we go below and have that picnic you brought?' he asked in a voice that had gone thick and husky.

'I am a bit peckish.'

'Then lunch it is.'

He called out to one of the crew to take over the wheel and after issuing the man instructions took her down to the yacht's main cabin.

Lunch was cold chicken, tomatoes, salad and apples. There was also château-bottled red wine. Nigel ate, tasting nothing. His eyes were riveted to Susan's, as hers, although a lot more coyly, were to his.

Susan enjoyed the wine. It relaxed her and put warmth in her stomach. When the meal was finished she languidly started to pack away what was left and in doing so turned her back on Nigel.

She stiffened a little as his arms encircled her and his hands cupped her breasts. She closed her eyes as he caressed her. He turned her to him and brought his mouth to hers. As he kissed her he dropped a hand to rub the front of her dress where her crotch was. Susan sighed and pressed herself against him. It was such a nice feeling.

He had to stoop a little in order to get his hand under her dress. When he rubbed the front of her knickers he could feel crinkly hair underneath.

'Oh Nigel,' she said, moaning.

His hand wriggled inside her knickers to find her. It was the first time she'd allowed him to get this far.

'What about the crew?' she whispered.

'They won't bother us.'

'Draw the curtains anyway.'

Reluctantly he withdrew his hand to comply with her wishes.

When the portholes were covered he turned back to her and she came into his arms.

'I want to make love to you, Susan,' he jerked out.

'No,' she replied.

'Please?'

'What if I got pregnant?'

'I have contraceptives with me.'

She smiled. 'So this was what you had in mind all the time?'

'I won't think any less of you if that's what's bothering you. I ... I ...' He trailed off.

'Go on,' she whispered.

He laid his head on her shoulder. His breath hot and rasping in her ear.

'I love you,' he said in a tiny voice.

Susan closed her eyes. It was the first time anyone had ever said that to her – and that included her parents. Not even as a little girl had they ever said they loved her.

'Do you really?'

'Yes.'

'You're not just saying it because you're after *that*, are you?'

'No,' he said in an anguished tone of voice.

'Oh my darling,' she replied. She wasn't sure whether she loved him or not, but she certainly liked him an awful lot. His hands fumbled with the buttons at the back of her dress. Susan knew if she was going to stop him going further this was the moment. Then she thought of what her father was always saying to her, which was that she should do everything in her power to consolidate her relationship with Nigel. Well, what could be more consolidating than letting him make love to her?

'Here let me,' she said, and reaching behind her deftly undid the buttons. Her dress slid to the floor and she stepped out of it. Picking it up she threw it across a table. Smiling, she then unhooked her bra.

Nigel tore off his clothes, which he left lying in an untidy heap. When he was naked he went to her and held her in his arms.

'I'm a virgin,' she whispered.

He reached down to fondle her, praying to himself that everything would go all right and that he'd be able to get it up and in.

Susan wasn't the first girl he'd been to bed with. Far from it. But unfortunately his first time he'd been so nervous he'd had trouble getting an erection, much to the girl's chagrin. And what he had managed hadn't been enough for him to get into her.

The girl hadn't said much after he'd given up but the look in her eyes had wounded him deeply, filling him with humiliation. The incident had scored itself deep into his psyche and now every time he went to bed with a girl for the first time he was more than half-convinced history would repeat itself. And so much did he worry about it, it often did.

Not that there was anything wrong with him physically. There wasn't. And after he'd managed it once he relaxed and usually had no trouble from there on in, albeit the fear was always there lurking just under the surface.

Because of this his lovemaking was invariably a hurried affair. For once he got it up he was in a hurry to get on with it in case his erection died on him and he couldn't get it up again.

They lay on the bunk side by side. 'Be gentle,' she whispered.

He stroked her flank and nuzzled her bosom, excitement mounting in him with the realisation he was getting hard.

'Hold me,' he said and guided her hand to him.

He spread her legs and worked frantically to make her wet. Come on, come on, he muttered under his breath.

Panic flared in him as he felt what erection he had begin to sag a little. Swiftly he crawled on top of her. If he could just get it in he'd be all right, he told himself.

Susan grimaced as he succeeded in entering her. She was still dry and what he was doing was sore. But because of her inexperience she thought the pain was due to her virginity.

He thrust and thrust. He wasn't going to fail after all. He was going to manage it with her first time. Uttering a groan he climaxed and then with a sigh laid himself gently on top of her.

Despite the initial discomfort Susan had enjoyed it, although she did wish it had gone on a bit longer. Gathering him to her she pressed his chest against hers. 'That was lovely,' she said.

'I'm not very good to start with but I get better as I go along,' he said.

'Then we must practise very hard.'

He laughed. 'Well I'm all for that.'

'You used the contraceptive, didn't you?'

His face was suddenly stricken. 'Christ I forgot!'

'Nigel!'

'In the heat of the moment it slipped my mind.'

'Well if I'm pregnant you'll just have to marry me.'

'I think I might marry you anyway,' he replied softly.

'Be careful what you say. I might hold you to it.'

'And I might want you to.'

They stared long and hard at one another. Then he bent down and kissed her.

Susan closed her eyes, happiness and sheer pleasure welling inside her.

A little later Nigel looked up as the boat started to turn to port. That meant they'd crossed the Sound of Bute and Sannox was in sight.

'We're on our way back,' he said. But he was talking to deaf ears. Susan had fallen asleep.

'Do you mind if we're excused, Father? Susan and I would like to go through and play some records.'

Geoffrey McBeth glanced across at his wife Fiona who smiled and nodded.

'Jean? Keith?'

'We don't mind at all,' Keith replied. 'Let the youngsters enjoy themselves. I can quite understand their preferring to play records than listen to the boring talk of old fuddy-duddies like ourselves.'

'Run along then,' Geoffrey McBeth said, giving a rather royal wave of his hand, 'but please keep the music down to a mild roar.'

'You won't hear a thing in here,' Nigel retorted.

Geoffrey raised an imperious eyebrow. 'I'd better not.'

Nigel held the door open for Susan and, laughing, they escaped the room.

Keith positively beamed after them. This was the second visit the Gibbs had paid to the McBeth household. The McBeths had been twice to them as well, and the foursome were rapidly becoming good friends, having discovered they had a great deal in common.

'If you don't mind my saying so, they make a lovely couple,' Keith said.

'They certainly seem to be very fond of one another,' Fiona replied.

Jean smiled and Geoffrey looked thoughtful.

'We've all taken to Susan,' Geoffrey said after a while.

Keith nodded.

'Very intelligent and sensitive young lady,' Fiona added.

30

Keith nodded again. The message was coming over loud and clear. The McBeths approved. Should Nigel and Susan decide they wanted to get married the McBeths wouldn't stand in their way.

'We enjoy having Nigel around,' Jean said. 'In fact we've almost come to think of him as our own son.'

'Always wanted a boy in the family. But unfortunately we weren't blessed,' Keith said.

'Well, who knows what time may bring?' Geoffrey replied.

'God can work in mysterious ways,' added Fiona, who liked to think of herself as a religious person and indeed regularly went to church, if that's anything to go by.

'He'll be working for you when he leaves university, I presume?' Keith asked.

'That's his intention, I'm happy to say,' Geoffrey replied.

Keith puffed with satisfaction on his cigar, that being very much the answer he'd wanted to hear.

'And Susan's going to be a vet?' Fiona said.

'She's always been fond of animals. Ever since a tiny thing. Can't think where she gets it from as it doesn't run in either of our families,' Jean said.

'Admirable quality that,' Geoffrey remarked.

'She'll make a marvellous mother and I *do* know where she gets that from,' Keith said, winking at Jean.

Everyone laughed.

'Have you ever been round a brewery?' Keith asked suddenly.

Geoffrey shook his head.

'Then perhaps you'd like to? Might interest you, if you can stand the pong.'

'I think I'd rather like that,' Geoffrey replied.

'Good we'll arrange it.'

There was a slight pause and then Geoffrey said, 'I'm taking a small party out on my yacht a fortnight this weekend. A run up to Oban and back with hopefully a spot of fishing on the way.'

'Sounds marvellous,' Keith said.

'Then we'll be glad to have you aboard.'

'Jean and I will look forward to it,' Keith replied.

'Let me get you another drink,' Geoffrey said, rising.

Seeing Fiona's attention was elsewhere, Keith flashed Jean a triumphant glance. Things couldn't be going better.

'Hell and damnation!' Hector swore. 'Nige is going to let us down. I just know it.'

'He is rather late,' Hector's girlfriend Mary said.

'I'm sure he'll be along,' Susan said. 'Something must've happened. Can't we extend our time on the court?'

''Fraid not,' Hector replied. 'I've already inquired and it's booked.'

'Is there anyone else around who could fill in for Nige?' Mary asked.

'No one we know,' Hector said. Then, clicking his fingers, 'Wait a minute, I did see someone in the changing room. Haven't a clue who he is but he might fancy a game.'

'No harm in asking him, whoever he is,' Mary said, reluctant to abandon the game, having been looking forward to it.

'Susan?'

'Why not?'

'All right, I won't be a minute.'

Hector loped off in the direction of the male changing room.

'I can't think what's happened to Nigel,' Susan said, worrying a fingernail.

Mary practised a few swings with her racquet.

'Well, we're in luck,' Hector said on reappearing. 'This chap's going to help us out.'

'Jolly good!' enthused Mary.

The chap gave them all a friendly smile.

'Kirk, meet Susan and Mary,' Hector said.

'Hello.'

'Shall we get on with it then?' Mary said.

Susan matched Kirk's smile. 'You'll be partnering me – if that's okay?'

'Fine by me,' he replied.
They walked on to the court.

KIRK

'For God's sake, stop nagging, woman!' Walter Murray pleaded. 'That's all you ever seem to do. Nag, nag, bloody nag!'

'It's the only way I can ever get you to do anything,' his wife Lizzie replied hotly. 'Left to your own devices, nothing would ever get done.'

Walter groaned and slumped further into his chair. He was dead beat having just come off duty at the restaurant His Lordship's Larder, where he was employed as a waiter. He'd had one difficult cover after another that day and the last thing he needed now he was home was for Lizzie to go on at him. Why couldn't she understand that all he wanted out of life was some peace and quiet!

And his lungs had been playing him up all day as well. He'd gone through two handkerchiefs with his coughing and spluttering. Once he'd had to stop and stand still for a full minute in order to get his breath back.

'Now I'm pregnant, it's our duty to the child for us to better ourselves. I want my child to be somebody. To get on and have money and position and mix with grand folk.' A fanatical gleam glinted in her eyes as she gazed inwardly at her own private vision of the life her child would lead when grown up.

If it was a girl, Lizzie saw her married to a professional man. A solicitor or banker, perhaps. Living in a big house with fine clothes to wear. And if it was a boy – well! He would go to a public school and on from there to university. And when he was qualified he'd be an accountant or a manager or something equivalent.

But that could only come about if the wee lassie or boy was given the right start in life. And it was up to her to see that's what happened.

'So what are you going to do about it?' Lizzie demanded, unconsciously rubbing the swell of her rapidly ballooning belly. She was five months gone but looked more.

'I'm a waiter to trade, Lizzie,' Walter said patiently. 'That's all I know. And at my age I'm too old to learn anything else.'

'Nonsense!' she retorted. 'That's defeatist talk.'

'It's being practical.'

'If we got the money together maybe we could run our own restaurant. You know all there is to know about running restaurants. You'd be bound to be a success.'

'Oh, I could do it all right,' he replied. 'The only problem, and an insurmountable one as far as I'm concerned, is the money. Where would I possibly get hold of the money it takes to buy and equip a restaurant? Not to mention the capital needed to keep it operational over the first few months until trade is established and it starts to make a profit.'

'You could go to the bank.'

'Which bank did you have in mind?' he asked, a tinge of sarcasm lacing his voice.

'I don't know. Any one.'

'As we live from week to week on what I bring home and have never had any previous dealings with a bank it would *have* to be any one. But let's say I did go to one. Put yourself in the manager's shoes. Would you lend anything to a waiter who wanders in off the street with no money of his own, and with no property or anything else like that either, who to boot has half his lungs burned away thanks to mustard gas inhaled in the trenches? Now be honest, Lizzie, what would you say to such a man who'd be asking to borrow hundreds off you?'

Lizzie sniffed.

'Well?'

'I'm not a bank manager. What do I know what he'd say?'

Walter smiled thinly. 'Well I know. It would be: there's the door, Jimmy, and please close it behind you on your way out.'

It was Lizzie's firm belief that if there was a will there had to be a way. The way was there, they just weren't seeing it, that was all.

'We'll just have to put our thinking-caps on,' she said, adding, 'The trouble with you is you've no ambition, no drive. No "get up and go"!'

She was right, he thought. He hadn't always been like this. In his youth he'd had plans and dreams like everyone else. But the war had done for those. He closed his eyes and thought back to France. How could anything ever seem important again after all that carnage and death and waste? To have come through it all alive had used up a whole life's ambition. Peace and quiet and an easy life were all he wanted now.

'I've just had an idea!' Lizzie said excitedly. 'Now listen . . .'

He forced himself to open his eyes and pay attention.

Walter sat patiently on the hard-backed wooden chair. He was dressed in his Sunday suit and best shirt and collar. His shoes had been so well cleaned they sparkled like black glass.

A glance at the clock ticking on the wall told him it was twenty-five minutes past his appointment time. He frowned fractionally but never dreamed of complaining. He was too grateful for being seen at all.

Thirty-five minutes past his appointment time a prim-looking secretary arrived to say Mr Gibb would see him now.

The owner of Black Lion Brewery was a dapper man in his early fifties. He had steel-grey hair parted in the middle and swept backwards. The steel in his eye matched that of his hair.

'Sit down, Murray,' Gerald Gibb said, picking up and rereading Walter's letter of application, 'And what makes you think you're suited to running one of my pubs?'

Thoroughly coached by Lizzie, Walter spoke his reply.

Christ, but he looks a hard and mean bastard, Walter thought to himself. He wilted a little when Gibb's penetrating gaze fastened itself on him.

'You'll be expected to live on the premises,' Gibb said.

'I understand.'

'And the hours are damn long. It means you wouldn't even see as much of your family as you do now.'

Walter smiled inwardly. Seeing less of Lizzie was an attraction as far as he was concerned. Not that he didn't love her – he did – but she was a gey, demanding woman with a tongue on her as long and sharp as a German bayonet.

'I want to get on,' Walter replied.

Gibb nodded his approval.

Gibb sat at his desk and pretended to reread Walter's application. Frankly he was in two minds. Walter just didn't seem physically tough enough for the pub he had in mind. And why did the man keep coughing like that?

'Mustard gas,' Walter replied when Gibb asked him.

Gibb grunted, softening a little toward Walter.

'I lost both my sons in France,' Gibb said, adding, 'At the second battle of Ypres.'

'I was there.'

'It was pretty horrendous from what I've been told.'

Walter nodded. 'I don't think anyone over here can really imagine just what it was like. Let's only hope and pray the world never sees its like again.'

There was a few minutes' silence during which both men sat lost in their own thoughts.

Gibb's eyes stole across his desk to where a small double-leafed leather-bound photograph holder stood. His two boys in uniform stared back at him. He remembered arguing at the time they shouldn't both join the same regiment but they'd insisted, maintaining they wanted to be together. And on the same day, in the same battle, within yards of one another, they'd both been mown down. Together they'd wanted to be and together they now were for all eternity.

Gibb named his sons' regiment but Walter had been in another, fighting with his lot further down the line.

Gibb made up his mind. If Walter wasn't suitable then he

could always replace him. But he couldn't find it in his heart not to give the man a chance. He would have done the same for anyone who'd been at Ypres.

'When can you start?' Gibb asked.

Walter blinked. 'I have to work a fortnight's notice.'

'Shall we say the first of the month, then?'

'That would be fine.'

'Consider it settled, then. You'll be contacted at home and given the relevant details. Good day to you, Mr Murray.'

'And good day to you, Mr Gibb.'

After Walter had gone Gerald Gibb again stared at the pictures of his two sons. Then, shaking his head in sorrow, he got back to the work in hand.

Lizzie was appalled. The inside of the pub was filthy dirty, and as for the living accommodation! She would've considered it a health hazard for pigs. Walter himself was disappointed. He'd been hoping for a lot better than this.

Lizzie stared out of a cracked window. The district was even worse than the one she'd left. Instead of going up in the world it seemed they'd actually come down.

She watched ragged urchins run up and down the street, only one of whom wore footwear and that carved wooden clogs. Her heart hardened within her. She'd move heaven and earth to ensure her child to come and any others that followed didn't end up like those ragamuffins out there.

With a shudder she remembered her own childhood. There had been times when there was no food at all and she, like the rest of her family and their friends, had got so thin their bones had stuck out like bare branches on a winter tree. She'd been nineteen years old before she'd owned a single article of clothing bought specifically for her and not handed down.

The fact she was plain to the point of verging on being downright ugly hadn't helped matters much, either. And for a long while it had been feared by herself and the rest of her family she was going to end up an old maid.

41

Then at the eleventh hour, so to speak, along had happened Walter Murray who, far from being the best catch in Glasgow, was certainly far better than none at all.

Lizzie dragged her attention back to the room she and Walter were now standing in. Hot water and soap would attend to the filth and dirt. Give her a month and she'd have this place sparkling like new from top to bottom.

'If we make a success maybe they'll give us a better pub in a better area next time,' she said.

'The cellar's a bloody mess,' Walter replied.

'Then fix it. You can, can't you?'

'Oh aye. It just needs some sorting out, that's all.'

She took off her coat and threw it over a chair. 'Then we'd better get started. You down there and me up here. As you say, there's a lot to be done.'

'Do you think we've made a mistake?' he asked slowly.

'No. Your job as a waiter was a dead-end one. This pub may be the bottom of the barrel but at least there's the opportunity to work your way up. And who knows? With a bit of luck there's no reason why we couldn't own our own one day. No reason why we couldn't own two or three, even.'

'Jings crikey, don't get carried away now girl,' he replied.

'Nothing's impossible, Walter,' she said. 'It all depends how much you want it in the first place.'

Which wasn't a great deal, he thought mournfully.

'Right then, let's get to it!' she said.

He made his way down to the cellar.

Walter wiped his hands on a towel and glanced at the clock on the wall. Lizzie had been upstairs in labour for twenty hours now. At the moment there was a doctor and midwife with her.

He'd leave it a wee while longer and then pop up again to see how she was. Despite assurances from both the doctor and midwife, he was beginning to worry everything wasn't as it should be.

He was in the middle of pulling a pint when the midwife appeared in the bar. The woman was smiling and nodding to him which immediately set his mind at rest. He called to George the other barman to take over.

'Well?' he demanded.

'A smashing big boy. A real whopper at ten pounds,' the midwife said.

'And Lizzie?'

'Fair played out but nothing a few days in bed won't cure.'

He shouted to George to give the midwife a gill and then, snatching up a bottle and two glasses, he rushed upstairs.

Lizzie's face was sunken round the cheeks and she looked totally exhausted. When she saw him she managed a wan smile.

'A boy,' she said.

'Aye, I was told. Would you like a dram?'

Slowly she shook her head.

'Well how about you, Doctor?'

'I won't say no. It's been a long hard pull. Or should I say push,' the doctor replied with a laugh. He hadn't been with Lizzie the entire time but had been popping in every hour or so to see how she was doing.

Walter poured two very large whiskies. 'Ach well, it's not every day you get a son,' he said and handed the doctor a glass. Walter stuck his chest out, pride oozing from every pore. 'To the baby!' he toasted.

'To Kirk,' Lizzie interjected weakly. 'That's what I want to call him.'

She pulled the wean even closer to her and gazed down at him adoringly.

She had plans for this big son of hers.

The years passed and Walter worked hard at running his pub but despite his efforts the pub never did really well. The sad truth was he just didn't have the sort of personality a good publican needs. And although he worked hard his heart was never really in it.

As Gerald Gibb had said, the hours were extremely long and taxing. Never in the best of health anyway since being

43

gassed, Walter soon looked pale and drawn, while his coughing grew more and more frequent.

Lizzie despaired. She hated the area and was mortified at the thought of her Kirk having to grow up here. She scrimped and saved every penny she could, with her mind always on the pub they would buy for themselves one day.

How different their life was to what she'd imagined. There was money in pubs, she'd always said that. The trouble was all the profit went to the brewery with them being paid a mere pittance by comparison.

Again and again she nagged Walter to ask Mr Gibb for a new pub and once Walter actually did write the man a letter. The reply had been curt in the extreme. There were no better pubs available from the brewery and that was that.

There were other breweries, she'd pointed out to Walter. Why don't they approach one of them? But Walter didn't want to know. He was in a rut and didn't want to move out of it.

Sexual relations between them deteriorated, to become non-existent. To begin with she'd hoped that by denying him she'd force him into taking a bolder stand, but as it had transpired, it hadn't bothered him to go without.

In the end she was the one who'd suffered most by the abstention. Not that she would have admitted it, mind you. And being as full of pride as a Highlander, Armageddon would come sooner than she'd make the first move to repair matters. She'd made her stand and that was where she'd stay until he capitulated. Lizzie Murray was a woman who never admitted defeat.

Kirk was eleven years old when Walter received a letter from Gerald Gibb saying he was going to be in the area on such and such a day and intended calling into the pub.

'You can't let this opportunity go,' Lizzie said at once. 'You must ask him again for a transfer. Perhaps a wee pub on the outskirts or a country pub. Just so long as it's not in a slum like this.'

Walter groaned. Did she never stop?

'Have you heard the way our Kirk's beginning to speak? I've done my best but it's those hooligans he's forced to associate with at school. He's starting to sound as common as they do.'

'He's working-class like me and you, Lizzie. How else would you expect him to speak?' Walter said patiently.

'Like the gentleman he's going to be someday.'

Walter shook his head. 'You live in a dream world, so you do. He's got about as much chance of becoming a gentleman as I do of going to the moon.'

'He'll be a gentleman all right and do well in life,' Lizzie snapped in return. 'I've promised him.'

'You shouldn't make promises you might not be able to keep.'

'I'd be able to keep them if you weren't the failure you are.'

'I do my utmost to make a success of this place,' he retaliated, making a vague gesture which took in the pub. 'I want Kirk to go to public school and university after that. We have to give him that chance. It's our duty. Why, you've heard his teachers yourself. They all say what a fine brain he's got. He's streets ahead of anyone else in his class.'

Walter had grudgingly to admit she was right. Kirk had ability, there was no doubt about that. But this public school and university she'd been harping on about for years. That cost money, a lot of it – he'd inquired – and was way and beyond their slender means.

'Go down on your bended knees if necessary,' Lizzie went on, 'but make Mr Gibb give us a better pub and preferably a bigger one. I'm not asking for my sake but for the boy's. He's your son too, after all.'

'You make it sound as if I didn't love the lad.'

'Then prove it! Talk Gibb into giving us a better place and with it the wherewithal to take Kirk out of that dreadful school he's forced to go to now.'

Walter sighed, 'I'll speak to Gibb when he comes.'

'And you'll do your best?'

'As best I'm able. You have my word.'

45

'Right then,' she replied. She was at the door when she turned. 'Would you like me to be there?' she asked. 'Would you shame me, woman, by speaking for me? I'm a man and can speak like one when I have to.' 'Aye, all right,' she said and left him to it.

The day Gerald Gibb arrived at the Murray's pub had been possibly the most traumatic of his life. He hadn't been feeling well of late, losing weight and off his food. Consequently, the previous week he'd been to the doctor's, who'd sent him to the hospital for some tests.

He'd been summoned back to the hospital that morning where a consultant had broken the news to him. He had cancer.

After learning this, a great anger had started burning inside him. There was so much left to do in life, minor things as well as major. He'd always wanted to go abroad and never had. He'd always wanted to go on a long sea cruise but due to business pressures and commitments had postponed it year after year. And now he would do none of these things. Putting off till tomorrow what he should have done today he had simply run out of time.

At least he was leaving a thriving business behind him, which was something. But what consolation was that, when he had no direct heirs to leave it to? Anger turned to bitter resentment and that in turn to a cold malevolent fury.

That was his mood when he entered the Murray pub.

Kirk was down in the cellar where he often played. Here among the beer barrels it was easy to imagine himself a knight in Camelot or a soldier in enemy terrain or a host of other characters in whatever situation those characters required.

The only trouble was he always played alone. His mother did not allow him to play with the boys from school, either out in the street or down here. Consequently, although used to his own company, he was often lonely, wishing there was some boy roundabout his mother would allow him to be pals with.

He was down on the cellar floor sneaking up on a couple of

46

imaginary Red Indians when he heard his father come down the stairs. He was about to jump up and make his presence known when he became aware there was someone with his father. When he heard the man addressed as Mr Gibb he froze and remained hidden out of sight.

'You'll remember I wrote to you asking for us to be considered for a new pub, Mr Gibb,' Walter said. 'And you replied saying there was nothing going at the time. Well, the wife and I were wondering if there was anything in the offing now? We really would be most grateful for promotion.'

Gibb turned a baleful eye on Walter. He had to vent his fury, at the card life had dealt him, on someone. And Walter, by unwittingly making his request at the worst possible moment, made himself the perfect target.

'I beg your pardon?' Gibb asked.

'The wife and I were wondering ...'

'What makes you think I would entrust you with a better pub when you've made such a hash of this one?'

Taken aback, Walter blinked. 'We haven't done that badly.'

'No?'

The look in Gibb's eye made Walter suddenly deathly afraid. He felt like someone who'd run on to what appeared to be a lovely sandy beach only to find himself, before he knew where he was, up to his neck in quicksand.

Gibb went on. 'I own four other pubs in this area. All of them in worse condition than this one and all of them taking more money. Why do you think that is, Murray?'

'I couldn't say,' Walter mumbled in reply.

'Well I'll tell you. Because as a publican you're a disaster.'

Walter cringed.

'And I rue the day I ever gave you the chance here. I've been through your figures and do you know something? At the moment you aren't even doing half the business my other four round about are.'

'I work hard, Mr Gibb, sir. Honest I do.'

'Sometimes hard work isn't enough, Murray. And for God's sake stop coughing and spluttering like that!'

47

'I can't help it, sir.'

'Well stand away from me then. I don't relish having your spittle all over my suit.'

Walter backed hastily away. 'I'm sorry, sir.'

Gibb's lips thinned. 'You're a horrible little man, Murray. Disgusting, I'd call you. No wonder the customers keep away from here. Who'd want to come and be served by that sour face and no doubt be coughed over half the time?'

Walter screwed his hands together. This was rapidly becoming a nightmare.

'What are you, Murray?'

'A horrible little man, sir.'

'That's right. And don't you ever forget it.'

'No, Mr Gibb, sir.'

Gibb took his time about lighting a cigar, enjoying watching Walter inwardly writhing in agony. He knew Walter now thought he was going to lose his job.

'The best thing I could do would be to have you replaced,' Gibb said.

Walter was appalled. Jobs were so scarce that at his age and in his condition he would probably never find work again.

'Please don't do that to me, sir. I have a wife and family to keep.'

A wife and family? It was more than he had, Gibb thought bitterly, Emmaline having died several years previously.

Tears squeezed out of Walter's eyes. Lizzie had told him to go down on his bended knees. Well so he would, only not for what she'd had in mind.

He sank to the floor. 'Please?' he pleaded.

The sight of Walter in such a state pleased Gibb. It made him feel better, for by making Walter suffer so, it was as though he was unloading some of his own pain.

'Please?' Walter repeated, and grovelled.

From his vantage point behind the barrels Kirk felt sick watching his father's humiliation. At that moment he didn't know whom he hated more, his father for allowing himself to be so humiliated or Gibb for doing it to him. For years he'd

48

listened to his mother's derisory remarks and comments about Walter but up until now he hadn't fully realised what a weak and pathetic creature his father was.

One thing was certain: no one would ever speak to him like that. No matter what the consequences.

He sank further back into the shadows and turned his face away. He didn't want to see any more. It was bad enough he had to hear.

Walter was sobbing now, a flood of tears rolling down his face from where they went spilling to the floor.

Gibb stared down at Walter. He wasn't being quite fair in saying his other four pubs in the area were on equal terms with this one. Each of them had factories and other small firms close by while this one didn't. It just proved Murray's stupidity for not realising that. The truth was this particular pub had always been a problem one and several times he'd considered selling it. But as long as it continued making a marginal profit he supposed it was best to hang on to it rather than give one of his competitors another outlet.

'All right man, get back on your feet,' he said.

Slowly Walter climbed upright. His lungs were hurting like hell, burning as though filled to overflowing with molten lava.

'I don't want to hear any more nonsense from you about promotion. Is that clear?'

'Does that mean I can keep the pub?' Walter asked eagerly.

'Lord knows why I'm being so lenient but I suppose you can.'

Seizing Gibb's hand Walter pumped it up and down.

'Thank you. Oh thank you, Mr Gibb,' he said.

Gibb shook him off and stalked to the stairs. Walter ran after him like a whipped cur after its master.

Kirk emerged from the shadows. The skin on his face was drawn tight and both his hands were clenched into fists. He stared down at a crate bearing the legend Black Lion Brewery stamped across one side. In place of the black lion insignia he saw Gibb's face.

His foot lashed out again and again.

Upstairs Gibb had just gone and Lizzie was eagerly confronting Walter. She fretted impatiently while he poured himself a large whisky which he gulped down. He poured himself another.

'Well?' she demanded.

In a harsh strained voice he related to her what had occurred in the cellar. When he had finished she sat, her ample backside spilling over the seat. She was numb through.

'Oh shite!' Walter jerked out. His coughing had started up again.

Lizzie looked at her man. But there was no sympathy in her expression. What had she ever done to be landed with the likes of him? she wondered. Well, whatever it was it must have been really dreadful for she was certainly paying for it now. Why, she was twice the man he was! Oh, if only she'd been born male she would have shown them! There would have been no holding her.

'There will be no public school now for Kirk,' she said, the words almost choking her.

'I'm sorry, girl.'

'Sorry! What good's that? It was a better pub and more money I wanted, not bloody sorry!'

Walter hung his head in shame. Why did everyone make life so complicated when it could be so easy? If they could just let him alone to get by without too much fuss or worry. All he wanted out of life was some peace and quiet. Surely that wasn't too much to ask?

'I've always said Gibb was a hard-hearted bastard but I've never seen him like that before,' Walter said.

'At least he's a man. Not some cowering wee mouse,' Lizzie retorted, her voice dripping venom.

'Let it be.'

'All my dreams, everything we've worked for out the window and you say let it be! Christ sake, have you no red blood in your veins at all, Walter Murray, or are you filled with nothing but piss and vinegar?'

He closed his eyes and thought of all his friends dead in the war. Men hanging on the wire, men drowned in mud, men with limbs and bellies and faces blown away, men shrieking in unbelievable agony, and the sanctimonious padres who tried to tell you in the middle of all that there was still a God! How could anything possibly be important after France? If only Lizzie could see how mean and petty everything she worried about was. So what if Kirk didn't get to public school? He was a bright and healthy lad, what more could anyone ask for?

He came out of his dwam to the realisation she was asking him something.

'If we can't afford public school at least let me send him to elocution lessons.'

He nodded. 'If that's what you want.'

'It's not much. But at least it's something.'

She rose to return upstairs. Half-way to the door she paused and turned. 'Did you really cry in front of him?'

'Yes,' he replied in a whisper. 'I thought for sure we were going to lose the pub and be out on the street. And where would I get another job, I ask you?'

Cynicism settled heavily on her mouth. 'And you're the man who can speak like one when he has to?' she said.

Laughing hollowly she left him alone.

When the time came for Kirk to leave school the war was over and Lizzie's fear that he'd have to participate in it laid to rest.

Of the twenty-seven applications for jobs Kirk lodged he got three interviews. Out of the three interviews, he was offered one position, that of a junior clerk in an import/export firm.

Lizzie was furious. This was a far cry from what she'd had in mind for her Kirk. But after discussing the matter at length between them it was decided he would accept the position. The plain fact of the matter was unemployment was high and jobs hard to come by.

During the time between leaving school and starting work Lizzie took Kirk into town and got him kitted out with clothes. To start with there was a suit, absolutely *de rigueur* for office

51

work. A stout pair of shoes to match the suit. A topcoat for the winter weather. And a trilby hat.

Some of the neighbours watched in amazement the morning Kirk left the pub to start his new job. He had this peculiar way of walking, what might be best described as a most pronounced swagger of the hips, which the neighbours found ludicrously pompous now that it had been combined with, or it might be said topped off by, a trilby hat.

'My God, will you take a look at that!' Mrs McMahon said, leaning out of her window.

'Help my Bob, what does he look like!' Mr McMahon said on joining her.

Mrs McMahon sniggered. 'Talk about having a big tip for yourself!'

'First day on the job and already he's dressing like a gaffer.'

'Ach well, he was always like that. Too good for the likes of you and me and the others around here. Say hello to him in the street and he nods down at you as though he was Lord God Almighty and you were something that had just been dug up.'

'Office work,' Mr McMahon, a riveter currently unemployed, sneered. 'Just right for our Kirk. He'll no' be dirtying his hands on that.'

'Kirk dirty his hands – don't talk daft, man!' Mrs McMahon replied.

And with a laugh they both came back into the house, closing the window behind them.

Out in the street Kirk swaggered on his way to the tramstop.

Kirk hadn't been working long when disaster struck at home. He returned to the pub one evening to find Lizzie in tears and his father sitting ashen-faced staring into space.

'What's wrong?' he demanded.

Walter shook his head, unable to speak.

Through her sobs Lizzie managed to get out, 'The new owner of the brewery's been here. A Major Gibb, Gerald Gibb's brother. He's given your dad the sack.'

'Holy Christ!' exclaimed Kirk.

Lizzie went on. 'It seems he's got rid of the board who's been managing the brewery since his brother's death. And now he's taken over personally he says he intends cutting away all the old dead wood.'

'When do we have to get out by?' Kirk asked.

'The end of the month. There will be a new manager installed by then.'

'What can I do?' Walter asked.

'Nothing,' Kirk replied. And he was right. As sole owner of the brewery Major Gibb could do as he damn well pleased.

Walter wrung his hands. 'Where will we go?'

'You'll never get another pub at your age so we'll have to find a house,' Kirk replied, adding, 'It's best you do that, Mum. And if you run into trouble then I'll just have to take a couple of days off my work to see what I can come up with.'

Lizzie nodded.

'There were no hints or prior warning,' Walter said. 'He just marched into the pub, announced who he was, took me round the back and came out with it just like that.'

'A military man,' Lizzie added. 'They don't beat about the bush.'

Bastard! Kirk thought. This Major sounded about as choice as his brother. A real nasty piece of work.

'Maybe I'll get a job as a barman. I don't see what else I can do,' Walter muttered.

'Either that or go back to being a waiter,' Lizzie said.

Walter buried his head in his hands.

Kirk stared angrily at his father. Weak as dishwater, he thought. Not one ounce of backbone. God, how he pitied his mother having to put up with him all these years. She'd deserved far better than the likes of that.

Walter started to cough. Wracking coughs that seemed to be coming from the very depths of his being. He covered his mouth with the large white handkerchief he was never without.

Kirk recoiled inwardly. You would have thought he would be used to his father's coughing by now but he wasn't. He still found it as disgusting and filthy as he always had.

'We might have to rely on your wages for a while till your father gets fixed up somewhere,' Lizzie said.

'Have you any savings?'

'A few pounds, that's all.'

'*Can* we get by on my wages alone?' he asked.

'We'll have to, son. Let's just hope and pray it won't be for too long,' Lizzie replied.

There was silence for a while after that and then Kirk said, 'What a bloody mess!'

Walter continued spluttering into his hanky.

It took Walter months to find another job, which he eventually did in a pub not that far away from where his own had been. When the regulars discovered why he coughed so much he was immediately nicknamed Mustard Murray. Walter took this in good part – not that he could have afforded to do otherwise – and soon became quite a favourite with the customers, something he'd never succeeded in doing in his own pub.

It was working simply as a barman and not having the responsibility of being manager which made Walter more cheerful in his dealings with the public. Although now making even less money than he had been before – and that had been little enough – he was far happier within himself.

The house Lizzie had managed to wheedle out of the Corporation factor was in the same area. The close they lived up was badly in need of repair and all the walls were damp. The communal toilets on the half-landings stank and were forever clogging up.

The first night in their new home Lizzie broke down and wept. Sitting by the fireside she cried buckets while Kirk did his best to comfort her.

Walter went through to the bedroom where he stood staring out the window. Some wee boys were playing 'kick the can' in the rubbish-strewn street. Some other wee boys were hurling round in a broken-down pram they'd found in a midgie somewhere. Above the tenements the chimneys belched

54

smoke into an already polluted atmosphere. Everywhere Walter looked he saw the colour grey. The buildings, the streets, the sky, even the faces of the wee boys.

'Ach, well, it could be worse,' he said, adding, 'At least we're alive, and that's the main thing.'

Having been brought up so much on his own, and continually dissuaded from making pals with any of the lads at school by Lizzie, Kirk continued being a loner now he was working. He would have considered making friends at the office but unfortunately there was no one there his own age, the closest to him being a man of thirty-two who was married with a family.

Therefore it was his habit to go on his tod to the Saturday night dancing up the town where he soon became an accomplished dancer.

Following the custom he would stop off at a boozer first where he'd sink a couple of pints before continuing on to the dance hall.

He lumbered, which is to say took home, quite a few lassies whom he later took out to the pictures and other dances. But none of these relationships lasted long, as his interest in the individuals concerned was always short-lived.

Till the night he met Minnie McKie, that is.

He knew the moment he saw her across the dance floor that he was going to ask her up. She was tall with close-cropped dark hair and finely chiselled features. A gem shining out from amongst the dross.

He strode forward, pushing his way through the standers till he was by her side.

'Would you like to dance?' he asked.

A half-smile lit up her face while she took a moment or two to study him. 'That would be nice,' she replied.

He was disappointed to hear her accent was quite broad. From the looks of her he'd been expecting something more refined.

Some young men find it difficult to chat up a girl, especially a particularly pretty one. But not Kirk. Lacking confidence

55

was a problem he'd never been bothered with.

She fitted easily into his arms and they moved well together. When the first dance finished he asked her if she'd stay up for the second. Soon he had her laughing.

'You've got good patter,' Minnie said.

'I'll take that as a compliment,' he replied.

She eyed him quizzically. 'There's something different about you. Maybe it's the way you talk, all posh like.'

Kirk talked 'posh' as a result of the long stint of elocution lessons he'd had as a child. Having failed to send him to public school Lizzie had made sure she'd had her way about that. She adored the fact he spoke with what she considered to be an upper-class accent. Others, unkindly, had described it as a plum in the gob.

'Then again, perhaps it's just me? What you might call a natural charisma,' Kirk replied.

'What's charisma?'

He smiled in what some people would have thought was a patronising fashion. 'A sort of magnetism,' he said.

'Well nobody could ever accuse you of being shy.'

'No,' he replied, 'that they couldn't.'

Sweat was running down both their faces as the hall was becoming more and more packed. Up on the platform the band was giving it big licks while from time to time a female vocalist went up to the mike and sang. Every so often lights were brought to bear on a many-faceted silver ball hanging twirling from the ceiling. The effect was to send blobs of light dancing over every available surface.

'What do you do?' Kirk asked.

'I work in a shipping office as a shorthand typist.'

'I'm with an import/export firm. It might be we deal with you?'

'Donaldson shipping?'

'Know them well,' Kirk replied.

Somehow that was a bond between them. Something to start off from and build on.

He asked her then where she stayed and was relieved to hear

it wasn't all that far from where he himself lived. With trams stopping relatively early it was always important to establish where a lassie lived in case you landed yourself with a long walk home.

They danced on to the last waltz during which he asked if he could see her back to her place.

'I'd like that,' she said, and laid her head on his shoulder.

During the tram journey home he discovered she lived with her mother and an older sister. Her father had been killed in the war. He didn't tell her much about his own family, preferring not to go into that.

When they got to her close he took her firmly by the hand and marched her round to the back where it was dark.

There they kissed and cuddled for a good twenty minutes before she said she just had to go in.

'Can I see you again?' he asked.

'If you like.'

'What about one night through the week?'

'Wednesday would be the best,' she said.

'That suits me fine. I'll meet you at your front close at seven.'

She took his face in her hands. 'I like you,' she said, well aware she was being awfully forward.

'And I like you too.'

'Till Wednesday then.'

She kissed him one last time before running up the stairs.

As he walked home through the gas-lit streets Kirk whistled a jaunty tune. It was good to be winching - which means taking out -- someone he had a real fancy for.

It was just a pity she was working-class, though. Otherwise she might have suited him in the long term just dandy.

After a couple of months of winching Kirk and Minnie started meeting one another at lunchtime. There was a cheap little restaurant they would go to while other times they would find a quiet spot to eat the sandwiches they'd agreed to bring with them.

It was during one such sandwich-eating session that Minnie said, 'My mum's boyfriend has come back from America and she's having a wee party for him at the house. Would you like to come?'

Kirk nodded. 'An American?'

'Aye, he's stationed over here with their Air Force. Hank the Yank we call him but his real name's Harry. I think you'll like him.'

'I'll look forward to it.'

'It'll also give you a chance to meet my mum and sister,' she said coyly.

Kirk grinned. 'Is this me getting my feet under the table?'

'See it as you like.'

'As long as you don't start talking about engagements,' he said.

Innocently she studied her sandwich. 'Oh it's far too early yet for that.'

Kirk told himself he was going to have to watch it with this one. Well he'd string her along for as long as he could. And if he played it correctly that could be quite some time.

He wondered if there would be some way he could get her alone at the party. He was getting awful fed up, and frustrated, by the restrictions of her back close.

Harry, whom all the Scots called Hank, Hydelman was a shortish, very hairy, American who looked like he had a lot of Italian or middle European blood in him. He laughed a great deal and was forever slapping people on the back – a habit which Kirk personally found very irritating.

Minnie's mother, Judy, looked to be in her mid-forties. Reasonably well groomed, she was still in good nick despite having had two children and lost a husband.

The sister Irene was an older version of Minnie but hadn't nearly such a nice personality.

'Have another Scotch,' Harry said and topped Kirk's glass up to the rim.

'Hey, go easy!' Kirk said, thinking it was something new to

see so much whisky being thrown around. Whisky was still as hard to come by as it had been during the war.

'How about you, Min?' Harry went on. 'There's plenty more where this came from.'

'Just a little one then,' Minnie replied, gasping when her glass got the same treatment Kirk's had done.

'Call that wee?' she said.

'It is in Texas, where I come from,' Harry replied with a laugh before moving on.

'Idiot!' Minnie smiled. 'He doesn't come from Texas at all. He's from Ohio.'

Kirk sipped his drink. Like most Glaswegians he wasn't a whisky connoisseur. As long as it was the real McCoy and came in a glass, that was fine by him. But he did know enough about whisky to appreciate that what he'd been drinking since arriving at the McKies' was deluxe quality of a standard he'd only ever tasted once before.

Music from a gramophone started up and he and Minnie danced. To show his manners he also danced with Judy and Irene – the former was already well on her way to being sloshed.

There were half a dozen Americans present, all of whom seemed amiable men eager to be liked.

Every time Kirk's glass was even half empty Harry appeared to fill it to the brim again.

'Enjoy! Enjoy! I like people to enjoy!' Harry called out.

'Quite a character,' Kirk said.

'Mum likes him.'

'Is marriage in the air?'

Minnie shook her head. 'He's already got a wife and kids in the States. That was why he was back there. He goes home to see them every so often.'

'What does he do in the Yank Air Force? Fly a plane?'

'No. He's in charge of the B.X. on their base.'

'What's a B.X?' Kirk asked.

'It's a big shop called a Base Exchange where the men and the families living on the base can buy things at a reduced price. According to Hank they've even got washing machines and fridges there, although I find that hard to believe.'

'Is that a fact?' Kirk said thoughtfully. 'And Hank's in charge of the whole kit and caboodle?'

'So he says.'

'Let's dance again,' Minnie added a few seconds later. George Formby singing 'Chinese Laundry Blues' had just been put on the gramophone and it was one of her favourites.

About an hour later Judy came up to Minnie. 'I'm getting a bit woozy so Hank's taking me out for a spin in his car. I'm just letting you know in case you can't find me and start worrying.'

Harry joined them. 'If we're late getting back don't feel you have to wait up,' he said.

'Fine,' Minnie said.

Judy kissed Minnie on the cheek and then she and Harry were making for the door.

Kirk smiled. He'd just been presented with a Heaven-sent opportunity. He gave Harry and Judy a good fifteen minutes to get under way before whispering in Minnie's ear he wanted to speak to her out in the hall.

Once there he said, 'Which is your bedroom?'

'Why?'

'Why do you think?'

She looked uncertain so he took her in his arms and kissed her.

'Just for a little while,' he whispered.

'All right then,' she said, and taking his hand led him to one of the several doors lining the hallway.

'Don't put the light on,' she said once inside.

There wasn't a lock on the door but there was a small chest of drawers close by. This Kirk lifted and placed in front of the door. If anyone tried to come in they'd get the message.

He kissed her and was still kissing her as he manipulated her on to the bed. Deftly he undid the top buttons of her dress so he could get at her breasts. Hot and sticky, she squirmed under him.

'Oh!' she said when his hands went under her knickers to find her.

Her knickers were half-way down her thighs when suddenly she stopped him. 'Tell me you love me,' she said.

'I love you, Minnie. I swear it,' he answered.

'I've never done it before, Kirk.'

'Neither have I.'

'I'm pleased about that.'

Her knickers slid off and then he pushed his trousers and underpants down to his knees.

She sucked in her breath and throwing her arms around his neck drew him close to her. 'Oh, my darling love,' she whispered.

He got on with it.

Lying in his own bed the next morning Kirk began to think about Harry Hydelman.

Harry was in charge of the B.X. and judging from last night this B.X. seemed to have an abundance of whisky, a commodity most sought after in Glasgow, being the Glaswegians' favourite tipple. There was some to be found in most pubs and occasionally to be bought over the counter but, since the war when the bulk of that produce had started to be shipped to America in return for warships, weapons etc., and latterly to repay some of the vast debt Britain had run up with the States, never ever enough to satisfy the demand.

It seemed to him this was a situation ripe for exploitation. The big question was, would Harry play ball? And if so what sort of quantities might be involved? It was an exciting thought and one he dwelled on over breakfast.

After the meal was finished he walked round to Minnie's where he was in luck. Harry had come back and stayed the night and had not yet returned to base.

Minnie welcomed him with a kiss and a knowing wink. In a whisper she said Judy was still in bed having the most God Almighty hangover. Harry was still with Judy.

Kirk said he would wait as he wanted a word with the American. Minnie and Irene got on with the clearing up while he sat by the fire and thought.

'It's all right for some,' Irene said, not entirely jokingly.

Kirk beamed her a smile and sat on.

Eventually there were sounds from the bathroom and a little later Harry appeared, having washed and shaved.

'Some party,' Harry said and whistled. Then noticing Kirk, 'You still here?'

'I've been home and come back again,' Kirk replied.

Minnie handed Harry a cup of coffee, which he accepted gratefully. She asked him if he'd like breakfast but he said no, the coffee was enough.

'It's you I've really come to speak with,' Kirk said to Harry. 'Perhaps we could take a walk while I explain what I have in mind.'

'Couldn't we talk here?'

Kirk smiled. 'I think it best we take a walk.'

Harry looked curious. He glanced at his watch and then nodded. 'Okay, I got a while before I'm due back on base. A walk it is.'

Kirk waited briefly in the hallway while Harry disappeared to have a word with Judy. Then Harry was back and side by side they descended the tenement stairs.

'You sure sounded mysterious up there,' Harry said when they were out on the street.

They passed Harry's flashy American car standing conspicuously at the kerb. Kirk wondered what the neighbours would make of that if it wasn't moved soon. But perhaps Judy McKie was the sort of woman who didn't give a damn what the neighbours thought. On reflection he decided that was probably the case.

'Minnie told me last night you're in charge of the B.X. out at your base,' Kirk said.

'That's right.'

'And amongst the other things you sell there is whisky.

62

Hence the liberal supply there was at the party.'

Harry came up short and his eyes narrowed. 'What are you getting at?' he demanded.

Kirk licked his lips which had suddenly gone dry. He wasn't at all sure he wouldn't get a punch in the face for what he was about to suggest.

'I was wondering if you'd be interested in us coming to some sort of arrangement? Literally any amount you can supply I can sell.'

They walked for a little while in silence, Harry's brow furrowed in thought. Every so often he glanced at Kirk.

'Supposing, just supposing mind you, I had a mind to sell the stuff off base, why go through you when I could do it myself?'

'For the simple reason you're an American and they stand out like sore thumbs here. You'd have everyone talking about you and what you were doing. I, on the other hand, am a local and I know the trade. I was brought up in a pub and it would be to pubs I'd be selling. Try it on your own and you'd be committing suicide. But with me on the inside, so to speak, there's no reason why we couldn't have a nice profitable little fiddle going without any of the authorities being any the wiser.'

'What sort of cut did you have in mind?' Harry asked.

'Fifty-fifty, straight down the line, as I believe you people say.'

Harry was tempted. But he needed time to think it through.

'I'll need a few days before I can give you an answer,' he said finally.

'Take as long as you need.'

Harry nodded. 'Okay then.'

They turned around and walked back to Harry's car, the door of which Harry opened.

'Aren't you going back upstairs?'

'Naw, I got to get back to the base. I have some paperwork I can't put off any longer.'

63

Harry climbed into the car, rolled down his window and stared straight into Kirk's eyes. 'Are you sure you could make your side of it work?' he asked.

'Absolutely positive,' Kirk replied.

'As much as I could supply you could sell?'

Kirk nodded.

'I'll be in touch through Min,' Harry said, putting the car into gear and driving off.

Kirk took a deep breath. His hands were trembling fractionally as he put them into his pockets.

He'd said he knew what he was doing. He just hoped he did.

Harry took his time about driving back to base. Kirk's proposition had been so unexpected that it had caught him off guard.

There was no doubt about the fact he could use some extra money. His elder boy was in college and the second one wanted to go too after he graduated from high school later in the year. He could manage both but it would be an awfully tight squeeze. And he had to remember it wasn't that long till he'd be leaving the Air Force. He still hadn't decided what he was going to do then but any additional dough he could get together in the meantime couldn't help but come in useful.

Could he trust this Kirk, though? What if the kid turned out to be all mouth or, worse still, tried some sort of double-cross?

But then why *should* the kid try a double-cross? He was the goose who'd be laying the golden eggs and it would be only stupid to try and screw him in any way. And Kirk hadn't struck him as stupid, in fact quite the reverse.

He smiled suddenly. It was a crazy notion, all right. Scotland making the goddamn stuff, selling it to the States, the States in turn sending it back to Scotland, then he, in tow with a Scotsman, selling it back to the Scots.

The idea appealed to him.

'I think the split should be sixty-forty,' Harry said. 'After all, as supplier I'm the one who could really be putting his ass in a sling.'

Kirk shook his head. 'We're both dependent upon one another. You need me just as much as I need you. Equal partnership or nothing.'

Harry pretended to consider that but his mind was already made up. 'Okay, it's a deal,' he said finally.

Kirk stuck out his hand and they shook on it.

'When can I have the first delivery and what sort of quantity will it be?' Kirk asked.

Harry got out a notepad and pencil. He wrote down a figure which he showed to Kirk. 'That's the cost per case to the B.X. Right?'

Kirk nodded.

'So you tell me what you'll be selling it for and we'll go from there.'

They got down to the business of hammering out the details.

The arrangement was Harry would deliver personally every Saturday afternoon, as this time suited them both.

Kirk found and rented a brick-built garage which was so situated it wasn't overlooked. This made it perfect for loading and unloading.

The first delivery consisted of ten cases. It was Harry's idea for them to start relatively small and see how they went from there.

That night Kirk started on the first of the independent pubs he'd decided to approach. Going up to the bar, he asked to see the publican, who turned out to be a Mr Fowler.

'I'm a rep, Mr Fowler,' Kirk said, shaking Fowler's hand. 'Is there somewhere private we can go? I'd like a confidential word.'

'This way,' Fowler replied, and led Kirk through to a back room.

'Now, what can I do for you, lad?' Fowler said.

Kirk opened his briefcase and pulled out a bottle of whisky

which he handed Fowler. 'I'm selling, if you're interested in buying.'

'What? The one bottle?'

Kirk smiled. 'By the case.'

Fowler sat down and regarded Kirk. 'It's knocked off, I take it?' he asked.

Kirk disregarded that. 'This isn't a one-off affair,' he said. 'Give me your order and I'll deliver it weekly.'

'What price?'

Kirk stated the price agreed upon between him and Harry.

'That's more than I normally pay,' Fowler said slowly.

Kirk shrugged. 'But not much more. And think how your business will pick up when it gets around you've got a regular supply of the cratur to sell. Why, I wouldn't be surprised if you doubled your beer profits, and what's a few extra quid against that?'

Fowler considered Kirk's argument. The truth was, he was desperate for more whisky. His customers were always moaning that there wasn't enough for their needs. Like every other publican he did his damndest to get more but inevitably he ended up with his quota and that was that.

'Can you do me five cases a week?' Fowler asked, blinking when Kirk said that was all right.

'Cash on delivery,' Kirk said.

'Fine by me.'

'I'll be round Monday night, then,' Kirk said. 'Delivery straight into the cellar just like any other.'

'I'll be expecting you,' Fowler replied.

Once he'd left the pub Kirk allowed a broad smile to light up his face. One up, one down. If the rest were as easy as that one had been, it would be like knocking ducks off the proverbial pond.

The second pub on his list was several streets away from the first. This one was a great cathedral of a place doing far more trade than the other.

When he emerged yet again into the night it was having taken an order for the second five cases and knowing the

66

publican would take an additional five when he could supply them.

As he strode for the bus to take him home, his swaggering walk was even more pronounced than usual.

He was most pleased with himself.

There was a wee man Kirk knew from the Black Lion Brewery pub his father had run as manager. John, the man's name was, and he owned a van.

The van was old but not so old as to be unreliable, dilapidated but not so dilapidated as to be particularly eye-catching. In other words just perfect; the sort of van seen every day making deliveries and which passers-by would never look at twice.

John was only too delighted to help Kirk out and a bargain was struck between them.

'You can rely on me, Mr Kirk,' John said with a leer and a wink. 'I'll not let you down.'

'We'll drink to that,' Kirk replied and, producing a ten-bob note, told John to away up to the bar and fetch another two pints.

Kirk sat back and watched John getting the order up. It was a good feeling to have other people obsequious to you and so keen to do your bidding. He liked the feeling a lot.

At the end of the first month Kirk was taking delivery of twenty-five cases a week and was supplying five pubs. Outlay was minimal. Just the rent of the garage and paying John for his muscle and the hire of his van.

After the divvy Kirk was already making more than twice what he earned from the import/export firm where he worked, and as far as he was concerned he and Harry had hardly even scratched the surface.

'A wee something extra for the housekeeping, Mum,' Kirk said that Friday night when he handed over what he paid for his keep.

Lizzie's eyes widened. 'Are you sure you can afford it, son?'

'Oh aye.'

Lizzie sat down and counted the money again. 'What are you up to then?' she asked.

He smiled and tapped his nose.

'You wouldn't be doing anything daft, would you?'

'Who, me?'

'Well whatever it is just make sure you take care.'

'Careful's my middle name,' he said, and crossing to her kissed her cheek.

She laughed suddenly. 'Have they made you managing director of that firm you work for?' she asked.

'You mean I forgot to tell you?'

'Get away with you!' she said, playfully punching his shoulder.

'It's just a wee deal I've got going,' he said. 'And as long as it's on, there'll be something in it for you every week.'

Moisture misted her eyes. 'I always knew you'd come up trumps, son. I always said someday you'd make it to the top. Right up there with all the big cheeses.'

'I've a long way to go before I'm that,' he replied, grinning. 'But let's just say I feel I've got my toe on the first rung. Now, do you mind if I get changed? I'm going out with my lassie tonight.'

'I'll lay out a clean shirt for you right away.'

A few minutes later as she was handing the shirt to him she said, 'And when are we going to meet this lassie of yours then?'

'Not this one, Mum. Maybe someday there will be one I'll bring home. But not this one.'

'I understand,' Lizzie said. And she did, perfectly.

While he knotted the new tie he'd treated himself to that day he thought of the night before him.

Judy and Irene were away out which meant he and Minnie would be left alone for a few hours, allowing them to have one of their 'sessions', as Minnie called them.

He was thoroughly enjoying sleeping with Minnie. The only trouble was he was beginning to find her a little hard-going when they had nothing else to do but talk to one another.

If things had been otherwise he would already have been on the lookout for someone else to replace her. But as her mother was being knocked off by Harry, and Harry and he had such a nice little thing going together, he didn't want to tempt fate by upsetting the applecart in any way.

The idea he had then caused him to stop what he was doing and stare at himself in the mirror.

Of course! Why not? With money starting to roll in it was a natural progression. If he could find himself a small flat, or a single-end even, that would give him a great deal more freedom than he now enjoyed. And how was Minnie to know what he was up to when she wasn't there?

The smile that curled his mouth upwards gave him the appearance of a friendly shark.

'Oh, you beast!' he said to his reflection.

Chuckling, he reached for the cologne bottle. He loved smelling nice.

Five months after they'd started, Kirk and Harry were selling a hundred and fifty cases a week to twenty-eight pubs.

Although Kirk had bought himself a small motor and learned to drive he retained the services of John, upping John's wages in accordance with the expansion of the amount of work involved for the man.

He'd also moved into a tiny but luxurious West End flat; an excellent address that pleased him no end.

Early one evening he was in bed with Minnie when there was a knock on the door.

'Who's there?' he called out.

'Harry.'

'Wait a moment.'

He slipped into his dressing gown before admitting Harry. It was the first time Harry had been in the flat.

'I hope you don't mind me barging in but I'd like to have a talk about the Scotch,' Harry said.

Kirk placed a finger over his mouth and gestured with a

69

sideways motion of his head towards the bedroom. Harry got the message.

'Minnie!' Kirk shouted. 'Get yourself dressed and come on out here.'

Kirk poured them both drinks and they talked about this and that till Minnie appeared. Neither she nor her mother, Kirk and Harry having decided it was prudent, knew the two men were doing business together.

'How about some fish suppers?' Kirk suggested, knowing full well that was Minnie's favourite food. Personally he found the meal somewhat vulgar.

'Great!' said Minnie and clapped her hands.

'Look, I've just poured Harry and me drinks so what about you toddling off down and getting them?' Kirk suggested.

'All right.'

He handed her a pound note and then he and Harry had to wait a further few minutes while she shrugged herself into her coat and made sure her hair was in place.

'Anything wrong?' Kirk asked anxiously once Minnie was on her way.

'Far from it. Quite the reverse in fact,' Harry replied.

'Thank God for that,' said Kirk sagging back in his chair. 'So what's this all about?'

'I've been having some correspondence with a couple of friends of mine stationed in England. Men who also run B.X.s. They're both open to an arrangement.'

Excitement surged in Kirk. Excitement that was tinged with a little fear.

'What sort of arrangement?' he asked.

'Well, I've reached a ceiling on what I can ask to be supplied to my B.X. If I was to up the ante any more it would only arouse suspicion.'

'The last thing we want,' Kirk said.

'Right,' Harry agreed. 'But if instead of being supplied by one B.X. you were supplied by three, then it's possible the amount you're currently offloading could be tripled. What do you think about that?'

'Four hundred cases a week!' Kirk said and gulped, his mind reeling at the thought.

'Can you handle it?'

'Yes,' Kirk said promptly.

'Are you sure? I don't want you to make a mistake about this. Rather we make do with what we've got than we blow it and end up in the hoosegow.'

'I can handle it,' Kirk said.

'Okay then. Of course our profit won't be so high on what we get from England. On those consignments it'll be a third each. You, me and the other party.'

'Agreed,' Kirk nodded. 'How do we get their stuff brought up here?'

'You leave that to them and me. Your problem is distribution this end.'

Kirk sipped his drink and thought furiously. John and the van would still be adequate but he was going to need more storage room. Furthermore, with the amount of time that was going to be involved now he would have to give up his job with the export/import firm so that he could distribute and collect cash during the day.

He would tender his notice at the first opportunity. And by God, how he was going to enjoy that! It was going to be marvellous to be rid of that dreary boring job.

Mentally he totted up what his share was going to be out of all this. The figure he arrived at caused his breath to catch in his throat.

He poured more drinks and raised his glass in a toast.

'To the United States Air Force and its most marvellous B.X.s!'

They drank to that and then Harry said, 'And here's to rye and bourbon and the fact that the vast majority of Air Force personnel in this country at the moment are drinking those rather than Scotch.'

'I'm not quite with you,' Kirk said. 'How does that affect us?'

'Because I have a natural in-built ceiling, as I've just told

71

you, beyond which I daren't go without running the risk of questions being asked. Now my ceiling is two hundred cases a week for the base, fifty of which is drunk by the personnel, and a hundred and fifty which comes to you. But if they wanted to consume a hundred cases then I'd have to give it to them, which would only leave us fifty. And so on. Savvy now?'

'I see,' Kirk replied. 'The less they demand the more for us?'

'On the button.'

'To rye and bourbon!' Kirk toasted.

'Amen,' added Harry.

Kirk grunted as he struggled out of bed. He went through to the bathroom and stared at himself in the mirror there.

There was flab on his shoulders and upper arms. The spare tyre round his belly filled both hands when he grasped it. His backside looked like two lopsided haggises filled to bursting. Too much booze and good food was taking its toll. He decided he was going to have to do something about it.

During that week and the next he made inquiries, the Hillhead and Kelvinbridge Sports Club being the one to emerge most highly recommended.

One afternoon he drove round there. He had difficulty at first finding it as it was most discreetly tucked away. He chatted to the club secretary who helped him fill out the necessary application form. When he said he didn't know a member of the club to sponsor him the secretary was only too happy to oblige.

Armed with a temporary membership card, until his proper one came through, he went on a tour of the facilities. The voices he heard were all very well spoken, the men and women they belonged to clean cut and obviously out of the top drawer.

Instantly he felt right at home. This was the sort of place where he belonged and the type of company he should keep.

There was a cool marbled pool which he swam in for half an hour before dressing again and returning to his flat.

He couldn't wait to get back.

EDDY

It was pay night and Frank King was having his usual celebratory bucket. He drained off his pint and then made his way through the press to the bar where he waited patiently till he could catch Sammy McCafferty, the barman's, eye.

'Remember the Boyne!' a drunken voice shouted, causing Frank to frown.

'Death to all Fenians!' another voice added. And a small roar of approval rose to batter the high ceiling.

Frank glanced round to see the knot of Orangemen who'd invaded the pub. All of them wore sashes and looked as though they'd been on the batter since early that day.

It was 12th July, the day the Orangemen took their annual walk. Wearing their sashes and playing their flutes they traversed Glasgow in a defiant show of strength against what they considered to be the Catholic menace.

Out on his coal-round that afternoon, Frank had seen a woman's accordion band, the noise from which had given his usually placid cuddy Damson a fright. And no wonder: the so-called music had been a dreadful din.

Frank slid his empty glass across to Sammy who gave him a fly wink. Sammy was also a left-footer.

'King Billy slew the Fenian crew at the battle o' Benwater ...' the Orangemen sang, banging their feet on the floor while several of them raised their clenched fists aloft. Frank decided it was time he was making tracks for home, which he would do as soon as he'd finished this last pint. He paid Sammy the correct money and then raised the beautifully headed pint to his lips. He was on his first swallow when the elbow dug savagely into his side, causing him to choke and splutter beer.

'What in the fuck do you think you're doing, Jimmy?' the angry voice demanded.

Frank caught his breath before turning to face the man addressing him.

The man was short with extremely broad shoulders and a face that was booze-flushed. His eyes were small and vicious-looking.

'You bumped into me,' Frank said quietly.

'Like fuck I did,' the man retorted, adding, 'You spat at me.'

Suddenly the atmosphere in the pub had changed. There was potential trouble afoot and everyone was aware of it.

'You jabbed me with your elbow, causing me to splutter. That's what happened,' Frank replied.

'Are you calling me a liar, pal?'

'I'm not calling you anything. I'm just telling you what happened.'

The man grunted and peered into Frank's face. He took in Frank's liquid brown eyes topped by a thatch of thick black curly hair. 'A fucking Mick,' he breathed.

The hubbub that had been all around quietened; it was as though the air had suddenly been shot through with electricity.

Frank was in deep trouble and knew it. Out of the corner of his eye he could see the Orangemen inching closer. He stood his ground for the simple reason there was nothing else he could do. The man and the rest of the man's Orange cronies were between him and the door.

'See the likes of you,' the man said and prodded Frank's chest with a stubby finger. 'You're a dirty lot who come over from fucking Ireland to work for cheap wages. You undercut good Protestants and put them out of work, so you do.'

A growl rose from the hovering Orangemen.

Frank kept his mouth shut. To say anything could only exacerbate matters. He reckoned in a man-to-man fight he might well be able to take his opponent, but tough and strong as he was, there was no way he could take on all the Orangemen and possibly win.

'No speaking, eh?' the man snorted, and prodded Frank again.

'There's a streak of yellow through all Micks,' the man added, underlining his point by hawking between Frank's feet.

Frank had been slightly drunk before but he was stone-cold sober now. His eyes flicked round the pub but he saw no help there. Most of the drinkers were studiously looking away, in fact anywhere but in his direction. They didn't want to get involved.

'Okay, break it up, break it up!' a new voice said.

The newcomer wore a black cotton jacket denoting he was someone in authority.

The man turned on the newcomer and snarled, 'This Mick cunt here spat at me.'

'Well that's worth a pint and a half-gill on the house any day,' the manager said, signalling to a barman to put it up.

'I'm still not satisfied,' the man said, still bristling.

'Look do me a favour, Jim, and let it go,' the manager said. 'Any trouble in here and I could lose my licence. You wouldn't do that to me, would you?'

The man instantly backed down a little. It would be a terrible thing to deprive another good Protestant of his living.

'Aye, well then,' the man said and reached for his free pint and whisky.

The manager took Frank by the arm. 'Right, come on you,' he said and hustled Frank toward the door.

Outside in the street the manager whispered, 'I know it wasn't your fault. Sammy told me. But I had to do what I did to get you out in one piece.'

'And I appreciate it,' Frank replied.

'See you another night,' the manager said before turning and bustling back into the pub.

Frank took a deep breath. Then he cursed himself for going into a boozer on Orange night. He should have had more sense. Hurrying down the street he headed for where he could catch a tram home.

To get to the tram stop he had to cut through an alleyway. Half-way up it and surrounded by darkness he became aware of the hurrying feet behind him.

There were five of them headed by the man from the pub.

'So you thought you'd get away with it, did you?' the man said as he swung the first punch.

An arm took Frank round the throat and seconds later his legs were kicked out from under him.

He landed heavily and as he did so the metalled working boots started to rain down on him.

There was a lot of pain until one lashing boot took him behind the ear.

Oblivion was instant.

Josie King was sitting knitting in front of the empty grate when there was a knock at the front door. Her sixteen-year-old son Eddy sat facing her, reading a cheap western novel he'd borrowed from one of his pals at the small repair shipyard where he worked as an apprentice boilermaker.

'I'll get it,' said Josie rising. She thought it was probably one of the neighbours round for a blether.

The two police constables both looked grim. One of them asked if they could come in.

A coldness swept through Eddy as he watched the two policemen enter the room. He dropped his book to the floor and stood up. Josie reckoned she knew what the trouble was. Frank had got drunk and been picked up. It had happened before but not for a couple of years now. He could be a wild man at times, her Frank.

'Mrs King?' the elder policeman asked.

Josie nodded.

'Wife of Francis Connelly King?'

Josie nodded again.

'I'm sorry to have to tell you your husband was in a fight of some sorts. A patrol found him and called an ambulance which took him to hospital. He died before he could get there.'

Numbness enveloped Josie. She couldn't believe what she'd just heard. 'What, do you mean he's dead?' she asked, her voice trembling.

The elder policeman looked at Eddy. 'I think you'd better make your ma a cup of tea, son,' he said. 'Or maybe something stronger if you have it in the house.'

'Oh my God!' said Josie. Tears welled from her eyes to run streaming down her face – a face that had suddenly gone milk white.

When Eddy didn't move the younger policeman went to the sink and ran water into the kettle, which he then put on the cooker.

Josie came apart. A strangled wail of anguish erupted from her mouth. She started to shake all over.

'Who did it?' Eddy asked.

The elder policeman shook his head. 'We've no idea yet. When your father was found he was alone in an alleyway. Whoever his assailant or assailants were, there was no sign of them.'

'You will find them though?' Eddy demanded.

'Oh aye.'

With that promise Eddy moved to comfort his distraught mother. Later she would want to see the body.

Summer dwindled into autumn, which in turn gave way to winter, and still the police failed to come up with anything. It was as though whoever had murdered Frank King had vanished into thin air, leaving the police completely mystified.

At first Eddy believed the promise the policeman had given him. But as time passed he came to realise the cynical view held by many of his Catholic friends was well founded. The reason the police weren't finding his father's killer or killers was for the simple reason they weren't pursuing their inquiries with much vigour.

A bastion of Protestantism, the Glasgow police didn't deem it worth their while, or in their best interests, to hunt down the

79

killer or killers of a Catholic murdered on Orange night. What was one Fenian more or less, after all? Good riddance to bad rubbish, they probably secretly thought.

With Frank dead and buried, Eddy's money wasn't enough to keep the house running so Josie had to hire herself out as a skivvy. She found two families of well-to-do Jews in the West End whom she did for six days a week.

Eddy hated the thought of his mother working but there was nothing else for it if he were to make ends meet. He considered it just as well he was an only child as he didn't know what they would have done had there been children younger than him.

It was unusual for a Catholic couple to have only a single offspring but as Josie had often said, God had only seen fit to smile on her and Frank the once.

Christmas was looming on the horizon when one Saturday, walking down the street, Eddy bumped into Sammy McCafferty.

'How are you then?' Sammy inquired, thinking Eddy looked a lot more grown up since his father's death. Before there had still been some of the boy in Eddy but there was no sign of that now. The boy had become a young man.

Sammy had been to the funeral but hadn't spoken to Eddy at the time. Nor had he seen Eddy since.

'How are the police getting on?' Sammy asked.

Eddy shook his head.

'I told them about that bastard who claimed your da the night it happened. I even called round at the station to tell them when he reappeared but whether they followed it up or not I couldn't say.'

'What bastard?' Eddy asked. This was news to him.

Sammy related to Eddy what had happened on the night of 12th July when Frank King had fallen foul of the Orangeman and his friends. He went on to say the Orangeman had been back into the pub three times now, twice on a Friday night and once on a Saturday.

Eddy considered going to the police and kicking up a stink.

But second thoughts told him he probably wouldn't get very far. Which left the ball in his court.

Of course there was always the possibility the police had spoken with this Orangeman, but somehow he doubted that.

He and Sammy walked a little way in silence. Finally he said. 'If I was to come into your pub the night would you give me the nod should this bloke appear?'

'Aye, sure, Eddy. Only be warned, he's a real mean sod if you're thinking of chiselling him yourself.'

Eddy wasn't at all sure of what he was going to do. He would play it by ear and see what happened.

'Just you give me the nod, Sammy. That's all I ask.'

When they parted on the corner Eddy called out, 'See you opening time, Sammy!'

And Sammy McCafferty waved back.

That night when the manager of Sammy's pub opened the front doors Eddy was one of those waiting to be let in.

He ordered up a pint and then found himself a corner in which to stand. And there he stood without even going to the toilet till closing time when last orders were called. Amongst the first in, he was last out. The Orangeman hadn't showed.

The next Friday and Saturday nights he was back but again had no luck. The following Friday he presented himself yet again. By half past eight his attention had wandered – he was half listening to a football conversation going on behind him – when suddenly Sammy was by his side.

'Him at this end of the bar trying to get a drink,' Sammy whispered out the side of his mouth, at the same time gesturing fractionally with his head.

Eddy sidled closer and took a long hard look at the man he'd come to find. And he didn't like what he saw.

Gloag, for that was the Orangeman's name, was still in his working clothes, having just knocked off. As he drank his pint he thought about the big Coventry Eagle motorbike he'd recently bought. He'd got it cheap as there was a lot of work needed doing on it. But he didn't mind that. He enjoyed working on bikes. He'd have the bike ready for when the good weather came again, Gloag thought. Then he'd take a run down to the coast, Saltcoats or Dunoon maybe. That would be grand.

For half an hour Gloag stood at the bar drinking pints and whiskies, then, turning abruptly, he carved his way through the crowd for the door and the street beyond.

It was bitter cold outside and snowing. Eddy huddled into his overcoat as he hurried after Gloag. He still hadn't made up his mind what he was going to do next.

The tramcar clattered out of the night and Gloag leapt aboard. His heavy boots rang on the metal steps as he ran upstairs. Eddy settled downstairs and bought a ticket for a maximum ride. His eyes were glued to the steps leading to the top deck as the tram rattled on its way.

Gloag got off the tramcar in a part of Glasgow Eddy had never been in before. There was a lot of bomb damage about including a church they passed which had only one wall left standing and, curiously enough, the font.

Gloag walked along a wasteland between two rows of houses. He paused by a snowed-over midden where he had a pee. Still doing up his flies he made his way behind the midden to vanish round the side of a wash-house.

For a moment or two Eddy panicked, thinking he'd lost Gloag. And he would have, too, if it hadn't been for the man's wet, clearly distinguishable footprints leading through a back close. Eddy followed the footprints up two flights of stairs to the door through which they'd disappeared. The name on the side of the door said 'Gloag'.

He now knew the Orangeman's name, which was a start. Standing outside the door he heard the thin cry of a wean from within, which told him Gloag was married with a family, which was something else.

But what should he do next? He went down to the front close where he stood watching the snow fall and thought about it.

★

82

Next morning Gloag woke with gummy eyes and tacky mouth. He thought of his Coventry Eagle which he would soon be working on, and smiled. Beside him his wife Margie snored with her mouth wide open. The teeth on view were without exception rotten.

Without any preliminaries Gloag hiked her nightie up and then rolled on top of her. Grasping her fat waist he savagely thrust into her.

Margie gasped and came awake. She was like sandpaper down there but knew better than to complain. To do so would have earned her a cuff round the chops. She closed her eyes again and tried not to grimace as he squeezed down on her breasts. She thought about the day's housework while he got on with it.

When it was over Gloag sat up in bed and scratched himself.

'Breakfast, woman,' he growled and headed for the sink to wash and shave.

After he'd eaten his bacon, eggs and fried bread he said he was off out. He didn't say where he was going nor did Margie expect to be told. A man's business was his own affair.

Outside in the street Eddy was stiff and cold through. He rubbed his hands and listened to his stomach rumble. He was dead-beat, almost dropping with tiredness having kept watch on Gloag's close all night.

He lit his last fag, more for something to do than anything else. It tasted like old socks in his mouth.

It was still dark, and would be for a good hour yet, when Gloag appeared in his close mouth. He was smiling at the prospect of what lay before him, as he headed up the street.

Eddy followed at a safe distance.

The garage where Gloag kept his motorbike was a ramshackle affair at the back of a stables. There were about a dozen horses kept in the stables which belonged to a local dairy. When Gloag arrived all the horses were out delivering the milk.

Gloag unlocked the garage door and let himself in. As there was no electricity he lit a paraffin lamp which cast a warm

83

friendly glow round its immediate vicinity.

Gloag was taking down his overalls when he became aware there was someone in the doorway watching him. 'Who the hell are you and what do you want?' he demanded harshly.

Eddy stepped forward a pace. Now he was face-to-face with Gloag, the numbing coldness that had seeped into his bones during his long night's virgil began to thaw. 'I've come about Frank King,' he replied.

'Who's he when he's at home?'

'The man you tried to pick a fight with in Chapman's pub last Orange night.'

Gloag's eyes narrowed as did his nostrils. He lifted the paraffin lamp so he could get a better look at Eddy. 'And who's this Frank King to you?' he asked.

'He was my da.'

Gloag smiled; a gruesome leer that lit up his face which, combined with the glow from the lamp, made it like an ogling Halloween lantern.

'The Fenain's brat, is it?' Gloag hissed.

Eddy knew then beyond all doubt Gloag had been in on his father's murder. Despite himself moisture misted his eyes. Anger like a ball of fire burst in his belly but for the moment he was able to keep it contained.

'Did the police ever bother to question you about the murder?' Eddy asked, his voice croaking a little.

'Why should they?'

'Don't play funny fuckers with me, Gloag. I'm telling you.'

'Oh you are, are you?' Gloag replied, laughing, adding contemptuously, 'I'd wait till I was fully grown before I start talking like that, sonny.'

Eddy swallowed hard. 'Were you alone or were there others with you?'

Gloag lit a cigarette which he drew on while studying Eddy. 'Why don't you piss off? You're beginning to annoy me,' he said.

'Why Gloag? Why? He never did you any harm.'

Gloag listened but there were no noises to be heard apart from his own breathing and Eddy's. He knew the pair of them were quite alone.

'Because he was a Catholic cunt and I hate Catholics,' Gloag said and spat. 'If I had my way I'd rid this country of every last one of the dirty swine. The answer to your question, sonny, is that your da got what he did because he was what he was. A dirty stinking Fenian who the world's well rid of.'

Gloag laid the paraffin lamp on the workbench and striding forward very quickly grasped Eddy by the lapels of his coat. He jerked Eddy up till Eddy was dancing on his tiptoes.

'And for two ha'pennies I'd do the same to you except it would spoil the pleasure I've been looking forward to of working on my bike. So why don't you do as you're told and fuck off while you're still in one piece.'

Having said that, Gloag threw Eddy from him. Eddy twisted to fall sprawling across the workbench.

With a contemptuous laugh Gloag turned to gaze lovingly at the Coventry Eagle thereby presenting his back to Eddy. It was the worst, and last, mistake he ever made in his life.

A berserk rage swamped Eddy. The ball of anger became a tidal wave which flooded through him in an instant. His hand closed over a heavy adjustable spanner.

The first blow split the back of Gloag's skull wide open. The second caused a section of bone to penetrate the brain killing Gloag were he stood.

The all-enveloping rage only lasted for a few seconds. When it passed Eddy found himself towering over Gloag's corpse, which lay huddled at his feet. Trembling, Eddy tottered over to the motorbike and sat on its pillion. He didn't have to examine Gloag to know the man was dead. That was blatantly obvious.

He sucked in a few breaths to steady himself while staring in fascination at Gloag's body. After a few seconds he rose and went outside to where he'd noticed a tap before entering the garage. The water was icy cold which was just what he needed.

He splashed handful after handful over his face till he was feeling better. Then he carefully washed the spanner and returned it to the workbench.

It was still very early but being a Saturday morning it wouldn't be long before people were out and about.

He crossed to the other buildings which a quick investigation revealed to be stables. Behind one of the buildings he discovered an evil-smelling pit three-quarters full of horse dung and dirty straw.

Returning to the garage, he grasped Gloag under the arms and dragged him to the side of the pit. Sitting back on his hands he put both feet against Gloag's and pushed.

There was a glopping sound as the corpse made contact with the pit's contents. The feet and legs were the first to disappear from sight, the horrible staring eyes and blood-matted head the last.

Eddy ran some more water from the tap and, using rags he found under the workbench, did his best to clean up the blood that was splashed over the garage floor. What stains remained he covered with oil and grease so that they were indistinguishable from the rest of the general muck and clart. The rags he wrapped round a half brick which then followed Gloag to the bottom of the pit.

Satisfied he'd done everything he could, he rehung Gloag's overalls on the peg where they lived and locked the garage door. This latter he achieved by simply snapping a padlock shut.

He then hurried out into the street and set off back the way he'd come.

Josie was worried stiff when Eddy didn't come home all night. Thinking something had happened to him, she was several times within an ace of going to the police but in the end decided to wait till morning before reporting the matter. It was lucky for Eddy she did.

'Where have you been?' Josie demanded angrily the

moment he let himself into the house. 'I've been out of my mind!'

He was pale and shaken and every few seconds his hands would tremble uncontrollably. 'I killed him,' he said.

Josie was taken aback. 'Killed who, son?' she asked.

'One of those who murdered my da.'

Josie could see from Eddy's face that what he said was true. 'Holy Mary, Mother of God!' she ejaculated, and having crossed herself sat down.

Eddy told his mother the whole story, starting from when he'd bumped into Sammy McCafferty right up to the bit where he'd dumped Gloag in the muck pit.

On completion Josie told him to get out of his clothes. With blood stains on them it was best they were burnt in the grate so they could never be used in evidence.

Eddy stripped down to the skin while Josie looked out a fresh set of togs. While he was putting them on she heaped those he'd just taken off on to the fire where they were soon consumed.

She then insisted he eat breakfast and much to Eddy's astonishment he found himself ravenous.

Over the meal they discussed what he should do. At no point did it cross either of their minds that Eddy should go to the police and meekly confess to what he'd done. That would have been tantamount to suicide. The options open to him were limited and clear. Either he stayed on and tried to bluff it out or he took to the road. He decided on the latter.

Josie packed a small case for him and from a secret place produced two five-pound notes which she made him take. This ten pounds was what she'd managed to save from her skivvying.

At the door she held him close but didn't cry. There would be time enough for that after he'd gone.

He promised to write but she said it was best he didn't for some time in case the police intercepted his letters and learned his whereabouts from them. He admitted she was no doubt right. If still free, he would drop her a note after six months and sign it as a fictitious relative. She could play it by ear from there.

Josie thought her heart would burst as she gave him a last kiss and told him to take care of himself.

On the half-landing he turned to smile and wave. Then he disappeared from view to go clattering down the rest of the stairs. Closing the door Josie went through to kneel before a statue of Our Lady. She prayed long and hard, at the conclusion of which hot scalding tears came.

'This is it,' the driver said with a yawn.

Eddy awoke and stretched as much as the confines of the lorry's cab would allow. He looked out the lorry window and liked what he saw. The surrounding houses were very alien in appearance to him but somehow they gave the impression of being friendly.

'Fulham,' the driver said. 'End of the line for me.'

'Thanks,' said Eddy and got out.

'There's a caf round the corner there if you feel like a wad. I can recommend it.'

Eddy nodded his appreciation and decided a bite was precisely what he needed.

He found the caf where the driver said he would and after a cup of tea and a couple of slices of bread and thinly scraped marg decided he would have a wander round the area.

As he walked he decided this would be an ideal place to settle in digs for a little while. After all, when the police did start looking for him, where better to lose himself than amongst this teeming humanity called London?

At the first newsagent's he stopped and bought a paper, which he anxiously scanned for news of a murder hunt. But there was nothing, which didn't surprise him unduly as it might well be months, if he was lucky, before that pit was dug out and Gloag's body discovered.

On the other hand, the police might well come looking for him sooner than later. When Gloag was reported missing, as was bound to happen in the next few days, some bright spark might well remember what Sammy McCafferty had reported and put two and two together.

A number of postcards were pinned in the newsagent's window advertising various items, one of which was board and lodging. Upon inquiring of a passer-by, Eddy discovered the address to be close at hand.

The woman who opened the door was tall and willowy. Eddy judged her to be in her late twenties or early thirties.

'Yes?' she asked, looking him up and down.

'I'm after digs,' he stated.

'Hmm!' she said. 'You'd better come through, then.'

The kitchen he was ushered into was neat and clean. He sat when she invited him to do so.

'You sound Scotch,' she said, eyeing him up and down yet again.

Eddy squirmed, embarrassed by the close scrutiny. 'Cumbernauld,' he lied, naming a small village outside Glasgow.

He accepted the cigarette she offered him.

'How long would you intend staying?' she asked.

He shrugged. 'That depends.'

'On what?'

'What sort of work I find. Whether I like it. A number of things.'

'So you haven't come down to a job?'

'No,' he said.

He was doing a bit of eyeing himself now. She was a good-looking woman of a finer, more delicate type than had been his experience up to now. The vast majority of Glasgow females might well have hearts of gold but they also had figures, to put it kindly, sufficiently padded to keep out the biting Scottish winter weather.

There was a leanness and breeding about Mrs Grimes which reminded Eddy of a picture of a racehorse he'd once come across in a book.

'Have you run away from home?' she asked suddenly.

Eddy had a winning smile when he cared to use it, which he did now. 'Not at all,' he replied. 'I just fancied coming to the big city. Who knows? After a while I might even go abroad.'

Mrs Grimes digested that. She'd taken an instant liking to this Scottish lad with the marvellous accent. There was something indefinable about him which excited her. Something wild and barbaric that was so utterly refreshing and new.

'There's not all that much work about at the present,' she said. 'Before the war ended there were jobs galore but when the soldiers came home these were all snapped up. Still, I'm sure there's something you can find. Do you have a trade or profession?'

He shook his head.

'So you're unskilled?'

'I'm afraid so.'

'Well you're young enough which'll probably be in your favour.' She paused, waiting for him to volunteer his age but he didn't oblige.

'Do I have digs then?' he asked.

She told him the rent and demanded two weeks in advance. He paid there and then.

En route to his room at the back of the house she said, 'I'll let you have your own key but on no account are you to try and sneak women in. Is that quite clear?'

She smiled inwardly when she saw he was blushing.

During the next four days Eddy tramped the streets of Fulham and nearby Walham Green to no avail. There was no work to be had, or if there was he couldn't find it.

Returning home discouraged, he threw himself on his bed and stared at the ceiling. He was still lying there when there was a tap on the door.

'Come in!'

Mrs Grimes entered, clad in her housecoat. 'How did you get on?' she asked.

He shook his head. 'Not a sausage.'

She looked at him thoughtfully. 'I had an idea this afternoon. Do you like cars?'

'Yes.'

'Can you drive?'

'No,' he replied. 'Although I'd love to learn!'

She smiled at his enthusiasm. 'I have a brother who sells used cars over in Warren Street. He mentioned about a week back he was going to have to look for someone to help him. Think that might appeal?'

'Sounds marvellous,' Eddy said.

'Then we'll go over there first thing tomorrow and see what's what. Mind you, I'm not promising anything. He might well have found somebody in the meantime.'

'I understand perfectly,' Eddy replied, adding, 'It's awful good of you.'

She sat on his bedside chair and crossed her legs, exposing a length of thigh in the process. She seemed blissfully unaware of this, although Eddy certainly wasn't, as she went on, 'The other thing is I need your ration book. I've been feeding you so far from the household rations which are short enough, goodness knows.'

This was an eventuality Eddy had been expecting and was prepared for. Rising from the bed he opened a drawer from which he extracted his book.

'Sorry the front's a bit of a mess,' he said apologetically. 'I spilled a cup of tea over it some time back.'

The name on the front of the book had originally read E.F. King. Eddy had doctored it since his arrival in London to read E.F. Kingsley which was the name he'd given Mrs Grimes.

As he handed the book over he couldn't help but see down the front of her housecoat. She wasn't wearing a bra which meant her small breasts were fully in view.

The breath caught in his throat. He had never seen a woman's breasts in the flesh before. The truth was he was still a virgin.

From the expression on his face Mrs Grimes guessed that to

91

be the case, thinking further that if he had any experience at all it was extremely limited.

'I'd better be getting on then,' she said. Standing she was only a fraction smaller than him.

This close and in such a confined space her personal scent was extraordinarily strong and sent Eddy's head whirling. He would have given anything in the world to be able to reach out and take her in his arms but of course he never dreamed of actually doing so.

'You can call me Annie,' she said, and with one last smile was gone, closing the door behind her.

Heart hammering, Eddy lay back on the bed. He tried to think about the job in Warren Street but instead his mind was filled with thoughts about Mrs Annie Grimes.

That night he slept fitfully, waking a little after midnight having dreamed he was back in the garage killing Gloag. He wiped sweat from his brow and then groped for his cigarettes.

He was half-way through his smoke when he heard the unmistakable patter of feet in the hallway. He knew from their lightness they belonged to Annie. A door softly opened and then just as softly closed again, causing him to frown. All the rooms on this floor belonged to lodgers, with the toilet downstairs where Annie's quarters were.

The room she'd entered was the one next to his and belonged to a Yorkshireman called Crosthwaithe. Besides himself and Crosthwaithe there were three other lodgers, bringing the grand total to five.

For a few minutes there was silence and then a bed began to creak. Soon the creaking changed to a rocking sound. There was no doubt in Eddy's mind what was going on through the wall and it surprised him how affected he was by the knowledge. Why should he be jealous? She was nothing to him, he told himself. But jealous he was.

He thought of Crosthwaithe and Annie making love together and the image conjured up in his mind brought the sweat back to his brow. He stubbed out his cigarette and buried his head beneath his pillow. But that didn't help much. He could still hear the rocking sound.

And then with a final bump it was over and silence reigned once more.

Later she left. The same pitter-patter of her feet on the linoleumed floor.

For what seemed like hours after her departure he tossed and turned before finally sinking into an exhausted and fervered sleep. He dreamed again, only this time Gloag killed him and it was his body the muck pit claimed.

Next morning at breakfast Annie was chirpy and full of beans whereas Eddy was morose and sullen.

Several times he threw baleful glances across the table at Crosthwaithe, whom up till the previous night he'd rather liked. He decided now the Yorkshireman wasn't at all his cup of tea, noticing for the first time several mannerisms of Crosthwaithe's which he found irritating.

After breakfast the other lodgers left immediately for work. He had to wait till Annie washed up.

While she was busy at the sink he sat smoking a cigarette and studying her back-view. He had to stop the latter when the same sweat he'd had the night before reappeared on his brow.

On the bus they had a fight over who would pay the fares. He insisted that as the man he should do so while she argued that was all very well but he was unemployed whereas she was earning an income.

In the end she let him have his way, smiling secretly to herself as he stared huffily out of the window. The more she saw of Eddy the more she liked him. Part of her mind thought of him as a son figure. But only part of it.

Gilbert Crabtree – 'Everybody calls me Gil!' – looked every inch the salesman he was. Exuding charm and confidence and *bonhomie*, he showed Eddy round the showroom after Annie had explained Eddy was looking for a job.

Eddy instantly felt right at home in the showroom. Running

a hand over a highly polished car he said if Gil would have him, he'd love to work there.

Behind the façade Gil Crabtree was an extremely shrewd and capable man. He was also an excellent judge of character. He could tell Eddy was honest and trustworthy, which counted for a great deal in his book. He could also see Eddy had a natural charisma, which was a potential customer winner.

'You start at the bottom. You understand that?' Gil asked.

Eddy nodded, eyes shining in anticipation.

'Thirty bob a week to begin with and we'll see how you go. Deal?' he asked, proffering his hand.

It was considerably more than Eddy had expected. 'Deal,' he replied. And they shook.

'When can you start?'

'Right away if you like.'

Gil laughed and put his arm round Eddy's shoulder. 'You and I are going to get on just fine, kiddo,' he said.

'I'll leave you two to it,' Annie said.

Gil saw her to the door where they stood talking for a few minutes. When she finally swung off down the street Eddy raised his hand in farewell but she never looked in his direction. He found that upsetting but didn't show it.

Eddy enjoyed the next few weeks more than any previous part of his life.

He missed Glasgow dreadfully and doubted if he'd ever get over the loss. In a way he felt the loss of Glasgow even more than that of his da.

But London was different: cheery and exhilarating. His time at work was spent either polishing and cleaning the cars or else answering the telephone when Gil was out.

He wanted to try and deal with some of the customers but Gil said it was too early for that. Selling wasn't as easy as it looked and Eddy would have to learn the art – for art it was, as Eddy soon discovered.

If he was happy during the day he was wretched at night,

however. He'd lie awake listening for the pitter-patter of Annie's feet on the linoleumed floor and all too often he heard it.

He began to hate Crosthwaithe, finding it increasingly difficult even to be civil to the man. He would dearly have loved to give vent to his feelings and punch Crosthwaithe on the nose.

In fact he often imagined that happening; Crosthwaithe lying vanquished on the floor with bloody nose with Annie looking on at him adoringly.

One night when Annie was in his bed and they were sharing a cigarette, having just made love, Crosthwaithe said, 'I don't know what I've done to offend young Eddy but he sure as hell hates my guts for some reason or other.'

This was news to Annie, who hadn't noticed anything untoward between the two.

'When I said hello to him this morning the look he gave me would have sunk a battleship.' Crosthwaithe had been in the Navy during the war and often used naval references and allusions.

'Do you want me to have a word with him?' Annie asked.

'If you don't mind. The bad feeling's getting on my wick.'

'And what a wick it is,' Annie said coarsely. And they both laughed.

She was padding back down the corridor when it suddenly dawned on her what the problem might be. She turned to stare thoughtfully at Eddy's door.

She knew of course that Eddy was daft on her. It was blatantly obvious, the way he looked at her. And she fancied him. The trouble was when Eddy showed up she'd already embarked on a most satisfactory affair with Crosthwaithe.

Perhaps if she shifted the rooms round that might help. On reflection she didn't think so.

She waited till the following Sunday afternoon when Crosthwaithe had gone to a cricket match and the other three lodgers were out, before confronting Eddy in his room.

She found him lying sprawled on the bed reading a western

95

novel. A type of literature she'd come to know he was fond of.

'Sit down, Annie,' he said, a smile lighting up his face.

She came directly to the point. 'What's between you and Crosthwaithe?' she asked. And when he didn't reply, she added, 'I won't have any bad feeling in this house. I can't stand atmospheres.'

He gazed sulkily down at the book in his lap, refusing to meet her gaze.

She smiled to herself, seeing he was wearing his petted-lip expression. When he looked like that he became so boyish she wanted to gather him in her arms and mother him.

'Well?' she demanded.

'I can't,' he mumbled.

'I think maybe it's my fault,' she said. 'It never dawned on me till the other night you might be able to hear.'

He shot her a glance and then looked hurriedly away again. 'Is that it?'

He nodded.

'I thought so.'

Eddy was the picture of abject misery. 'Maybe I should find other digs?' he suggested, although it was obvious from his voice that was the last thing he wanted.

'I don't think it's necessary to go that far,' Annie replied. 'It's awful hearing you two at ... through there.'

'I can imagine.'

At that moment he was despising himself for a weakling. Men didn't behave like this in front of women where he came from. He was acting like a big softie. If his pals at home could have seen him they would have had a right good laugh.

But there was something different about Annie Grimes. Something he'd never seen in any of the women he'd been friendly with in Glasgow. Perhaps it was her age or her Englishness. But he didn't think it was either. It was something, a quality, in the woman herself. A sort of added dimension that kept giving him the feeling she knew something he didn't.

Annie realised she was going to have to make a decision.

And the time to make it was here and now.

'Eddy?'

There was a throatiness in her voice which made him look up instantly.

'Do you want me?'

He couldn't believe his ears. 'Do you mean . . . ?'

'That's precisely what I mean.'

'Oh Annie,' he said, but still didn't move.

She stood up and crossing to the door turned the key in the lock. Then she closed the curtains as the window was overlooked.

Standing by the bed she smiled staring down at him. 'Well?' she asked.

He took her into his arms awkwardly and clumsily, still not able to believe this was actually happening. Their mouths met and when their tongues touched he literally staggered as his legs seemed to turn to jelly.

'Take your clothes off,' she whispered in his ear.

He tore at his pants and shirt while she regarded him with amusement.

'Don't look at me like that,' he said.

'I'm sorry. I didn't mean to.'

'Do you find me funny because I'm so much younger than you?'

'You mustn't take offence,' she replied. 'There's none meant.'

'All right then,' he said. 'But don't laugh at me again. I don't like it.'

'I was smiling not laughing.'

'You know what I mean!' he said.

'I know,' she replied and took off her blouse to reveal she wasn't wearing a bra.

Her skirt slid to the floor to be kicked to one side. She sat to remove her stockings, garter and belt and pants.

Eddy was suddenly embarrassed and shy. The last woman to see him with his clothes off had been his mother and that had been years ago when he was a wee boy.

Annie could tell she'd been right about his lack of experience. 'Have you had many women?' she asked teasingly.

'Oh aye, lots,' he lied.

'I see.'

His eyes devoured her as she moved to the bed. Her personal scent was stinging his nostrils and he suddenly knew what it reminded him of. She smelled just like gin. A peculiar odour but an attractive one.

She could see how nervous he was. His chest was rising and falling while the skin on his upper arms rippled from time to time. His expression was studiedly casual as though this sort of thing happened to him every other day.

She circled his neck with her arm and drew him to her. His hand came up to cup her breasts.

She gasped in astonishment as he leapt on top of her. His hips ground against hers as he desperately, and with no success at all, tried to enter her. She knew then she was his first woman.

'Hold on a minute,' she whispered.

He was panting while sweat slicked down the side of his face and along his nose. He jerked when she took him in her hand to help him.

And then he was off as though it was something that had to be done as quickly as possible and he was out to break the world record.

The way he leapt up and down causing the bed to bang convinced Annie they were going to break it. Talk about being heard in the next room! The way he was carrying on they'd be heard in the next bloody street!

When it was all over Annie said, 'I can honestly say no one has ever made love to me like that before.'

'I thought it was good, too.'

She lifted herself on to one elbow to stare into his face. He looked like a cat who'd fallen into a bowl of cream. 'There's no need to go at it like an express train,' she said.

Instantly his face fell. 'Did I do something wrong?'

98

'Not exactly wrong.' Then teasingly, 'Have none of your other girls ever said anything?'

'No,' he said hesitatingly. Very unsure of himself now.

'Well they should've done. They should have told you to relax and enjoy it more. Draw it out. Make it last.'

He thought about that. 'That's decadent,' he said finally.

She couldn't help the guffaw which erupted out of her. 'You're in a class of your own, Eddy. You're absolutely priceless!' she said.

'Are you laughing at me again?'

'Yes. What are you going to do about it?'

'I could, eh ...'

She laid her hand on his thigh. 'Biff me one, is that it?'

'I never said that.'

'You Scotchies are all so tough. Tartan terrors, all of you,' she said, tongue in cheek.

He liked the image of that. Like most working-class Glasgow men he fancied himself as a hard man.

'I could tell you things that would wipe the smile off your face,' he retorted, thinking of Gloag.

'Then go ahead.'

He shook his head and wouldn't be drawn. That was a secret iron bars wouldn't have prised out of him.

She caressed him, thinking what a magnificent raw animal he was. Nor did she mean that in a derogatory way. He wasn't stupid, far from it. But his mind was still very unformed, amorphous in its lack of experience and sophistication. He thought he knew a lot but in reality he was still a child.

There was also an arrogance about him which was deeply rooted in the Glasgow thing. Annie saw, and was attracted by, the manifestation of this arrogance but was wrong in thinking it a personal trait. The root-cause went far deeper than her understanding of it.

She fingered the small crucifix dangling from his neck. 'Are you a Catholic?' she asked.

He nodded, suddenly wary. 'Why?'

99

'Nothing. I just wondered.'

'Does it make a difference that I am?'

She frowned. 'Why should it?'

'Where I come from it might.'

'You get all sorts round here,' she said. 'All religions and colours of the rainbow. We don't bother too much about it. The rule is if they don't bother you, you don't bother them. Live and let live.'

Eddy sighed. 'Where I come from you can end up dead for kicking with the wrong foot.'

'Kicking with the wrong foot?'

'Catholics with the left and Protestants with the right. It's a saying.'

'You're exaggerating, surely?'

He thought of his da done to death in an alleyway. And for what reason? No other than he'd been a Mick on Orange night.

'No exaggeration,' he said softly.

There was a wistfulness in his voice which reached deep inside to touch her. 'Why don't we try again?' she asked.

The surprised look on his face told her he hadn't thought of a second time.

'Just relax,' she said soothingly. 'Leave it all to me.'

This time the bed was only in half the danger of being broken.

For years now Annie had been sleeping with a succession of her lodgers, having been lucky in as much as there had always been one who'd taken her fancy and vice versa. But this was the first time she'd actually taken up with a new one while the old was still in residence.

That night she told Crosthwaithe to stay behind in the communal sitting room after the others had gone to bed. She wanted to speak to him.

When they were alone she took him through to the kitchen and made a pot of tea. Handing him a cup she said bluntly, 'I'm afraid you're going to have to find another place to stay, Eric.'

Crosthwaithe was flabbergasted. 'What do you mean?'

'What I said. I want you to find another place to live. It's all over between us.'

Crosthwaithe's face twisted into an ugly scowl. He wasn't a man who took kindly to being chucked over.

'Is there someone else?' he demanded.

Annie shrugged. 'That's none of your business.'

'And what if I make it so?'

'There would be no point. It's finished, Eric. Now let it go. I know of a few places round about that are nice and comfortable. I'll put in a good word for you.'

But Crosthwaithe had no intention of letting the matter drop. Reaching out, he grabbed Annie's arm, twisting it so that she cried out.

'That hurt!' she said.

'Where do you get off thinking you can treat me like this?' he demanded. 'Why, you're nothing but a bloody slut!'

Using the open palm of his free hand he cracked her hard several times across the face. On one of her cheeks he left a red-wealed imprint.

'Let me go, you bastard!' she hissed, badly shaken. She'd known he had a temper but had never figured this to happen.

'You heard her,' a new voice called from the doorway. 'Let her go.'

Crosthwaithe turned to find himself staring at Eddy, who was clad only in pyjamas. He barked out a laugh. 'Get lost, kid,' he said.

Eddy closed the door and moved closer to where Annie was struggling in Crosthwaithe's grip. 'I meant what I said. Let her go.'

'Or else what?'

Eddy picked up the bread knife. It was a vicious-looking weapon that had been sharpened so many times it was hooked slightly in the middle of the blade giving it a scimitar-like appearance.

'I'll stick this in you,' Eddy said simply and quietly.

Crosthwaithe laughed again, but this time the laugh died

101

somewhat. There was an expression in Eddy's eyes which told him Eddy meant precisely what he said.

'So *you're* the new one, are you?' Crosthwaithe said in a taunting voice. 'Well, you're only the latest in a long line. And I mean a *long* line. She's anybody's who'll give her the time of day.'

Annie sobbed at that and averted her head.

Eddy desperately fought to keep his rage under control. He'd already murdered one man. The last thing he wanted was to up his tally.

'No wonder you've been giving me such filthy looks of late,' Crosthwaithe went on at Eddy. 'Christ, was I slow! I should have guessed marmalade thighs had been at you.'

Eddy frowned, not understanding the allusion.

A cruel smile stretched Crosthwaithe's mouth. 'Why marmalade?' he asked. 'Because it's a well-known early-morning spread.'

Annie cringed and seemed to shrivel where she stood.

'Pack your bag and go. Tonight. Now,' Eddy said, his grey Glasgow-accented voice thickening when he added, 'or so help me God, you're a dead man. I swear it.'

Crosthwaithe released Annie, who staggered away from him. She stood with her face to the wall and her back to both men.

Eddy gestured with the knife towards the door. 'You've got five minutes,' he said.

Wearing a contemptuous leer Crosthwaithe walked stiff-legged from the kitchen.

'Annie?'

'Not yet. Wait till he's gone.'

'I understand,' Eddy replied.

Tears ran down Annie's now red cheeks to fall splashing to the floor. She looked years older than she normally did.

Eddy stood by the outside door with the knife held ready in his hand. His breath was laboured as though he'd been running. The fire in his belly was like a red-hot cone trying to burrow its way through his flesh.

When Crosthwaithe appeared with a battered suitcase in his hand nearly a quarter of an hour had passed since he'd left the kitchen.

Eddy didn't say anything about that. The important thing was Crosthwaithe was going. He stepped aside to allow Crosthwaithe access to the door. 'One other thing,' he said. 'You bother Annie again after this and I'll come looking for you. And it won't be a knife I'll have. It'll be a brace of razors.'

Crosthwaithe blanched and some of the defiant cockiness oozed out of him.

Eddy went on. 'I'll carve you so badly there's not another woman will ever look at you.'

Crosthwaithe opened the door and walked out into the night.

Back in the kitchen Eddy tried to take Annie in his arms but she'd have none of it. She dabbed her tear-streaked face with a tea-towel. She felt old and horrible and, above all, dirty. If the water had been hot she would have had a bath. As it was she would have to make do with dousing herself with perfume when she went through to her room.

'I'm sorry you had to hear that,' she said.

'The man's a pig.'

She nodded her agreement.

He laid the knife on the table and helped himself to two of her cigarettes. She mumbled her thanks when he pressed one between her cold and colourless lips.

Again he tried to take her in his arms and again she broke away from him.

'Maybe it would be best now if you left as well,' she said.

'I don't want to, Annie.'

'Even after what you heard?'

'Was it true?' he asked.

Her eyes were full of pain. 'Yes,' she whispered in reply.

He drew heavily on his cigarette and then bit his lip. 'It's different now I'm here,' he said after a while.

The ghost of a smile lit up her face. 'You're lovely, Eddy. Truly lovely. Perhaps things might have been different if I'd met you years ago instead of now. But I didn't.'

He said awkwardly. 'I know you're a lot older than me but we can still make a go of it, can't we?'

'There's a lot you don't understand, Eddy. A lot I haven't told you.'

'Then tell me now.'

'No. Tonight isn't the right time. Certainly not the way I'm feeling.'

'Can I come to your room?' he asked.

She came to him and laid her hand on his cheek. 'You really would have killed Eric, wouldn't you?'

'Yes.'

She shivered, then kissed him on the side of the mouth. 'Thank you for being my protector. My knight in shining armour.'

'I'd do anything for you, Annie,' he said – and meant it.

'Not tonight, Eddy. Tomorrow night if you still want me. But not tonight.'

'I'll want you all right.'

'Then I'll come to you.'

'Promise?'

'I promise,' she said.

He felt a tremendous warmth and affection for this woman called Annie Grimes. He'd only known her a short time and yet already he couldn't imagine life without her. It was as though he'd known her always.

He went to sleep alone but smiling.

The following week Gil announced it was high time he learned to drive. After all what damn good was a car salesman who couldn't demonstrate the vehicles!

Eddy was therefore given time off from the showroom to go and apply for a provisional licence, and the night of the day it arrived Gil personally gave him his first lesson.

Eddy found he loved driving. There was a thrill about it he found exciting in the extreme. Furthermore it turned out he was a good driver, having a natural rapport and feel for cars.

104

Gil also started teaching Eddy the administrative side of the business, showing him how to keep the accounts and fill out the various forms that bureaucracy demanded.

At the end of the month Gil was so pleased with the speed of Eddy's progress he increased Eddy's wages to two pounds ten shillings a week. Eddy was naturally delighted, saying he felt like Carnegie with all that loot.

Annie was insistent he save some of it which he did by opening a Post Office book. He considered sending some of it home to Josie but after a great deal of thought decided against that. It had been agreed between him and his ma he wouldn't contact her for six months, so that's the way he'd leave it.

He still hadn't got over the daily fear of having his collar felt at any moment. But as time went by and nothing happened his fear began to die down a little.

He was amazed to discover Annie could drive – he'd never heard of any woman in Glasgow capable of that! – and several weekends Gil lent them a car which they drove out into the country.

On one such occasion Annie took along a picnic which they had to eat in the car as the weather was still cold.

He asked her to tell him about the things she'd promised to tell him the night of Crosthwaithe's departure but she demurred, saying not yet. He was left wondering what deep and dark secrets she had that she was so loath to confide to him.

Every night she came to his room and into bed with him. Most nights they made love but not every night. Sometimes it was sufficient for them to have a cuddle and just be with one another. Several times he asked to come to her room but she always refused. That was her private place, she said. Her sanctuary. Her Holy of Holies.

Once when he was home alone he was tempted to go into her room and have a look around. In the end he decided against it. It would have been betraying her confidence as well as his love for her which daily grew more and more strong.

He firmly believed she loved him in return.

The shock was therefore profound when one night she took him into the kitchen to announce her husband was coming home that Sunday.

He'd known right from the start she was a 'Mrs' of course, but somehow he'd assumed she was divorced or her husband had been killed in the war. There was enough of the latter, by God, war-widows being thick on the ground.

'His name's Toby,' she said. 'And he's an actor.'

'An actor!' Eddy exclaimed. That was the last thing he'd expected. The only actors he knew anything about were those he saw at the pictures, like James Cagney or Errol Flynn. And what chance did he have up against a man like Errol Flynn!

Annie laughed when he mentioned Flynn. 'Toby's not at all like that,' she said. 'He's a theatre actor, which is a different breed entirely. He's about your height, not at all good-looking and certainly not dashing. He plays character parts, which means he's forever having to be an old man or a hunchback or something.'

'And you mean you two are still together?'

'Yes. Although he spends most of his life away in rep while I keep the house running.'

Eddy was mystified. To him, a husband stayed with his wife, or if he absolutely had to go away, like a soldier or a sailor, he wrote or kept in touch or came home at every opportunity, which certainly wasn't the case between Annie and this Toby.

'Tony's hobby is betting on the horses,' Annie explained. 'That's why he only ever does seasons at reps like Cheltenham or Windsor or Wolverhampton where there's a racecourse nearby. Even between seasons he often stays on just to be at the track. If it wasn't for acting, which he's also mad on, I do believe he'd spend twenty-four hours a day there.'

Eddy was angry. She should have told him about all this when they started. Not left it to what was almost the last minute before the husband arrived back.

Anger and resentment churned together. He felt he'd been played for a mug although in his heart of hearts he knew that wasn't so.

106

'How did you meet an actor?' he asked.

'He was in rep in Worcester, where I come from, and where there's a track of course. I had a girlfriend who worked at the theatre, and who invited me to a first-night party. At the party I met Toby, he asked me out, and it all snowballed from there.'

'Did you love him?'

'I wouldn't have married him otherwise.'

Hopefully, 'But you don't any more?'

'I'm afraid I do, Eddy. And I always will.'

He felt dreadful when he heard that. Each word was a spike driven into his brain. 'I see,' he mumbled.

Annie stared into space, a peculiar lopsided smile disfiguring her face. She was seeing the past, reliving old memories.

'At our first anniversary I discovered I was pregnant. We were both overjoyed and decided to establish ourselves in a permanent base. This house was it. We settled in and got it all sorted out and then six months into the pregnancy I lost the baby. Right here in the kitchen.'

'I'm sorry, Annie.'

The lopsided smile grew deeper and even more pronounced. Lines Eddy had never noticed before appeared round her eyes and mouth.

She went on. 'It happened and we got over it. He went into the Army but not before I was pregnant again. I had to write to him telling him I'd lost that one at five months. Eighteen months later, after he'd been home on leave, I got pregnant yet again. I kept that one for twelve weeks before I miscarried. The doctor at the hospital told me I'd never be able to get pregnant again. Which was just as well, I suppose, as it seemed I just couldn't hold on to them.

'When he came back from the war we were both changed. He more than me to begin with, though. The loss of the children coupled with what he'd been through had affected part of his mind. Oh he wasn't crazy or anything like that! He just didn't want to know about sex any more.

'At first I held out hope he would get over it. But he never has. Believe me, I tried everything I could think of, and I'm quite inventive that way when I want to be, but nothing worked. He's utterly and totally impotent.'

There was a long pause during which Eddy stared at Annie and she continued to gaze into space. Finally she went on.

'I wanted to go with him when he went back to acting but he wouldn't have that. He said it wasn't fair on either of us. And I suppose he was right. So now he keeps away for most of the time and I stay on here.'

Eddy didn't know what to say. He couldn't think of any words which seemed adequate.

'I won't sleep with you while he's at home,' she said.

'I understand.'

'Which won't be for long. It never is.'

'I'm glad you told me,' Eddy said. 'All of it, that is. I might have hated him otherwise.'

Annie sent Eddy to bed early after that. She sat for a while alone in the kitchen thinking of the early days with Toby when they'd been happy together.

Then she went to her own bed in the room no man other than her husband was ever allowed to enter.

On the Sunday, Toby appeared, having taken a taxi from the station. He was just in time to join Annie and the lodgers at the communal supper table.

He didn't look much like an actor, Eddy thought. And certainly nothing at all like Errol Flynn! Annie had been right about that.

He had an anonymous sort of face which looked vaguely pale and drawn. He was slim and rather athletic in his movements, with eyes which had a rather brooding quality about them. He alternately smoked and chewed a pipe, or its stem rather. And except at meal-times this pipe was more or less a permanent fixture in his mouth.

After supper, which was a rather subdued affair, Annie and Toby disappeared into her bedroom, leaving Eddy feeling wretchedly alone.

108

He lay on his bed trying to read a western but just couldn't settle to it. He desperately craved Annie's company but that would be denied him at night from now on until Toby went back into rep again. And judging from what Toby had said at supper he had no immediate prospects.

Rather than lie there fretting Eddy decided to go down to the local pub for a drink. So he consequently put on a collar and tie and took himself off.

He enjoyed English boozers, finding them as different as chalk and cheese to their Scottish counterparts. The atmosphere was generally more friendly and relaxed and you could take your ease over a drink without having to worry about very early closing time.

He ordered a pint from a new bird behind the bar. At least she was new since the last time he'd been in which was a few weeks back.

'One for yourself?' he asked.

She smiled and thought about it. 'A half of shandy would be nice,' she said.

He laid the money on the counter.

The pub wasn't too busy so they had a chance to talk. At first she was reluctant to be drawn but using all his charm on her – the same charm Gil was so impressed with when it came to dealing with customers – he soon had her chatting.

Her name was Michelle and she lived nearby. During the day she was a shorthand typist but was doing this evening job in order to save up enough money to buy a car. She softened towards him considerably when he told her he was a used-car salesman and might be able to put something worthwhile at a reasonable price her way.

She offered to buy him a drink in return but he refused. A man should always pay for the drink, he said, muttering into his beer the English had some bloody queer notions about what was proper, right enough.

After a while business picked up and he decided to head for home. He paused by the door to give her a wave and got one in return.

That went a long way to making him feel a lot better.

The next night he returned to the pub and the night after that. During a lull when they were able to talk he asked her if she'd like to come to the pictures with him.

'There's a new Humphrey Bogart movie on,' he said.

'Marvellous,' she replied.

'In here or outside the picture house?' he asked.

'Outside the picture house.'

'When?'

'It'll have to be next Monday night. That's my only night off.'

'Next Monday at seven-fifteen outside the Odeon.'

'It's a date,' she replied. And they both laughed.

She showed up promptly to find him already waiting in the queue. He said it would only be another couple of minutes and they'd be allowed in.

She wore a lot more powder and paint than Annie did. And he couldn't help but think how much younger than Annie she was. He later found out she was eighteen, a few months older than himself.

Although the picture was later hailed as a classic, Eddy remembered little of it. They sat in the back row where the lovers went. And, after holding hands for a few minutes, started to kiss. The kissing went on almost non-stop till the end of the programme.

She lived in a house the exact same type as Annie's. He took her round the back and behind a garden shed.

They kissed some more and then he put his hand on her breast. When he tried to undo her bra she objected, asking him what he thought she was? It was their first time out, after all.

He apologised immediately while cursing inwardly at not being able to go any further. First dates and having to sneak behind garden sheds had never been a problem where Annie was concerned, he thought ruefully. He kissed her one last time and said he'd see her in the pub the next night. When she was indoors he trudged off home.

He found Annie in the kitchen making some cocoa.

'Toby's already in bed,' she said.

He was still excited from his encounter behind the garden shed. Hungrily he eyed Annie, desperately wanting her.

'Would you like a cup?' she asked.

Her gaze flickered from his face to his neck and she frowned. 'You're bleeding,' she said.

'Eh?'

She hurried to his side and touched what she'd thought was a wound. But it wasn't blood that stained her probing finger.

'Lipstick,' she said.

He was thrown into confusion, cursing inwardly for not having had the sense to go to the bathroom first to check for tell-tale marks.

Annie was upset and looked it. Biting her lip she turned away.

'Annie, I ...'

'You don't have to say anything,' she cut in frostily. 'I have no claim on you, after all.'

'You've got it all wrong.'

'Have I?'

He tried to but couldn't meet her gaze when she swung it on to him.

'What's her name? Or don't you know?' she asked. Her voice dripping acid.

'Michelle.'

'Pretty?'

'Not as much as you,' he replied gallantly.

Annie's features settled into an inscrutable mask. 'You weren't able to wait very long, were you?'

He felt like a little boy caught in the biscuit tin. He was flushing and that made him furious with himself.

'I got the impression Toby's going to be home for quite some time,' he mumbled.

'That still shouldn't have made any difference,' she replied softly. 'Even if your assumption was true – which it isn't. I've already told you, he never stays for any length of time and there's no reason to believe this visit will be any different from the others. He always makes out that it'll be ages before he gets work again. Actors are all like that. No matter how good or successful they are they all have this terrible fear they're going to be sitting on their backsides for goodness knows how long if indeed they'll ever be re-employed again. From the work point of view, the acting profession is the most insecure race there is.'

'I didn't know that,' Eddy muttered; then suddenly erupting, 'What difference does it make who I go out with anyway? It's *him* you love, not me!'

'Maybe I was expecting too much,' Annie replied. 'But you're wrong too. You should stop seeing everything as either black or white. It's not. There's a whole spectrum in between.'

Eddy thought he understood what she was saying but he didn't really.

Annie poured two cups of cocoa which she put on a small tray. 'Goodnight then,' she said.

'Goodnight.'

She gave him the briefest of smiles and then left, carrying the cocoa.

He made his own which he couldn't drink because he felt so sick.

'Eddy, have you got a moment?' Toby inquired, smiling behind his belching pipe.

Eddy was just getting ready to leave for the pub. He'd arranged to take Michelle home after she'd finished behind the bar.

'Sure, what can I do for you?' he replied.

'I'm taking Annie to a party in Kensington Sunday night. Actors, directors, angels, that sort of thing.'

'Angels?'

The smile widened. 'People who back plays. They're called angels.'

'Oh!'

'Anyway I was wondering if you'd like to come with us. You might find it amusing.'

Eddy hesitated. 'Did Annie suggest I come?' he asked.

The minutest hint of steel crept into Toby's smile. 'No, it was my idea,' he replied.

Thinking about it, Eddy decided he liked the idea of mixing with theatricals. The prospect was an exciting one. 'I'd love to come,' he said. 'I'll look forward to it.'

'No need to get overdressed. Actors and the like aren't noted for their formality.'

Eddy didn't detect the tinge of mockery in Toby's voice.

He left for the pub in high spirits determined that tonight was the night he was going to make Michelle behind the garden shed. But he was wrong.

'Not here,' she hissed, pulling his hand down from where it had been up her skirt.

'Then where?' he demanded.

'I don't know,' she replied. 'But certainly not outside like this, like some common street woman. You might have a bit of respect.'

'But I do respect you!'

'Well you don't show it when you act like this.'

Eddy boiled over with frustration. 'There must be somewhere we can go. Don't your parents ever go out at night?'

She shook her head in the darkness.

'Fuck it!' he swore.

'That's what you've been trying to do,' she giggled.

Her giggle caused him to laugh, allowing some of the tension to ease out of the situation. He drew her to him. She was incredibly well-built, busty with lots of delightful curves that rarely failed to draw an appreciative ogle from the male customers in the pub. Her flesh had a spongy quality about it so that it gave easily to the touch. Cuddling her was rather like embracing a large soft cushion.

'I like you,' he said.

'I should hope so too when you've just been feeling me tits and had your hand up me knickers,' she retorted.

He laughed again.

'I wish you had more nights off,' he said.

'You and me both.'

'Pictures again on Monday?'

'Unless you can think of something you'd rather do?'

He chuckled. 'Oh I can think of something I'd rather do, all right. It's finding the place to do it.'

'You're sex mad,' she teased.

'If I'm mad it's from the lack of it.'

'Go on, I bet you say that to all the girls.'

'Only the pretty ones,' he replied.

'Flattery will get you everywhere. But not here.'

'I'll think of something,' he said. But for the moment anyway it certainly seemed an insoluble problem.

He explained then he wouldn't be in the pub Friday night as he was going to a party with his landlord and landlady.

When he told her the 'do' was in Kensington she made a remark about his going up in the world now he was mixing with the toffs.

He kissed her one last time on her doorstep, leaving her squealing with indignation as he had a final quick feel of her bum.

The block of flats where the party was being held was very grand. There was a doorman and a reception desk, both of which impressed Eddy no end.

He was dressed in the suit he'd bought for the showroom, which Annie had assured him was the right thing to wear. He was a bit mystified by that, not seeing how a suit could be classed as informal. But then he'd never heard – as Toby had so rightly guessed – of black tie.

'Darlings!' spouted a stunningly good-looking lady who was introduced to Eddy as Milly Tilson their hostess. He was later told she was a well-known West-End actress.

Eddy tried not to gape at the furnishings and decorations. He'd never been so close to anything so splendid. He kept thinking it must be something like this inside Buckingham Palace.

Annie's apprehension as she watched Eddy's reactions was coupled with concern. Although nothing had been said she knew Toby had cottoned on to the fact Eddy was, or had been, her latest lover. She also knew Toby was setting Eddy up in the hope Eddy would make a fool of himself. It was Toby's revenge for Eddy's being able to do what he couldn't.

In different circumstances she would have warned Eddy and possibly persuaded him not to come. But she was still hurt and smarting over the fact Eddy had so quickly gone and found himself another woman.

One part of her wanted Eddy to fall into Toby's trap. Another part of her didn't.

For what she realised about Eddy, which few other people did, was how sensitive he was. Behind the hard Scottish exterior there was a quite different person to the outward portrayal.

'Darling, wasn't it absolutely divine! I thought I would corpse rigid when the old roué whispered that in passing.'

Eddy wondered what a roué was and why did they call one another darling all the time? And by God if there wasn't two pansies over in the corner actually holding hands! He tried, but couldn't take his eyes off them till they moved away and were lost to his view.

He stood by an oaken sideboard and stared at it in open admiration. It was beautiful and must have cost the absolute earth. His mother loved good wood and in a flight of fancy he imagined turning up on her doorstep with this very sideboard as a present.

'Are you in antiques?' a voice beside him asked.

He turned to find himself staring at an extremely distinguished-looking elderly gentleman.

'Not me.' Eddy replied. 'I deal in used cars.'

'But you obviously have an eye for beauty.'

Across the room Eddy could see Annie staring at him. 'I know what I like,' he replied.

The man regarded Eddy quizzically. 'It's a Glasgow accent, isn't it?' he asked.

Eddy was suddenly wary. 'A little place just outside,' he replied.

'One of the most difficult accents for an English actor to do, you know, especially southern English. The voice placing is so different.'

'Is that so?' Eddy said, wondering what in hell a voice placing was. 'I take it you're an actor, then?'

'That's correct.'

'I'm afraid I don't know much about the theatre. Films are about my limit.'

'Nothing wrong with films,' the man said; then, glancing round, 'although I'm sure there are many of my colleagues who wouldn't agree.'

'Snobs, eh?'

The man chuckled. 'Precisely.'

'It's all entertainment surely, whether it's Shakespeare or the Keystone Kops?'

The man regarded Eddy with new interest. 'Wisely put, if I may say so. Have you ever seen any Shakespeare?'

Eddy laughed. 'Christ, no. But I have been to the theatre once.'

'Ah! And what did you see?'

'Harry Lauder. He was very good.'

For a moment or two the man wasn't sure whether or not Eddy was pulling his leg. But the straight face Eddy kept finally convinced him he wasn't.

'Harry Lauder's what we call variety. Have you ever seen a straight play?'

Eddy shook his head. 'Where I come from people want a good laugh not culture.'

'But you can get a good laugh as you call it from a straight play. A comedy play, that is.'

'I'm sure you're right,' Eddy said politely.

The man looked thoughtful. 'Why don't you come to the theatre next week as my guest?' he asked finally. 'You can bring a partner if you like.'

Eddy was taken aback. 'That's very kind of you,' he replied.
'I think I'd like that. Is it Shakespeare?'

'No, a comedy.'

'Better still.'

'What's your name?'

Eddy became wary again. 'Why?'

'So I can leave tickets for you at the box office.'

'Oh! Eddy Kingsley.'

'Fine,' said the man, noting the name in a small black
pocketbook he'd produced.

'Can you make it tomorrow? Monday's the only night my
girlfriend get's off.'

'Tomorrow it shall be,' the man said.

They both looked round as Toby joined them.

'Everything all right?' Toby asked.

'Would you believe this fella's never seen a play in the
theatre? Extraordinary!' the man said. 'Coming as my guest
tomorrow night.'

'Well, well, well,' Toby said, lost for words.

'And come round after for a drink, dear boy,' the man said.
'I'll tell the stage doorkeeper to let you through.'

And with that the man was off to talk to someone else at the
other end of the room.

'Nice old duffer that,' said Eddy.

Toby rolled his eyes heavenwards. 'That "old duffer", as
you call him, happens to be one of the most important
respected actors in British theatre.' And he went on to name a
name even Eddy had heard of.

'Bloody hell!' exclaimed Eddy; then, remembering the man
had been to Hollywood before the war to make several
pictures, 'I wonder if he knows Errol Flynn.'

Toby stood, looking totally baffled.

The play was by Noel Coward and Eddy didn't think much of
it, probably due to the fact it was set against a social
background he knew nothing about.

117

Michelle thought the play marvellous, however, and sat enraptured for the duration, eyes wide, drinking everything in.

As promised, the stage doorkeeper was expecting them and gave them explicit instructions how to get to number one dressing room.

'Dear boy, I'm so glad you could make it!' the knighted actor said. He had already changed out of his stage costume and was now wearing a magnificent gold robe over his own clothes.

'Do help yourself to champagne while I take my slap off.'

Slap, it transpired, was his make-up.

Eddy felt it only right he said he enjoyed himself. But if there was any reticence in his praise it was more than made up for by Michelle, who fairly gushed compliments.

There was a second glass of champagne to follow the first and then the knight was ready to leave.

At that moment there was a knock on the door and the stage doorkeeper handed in a note.

'Dash!' said the knight, having read it. 'I've been let down.'

'Anything I can do to help?' Eddy asked.

The knight considered that. 'Yes, there is,' he said, having come to a decision. 'I was supposed to be taking several friends out to supper and now they can't make it. And as I was looking forward to it and the table's already booked, how about you two joining me in my other friends' stead?'

Michelle gasped.

'Oh we couldn't!' Eddy said.

'Why not?'

'Well, eh ...'

'Have you anything else planned?'

'No, we haven't,' said Michelle quickly.

'Then supper it is,' the knight said. 'And I'll brook no further argument.'

All the way to the restaurant Michelle beamed fit to burst.

The Ivy wasn't far away and was, the knight confided to them, a great haunt for actors.

Having been shown to a table, the knight ordered a bottle of French wine which he said he hoped they would enjoy.

Eddy gazed around, the same open admiration stamped all over his face as had been there when the knight had caught him staring at the sideboard. This sort of lifestyle was about as far removed from what he'd been brought up to in Glasgow as the Gorbals is from the moon. The tablecloths were crisp white linen, the cutlery heavy silver. Everything screamed taste and quality and money.

He was suddenly aware how cheap his suit looked compared to the one worn by the knight. A discreet glance confirmed the rest of the male diners were as well and expensively attired as the knight.

And as for Michelle! Alongside the ladies present she appeared coarse and vulgar. She was wearing far too much make-up and her dress looked positively gaudy. But the worst thing was when she laughed. He'd never noticed her laugh being particularly different before but now he could hear it was more of a strident cackle than a laugh. He hoped and prayed it was just his imagination that several of those diners closest to them had glanced disapprovingly their way.

He wouldn't have felt like this if it had been Annie he'd come with, he thought. She had class and would have been right at home here.

The wine when it arrived was delicious, an absolute delight on the palate, as were the fish he had for starters and the beef he had to follow. The pudding was a caramel and gâteau concoction and absolutely out of this world.

At the end of the meal Eddy felt like someone who'd just spent an hour and a half in fairyland.

If he thought he and Michelle were out of place it certainly didn't seem to bother the knight, who maintained a steady flow of sharp and witty conversation.

For a while the knight quizzed Eddy about Glasgow and its people, saying that the two times he'd played Glasgow he'd died the death.

'And such antagonism everywhere you go,' the knight said.

119

'You can almost feel it crackle in the air like an electrical force. Antagonism and violence.'

'The antagonism was probably because you're English,' Eddy said; then quite simply, 'they hate the English.'

'Even yet?' the knight asked wonderingly.

'Even yet.'

The knight shook his head in amazement.

'And they'd hate you even more because you're upper-class English,' Eddy added.

The knight chuckled. 'If only they knew.'

'What do you mean?'

'I was born and bred in Stepney,' the actor said.

'Never!' Michelle exclaimed. 'You don't arf talk posh now.'

The knight smiled enigmatically. 'Marvellous institution, the theatre. You can be anything you want in it. A king, a prince, a knight of the realm.'

'But you *are* a knight of the realm,' Eddy said.

The smile deepened. 'That's what is so particularly nice about the theatre. Sometimes the fantasy becomes reality.' His eyes twinkled. 'But it all started in Stepney and I never allow myself to forget that.'

For the first time in his life it consciously came home to Eddy that just because you had been born in the slums didn't mean that had to be your lot for life. There were ways and means of self-advancement. What the knight had just told them proved that.

He weighed the silver knife and fork in his hand and stared appreciatively at the crisp linen table cover. The food he was eating and the wine he was drinking were far superior to any he'd ever eaten or drunk before.

Yes, he decided. He could get to like this way of life. He could get to like it a lot.

After the meal the knight drove them home in his Rolls which had been parked close by the restaurant.

Eddy and Michelle were profuse in their thanks. The knight replied saying the pleasure had been all his.

After the Ivy the last thing Eddy wanted was a quick grope

and cuddle behind the garden shed so he said goodbye to Michelle on her doorstep. She reminded him about the promise he'd made her the night they met about his getting her a car. He said he hadn't forgotten and was merely waiting for the right sort of vehicle to show up.

As he walked slowly back to the Grimes' house he thought again how out of place Michelle had looked in the Ivy. Like a lump of coarse clay set against best Dresden.

His trouble was, he concluded, Annie had spoiled him. And he cursed himself for being so stupid and hasty in taking up with Michelle when he could have had Annie back in his bed again if he'd only had the patience to bide his time.

The trouble was, and what had motivated him to take out Michelle in the first place, he loved Annie but she loved her husband.

How could he ever have made love to her again knowing she loved somebody else? That he was merely a sex substitute for Toby who couldn't do it any more?

Feeling miserable as sin he went to bed, where it was a long time before he fell asleep. Going to bed miserable and having difficulty getting to sleep was becoming a habit with him.

A few days later Toby announced he and Annie were going to spend the weekend with his parents.

Eddy was half way to work before it dawned on him that meant he would be able to bring Michelle back to his bedroom, which he naturally hadn't been able to do with Annie in residence.

That very afternoon they got a car in which he knew was exactly what Michelle was looking for. He spoke to Gil about the price and Gil said he would be happy to let Michelle have it for what he'd paid for it with only a few nicker on top to cover overheads.

He kept the car at work till Friday when after knocking-off time he got Gil to drive it round to Michelle's pub, where Gil parked it outside the front door.

He had to make his own supper that evening, as had the

other lodgers, Toby and Annie having caught a late-afternoon train.

After supper he went out and bought a bottle of whisky which he placed by his bedside along with two glasses and a jug of water.

Humming, he set off for the pub. With access for the pair of them to his bedroom and a car to hand over to Michelle, tonight couldn't help but be the long-awaited night!

He kept the news of the car secret till closing time when he announced to Michelle that he had a surprise for her. When she was cleared from her duties he took her outside where he handed her the keys and logbook.

'Yours,' he said indicating the car with a flourish.

Michelle squealed with delight, squealing again when he told her the price, which was well within the limit she'd allowed him.

'Oh Eddy!' she said throwing her arms round his neck. Her kiss was one of excitement rather than passion.

'Let's go for a little drive,' she said, having settled herself in the driver's seat.

But he had other plans. 'You can drive us round to my place. I have another surprise for you there.'

'Another surprise?'

'A big one,' he said and smiled.

En route he told her about Annie and Toby's being away for the weekend.

Once they were in the bedroom he closed and locked the door.

'Are you sure no one will disturb us?' she asked.

'I'm positive.'

She came into his arms, shivering a little as his hands cupped her backside.

'Let's get stripped,' she whispered.

He was only too happy to agree.

Naked, she was a magnificent female animal. A cat who stretched out lazily on his bed before beckoning to him.

The weeks of pent-up sexual frustration welled up within him.

'I see what you mean about it being a big surprise,' she joked.

He lay down beside her and soon joking was the furthest thing from both their minds.

He came back to sit on his bed having seen her out to the car. He poured a large whisky which he knocked back in one. Then he poured himself another.

It hadn't been a success. Not that anything exactly had gone wrong. It hadn't.

For him it had just been nowhere near as good as it was with Annie. More of a base metal experience than the gold making love with Annie was.

In bed as well as out, Annie had that indefinable something which put her in a far different and higher league to the one Michelle was in.

He drank more whisky and lit a cigarette. He thought how strange the house seemed without Annie in it. Lacking her presence it was as though the house was a dead thing, a mere shell, empty and lifeless, waiting forlornly for her return.

He lay back on the bed, which now smelled of Michelle. How often that self-same bed had smelled of Annie and how he had taken for granted that which had been something extraordinarily worthwhile in his life.

He didn't realise it but he was going through the painful process of mentally growing up.

Annie Grimes was his catalyst.

A few weeks after the visit to his parents, Toby secured himself another job in rep. He left almost immediately, having said he would he gone for at least six months.

With Toby's departure Eddy hoped things between him and Annie might go back to what they had been before. But she would have none of it.

123

His great fear, in fact it made him sick just thinking about it, was she'd take another lover from the ranks of the other lodgers. But much to his relief she didn't.

He'd dropped Michelle as soon as she'd paid for the car and now stayed home most nights reading. His tastes in that department had begun to widen and he found himself ploughing through writers of the calibre of Thomas Mann and James Joyce. True, he didn't understand an awful lot of what they said but he persevered and as time passed more and more began to sink in.

During this period Annie was friendly enough towards him but that was as far as it went. There were no nightly visitations although once he lost control of himself to actually plead with her.

'I don't think it would be for the best,' she'd replied firmly. And that was that.

He'd been left feeling extremely embarrassed and hating himself for having pleaded with her.

Then one evening he'd come rushing home with the news he'd passed his driving test at the second attempt. He was quite beside himself with excitement, and on finding her in the kitchen swept her off her feet and whirled her round.

'I've passed my driving test!' he exclaimed and then whooped like a Red Indian.

'Oh Eddy, I'm so pleased for you!'

'Isn't it bloody marvellous?'

Setting her down again he did a funny little jig to the accompaniment of a strangulated vocalisation which was supposed to sound like bagpipes.

Annie laughed. 'You're daft as a brush,' she said.

'We must celebrate. Will you come out with me for a drink?'

'Depends which pub you have in mind.'

He recognised that for what it was: a dig at his relationship with Michelle.

'That was all over ages ago, Annie. I swear.'

'So you say.'

'I give you my word.'

'All right. Accepted.'

He took hold of her hand. 'Michelle was merely a reaction against you having told me you still loved Toby. That went deep, very deep.' He paused before continuing. 'Anyway, aren't you being just a little bit selfish about all this?'

'How do you mean?'

'You love Toby but you wanted me as well. When Toby came back I was supposed to sit meekly on the sidelines while you took up with him where you left off.'

'Hardly "taking up" when there's no sex involved!' she exclaimed.

'Well I for one certainly wouldn't agree with that. You both love one another so whether there's sex or not it's taking up again as far as I'm concerned.'

She bit her lip and frowned.

Eddy continued, 'And when I react by going out with someone else you pull the rug from under my feet as if I was the one who'd promised to love and cherish you till death us do part.'

'Did you sleep with Michelle?' Annie asked.

'Yes.'

'So there you are! You betrayed me, us.'

'Did you sleep with Toby?'

The frown returned to her face. 'We were in the same bed together, that's all.'

'Then answer me this. If he was still capable of getting it up, would you have had it off with him?'

'That's hypothetical ...'

'Would you have had it off with him, Annie?'

She looked at the floor. Then nodded.

'So the only reason you didn't betray me was because it wasn't possible to do so. How then can you justify your attitude towards me?'

When she looked up at him there was new respect in her eyes. This was a far more mature Eddy than the one she'd known to date. She began to appreciate just how traumatic an experience her disclosure that she was still in love with Toby,

125

and their consequent break-up, had been to him.

Eddy had only reacted in the way any red-blooded man would have done. And in the light of what had just been said, if there was a villain in the piece, wasn't it her?

'I think we should go and have that drink,' she said.

He knew then he'd won her back. Furthermore he'd come out of all this a far stronger and more knowledgeable person than he'd been before, which pleased him greatly.

Later they returned to the house and went straight to his bed where she remained all night.

Their lovemaking wasn't quite the same as it had been before, the subtle difference making it even better.

For the first time Eddy felt he was the more dominant one. He liked that. He liked it a lot. A man should be on top.

And when next morning going to work he thought of the *double entendre* contained in that last bit, he laughed long and loud.

Six months to the day he'd fled Glasgow, he wrote home to his mother. In his letter he pretended to be a relative who'd just heard his father had died and was writing to tend his condolences.

Josie's reply came by return of post.

First of all she was desperately relieved to hear from him and know he was all right. With regard to the Gloag matter, whatever inquiry there had been, if there had been one at all, certainly hadn't involved the police questioning her. Nor had there been anything in the papers. To the neighbours and the yard where he'd worked she'd said he'd had a sudden opportunity in Canada which he'd had to take up on the spot otherwise he would have missed it.

This explanation of Eddy's overnight departure had been accepted without undue comment, Glaswegians having a long tradition for grabbing opportunities whenever and wherever they arose.

Eddy read his mother's letter through several times and then sat back to think about it. It seemed to him more or less

126

certain that Gloag's body hadn't yet been discovered. For it if had there would surely have been something about it in the papers.

This was excellent news as far as he was concerned. The longer that body remained in the muck pit the less likelihood the police would tie it in with him.

Of course he wasn't in the clear yet. Far from it. But he could now afford to entertain a lot more hope than he would have dared up to now.

From then on in he kept in constant correspondence with Josie, both of them having agreed it was best he remain in London for the present just to be on the safe side.

During the next eighteen months Eddy learned all Gil could teach him about selling cars. His earnings rose considerably, allowing him to send money home to Josie every week, which was just as well as she had to give up work due to failing health.

His relationship with Annie settled into a regular pattern. She slept with him most nights, the exception being when Toby returned from rep as he did four times during the eighteen months.

He and Toby even came to like and respect one another. And he got the definite feeling, although he never asked Annie if he was right, that Toby approved of him as Annie's lover.

He desperately loved Annie but was reconciled to the fact she would never fully be his woman. The reconciliation had been a hard one but he'd managed it in the end.

Then one day when he returned home from work there was a letter waiting for him from Josie telling him if he ever received it it meant she was dead.

Practical as ever, Josie had arranged for a neighbour to hold on to the letter with instructions to send it at the appropriate time.

The letter was addressed to Mr Kingsley so the neighbour didn't know it was going to Eddy.

Eddy was deeply upset to hear of his mother's death. Although he'd known her health was bad enough to stop her working, he hadn't realised her condition might be terminal. Thinking about it in the past he'd imagined her to have ten or fifteen years left to her at least.

This meant he would have to make a trip back to Glasgow. Josie would need burying and, as her only surviving relative, the task naturally fell to him.

He ate a hurried supper while Annie packed his case. Then together they went to Euston where he bought a ticket on a sleeper.

It was a brief parting and an unemotional one as he only intended being gone a few days.

They kissed and she told him to take care. He didn't even bother to watch her while she walked back along the length of the platform.

He was already asleep when the train pulled out. When he awoke he was back in Scotland.

It was like slipping into a much-loved old garment which had been misplaced and then refound. Or meeting an old friend whom you hadn't seen for a long time.

Slowly he drew in a deep breath. Dirt, soot, salt air and a dozen other things which combined to give Glasgow its distinctive smell filled his nostrils.

An enormous love and warmth for this place, this horrible dirty city straddling the Clyde, swept through him.

A lump rose in his throat. Time and Annie Grimes had combined to make him forget how much he missed Glasgow. But now he was back it was all too apparent to him. This was his true home and no matter where he was forced to roam or had to go, this was where he really belonged.

He caught a taxi which took him back to the grey lowering tenement he'd been born in.

The next-door neighbour – the same one who'd sent the letter to him without realising it was him she was sending it to – had the keys of the house and was also able to tell him Josie's body had been taken off to the city mortuary.

At the mortuary he told them he'd be having Josie buried

privately and they were good enough to recommend an undertaker. He therefore duly went on to the undertaker's where it was arranged the burial would take place two days thence, from the funeral parlour.

She was to be laid to rest beside his father as she would've wanted to be.

He returned back to the house after that, from where he put it about to the neighbours that he'd returned home from Canada because of his mother's failing health and it had been a shock on arrival to learn he was too late and she was already dead.

That afternoon he returned to the city centre to attend to a few matters relating to the forthcoming funeral. After which he felt he'd well and truly earned a drink.

The boozer he chose was a little one just off Argyle Street.

'Pint of bitter,' he said to the man behind the bar, making the mistake because his mind was on other things.

'We call it heavy here, Jim,' the barman retorted.

Eddy smiled. 'Oh aye, of course. Sorry, I've been away.'

'Just come back, then?

Eddy nodded.

'You'll be pleased to be home?'

He sipped his pint appreciatively. 'I never realised how much I'd missed the place till I got off the train this morning. That was when it hit me.'

'I was away from Glasgow for four years at one point during the war. Fighting the Jerries was nothing. It was the homesickness that got me. The day I arrived back I swore I'd never leave again and I never have and I never will.'

Eddy raised his glass. 'To Glasgow!' he toasted.

The barman smiled and a loving expression appeared on his face. 'You'll not find a better place anywhere, pal. I tell you.'

Eddy drank to that.

The morning after the funeral Eddy received a letter from Annie. In it she said she thought it best their relationship be ended and this seemed an ideal opportunity for a clean break to be made. She went on to say how fond she'd become of him and that their two years together would be something she'd remember for the rest of her life.

But it was because she'd been so selfish to him in the past that she was trying not to be now. As she'd made clear all along, she was Toby's woman and always would be. She couldn't expect him to continue playing second fiddle with no hope of becoming number one in her life.

With the break he'd be free to find his own woman who would love him the way she loved Toby. And she fervently hoped and prayed he'd find that woman soon.

As for her, the last two years had been most therapeutic and it was directly thanks to him this was so. She only hoped she'd given him as much as he'd given her.

She'd come to accept the fact of Toby's impotence and that she wouldn't have any children. From now on she would travel with Toby round the reps, the pair of them living together on a full-time basis as man and wife.

Eddy was her last affair. Perhaps with them back together again Toby might regain his sexual potency; if not, she'd do without. But that there would be no more men outside the marriage bed she was certain. Her mind was fully made up on that.

In the last paragraph, she wished him all the luck in the world for the future.

He read the letter through twice, then folded it carefully and put it in his wallet.

In his heart he knew what Annie said was right. Things couldn't have gone on for ever as they had. This way was best.

Best, but not easy.

For a while he sat in darkness crying his eyes out. When he'd brought the crying under control he washed his face. Then he went into town to the pub with the friendly barman where he got drunker than he'd ever been in his life before.

He'd been home a week before he managed to screw up the

courage to do what he had to. Namely return to the scene of the crime.

He caught the same tramcar out to the stop where Gloag and he had alighted and there got off. He then retraced his steps to Gloag's house, having trouble doing so as much of the area had been earlier rebuilt or was in the process of being so.

He recalled then the extensive bomb damage he'd noticed the night he'd followed the Orangeman home. It seemed since his last visit the majority of the damage had been cleared and a large rebuilding programme got under way.

He came up short when he came to where the dairy and ramshackle garage had been.

For a moment or two he thought he'd come to the wrong place but a quick recheck convinced him he hadn't. The dairy and garage had fallen victim to the planners. They were now gone and in their place stood a long line of brand new shops.

As best as he could work out, and his calculations were very rough indeed, where the muck pit had been was now underneath the back of a fruiterer and greengrocer's.

Eddy just didn't know what to make of it. Surely some sort of foundations had been laid down in which case the muck pit must have been dug up? Or had it been filled in?

Well whatever had happened, Gloag's body hadn't been discovered. Or if it had and had further been identified then no suspicion had fallen on him.

He ran a hand over his face and then lit a cigarette. The weight that had just been taken from his shoulders was an enormous one.

He'd got away with it. Of that he was absolutely certain.

There was now no reason why he couldn't remain in Glasgow. He wasn't only home. He was home to stay.

He'd managed to save quite a bit from his job with Gil and this he now put to use. He scoured various parts of the city until he found what he wanted. A centrally situated lot that would be ideal to sell used cars from.

131

He then went to the motor market and bought six cars all at excellent prices.

He was now in business for himself.

It was in his third week of trading that a rather posh-looking bloke with a plummy voice asked if he thought he could get hold of a particular Alfa Romeo which the bloke wanted.

Now Eddy didn't think there would be many Alfa Romeos knocking around Glasgow, which was obviously why the bloke was having difficulty getting hold of one, but London was a different kettle of fish entirely. He was pretty certain he knew where in London he could lay his hands on the particular Alfa the bloke was after. What he would do would be to get Gil to buy it and send it up by train, for which trouble Gil would receive part of the profit.

'I think I can get the car you want but it'll take me at least forty-eight hours to verify it,' Eddy said.

'Fine,' the bloke replied. 'When you know you can contact me here.'

He handed Eddy a card upon which various details were printed.

The name above the address was Kirk Murray.

KEITH AND JEAN

THE YEAR 1911

Keith Gibb was just dozing off when the first shot banged out. Sitting up in bed he rubbed his eyes, wondering if he'd fallen asleep without realising it and had dreamed the shot. Then the second one boomed and he knew it had been no dream or figment of his imagination.

Long and lean he slipped from beneath the covers and hurriedly shrugged himself into his dressing gown. The thought uppermost in his mind was that burglars must have broken in and father was taking pot shots at them with one of the several shotguns the family owned.

Snatching up a spike-ended shooting stick and carrying it like a sword, he ran from the bedroom. At the head of the stairs he met Ferguson the butler, who was incongruously clad in his black jacket hastily thrown over thick flannel pyjamas. Ferguson was out of breath, having just come galloping up the stairs.

'I think the shots came from Master Gerald's old room,' Ferguson gasped, his chest heaving like some ancient bellows.

'Right then,' Keith replied, grasping the shooting stick even tighter. 'Let's take a look then.'

Slowly Keith stalked forward, with Ferguson following a few paces behind. The lights were already on.

At what had been Gerald's room he stopped and placed his ear against the door. There was no sound from within. Gripping the door handle he counted to three, then threw the door wide open. Flicking on the light switch he strode forward with the shooting stick held waist high before him.

A quick check of the various cupboards and under the bed revealed the room to be quite empty.

'Well it sounded like it came from here,' Ferguson said.

Keith grunted. His parents' bedroom was across the hallway. That was where he'd go next.

The door was locked. 'Father? Mother?' Keith called out, rattling the doorknob. But there was no reply.

He placed his ear against the door and listened. As in the previous room, all he heard was silence.

'Father, are you in there?' he called out, rattling the doorknob again.

He suddenly had a terrible thought. What if the burglars were in there holding his parents captive? His father might have been overcome and had the shotgun taken from him, in which case that very gun might well now be pointed at the door. His mouth was suddenly desert dry.

'What are you going to do?' Ferguson whispered. He'd had the same thought as Keith.

'I'm going to break the door down,' Keith whispered in reply. 'You stand back and give me room.'

Ferguson scuttled out of the way.

Keith threw himself against the door, only to bounce off it. He prepared himself for another charge, trying not to think of the third shot, which might ring out at any moment.

On the fourth attempt the lock gave and the door crashed open. Carried on by his momentum Keith stumbled into the room, got tangled up with his shooting stick and went tumbling to the floor. He cursed volubly as he rolled on the carpet.

In the doorway Ferguson stood rooted, eyes bulging as he stared at the bed.

Keith came to his feet and seeing Ferguson's expression whirled round to face his parents' bed. 'Oh my God!' he whispered at the sight which greeted him.

Numb with shock he walked to the side of the bed and gazed down at its contents.

The sheets, blankets and headboard were covered in blood

136

and a pinky-greyish matter which he took to be brains. His mother was lying on her side with the back of her head shot away. His father was sprawled across her, the entire top of his head completely blown off.

Obscenely the shotgun still dangled from his father's big toe, the latter obviously having been used to fire the piece's second barrel.

Keith sat on the edge of the bed, picking a tiny triangle that miraculously wasn't spattered with blood and gore.

'Why?' he asked the two bodies. 'Why?'

Only several hours previously they'd all been downstairs together enjoying a marvellous dinner. His father had been in a particularly good mood that evening, laughing and joking like some music-hall comedian.

Mother had been a little restrained, that's true. But then a quietish woman by nature, that was nothing exceptional or out of the ordinary for her. Neither had given even the slightest hint that they were contemplating suicide. For suicide was what it clearly was.

With tears streaming down his face Ferguson came to the bedside to lift the turned-down covers and gently drape them over the corpses. He'd been in Roderick Gibb's employ for over twenty-five years.

Keith forced himself out of his reverie. His brain started to function again as he watched Ferguson remove the shotgun and lay it on the floor beside the bed. The first thing he had to do was ring his brother Gerald. And after that, the police.

'You stay here with them, Ferguson. I won't be long,' he said.

Then, rising, he padded downstairs to the telephone his father had installed only the year before.

'Where are they?' Gerald said, bursting into the bedroom. Keith turned to face his elder brother who'd already come up short on having seen the bloodstained and gore-covered bedclothes.

'Sweet Jesus,' Gerald breathed.

He walked to the bed and drew back the coverings, gagging at the sight of what lay underneath.

'They couldn't have killed themselves. You must be wrong,' he said.

Keith shook his head. 'Father shot Mother first then himself. There's no doubt about it.'

'But why?'

'That's precisely what I've been asking myself since I broke in here.'

Gerald took a deep breath and then replaced the covers. 'Where's Ferguson?' he asked.

'Below stairs trying to calm the servants. He's already broken the news to them.'

'Sweet Jesus,' Gerald repeated.

Keith shivered. The shock of the night's events was beginning to seep into his very bones. He felt cold all the way through.

'You say you've informed the police and they're on their way?' Gerald asked thoughtfully.

'Yes.'

'Well when they arrive you'd better let me do all the talking.'

Anger flared in Keith. It was just like Gerald to try and take over. There might be a huge gap between them but that was no excuse for Gerald's always treating him as though he were still a child.

'As I found them and I still live here, and you don't, I think it's best I handle this,' Keith replied.

Gerald blinked. 'Now look, young Keith ...'

'Don't you young Keith me. I'm twenty-one now and have attained my majority, don't forget! I won't be patronised by you or anyone!'

Gerald lit a cigar, taking his time about doing so. He sometimes forgot how touchy Keith was about his age and the difference there was between them. After all, his own two boys were contemporaries of Keith's, being two and three years respectively younger than his brother.

138

The voice of Agnes, one of the maids, came from out in the hallway. 'Please Master Gerald, Mr Ferguson has sent me up with a decanter he says you might be wanting to use. He also said I wasn't to come in.'

'I'll get it,' Keith said, and strode to the door.

The decanter contained Glayva, which had been a great favourite with his father – and indeed he and his father had drunk a glass each after dinner.

He poured large ones, a lump sticking in his throat at the memory of having seen his father do precisely the same thing with the same decanter and glasses so many times before.

'There was no hint at all, you say?' Gerald asked.

Keith shook his head. 'None. What about you?'

'Nothing.'

There was a pause and then Keith said, 'Do you think maybe they were ill or something?'

'That's possible.'

'I can't think of any other reason. At least none that makes sense.'

'There was no note?'

Keith frowned. 'I haven't seen one. But then neither Ferguson or I thought to look.'

Together Keith and Gerald searched the obvious places in the room and then the not so obvious. On turning up nothing, Gerald went downstairs to search various rooms there. But of a note there was no sign.

Gerald was on his way back up the stairs again when the police arrived.

'What!' Gerald exclaimed. 'Surely you must be wrong?'

Dan Ritchie, the family lawyer, shook his head. 'I'm afraid not,' he replied.

Keith sat dumbfounded, for the moment unable to speak. What remained of his world following the death of his parents had just collapsed around his ears.

'I think you'd better tell us how it happened,' Gerald said.

Ritchie leaned forward on his desk and made a pyramid with

139

his hands. He spoke slowly and evenly as he always did. He was a dour, dreich sort of a man.

'Your father had been speculating heavily in the past year as well as investing a considerable amount of capital in various overseas projects. All of which, I'm unhappy to say, proved to be disasters. He could've ridden these out, mind you, if they hadn't coincided with a long, bad run he was having at the tables. In the end it was gambling, your father's little weakness, that did for him, gentlemen.'

'Not so little,' Gerald said bitterly.

'Aye,' said Ritchie, nodding. 'You have a point.'

'How much is left?' Keith asked, his voice a croak.

'Virtually nothing. There are debts as well, you see ...'

'Debts!' Gerald exclaimed.

'Gambling ones. Not legal, mind you, if you feel you don't want to pay them.'

'We'll pay,' Gerald said. 'I won't disgrace his name. Right Keith?'

Keith nodded.

'Well then,' Ritchie went on. 'Once those are met, all that will be left which is yours is the Black Lion Brewery.'

'What about the house?' Keith asked.

'That'll have to be sold as well, I'm afraid.'

'Can't we sell the brewery and keep the house?'

'No!' Gerald said emphatically. 'Neither you nor I, having no income of our own, can afford the upkeep of the house. The brewery on the other hand gives us the means to earn something.'

'What do you know about running a brewery?' Keith asked scornfully.

'Nothing. But I can learn. After all, Father knew nothing about breweries either and yet it made money for him.'

'Not a lot,' Ritchie said, 'and I always blamed the fact your father never took a personal interest in it as the reason. A business like that needs personal handling if it's really going to amount to anything.'

140

'So we'll both be working at this brewery then?' Keith asked.

'Certainly. If you don't mind me being boss,' Gerald replied.

'Why should you be boss?'

'For the obvious reason. I'm nearly twenty years older than you. Also, as elder brother, it's my right.'

Keith hated the idea of having to take orders from Gerald. That would be too much. All his life he'd lived under Gerald's shadow, at home, at school, everywhere. The wonderful Gerald, who was so clever, so witty, who at school had been such a marvellous sportsman, not to mention head boy.

He, on the other hand, wasn't clever, nor was he witty or good at games. And when it came to sheer personality he wasn't a patch on Gerald, who could tell such fabulous stories – risqué and otherwise – in company, while the best he could do was blush and stammer and invariably fall over his words. Especially if there were young women present.

'Then you can count me out,' Keith replied. 'For I'm not working under you and that's that.'

'I understand,' Gerald said. And he did.

'You'll have to make some remuneration to your brother in that case,' Ritchie said, 'the brewery being left jointly between you.'

'Half whatever profits I make suit you?' Gerald asked.

'That would be fine,' Keith replied, pleased with himself for having taken such a positive stand.

Gerald sat back in his chair. 'Having to work for a living for the first time at my age!' he said. 'What a turn-up for the book that is!'

For up until that moment both Gerald and Keith had led lives of leisure as befitted gentlemen of their social standing.

Keith frowned, thinking about that. Even with some money coming in from the brewery – and Ritchie warned him that certainly for the next few years it wouldn't be all that much – it was going to be impossible for him to maintain himself in even

141

a semblance of his present lifestyle.

But what to do? Working for a wage seemed demeaning. And especially in the south of Scotland, where he was well known.

There was the law and medicine, of course, both honourable professions he could go into. But neither appealed. Nor was he certain he had the particular talents required for either. Then the idea came to him, bringing a smile to his face. It would be the Army for him!

The Army was the ideal solution, he thought. The perfect answer to his problem.

And there and then he resolved to take up a commission.

Gerald was also thinking, but about his wife Emmaline. She was beautiful and came from a proud old Scottish family. Sadly, however, the family were also poor as church mice which hadn't bothered him one bit when he married her but which he now slightly rued.

After all, there had been so many beautiful women he'd been attracted to, and they to him, it was a pity, seen now in hindsight, that he'd chosen one without money of her own.

He shrugged mentally. There was no use crying over spilt milk. What was done was done and that was that. And hadn't Em given him two fine boys of whom he was inordinately fond? He wouldn't have traded either for a fortune. They were going to find things tough going also from now on in but like him, no matter how painful, they were going to have to learn to adapt.

Thank God his own house was bought and paid for. A present from his father years ago. That at least was something to be thankful for.

And Em had a few bits and pieces of jewellery that could go to tide them over the first few years until he got this brewery really onto its feet and providing a substantial living for them.

What an amazing occurrence this was to happen at his age, he thought. And beer of all things for him to get involved with. Not only hadn't he a clue how it was made, he positively loathed the stuff as a drink!

Second Lieutenant Gibb was in the ward-room of a troop-ship bound for India drinking pink gin with other officers of his regiment, when the news came through.

The ship's captain was handed a radio message which he read from beginning to end twice before looking up. Crossing to the Colonel of the regiment, he handed him the message.

'Gentlemen,' the Colonel said, having, like the ship's captain, stared long and hard at the message. 'I have an announcement to make.'

The hum in the ward room stilled as every eye was turned to the Colonel.

'Yesterday the Germans invaded Belgium and as from that date we are at war with Germany.'

Pandemonium broke out in the ward-room as neighbour excitedly turned to neighbour.

'The King!' someone shouted.

'The King!' the gathering toasted.

Spontaneously they began to sing.

'God save our gracious King ...'

The date was 4 August, 1914.

Keith took to India the way a duck does to water. He loved its heat, smells, alienness, its colour and inherent treachery – the latter both of the land itself and the indigenous peoples inhabiting it.

Fort Victoria was north of Peshawar and south of the Khyber Pass. The billets and other various buildings were made of local brick, the compound surrounding them of stone.

In the distance the hills loured, brooding and menacing. Hills filled with hostile natives who'd never made their peace with the Raj.

The regiment's brief, as had been the regiment's before them and the regiment's before *them*, was to be the continued British military presence in the area, stopping the wild hill brigands from sweeping down to rape and pillage the broad lands of the Punjab.

★

'The Gay Gordons, if you please!' Captain Rintoul called out, smiling broadly at the company.

The various dancers formed into two lines and the band struck up. Several wheeches rent the air as the dance got under way.

Keith Gibb stood not far from the punch bowl, talking to another second-lieutenant with whom he shared a quarter.

'Surely they won't keep us festering out here much longer,' Second-Lieutenant Dick said. 'It's been four months, now, after all.'

'Who knows how they think?' replied Keith.

'Och man, we're a Jock regiment. We should be in the thick of it giving those Jerries what for.'

It was a conversation every soldier in the fort had already been through a thousand times or more.

'They say the casualties are dreadful,' Keith said.

'Aye. I hear the lads are taking awful punishment.'

'Well for every one of ours that gets it, we're getting two of theirs,' Keith said, repeating what an officer had told him.

Dick smacked his palm with a clenched fist. 'It's damnable being out here nursemaiding brownies when we should be in France where the action is. They say promotion is so quick out there you can go up several ranks in a week.'

Keith shook his head in wonderment.

They both sipped some punch and then Dick said, venomously, 'I hate India. It's a filthy place. Nothing but flies and the pox.'

'I like it. Could live the rest of my life out here and be quite happy.'

'Really?'

'Yes.'

'No accounting for taste, is there,' Dick replied. 'And talking of taste, what do you think of Miss Jean Ogilvie? That's her over there.'

Keith gazed at the female in question. He'd never seen her before.

144

'Major Ogilvie's daughter. Came out with us but went on to Poona where the family have friends. Only joined us at the fort last week.'

Jean Ogilvie was a somewhat dumpy girl who could never have been accused of being beautiful. Homely and saucy was the best description for her.

Keith didn't particularly like beautiful girls, finding their beauty off-putting. Besides, all the handsome young men monopolised the beauties, which meant he, shy and awkward, never got a look in.

The more homely variety was far more up his street. With them he didn't feel nearly so bumbling or thick-tongued.

'Not bad,' he said.

'If you like her, away and ask her up, man! She's free now but won't be for long I shouldn't think.'

Keith considered the matter, rarely making decisions on impulse.

'Aye, why not?' he said, after thinking it over.

He laid down his punch glass, minutely adjusted his uniform and then moved towards where Jean Ogilvie was standing watching the dancers.

'Would you care to go on the floor?' he asked, bowing slightly from the waist.

Her eyes took him in. And then a soft smile curled her mouth upwards. 'I'd love to, Lieutenant,' she replied.

He didn't dislike dancing, but then he didn't particularly like it either. He moved swiftly and without grace.

Jean thought Keith gauche but pleasant. When it soon became apparent he wasn't very good at small-talk, she chattered on. And the onus of having to make the conversation flow lifted from him, he relaxed considerably.

At the end of their third dance together it was obvious to both of them that they'd clicked. At his suggestion they took some refreshment, after which they strolled out on to the verandah.

There, under her gentle probing, he started telling her about himself. Her face expressed concern and sympathy when he related how his mother and father had killed themselves in a joint suicide pact.

She was the first person he'd confided that to since joining the Army.

'How awful,' she said.

'It was rather. Even more so when my brother and I discovered the family fortune was no more. Still, one has to make the best out of things, eh?'

'I think you're very brave,' she said.

He pushed his chest out a little. No one had ever called him that before. It brought a warm glow to his insides.

'I say,' he said. 'Do you think I could see more of you after tonight?'

'I don't see why not.'

'Can you ride?'

'I was brought up on a horse.'

'Good,' he said, smiling. 'Then riding it is.'

They talked some more and then went back to join the others.

Jean laughed as her horse broke into a full gallop. She felt gloriously alive as her hair streamed out behind her like a banner in the wind.

Keith urged his mount forward but try as he might he just couldn't catch Jean. Being lighter than him and with the better horse was proving an advantage he just couldn't overcome.

By a grassy knoll Jean drew rein and there she had to wait for a few seconds till Keith caught up.

'Slow coach,' she teased.

Keith dismounted and then helped her to the ground. They held hands as they walked their horses a little distance.

'I've got a new job,' Keith said, pulling a face. 'They've given me a desk and put me on to the administrative side of things. It's excruciatingly boring.'

'I wouldn't have thought of you as being good at that sort of thing,' she replied. 'You seem to me to be far more the man of action.'

'Some man of action who can't even catch up a lassie on a horse!' he joked, causing her to grin.

He stared at the hills and then slowly took in the surrounding terrain. Out here away from the fort it always paid to be careful. There were standing rules about that.

'Do you wish you were in France?' she asked suddenly.

'Of course.'

Jean looked sad. 'So many good men gone already. The papers seem filled with endless lists.'

'The Navy's doing well anyway.'

'Are they? I wouldn't say so, with the *Good Hope* and *Monmouth* being sunk.'

'Ah well ... perhaps you're right. At least the Turks have been defeated in the Caucasus which is something.'

'I know it's a terrible thing to say, but I hope the regiment never gets sent to France,' Jean said.

'You're thinking of your father?'

'Yes. But not only him.'

'I see,' Keith replied, squeezing her hand.

When the horses had had their breather he helped her to mount. But not before shyly taking her in his arms and kissing her.

When they raced back to the fort she allowed him to win.

A year passed, during which Keith and Jean continued seeing one another. Their relationship went from strength to strength as they grew closer and closer together.

In the May of that year Keith had learned of the deaths of Gerald's two sons at the second battle of Ypres. He'd written Gerald and Emmaline a long letter expressing his condolences. He'd been fond of Michael and James, who in a way had been more like brothers to him than Gerald ever had.

Gerald's reply said he and Emmaline were distraught but were somehow coping, he mainly by throwing himself into his work at the Black Lion Brewery, whose business and profits were expanding all the time. Keith was naturally pleased about the latter, as the more profit the brewery made the more money was credited to his bank account.

Financially his fortunes were beginning to revive somewhat, although still far from what they had been before his parents' death.

And then one morning the word spread round the fort like wildfire. The regiment was being posted to France. Once off duty he went straight round to see Jean, finding her sitting crocheting with her mother. He could tell at once from the expression on her face that she'd already heard the news.

'Tea?' Mrs Ogilvie asked. And diplomatically left the room.

'Daddy came home an hour ago to tell us,' Jean said. 'They say we're shipping out within the fortnight.'

Jean nodded. 'That was what Daddy said.'

'We're going straight to the front, apparently.'

Jean's eyes filled with pain. 'Yes. So it seems,' she said.

'There will be plenty of scope for promotion.'

'I've no doubt,' she replied softly, turning her face away so he didn't see the look of anguish which twisted her features.

He was suddenly embarrassed, clumsy and awkward again. Nervously he twisted his fingers. 'Jean ... I ... eh ...'

'You want me to marry you, don't you?'

'How did you know that?' he asked surprised.

'You've been working yourself up to ask me for some time now. And don't look at me as though I could read minds or something. It was quite obvious really.'

'Well? What do you say? I think we're made for one another.'

She rose and crossed to a window to stare out. Her mind was a turmoil. Finally she said, 'If it was peacetime, Keith, I'd marry you gladly. But it's not. And now the regiment's off to fight in France.'

Sick with disappointment, Keith lowered his eyes.

'I'm sorry, Keith. But that's the way I feel. If you're still alive and want to ask me again when the war's over, then I'll say yes.'

148

'I understand,' he said miserably. 'It was selfish of me to ask.'

'No. It's selfish of me to refuse.'

He went to her and circled her waist with his arms. 'I love you, Jean,' he whispered.

Tears filled her eyes. 'And I love you too.' Breaking from his grasp she fled the room.

Keith couldn't believe it. 'Are you sure?' he demanded.

Second-Lieutenant Dick nodded. "Fraid so, old chap. The entire regiment with the exception of second battalion is off to jolly old France. We're staying behind to maintain the British presence in the area.'

'Well I'll be a son of a gun,' Keith said.

'Feel the same way myself. Let's just hope it won't be long before we join the others over there. I'm itching for action, I can tell you.'

'But we can't patrol this entire area with only one battalion,' Keith said. 'That's impossible.'

'We're being reinforced with a battalion of brownies. Gunga Din, what?'

'That makes it more reasonable then.'

'Brownies,' Dick said in disgust. 'I want to scratch every time I'm near one.'

'Oh come on, they're not that bad!'

'Tell me that again after you've had a faceful of curried breath.'

Keith laughed. 'Well, that *can* be a bit much at times.'

'My aunt Sally and it can!'

Keith picked up his hat and swagger stick. He must get over to break the news to Jean right away.

'So you'll be staying on then,' Keith said.

Jean nodded. 'Daddy says that would be the safest thing for Mother and I, what with the U-boat menace and all. He says it's best we remain in India until the war's over.'

'I quite agree. It's by far the most sensible thing to do,' Keith replied.

'From what Daddy's been told we'll be allowed to remain in the fort – all the families who wish to stay on, that is – as with the number of personnel greatly reduced there'll be no trouble about quarters.'

'There's tremendous excitement in the regiment,' Keith said. 'They're positively champing at the bit, dying to get to grips with Jerry.'

'You're sick at not going, aren't you?'

'Yes.'

She took his hand. 'Well, I'm glad you're not. It's bad enough Daddy's got to go without you as well.'

'Well if I have to remain on here with the battalion the fact you're staying on too is the best consolation prize I could have. Are you sure you won't change your mind?'

'About what?'

'Marrying me.'

Her face clouded over. 'Not till the war's over, Keith. I'll never change my mind about that.'

'Then I'll just have to wait.'

She kissed his cheek. 'Let's just hope it's over soon.'

'But not too soon. Otherwise I might not get a chance to get into it.'

'Men,' she said reproachfully. 'What children they all are!'

News of the big battle came over the telegraph on the direct line with Peshawar and being on duty and in administration Keith was one of the first to know.

He and Second-Lieutenant Dick stood looking at one another, aghast at what they'd just heard.

Captain 'Robbie' Roberts repeated what he'd just read out.

'The regiment was decimated,' he said. 'Overall British losses were approximately four hundred thousand men.'

'Four hundred thousand,' Dick said, and shook his head. It was a mind-boggling figure.

'How many of our regiment came through?' Keith asked.

Roberts scanned the message. 'Two hundred and fourteen,' he replied.

All those in the room looked from one to the other, each thinking of the many friends and comrades-in-arms they'd never see again.

'Do we know who these two hundred and fourteen are?' Keith asked.

'That's coming through in a later message,' Roberts replied.

'All those bonny lads,' said McPherson, an old sergeant who'd been in the Boer War. There were tears trickling down his stone face as he rose and stalked from the room. Keith thought of Jean and her mother. It was best he told them himself what had happened.

It was late that night before the second message came humming over the telegraph.

For hours the families who'd remained behind mixed with many of the soldiers standing outside the telegraph hut waiting to find out who'd survived.

For a long time they sang hymns, 'Abide With Me' and 'Rock Of Ages' being repeated several times.

But eventually the singing ceased and those gathered waited on in a stolen silence only broken by night sounds.

Finally the message came through and a notice was pinned to the door of the telegraph hut. The notice contained a list of the names of the two hundred and fourteen survivors.

Major John Fergus Ogilvie was not among them.

'The regiment's being reformed in Scotland but still we're to remain here!' Second-Lieutenant Dick said in disgust.

'Surely not!' Keith exclaimed.

'So the orders say.'

'And what about promotion?'

'If you mean for us, then forget it. It'll be the usual slow grind for you and me, just as though there wasn't a war on.'

'But that's not fair!' Keith said angrily. 'In France there are chaps our age who are majors by now.'

'So when was the Army ever fair? Anyway, France is France and India is India.'

'But we should be forming the nucleus of the new regiment.'

'That's not how the War Office sees it, apparently,' Dick replied.

Keith sat and sulked.

After a while he rose and strode out in the warm sunshine. A good ride was what he needed to blow his anger and frustration away.

'If the regiment's gone back to France then there must be a new offensive brewing,' 'Robbie' Roberts said.

Keith chalked his cue. He and Roberts were playing billiards. He lined up his shot and potted well.

'Good shot!' said Roberts. And swallowed some port.

'I'm dying to see what these new tanks are like,' Keith said. 'They sound quite something.'

'First gas and now huge metal monsters that crush a chap to death,' Roberts sniffed. 'War's becoming dashed uncivilised, what?'

'All that matters in the end is winning,' Keith replied thoughtfully. 'Nothing else.'

His cue stroked forward and another ball disappeared.

There was a new look in Robert's eye as he stared at Keith. It was as though he was seeing Keith for the very first time.

Face flushed, Keith burst into the room. 'We're going at long last!' he said, and taking Jean in his arms whirled her round.

'I don't have to ask where,' Jean replied when she'd finally caught her breath. 'It can only be France.'

Keith nodded excitedly.

'Well, I suppose it was inevitable,' she said in a resigned tone of voice.

'Aren't you thrilled?'

'Don't be stupid,' she retorted bitingly. 'How could I possibly be thrilled about you being sent to that slaughter-house?'

'I'm sorry,' he said, calming down. 'I suppose that was thoughtless of me. I mean, your father and ...' He trailed off.

Her eyes filled with tears. 'I know I shouldn't say this but if you go I know I'll never see you again. It'll be just like Daddy. A final wave at the railway station and then with a toot-toot of the engine you'll be taken out of my life forever.' She dabbed her eyes with a handkerchief. 'I've just read the names of four boys I knew back home in the last papers which arrived this morning.'

'All dead?'

She nodded.

'I'm sorry.'

'Oh, Keith!' she said rushing into his arms and hugging him tight. 'What did we do to deserve what's happening in the world today?'

'God alone knows,' he replied softly.

And in silence they stood hugging one another for a long time until finally Mrs Ogilvie appeared, when they broke apart.

'It's unbelievable!' Second-Lieutenant Dick said, taking off his cap and throwing it on to his bed from where it slid to the floor.

'Word came through less than an hour ago,' Keith said. 'Our orders are cancelled. We're not going to France after all.'

'The blooming Ruskies have had a revolution you say?'

'So it seems – which makes this area even more strategically important than before. The War Office must think there's the possibility that whatever government comes into power might try and sweep down to have a go at taking India from us. Which would be easy enough for them when you consider that due to the war in Europe our army in India is probably at its lowest strength since the beginning of the Raj.'

Dick lit up a cigarette, having first carefully placed it in the ivory holder he affected. 'If they do come we certainly don't have enough troops here even to attempt a holding action. It would be like a gnat trying to stave off a vulture.'

153

'We're to be reinforced,' Keith said.

'More brownies?'

'No, troops from Blighty. An English regiment but we don't know which one yet.'

'Well that's something at least,' Dick replied.

'We'll never get to France now,' Keith said. 'That was our last chance.'

'Bloody bolsheviks!' Dick swore.

At long last it was all over. The Kaiser had abdicated and escaped to Holland. The Armistice had been signed by the Germans.

Keith took Jean out into the velvet night and together they strolled, hand in hand.

'You said I was to ask you again when the war was finished,' he said. 'So I am. Will you marry me?'

'As soon as you like, my darling.'

He caught her in his arms and kissed her.

'Keith! Someone might see!'

'Let them. Who cares?'

'I do, for one!'

'Isn't a man allowed to kiss his fiancée?'

'Yes. But not out here where everybody can see! One has to be discreet about these things. And as a second-lieutenant you have to set an example to the men.'

'That's the other good news,' he said. 'It's now Lieutenant.'

'Oh Keith! I'm so happy for you.'

'For *us*, Jean. From now on it's us.'

She smiled and slipped her hand back into his. She thought she'd never been more happy or contented.

For the umpteenth time Keith cleared his throat and then examined his appearance in the mirror. He was more nervous than he'd ever been in his life before.

There were places in Peshawar where one could go to learn these things but he never had. Nor had he done it before joining the Army and coming out to India.

Tonight, his wedding night, would be his first time ever.

He sipped some gin and then glanced yet again at his watch. She'd had half an hour on her own through in the bedroom to get ready. Was that enough time or should he wait a while longer?

He sipped more gin and then started to pace.

In his mind he went over all he knew about lovemaking.

It didn't take long.

Through in the bedroom, Jean lay propped up in bed waiting for Keith to come to her. If anything she was even more nervous than he was. Her hand crept behind one of the pillows supporting her to touch the large white hanky she'd placed there. Although what on earth she was going to need it for she didn't know.

But that had been her mother's sole advice to her when she'd blushingly asked about sex.

'Just keep a large white handkerchief under your pillow, my dear,' Mrs Ogilvie had said, as embarrassed about the subject as her daughter was.

And that was the end of that conversation.

The door to the bedroom opened and Keith entered, looking splendid in his silk pyjamas and silk dessing gown.

'Everything all right?' he asked.

'Fine, fine,' she replied, trying to sound casual.

'You don't mind if I join you, then?'

'No, of course not.'

He cleared his throat. 'I thought everything went jolly well today, don't you think?'

'Yes.'

'Dick was a laugh.'

'Always is at a party.'

Keith inched slowly towards the bed, very conscious this was the first time he'd ever seen Jean in her night attire.

'Thought the chaplain made a good speech after,' he said. 'Quite witty which surprised me.'

'Me too.'

'The chaps were trying to get me sloshed, you know, but I

was having none of it. Wouldn't do to be stinko on one's wedding night, what?'

Jean smiled.

He knew he was prattling on but felt he had to. Silence would have been even more disconcerting and embarrassing.

Taking off his dressing gown he threw it across a chair, at the same time saying, 'Dashed decent of the C.O. to lay on the champagne, I thought.'

'Yes, I thought so too.'

He slid into bed beside her. 'Well then ...' he said, and cleared his throat.

It wasn't till morning that it dawned on Jean what the hanky was for.

'Keith! How marvellous to see you!' Gerald said. 'And this must be Jean.'

Jean and Gerald shook hands. Then he ushered her and Keith through to where Emmaline was waiting.

'First time home in ... how long is it?' Gerald asked.

'Eight years,' Keith replied.

'Is it really?' Emmaline said, shaking her head.

Gerald had aged considerably, Keith thought. And so had Emmaline but she was still an incredibly beautiful woman all the same.

Gerald passed round sherry.

'How long are you home for?' Emmaline asked Jean.

'Four months, and then it's back to India.'

'You like it there, I believe.'

'Yes, we both do.'

'It has a way of getting into the blood,' Keith said. 'We'll both be upset when we have to leave.'

'Is that likely?'

'Oh yes. As you know my regiment was posted back there after the war but we're due to be moved on again any time now. Singapore and the Far East I should think.'

'Sounds terribly exciting,' Emmaline said.

156

Keith smiled. 'There's a lot to be said for the Army. It's certainly been good to me.'

'Kept you out of the war, eh?' Emmaline went on, the merest hint of wickedness in her eyes. When she saw the expression on Keith's face she added hastily, 'I don't mean you to take that the wrong way. I only wish our Michael and James could have sat it out in India. They'd be alive today if they had.'

'If I didn't get to France I can assure you it wasn't for the lack of trying,' Keith said.

'Of course. I didn't doubt otherwise.'

'More sherry?' Gerald asked.

'Yes please,' Jean replied emphatically.

'Losing the boys was a terrible blow,' Gerald said. 'And one we haven't recovered from yet.'

'If we ever will,' Emmaline added.

'It's a pity you're too old to have had another family,' Jean said.

Emmaline turned an icy stare on to Jean. 'Yes, it is rather. But what about you two? Surely it's high time for a son and heir?'

Bitch, Jean thought.

This was a sore point with Keith. He'd hoped Jean would fall pregnant soon after their marriage but so far nothing had happened in that direction.

He glanced across at Gerald. That was another thing Gerald had scored over him, he thought bitterly. Michael and James had come quickly after Gerald had married Emmaline.

Gerald smiled back, as though aware of what Keith was thinking.

'It won't bother us not to have a family for a year or two yet,' Keith lied. 'That sort of thing is always difficult when you're in the Army and abroad a lot.'

'Quite,' Gerald agreed.

The death of her two sons had turned Emmaline into a shrew, Keith thought. Underneath that still beautiful face she was as sour as acid.

157

Mind, you, to be fair, he had some sympathy for her. He hated to think what he'd have been like had he lost two sons in the conflict.

Plain as a suet pudding, Emmaline was thinking, while smiling at Jean. Typical of Keith to marry a woman like that. A proper little *hausfrau*.

Turning to Keith she said, 'And what rank are you now?'

'Still Lieutenant.'

'Really? I would've thought you'd be a Field Marshal at least!' And having said that she gave vent to a derisory cackle.

A blush crept over Keith's features while Jean's lips thinned in anger.

'She's only teasing,' Gerald said. 'A great one for that, my Em. There's no harm meant by it.'

Like hell there isn't, Keith thought.

'Promotion's very difficult in the Army at the moment,' Jean said.

'You mean so many young officers holding comparatively high rank with still the great lump of their military career stretching before them?' Emmaline asked sweetly.

'Precisely,' Keith replied.

'Those young officers were promoted on the battlefield,' Jean said, determined to get it in before Emmaline did.

'That must be very frustrating for you,' Gerald said to Keith.

'It is.'

'Enough to make you pack in the Army?'

Keith shook his head. 'No.'

'How do you feel about that, Jean?' Emmaline asked.

'I'm only too happy to agree with whatever Keith wants or thinks is best. I believe very firmly in family loyalty, you see.'

Emmaline disregarded the barb. 'But doesn't it upset you, never having a permanent place of your own? I know it would me.'

'One has to make sacrifices in life,' Jean replied. 'I thought we all learned that in the war.'

'Oh well, there's always a job for you at the brewery any time you want it,' Gerald said to Keith.

'No, thank you.'

'Well it's always there, should you ever change your mind.'

'I don't think I will,' Keith said softly and emphatically. In fact I'd rather sweep the streets first, he added under his breath.

A maid arrived to announce dinner was ready to be served. They all smiled at one another as they went through.

'What do you think then?' Gerald demanded.

Keith shrugged. 'I never saw it before so I can't really say.'

'Production's up three hundred and fifty per cent since I took over,' Gerald said proudly. '*And* I've doubled the number of pubs I own.'

'*We* own,' Keith corrected.

'Of course. That's what I meant.'

His brother was obviously extremely good at the business of running the brewery and that rankled with Keith. Why did Gerald have to be so damn good at everything he did!

'You do check how much goes into your personal account every month?' Gerald asked just a trifle sarcastically. He had been expecting Keith to be just a little bit more enthusiastic.

Keith nodded.

'Then you'll appreciate how much the profits have increased.'

Keith was damned if he was going to say 'well done' or anything like that.

'What are your plans for the future?' he asked instead.

'Keep on expanding, I suppose.'

'Why not?' replied Keith somewhat vaguely, and was delighted when a flash of irritation crossed Gerald's face.

They walked along a gantry overlooking some fermenting vats. Keith walking ramrod stiff, every inch the officer and gentleman. It amused him to note Gerald had become round-shouldered and developed something of a slouch.

'Mind you, I suppose running a brewery isn't all that difficult. I would imagine the stuff almost sells itself,' he said.

'It's not quite as easy as that,' Gerald replied disdainfully.

'No?'

'*No*,' Gerald said with emphasis.

'That surprises me,' said Keith.

They stopped by a set of metal steps descending to the floor below.

'I don't suppose you'd be interested in selling your half of the place?' Gerald asked hopefully.

''Fraid not, old bean,' Keith replied, a soft smile curling his mouth upward. 'I'm very happy with things the way they are.'

Using his swagger stick he touched Gerald on the lapel. 'Very happy.'

He used his swagger stick again to gesture that Gerald could lead the way down the metal steps.

Should an accident occur, and he fell, he wanted Gerald below him.

The regiment spent six years in the Far East and two in southern Africa before finally being shipped home to Glasgow's Maryhill barracks.

During this time Jean visited a number of doctors, all of whom told her the same thing. There was no physical reason whatsoever for her not to have a child.

Secretly Keith feared he was to blame, thinking there must be something wrong with him.

Until one evening he returned home to their quarters to find a bottle of champagne cooling in a bucket and a special dinner laid on.

'What's all this for?' he asked, having hastily confirmed to himself that he hadn't forgotten either her birthday or their anniversary.

Jean produced two glasses and told him to open the champagne. When their glasses were charged she clinked hers against his and then said, 'Here's to the three of us!'

Keith frowned. 'What three?'

'You, me and the baby.'

'What baby?'

'You're not being very quick on the uptake, Keith.'

A few seconds passed and then his frown cleared. 'You mean ... ?'

'Yes. I'm pregnant.'

'You're sure? Absolutely?'

Smiling she nodded.

'Oh Jean!' he exclaimed, and, taking her in his arms, kissed her.

'After all these years it just happened,' she said excitedly.

He drank off his champagne and then poured himself some more. His eyes were shining fiercely with pride.

'I'd almost given up hope,' he said; then, 'Dammit, I *had* given up hope!'

'I'm three months gone and the doctor says everything's just as it should be. It should be a straightforward birth with no complications.'

'I'm going to have a son!' he said and whooped.

'Now hold on, Keith. I can't promise that.'

'Don't be daft, woman! Of course it'll be a boy. They run in the family. Didn't my father have two and didn't Gerald?'

'Still ...'

'There's no "still" about it. A boy it'll be. Anything else would be unthinkable.'

He paused and his eyes gleamed. 'A boy, who'll turn out to be a better man than any of us. Better than me, Gerald, Michael and James. A man who'll restore the family fortunes to what they once were!'

Chest heaving, he sat down. He was quite overcome with the vision he saw.

'A son,' he whispered. 'A son!'

Jean bit her lip.

Keith paced up and down the hospital corridor, a tall slim man of what had become in the past few years a hawkish appearance.

161

He glanced at his watch. God, how much longer? he thought. And continued pacing.

Several nurses hurried by. He searched their faces for some sort of sign as to how things were going. But they knew nothing.

'Keith?'

He turned to find Gerald standing beside him.

'Any news?'

'Not yet.'

'She's certainly taking her time about it. I expected it to be all over by now.'

Keith grunted, sure from Gerald's tone that was an intended jibe.

Gerald went on, 'We were lucky with Em's births. Both were short labours.'

They would be! Keith thought. Out loud he said, 'And how is Em?'

'Fine. You know you and Jean really should try and manage to come over more often.'

'We keep meaning to,' Keith lied. 'But you know how things are. What with Jean being pregnant and one thing and another.'

'Well, maybe after the baby's born?'

'We'll try and arrange something,' Keith said, having absolutely no intention of doing so. Then to change the subject, 'How's the brewery doing?'

'Excellently. Profits up again. Can't complain about that, eh?'

Keith knew fine well profits were up as he kept a close watch on what was deposited every month in his bank account. 'No, we can't,' he agreed.

A door opened and the Ward Sister appeared. 'Captain Gibb?'

Keith hurried to her side.

'I'm happy to tell you you've got a smashing wee daughter. Both she and your wife are doing fine.'

162

Keith blinked. 'There must be some mistake,' he said quickly. 'We were expecting a boy.'

The Ward Sister smiled.

Keith realised what he'd said and how ludicrous it must have sounded. 'What I mean is . . .' he stumbled on.

'Congratulations Keith!' said Gerald, clapping his brother on the back.

'We were just convinced it was a boy,' Keith said lamely to the Sister.

'As long as the baby's healthy that's the main thing,' Gerald said.

'Quite so,' the Sister added.

Keith was completely shattered. It just hadn't crossed his mind that it wouldn't be a boy. They'd chosen the name months ago. Roderick Keith Gibb. They hadn't even thought of one for a lassie.

'Cheer up!' Gerald said. 'I'm told anyone can produce a boy but it takes a man to produce a girl.'

For two peas Keith would have belted Gerald then. Instead he forced a smile on to his face – it came out as something of a grimace – and nodded.

'When can we see mother and daughter?' Gerald asked.

'In about half an hour,' the Sister replied.

'Right! That gives us time for a wee celebratory dram first. Eh, Keith?'

'Half an hour?' Keith said, looking at his watch. 'All right then.'

They went to a pub round the corner which, being owned by Black Lion Brewery, meant Gerald was received like Lord God Almighty.

To Keith that was like rubbing salt into an open wound.

The regiment was going abroad again and Keith, still bogged down in the administrative job he loathed, was naturally going with it.

As usual Jean would accompany him.

'If we have to leave Susan behind she could stay with Gerald and Em,' Jean suggested.

'Do they know we're going yet?'

'No, I haven't told them.'

'Fine,' said Keith, nodding. 'We can't take the lassie with us, it just wouldn't be fair to her where we're going. And I'm not having Gerald doing a takeover bid on her. Susan's ours and she's going to stay that way.'

'So what do we do then?'

'There's a school I've heard of in Kelvinside. Miss Buchan's School For Young Ladies. It has an excellent reputation and I thought she might go there as a boarder.'

'But she's only four!' Jean said, feeling absolutely wretched.

'I appreciate that, woman, but what else can we do? She'll be well looked after, a home away from home, they say. And so it should be at the price they charge.'

'I can't help feeling it's wrong somehow,' Jean said, wringing her hands. 'She's such a wee mite, after all.'

'Do you have any other suggestions?'

Jean shook her head.

'Well then?'

'I suppose it'll have to be ... What did you call it?'

'Miss Buchan's School For Young Ladies.'

'Miss Buchan's it is, then. But I can't say I feel happy about it.'

'Neither am I. But everything in life doesn't just go as we would want it, as you well know.'

'I'll have to see the place and meet this Miss Buchan and her staff before I agree, Keith.'

'Naturally,' he replied. 'I wouldn't have expected otherwise.'

Outside, it was typical Glasgow weather. Grey and dreich with soft rain smirring down.

'I can't wait to get back to the sun,' Keith said.

Jean sighed. She missed the sun dreadfully as well.

SUSAN AND KIRK (1)

'What's your game then, Jim?' the publican demanded.

'I'm only trying to sell you some whisky, that's all,' Kirk replied.

'And where would you get whisky when most of us can't get the bloody stuff for love or money?'

'That's my business,' Kirk replied.

The publican was a small man with an inturned eye. There were two very old razor scars down his left cheek.

'Fell off the back of a lorry, I suppose?' the publican said sarcastically. Then suddenly reaching forward he grabbed Kirk by the lapels of his coat. 'Are you trying to get me back in the Bar-L?' he demanded, referring to Barlinne Prison.

'Why should I do that?'

'Because you might be the polis. What with your fancy clothes and la-de-da accent and flashing bottles of whisky under me snoz with the promise as much as I need to come if only I'll give you an order. Do you think I came up the Clyde on a bicycle or something?'

'I'm not the police,' said Kirk, beginning to sweat a little. This was turning ugly.

'Sez you!'

Kirk picked up his sample bottle of whisky and slipped it into his briefcase.

'I think I should go now,' he said.

'Damn right,' the publican replied angrily. 'And don't come back again. Neither you or any of your pals. And you can tell them from me there's no way they're going to get me back inside again. I'm going straight. That's the word. Got it?'

'Got it,' Kirk replied.

'Now fuck off!'

The publican followed him through the saloon to the door and closed it firmly behind him.

Kirk walked down the street a little way before stopping and drawing in several deep breaths. He might well be making a lot of money but by God there were times when he didn't half earn it. For a few moments back there he'd thought the skelly-eyed nutter was going to carve him. The bugger might have been wee but often the smaller they were the more dangerous they were.

He was suddenly aware he was soaking wet under his arms and all around the crotch. He'd had quite a fright back there. Quite a fright indeed.

He decided to call it a night. He'd more or less made the calls he'd set out to make anyway.

Half-way back to the flat he suddenly thought it would be a marvellous idea to go to the sports club and have a swim. The way he felt now that was just what he needed.

He stopped off at the flat to pick up his trunks and other sports equipment, then continued on out to the club.

The place was less busy than usual and the pool was empty. He swam contentedly for a while and then, coming out, went through to the male changing room to put his clothes back on again.

'I say, you wouldn't care for a game of badminton, would you? We were supposed to have a mixed foursome and the other chap hasn't turned up.'

Kirk looked up at the young man poking his head round the changing-room door. 'Badminton?' he queried.

'It would be awful for us to come out and then not get a game. Won't you help?'

Although Kirk had never actually played badminton he knew the rules, having watched a number of matches since joining the club.

'All right,' he replied. 'I'll be out in a minute or two.'

'Jolly good,' said the chap and disappeared from view.

It was the first time Kirk had been asked to join in any of the activities since taking up his membership, so he thought it a good idea to show willing. The sooner he got to know some of these people the better.

The chap was called Hector and Hector introduced him to the two girls, one of whom was Mary and the other Susan.

His partner was Susan.

She was a girl he judged to be roughly the same age as himself, with shoulder-length blonde hair and warm blue eyes. She wasn't beautiful as such, or a stunner even, but she was certainly attractive and he found himself drawn to her right away.

'I hope I don't let you down,' he said. 'I'm afraid my experience is strictly limited.' He thought it best not to mention he'd never played before.

'That's all right.' She smiled. 'As long as we can get a game in, that's the main thing.'

The other three played expertly while he sort of lumbered along doing the best he could. Fiercely competitive by nature, he hated it when he lost points and made errors. And the more graceful Susan and her companions seemed, the more cumbersome he felt by comparison.

'Well, we didn't do too badly,' Susan said politely when it was all over. Actually she and Kirk had been thrashed by the other two.

Kirk felt like a limp rag. He hadn't had so much exercise in a long time and felt the better for it.

'I could use a drink after that,' he said.

'Well we usually have one in the bar afterwards. Won't you join us?'

'I'd love to,' he said, smiling.

'We'll see you and Hector there in about fifteen minutes then,' Susan said.

She and Mary marched off to the ladies' changing room while he and Hector went to the men's.

After they'd showered Kirk established from Hector that it

was Susan's boyfriend, somebody called Nigel, who'd failed to show earlier on.

When he and Hector arrived in the bar, feeling it was the proper thing to do he placed the first order, extending the order when the girls showed up.

He'd just started to chat to Susan when suddenly there was a shout and a halloo! from the entrance to the bar.

'Nige, old son!' Hector called and waved.

'I'm frightfully sorry, Susan,' Nigel said when he joined them, 'but my flaming bus went and conked out miles from anywhere and it's taken me till now to get here.'

'Nigel, Kirk. He very kindly stepped in to make up the foursome.'

Kirk shook hands and forced a smile on to his face. He could have seen Nigel far enough, for by now he'd decided he fancied Susan.

'New to the club, are you?' Nigel said in a friendly manner.

'Yes.'

'It's a good old place, eh?'

'I like it. The club itself, that is, anyway. I'm afraid I don't know anyone here yet.'

'Well, now you know us,' said Susan.

'That's true,' he replied, looking her straight in the eye and smiling.

Nigel frowned fractionally when he saw that.

'I'm not really keen on badminton myself,' Nigel said after a few moments. 'Always considered it more of a ladies' game than anything else.'

'He's a squash man,' Hector said. 'One of the best players in the south of Scotland.'

'That a fact?' said Kirk.

'Squash is a man's game,' Nigel said. 'Do you play?'

Kirk shook his head.

'Pity. I would have liked to have got you on the court.'

Kirk knew then Nigel was aware he fancied Susan. 'Maybe someday,' he said softly.

'I'd like that,' Nigel replied.

170

Susan's gaze drifted from Nigel to Kirk and back again. The hint of a smile lifted the corners of her mouth.

While Hector was ordering another round Mary asked Kirk where he lived.

'With your parents?' she asked.

'No, I have a small flat of my own.'

'How lovely!' said Mary. 'I wish I had one.'

'Do you live with your parents?' Kirk asked Nigel.

'Yes.'

Kirk nodded in such a way as to give the impression to Nigel he found that secretly amusing.

Nigel looked furious.

'Who does your cooking?' Susan asked.

'Me.'

'Really?' she said surprised.

'I'm actually quite good at it. But then one usually is quite good at what one enjoys doing.'

Nor was it cooking he was talking about now, as she well knew. She blushed a little and turned her attention back to Nigel who was looking as though he would love to have a go at Kirk.

Susan thought she liked Kirk, although she found him somewhat brash. But there was no doubt there was something very exciting about him. Something extremely vibrant and alive. And he had wicked eyes. There were moments when he was looking at her when she knew precisely what was in his mind.

'I think we should be getting along. Look at the time,' said Nigel.

'Where's the car parked?' asked Susan.

'It isn't,' replied Nigel. 'At least not round here. I had to leave it where it broke down and thumb a lift in part of the way. The rest I came by public transport.'

'I can't take you both home,' said Hector. 'I haven't got enough petrol in my tank and I'll never find a garage open this late.'

'Then you'd best take Nigel as you three live relatively near one another and I'll either catch a tram or a bus,' Susan said.

'I won't hear of it!' said Nigel.

'If you take me home then how will you get back?' Susan asked.

Nigel chewed his lip. He had no answer to that.

Kirk thought the gods must be smiling on him that night. It was a heaven-sent opportunity.

'I could drive Susan home if she'd like,' he said casually.

Nigel opened his mouth to object but before he could speak Hector said, 'That would solve everything!'

Kirk turned to Susan and raised an eyebrow.

'All right then,' she said. 'It seems the easiest way out of the problem.'

When he heard that, Nigel put a brave smile on his face. But he seemed to be having difficulty swallowing.

At the front entrance to the club they split into two groups. Hector, Mary and Nigel going off in one direction, Kirk and Susan in another.

'It's not much of a car,' he said apologetically when they arrived at his motor, 'but at least it goes.'

Susan laughed when he said that.

Once inside the car she gave him her address and they moved off. It was a small car so they were squashed together. When he shifted gear he couldn't help but occasionally brush her leg.

Once, she looked at him to see if he was doing it deliberately. Deciding he wasn't, she turned her attention back to the road and the directions she was giving.

He parked the car and turned to her. 'Can I see you again?' he asked.

'I don't know you.'

'Go out with me and you'll get to know me.'

'You're quite a pushy person, aren't you?'

'I've had to be,' he said in the darkness.

He put his arm round her and drew her to him. She didn't resist but then again she didn't exactly melt in his arms either. He kissed her long and hard, enjoying the experience. When

172

he put his hand up to touch her breast she pushed his hand away.

'How long have you been going out with Nigel?' he asked.

'A little over a year now,' she replied.

He caressed the side of her face. Drawing a finger slowly along her cheekbone.

'You're a ladies' man, aren't you?'

He laughed. 'What does that mean?'

'Amongst other things, you're not scared of them in any way.'

'No,' he said, 'I'm not.'

'Nigel is. He tries not to show it but deep down he's scared of women.'

'A lot of men are. I could never see why myself.'

'What do you do?' she asked.

'I'm in business.'

'What sort of business?'

'My own.'

'You're not exactly forthcoming, are you?' she said.

'There's not a lot to be forthcoming about. I have a small business from which I earn my living. I'm what you might call a middle-man.'

'You make it sound mysterious.'

He laughed. 'I don't mean to. And what do you do?'

'I'm at college studying to be a vet.'

'I'd never have guessed that,' he said, surprised. 'You don't look the type.'

'And what *is* the type?'

'Big and butch or horsy. That's hardly you.'

'And what's me?'

'Extremely feminine and attractive,' he said, and kissed her again. This time she responded more, putting her arms round him and returning his kiss.

When they broke apart they were both breathing more heavily than they had been.

She studied what she could see of his face in the darkness.

'I think you're dangerous,' she said after a while.

'In what way?'

'I'm not sure yet.'

'You mean you think I might be a homicidal maniac?' he said jokingly.

She laughed. 'No, I mean towards women. What is usually referred to as a right proper bastard.'

'Why don't you go out with me and find out?'

'Maybe.'

'That's neither yes nor no.'

She fumbled in her pocket to produce a lighter which she flicked into flame. She wrote in a small diary, tearing the page out and handing it to him.

'I'll be home tomorrow night. If you still want to take me out ring me and we'll talk about it.'

She got out of the car and closed the door.

He rolled down the window.

'I'll ring. You have my promise on that,' he said.

'Thanks for the lift home.'

'My pleasure.'

He watched her walk across the pavement and into the drive which led to her house. He couldn't see much of the house because it was screened by some trees. But what was visible was imposing and very, very large.

'She's worth a few bob,' he thought to himself as he drove away.

He would telephone all right.

He racked his brains to think of somewhere different to take her, wanting them to get off to the best possible start. Idea after idea was discarded until a possible solution suddenly dawned on him.

He drove to the BBC where he was in luck. His inquiry procured him two tickets for a well-known wireless comedy programme several days thence. They would be part of the audience.

He rang as he said he would and told her about the tickets.

She said she'd love to see the show as she listened to it often. It was a date.

Their evening out together was a huge success, and in more ways than one.

The episode with the skelly-eyed publican had put the wind up Kirk and had been worrying him ever since. And thinking about it he realised he was bound to run into the odd nutcase from time to time. But how to protect himself?

The solution was suggested to him in a hilarious sketch about the infamous old-time gang called The Billy Boys who terrorised Glasgow in the twenties and early thirties. He would hire himself a bodyguard, and what's more he knew just the right man for the job.

After the show Susan declared she'd thoroughly enjoyed herself. He suggested they go for coffee. They found a small café that was open and having bought their coffee settled themselves at a wooden table.

'I don't even know your last name yet,' he said.

She smiled. 'Gibb.'

'Susan Gibb?' he said. 'I like it. It has a nice ring about it.'

'Susan *Euphemia* Gibb. But I'm not too keen on the Euphemia part.'

'I'm not surprised,' he said.

And they both laughed.

They sat staring at one another in silence for a few seconds while in the background the Italian proprietor's voice could be heard issuing melodic instructions to his staff.

'Will you go out with me again?' Kirk asked.

'If you like.'

'I like.'

'There's a dinner-dance I've been invited to next week. A small thing my father's throwing for some members of his firm. Nigel was supposed to be taking me but he's had to cry off. Some squash fixture or other that was originally postponed and has now been rescheduled for that night, which he says is just impossible for him to break.'

175

'Sounds like Nigel's loss is my gain.'

'You'll take me then?'

'I'm already looking forward to it,' he said.

They made the arrangements there and then, after which he said, 'Now, tell me about studying to be a vet. I'm absolutely fascinated.'

'Are you taking the mickey?'

'Who me?'

He tried to keep a straight face but couldn't.

She joined in his laughter.

Kirk felt decidedly nervous as he chapped the tenement door. The man he'd come to see had a reputation a mile long. Amongst all the city hard men, he was one of the – if not *the* – hardest.

'Who is it?' a gruff voice demanded from behind the door.

'My name's Kirk Murray and I've come to see Mr McGhie.'

'What about?'

'I have a proposition which might interest him.'

'Who did you say you were?'

'Kirk Murray.'

'Never heard of you.'

'You're quite right, we've never met.'

There was a fractional pause. Then, 'Are you alone?'

'Yes.'

'Just wait a minute. I've got to get my clothes on.'

Kirk took a step backward from the door. Further along the front close a marmalade cat had its tail up and was having a pee against the wall. He watched that with interest.

'Turn round very slowly, Murray, and keep your arms by your sides,' the voice that had come from behind the door said now from behind him.

He did as he was told and inched round.

The man confronting him was in his early thirties with a face like a bashed-in turnip. His hair was cut extremely short and there was a small puckered scar on his chin. He was wearing a blue shirt and waistcoat, two ivory-handed razors clearly

176

protruding from the top pockets of the latter.

The eyes that took Kirk in were palest blue and had a dead, glacial quality about them. Kirk looked into those eyes and found them absolutely terrifying.

With a shrug McGhie dismissed Kirk. Here was no threat. 'Can't be too careful you understand,' McGhie said. 'There are some right bampots around.'

As McGhie's house was on the ground floor, Kirk presumed McGhie must have climbed out a back window and come round on him that way.

'Can we talk inside?' he asked.

'Aye, sure. Proposition, is it?'

Kirk nodded.

McGhie opened the door and led the way.

Kirk was well acquainted with the stink of tenement houses but even so this one was worse than usual. It was like walking into a long-unwashed underarm.

Mrs McGhie was a lot younger than her husband and pretty in a common way. There were two half-naked children crawling round the floor.

'What can I do for you, Murray?' McGhie asked, sinking into a fireside chair that had seen better days. He gestured for Kirk to sit.

Mrs McGhie collected the two children and dragged them squawling from the room. She wouldn't return until her husband shouted for her.

'What I have in mind, Mr McGhie, is this –'

'Call me Turk. Everyone else does.'

Kirk started again. 'Are you working, Turk?'

'Hell no! Who'd employ the likes of me?'

'I might. If you were interested.'

McGhie leaned forward. 'Doing what?'

'Hopefully nothing more than just keeping me company. I'm looking for a bodyguard.'

Turk McGhie smiled. 'I like the sound of that. A bodyguard? Against whom?'

'Nothing professional. Just the odd headcase who might

177

want to have a go at me. And who I'm hoping won't because you'll be there.'

'Sounds like money for old rope. What sort of wages did you have in mind?'

Kirk mentioned a figure he'd already decided on, adding, 'Cash in your hand every Friday night and no one the wiser. What do you say?'

'When do I start?'

'Tonight if you can.'

'Just tell me where and when and I'll be there.'

They shook hands on the arrangement and Kirk left the house feeling hugely pleased with himself. As far as he was concerned, employing Turk McGhie had been inspirational on his part. For now his personal safety wasn't only assured, it also meant he was in a position to bring a certain pressure to bear on those publicans he was dealing with.

He was thinking of expanding his empire, and his plans, although dependent upon the whisky Harry Hydelman and Harry's friends down in England were supplying, did not include them.

The whisky was his cake. Give it a few more months for the English side of things to reach full capacity and he would start going for the icing, which would be his and his alone.

After all, Lizzie had always drummed it into him that if he was going to think at all then he should always think big.

Which was precisely what he intended doing.

The dinner dance was held at the Covenanters' Inn in Aberfoyle. The décor was Jacobean; tartan and weaponry were everywhere.

Kirk was looking forward to the evening ahead of him as he escorted Susan through to the roped-off area reserved for her father's party. This sort of 'do' was right up his street.

'Kirk, I'd like you to meet my father, Major Gibb,' Susan said.

Major Gibb was a tall slim man with a definite military

bearing about him. He spoke in clipped tones and everything he said somehow sounded like an order.

Mrs Gibb was a pleasant, faded sort of lady who might have at one time in her life spent too long in the sun and consequently dried out as a result.

'Let me introduce you around, my boy,' Major Gibb said. 'Then we'll all have another drink before we sit down.'

And still it didn't click with Kirk. Nor did it until he was about to sit down at the table when his eye was caught by a piece of white cardboard leaning against a pepper pot.

The cardboard bore the legend, 'Reserved for Black Lion Brewery'.

He felt as though he'd been doused with ice-cold water.

'They've got venison on tonight. I just love it, don't you?' Susan said at his side.

Kirk stared at the man who'd so cold-bloodedly sacked his father and whose dead brother, Gerald, had once dreadfully humiliated Walter that afternoon long, long ago in the cellar of what had then been Walter's pub.

'Kirk?'

He turned to her. 'Sorry. Did you say something?'

'Your eyes have gone all poppy as though you'd just seen a ghost.'

He smiled. Unwittingly she'd just come up with the perfect allusion. 'In a way I have,' he replied.

'How so?'

He continued smiling and didn't reply.

For the rest of the meal he was strangely silent, often staring quizzically at Major Gibb and occasionally sideways at Susan.

Once, she asked him what he was thinking.

'That it's a small world,' he replied. And although she pressed him he wouldn't elaborate.

After the meal came the dance part. More drinks were brought while the table was cleared. In another part of the room a small band struck up.

By now Kirk had established that the majority of men in the

party were senior personnel with Black Lion Brewery while the others had outside connections.

One of these was a man called Andy White who worked for a small distillery which supplied a variety of spirits to the pubs owned by Black Lion Brewery. Although whisky was in short supply there was no shortage of other spirits such as gin and brandy, and it was mainly these Andy White, the area rep, supplied to Black Lion.

Kirk made a point of chatting at length to White, saying confidentially he would like to talk to White at a later date on a business matter. On hearing that, White was only too pleased to give Kirk his card. Kirk said he would phone White the following week.

Kirk had been planning to contact a distillery soon but up until that evening hadn't decided on any particular one. Now that he'd met White it would have been foolish of him not to have taken advantage of the fact.

He and Susan had a few dances together after which they were summoned over to where Major and Mrs Gibb were sitting.

'It's most kind of you to escort my daughter when Nigel couldn't make it,' the Major said. Then, turning to Susan, 'You did say he'd met Nigel, didn't you?'

'Yes,' Susan replied.

'Marvellous fellow, Nigel,' Major Gibb went on. 'Very fond of him.'

Kirk could see only too clearly which way the wind was blowing. Nigel was favoured and the Major was letting him know it.

Mrs Gibb said, 'He comes from a very well-connected family. They're in shipping, don't you know.'

'No, I didn't,' Kirk replied.

'And what is your family in?' the Major asked.

It was on the tip of Kirk's tongue to say his father had been killed in the war or come out with some other fanciful, and acceptable, story. But at the very last moment he changed his mind.

Very slowly and with a smile on his face he said, 'Actually my father works as a barman in a pub. He used to run a pub of his own once but the owner sacked him.'

'And which brewery owner was that?' Major Gibb asked.

Kirk's smile thinned. 'You,' he replied softly.

Susan looked quickly at Kirk but he kept his gaze riveted on the Major, who now suddenly looked quite put out. A blush crept into Mrs Gibb's cheeks and her hands fidgeted in her lap. Kirk sipped his drink, said nothing and waited.

'I hope there are no bad feelings?' the Major said after a while.

'From my dad or myself?'

'Both of you. Business is business, after all.'

'Well, there's certainly none from me,' Kirk lied, adding a trifle acidly, 'as you say, business is business.'

Susan placed a hand on his arm. 'Shall we have another dance?' she asked gently.

'Why not?' he replied and led her back on to the floor.

'You're certainly a cool one,' Susan said when they were dancing.

'Do you want me to go?'

'Not unless you feel you want to.'

'I didn't know who your father was until tonight,' he said.

'I know that,' she replied. 'Do you hate him?'

'He put my mother, father and myself out on the streets so I'm not exactly enamoured of him. But if I hated anyone in your family it was your Uncle Gerald, who owned the brewery before your father. He was a real choice specimen.'

Susan registered surprise. 'You knew him!'

'No. But I had first-hand experience of him at work. He once humiliated by father like you wouldn't believe. Made my father beg like a dog. There was no need for that, none at all. Neither of them was aware that I overheard.'

'I'm sorry,' Susan said. 'It must have been awful for you.'

'I've never forgotten the incident. Things like that leave a mark on you.'

'Did your father deserve to be sacked?'

181

'To be honest, he wasn't exactly the best publican in the world. But he didn't deserve that sort of treatment, not after the years he'd put into that pub. Your father could have at least placed him elsewhere as a head barman or something.'

'And now he works as an ordinary barman?' she asked.

Kirk nodded. 'He was far too old to get another pub. Especially having been sacked, which meant he didn't have any references. He was idle for quite some time during which we lived off my wages till he landed the job he's got now.'

They danced for a while in silence. Then Kirk said, 'I got the message loud and clear from the Major that he more than approves of Nigel.'

'He wants us to get married.'

'And will you?'

'I haven't made up my mind yet.'

Kirk smiled. 'Shipping and beer. It could be the foundation of something really colossal.'

'I rather think my father sees it that way too.'

'I thought he might.'

'But when I marry it'll be because I want to and not because he's forced me into it.'

'And how does Nigel feel about all this?' Kirk asked.

'He loves me.'

'But you don't love him?'

'I never said that.'

Kirk smiled. 'You didn't have to. It's obvious from the way you speak about him.'

Susan furrowed her brow and looked thoughtful. 'I like him, there's no doubt about that.'

'But liking isn't loving. There's an awful big difference between the two.'

'Have you ever been in love?' she asked, looking up at him.

'No.'

'Not even a little bit?'

He gently squeezed her waist. 'Is that supposed to be a leading question?'

'Of course not. How could you even possibly begin to feel

that way towards me? You've only known me five minutes.'

'Precisely,' he replied.

'I suppose I was just trying to pry into your past,' she said.

'There's no one else, if that's what you're trying to find out,' he lied smoothly. God, Minnie would've had a fit had she heard him say that!

Susan smiled and seemed to put more vigour into her dancing.

They stayed for a further hour and then Kirk suggested they go, to which Susan agreed.

'Thank you very much for the evening,' he said to Major Gibb. 'I thoroughly enjoyed myself.'

'It was a pleasure to have met you,' the Major replied, looking as though it was anything but.

Kirk shook hands with Mrs Gibb and then moved away to wait until Susan had said her goodbyes.

Once in the car Susan snuggled up to him. The drone of the engine and the darkness all around soon took their effect by sending her off to sleep.

As they headed for Glasgow, Kirk had time to reflect on the evening. To begin with he thought he'd been a bloody fool to come clean with Major Gibb the way he had. But thinking on it further he came to the conclusion his reaction had been the right one. If he was going to continue to see Susan, and he certainly had every intention of trying to, then to have lied would only have got himself horribly enmeshed in a skein of untruths which could have unravelled at any time very much to his detriment.

'We're here,' he said later, shaking her by the shoulder.

Susan blinked and sat up. 'Where are we?' she yawned, looking out the car window.

'Outside my flat. I thought you might like a cup of coffee.'

'Coffee?' she mocked gently.

'Genuine Blue Mountain. You can't get better than that,' he replied, pretending not to have picked up her inference.

He held the door open for her while she got out, then, taking her hand, led her upstairs.

Once in the flat she gazed around. It was the first time she'd ever been in a bachelor flat.

'What do you think?' he asked, taking her coat from her.

'It could do with a bit of redecoration.'

'Couldn't agree more. Unfortunately I just don't seem to have had the time.'

'It's a bit plebian as it stands now.'

He treated her to a mocking smile. 'But you've forgotten. My secret's out. I *am* plebian.'

'Nonsense. You might have come from the masses but you're not one of them.'

Busy getting out the coffee, he said over his shoulder. 'If my mother could hear you say that she'd go down on her knees and kiss your feet.'

'You sound like you're fond of her.'

'I am. She's the original pillar of strength. If she'd been born a man she could've become Prime Minister.'

'And what about you, what do you want to become?'

'Rich,' he said and laughed. 'Filthy stinking rich. I have an aim in life: to be top dog.'

'Top dog at what?'

'Whatever I'm doing,' he replied.

'That's quite an aim,' Susan mused. 'And you know something?'

'What?'

'I think you'll probably succeed.'

He laid out two cups. 'If I don't, it won't be for the lack of trying, I promise you.'

Susan sat and regarded him steadily until the coffee was made. They drank in silence, each watching the other, both knowing what was coming next.

When their cups were empty he took hers and placed it along with his on the side of the sink. He liked to be tidy, that being something else Lizzie had instilled in him.

He crossed back to Susan and hoisted her into his arms. He kissed her while at the same time caressing her body. She moulded herself against him and moaned deep in the back of her throat.

He pulled his lips from hers and gazed into her eyes. He saw assent there.

In the bedroom he took his time stripping her. As he worked, she stood staring at him, the bird hypnotised by the stalking cat.

When she was naked he laid her across the bed and caressed her some more. She twisted and writhed under his knowing fingers.

'Get your clothes off,' she gasped, perspiration dotting her brow.

The waiting was almost unbearable for her as he slowly undressed and then carefully folded his various articles of clothing over a nearby chair.

When he finally came to her she'd worked herself up into a fever pitch. Eagerly her hands grasped him, urging him on.

But Kirk had learned a great deal with Minnie, part of which was that he had a natural talent for sex. Instinctively he knew what to do and how to go about it. Nor did he ever allow himself to become totally subjective during the preliminaries and the act. There was always that part of him he kept apart.

He soothed her now. Tamping down the fires he had lit and her imagination had fanned into a roaring furnace.

When she was calm and once more in control he started again, secretly amused and pleased with himself at having such power over the female body.

When her flesh was burning to the touch and her neck was stained with passion he went into her. Slowly, deliberately, the maestro putting bow to his violin.

And all the time he made love he smiled like some benign god looking down from on high.

Later that night, Susan sat before her dressing-table mirror thinking of Kirk and his lovemaking.

What he'd done to her, and how he'd made her feel, had

been absolutely fantastic! Right out of this world! Compared with him Nigel was a ham-fisted clod.

Goose-bumps played up and down her spine at the memory of the orgasms she'd had. What she'd experienced previously were mere minor sensations, not even in the same league as those which had racked her body causing her to cry out in exultation and ecstasy.

Earlier, she'd talked to him about love. Well surely what she and he had experienced on his bed was love. What else could it be?

And it was glorious.

'Pleased to meet you again, Kirk,' Andy White said, rising from behind his desk, where he'd been busy with paperwork. 'Now, how about a dram?'

'Bit early for me, thanks all the same,' Kirk replied. It was ten in the morning.

'Tea or coffee, then?'

'Tea please.'

'Right. I'll just send the girl to make it.'

Andy left the room and Kirk gazed around. The Carswell Distillery was situated on the outskirts of Glasgow and dealt mainly with Glasgow and the surrounding area. Still small, it nonetheless was ambitious and was trying to muscle in among the larger distilleries with the intention of one day being counted as such itself.

To Kirk's way of thinking, this made them ideal for his purpose as it meant he stood a far better chance of getting a better deal with Carswell's than he would with its larger competitors.

'Now, what can I do for you?' Andy White asked on his return.

'I want to know the discount terms you'd give me if I bought from you in bulk?'

White smiled just a little patronisingly. 'Whisky's very tight, if that's what you're after.'

'I want everything but. Whisky doesn't interest me.'

186

'And what sort of size order did you have in mind?'

Kirk handed White a sheet of paper on which he'd written his weekly requirements.

The smile vanished from White's face as he read the paper.

'That's only for starters,' Kirk said. 'I hope to double and then triple it within the month.'

'That's a lot of drink,' White said.

'I'm dealing with a lot of thirsty people.'

White fiddled with a pencil. 'What sort of discount did you have in mind?' he asked.

'Twenty-five per cent.'

White looked up, shocked. 'That's ludicrous!'

'Oh, I don't think so. It still leaves you enough to make a fair whack out of it. And don't forget it's your product that'll be going into the pubs and once people get used to a certain product they tend to keep on using it. Off-sales, that sort of thing.'

'So this would be going into pubs, then?'

'Yes.'

'That makes a difference.'

Kirk smiled gently. 'I thought it might.'

'Do you ... eh ... own these pubs?'

Pub ownership had never occurred to Kirk before. He decided he liked the idea.

'No,' he replied. 'Let's just say I have influence with them.'

'It's a helluva big single order if you manage to triple it,' Andy White. 'It would make you our second largest customer.'

'Who's the largest?'

'Major Gibb's Black Lion Brewery.'

'Second to them, eh?' Kirk said. That was another idea he liked.

'Of course you realise I can't give you an answer on this myself. I have to put it higher up.'

'How long before you can tell me?'

'A couple of days. Shouldn't be more.'

'Fine. I'll wait to hear,' Kirk replied.

The tea arrived and for a while they talked about football. White, it turned out, was a Clyde supporter.

'Masochist,' said Kirk.

With Turk McGhie bringing up the rear, Kirk entered the pub. This was the last on the long list of those he supplied whisky to. The owner was a man called McAlpine. McAlpine was behind the bar, and when he saw Kirk come in through the door he gave him a friendly nod and gestured towards the back room. When he saw Turk was with Kirk, a nervous expression flitted across his face. Turk tended to have that effect on people.

'This isn't your regular day,' McAlpine said, breaking open a bottle. He poured three half-gills which he handed round.

Turk downed his in a single gulp. As far as he was concerned, whisky was for swallowing and not for playing with.

'How's business?' Kirk asked.

McAlpine was no fool. He knew something was coming. 'Can't complain,' he replied.

'I've been in a few of the boozers round about. You're doing better than them.'

'Aye, I'd say that was probably so.'

'Can you say why?'

He's going to put up the price of his bloody whisky, McAlpine thought bitterly.

'Because I've always got whisky and they haven't,' he replied looking grim.

Kirk nodded. 'Quite.'

'How much a case?'

Kirk looked puzzled. 'Pardon?'

'How much are you putting it up a case?'

Kirk grinned. 'No, no, you've got the wrong end of the stick entirely, Mr McAlpine. My price stays the same. But whether the whisky stays with you is another thing entirely. Tell me, what do you pay for a case of gin?'

McAlpine mentioned a price.

188

'Aye, that's about right. You see, what I want you to do is buy all your spirits from me. Same price as you're paying now, so you're not out of pocket any. The only difference, as far as you're concerned, would be that I'd be your sole supplier, instead of me and the other people you're dealing with now.'

'Same price on everything?' McAlpine asked, wanting to hear Kirk say it again.

'You show me your invoices and I'll match the prices. Of course, if you don't scratch my back here then I won't feel obliged to continue scratching yours. In other words, there'll be no more whisky.'

McAlpine was over a barrel and knew it. He was one of four pubs supplied whisky by Kirk in the district and all of them were doing far better than their competitors. He'd be cutting his own throat not to agree. And as Kirk had pointed out, it wasn't going to cost him anything.

'You're on,' McAlpine said.

Kirk sighed. That was the last pub wrapped up and not a bit of difficulty in convincing any of them.

'Another half?' McAlpine asked.

Kirk nodded. 'And while I'm drinking it I'll read through your invoices so I can make a note of what you're now paying.'

While McAlpine fetched the invoices, Kirk thought about how much more money all this was going to mean for him.

On top of his whisky profit he was going to collect a cool twenty-five per cent on every other bottle of spirits supplied by him. At the very minimum his income was going to increase by at least seven hundred and fifty per cent. It was a staggering thought.

There was no use leaving that amount of money lying in a bank collecting a derisory interest. He had to make it work for him, and Andy White had given him the idea of just how to do it.

It was time he bought his own pub, which would be even more grist to his spirits mill.

It was true what was said about money, he thought. Once you had it you couldn't help but make more.

But first he was going to give himself a well-deserved treat. He'd taken Susan to the pictures the other night and one of the films had featured an Alfa Romeo which she'd enthused about.

He'd find and buy one of those. And he'd start looking in the morning.

Kirk lay in bed with Minnie snoring gently by his side. God, he was bored to tears with her, he thought. He knew it to be his imagination but daily her empty chatter seemed to get more and more inane.

He was finding it damned difficult running two birds at the one time though he was managing it. The trick was to make sure neither came up to the flat unless specifically invited. Both had strict instructions to telephone rather than call round if they wanted to speak to him.

The other problem was that for a large city Glasgow had an amazingly small centre which was where most of the amenities were. It always worried him that when out with one he'd bump into the other.

Still, that was a risk that had to be run, for he had no intention of giving up either – for the time being, that was.

He put his hands behind his head and pictured Susan. She was still seeing Nigel but, so she assured him and he believed her, only at her father's insistence. The Major still wanted to marry beer to shipping.

'Black Lion Brewery,' he said out loud. Christ, what a coup it would be to marry Susan and fall heir to the whole shebang!

For Susan was the Major's only heir and when he popped his clogs the brewery would come to her, and through her to whoever she was married to.

What a magnificent opportunity there was for him here if only he played his cards right. The Major was dead against him of course, wanting the merger with Nigel. And he daren't alienate the Major, who might spike his guns – should he succeed in marrying Susan – by putting all sorts of complications in his way.

That meant that anything sudden and without the Major's blessing, like an elopement say, was definitely out.

He hadn't proposed yet but he would soon. And when Susan accepted, as he had no doubt she would, they would then both have to work at getting her old man to agree.

That might take quite some time and would depend entirely on Susan's sticking to her guns and not giving in to pressure to marry Nigel instead.

This time-lapse suited his purposes admirably. For the goose that for the moment was laying such marvellous golden eggs for him wouldn't be around forever. And when the goose flew back to America his entire spirit empire would collapse virtually overnight.

He'd already spoken to Harry about continuing with the blokes who man the P.X.s down in England but they'd turned down the idea. They'd only work the fiddle through Harry because they knew and trusted him.

When that happened he could get shot of ratbag snoring beside him, her usefulness being ended, and get on with marrying Susan.

'Black Lion Brewery,' he said again out loud. What a perfect revenge on that sod Gerald Gibb who'd humiliated his father so badly and cruelly. And what a deliciously ironic twist against the Major, that the son of the man he'd fired so callously would end up in the Major's seat.

It was a lovely dream but there was still an awful lot could go wrong. In the meantime he must get on with investing the substantial amount of money he was earning. And in fact he was going to see a pub in the morning that had been recommended to him as a good buy.

The other thing was to get hold of the Alfa he'd promised himself. He'd tried a dozen dealers so far and not one of them had come up with the particular model he wanted.

He remembered then passing a new used-car lot that had

191

only opened recently. As it was on the way to the pub he had to go and see, he would stop in there.

Whoever ran it couldn't do any worse than the other dealers he'd tried.

'What?' Walter Murray exclaimed, and sat down.

'I've bought a pub and I want you and Mum to run it for me,' Kirk said.

'You mean you actually own it?'

'Lock, stock and water engines.'

'Since when?'

'This afternoon.'

Pride blazed from Lizzie's eyes. 'You're on your way, son. You're on your way,' she said, and going to him hugged him tight.

Walter scratched his head. This was the last thing he wanted. He was happy being an ordinary barman. No worries, no problems, just pulling pints and letting life roll over him.

'I thought I'd run you over to see the place. What do you say?' Kirk asked.

Walter shifted uncomfortably. 'I've got to be on duty soon. It's not really all that convenient at the moment.'

'To Hell with your shift!' Lizzie exclaimed. 'This is far more important. Walter, you're going to be running your own pub again! Just think of it!'

'Aye,' he replied miserably. 'I am.'

'When do we take over, son?' Lizzie asked.

'I've given the chap I bought it from a few days to move out and you can get in directly he's away.'

'Is it a big house?' Walter asked.

Kirk grinned. 'Huge.'

Walter groaned inwardly.

Kirk wasn't surprised by his father's reluctance. He had been expecting it. En route to the pub in his car, he stated it was his idea for it to appear that it was Walter who was running the pub while in actuality it would be Lizzie who'd be pulling the strings from behind the scenes. Walter would be out front managing the bar itself, while Lizzie would be doing all the paperwork and actual management.

Walter brightened considerably when he heard that. Lizzie nodded her approval. This arrangement would suit her down to the ground.

As Kirk had said, the pub was huge – barn-like; there was a predominance of tiles everywhere, which gave it the appearance of a public toilet.

As far as Lizzie was concerned, the biggest mark in its favour was that it was situated in a part of the city that, although still working-class, was definitely far superior to the area they were in now. Definitely several steps up, she said, nodding her approval.

While Lizzie and Walter were being shown round by the man who up until that afternoon had been the owner, Kirk took himself down to the cellar, wanting to see again the extremely large storeroom situated at its rear. It was this storeroom which had clinched the buy for him. There was plenty of room to store his spirits, whisky and otherwise, prior to their distribution. And with his mother and father above the storeroom, like two dogs guarding a buried bone, his spirits were as safe and secure as drink can ever be said to be in a city renowned for an extremely high incidence of alcohol thefts.

Whistling, he made his way back upstairs. If the result of today's work didn't call for a celebratory drink, then nothing did.

'Oh my God, my God . . . my God!' Susan gasped, her body convulsing.

Breath hissed from beneath Kirk's teeth as he collapsed on to her.

Her face was awash with sweat, various strands and locks of her hair wet and plastered to her skin.

'Ooooohh!' she groaned. The sound seemed to come up from her very toes.

Kirk lay where he was for a few seconds and then gently pulled himself away.

'That was the best yet,' Susan said.

'Happy?'

'Hmm. You?'

'If you are, I am.'

There was a pause and then she said, 'I never knew it could be like this. So ... so satisfying.'

'I love you, Susan.'

She rolled over to face him. 'And I love you, too.'

He smiled in a way he knew she found disarming. 'Fancy getting married?'

She blinked, caught off guard. 'Pardon?'

'Would you like to get married?'

'Is that a formal proposal?'

'As formal as you'll ever get from me. What's wrong? Was I supposed to go down on one knee or something?'

She shook her head. 'I'm just ... I don't know what to say!'

'The customary reply is yes or no.'

'Of course it's yes! What I meant was, it was a bit of a shock coming out the blue like that.'

He drew her to him and kissed her on the mouth. Putty in his hands, he thought. Sheer bloody putty.

'I think I knew the moment I first saw you it was going to end up like this,' he lied smoothly. 'There seemed a sort of inevitability about us. As though it had been decreed from on high.'

'Mrs Kirk Murray,' she said aloud, but as though talking to herself. 'I like the sound of it.'

'When shall we tell the Major?'

Susan frowned. 'That isn't going to be easy. He won't be exactly mad on the idea.'

He stroked her flank causing her to shudder. 'If he does make strong objections, the thing is for you to stick to your guns. It may take a while, and there's no great rush for us to get married, after all, but we must bring him round to seeing it our way in the end.'

'He's going to be awfully disappointed. He has his heart set on my marrying Nigel.'

'His heart or his sporran?'

Susan laughed. 'That's wicked!'

'But true. And you know it.'

She looked wistful. 'He so desperately wants to be a big success in business like his older brother Gerald was. He was always under Gerald's shadow, as far as I can make out, the way some younger brothers are. He sees my marrying Nigel as laying the foundations for something far larger and grander than anything Gerald achieved.'

'Well we must persuade him your happiness is more important than empire building,' Kirk said.

'We can try.'

'And we'll succeed. You leave it to me.'

'I don't care about anything else, Kirk. Just so long as I have you,' she whispered.

'That's how I feel about you. But we must be practical. I mean, there's no use being silly about these things. Besides, it would hurt me to think I'd caused any sort of rift in your family. That would be getting off to a bad start and I don't want that for us.'

'When shall we tell him, then?'

'If he's in, why not tonight? There's no use putting off till tomorrow what we can do today.'

Her leg curled round his and she reached down to stroke him. 'I couldn't agree more,' she said.

He laughed before saying, 'And before we go to see him I've a surprise for you I've got to pick up.'

'What sort of surprise?'

'Wait and see.'

'Oh! That's unfair!'

He rolled over on top of her, pinning her to the bed. Slowly he sank on to and then into her.

Within a minute she'd forgotten all about the surprise.

'It's absolutely beautiful, Kirk!' Susan exclaimed, clapping her hands in delight.

'She's a beauty right enough,' Kirk said. 'Just what I had in mind.'

Eddy King smiled. There was nothing like a happy, satisfied customer.

'The engine's in excellent nick,' Eddy said. 'I've checked it out myself so you can take my word on that.'

'How clever of you,' Susan said to Kirk. 'It's just like the one we saw at the pictures.'

'I'm glad you like it. It was a bit of a problem getting hold of one but seeing your face now makes it all worthwhile.'

'Are you taking it with you?' Eddy asked.

'Of course,' Kirk replied, extracting a packet of money from a side pocket. He already knew the price, having been told by Eddy on the telephone earlier.

'What about my old car?' Kirk asked. 'Will you take that off my hands?'

Eddy crossed to the car and looked at it. He named a sum he thought fair in the circumstances, which Kirk accepted on the spot.

After money and log-books had been exchanged, Eddy waved to Kirk and Susan as they drove off in the Alfa Romeo.

Not a bad-looking bit of skirt that, Eddy thought to himself after the Alfa had disappeared from view.

What looked like a potential customer appeared on the lot to stare at an old Lanchester. Eddy hurried over, Kirk and Susan already fading from his mind.

Major Gibb stared long and hard at Susan before turning his gaze to Kirk.

'Naturally we want your blessing, sir,' Kirk said.

'Do you, now,' the Major replied, his voice steely with overtones of anger.

Susan bit her lip.

'We love one another very much,' Kirk added.

Major Gibb poured himself a small whisky, which he sipped, rather like a bird of prey delicately tasting blood. He didn't offer a drink either to Kirk or his daughter.

Inside he was fuming. How dare this ... this upstart, this guttersnipe, propose marriage to Susan! And how dare she

196

accept him when she knew damn well it was his dearest wish she marry Nigel.

'What do you say, sir?' Kirk asked.

Major Gibb stared straight ahead and didn't reply. The tension in the room mounted and mounted.

Kirk looked at Susan, who pulled a face. He shook his head and gestured everything was going to be all right, doing that to calm her more than anything as she was obviously becoming very agitated.

'Susan?' the Major said at length. 'Do you trust me?'

'Yes, Daddy.'

'And have I not always tried to do my best for you?'

She nodded.

'Then listen carefully to me now. I'm a lot older than you with far more experience in life. What you feel for this man here is mere infatuation that will soon pass as all these things do. A marriage with him would be a disaster. He has no stock, no breeding. In other words, albeit he might speak like a gentleman, he's as common as muck.'

Kirk went white. He'd been expecting a set-to but this was below the belt.

'What's he got to offer you apart from this infatuation, eh? Well the answer's nothing.'

'I own a pub of my own!' Kirk said hotly. 'And I have other interests.'

'A pub,' the Major said scornfully. 'One pub. And what are these other interests?'

'Spirits,' Kirk replied. 'I buy and sell in bulk.'

'That's interesting. So you deal in spirits and own a pub. And of course I own a brewery plus a great many pubs, all of which Susan will inherit one day. I don't suppose that ever crossed your mind, did it?'

'We love one another and that's why we want to get married,' Kirk insisted.

The Major smiled. 'I met lots like you in the Army, young man; you're a breed I know well. Adventurers, we used to call them. They'd do anything to get on.'

Kirk was furious now. He hadn't expected the old fart to see through him like this - at least not quite so clearly.

'Father I ...'

Susan was forced to shut up when the Major interrupted her. 'Has it crossed your mind, my girl, that it could well be your inheritance he's after?'

'Not Kirk, Daddy. Honestly, he's not like that.'

He smiled patronisingly. 'What a naïve child you really are!'

'I am not a child, nor am I naïve!'

'If you're not a child then stop acting like one. Can't you see he's trying to take you in?'

'It's just not true!' Kirk said.

'So you say,' the Major replied. 'But I don't believe you.'

'You can't make me marry Nigel,' Susan said.

'No, that I can't.'

'And I won't, Daddy. Not now I've met Kirk. He's the one who's right for me.'

'How can you be so sure about such a thing at your age?'

'I just can,' she replied defiantly.

The Major went on, 'Nigel's people have position, power, status. They're one of Scotland's leading families. You'll never do better than that.'

Kirk barked out a laugh. 'And you accuse *me* of being an adventurer! What do you think you are? Why, you're trying to do exactly the same thing you're accusing me of!'

'It's not the same,' the Major replied coldly.

'Why not? Because I'm common as muck, as you put it, while you're a few rungs higher up the social ladder? Christ, but that's the most two-faced, hypocritical attitude I've ever heard.'

'What I'm proposing is a marriage between social equals,' the Major said, 'with advantages to both sides. The way these things have always been done. I will not, repeat, *not*, have Susan marry beneath her and to someone who is so obvious and blatant an opportunist and adventurer.'

Kirk clenched his hands into fists. The last thing he'd

wanted was for this to happen. His bitter retort died in his mouth as Susan suddenly burst into tears. Going to her, he took her in his arms.

As Susan sobbed on Kirk's shoulder and the Major glared at them, the door opened and Mrs Gibb entered. She'd been out and had just that minute returned.

'What's going on here?' she demanded.

'He's proposed to Susan,' the Major said.

'Susan hasn't accepted, has she?'

'She has.'

'Quite impossible. Completely out of the question.'

On hearing that Susan burst out wailing.

'Precisely what I've been telling them,' the Major said jubilantly.

At that moment Kirk saw himself back in his father's pub cellar and heard his father being cruelly humiliated by Gerald Gibb. And now the same thing was happening again, only this time he was the one on the receiving end. Well, the Gibbs wouldn't find him such an easy mark as Walter. By God and they wouldn't!

The intense hatred he'd felt towards Gerald Gibb when he was a boy was born in him again, only this time it was directed at Gerald's brother, the Major.

'There there, lass,' he crooned, stroking Susan's hair. 'They won't break us apart. You have my word on that.'

'Your *word!*' the Major sneered. 'The word of a guttersnipe.'

'If you weren't an old man and Susan's father I'd punch your head in for some of the things you've just been saying.'

The Major stuck out his chest. 'Don't let my age deter you. I'm more than capable of looking after myself.'

'Right then!'

He tried to let Susan go but she clung on to him. 'Please Kirk, not that. Please!'

Her pleas made him pause.

'Hiding behind a lassie's skirts now, eh?' the Major taunted.

199

With a roar Kirk tore himself from Susan and leapt forward. All deviousness and previous good intentions were swamped by anger.

As Kirk charged at him the Major leant down and picked up an object that had been standing against the back of a chair.

'No!' Susan screamed.

The Major's hand flicked and there was a brown blur through the air.

Kirk's cheek was opened from ear to mouth as neatly as though a scalpel had been run along it. Blood spurted to blind one eye.

The Major darted to one side and the brown object blurred through the air again.

This time Kirk managed to get a hand in front of his face. He grunted in agony as a section of skin was flayed from the side of his hand.

The Major raised his swagger stick to strike again but that blow never landed. He staggered backward as Kirk's head took him full in the chest.

Kirk and the Major tumbled to the floor with Kirk managing to get himself on top of the Major. His undamaged hand grabbed the swagger stick and tore it from the Major's grasp.

Kirk was dimly aware of Mrs Gibb pounding on his back as he raised the swagger stick to strike. Beneath him the Major struggled, but to no avail.

'Kirk?'

Susan's hand closed around his. 'Please don't. For me.'

He swallowed and then took a deep breath.

'Please?'

He took another deep breath and then another. Blood from his cheek fell splashing on the Major and the carpet.

'All right,' he said, his voice trembling. 'I won't touch him.'

Very slowly he brought the swagger stick down till it was resting across the Major's throat.

'You've just made the biggest mistake of your life,' he said.

The Major's look was one of contempt.

Kirk rose to his feet, leaving the swagger stick across the Major's throat, where it rested for a few seconds more before the Major snatched it away.

Susan peered at the wound on his cheek. 'You'll have to go to the hospital with that. It needs stitches,' she said.

'Get out of my house,' the Major said, coming to his feet.

'You riff-raff are all alike. Cause trouble wherever you go,' Mrs Gibb spat.

Susan found a hanky which she pressed to Kirk's cheek, and for the present anyway this stopped the flow of blood. There was also blood dripping from Kirk's hand, the damaged part feeling as though it had been immersed in boiling water.

'Will you come with me to the hospital?' Kirk asked.

Susan nodded.

'You'll stay here! I forbid you to go!' the Major said.

'Susan dear, Daddy knows best,' Mrs Gibb added.

Susan looked undecided.

'Well?' Kirk demanded softly.

Susan made up her mind. She knew if she deserted Kirk now their cause would be lost forever.

'I'll get the coats,' she said. And without looking at either of her parents she left the room.

Kirk stared hard at the Major, as though trying to imprint the man's face in his memory for all time, the hatred between them so strong it almost seemed a physical entity.

'You sacked my dad but you'll never sack me,' Kirk said.

'Peasant,' Mrs Gibb commented after he'd gone.

'Now just try and relax,' the doctor said, priming the hypodermic.

Kirk stared at the needle in fascination, his insides turning as the doctor brought it close to his flesh. He closed his eyes and waited for it to bite.

Within seconds the anaesthetic took effect and his lacerated cheek grew numb. While this was happening, nimble fingers

201

were cleaning and bandaging his hand. 'This'll be as right as rain again in a few weeks,' the pleasant-faced nurse said as she worked on the hand.

Kirk mumbled his thanks.

'Right then, let's get you sewn up,' the doctor said.

After a while Kirk asked, the words coming out most peculiarly due to one side of his face being frozen, 'Will there be a scar?'

The doctor stopped what he was doing and took a step back. His eyes locked on to Kirk's.

'I'm doing my absolute best but I'm afraid there will be. I'll try and make it as fine a one as possible though.'

'Thank you,' Kirk replied. He closed his eyes again and let the doctor get on with it.

In his mind he conjured up the image of Major Gibb. One way or another he'd get that bastard, if it was the last thing he ever did. On his mother's life he swore it.

He'd marry Susan, not because it was a way at getting the brewery but because it would hurt the Major and his dreadful wife. They desperately wanted Susan to marry Nigel. Well, he would deny them that.

And that would only be the start.

Susan dropped him off at the flat in a taxi.

'You'd better not come up,' he said. 'All I want to do is go to bed and sleep.'

'I understand. Oh, my poor Kirk,' she said laying her hand on his injured cheek.

'It only hurts me when I laugh,' he joked. And they both smiled in the darkness.

'I'll ring you in the morning,' she said.

She kissed him on the lips and then sat back in the seat as he climbed stiffly from the cab.

The first thing he did when he was inside the flat was to pour himself a large drink. He drank that off as though it was lemonade and poured himself another. The alcohol went straight to his head, making him feel woozy. He swayed and

202

had to catch on to the mantelpiece to steady himself.

There was a mirror above the mantelpiece which he now gazed into. Although no Adonis, he'd always been proud of his looks, knowing himself to be a little bit more handsome than the average. Well, that was all changed now that he was to bear a scar for the rest of his life. What hurt most was the fact people would be bound to think it was a razor scar, the mark of the criminal and lower classes.

His reverie was broken by a knock at the door. 'Who in hell's that?' he said to himself, seeing off yet another drink.

When he opened the door a smiling Minnie stood revealed.

'Hello, love,' she said, her smile turning to a frown when she saw his bandaged cheek and hand.

'What happened to you?'

He gestured her inside. 'I got done over and robbed by a gang,' he said, that being the story he'd earlier decided to tell everyone.

'Did they put the boot in?'

'Aye,' he said pouring himself yet another drink and one for Minnie. He suddenly rounded on her as a thought struck him.

'What do you mean coming here without ringing first? You know I told you never to do that.'

'I was just so excited,' she replied eagerly. 'I just had to come right up and tell you the good news.'

'What good news?'

'I'm expecting a wean.'

The words hit him like a thunderbolt. 'Hell's teeth!' he exclaimed. He swallowed his drink and poured himself another large one. His head swam and Minnie went out of focus. He remembered then the nurse had told him not to drink on top of the pills she'd made him take.

'Are you sure?' he demanded.

'Aye. There's no doubt,' she nodded.

Minnie came to him and took him in her arms. 'Now you're doing so well there's no reason we can't get married is there?' she asked.

The laughter rumbled out from deep within him. 'Marry

203

you?' he said contemptuously, breaking away. 'Don't be so bloody daft!'

Minnie caught her breath, the beginnings of tears in her eyes. 'Why not?'

The alcohol rose up and swamped him. All his pent-up fury and rage exploded. He wanted to hurt someone, to humiliate them the way the Major had humiliated him.

He lashed out verbally, hardly conscious of what he was saying.

'Because you're hairy Mary, that's why. A bloody hairy who lives with her slag of a mother in the gutter. Do you actually think I'd marry the likes of you? Why you must be out of your effing skull, woman! I never said I intended marrying you. And as for this brat you say you're carrying, how do I know it's mine, eh? Answer me that!'

'Oh, Kirk,' she whispered, standing transfixed.

He raved on. 'I've no guarantee that I'm the father, after all. God knows who could've been through you, the whole male population of the district for all I know. And anyway how *can* you be up the clout? You always told me you took precautions.'

'Something must've gone wrong,' Minnie mumbled.

'I'll bet it did. Gone wrong intentionally. Well, if you think you're going to nail me with this brat you say you're carrying, you've another think coming.'

He stumbled to the bottle and poured himself another, slopping quite a bit on the floor in the process.

'Now get out!' he said, reeling where he stood.

For the space of a few seconds Minnie stood staring at Kirk. Finally she said, 'May God forgive you for tonight because I never will.'

Then with great dignity she walked from the flat, pulling the outside door quietly closed behind her.

Kirk stumbled through to his bed and fell across it. 'I'll never marry hairy Mary,' he muttered thickly. 'It's the Gibb lassie for me.'

His snoring filled the room.

When Susan returned from the hospital she found her parents waiting up for her. She knew right away from her father's flushed face he'd been drinking more than usual.

'The doctor told Kirk he'll carry a scar for the rest of his life,' she said accusingly.

'Marriage with him is, as your mother said earlier, *completely* out of the question,' Keith thundered. 'Can't you see that?'

'You'd live to regret it, dear,' Jean said, a pleading tone in her voice.

Keith went on. 'Nigel is such a nice boy ...'

'I'm not disputing that,' Susan cut in. 'But it's Kirk I happen to love.'

'Love!' Keith spat scornfully. 'What do you know about love at your age!'

Susan coloured a little. 'I'm not a child any more ...'

'Then stop behaving like one.'

'I would say you were the one doing that, Father.'

His hand flashed to crack against her cheek. Crying out, Susan staggered backwards.

'I won't be spoken to like that by anyone, far less you,' Keith said.

'Perhaps you'd like to take your swagger stick to me as well?'

'Susan!' Jean warned.

'I never realised before tonight what a bully you really are. That and selfish through and through.'

Keith advanced a step, his face suffused with anger. 'When I think of everything we've done for you ...'

'Like what?'

'You've had nothing but the best in life.'

'Oh sure! Except my parents when I needed them.'

'Don't talk nonsense,' Jean said guiltily.

'You abandoned me when I was four years old. Twice I saw you, twice only between then and the beginning of the war.'

'It was unavoidable,' Jean said. 'Your Daddy was in the army ...'

'My "Daddy" wanted a boy. What he didn't want to know was me.'

'That's just not true,' Keith said.

'When have you ever shown any affection for me? When have you ever shown you loved me? Well, I'll tell you. Never! Not once!'

At long last the dam had well and truly burst and all the bitter years of loneliness and frustration came pouring out. Tears ran down Susan's face washing her make-up away. Her eyes took on a peculiar staring quality.

'Neither your mother nor I are particularly demonstrative,' Keith said. 'You must have realised that.'

'You managed to be demonstrative with one another, all right. It was only when it came to me that you were suddenly unable to be.'

'We did, and still do, love you very much,' Jean said.

'Then why did you never tell me?'

Jean hung her head in shame.

Susan rounded on Keith. 'And the only real interest you've ever taken in me is since I've met Nigel. And why is that, I ask? As if I didn't know.'

'He's the perfect match for you,' Keith said.

'You mean his money and assets are the perfect match for ours.'

'Think of the children you'll have. Think of the marvellous position they'll be in,' Keith urged.

'And what about *me*? Don't I count?'

Keith threw up his hands in exasperation. 'Everything was all right until this Kirk Murray appeared!'

'You'll break your father's heart if you don't marry Nigel,' Jean said softly.

'Both you and he broke mine often enough when I was a child.'

Jean had no answer to that.

Susan continued. 'I like Nigel well enough and if Kirk hadn't happened along I no doubt would have married him. But I did meet Kirk and love him, and no one, not you,

Mother, nor you Father, is going to make me give him up. As far as I'm concerned he's the only decent thing that's happened to me in this life and I have no intention of sacrificing what we've got together merely to further Father's family ambition.'

All Keith had dreamed of since Susan met Nigel was collapsing round him. He just couldn't believe it was actually happening.

'We gave you everything,' he said in a piqued tone of voice.

'You gave me pocket money and Miss Buchan's School For Young Ladies,' Susan replied.

Jean was crying as Susan left the room.

Kirk groaned as he came awake. His mouth felt like a sand-pit and his head was filled with cotton wool inside which someone was playing a big bass drum.

'Christ!' he said, sitting up. He had a thirst on him he felt the entire Clyde wouldn't slake.

It was his own fault, of course. He shouldn't have forgotten the nurse's warning about taking alcohol on top of the pills.

Then he remembered Minnie's visit and slowly, in bits and pieces, what had been said came back to him.

Groaning again, he buried his head in his hands. First the Major fiasco and how he'd gone and bombed out Minnie. Not that he gave a monkey's about her but if he was to lose Harry Hydelman because of it then his entire business would vanish down the plughole virtually overnight.

He mustn't let that happen without at least trying to save the situation. He'd explain to Minnie about the pills and how, combined with the alcohol, they'd put him out of his mind.

He'd tell her he hadn't known what he was saying. Anything, as long as it gave him a chance to continue stringing her along until Harry was due to return to the States. The kid was going to be a problem but that was something he'd worry about once he was reconciled with Min.

He washed some aspirin down with tea which made him feel fractionally better. Then he set about getting dressed, not an easy task, feeling the way he did and with a bandaged hand to boot.

Minnie's elder sister Irene answered his knock. 'Is Min home?' he asked, forcing a smile on to his face.

Irene looked daggers. 'Aye, she is. Away ben.'

Minnie was in bed, with her mother, Judy, sitting on a chair beside her.

'Oh, it's you,' Judy said scornfully.

'Is she having a long lie or something?' Kirk asked.

At the sound of Kirk's voice Minnie's eyes flickered open. Slowly she turned her head to stare at the wall.

'I'm sorry about last night,' Kirk said. 'I'd taken these pills at the hospital you see and ...'

'You meant every word you said. I could see it in your face,' Minnie said.

'That's not true. Honest!'

'Don't lie, Kirk. Not ever again.'

'Hairy Mary?' Judy said. 'Oh, you sod!'

'Listen, about the baby ...'

'There is no baby now,' Minnie said, tears welling from her eyes.

'But you said ...'

'There was one last night. But not this morning.'

'She went to an abortionist,' Irene said from the doorway.

'Oh, God Almighty!' Kirk said, holding his head which was still throbbing violently.

'The first we knew of it was when she came home bleeding like a stuck pig. I know well the butcher she went to and it's a wonder she survived,' Judy said.

'He uses a knitting needle,' Irene added.

Kirk felt sick then. Bile rose in his throat but he managed to swallow it down again.

'Is there anything I can do?' he asked.

'It cost a fiver,' Judy said.

'I don't want his rotten money. Let him stuff it,' Minnie said vehemently.

'It's the least I can do,' he said fumbling for his wallet.

'I tell you, I don't want it!' Minnie yelled, half rising from the bed. With a sob she fell back again.

'There, there, lass,' said Judy.

'It's all a horrible mistake,' said Kirk.

Minnie wiped tears from her eyes. 'I never ever want to see you again. Do you understand?'

'You'll change your mind. You're naturally fraught,' Kirk replied hopefully.

'No. You and I are finished. Just the thought of you ever laying your hands on me again makes me want to vomit.'

'All right then. I'll go.'

'And don't ever come back! As far as I'm concerned, from now on in you're as dead as the wean that man howked out of me.'

Having said that, Minnie pulled the blankets over her head and gave herself over to her grief.

At the door Kirk handed Irene two fivers. 'To pay for the abortionist,' he said.

Irene handed one of the fivers back and without saying anything further shut the door in his face.

He walked downstairs to stop at the close mouth. What a bloody shambles! Yesterday he had everything, today ...

I must ring Harry, he thought. Maybe I can still salvage something out of all this.

But knowing how thick Harry and Judy were, he didn't hold out much hope.

They met in a café not far from the base where they'd met several times previously. Kirk arrived first and had already got through two cups of coffee by the time Harry showed, dead on three o'clock as agreed.

'Now what's the panic?' Harry demanded once he'd got himself a coffee and sat down facing Kirk.

'It's about Min and I,' Kirk replied, and went on to tell Harry a version of what had happened.

Harry listened attentively while puffing on a stogie he'd lit up. During the entire story his eyes never once left Kirk's face.

As Kirk talked he sweated, under the arms and between his legs. His stomach felt as though there was a pound of lead sitting on it.

'So there we are then,' he said, coming to the end of his tale.

'A bad business,' Harry said.

Kirk nodded.

Carefully Harry knocked ash into the ashtray. 'So why come all the way out here to tell me? What's your reason, Kirk?'

'I want to know how this affects us. Judy and you being so close and all.'

'Hell, shit! She's just a handy piece of ass as far as I'm concerned. There's certainly nothing she would say to me would affect what you and I have got going.'

A tidal wave of relief surged through Kirk. Grinning, he said, 'And there I thought it was love between you two.'

'That's what she thinks as well,' Harry smiled. His smile broadened when he added, 'Truth is, I wanted to dump her a few months back but decided against it, thinking it might upset you in some way. You see I thought *you* were in love with Minnie. The real thing, wedding bells and all that horse manure.'

'You thought ... ?'

'I guess we were both wrong,' Harry said.

Kirk sat back in his chair and shook his head. 'Bloody hell!' he said.

Harry continued, 'So now you've split with Min that leaves me free to give Judy the heave. You see, I got the sweetest little soldier lady back at the base. A real hot momma who just can't get enough of ole Harry here!'

'So things can go on between us just as they have been?'

'Darned tooting, kid. Darned tooting!'

This was unbelievable luck, Kirk thought. Just when he'd thought everything was lost the tables had turned and he'd come out ahead – for that's how he saw getting rid of Minnie.

Of course, he was still losing, as far as the Major and Black Lion Brewery were concerned, but he'd just have to live with that for the moment. The important thing was the whisky fiddle was still secure and in the short-term that mattered above all else.

He felt a tinge of regret that the child was gone; he rather fancied himself as a father, but what the hell! There was plenty of time ahead of him for babies. Ones that Susan would give him.

And now that Min was off the scene there was no reason from his point of view why he and Susan couldn't get married more or less right away.

Of course this went totally against all the plans he'd had in that direction but it was just impossible for him to carry those out after his scene with the Major and Mrs Gibb.

He'd put it to Susan first chance he got, he decided, which turned out to be sooner than he'd imagined. When he got back to the flat, she and several suitcases were on the doorstep waiting for him.

She'd left home, and come to move in.

'It's working out a treat,' Kirk said, closing the books his mother kept on the running of the pub.

Lizzie folded her arms under her substantial bosom. 'I enjoy it. As does your dad not having any worries other than managing the bar.'

'Good,' he nodded.

'Mind you, I am a wee bit disappointed.'

'In what way?'

'We're doing well but not as well as I thought we would've.'

'And why's that?' he asked.

'It's that pub, the Belle Vale, round the corner. Because they're so close to the subway station they get all the people coming home from their work. Friday nights between six and eight that place is a wee gold mine.'

'Is that a fact?' Kirk said thoughtfully.

'If we could just get that trade our figures would be up fifty to seventy-five per cent at the end of the week. But there's no hope of that, I suppose. After all, the Corporation's hardly likely to move the subway just to oblige us!'

Kirk laughed with his mother. 'Hardly!' he agreed. 'But then if the mountain can't come to Muhammad, then it might just be possible for Muhammad to go to it.'

'I don't follow you, son.'

'Is the pub brewery owned or independent?'

'Independent,' she replied.

Kirk smiled. 'Well you know the old saying, if you can't beat them join them. Or better still take them over.'

'They'd never sell,' Lizzie replied, pursing her lips.

'You never know until you ask them, do you?' Kirk said. And left it at that.

He waited till early Friday evening before paying a visit to the Belle Vale and it was just as Lizzie had said. The place was packed to the gunnels, with the four barmen on duty working flat out.

He left, to return early Saturday morning, ordering a soft drink and asking to see the owner, who turned out to be a Mr Muir.

'What can I do for you?' Muir asked. Although well on his way to seed he still had a hard look about him.

Kirk introduced himself and shook Muir's hand. Then, coming directly to the point, he made a gesture which took in the Belle Vale.

'I was wondering if you'd be interested in selling?' he asked.

Muir shook his head. 'Not a hope. I like the place fine.'

'I'd give you a good price.'

'The answer's still no.'

Muir stood up to walk away but Kirk restrained him by placing his bandaged hand on his arm.

'Why don't you think it over? There's no harm in that.'

'The answer's still going to be no, Jim, even if I think it over till kingdom come. Now do you mind? I've got work to be getting on with.'

Pity, Kirk thought as Muir strode away. For now he would have to send in Turk McGhie.

On the previous night he'd decided he was going to have this place.

212

*

It was just after closing time and Muir was out the back of the pub stacking crates of empties for the early morning pick-up. He looked up as a figure loomed out of the darkness.

'Mr Muir?'

'Aye, what is it?'

Muir screamed as the bicycle chain wrapped itself round his head. He screamed again when the chain was savagely jerked, causing its many sharp edges to rip his face to shreds.

He fell to his knees, desperately tearing at the chain. Breath whooshed out of him as the boot went into his kidneys. Knocked off balance, he fell forward to land sprawling in a puddle.

Many men would have been finished then but Muir wasn't. Blinded by blood and chain he none the less rolled over and tried to climb back to his feet.

He grunted as his legs were kicked from under him and again he fell sprawling into the puddle. A hand grabbed the hair on the back of his head and pushed. His nose and mouth went under water.

Just when he thought he was going to lapse into unconsciousness his head was pulled clear of the water and life-giving air rushed into his lungs. The effect was to make him cough and splutter.

A voice in his ear said, 'This is only the start. Things can get a lot worse, I promise you. We'll wreck your pub, drive your customers away, and with my razor here I could carve your bonnie wife just like a Christmas chicken. And if you went to the polis, well . . . nothing would happen for a while like and then she'd just disappear one day. For ever. Get my meaning?'

Muir nodded.

'Good. So why don't you just save yourself all that trouble by talking sensibly to my friend Mr Murray when he calls to see you again? He's the one who wants to buy the Belle Vale, remember?'

Muir nodded again.

'He'll give you a fair price so you can buy another boozer

elsewhere. It's just that he's decided he wants the Belle Vale for himself. Understand?'

'Yes,' Muir croaked.

'Right then,' Turk said.

And to make sure the point was fully driven home Turk drew back his foot and kicked Muir full in the testicles.

Muir was howling and scrabbling on the filthy ground as Turk faded back into the night.

'You've got to carry me over the doorstep,' Susan said. 'It's traditional.'

'Bloody hell!' exclaimed Kirk. 'Carry a big fat lump like you!'

'Beast!' replied Susan, laughing.

'You haven't even begun to see the beast in me, Mrs Murray. That comes once we're inside and I can have my wicked way with you.'

'Oooh!' she said, pretending to be frightened. 'I think I might like that.'

He swung her into his arms and kissed her first before carrying her into the house. Once inside he unceremoniously dumped her into a chair.

'Now, how about some of that champagne I paid an absolute fortune for?' he asked.

'Yes, please.'

He popped the cork off the ceiling and then proceeded to pour more champagne over the floor than he actually got into the glasses.

'Some publican you are,' Susan sniffed.

'Champagne isn't my normal line. I'm more used to pouring pints of heavy,' he retorted.

'Then we'll have to ensure there's more champagne from here on in.'

'Damn right!' he said.

He handed her a glass. 'To us!' he toasted.

'To us!'

He sipped appreciatively, absolutely adoring champagne.

'Are you upset your folks didn't come?' he asked.

'I didn't expect them to. Did you?'

He shook his head.

'They'll get over it. In time.'

Kirk's eyes glittered. 'I don't think so somehow. To put it mildly, they hate my guts.'

'I thought it was nice of Nigel to send a telegram to the registry office.'

'Maybe we should have had a church wedding, but with your folks acting the way they've been, a ceremony in the registry office seemed the best thing in the circumstances.'

'The main thing is we're married,' Susan said. 'That's all I wanted.'

'Me too.'

He poured more champagne and then, kneeling beside her, said, 'Bed?'

'But it isn't even noon yet!'

'Spoken like a good Protestant,' he said.

She uncurled herself from the chair and stood up, drawing him with her. 'I love you,' she said simply.

'And I love you too.'

He led her to the bedroom, his mind already on the appointment he had later that afternoon when he was to sign the final papers transferring ownership of the Belle Vale to him.

He'd done down the Major and acquired his second pub at a rock-bottom price all in one day!

Starting to undress Susan, he thought that what he was about to do to her wasn't the only screwing he excelled at.

'That's it then,' said Harry Hydelman. 'I fly back Stateside middle of next week.'

Kirk sighed. It had been a damn good run and now it was over. The shipment of whisky Harry had just delivered was the last one.

He opened a bottle and poured them both a stiff one. 'We couldn't have gone on much longer, anyway,' he said. 'More and more whisky's being made available. A few more months and who knows? The publicans and the punters might well be able to get as much as they want just for the asking.'

'It's good to take it philosophically,' Harry said.

Kirk stared into his drink. He had an Alfa, a house and four pubs. What did he have to complain about? And the pubs were coining it in for him. Jesus, but they were money-spinners!

He and Harry talked for a little while longer and then Harry took his leave.

'Goodbye, kid,' Harry said at the door.

'Goodbye, Hank the Yank.'

He closed the door and Harry Hydelman went out of his life.

Another week, he thought, and that would be the end of his spirit business. He grinned, thinking Harry had never found out about the deal he had going with Carswell's Distillery.

Harry might have made on their fiddle, but he'd made an awful lot more.

He picked up the latest letter he'd received from the Army and read it through again. For over a year now he'd been successfully using one excuse after another to postpone his call-up. He would have considered it an unmitigated disaster to have had to go while Harry was still in Britain.

But with Harry now going home there was no reason for him to keep up his delaying tactics. He'd notify the Army in a fortnight's time and let events take their course from there. It was a real bitch that he had to go but since the Army medic had logged him A1 fit he'd known it was inevitable.

He'd put his mother in overall charge of his pubs while he was away. She'd see no fast ones were pulled on him by any of his managers or staff. And if anyone tried, well . . . there would be Turk McGhie to back her up.

He made a mental note to increase Turk's wages. He needed the hard man's loyalty while he was away and as far as he was concerned nothing secured loyalty better than money.

'You'll write to me as soon as you can?' Susan said, dabbing at her tears with a handkerchief.

'The first moment I get. I promise.'

'Oh Kirk, I'll miss you.'

'I should get leave after basic training and anyway two years isn't for ever.'

'At this moment it seems like it.'

He held her close and whispered in her ear, 'I know what it is you'll be missing most. Old Henry one eye.'

'Don't be crude,' she said. But his joke had brought a smile to her face.

'Now away with you. And I'll write the first moment I get.'

He kissed her and then propelled her from him. He gave her a wave before turning abruptly into the door of the assembly point. He reported to a sergeant who told him gruffly to sit down. He chose a bench on which a solitary figure sat hunched.

The figure straightened and lit a cigarette.

'I know you,' Kirk said. 'But I can't put my finger on it for the moment.'

Eddy King smiled. 'I sold you an Alfa Romeo. How's it going?'

Recognition flooded Kirk's face. 'The Alfa, of course. It's still going well.'

'Glad to hear it.'

They shook hands and reintroduced themselves.

'It's good to see a friendly face in a situation like this,' Kirk said.

'Aye, it is that,' Eddy agreed.

Susan walked away from the assembly point looking neither left nor right. She might have been a zombie or a robot.

She didn't know how long she walked for but suddenly she was aware she was standing outside a teashop. She went inside and sat at a table.

'A pot of tea and a cake please,' she said to the waitress.

She looked at the faces around her and saw nothing. All she could think of was that Kirk had gone away and for most of the next two years she was going to be on her own again.

She was still attending college, which would help fill the days and her mind. But the nights. Oh, the terrible nights that lay ahead of her.

The loneliness she remembered only too well from her childhood settled back on her, causing her shoulders to sag a little.

Without Kirk's presence and lovemaking it would be as though she was dead. For these two things were very life-blood to her.

Rising, she made her way through to the toilet where, once in the cubicle, and having locked the door behind her, she bent down into a squatting position.

She threw up into the bowl.

KIRK AND EDDY

'Mean by name and mean by nature,' the corporal spat, drawing himself up to his full five feet two inches. His eyes, like something out of the reptile house, swept round the room taking in everyone and everything.

'We've got a right one here,' Kirk muttered to Eddy who was standing beside him.

'Silence!' Corporal Meany bellowed. 'Anyone utter again and I'll have all your guts for garters.' He paused before adding spitefully, 'And maybe I'll have them anyway. Just to keep in practice, like.'

Stiff-legged, he stalked forward. The men of his previous section had given him a nickname. They'd called him the meanest poison dwarf of all. It summed him up precisely.

There were eight in the section and they'd all just arrived in from Scotland, having completed their basic training. Billeted at Schloss - which is to say 'castle' - Schwartzberg, they now formed part of the BAOR, or British Army of the Rhine.

Meany stopped in front of a soldier. 'Name?'

'McKenzie, sir.'

'You're a horrible shite of a man, McKenzie. Know that?'

'Yes sir.'

'Now what are you?'

'A horrible shite of a man, sir.'

'Good.' Then very softly, 'And don't you ever forget it.'

Meany passed the next man and then stopped at the next. 'Your name?'

'Napier, sir.'

221

'You sound Edinburgh.'

'I am, sir.'

Meany grinned. 'Well you must be a poof then. Only poofs ever come out of Edinburgh.'

A man laughed.

'Shut up!' Meany screamed.

The man stopped laughing instantly and swallowed hard.

Meany turned his attention back to Napier. 'What did you do in civvy street? I take it you are a conscript?'

'Yes, sir. I was a musician, sir. Played clarinet.'

'Clarinet, eh? So I was right. You are a poof.'

'No sir.'

'Are you contradicting me?'

'No sir. I'm only ...'

'Only what?'

Napier started to look scared. 'I'm not a poof, sir,' he said in a voice that was little above a whisper.

Meany brought his face to within inches of Napier's. 'If I say you're the fucking abominable snowman then the abominable snowman you are,' he hissed.

Napier nodded.

Meany moved on.

'Now what have we here?' Meany said, stopping in front of Eddy. 'Name?'

'King, sir.'

'King, is it? Not Dunphy or O'Toole or O'Houlihan?'

Eddy stared straight ahead, not rising to the bait.

Meany went on. 'The map of Ireland written all over your face. A Mick, is it? A Fenian? A fucking left-footer?' He waited a few seconds and then screamed, 'Well?'

'I am a Catholic, sir.'

'Aaahhh!' breathed Meany. 'One of those. Well, well, well.'

Pursing his mouth, Meany walked round to the side of Eddy's bed where his kit was stacked.

'Show it to me. I don't want to touch it,' Meany said.

Eddy did as he was bid. Holding each piece of kit up for inspection.

222

'Dirty,' Meany said. 'Dirty ... dirty ... dirty ... dirty ...'

Meany drew in a deep breath. 'Your entire kit's dirty, King. Almost crawling, you could say.'

With a sudden motion his arm swept sideways to send Eddy's kit clattering over the bare wooden boards that comprised the floor.

Meany grinned viciously. 'You have an hour, soldiers. When I come back I want to see your kit shining, and I mean shining. And of course the floor will be filthy now, thanks to King's kit contaminating it, so that will have to be cleaned. You, King, that will be your responsibility. Floor and kit for you. Kit for the rest of you.'

He paused and his grin grew even wider. 'One hour. Precisely.'

Humming jauntily, he strode from the room, slamming the door behind him.

The men slumped where they stood.

'Welcome to Germany,' Napier said.

'That man's unbelievable,' McKenzie said.

Norrie Smart nodded his agreement.

'I suppose we'd better get on with it,' Kirk said.

Eddy looked in dismay at his kit strewn across the floor. He was thinking of his father and Gloag and praying history wasn't about to repeat itself.

'I'll never get all this done in time,' he said.

'Yes you will,' Kirk said. 'We'll divide your kit amongst the rest of us which will only leave you with the floor.'

'Hold on a minute,' Pete Rennie said. 'I don't see why in the hell I should help him out.'

Eddy blushed. 'I'll do it all myself then.'

'No, no!' Kirk said, waiting till the full attention of the section was focused on him. He then went on.

'The way I see it is this. We've been unlucky to draw a first-class bastard for corporal. Well, that's tough on us. But if we don't all pull together as a unit it'll be even tougher. One for all and all for one like the musketeers, that should be our motto. Because you see, Rennie, it might be Eddy here just now but

223

who's to say who it'll be next week? It might be you, pal. Or you McKenzie or you Kirkwood.'

'I think what you say makes sense,' said Napier. 'I'm certainly willing to help Eddy if he helps me. If Meany doesn't like Catholics, he certainly doesn't like Edinburgh folk either.'

'One for all and all for one,' Smart said approvingly.

'Well?' Kirk demanded.

Napier nodded. 'I think maybe you're right.'

'I *know* I'm right.'

'Let's get on with it then,' Ogle said, picking up a piece of Eddy's gear. 'Time's a-wasting.'

The men galvanised into action, Eddy hurriedly starting to change before making for where the buckets and hot water were kept.

In the midst of all this, Ogle said suddenly. 'Tell me, Napier, are you really a poof or do you just walk that way natural, like?'

'Get me a bird and I'll show you whether I'm bent or not!' Napier retorted.

Everyone burst into laughter.

On time to the minute the door to the room opened and Meany strode in. He came up short and his eyes slitted when he saw the men were standing to attention by their beds.

The inspection was thorough, done by an obvious expert.

'Hmm!' said Meany, grudging approval in his tone, when it was all over.

The men stood rigid, staring straight ahead. Not a muscle moved or eyeball flickered.

'When did you last sleep?' he asked Smart.

'Over twenty-four hours ago, sir.'

'Well then, big hard men like you won't be tired yet, will you?'

Smart wasn't sure whether to reply or not.

'Will you?' Meany barked.

'No sir.'

'I'm glad to hear it. Because in an hour and a half we leave on all-night patrol. I suggest you get yourselves something to eat in the meantime. You're going to need it.'

Chuckling he quit the room.

'Bastard!' said Smart.

'But an NCO,' Kirk said.

Muttering and grumbling, the section left for the cookhouse where Sergeant McQuarrie – affectionately known as the Glasgow poisoner – held sway.

The pine forest was dark as the inside of a coal bin. In single file, with Meany in the lead, the section moved forward.

'I can't see a bloody thing,' Eddy whispered.

'You're not alone,' Kirk's voice came whispering back out of the blackness.

'Damn!' said Ogle, who'd just fallen over a tree stump.

'Quiet!' Meany's voice scythed through the night air from ahead.

Eddy's eyes were drooping and his eyelids felt as though there were grains of sand under them. It was bitterly cold, which was affecting him even more than it normally would have done, due to lack of sleep.

The thought uppermost in his mind was that if they didn't get a break soon he'd drop in his tracks. And he shuddered to think what Meany would do to him should that happen.

Soon the trees started to thin and then they disappeared altogether. The section found themselves moving along hillside with thick bracken underfoot.

The moon was a pale sliver high in the sky. The clouds were low, many and scudding in the biting wind that had sprung up.

Meany stopped and waited till the section had come alongside him. Using his sten he pointed to a clump of trees several hundred yards away.

'The boundary between us and the Russian sector,' he said. 'Cross over and you'll have Ivan breathing down your neck *tout de suite*.'

All in, the men leaned on their rifles. Breaths rasped as they tried to catch their wind.

'Not tired, are we?' Meany taunted in a low voice. He was

still fresh, thanks to the full eight hours he'd had the previous night coupled with the fact he was used to this patrol having been doing it for the past eighteen months.

The men kept silent, deeming that the best policy.

Meany chuckled. 'Only another couple of miles and then I'll let you have a smoke. All right?'

Kirk, who was closest, nodded.

'Then let's go.'

To try and keep himself awake Eddy thought of Annie Grimes as he walked. A smile came to his face as he remembered the good times they'd had together. He didn't think he was ever going to find another woman like her.

Kirk was idly thinking about Susan, wondering how she was getting on.

He'd been home on leave the previous week, a forty-eight hour pass and his first since coming into the Army, which had been marred by Susan being down with a bad attack of the flu.

That had been a big disappointment to him as he'd been looking forward eagerly to those two days. She'd told him to go out and enjoy himself, but apart from checking round his pubs, which were all doing very nicely thank you, and having a few drinks here and there, he hadn't bothered.

When he left her her face was still all puffed up, her nose red and streaming. A repulsive sight, he'd thought, but had naturally refrained from saying so.

The worst thing of all was he hadn't been able to have sex with her. She had offered but quite frankly she was in such a state it would have been a form of sadism, and masochism on his part, to have gone ahead with it.

He couldn't remember when he'd been so randy and couldn't wait to get amongst the Kraut fräuleins, or 'frats', as he'd heard they were called.

One thing was certain. Irregardless of what he'd said to Susan, he wasn't going to be going without while he was over here. The very idea was ludicrous. If he had to be in Germany then he was damn well going to make the best of it ...

There was a secluded dip in a hollow and this was where

Meany led them. From beyond the dip could be heard the sound of running water.

'We'll have a brew up,' Meany said, slumping to the ground. 'Ogle, you go up to the top there and watch. I'll have your char brought to you. Napier, you go down to the burnie over by and fill the kettle.'

There was a rattle and then a clank as a small kettle came tumbling over the ground to land at Napier's feet.

'All the comforts of home,' Meany added.

With a sigh, Eddy sank on to his backside. He couldn't remember when he'd been so whacked.

'King? What do you think you're doing?'

Eddy was instantly wary. 'Taking a break, Corporal.'

'Wrong, Mick. You've got a job to do.'

Eddy struggled to his feet. He was coming to hate Meany albeit their acquaintance had been a short one to date.

'What do you want me to do, Corporal?'

Meany took his time lighting a cigarette. He sighed with satisfaction as he blew smoke into the air.

'I want you to cross that burnie and report back to me what's on the other side.'

'What sort of thing am I looking for, Corporal?'

Meany smiled in the darkness. 'I've been wondering for some time whether or not the Ruskies have mined the far bank. Now seems as good a time as any to find out.'

Eddy's mouth went dry. 'Mines?'

'Aye. You know the things? When you step on them they go bang.'

Eddy wasn't at all sure whether Meany was having him on or not, playing games with him.

'That's a direct order,' Meany said softly.

'Right then, Corporal,' Eddy replied, now very wide awake.

'Then get on with it.'

Meany closed his eyes and lay back. 'Murray and Rennie can make the fire,' he added as an afterthought.

Eddy glanced at Kirk, who looked back sympathetically. Hefting his rifle he headed for the burn.

He found Napier just straightening up having filled the kettle. 'I've to go for a walk on the other side to see if it's mined,' he said.

'The man's a bloody headcase,' Napier replied.

Eddy couldn't have agreed more.

He stared at the burn, realising with a shock it was more than that. It wasn't exactly a river but neither was it a burn. Fast-flowing, it had the breadth of a British canal.

He went in tentatively, feeling with his feet to see what sort of bottom it had. Holding his rifle above his head he waded out towards the middle.

The water came up to mid-thigh and then stopped. The surface beneath his feet was still fairly solid as he continued across.

Then it happened. His right foot came down, only instead of being arrested it continued going down and down. With a muffled cry he pitched forward.

Water closed over his head as he sank feet first. Despite his alarm he had wits enough to hang on to his rifle.

He kicked for the surface, using his free hand to make a doggy-paddle sort of movement. He gasped in a huge lungful of air as his head broke water.

The flow of water carried him a few yards by which time he was able to reach out and grab hold of the grassy bank. Digging his fingers in, he managed to drag himself up on to the bank where he collapsed, coughing and spluttering.

When he'd caught his breath he'd have given anything for a cigarette but his packet was sodden. He cursed through clenched teeth.

He allowed a few minutes to go by before coming to his feet. Carefully keeping close to the bank he walked upstream. As far as he was concerned, this bank was as far as he was going. He found the broken branch of a tree which he used to test the depth of the water for nearly a hundred yards upstream, from where he'd landed. But nowhere was the water as shallow as it had been on the other side. Finally he decided there was nothing else for it but to swim back across to where the water became shallow again.

He slung his rifle round his shoulders before sitting on the bank. He submerged his feet in the water and then sort of slipped and slid in. He struck out strongly, doing the breaststroke. In less than a minute he was clambering to his feet, having come again into shallow water.

'Dear, dear me,' said Meany when he saw the dripping and bedraggled Eddy looming out of the darkness. 'And what happened to you, soldier?'

'Nobody told me your burnie was deep at the far end,' Eddy replied.

'Is that a fact?' Meany said, pretending to be surprised. 'I'll have to make a mental note of that for future reference.'

'Were there any mines over there?' Smart demanded eagerly. Intellectually he was the complete opposite to his name.

'Oh aye, hundreds and thousands of them,' Eddy replied sarcastically. 'Didn't you hear them going off?'

'Oh!' said Smart. The penny dropping.

'How far over the other side did you go?' Meany asked casually.

Eddy squatted by the small fire and tried to warm himself. His teeth were chattering.

'I went up and down a hundred yards and in about a hundred feet,' he lied smoothly.

'So we can safely say it isn't mined,' Meany said.

'Or else he was lucky,' Kirkwood added.

'Are we all going over?' McKenzie asked anxiously. The last thing he wanted being to end up soaked through like Eddy.

'Here,' said Kirk putting a steaming mug of tea into Eddy's hands.

'No we're not,' said Meany, replying to McKenzie's question as he rose to his feet. 'And there's no time for that now, King,' he added. 'You can use it to put out the fire.'

Eddy trembled, and it wasn't from the cold either.

Kirk reached out to place a restraining hand on Eddy's arm. 'Do as the man says,' he said gently.

Eddy upended his mug, causing the small fire to expire in a billow of steam and angry hisses.

'Right then, single file as before,' Meany said. 'And I think we'd better double it up so King here doesn't catch cold. You look the delicate type to me – are you, King?'

'Not particularly, Corporal.'

'We'll double it up anyway. Nothing like getting the old blood coursing, especially on a cold morning like this.'

Clutching his sten in front of him, Meany led the way at a trot.

'Can you make it?' Kirk asked quietly.

'Do I have an alternative?'

Kirk grinned. 'That's the lad.'

'Besides, if I stood still I'd probably freeze to death.'

The rest of the section had now started after Meany.

'I'll bring up the rear,' Kirk said.

Unslinging his .303 Eddy followed the dim shape of Ogle while behind him the still overweight Kirk was soon puffing and panting.

Before long, the run began to take on a nightmare quality for Eddy. A cold, clammy perspiration appeared on his brow and his breath became harsh, like sandpaper, in his throat.

Weakness settled on him, sapping his strength and will. To combat it he thought again of Annie Grimes. Talking to her, laughing with her, the pair of them making love together. And when that was exhausted he thought back to his young days in Glasgow. Going guising at Halloween. Playing street-games of which there had been a multitude. The first time he'd kissed a lassie down a back close dunny.

He thought of his father, whom he'd idolised and whom that bastard Gloag had murdered for no other reason than his father was a Catholic. In his mind he tried to conjure up a picture of Gloag but the face he saw was Meany's. A man he hadn't even known existed until the previous day.

His feet pounded beneath him while his senses swam. He

230

knew he had a temperature and guessed he was either already delirious or else well on the way. The heat of his fevered body was causing his clothes to steam, the steam puffing off him in wisps and clouds.

From somewhere ahead a voice began to sing and amazingly was allowed to continue to do so. The voice was Norrie Smart's.

'Three German officers crossed the Rhine,
Parlez-vous?
Three German officers crossed the Rhine,
Parlez-vous?
Three German officers crossed the Rhine,
Fucked the woman and drank the wine.
Inki pinki parlez-vous?'

Napier, in a most untuneful voice for a professional musician, sang the next verse.

'Oh landlord have you a daughter fair?
Parlez-vous?
Oh landlord have you a daughter fair?
Parlez-vous?
Oh landlord have you a daughter fair,
With milk white tits and curly hair?
Inki pinki parlez-vous?'

Up ahead Meany started to laugh as it began to rain.

'Jesus Christ Allbloodymighty!' Kirkwood said, collapsing on his bed. 'I never ever want to go through the likes of that again.'

Eddy sat on the edge of his bed. He was wide-eyed and staring.

'The best thing is for us all to get stripped off and towelled down,' Kirk said, to which there were murmurs of agreement.

'See that Meany!' Ogle said. And a few of the section

laughed when he mimed strangling the corporal.

Kirk threw off his top clothes and then turned his attention to Eddy. 'Come on, let's be having you,' he said.

Eddy grinned weakly but didn't move.

'You feel as though you're burning up,' Kirk said, having felt Eddy's brow.

'Perhaps we should report him sick?' Ogle suggested.

Eddy shook his head. 'I won't give him the satisfaction. Just help me get into my kip, Kirk, and I'll be all right.'

'I have a couple of aspirins,' Pete Rennie said, crossing to his locker.

Kirk helped Eddy strip down to the buff. Then, using a thick coarse towel, he rubbed Eddy vigorously from head to toe. Eddy stood as though in a dream, shivering and occasionally shaking. Even after the rub-down his flesh was still bluish and mottled.

Kirk assisted Eddy into pyjamas after which Eddy gulped down the aspirins Rennie handed him.

'Bed and sleep,' Kirk said.

Eddy's head touched the pillow and his eyes closed. Before Kirk had finished drawing the bedclothes up over him he was snoring.

'Rise and shine, you horrible lot. Come on, out your stinking pits!' And walking down one line of beds, Meany pulled the covers from each. He repeated this when he walked up the opposite line of beds.

'Come on, come on, come one!' he yelled with relish. 'What do you lot think this is, a holiday camp or something?'

Eddy's eyes flickered open. His fever had gone, leaving him still weak, but apart from that he was all right. Constitution of a bloody horse, he told himself as he swung his legs out of bed.

Meany strode down the room to stand in front of Eddy. 'And how's our intrepid swimmer this morning?' he asked.

Eddy stared up at Meany, thinking of Gloag. 'Intrepid, Corporal? I'm afraid that's too big a word for me,' he replied.

Meany's eyes glinted. He knew he was being got at.

'A smart bastard, eh?' he hissed.

Eddy smiled. 'That's the point, Corporal. I'm not. I never had the advantages of education you've so obviously had.'

A hint of a red flush crept up Meany's neck. 'I went to the ragged school, sonny, where we knew how to deal with the likes of you.'

'I'll bet you did,' Eddy replied softly.

'Where I come from in Glasgow we had Catholics for breakfast,' Meany said.

'Where I come from in Glasgow we were lucky to get breakfast,' Eddy retorted.

'Oh, so you think yourself a bit of a hard man, do you?'

'Not me, Corporal. I leave that for the bampots and headcases. Life's hard enough without added aggravation.'

'You haven't even begun to understand what aggravation is, sonny.'

'Are you trying to tell me I'm about to find out, Corporal?' Eddy asked, a trace of insolence in his tone.

'I think you could take my word on that.'

Eddy nodded. The position was crystal clear.

Meany strode into the centre of the room. 'We go out on patrol every other night,' he said. 'Always covering the same ground we did last night and this morning. Understand?'

Smart grunted something in the affirmative.

'Now, it became obvious to me during last night's patrol that despite your basic you're all still soft. And it's going to be my task, indeed pleasure, to toughen up you load of namby-pamby jessies and poofs.'

He paused to puff out his chest and stride up and down a few steps before continuing.

'First off, I think we'll start with PT, as I'm sure you're all stiff after your wee stroll out there in the German countryside. So you've got forty minutes for ablutions and something to eat before reporting to me on the exercise yard. Right then, get to it!'

Heels drumming a tattoo on the wooden floorboards, he marched from the room.

233

'I wouldn't push him if I were you,' Kirk said to Eddy. 'Don't forget he's got the stripes up, which gives him the power of God as far as we're concerned.'

'Aye, I shouldn't let him rile me,' Eddy agreed.

'How are you feeling?'

'Well, not exactly fit to take on the world but an awful lot better than I was last night.'

'I really thought you were going to come down with pneumonia or something. You looked dreadful.'

'And I felt it too, I can assure you.'

Kirk fingered the scar on his cheek. It was something he often did when he was thinking. 'You were lucky,' he said.

'Lucky? To have been landed with a corporal like Meany? That's hardly what I'd call it.'

'You have a point there,' Kirk admitted, as side by side they headed for the ablutions.

'I hope there's hot water,' Eddy said.

There wasn't.

Punctual to the second, Meany strode on to the exercise yard. Like his section standing waiting for him, he was dressed for PT.

'Flat on your faces, you load of nancies,' he shouted. 'And we'll begin with push-ups. Thirty to start with and then in batches of twenty. And if any man stops before I give the order, he has to start all over again.'

Meany threw himself flat on the ground. 'Arms – raise!' he said. Then, counting out the push-ups, 'Hup ... hup ... hup ... hup ...

'All right, come to your feet and run on the spot.'

Kirk came slowly erect. Never an athletic person at the best of times, the push-ups had just about done for him.

Weak to start with, Eddy considered it a miracle he'd got through that first exercise. Gritting his teeth, he ran where he stood. He would drop before he gave in.

The exercises went on and on till finally, with a groan, Napier keeled over.

'Get up!' Meany screamed.

Napier shook his head. 'I can't Corporal. Honest!' he somehow managed to get out.

'The poofs always give in first,' Meany smirked to the rest of the section. 'No guts, you see. No stamina. No backbone.'

He paraded up and down in front of them. 'Now, look at me and you'll see a man and a soldier. And that's what this army's all about. Men and soldiers. Which, God help me, I'm supposed to turn you lot into.'

Smart reached down to help Napier back to his feet.

'What do you think you're doing?' Meany demanded.

'I just thought I'd . . .'

'You're not here to think! You're here to do as you're told. What I tell you. That and nothing else! Understand?'

'Yes, Corporal.'

'And come to attention when you talk to me!'

Smart snapped to attention.

Napier dragged himself to his knees. His face had gone a pasty colour and veins stood out on his arms and legs.

'Smart!'

'Yes sir?'

'As you've got so much energy you may as well wear some of it off. Ten times round the exercise yard, starting *now*! Double time! Double time!'

Smart doubled off to sympathetic looks from the rest of the section.

'And what are we going to do with you, clarinet player?' Meany mused.

Napier climbed to his feet, his thin chest heaving.

'What a specimen,' Meany said scornfully. 'Typical Edinburgh, all pish and water.' Rounding suddenly on Kirkwood, he said, 'And just what do you think you're staring at?'

'Sorry sir. I didn't realise I was staring.'

'Well, you were, you nasty little shit. What are you?'

'A nasty little shit.'

'A nasty little shit, *sir*.'

'A nasty little shit, *sir!*' Kirkwood echoed.

'And don't you ever forget it!'

'No sir!'

Meany walked up and down in front of them several times and then glanced at his watch.

All eyes were on Smart as he doubled past.

'Faster! faster! faster!' Meany shrieked.

Smart positively sprinted on his way.

Meany turned to the rest of the section. 'You've got half an hour and then I want you on the training compound, kitted out for armed combat. Got that?'

'Yes sir!' the section chorused in unison.

'Attention!'

They came smartly to attention.

'Right turn. Dismiss!'

'Phew!' said Kirk when he and Eddy were out of range of Meany's hearing.

'Between last night's patrol and now this, I feel as though I've tangled with a road roller and lost,' Eddy said.

Kirk gave a small grin. 'I know exactly what you mean.'

A few minutes later, as they were changing, Kirk added, 'You know, that man's not only off his chump, he's downright bloody dangerous as well.'

'My da once met someone who I'm sure was just like Meany,' Eddy said, pausing and staring off into space.

'What happened?'

'He murdered my da.'

'God above!' exclaimed Kirk softly. 'Was he caught?'

'He paid the penalty all right,' Eddy replied in a peculiar tone of voice.

Kirk was fascinated by the strange expression on Eddy's face. It sent shivers up and down his spine, as though someone was walking across his grave.

Meany was already waiting for them when they arrived at the training ground, which was situated at the rear of the castle behind the kitchens and stores.

The castle itself was a towering Gothic edifice built on a sort

236

of black rock, the latter giving it its name, Schwartzberg, meaning literally 'black mountain'. There was a magnificent view from the ramparts. On one side there was a sheer drop to a tree-studded valley, while on the other side a rolling plain stretched for several miles until it ran into tree-covered foothills. In the far distance there was the silver glint of water.

The road from the castle gates ran downward until it became the main thoroughfare of the small town of Welsdorp.

'Now, as you all know, this is a rifle,' Meany said, brandishing a .303. 'And this is a bayonet, the bayonet being affixed to the rifle so.'

There was a click as the bayonet slotted into place. Levelling the rifle, Meany brought the tip of his bayonet on to a level with Kirk's belly.

'I think I'll have you to start with, Murray,' Meany said.

Without taking his eyes off Meany, Kirk fixed his bayonet.

'That's a clever laddie. Now come at me.'

Kirk advanced tentatively.

'Not like that, you stupid great nana. Come at me like you meant it. Like you intended doing me some damage.'

Kirk's mouth twisted into a leer. That was going to be easy.

The two men circled one another, eyeball locked to eyeball. Suddenly, and shouting the way he'd been taught, Kirk lunged.

The bayonet stabbed forward, but where only moments before Meany had been standing there was now only empty air. Kirk stumbled by, grunting as the butt of Meany's rifle rapped him in the side.

'You're dead,' Meany said.

Kirk lumbered round, ready to have another go. But Meany waved him back to join the others.

'Now, how about you, Rennie? Let's see if you can do any better.'

Rennie couldn't, being, if anything, slower and more awkward than Kirk.

'Ivan would have you lot on toast,' Meany said scornfully. 'A bunch of bloody Girl Guides could do better.'

For a full five minutes Meany demonstrated, using Smart as an opponent and foil, the intricacies and techniques of the bayonet in close combat.

'Think you've got any of that?' he asked when he'd finished his demonstration. And when there was no reply, 'I said have you got that, you load of imbeciles!'

'Yes, sir, Corporal!' the section chorused.

'Well, let's see if you have then. King, step forward.'

Eddy fixed his bayonet and then stepped towards Meany.

Meany grinned. 'Now if there's one man in this section who looks as though he'd really like to use his sticker, it's you, Mick. Present!'

Eddy levelled his weapon, the tip of his bayonet about six feet from the tip of Meany's.

'Come on then, sonny Jim,' Meany said, crouching fractionally.

Eddy went in slowly. They circled one another, first one way and then the other.

Kirk and rest of the section looked on anxiously. During the last few minutes the atmosphere had changed to become taut and charged.

'Papishers, if I had my way I'd shoot the lot of them,' Meany whispered just loud enough for Eddy to hear. 'I've never yet met one who was worth a monkey's wank.'

Eddy blanked out what Meany was saying, keeping his concentration fixed on waiting for an opening. The tip of his bayonet wove a small figure of eight in the air in front of him.

'And they're usually cowards. Back stabbers,' Meany whispered.

Eddy lunged fractionally but didn't follow it through. Meany danced out of the way.

Meany was certainly quick on his feet, Eddy thought. The man would have been a big hit in the Locarno in Sauchiehall Street any Saturday night.

'What's the matter? Want me to tie a hand behind my back?' Meany whispered. And having said that, he laughed.

Eddy gritted his teeth. He was damned if he'd be drawn. Let the bastard come to him.

'*One, two, three, O'Leary, I saw Wallace Beery,*
Sitting on his bumbeleree, kissing Shirley Temple-O!' Meany sang, and waggled his rifle.

Eddy started to circle again, his concentration homed on Meany's eyes.

'What's the matter? Don't you want to play?' Meany whispered.

Eddy didn't reply, biding his time. As far as he was concerned he could go on like this just as long as it took.

Irritation flashed across Meany's face. He was beginning to get annoyed.

'Come on, you stupid Mick,' Meany said.

Eddy went back to making a figure eight pattern with the tip of his bayonet. He could see his continued silence and refusal to make the first move was getting through to Meany.

'Oh all right then!' Meany said, straightening up and bringing his rifle into a vertical position.

Heaving a sigh of relief, Eddy brought his .303 into the same position, which was a mistake. Too late, he realised Meany had conned him.

'Ha!' cried Meany jubilantly, viciously swinging the butt of his rifle round and lunging forward at the same time.

Breath whooshed out of Eddy as the rifle butt took him full in the kidneys. He pitched to the ground when the rifle barrel smashed across the back of his neck.

He hit the ground with a jarring thump, his own rifle flying from his hands to clatter away. He was trying to struggle on to his knees when the cold metal of Meany's bayonet came to rest against his right cheek. He immediately froze.

'You're dead, King. What are you?' Meany said.

'Dead, Corporal.'

'In combat never ever trust the enemy. No matter what he does or says. Anything could be a feint or ruse to give him the advantage. And once he gets that you end up just so much meat. Got all that into your thick skull?'

'Yes.'

'Yes, *sir!*' Meany screamed and lashed out with his foot.

Eddy groaned as Meany's foot smashed into his side. For a brief instant he saw red and an awesome fury started to envelop him. But luckily, before the fury could overcome him, he remembered Kirk's words about the corporal's stripes making the man God as far as they were concerned. Biting his lip, he brought himself back under control.

'Well?' Meany demanded.

'Yes, *sir*,' Eddy croaked.

'Now stand up.'

Slowly Eddy came to his feet.

'Pick up that rifle.'

Eddy did as he was bid.

'Let me see it.'

Eddy handed the rifle over.

'This is filthy, King. In fact I've never seen a rifle so filthy. What have you been doing with it? Kicking it round the parade ground?'

Eddy came to attention and stared straight ahead.

'Answer me, you horrible shite of a man!'

'I dropped it, sir.'

'Tch! Tch! Very careless of you, King. The Army doesn't like its property being treated in such a manner. In fact it gets downright upset. These ...' and he waggled the rifle under Eddy's nose, 'cost money, a great deal of money, which the Army is very short of. So Army property has to be treated with the utmost respect. Is that clear?'

'Yes sir!'

'I think you'll have to make up for your carelessness, King. Report to Sergeant McQuarrie after I've dismissed the section.'

'Yes sir!'

Meany thrust the rifle at Eddy so that it banged hard against his chest.

'And after McQuarrie's through with you you'll clean and

polish that rifle like you've never cleaned and polished it before.'

'Yes sir!'

'Right then, rejoin the section.'

Meany strode up and down, his eyes glittering as he surveyed the men standing before him.

'You're a slovenly lot. A horrible, nasty, slovenly bunch who need their arses kicked from here to kingdom come and back. And I'm just the corporal to do it. God knows what I've done to deserve eight misfits like you but having drawn you I'm going to make something out of you. And do you know why? Because I've a reputation to think about. A reputation, I may add, that took me a long time and a great deal of sweat to acquire. And no bunch of clarinet-playing Edinburgh poofs and left-footed morons are going to bugger it up for me.'

He paused to take a deep breath. 'You're a bunch of fucking toerags! What are you?'

'A bunch of fucking toerags, sir, Corporal!' they responded in unison.

The man's demented, Kirk thought.

'What are you smirking at?' Meany demanded.

'I wasn't aware I was, sir,' Kirk replied.

'I don't like the way you talk,' Meany said. 'You speak with a plum in your mouth like an officer. So why aren't you one?'

'I don't want to do any more than two years, sir!'

'I suppose you're one of those born with a silver spoon in your mouth? Daddy with a Rolls and cucumber sandwiches for tea?' Meany laughed, finding himself amusing.

'My father manages a pub,' Kirk replied. 'And before that he was a barman. And there was no silver spoon, sir.'

'So why do you talk that way?'

'I had elocution lessons when I was young, sir.'

'Elocution lessons!' Meany exclaimed, and guffawed. 'Help my bob, another poof!'

'It was my mother's idea, sir. Not mine.'

'A right little mother's boy, I'll bet you were. Did you wear a sailor suit when you went to your elocution lessons?'

241

'No, sir.'

'My, my, this mother of yours must have cried when someone razored your pretty face.'

'I wasn't razored, sir. I had an accident. And yes, she wasn't very happy about it. In fact she was quite upset.'

'I'll bet she was. What sort of accident was it then?'

'I prefer not to say, sir.'

Meany glowered. 'When I ask you a question you'll answer it.' Adding onimously, 'Or else.'

Kirk racked his brains for something to say, having absolutely no intention of telling what had really happened. Finally he said, 'I was in a car crash. The windscreen shattered and it was that which ripped my face.'

'Hmm!' said Meany, thinking that was plausible enough.

Eddy glanced at Kirk. He'd been wondering, since meeting Kirk again how he had come by that scar. He'd never asked and Kirk had never volunteered the information. He didn't believe the explanation Kirk had just given Meany.

'You're pals with King here, aren't you?'

Kirk was wary. 'Our beds are next to one another, if that's what you mean, sir.'

'Don't play at words with me, sonny,' Meany replied threateningly.

'I wasn't trying to, sir. I mean I wouldn't presume as much. I was only trying to answer your question. You see, we're all pals together in the section. We all get on.'

Meany came forward to tap Kirk on the chest. 'I get the feeling from you sometimes that you're trying to take the piss. Well don't. It would be a big mistake on your part.'

'Yes sir!'

'And just so you've got time to think about that, you'd better join King when he presents himself to Sergeant McQuarrie at the cookhouse.'

'Yes sir! Thank you, sir!' Kirk snapped.

Meany's eyes narrowed. He suspected Kirk was taking the piss again. And he was right.

'Section, attention!'

Sixteen feet came smartly together and eight backs went ramrod straight.

'Right turn! ... Dis – miss!'

When they were out of Meany's hearing, Kirk came alongside Eddy. 'How are you?' he asked.

'Sore. That was a belter I got in the kidneys. And the kick I got in the side wasn't too helpful, either.'

'There was a moment back there when I thought you were going to haul off and hit the sod.'

Eddy nodded. 'There was a moment I thought so too.'

'Well don't ever do it. No matter what the provocation. Believe me, you'd be playing right into his hands.'

'That's what I keep trying to tell myself.'

'I have a suspicion we're both going to be prime targets from now on in,' Kirk mused. 'As you heard, he doesn't like the way I speak.'

Tongue in cheek, Eddy said, 'He's a horrible little shite of a man. What is he?'

'A horrible little shite of a man!' Kirk replied.

And they both laughed.

'You can wash, Murray, and you, King, can dry,' Sergeant McQuarrie said. He was large and fat with only a few wisps of hair to cover an otherwise bald head. He smiled a great deal and was extremely popular with the men.

Kirk groaned when he saw the mountain of dishes confronting him.

'And when you get through with that lot there's more to come,' McQuarrie added.

'We haven't eaten,' Eddy said hopefully.

McQuarrie nodded. 'I'll see you don't starve.'

'Thanks, Sarge.'

'Here we go then,' Kirk said, plunging his hands into a huge sinkful of steaming water.

Eddy picked up a drying-cloth.

For the next two and a half hours they worked flat out, no sooner clearing away one pile of dirty dishes, pots and pans, than another took its place.

McQuarrie appeared every so often to check up on how they were getting on, once instructing Kirk to fill a very badly crusted pot with water and leave it to steep – for which Kirk was most grateful, having been scrubbing away at the pot for a good ten minutes.

Finally it was all over; the last dish and item of cutlery had been dried and put away.

'You did well,' McQuarrie said. 'Now come away through and mess with the rest of us.'

There were eight of them round the table over which McQuarrie presided, sitting at its head.

Kirk goggled when he saw what was served up. He hadn't seen food like this since joining the Army.

'Perks of the job,' McQuarrie said, attacking a huge piece of steak.

'Wine?' a cook asked Eddy, proffering a bottle.

'Yes, please,' Eddy replied eagerly.

'Breakages from the Officers' Mess,' McQuarrie said, giving them a sly wink. 'It's just amazing how butter-fingered some of our boys can be.'

A general laugh ran round the table.

As a man who loved his food, Kirk was most appreciative of the spread he was now tucking into. 'I could almost forgive Meany anything for this,' he said.

'Aye, of course it was Meany who sent you to me,' McQuarrie said. 'What did the pair of you do?'

'He doesn't like me because I'm a Catholic,' Eddy replied.

'Nor the way I speak,' Kirk added.

'Well, he certainly doesn't like Catholics,' McQuarrie said. 'Which means we'll be seeing a lot of you here.'

'Is he an Orangeman?' Eddy asked.

'No, I don't think so.'

'So why does he hate Catholics?'

McQuarrie poured himself a huge glass of hock. The

redness of his nose gave it away that he was a man fond of his drink.

'There was an incident some years back. The good corporal came home one night to find a note from his wife telling him she'd run off with some bloke called O'Malley. Don't ask me what O'Malley did or how she came to meet him, but ever since then Meany's had a down on Catholics. What's your name?'

'King.'

'Just thank your lucky stars it isn't O'Malley. If he's bad on you now he'd be ten times worse then.'

'He certainly takes liberties with his men,' Kirk said.

McQuarrie leaned forward to emphasise his point. 'You'd better understand this. Meany is well liked and respected by the officers. He turns out good soldiers, whatever his methods, which is what the officers like. If he is a bit overenthusiastic at times, the officers turn a blind eye towards it. You see, there's a lot of them, regulars who fought in the war, think the Army's becoming too soft and would like to see it toughened up again back to wartime standards.'

'He's a sadistic sod all the same,' Kirk said.

'But *careful* with it,' McQuarrie added. 'He'll never be caught out because he's far too fly for that. Anyway, the officers *don't want* to catch him out which gives him an awful big advantage.'

'So what you're saying is no matter what happens we can never complain about him?'

McQuarrie pulled a face. 'Murray, the last thing you ever do in the Army is complain. It just isn't done.'

One of the cooks sang dolefully, causing them all to smile,

'They say that in the Army the prunes are mighty fine,
A prune fell off a table and killed a pal of mine.
Oh, I don't want to lead an Army life,
Gee ma, I want to go, but they won't let me go,
Gee ma, I want to go home!'

'Bugger it!' Eddy said when he and Kirk got back to the room where the section slept. He'd just remembered he still had his rifle to clean.

'No rest for the wicked,' Kirk said, starting to pull off his clothes.

'I wouldn't do that if I were you,' a voice said from the doorway.

They turned to find Meany staring at them. The rest of the section were already fast asleep.

'We're just this minute back,' Eddy said.

'I know that, sonny. I've been waiting for you.'

Eddy picked up his rifle and sat on his bed. With Meany watching him he started disassembling it.

'You want me for something, Corporal?' Kirk asked.

'I thought your friend King here might get lonely so I've decided you can keep him company. Go through to my room, pick up my gear which is stacked on my bed, bring it back here and clean and polish it.'

'Now?' Kirk asked.

'*Now*,' Meany replied, a faint leer twisting his mouth upwards.

Meany's room was down the corridor. As Meany had said, Kirk found the gear ready and waiting for him.

When they were alone Kirk said to Eddy, 'I don't know how, yet, but we're going to have to deal with that man because there's just no way I'm going to take two years of his riding me.'

'That's also been in my mind,' Eddy replied. 'But like you, I haven't yet thought of a way without landing myself in it.'

Kirk spat and buffed. 'My mother used to always say "where there's a will there's a way". It's a problem we'll just have to think about long and hard. And if we do we'll find the answer in the end. I promise you.'

An hour later Meany returned to find Eddy finished but Kirk still hard at work. He picked up Eddy's rifle and minutely examined it.

'Call this clean?' he said scornfully. 'Why, I've seen

246

middens cleaner than this. It's an absolute fucking disgrace! What is it?'

'An absolute fucking disgrace, sir!' Eddy chorused.

Meany threw the rifle at Eddy who caught it deftly. 'Now try again and let's hope you get it right this time otherwise you'll be up on a charge.'

Grinning malevolently he turned and strode from the room.

'The answer will come,' Kirk said softly, staring at the door through which Meany had vanished. 'It just needs lots and lots of thinking on.'

'Can't a bloke get some sleep around here!' Ogle grumbled from his bed.

'Piss off!' replied Kirk.

Spitting, he buffed some more.

'Right wheel! Left right ... left right ... left right ... left right!' Meany shouted.

Although it was bitter out, the sweat was pouring from Eddy as he marched and counter-marched to Meany's orders. The section had been on the parade ground for two and a half hours now and the strain was beginning to tell.

'Right turn! ... right face! ... Halt! ...' And before they had time to even catch their breath, 'By the left ... quick march! Left right ... left right ... Pick up your feet, Rennie, it's the British Army you're in, not the bloody American one! Left right ... left right ... Shoulders back, Kirkwood! You look like the hunchback of Notre Dame! ... left right ... left right ... Right wheel! ... left right ... Squad halt! ... Squad present arms! ... Squ ... aadd slope arms! ... Squaaddd ...'

Eddy glanced at Kirk, who shot him a weak grin. Then he was doubling up, the pack on his back feeling as though it weighed a ton. He sought solace in thinking about his bed, frowning when he remembered they were on patrol tonight. It would be tomorrow morning before he'd get some kip.

'Double up! Double up! Double up!' Meany screamed.

Eddy groaned.

*

247

There was no moon in the sky, which rendered the night black as pitch. The section was in a pine forest, Eddy hurrying along behind Kirk knowing if he once let Kirk out of his extremely limited vision he'd be lost and have to call for help – Which was the last thing he wanted as it would give Meany an excuse to punish him some more. If Meany needed an excuse, that is.

Twigs snapped underfoot as he pushed forward. It was eerie in the forest. Trees and branches making weird and grotesque shapes. He kept telling himself not to be so bloody silly but despite that he couldn't help but keep imagining the shapes were, or concealed something, waiting to pounce on him.

He wouldn't have been at all surprised if a whole battalion of Ruskies had suddenly materialised, tanks and all.

'Corporal? Corporal, where are you?' Napier's voice said from somewhere ahead. Napier had been behind Meany who'd been in the lead.

Eddy came up short, as ahead of him Kirk stopped.

'Corporal, can you hear me?' Napier called out, this time more urgently.

Eddy was just about to move up and join Kirk when suddenly a kick in the backside sent him sprawling. He yelled as he nose-dived into a soggy mixture of wet leaves and earth.

'Ivan!' he thought, rolling to one side. He desperately tried to scramble to his feet only to be knocked sprawling again by a boot kicking him in the belly.

Lying on his side, doubled up with pain, he stared in fascination at the sten's muzzle inches away from his forehead and pointed straight between his eyes.

'Asleep on our feet, were we?' Meany asked jovially. 'Or just lost in thought?'

Kirk and Rennie appeared, to stand staring at Meany.

'I didn't hear you,' Eddy replied.

'Oh I know that!' Meany said sarcastically. 'Otherwise you wouldn't be lying there like the stupid tit you are. What are you, King?'

'A stupid tit, sir.'

'Well, if it's any consolation to you, you're only one tit

248

among eight. What were you dreaming of, eh? Answer me!'

'I wasn't, Corporal.'

'Don't lie to me. Of course you were dreaming, for you sure as hell didn't have your mind on what you were about.'

By this time the rest of the section had gathered around. Meany swung on them. 'None of you did. You were all content to play follow the leader with what you laughingly call your minds elsewhere.' He sighed. 'Make soldiers out of you lot? I'm beginning to think it's impossible.'

Somewhere an owl hooted, causing Napier to jump.

Meany laughed when he saw that. 'Frightened of being out in the dark, poofter?' he asked.

'No sir.'

'What about you, plum in the mouth?'

'How could I be scared when you're with us Corporal?' Kirk replied.

Meany's eyes slitted fractionally. 'I told you before, don't try and get funny with me or by God you'll live to regret it.'

'It was a statement of fact, sir. Nothing else,' Kirk lied.

Meany came up close to Kirk. 'I don't trust you, Murray,' he said. 'You're a devious bastard who thinks he's more clever than he is. I know the type.'

Kirk stared into Meany's eyes and didn't reply.

'Just watch it, that's all. Especially your mouth. I suggest from now on you keep a tight rein on it.'

They stared at one another for a few seconds and then Meany swung round.

'Right, you dozy bunch of diddies, that was your smoke break. Now let's get cracking again. And this time try and keep awake!'

'I could get to hate that man,' Ogle muttered to Eddy.

'You wouldn't be alone, mate,' Eddy whispered back.

When the patrol was finally over they made their way back to their room in the castle where they all collapsed on to their respective beds. It seemed no time at all before Meany was striding into the room crying, 'Rise and shine! Rise and shine!' and, as he always did, pulling the covers from their beds.

'Atten ... tion,' Meany shouted, and waited till they'd done so at the end of their beds before continuing.

'What day is it, Kirkwood?'

'Saturday, sir.'

'Correct. But it's also something else. Rennie?'

Rennie screwed his face up in a frown. 'I don't know, sir,' he replied eventually.

Meany beamed. 'Of course you don't because I haven't told you yet. Funny eh?'

They all dutifully laughed, knowing it was expected of them.

'Well I'll tell you. It's not only Saturday, it's your day off. What is it.'

'Our day off, sir, Corporal!' they chorused.

'Did I hear "For He's A Jolly Good Fellow"?'

Smart led the singing *'For he's a jolly good fellow, for he's ...'*

When the song was over Meany went on, 'Now I suppose most, if not all, of you will be going down to Uelsberg. Right?'

'Yes sir, Corporal.'

'So what I want to say to you is this. If anyone is naughty or misbehaves himself in any way, which would reflect on me as your NCO, I will personally make his life not worth living. And that, I can assure you, is no idle threat. Now gather round for your passes.'

Meany manipulated it so that Eddy and Kirk were last in line. When finally it was Eddy's turn he said. 'Ah, King! I'm afraid you won't be going along.'

Eddy's heart sank.

'Nor you, Murray. I was asked for two volunteers for a most demanding job and you two are them.'

He cupped his hand to his ear. 'Did I hear you say something? Like, "I volunteer, Corporal"?'

'I volunteer, Corporal,' Eddy said dully, the others looking at him and Kirk in sympathy.

'Murray?'

'I volunteer, Corporal.'

'Lovely!' said Meany rubbing his hands together. 'I'll be back in ten minutes and I'll expect you to be dressed for a dirty job.'

'Don't we get time for something to eat, Corporal?' Eddy asked, adding, 'I'm starving.'

'Plenty of time for that afterwards,' Meany replied, pausing by the door to say over his shoulder. 'Nine minutes, now.'

'Hard luck,' said Ogle when Meany was gone.

'We'll tell you all about it,' Rennie said.

'Thanks a lot,' Eddy replied sarcastically. 'That's just what I need, a lurid account of your day off to keep me going.'

He and Kirk began dressing for a dirty job.

Prompt as usual, Meany strode into the room to find Eddy and Kirk waiting for him. He checked that they'd washed and shaved before telling them to follow him.

He led them to another part of the castle which was the officers' quarters. Stopping by a door he opened it and a toilet was revealed. He ushered them inside.

The stench was appalling, causing Eddy to gag. He didn't have to be told to know what was coming. Meany told him anyway.

'Your job's to unbung this lot and when you've done that I want the bowls, the floor, everything, cleaned out like new.' He gestured across to where various buckets, brooms and tools were either lying or propped against a wall. 'I think you'll find everything there you need,' he added.

Eddy glanced at Kirk, who looked as though he was going to throw up. He felt that way himself.

'I'll be back in a while to see how you're doing. Any questions?'

Eddy shook his head and Kirk did likewise.

Meany made to go and then paused. 'Oh!' he said, pretending he's just remembered something. 'Happy day off!'

Chuckling, he left them to it.

Eddy cautiously approached the first bowl. Water and urine

251

were dripping down its sides on to the floor. Its inside was filled with what looked like diarrhoea. Close up the stench was, if anything, even worse.

'Any ideas about how to go about this?' he asked.

'Not a clue,' Kirk replied.

Eddy crossed to the tools and picked out a plunger. 'I suppose this is as good as anything to start with,' he said.

'Christ!' exclaimed Kirk a little later when some of the mess slopped over his boots.

Trying not to be too aware of the smell they both got on with it.

Two hours later a grinning Meany arrived back in the toilet. Hands on hips he surveyed what they'd done.

Eddy and Kirk were down on their hands and knees scrubbing the floor. The toilets were unbunged and functioning properly.

'Not bad,' Meany said grudgingly.

'Phew!' said Eddy when they were finally all finished. 'I stink like a pig.'

'You stink *worse* than a pig. We both do,' Kirk added.

Meany laughed.

Kirk stared at the corporal, careful not to let what he felt about the man show in his eyes. Just keep on thinking, he told himself. Just keep on thinking.

When they'd stacked the buckets, brooms and assorted tools, Meany told them to fall in behind him and with him leading the way they marched back to their room. Once inside, Meany picked up Eddy's rifle and threw it to him. 'I believe that's still dirty from last night. What are you going to do about it?'

'Clean it, Corporal.'

Meany nodded. 'You're an awful one for getting your rifle dirty, King. I've never known the like.'

'Perhaps I'm accident-prone?' Eddy suggested.

'Perhaps. In which case you should pray to one of those plaster saints of yours.'

'I might just do that, Corporal, seeing as how you've suggested it.'

'You do that, sonny. For all the good it'll do you.'

Meany took two passes from his pocket and threw them on to Eddy's bed. 'The rifle gets cleaned first,' he said. 'And be sure you're back by twenty-three hundred.'

Eddy picked up the passes, gaping at them in astonishment. This was the last thing he'd expected and, judging from the incredulous look on Kirk's face, the last thing Kirk had expected as well.

'One last thing,' Meany said, 'whatever you do, don't go to the Blue Pig bierkeller. It's not off bounds or anything like that. I just don't recommend it.'

When Meany was gone Eddy said, 'Well I'll be a son of a gun! He gave us passes after all. Do you think we've misjudged him?'

'Not a chance,' Kirk replied. 'He's a bastard through and through. If he gave us those passes then he had a reason, and one that suited him, not us.'

'Well, I'm not looking this gift horse in the mouth.'

'Me neither.'

Eddy's face fell. 'Bloody rifle. That'll take a good half-hour.'

'Quarter of an hour. I'll help you.'

'Thanks, mate.'

'One for all and all for one, eh?'

'Pass the cleaning gear, D'Artagnan,' Eddy said, grinning.

Once out of the castle they hurried down the road that led straight into Uelsberg. Both were excited and champing at the bit to enjoy themselves.

'First thing I want is a beer,' Eddy said.

'What I want is me hole. Us married men miss that sort of thing you know.'

'I wouldn't say no myself.'

'I'll bet you wouldn't, you randy bugger. Did you have someone at home?'

Eddy shook his head.

'Footloose and fancy free?'

'That's one way of putting it.'

A gleam came into Kirk's eye. 'Before getting married I had a bit called Minnie. A real looker, and Christ could she screw! I get horny just thinking about it.'

'I had a woman down in London when I was staying there. My landlady. She and I ... well ... we were having it off together.'

'You sound like you were fond of her?'

'I was. There was only one problem. She was married and still loved her husband.'

'Too bad,' Kirk said sympathetically.

'Her name was Annie and she was quite a bit older than me. Tall, slim, dark-haired.'

'Do you write to her?'

'No point,' Eddy said softly.

They walked for a little while in silence, Eddy's initial excitement having turned to introspection.

Kirk gazed about, taking everything in. He was loving this.

'My first time abroad,' he said. 'You?'

Eddy nodded.

'I miss Glasgow, mind you. I even dream about it at nights.'

'You'll miss the wife more than anything I'd imagine?'

'Oh aye, her as well,' Kirk replied, eyes riveted on a girl passing on the opposite side of the road. 'Look at the bum on that!' he exclaimed.

'I'm still starving,' Eddy said. 'Don't forget we haven't had anything to eat yet.'

'Food and beer first. Then, when the inner man's satisfied, we'll see what we can do about the rest of us.'

They found a small bierkeller which served them frothing steins of lager, after which they had lavish helpings of sausage and sauerkraut.

Kirk ogled the waitress who was blonde, buxom and dressed in a traditional peasant-type outfit cut low at the top.

When she returned to clear away their dishes he tried to chat her up but she would have none of it.

'Can't win them all,' he said as she swayed away from them.

They paid at the bar and then made their way out into the street. 'What now?' Eddy asked.

Kirk smiled. 'I can't help wondering why Meany didn't want us to go to this Blue Pig. Probably because it's the best place in town.'

'You could be right.'

Kirk stopped a passer-by and asked for directions.

The Blue Pig turned out to be a subterranean dive at the end of an alleyway. They ordered beers and then settled themselves at a table.

'More like it,' said Kirk. 'Look at the spare bint flying around.'

There were a number of unescorted girls sitting at tables, standing at the bar and even dancing together on the small dance floor.

There were roughly a dozen other soldiers about, all of them with girls whom they'd obviously picked up there.

'This place is a whore house,' Kirk said. 'No mistaking it.'

Eddy gazed about him with renewed interest. He'd never been in a brothel before.

'Either of you two gentlemen spare a lady a cigarette?'

Kirk and Eddy stared up at the female standing beside their table. She was no Rita Hayworth but then she wasn't exactly ugly either.

Eddy held out his cigarette case. 'Be my guest,' he said. He suddenly felt nervous and a bit embarrassed.

The female helped herself to a cigarette, put it between scarlet painted lips and waited for a light. Eddy obliged.

'You're new, aren't you?' she said.

Kirk nodded. 'How do you know that?'

She smiled secretly. 'It's not difficult to tell. My name's Gottfried.'

Kirk rose to his feet. 'Perhaps you'd care to join us for a drink?'

She looked from one to the other. 'I have a friend,' she suggested.

'Which one?' Kirk asked.

Gottfried pointed out a girl sitting a few tables away. 'Magda,' she said. 'Very nice.'

Kirk glanced at Eddy, who nodded.

'Fine,' he said. 'Perhaps you'd like to ask her over.'

Gottfried smiled and moved away.

'We've cracked it!' Kirk said enthusiastically.

Eddy was still nervous. 'I'm not so sure,' he said.

'What do you mean you're not sure?'

Eddy cleared his throat. 'I've never ... I mean a whore before.'

'Me neither. But there's always a first time for everything. And the way my hormones are jumping I don't care what she is as long as I get it up her.'

'Well if you think it'll be all right ...'

'Of course it'll be all right. If it wasn't, those other blokes wouldn't be here.'

'That's true,' Eddy murmured.

They both rose as Gottfried and Magda joined them.

Introductions were made all round and they sat. Kirk waved to a passing waiter, who came instantly to their table. The order was four beers.

'Can Magda have a cigarette as well?' Gottfried asked.

'Of course,' replied Eddy and again proffered his case.

Magda took the cigarette hungrily, smiling gratitude to Eddy when he lit it for her.

'So ...' said Gottfried. 'You are new up at the *Schloss*, yes?'

'Yes,' said Kirk.

'And this is your first time into Uelsberg?'

'Right again.'

Gottfried's eyes gleamed. 'The price is two packets of cigarettes or half a pound of coffee. *Each*,' she said.

Kirk blinked. 'What happened to good old-fashioned money and army vouchers?'

'Money and vouchers no use unless you have sterling. In which case it is two pounds.'

'Each,' said Kirk.

'*Each*,' she replied emphatically.

'What's all this cigarettes and coffee business?' Eddy asked.

'Everything is cigarettes and coffee nowadays,' Magda said.

'Christ, look who just came in!' Eddy exclaimed.

Kirk glanced up to see Meany staring at them.

'We're for it now,' Eddy added. But he was wrong.

Meany continued staring at them for a few seconds before making his way to the bar where he stood with his back to them.

'What's he up to?' Kirk said quietly. 'Because I'm certain the bugger's up to something.'

'Well, he only said he didn't recommend we come here,' Eddy said.

Magda laid her hand across Eddy's. 'I like you. You're nice,' she said.

'You've got an American accent!' Eddy said in surprise, having just noticed it.

She caressed his hand, stroking it as though it was a thing of great beauty.

'I lived in the American sector for some years. I have only recently moved to Uelsberg.'

Kirk brought his attention back to Gottfried. 'As I don't smoke I haven't any cigarettes on me, so it'll have to be sterling,' he said.

'Fine.' She nodded.

'And you?' Magda asked.

Eddy had picked up his Naafi ration the previous day and consequently had a number of packets on him. 'I'll pay in fags,' he replied.

'What about a bottle to take upstairs?' Kirk asked.

'We can get slivovitz but that would mean more cigarettes.'

'How many?' Eddy asked.

'Twenty.'

He shook his head. 'No can do. Another ten's my limit.'

'For that you get half a bottle.'

Eddy passed ten cigarettes across to Gottfried and while she went to the bar he, Kirk and Magda made their way to a door beyond which Magda had told them were the stairs to their rooms on the upper floors.

En route, Kirk caught a glimpse of Meany watching them in a large ornate mirror. Meany was smiling.

'What's slivovitz?' Eddy asked as they climbed the stairs.

'A sort of plum brandy,' Kirk replied. 'I've heard of it but never tasted it.'

'I would have preferred whisky myself,' Eddy grumbled.

Magda laughed. 'It is very rare to see a bottle of whisky. And to buy it would be very, very expensive.'

'How many fags?' Kirk asked, curious.

Magda shrugged. 'Two hundred maybe. Maybe more.'

Kirk thought of all the whisky he'd had from Harry Hydelman. Christ, if he could have pulled that stunt again he could really have cleaned up here.

The room Magda told him to wait for Gottfried in was small and cramped. There was a large quilt on top of the bed, which looked as though it had already been put to use, and not long since either. The thought didn't put him off at all.

Gottfried arrived to say she'd given half of the half-bottle to Eddy and Magda.

What was left she poured into two tumblers and handed Kirk one.

'*Prosit!*' she toasted.

'*Prosit!*' he replied.

She sipped hers appreciatively.

He swallowed some and then coughed. He thought it must be like drinking bloody paraffin.

Gottfried laid her glass down and immediately started to strip. She did this in a clinical way and without any overtones of sex whatsoever. When she was totally nude she turned to Kirk.

'Now we have the fuckings!' she said gaily.

258

'Now we have the fuckings,' he agreed.

Later that night Kirk and Eddy lay in their own beds in the darkness.

'I certainly enjoyed that,' Eddy said. 'Just what I needed after a week of Meany. Mind you, I'm not looking forward to the morning. That bastard will take it out on us for going to the Blue Pig after he advised us not to.'

'Cigarettes, coffee and whisky. There's a fortune to be made out of those, it would seem.' Kirk's mind ticked over with the possibilities.

'Unless you've got an outside source, you can't get enough of either to really make it worth your while,' Eddy replied.

Kirk smiled. 'So you were thinking along those lines as well, eh?'

'Once a dealer always a dealer,' Eddy replied, going on to say, 'Magda told me the redcaps are sheer murder on anyone trying to deal in the *schwartz*, as she called it. That's the black market to you and I. She says several of the lads have tried in the past but the redcaps quickly got hold of them. Uelsberg's a small place and is already carved up by one or two local operators. It seems if competition tries to start up the redcaps quickly get to hear of it, or are given heavy hints, that sort of thing.'

'And if the competition's civilian?'

'The operators deal with it themselves. And from what Magda said, they tend to be heavy-handed in a fatal sort of way.'

'It's still a thought,' Kirk mused.

'But where would you get the commodities?'

'Where there's a will ...'

'... there's a way,' Eddy finished for him.

They both chuckled.

'I hate to see an opportunity go by,' Kirk said. 'It upsets me.'

'I know what you mean. And you were rooked tonight. Two packets of fags against two quid!'

'I won't be caught short again,' Kirk said. 'From now on I'll be taking up my Naafi ration. Too right and I will.'

The next thing he knew Meany's voice was shouting that it was time to get up. He shivered as his coverings were whipped from his bed.

'Rise and shine! Rise and shine, you horrible lot of shits. What are you?'

'A horrible lot of shits sir, Corporal!' the section responded.

'Aaatten ... tion!' Meany yelled.

The section scrambled to the end of their beds, where they lined up.

Grinning, Meany walked up one line and then down the other.

'Did we enjoy our day off?'

'Yes sir, Corporal!' they chorused.

'Good! I'm glad to hear it.' He paused before saying, 'Murray, King, one step forward, march!'

Here it comes, Eddy thought.

'Who were naughty boys, then? Who went to the Blue Pig when nice Corporal Meany told them not to?'

'We didn't realise that was it until we left,' Kirk lied.

'A little mistake, was it?'

'Yes sir,' Kirk said.

'A bigger mistake than you realise,' Meany said with relish.

Kirk frowned. There was something here he was missing. And from the look on Meany's face he was about to be enlightened.

Meany was enjoying this so he teased it out.

'Do you know why I recommended you didn't go to the Blue Pig?' he asked.

'No sir,' Eddy replied.

'Murray?'

'No sir.'

'You did appreciate I must have had a reason though, didn't you?'

'Yes, sir,' Eddy said.

'And yet you elected to disregard my advice. Very foolish, King. Not very clever, Murray.'

He chuckled, his eyes twinkling with amusement.

'Get your nookie?' he asked.

Ogle tittered.

'Well?'

'Yes, sir,' Eddy replied slowly. He knew there was no use pretending otherwise. Meany had seen Kirk and him go upstairs with the two whores.

'And you, Murray?'

'Yes, sir.'

'Oh dear, oh dear me!' Meany said, grinning from ear to ear. He stepped back a pace as though wanting to put distance between himself and them.

'Been to the bog yet this morning?' he asked.

Eddy glanced at Kirk. He couldn't think what all this was leading up to. But a glimmer of light was beginning to dawn with Kirk.

'No, sir,' they both answered.

'Then you'd better go now. Come on, hurry up. I'll be waiting for you when you get back.'

Eddy and Kirk left the room and made for the toilet where they both relieved themselves.

'What's this all about?' Eddy asked.

'I just hope to God I'm wrong. But I think I might know.'

'Well come on, tell me!'

'How's your pee?'

Eddy stared in astonishment. 'What do you mean how's my pee! Same as it always is.'

'Then let's just hope it stays that way.'

'I'm still not with you.'

'Don't be dense, Eddy. We went out with two whores last night and now Meany's getting us to slash. Put two and two together.' And when Eddy still looked blank. 'VD man!'

'Oh Christ!' exclaimed Eddy.

'It must be that. What else?'

Eddy hastily examined himself but it looked the same as it always did. 'How about you?' he asked.

'Normal. No sensation of pissing over broken glass, which I'm told is how it feels.'

'Oh that bastard! He watched us climb those stairs.'

'And he was smiling all the time,' Kirk added.

They took themselves back to their billet, both angry and a little scared.

'Everything all right?' Meany asked when they entered the room.

'Yes Corporal,' Kirk replied.

'Ah!' Meany said, nodding at some private thought. After a few suspenseful seconds he asked, 'Penny dropped yet?'

'You think we've caught a dose, sir,' Kirk replied.

'I don't know for certain, mind you. But I'd say the chances are fairly high. You see I'm rather friendly with the particular medic who deals with these things. And he told me yesterday morning that it had been confirmed to him only hours previously that the recent run of VD cases he's had have all been traced back to the one source: the Blue Pig.'

Eddy sucked in a breath.

'Bloody hell!' exclaimed Rennie.

Meany went on, 'The civilian authorities will have been informed by now and by tomorrow the place will have been closed down. The thing is, were only some of the girls infected or were they all?'

'Is there some way of finding out?' Eddy asked. 'I mean surely they'll be examining every female who worked there?'

Meany smiled sadistically. 'That's got nothing to do with the Army, King. I presume you're asking me to inquire about the two you and Murray were with?'

Eddy nodded.

'No can do, sonny boy. Right out of my jurisdiction.'

Oh you're really lovely, Kirk thought. A real gem.

'So I suppose you'd better make your way to the medic for the cure. Which I am assured is most painful. Socking great jabs of penicillin up the arse two or three times a day. I've heard it said strong men have broken down and cried during the treatment. Needle like a bicycle spoke, I'm told.'

Eddy blanched. He had a thing about injections.

Meany went on, 'Just one other item. Once it's been established you have a dose, you're put on a charge. Ten days in the guard house at the tender mercy of Sergeant Marnoch. Who also is a great friend of mine, by the way. I know a word from me to him will ensure things are made interesting for you.' Meany rocked back on his heels and sighed. 'So there we are then. You see, you should have listened to what I told you.'

Kirk was thinking furiously. If the medic was a friend of Meany's, what guarantee was there, knowing how devious and underhand Meany was, that Meany wouldn't have fixed it with the medic to say they had contracted VD, whether they had or not? It was a risk he was damned if he was going to take unless he absolutely had to.

'Are you ordering us to go to the medic?' Kirk asked.

'Noo ... oo,' Meany replied slowly. 'Merely advising it.'

'Then I prefer to wait until there are some definite signs.'

Meany pursed his lips and frowned. 'And you, King?'

Eddy glanced at Kirk who imperceptibly shook his head. 'I'll hang off as well,' he replied.

Meany regarded the pair of them thoughtfully. Suddenly his brow cleared and he was smiling again. 'It'll take six months for you to be absolutely certain,' he said. 'And in the meantime if you do have it it'll be getting deeper and deeper into your system. And the deeper it gets the harder, and more painful, it is to cure.'

Kirk knew Meany was right and that he was taking an awful risk. But he still preferred that to the almost certainty of a cure followed by ten days hell, if ten days was all it was, at the hands of Sergeant Marnoch. He'd heard tales of men who'd gone into the guard house for a week and hadn't reappeared till months later, it having been alleged they'd been 'difficult' while inside. Men who'd come out relatively fine in body but completely broken in spirit.

'I'll chance it,' Kirk said.

'King?'

Eddy knew Kirk had to have a good reason for making this decision. 'Me too, sir,' he replied.

'Right then. I'll leave you two lepers and the rest of you to get on with it then,' Meany said, throwing over his shoulder at the door, 'You've got an hour and then it's outside for drill.'

When Meany was gone the section relaxed. Eddy sat on the edge of his bed and Kirk on his.

'Why?' Eddy asked. And Kirk explained his reasons, which Eddy was forced to agree with.

'Why don't you go and see a civilian doctor?' Smart asked.

Kirk replied. 'You don't think he's going to let us out the castle, except on patrol, until this is all over, do you? He must know we'd think of that.'

'I'm sure six months is wrong,' Kirkwood said.

Ogle said, 'There's a chap down the corridor, Randy Ronnie Ralston they call him, who I was told has had a dose several times. Why don't we check with him to see what he knows?'

'Good idea,' Eddy nodded.

'I'll see if I can catch him before he goes to breakfast,' Ogle said and left the room.

'That Sergeant Marnoch is terrible,' Rennie said. 'Some of the lads were talking about him in the Naafi the other night. He's real bad news.'

Eddy sat fretting until Ogle returned with Randy Ronnie, who turned out to be a small ferret-faced man.

'Meany's talking a load of garbage,' Randy Ronnie said straight off. 'Three weeks is absolute maximum for it to show itself. After that your worries are over.'

Kirk heaved a sigh of relief. That was something, anyway. There was one helluva big difference between six months and three weeks.

'Good luck, mates,' Randy Ronnie said and left.

Napier said, 'Look I don't want this to be misconstrued or anything. But while you two don't know, is it safe for us? Sharing a room with you and all, I mean?'

'That's a point,' Kirk said.

'How about if Kirk and I keep to ourselves. And you lot just make sure you don't touch anything of ours,' Eddy suggested.

'What about the bog? Aren't you supposed to be able to catch it from toilet seats?' Smart asked.

'When we have to go we'll make sure we never actually touch the seats. All right?' Kirk said.

Smart nodded, but reluctantly.

'What a hell of a fix,' Eddy said miserably.

'We'll get our own back. Somehow, some way. It just needs . . .'

'. . . thinking on. So you keep saying,' Eddy said.

Kirk suddenly smiled. 'Well come on, cheer up. It isn't exactly the end of the world!'

'You won't say that when your dick falls off,' Eddy replied miserably.

The next three weeks were sheer murder for Eddy and Kirk. Every time they went for a pee they held their breath, waiting for the tell-tale burning sensation. And every morning when they woke, the first thing they did was examine themselves to see if they'd had a discharge during the night.

The rest of the section were pleasant enough about it but naturally and sensibly kept their distance.

The result of this was that Eddy and Kirk spent the whole of their free time together, becoming, in their plight, even closer than they'd previously been.

Finally the great day dawned when their three weeks was up and neither of them had shown any signs of infection whatsoever.

To celebrate, the entire section went along to the Naafi, where they had a few beers. And that was where Meany found them.

'What's all this in aid of then?' he asked.

'The three weeks are up, Corporal,' Eddy replied.

'What three weeks?'

'You were mistaken, sir. The waiting period is three weeks, not six months.'

265

Meany frowned, his gaze travelling from Eddy to Kirk and back again. 'Who told you that nonsense then?' he asked.

'It's general knowledge, sir,' Eddy replied. 'Quite a few of the men told us.'

That wasn't true. Randy Ronnie was the only one they'd consulted.

Meany's frown deepened. He knew then he should have ordered them to go up before the medic. It had been a mistake on his part for him not to have done, but then he'd been convinced they'd both caught a dose.

'You were lucky then,' he grumbled, admitting defeat.

Smiling, Eddy lifted his glass and swallowed off the remains of his beer. The glass had been almost full.

'I'd be careful if I was you. That stuff's alcoholic,' Meany said scathingly.

Like most male Glaswegians Eddy couldn't bear any slur on his drinking ability. 'It would take a lot more than that to get me even slightly pissed,' he retorted.

'*Sir!*' Meany warned.

'Pissed, sir,' Eddy said hastily.

'Fancy yourself as a drinker then, do you?'

'I can hold my own.'

'Amongst boys maybe. But what about up against a man?'

Eddy realised he was being goaded but couldn't help himself. 'What man did you have in mind, sir?' he asked.

Meany glanced around to make sure their conversation wasn't being overheard. 'How about me?' he suggested.

'You, sir?'

'Aye, me. I say I can drink any stinking Fenian under the table and what's more I'm willing to put my money where my mouth is.'

Hush fell round the table as every pair of eyes came to rest on Eddy's face.

'How much were you thinking of?' Eddy asked.

'What can you afford, sonny boy?'

'How about twenty?'

'Pennies or shillings?'

'Pounds,' Eddy said.

'Wow!' said Smart. It was an awful lot of money.

'You're on,' Meany replied. 'Tomorrow night at nine in the cookhouse. I'll tell Sergeant McQuarrie to expect us.'

'What about the drink?' Kirk asked.

'Don't worry about that. Whisky. And I tell you what, I'll even supply it myself. How about that?'

Eddy nodded.

'Twenty quid, eh?' Meany said and laughed. 'I'm going to enjoy this.'

Chuckling to himself he left the Naafi.

Eddy sat and stared into his empty glass.

'That might have been foolish,' Kirk said.

'Would you have backed down?'

Kirk pulled a face. 'You're right, I wouldn't.'

With the exception of Napier, they were all Glaswegians round the table and they all understood. Their attitude to drink had been instilled into them since they were wee. A man was expected to drink hard and often. To have turned down a direct challenge of the sort Meany had issued to Eddy would have been a jessie thing to do.

'You must drink at least a pint of milk beforehand,' Napier said. 'It lines the stomach.'

'And have a good meal before as well. That absorbs it,' Smart added.

Suddenly suggestions were being offered from all directions as everyone in the section put forward tips they thought might help.

The next morning they were drilling on the parade ground when an officer called Lieutenant Gilzean came striding up.

Meany immediately called the section to attention and saluted.

'I need four men for a job,' Lieutenant Gilzean said.

'I'll take him, him, him and him,' he said, his pointed finger stabbing the air. Eddy and Kirk were two of those singled out.

267

Meany gave the appropriate orders and soon the four of them – Smart and Ogle were the other two – were marching along behind the lieutenant.

When they reached a parked lorry Gilzean told them to climb aboard. He got in front with the driver and the lorry moved off.

They rattled out through the castle gates, heading towards Uelsberg. When they entered the town it was the first time Eddy and Kirk had been back since their night out at the Blue Pig.

The lorry drew up at the railway station and Gilzean ordered them out. He said they could have a smoke while he went to see what was what.

'Seems a decent sort of bloke,' Ogle remarked once the officer had gone.

'Unlike a certain NCO I could name,' Smart said. Then, turning to Eddy, 'How do you feel for tonight?'

Eddy shrugged. 'All right, I suppose.'

'There'll be no holding Meany back if you lose,' Ogle said.

'But what'll he be like if Eddy wins?' Kirk asked.

Ogle grimaced. 'I hadn't thought of that.'

'We can't win either way,' Smart added.

Gilzean reappeared and they came to attention.

'Stand easy,' Gilzean said. 'We're here to pick up a load of supplies but it seems the train is late. Just how late they're not sure yet. They're telephoning down the line now and somebody will be out to tell me as soon as they have a definite answer. So we'll just have to hang around for the moment. Sorry about that, chaps.'

Five minutes later the station master hurried out of the station. When he saw him Gilzean got out of the lorry cab where he'd spent the interim reading some official-looking documents.

The station master and Gilzean spoke briefly. Then with gestures of apology the station master made his way back into the station.

Gilzean called the men together. 'The damn train is going to be at least an hour and a half late which is a real piece of nonsense,' he said. 'Rather than return to the castle and then have to come all the way back again I think it best if we disperse and then meet up here again in exactly an hour and a half. That meet with everyone's approval?'

The four of them were quick to say that was fine and dandy with them.

'Thought it might be,' Gilzean said drily. 'All right then, hop it. And don't be late back!'

'There's a stroke of luck!' Smart said.

'How about a beer?' Ogle suggested.

But a thoughtful-looking Kirk had other ideas. 'You two go on,' he said. 'Eddy and I have a little something to attend to.'

Eddy turned in surprise to Kirk. This was news to him. But he went along with it.

'What do you have in mind?' Eddy asked after Smart and Ogle had hurried away.

'What sort of chance do you really give yourself up against Meany tonight?'

Eddy shrugged. 'I honestly don't know. I'm a pretty fair drinker when it's called for but who knows what Meany's like? He may well be the original hollow legs.'

Kirk stroked his scar. 'There's just the possibility, and it's a long shot at the moment, that we can turn tonight to our advantage. But to do so you've got to drink the sod under the table.'

'I'll certainly be trying my best.'

'I've no doubt about it. But why don't we see if we can get you some help, make the odds a little more in your favour, so to speak?'

'How?'

'Well, maybe I'm barking up the wrong tree but perhaps there's something medical that would help. A pill or something, I don't know. It's just an idea but one I think is worth looking into now that we've got this hour and a half to ourselves. What I suggest we do is find a doctor who can speak English and put it to him.'

269

'It's a helluva long shot but why not?' Eddie replied. 'I've nothing to lose after all.'

'And if it works out possibly everything to gain.'

'What haven't you told me, Kirk? I know that funny look you get in your eye. It means you're up to something.'

Kirk laughed. 'First things first. Let's find the quack and we'll go from there.'

They made inquiries round about for a doctor who spoke English and the name they came up with was that of a Doctor Kruppermann whose address was close by. They hurried there at once.

The receptionist was a middle-aged lesbian type who primly told them to wait and the doctor would see them as soon as it was convenient.

'Leave the talking to me,' Kirk said.

Ten minutes later, they were ushered into the presence of an extremely good-looking blonde in her mid-thirties sitting behind a desk.

'We're looking for Dr Kruppermann,' Kirk said.

The woman smiled. 'I am she.' Then seeing their looks of bewilderment. 'Don't you have women doctors in England?'

'Scotland,' Eddy replied quickly. 'We come from Scotland.'

'I suppose we do. It's just I've never experienced one before,' Kirk added, thinking she wasn't a bad-looking bit of gimp at all.

'Now which one of you is sick?' Dr Kruppermann asked, waving them to seats.

'Neither of us,' Kirk replied.

The doctor frowned.

Kirk hurried on, 'The reason we've come to see you is because my friend here . . .' He paused and then said. 'Oh hell! I was going to give you a cock and bull story but I think the truth's far better.'

She nodded and he smiled inwardly. He knew women always found that line disarming.

And then he went on to explain why they'd come to see her.

When Kirk was finished Dr Kruppermann sat back in her

chair and gave a soft laugh. Her washed-out blue eyes twinkled
with amusement.

'Can you help us?' Eddy asked eagerly.

'I don't know. Let me think,' she replied.

Silence reigned in the room while the two men sat looking
expectant.

'Hmm!' she said eventually, and, rising, crossed to a
bookcase from which she extracted a book.

'Naturally we want something that's safe. If it exists at all
that is,' Eddy said.

'Naturally,' she replied.

Sitting again at her desk, she opened the book and for the
next few minutes pored over it.

Kirk glanced at his watch. He and Eddy still had a
considerable amount of time left before having to report back
to Lieutenant Gilzean.

'Ah!' said the doctor, and then again, 'Ah!'

'You've found something?' Kirk asked.

She looked up at them. 'I thought I remembered something
from my early medical studies. And here it is. Fructose is what
you want.'

'Fructose?' Eddy queried.

'Fruit sugar.'

'How does that help?' Kirk asked.

'It changes the metabolic rate by up to twenty per cent,
which means alcohol consumed during that period is burned
off more quickly. In other words someone having taken
fructose will be able to drink more than normal.'

'And it's safe?' Eddy asked.

'Oh yes. Quite.'

'Well I'll be . . . !' Kirk said, looking extremely pleased with
himself. 'Fruit sugar, eh?'

'I won't even have to give you a prescription. You don't
need one to buy it.'

'Doctor, you're lovely,' Kirk said.

Kruppermann laughed, 'I'm glad to be of assistance.'

When Kirk and Eddy arrived back at the railway station

271

they had a bottle of fructose with them and full instructions on how and when to take it.

The entire section reported to the cookhouse at nine o'clock to be ushered into a back room where they found a trestle table and chairs had been set up.

Eddy felt marvellous, psychologically as well as physically. He was well primed with fructose.

A few minutes later Meany arrived. 'Is the lamb ready for the slaughter?' he demanded and laughed.

One of the cooks shook his head, confiding to Napier, 'He pulls this stunt every time he gets a new section and he's never lost yet. The man's capacity is phenomenal.'

Meanwhile Meany had started needling Eddy. 'How about upping your bet, Fenian? Or have you got cold feet already?'

Eddy stared hard at Meany, hating this man who in many ways reminded him of Gloag, whom he'd killed all those years ago. He would have given anything to be able to have a go at Meany in a fair fight. But of course that was impossible.

'You look right scared, sonny boy. Green round the gills and you haven't even had a drink yet.'

Having said that Meany laughed cruelly, at the same time fishing in his pocket for money. He slapped notes on the table in front of him.

'Twenty pounds, I believe you said. Well there's mine. Where's yours, King?'

In reply Eddy laid four fivers beside Meany's notes and then held up two more. 'Did you say you wanted to up the bet?' he asked quietly.

Meany chortled. This was getting better and better. 'Done!' he replied. And laid another ten singles out to match Eddy's two extra fivers.

Napier and the rest of the section looked on wretchedly. By now, it had passed among them what the cook had told Napier and they believed Eddy didn't have a snowball in hell's chance.

'Any more bets? I'm willing to cover them all,' Meany said.

Neither Napier nor the rest of the section were having any. With the exception of Kirk, that is. He was willing to have a flyer, knowing what he did.

'I'll match Eddy's thirty. If that isn't too much for you, Corporal?' he said blandly.

'Let's see your cash, plum in the mouth.'

Kirk laid his money on top of Eddy's.

'Consider it a bet!'

Meany covered Kirk's amount. 'Any more for any more?' he asked.

There were no takers.

The same cook who'd spoken to Napier shook his head. 'Suckers,' he mumbled.

'I think Sergeant McQuarrie should hold the money,' Kirk said. 'Just so there's no problem after.'

'There won't be any problem, I assure you,' Meany said, laughing yet again.

McQuarrie picked up the money, counted it to confirm it was all there, and then slipped it into a trouser pocket. He then went to a cupboard from which he produced two bottles, neither of which bore a label.

'What's this then?' Kirk asked.

'I said I'd supply the whisky and that's it,' Meany replied. 'Heather Dew, McQuarrie's own.'

Kirk uncorked the bottle and took a sniff. He then tipped some into his mouth. It was very strong and smoky-flavoured, rather like some of the highland malts, he thought.

'You make this, Sergeant?' Kirk asked.

'I used to work for a distillery before I joined the army,' McQuarrie replied. To Eddy he added, 'Don't worry, it's good stuff. But it's about a hundred proof.'

'If you back out now you forfeit your bets,' Meany said quickly.

'Poteen,' Eddy said.

'Which will soon separate the men from the boys,' Meany added, pleased at the flanker he'd pulled.

Kirk looked at Eddy, who nodded. He was willing to go on.

'I doubt if you'll need more than a bottle each,' McQuarrie said. 'No one's ever drunk more than that.'

'Right. Let's get on with it,' Kirk said.

McQuarrie took charge. 'I do the measuring and pouring out, gentlemen. It's half-gill at a time and both have to finish before the next tot is poured. Is that clear?'

Eddy and Meany nodded.

'The contest ends when one of you either flakes or else says he's had enough. Is that clear?'

Eddy and Meany nodded again.

'And when I declare a winner that's final. There'll be no argy-barging after or tomorrow or whenever.'

'Get on with it, man. I'm bloody thirsty,' Meany said.

McQuarrie used a proper pub measure, pouring each from the same bottle.

Meany took his first and threw it back. He smacked his lips with relish. 'Mother's milk,' he declared.

Eddy tasted his tentatively; appreciating the strength of it from the bite in his palate.

'Swallow it, don't play with it,' Meany gibed.

'There are no time rules so why don't you just shut up ... *Sir*,' Eddy replied.

Meany looked murderous, his lips thinning into a vicious downward hook.

Eddy slowly drained his glass and then nodded to McQuarrie that he was ready for another.

McQuarrie poured out two fresh measures.

Meany took more time over this one having got the message he wasn't going to pressure Eddy into drinking quickly.

The minutes ticked by and two glasses each became three and then six.

Eddy smoked, his eyes fastened to Meany's. Meany glared back, having now lost his initial jocularity.

Eddy pushed his glass forward for a seventh tot. 'Mother's milk,' he said, repeating what Meany had said earlier. As he'd guessed it would, he saw that infuriated Meany.

The alcohol was taking effect on Eddy now. His brain was

beginning to numb and he was getting a little lightheaded. But he felt he could go on for a long while yet.

At ten o'clock they were on their fifteenth drink and both men were swaying slightly where they sat. The inside of Eddy's head felt as though it was a block of ice. He had to concentrate to keep his vision sharp.

'And again, sergeant,' he said. As usual he'd finished after Meany.

Meany's face was flushed and there was sweat on his brow. Every so often he made a sort of sighing sound at the back of his throat.

McQuarrie held up the second bottle, which was now empty.

'Well there's a first time for everything,' he said wonderingly.

The rest of the section and the cooks looked on in awe.

In the functioning part of his brain Eddy was thinking that without the fructose he'd have been gone long before now.

His skin was cold on the outside but was raging hot underneath. He guessed that to be his metabolism working overtime in burning up the alcohol.

He brought the glass to his lips and drank. The smoky-peat flavour was heavy in his nostrils and a fog of it seemed to have gathered at the back of his throat. It was a taste and smell he felt would be with him for the rest of his life.

'Catholic whoor!' Meany said venomously; adding, 'the only good papisher's a dead one.'

'It's nice to be liked,' Eddy replied, and without realising what he was doing drained his glass. It was the first time he'd finished before Meany and when it dawned on him what he'd done he grinned.

'I'm waiting, Corporal,' he said.

Meany blinked and stared at Eddy's glass.

'It's empty,' Eddy said.

Meany seemed to shrink even further in upon himself and Eddy knew then he'd scored heavily psychologically.

'Fill 'em up!' Meany said with bravado, having finished his

drink. But there was something empty in his voice as though the spirit had gone from it.

The end came two drinks later. With a moan Meany's head slid sideways and he started to slip from his seat.

'Have you had enough, Corporal?' McQuarrie asked.

'Away to hell! All of you bastards!' Meany jerked out. His hands desperately clawed at the table to try and stop himself, but he couldn't. He went crashing to the floor.

Slowly and emphatically Eddy emptied what remained in his glass down his throat.

'I declare King the winner!' McQuarrie said.

The section cheered while Kirk hurried to Eddy's side. 'How do you feel?' he asked.

'Bloody.'

'I'm not surprised.'

Eddy's face broke into an expression of sheer delight. 'I beat the sod. I beat him!'

'You did that,' Kirk said.

'That was just amazing,' McQuarrie said, handing their winnings over. 'Just amazing.'

Eddy started to retch.

Kirk gestured Smart and Ogle over. 'Take him to the bog, will you. Napier and I will see to the Corporal.'

'Aye, of course. Sure,' Ogle replied.

If anyone thought those arrangements unusual or that Kirk was suddenly showing concern for Meany, they never said so. Smart and Ogle each took one of Eddy's arms and draped it round their shoulders. He managed a few steps and then staggered, his feet buckling under him.

'Hurry for Christ's sake!' Eddy mumbled. His cheeks ballooned as vomit burst from his throat into his mouth.

A cook held the door open as Smart and Ogle broke into a run with the hapless Eddy being dragged along between them.

Meany's eyes opened and closed, his lips drew back in a snarl. His body twitched involuntarily as though he had St Vitus' dance.

'What a state,' Kirk said, grabbing hold of Meany's front.

With Napier helping him he got the Corporal upright.

They held Meany the way Smart and Ogle had held Eddy. 'We'll get him into his beddy bydoe where he can sleep it off,' Kirk said.

Meany sagged suddenly between them as he flaked out.

'The sooner he's in kip the better,' McQuarrie said. 'And I'd put a bowl by the side of the bed if I was you.'

'Bugger that. Let him wallow in his own spew,' Napier retorted.

McQuarrie sighed. None of the men ever liked Meany. Which wasn't all that surprising considering how Meany treated them, he reflected.

'We're away then,' Kirk said. 'And thanks for the facilities.'

'I wouldn't have missed it for the world,' McQuarrie replied. Then, shaking his head, 'More than a bottle each. Bloody hell!'

Once outside in the cold night air Meany showed signs of reviving, which suited Kirk just fine. He didn't want the corporal totally zonked out.

'Where are you going? His billet's this way,' Napier queried. Kirk was pulling them in another direction.

'I'm going to have a go at fixing this sod,' Kirk replied. 'Will you help me?'

Napier pulled up short. 'What do you have in mind?' he asked suspiciously.

Kirk laughed softly at the expression on Napier's face. 'Well, I'm not going to stick a bayonet between his ribs, if that's what you're thinking.'

Napier nodded. 'Anything short of murder and I'm your man.'

'Right then. Let's make tracks for the Officers' Mess. And we'll keep in the shadows in the hope nobody sees us.'

'Wherewegoing?' Meany muttered, his eyes flicking open and then closing again.

'Don't worry about a thing, Corp,' Kirk replied soothingly. 'We're going to see you right.'

'That'shelluvagoodofyou,' Meany said. And a second or

two later his head dropped forward again.

When they came to the Officers' Mess they came round the side of it. Napier held on to Meany while Kirk confirmed the coast was clear. En route he'd given Napier his instructions.

The Officers' Mess was ablaze with light and the muted hum of voices could be heard.

As Kirk and Napier dragged Meany up the steps leading to the Mess, Kirk whispered in Meany's ear, 'Eddy King's coming for you, Corp. The Fenian bastard says you're nothing more than a yellow-livered snake and he's going to sort your hash once and for all.'

Kirk held Meany upright while Napier pounded on the Mess door.

'You're all a bunch of cunts!' Napier yelled. 'A bunch of fucking horrible toerags and if just one of you will step out here I'll give him what for!'

'He's coming,' Kirk whispered. 'He says he's going to give you what for!'

'Like fuck he will!' Meany snarled.

Kirk draped the Corporal over a wooden rail.

'Someone's coming!' Napier whispered urgently.

'Get on your feet man! Get on your feet!' Kirk urged.

Meany grabbed hold of the rail and stood there swaying. 'Where are you, King? Where are you, you Catholic whoor!' he slurred.

'Come on!' cried Napier vaulting over the railing.

Kirk stayed long enough to pound on the door one last time, then followed Napier over the railing.

Napier scurried round the side of the building to be joined almost instantly by Kirk.

'What's all the racket?' a voice queried.

'Let me at you, you whoor!' Meany's slurred voice replied.

There was the sound of a scuffle.

Kirk crossed his fingers.

'Having trouble, steward?' a new voice asked.

Kirk recognised the voice immediately. 'Lieutenant Gilzean,' he whispered.

'I'm afraid the Corporal's had a bit too much, sir,' the steward replied.

Meany stood swaying, blinking his eyes as he tried to focus. His hands were balled into fists.

'Now there's a good chap. Get yourself back to your billet before you're put on a charge,' Gilzean said kindly. Coming to Meany he tried to put his arm round Meany's shoulders with the intention of assisting the corporal down the short flight of steps leading to the ground.

With a roar Meany swatted Gilzean's arm away. 'Don't touch me, you Catholic whoor!' he cried. And roaring again punched Gilzean full in the face.

Blood spurted from Gilzean's nose as he staggered back. Blood that fell to spatter the front of his tunic. The steward leapt forward to Gilzean's aid but Gilzean shrugged him aside.

The door banged open to reveal the portly figure of Lieutenant-Colonel Boswell. 'What the deuce is all this, Lieutenant?' he demanded.

Gilzean, blood still streaming down his face, came to attention and saluted. In a few terse sentences he explained the situation.

Boswell's eyes blazed. 'Striking an officer, eh?' he said in an ominous tone of voice. 'All right, Lieutenant, carry on. You know what to do.'

'Yes, sir!' Gilzean replied, saluting again.

Meany shook his head. Something was desperately wrong but he couldn't think what. And where was King? The bastard had been here only seconds ago.

He blinked his eyes but still couldn't focus. All he could make out were blurred images in khaki.

Then suddenly there were more khaki figures and hands were grabbing hold of him. He was dimly aware of his feet scraping the ground.

Kirk and Napier shrank further into the shadows as the guard hauled Meany away. Kirk was jubilant; that a Lieutenant-Colonel had been involved was far far better than

279

anything he'd dared hope. Meany would have the book thrown at him.

'Come on,' he whispered, 'let's get out of here.'

When they were a safe distance away Kirk turned to Napier and said, 'We must keep stum from the rest of the section about what we've just done. I know they wouldn't do it intentionally but should one of them ever blab and it got back to the other NCO's, you and I would in for the high jump.'

'My mouth is sealed,' Napier replied. Then said excitedly, 'Jesus, what do you think they'll do to him?'

'I'm not quite sure but whatever it is it won't be pleasant. Of one thing we can be certain. He's finished as a corporal.'

'Poor sod. I almost feel sorry for him in a way.'

'Don't,' Kirk replied. 'He sure as hell wouldn't if the positions were reversed.'

Napier sniffed. Kirk was right.

The next morning the section had the unbelievable luxury of a long lie in.

It was gone half past nine when the door banged open and Corporal Forbes marched in. 'Wakey wakey!' he shouted. 'The holiday's over.'

Eddy groaned and covered his head with his hands.

'Which one of you is Murray?' Forbes demanded.

My God, Meany's remembered it was me set him up, Kirk thought. He glanced across at Napier who was looking grim and not a little scared.

'I am, sir!' he said, crawling out of bed and coming to attention.

'Troop Commander wants to see you right away so get washed, shaved and dressed as quick as you can.'

'Yes, sir!'

'The rest of you clean this room out. Further orders will be forthcoming.'

'Yes, sir!' came the ragged reply.

Turning on his heel Forbes marched from the room.

'I'm dying!' Eddy moaned. 'I really think I'm dying.'

'You look terrible,' McKenzie said cheerfully.

'Like a corpse all set for interment,' Kirkwood added.

'I'll never drink again,' Eddy groaned.

'That's what they all say,' Smart said, pleased that it raised a laugh.

'What's happened to Meany?' Ogle asked.

'Must be laid up with a hangover,' Smart replied.

'I hope the bastard suffers,' Rennie said.

'I'll drink to that,' Kirkwood said, and again everyone laughed.

Napier sat on Eddy's bed. 'Can you get up?' he asked.

Eddy's face was white as cream and his eyes were bloodshot. 'I did win, didn't I?' he husked.

'You did.'

'Where's Kirk?'

'Off getting washed. The Troop Commander wants to see him.'

'What about?'

'I've no idea.'

Eddy groaned. 'I've never ever had a hangover like this one. My head feels as though a grenade's gone off inside it.'

'A couple of pills and a shower's what you need,' Napier said.

'I don't think I could manage that on my own.'

'Don't worry. I'll help you.'

Looking like death itself, Eddy was helped out of bed and to his feet.

Ogle started to sing and the others joined in.

'For he's a jolly good pish artist,
For he's a jolly good pish artist,
For he's . . .'

'Very funny,' said Eddy.

Twenty minutes later the section were sitting on or by their beds waiting for the further orders they'd been promised.

Eddy was still in a dreadful state but feeling a lot better than

281

he had been. His skin was clammy and oily still despite the shower, and every time he swallowed it was as though his windpipe had been scalded by boiling water.

Napier sat nervously watching the door. He couldn't think why Kirk might have been sent for other than in connection with the previous night's incident. He started sweating profusely under the arms.

Napier was first on his feet when the door opened and Kirk entered. Kirk wore a bemused expression.

'Well?' Napier asked.

Kirk smiled as he surveyed the section. 'It seems Corporal Meany disgraced himself last night,' he said. 'In fact he disgraced himself so badly the Corporal will shortly be a corporal no more.'

Relief surged through Napier. He knew from the quick look Kirk had shot him that they were in the clear.

'What happened?' Rennie demanded.

Kirk went on, 'Well, as you all know, Napier here and myself took Meany back to his billet after the drinking contest. We didn't undress him or anything, just dumped him on his bed and left him to it. Only it seems Meany didn't stay there but somehow got up again and went for a walk.' He paused before adding, 'To the Officers' Mess.'

Ogle whistled.

'I like it so far!' Kirkwood said.

'And ... ? And? ...' Smart demanded.

'Nobody knows why but apparently he started banging the Mess door and shouting obscenities. And when a steward and Lieutenant Gilzean tried to talk him into quietly going back to his room, he thumped Gilzean.'

'Ah!' said Kirkwood, bliss written across his face.

'Bloodied Gilzean's nose,' Kirk added.

'Ah!' Kirkwood repeated.

'At which point Lieutenant-Colonel Boswell appeared on the scene and Meany was marched off to the guard house.'

'What are they going to do to him?' Napier asked.

'He's to stay in the guard house till tomorrow when he's

being flown back home. He'll be doing his detention in the Military Correction Training Centre at Colchester. Fifty-six days' worth.'

The section looked from one to the other. They'd all heard about Colchester and what allegedly went on in the MCTC there.

'What happens to him after that?' Ogle asked.

'He'll certainly be reduced to ranks, although whether that happens before or after, I'm not sure, and then he'll be returned to the regiment.'

'So we could meet up with him again, only this time on equal terms?' Smart said, a speculative gleam in his eye. 'I doubt that. From what the Troop Commander said, I definitely got the impression he'll be posted to another battalion.'

'Pity,' replied Smart, his voice heavy with disappointment.

'So with Meany gone, who's our new corporal?' Rennie asked.

'Stand to attention and salute when you talk to me, you horrible little shite of a man!' Kirk barked out, adding with a twinkle in his eye, 'What are you?'

'You don't mean . . . ?'

'I'm afraid so,' Kirk replied. 'I did my best to talk them out of it but you know how it is when one is so obviously head and shoulders above the common herd.'

'I'll give you common herd!' Smart said indignantly.

'He's pulling your pudding, Norrie. Don't rise to the bait,' Napier said.

'Oh!' replied Smart, then, 'I knew that!'

McKenzie and Ogle both groaned and Rennie said scathingly, 'Of course you did!'

'Life suddenly looks an awful lot rosier than it did a few minutes ago. Congratulations . . . Corp!' Napier said, crossing to Kirk and pumping his hand.

The rest of the section crowded round, eager to slap Kirk on the back and get in on the hand pumping. The only one not to do so was Eddy, who was lying curled up on his bed with his back to Kirk.

Finally Kirk broke away from his well-wishers and, crossing to Eddy's bed, sat. 'Well what have you got to say to your new corporal?' he asked.

His reply was a combined grunt and snore. Eddy was fast asleep.

'I think we'll let this David kip,' Kirk said quietly and tenderly. 'It took a lot out of him beating Goliath.'

'What the hell's he talking about?' Smart whispered.

Ogle withered Smart with a look.

'Well I can't have seen every picture that's ever been made,' Smart replied waspishly.

It was the section's twenty-third patrol with Kirk as leader. It was three o'clock in the morning and they were taking their second break.

McKenzie was acting as lookout while Rennie brewed up. Smart had built the small fire which crackled fiercely. When it came to building fires there was no one in the section to touch him.

Kirk and Eddy sat side by side, both with steaming mugs in their hands. Eddy was smoking.

'Just stay where you are, gentlemen, and don't move!' a voice said, coming from the darkness beyond the fire.

Everyone froze with the complete unexpectedness of it.

'MacKenzie?' Kirk called out.

The reply was muffled and indistinct.

'Who are you?' Kirk asked, gesturing to Smart to stay where he was.

'Throw your weapons behind you, please,' the voice instructed.

'No,' said Kirk emphatically. 'I'm afraid we can't do that.'

'Then I might have to shoot you.'

'For what reason?'

'An armed incursion into Russian territory.'

Kirk frowned. The voice had an English accent. 'You don't sound Russian to me,' he said.

284

A sentence in Russian rapped out and there were vague rustlings all around.

'Okay, I believe you,' Kirk said. 'But tell me, when did the Russian sector become Russian territory?'

The voice chuckled. 'The moment we Russians took it over. We're very possessive, don't you know?'

'If we are in the Russian sector, and according to my map we aren't, then it's a genuine mistake. So rather than shoot holes in one another why not join us for a cup of coffee instead? I don't know how many men you've got but I'm sure we can cope.'

There was a brief pause and then the voice said, '*Real* coffee?'

'As real as you'll get anywhere.'

Again there was a brief pause and then the voice rapped out what could only be an order.

McKenzie stumbled out of the darkness looking sheepish and embarrassed. 'I never heard a thing,' he said.

'Did they hurt you?'

'No. Just a hand over the mouth, that's all.'

'Ivan!' Ogle whispered excitedly.

The man who came towards them was short and stocky. He was dressed in the uniform of a Red Army officer.

'Good morning,' he said.

Kirk rose and extended his hand. 'Corporal Murray,' he said, then gesturing around, 'my men.'

The Russian nodded pleasantly to the section before turning his attention back to Kirk. 'I am Captain Turushev and you said something about coffee?'

Eddy poured some into his own mug which he passed to Turushev, who accepted it gratefully.

'Sugar and milk?' Eddy asked.

Turushev laughed softly. 'All the pleasures of home.'

'What about your men?' Kirk asked.

'They can stay out there.'

'How many of you are there?'

'A lot more than you, Corporal.'

The section relaxed. Most eyes fastened on Turushev, others were drawn to the surrounding darkness and the Russian soldiers whom they couldn't see but who could see them.

'Ah!' sighed Turushev after he'd taken a swallow. 'It's been such a long time since the real thing.'

'Your English is very good,' Kirk said.

'I was posted in London for two years after the war. That was where I learned it.'

'You sound just like an Englishman,' Eddy said.

'I'll take that as a compliment. Although being Scottish perhaps you didn't mean it as one. The Battle of Bannockburn, Scotland v England at Hampden Park and Wembley.' And having said that, Turushev laughed.

'Did you like England?' Kirk asked.

'Loved it. I was connected with the Embassy there, which meant I attended a great many parties and then functions. I had some marvellous times I can tell you. Especially with the English women.' He leaned forward confidentially. 'Whoever said English women are cold doesn't know what he's talking about. You can take my word for that!'

Kirk smiled. 'Eddy here's our expert on English women. Had one in London for some time himself.'

That annoyed Eddy a little. He didn't like Annie talked about that way. Somehow it cheapened her. To change the subject, or to try and get away from it anyway, he pulled out his packet of cigarettes and offered the Russian one.

Turushev delicately picked out a cigarette and held it up so he could admire it. 'Senior Service,' he said. 'I haven't had one of these since I left England.'

'I thought Russian fags were supposed to be good,' Eddy said.

'Camel dung. Or if it isn't, that's what it certainly tastes like. But you can find out for yourself.' And having said that he passed one of his own cigarettes over to Eddy.

Eddy flicked a match and they both lit up.

'Christ Almighty!' said Eddy coughing. 'You're right.'

'And this is sheer bliss,' Turushev replied, drawing smoke deep into his lungs.

Kirk caught Eddy's eye and gave a slight gesture of his head to indicate Eddy's packet which was still out. Eddy got the message.

'Here, you'd better have these,' Eddy said. 'I've got more back at the billet.'

Turushev didn't need to be offered twice. 'You're most kind,' he said, accepting the packet as though it was some priceless item.

'Now, about this little mix-up,' Kirk said. 'According to my map we're still in the British sector.'

'Show me,' Turushev said.

Kirk unfolded his map and spread it on the ground. Using his finger he pinpointed what he thought to be their position.

Turushev shook his head. 'This is where you really are, right here!' he said.

'Are you sure?'

'Absolutely.'

Kirk chewed his lip. 'Map-reading never was my strong point,' he admitted.

'It's easily done on a night like this in country which is very similar for miles around,' Turushev said generously, adding with a wink, 'actually I've been over on your side several times myself when I shouldn't have been.'

Kirk knew then it was going to be all right. 'More coffee?' he asked, seeing Turushev's mug was empty.

'If you could spare it.'

'Our pleasure,' Kirk replied.

As Eddy was filling Turushev's mug, Kirk said, 'How about a wee dram to go with it?'

Turushev's rather slanted eyes opened wide. 'You don't mean whisky, do you?'

Kirk produced a small flask, which he always took along on patrol with him. It contained Sergeant McQuarrie's Heather Dew, which he rather liked and which was only a fraction of the cost of a bottle of Scotch – when Scotch was available that is, which was rarely.

'Tell me what you think of that,' he said, handing over the flask.

Turushev took a deep swig.

'And again,' Kirk said.

The second swig was even deeper than the first.

'Well?' Kirk demanded.

'Excellent. Highland malt, if I'm not mistaken?'

It was on the tip of Kirk's tongue to say he also thought it tasted like Highland malt when in actual fact it was poteen, but something stopped him from doing so.

'Real coffee, good cigarettes and malt whisky,' Turushev said. 'My lucky night.'

Kirk glanced at his watch. Time was passing, the section really should be on its way.

Turushev noted the glance and realised what it meant. 'I too must continue my patrol,' he said.

'Is this your regular beat?' Kirk asked.

'Yes. Every night.'

'We do turn about with another section.'

'One on, one off. You're very lucky,' Turushev said wistfully.

Turushev finished his coffee and the remainder of the whisky, after which hands were shaken all round. Turushev was about to stride back into the darkness where his men were patiently waiting, when suddenly he paused as a thought struck him.

'Can we talk privately for a second?' he asked Kirk.

'Sure,' Kirk replied. And the two of them moved away from the others.

Turushev said, 'I was wondering if you could get me a few bottles of that excellent whisky. I'd be willing to pay handsomely of course.'

Kirk rubbed his scar. Why not do the Russian a favour? he thought. It was no skin off his nose.

'Roubles are no use,' he said.

'Naturally. But I think I can lay my hands on some sterling or Deutschmarks.'

Kirk nodded. 'It is a bit pricey, you appreciate?'

'How much in sterling?'

Kirk knew how much it cost to buy a real bottle of Scotch on the German black market, which was the price he now stated.

'Fine.'

'Half a dozen bottles too many?'

Turushev sucked in a breath. 'You can get me as many as that?'

'No problem.'

'Then half a dozen bottles it is. Now, when and where?'

'Night after next? Same time, same place?'

'I'll be looking for you,' Turushev said. 'Till then, Murray.'

'Till then, Captain,' Kirk replied.

After the Russians had gone, the section proceeded on its way. The men of the section had strict instructions from Kirk that they weren't to mention to anyone about their encounter with the Russians.

The men were only too happy to comply.

A smiling Turushev strode out of the darkness. 'Good morning,' he said.

'Good morning,' Kirk replied, handing Turushev a mug of coffee.

The Russian accepted a cigarette from Eddy, which he allowed Eddy to light for him before turning to Kirk and raising an eyebrow.

Kirk opened his knapsack and passed over half a dozen bottles of Heather Dew.

'No labels?' Turushev asked, examining one of the bottles.

Kirk shrugged. 'It's what's inside you're drinking, not the label.'

'Quite true,' Turushev replied, and taking the top off the bottle had a swig.

'There's no mistaking true Highland malt,' Turushev said.

Kirk nodded, thinking, like hell there wasn't!

Turushev pulled out his wallet and he extracted a wad of notes. These he handed to Kirk. 'I think you'll find that right,' he said.

'You don't mind if I count it, do you?'

'Of course not.'

The money was in Deutschmarks and correct.

'It's a pleasure doing business with you,' Kirk said.

Turushev packed the bottles away in a haversack he'd brought with him and then returned to his coffee, which Eddy had topped up. He squatted, facing Kirk.

'Is there any chance you can get me more?' he asked.

Kirk regarded the Russian thoughtfully. This was beginning to get interesting.

'How many bottles would you want?' he asked.

'As many as you can get me.'

Excitement fluttered in Kirk's insides. It was the same sort of excitement he'd experienced when he'd heard about Harry Hydelman and the B.X.

'Are we talking in terms of a dozen now, or in cases?' he asked.

'Cases if you can do it.'

Kirk rocked back on his heels. It had been galling him that he hadn't been able to deal in the Uelsberg black market. The people who did so had registered their disapproval of soldiers trying to butt in only a few weeks previously, when a soldier who'd tried to set up in silk stockings had been beaten within an inch of his life. And Kirk was damned if he was going to get mixed up in proceedings like those without a Turk McGhie to back him up.

But dealing with a Russian for a Russian market was a different kettle of fish entirely. And one that smelled hugely of profit.

'What about money?' he asked. 'Can you lay your hands on large sums of sterling and Deutschmarks?'

'I can do better than that,' Turushev replied mysteriously. 'Come, let us take a walk, you and I.'

The two men rose and strolled a little way off.

'What do you make of that?' Turushev asked, handing Kirk a small hard object.

Turushev flicked a lighter into flame and held it close to Kirk's palm so Kirk could see what it was that lay nestling there.

Yellow metal glinted in the light from the flame. Metal that had been cast into a small bar.

'Gold!' whispered Kirk through suddenly clenched teeth.

'Eighteen carat,' Turushev added.

Kirk weighed the gold in his hand. For such a small amount it was surprisingly heavy. Reluctantly he handed it back to Turushev, who was grinning in the darkness.

'How much is that worth?' Kirk asked.

'That, and the box of bars it came from, is valueless to me because I can't cash it in,' Turushev replied with a shrug.

'Why not?'

'Because all spoils of war go direct to the State. Yes, my friend, this was Nazi gold. A small cache which I was lucky to stumble upon.'

The picture was beginning to clear for Kirk. 'Gold you can't sell but whisky you can?' he asked.

'When I was in London I committed a small indiscretion, as a result of which I will never be allowed to set foot in the West again. So the gold, as I've already said, is valueless to me now and in the future. But if I could exchange it for whisky, I would then be in a position not only to further my career – "bribery and corruption", I think is the appropriate English phrase – but also to feather my nest at the same time. The latter, of course, providing we can deal in quantity.'

He paused to light a long Russian cigarette before going on. 'I take it you are acquiring your whisky from the German black market?' he asked, eyes slitted and intent upon Kirk.

'Yes,' Kirk lied.

'So you will act as middleman between them and me for which, naturally, you will make a substantial profit.'

Kirk's mind was whirling. The trouble was he didn't know what McQuarrie's still was capable of or even if McQuarrie would agree to sell to him in bulk. He needed time to think and make inquiries and work everything out.

'Look,' he said slowly. 'The contact I have is only a small one and frankly I don't know what sort of amounts he can handle. Let's agree to meet four days hence, which is my patrol after next, and I should be able to know more then. Whatever happens I'll bring you another half-dozen bottles.'

'That arrangement is satisfactory with me,' Turushev replied, handing Kirk the gold bar.

'In the meantime have that on account, as I presume you will want to have it assayed and establish its value.'

Kirk fingered the small bar lovingly before slipping it into a pocket where it would be safe.

'Now, what about coffee and cigarettes? Can you do anything for me there?' Turushev asked.

Kirk knew there would be nothing like the profit in those that there would be in the whisky. But a profit was still a profit, after all.

'I'll give you an answer on those next time as well,' he replied.

Turushev nodded his approval.

Kirk stroked his scar, his mind tumbling over at a rate of knots.

Sergeant McQuarrie sat on the edge of a table and looked long and hard at Kirk. 'Just what have you got yourself mixed up in?' he asked.

'Something that can make some extra change for both of us,' Kirk replied.

'If you're selling round about, those German black marketeers will cut your balls off, you know that, don't you?'

'I won't be selling round about.'

'Then where?'

'That's my business, Sergeant.'

McQuarrie looked sceptical. 'Now let's go over this again. You want me to up my production and you will buy the lot?'

'As much as you can sell me.'

'At the same price as usual?'

Kirk laughed softly. 'I'm not asking for bulk reduction if that's what you're thinking!'

'I was thinking more of an increase actually,' McQuarrie replied.

'How much per bottle?'

'An added one and six.'

Kirk pretended to consider that, finally saying reluctantly, 'You drive a hard bargain, Sergeant. But it's agreed.'

Rising from the table McQuarrie beckoned Kirk to follow him. He led Kirk through various rooms to the very back of the cookhouse area, all of which was his exclusive domain.

When they reached the room where the still was, McQuarrie locked the door behind him. Kirk stared in fascination at the still; it was the first he'd ever seen.

'Where on earth did you get it from?' he asked.

'I didn't. It was already here when I arrived. The Wehrmacht were billeted here during the war so I can only presume they had it installed.'

Kirk regarded the steady drip of alcohol, which was rapidly filling up a two-gallon jar. The air was pungent with the smoky odour he'd come to associate with Heather Dew.

McQuarrie went on, 'When I came across it, it had been shoved back here out the way and quite obviously hadn't been used for a number of years. Well I got to thinking. It seemed there was never any whisky available in the Mess and of course the black market stuff was way beyond what I could afford. The next step seemed inevitable, me having worked in a distillery and all and knowing how to go about making it.'

'What amazes me is how much like Highland malt it is,' Kirk said. 'I've been around pubs and whisky all my life and honestly I couldn't tell the difference.'

'It's a very high-quality poteen, and that's because I know exactly what I'm doing. But there's more to it than that. So much of the flavour and body of a whisky depends on the water used to make it with. And the water round here seems to be similar to that found in many parts of the Highlands.'

Kirk shook his head. 'Amazing!' he said.

'But there's a lot about whisky-making we don't know. Why is it, for example, that two distilleries across the road from one another and using the same stream can turn out two quite different-tasting malts? No one's discovered the answer to that one yet. It's simply one of the mysteries.'

'As far as I'm concerned, the big question is how much can you turn out per week?' Kirk asked.

'I'm not sure. At the moment I'm only producing enough for myself and a few of the lads I sell it to, which amounts roughly to about two dozen bottles a week.'

'Could you do a dozen cases?'

'Oh aye, easy. If I can get the grain that is.'

'Where do you get it from now?'

'From the supplies brought in, man. I just syphon off what's required and that's that.'

'What about enough for full production?'

McQuarrie frowned. 'That could be tricky. I don't see how I could explain how I suddenly needed that amount when I've been getting by on what I have for a number of years now.'

'All right, that's a problem I'll have to solve,' said Kirk thoughtfully. 'You just write down what you need and I'll see to it.'

'Then there's bottling,' McQuarrie went on. 'What about that?'

Kirk picked up a distinctive green bottle waiting to be filled with Heather Dew. McQuarrie always used the same type bottle for his poteen.

'Where do you get these from?' Kirk asked.

'From the laundry. They're old bleach bottles.'

Kirk raised an eyebrow. 'And you're telling me you can't get enough from the laundry if, or should I say when, we go into full production?'

'That's it.'

'Leave that to me as well, then.'

And labels, Kirk thought. He'd have to do something about

those. If he was going to do this thing he may as well do it properly.

'Right then!' said Kirk, smacking his hands together. 'I'll need half a dozen bottles for three days from now and in the meantime I'll get on with my side of things.'

'I just hope you know what you're doing,' McQuarrie said.

Kirk remembered that was a question he'd been asked once before. Well that had worked out all right, so why not this?

'Trust me Sergeant. Just trust me and I'll put an added bit of jingle in both our pockets. Making money's a talent I have.'

Humming, he went in search of Eddy.

'There you are, sir,' the jeweller said, counting the notes out into Kirk's hand.

Kirk stared at the pile of Deutschmarks in amazement. It was far, far more than he'd expected.

'Pleasure to do business with you, sir. Call again any time,' the jeweller said.

Kirk nodded and, turning, left the shop.

Outside Eddy was waiting for him. Together they walked down the street.

There was an enormous profit to be made here, Kirk thought. He would be buying whisky from McQuarrie for a pittance, selling it at black market prices plus some. And now there was the value of the gold which he could further juggle to increase his profit.

'Want in?' he asked Eddy, aware that Eddy knew full well what he was up to.

'Why not?' Eddy replied.

'I'll need a partner. It's a two-man operation, the way I see it.'

'If I'm a partner then that's fifty-fifty, I take it?'

Kirk smiled. 'It's my idea so I get extra for that. But I'll tell you what, seeing how I like you and we've been such good mates, how about sixty-forty?'

'You're on,' Eddy replied. And they sealed the partnership by shaking hands.

A few steps further down the street Eddy said, 'What about the rest of the section? One for all and all for one, as you put it?'

'This is money we're talking about. There's no one for all when it comes to that,' Kirk replied.

Eddy laughed. 'Jesus, you're a hard bastard,' he said.

'Not as hard as some I could name. But I'm getting there.' Kirk replied softly.

He was thinking of Major and Gerald Gibb.

Eddy was well pleased with himself as he stepped out of the printer's office. He'd got a good price on the labels for Heather Dew which he'd placed with the printer and which the man had promised him would be ready in two days' time.

He glanced at his watch. He had some time to kill before making his way back to the castle. He was supposed to meet up with Kirk who was somewhere at the other end of Uelsberg talking to a grain merchant.

He knew the coffee in the coffee shop was ridiculously overpriced and not very good either but for the moment he couldn't think of any other way to pass the next half-hour.

After buying his coffee he looked for a seat, spying one beside a solitary woman. He'd sat beside her and started to spoon into his cup before he recognised her.

'Dr Kruppermann, isn't it?' he queried.

She looked up to stare at him blankly.

'I came to see you some time ago about an alcohol problem I had.' Then, blushing when he realised what that must sound like, he blurted out, 'Fructose?'

'Oh yes! Now I remember!' She laughed. 'The drinking contest.'

He nodded. 'I won.'

'I'm pleased to hear it.'

'The fructose made all the difference. I couldn't have done it without it.'

She smiled and sipped her coffee, crow's-feet crinkling the corners of her eyes and mouth.

Eddy was enjoying the experience of being alone with a good-looking woman, the last having been the whore Magda. Suddenly he was self-conscious and ever so slightly embarrassed.

'Cigarette?' he asked, offering his packet.

'Thank you.'

He lit it for her and for the next few seconds they smoked in silence.

'Are you married, Doctor?' he asked, then wondered what had prompted him to do so. It was terribly forward.

What could only be interpreted as pain edged into her eyes. 'I was once,' she said, 'but no more.'

'The war?'

She smiled again, only this time there was a bitter quality about it.

'The Russian Front,' she replied.

'I'm sorry.'

'Why should you be? You never knew him and he was your enemy.'

'The worst thing about war is the ones who're left behind. Wouldn't you agree?' he said after a while.

'Yes, I would,' she whispered.

'I was lucky to miss it.'

Annie Grimes, he thought. That was who Dr Kruppermann reminded him of. They weren't physically alike at all, Annie being tallish, brunette and slim while Dr Kruppermann was quite short with blonde hair and, from what he could see, a well-padded, curvaceous figure. But they both had the same quality of femininity which he recognised but couldn't have described in words. He judged the doctor to be a few years older than Annie.

Seeing her cup was empty, he said, 'Would you like another?'

She looked undecided.

'I'd really appreciate the company,' he said.

There must have been something in his tone for she looked at him strangely and quizzically.

'I'll get the coffee,' he said and taking her cup rose and made for the counter.

On his return she said, 'Are you a regular soldier?'

'No. National Service.'

'It must be difficult for a young man like you to be away from home. You must be homesick for your parents and sweetheart, perhaps?'

He shook his head. 'There's no one.'

'No one at all?'

'Nobody,' he said, and stared into his cup.

'Me neither,' she replied. 'I was the only one of my family to survive the war.'

'We've got something in common then. Being alone in the world, that is.'

After a little while she said wistfully, 'Such strange and sad times we live in.'

His heart went out to her, and although he'd only known her a few minutes, and despite the fact she was considerably older than he was, he wanted to reach out and touch her, to take her in his arms and comfort her.

'Was your husband a doctor?' he asked.

'No, not Willi!' she laughed. 'He had his own business.' She laughed again. 'Anyone less like a doctor I can't imagine.'

They stared at one another, she cool and very self-contained.

'And what did *you* do before they made you a soldier?' she asked.

'I also had my own business.'

'Oh!' she said, surprised. 'You look too young for that.'

'Mind you,' he added, 'it wasn't all that much of one. I sold used cars. But they were my cars on my lot and that was the main thing.'

'You sounded very proud when you said that.'

He shrugged. 'I suppose I am. Where I come from that would be considered something of an achievement.'

'Oh, *ja!* The Scottish man, I'd forgotten that,' she said smiling.

'Not just Scottish. I'm from Glasgow, a Glaswegian.'

She laughed softly. 'Your eyes shoot fire when you say that. Say it again.'

'Glaswegian?'

'There we are. Shafts of fire!'

He cocked his head and looked at her. 'Are you taking the mickey?' he asked.

'No, I wouldn't do that to you. But tell me about this Glasgow of yours which brings such fire to your eyes.'

'Ach - it's a dump. A real hole in the ground. Dirty big tenements, most of them with outside cludgies ...'

'Cludgies?'

'Toilets.'

'That's awful,' she said.

He went on. 'Chronic unemployment. Terrible housing. Why, I've known whole families of six and seven crowded into a room and kitchen with the room hardly big enough to swing a cat in.'

She shook her head.

'And a terrible place for drink. Friday night, pay night, you'll see them crawling home along the gutter. A couple of screwtops in their jacket pockets, a half-bottle in their back one, and pissed as ... well, "farts", the expression is. If you'll excuse me.'

'And you like this place?'

'Oh aye. It's wonderful.'

She shook her head in amazement.

He groped for words, trying to explain. But he wasn't really articulate enough. 'It's the people, you see. They're different ... they're ... well, there's just nobody like Glasgow folk, except perhaps those in Liverpool, but I've never been there so I can't say.'

He offered her another cigarette, which she eagerly accepted. She didn't seem to have any of her own. They both lit up.

299

'And it's a violent place,' he said, continuing. 'Stabbings, razorings, broken bottles, hatchets. You never know what you might be up against if you get into a barney with someone.'

'And these are your marvellous folk?'

'I know, it does sound a bit funny when it's put that way,' he replied ruefully.

'Funny?'

'Peculiar. Odd.'

'I agree,' she said.

'But it's a wonderful city all the same. You'll not find a better anywhere, not in the whole wide world.'

Leoni Kruppermann decided she liked Eddy. She liked his youth and vitality, but above all she liked the raw enthusiasm he exuded. So different, and uplifting, to the cynicism and deep-rooted weariness of herself.

Sighing, she drained her cup. 'I really must be getting on,' she said. 'I have several calls to make, important ones. Thank you for the conversation and cigarettes. And the coffee of course.'

He didn't want her to leave. Being with her had brought back that warm glow he'd once felt with Annie Grimes and hadn't experienced since.

'I, eh ... eh ...'

'Yes?'

'There's an English picture on at the weekend. I ... eh ... don't suppose you'd like to go and see it, would you?'

He looked like an overgrown schoolboy, she thought. And his lack of sophistication was absolutely charming. So different to what she'd been used to in the past.

He was very young of course. She was probably old enough to be his mother. Well ... perhaps not quite, she pretended. And she could do with a night out. Some laughter and gaiety.

'If you're already busy I'll understand perfectly,' he said.

'I'd love to go,' she replied.

Relief, tinged with excitement, welled through Eddy. 'That's great,' he said.

She produced a pocketbook and pen, scribbling a few lines

300

in the former. 'That's my home address,' she said, tearing out a page and handing it to him. 'Telephone the surgery and leave a message as to what time you'll pick me up.'

He stood and gazed down into her face. 'I'll be looking forward to it,' he said.

'I also.'

They shook hands in the continental fashion and then she was hurrying away. He watched her through the large coffee shop window until she'd disappeared from sight. He looked at his watch and with a start realised he'd been so engrossed he'd forgotten the time. He too would have to hurry if he was going to meet Kirk.

'What kept you?' Kirk said when Eddy arrived at the appointed place.

'Oh, I just met someone, that's all.'

'Sounds mysterious.'

'Not really. How did you get on with the grain merchant?'

They started walking in the direction of the castle. 'Expensive sod, but he'll supply what we need,' Kirk replied. 'And you?'

'We can have the order in two days' time.'

Kirk nodded. 'That only leaves the bottles to sort out, which is being more difficult than I'd anticipated. The bleach is made and bottled in Düsseldorf, apparently, which rules out a direct approach. I'll just have to think of something else, that's all.'

'Life's tough at the top,' Eddy said and laughed.

'You'd better believe it. And what's got into you suddenly? You're all bright-eyed and bushy-tailed, as the Yanks say.'

'Can I have a pass for Saturday night, Kirk?'

'Sure. I thought we all might go into town anyway and have a few beers.'

'I actually want to meet somebody.'

Kirk stopped dead. 'A bird, is that it? I should have known.'

'She's helluva nice. I like her.'

'Not one of the brasses I hope?'

301

'No. Doctor Kruppermann. Remember her?'

'You fly bugger! She was quite a classy piece of skirt, as I recall.'

'Yes, she is good-looking.'

'Not too old for you? Sure you can handle her?' Kirk teased.

'I can handle her,' Eddy replied emphatically.

Kirk laughed as they continued on their way to the castle.

'Well?' Eddy demanded a little further on.

'Well what?'

'The bloody pass, Kirk!'

'Of course you can have it. Would I stop a pal, and business partner, getting his hole?'

'It's not like that,' Eddie said quietly.

Kirk smiled mockingly and snorted, bursting out laughing again when Eddy turned and good-humouredly hit him on the shoulder.

Kirk and Turushev strolled a little way off from the section. Both held steaming cups of coffee. As usual, the Russian's men remained hidden.

'Your gold is genuine all right and my contact has given me the go-ahead for two dozen cases a week. All that remains now is for you and I to haggle out a price,' Kirk said.

'Two dozen cases!' Turushev mused. 'Excellent!'

'Which I suggest I don't deliver every week but rather do a monthly delivery of eight dozen. It would be a lot easier for me that way, if it's all right by you.'

'Fine. That suits me down to the ground.'

'And with the monthly shipment there'll be five thousand cigarettes and a hundred pounds of coffee. That all adds up to quite a load so I suggest you have some sort of transport available.'

Turushev shook his head. 'Not necessary. My men are yellow-faces from Kazakhstan and Uzbekistan, peasants well used to carrying heavy loads. They could hump double that amount if needs be.'

'Suit yourself,' Kirk said shrugging. 'Now, I had the gold bar you gave me assayed and valued. Going on that value, and not forgetting I have to make a profit out of all this, what I propose is . . .' And he went on to state just how much whisky, cigarettes and coffee he was prepared to give against each gold bar.

When he was finished Turushev said cynically, 'You do like to make your profit, don't you?'

'I'm taking an awful risk, Turushev. And risks cost money.'

'All right then. It's agreed. And as we're going to be doing business from now on, you can call me Kolya.'

'And I'm Kirk.'

They shook hands.

'Now let's arrange a time and place for the first meet,' said Kirk, all business once again.

It was evening and Kirk and Eddy were in the still-room bottling Heather Dew. Kirk held a two-gallon jar of poteen and Eddy a metal funnel as they carefully filled bottle after bottle. Several other brimming two-gallon jars lay stacked nearby.

'So how are you getting on with your doctor then?' Kirk asked.

'All right.'

'What does that mean?'

'Precisely what it says. All right.'

'Got your end away yet?'

'To hear you, you'd think sex was the most important thing in the world,' Eddy retorted.

Kirk looked thoughtful. 'Well, – it's a toss-up between that and money. I'd hate to have to choose.'

'There are other things in life, you know.'

'Which I suppose means you haven't got there yet?'

Eddy mumbled something.

'What's that? Speak up! I can't hear you.'

Eddy mumbled again.

'I still can't bloody well hear you!'

'*No I haven't!*' Eddy yelled.

'All right, all right! No need to blast my eardrums to bits. What's wrong with you then? Lost the notion?'

'I haven't got round to it yet, I suppose.'

'So what do you do, these nights you take her out?'

'The pictures. Music. We take walks. Discuss art ...'

'What the hell do *you* know about art?' Kirk exclaimed, obviously amused.

'Not a lot. But I'm learning. Matisse, Gauguin, Rembrandt, Picasso. Leoni has books with pictures in them, pictures of paintings and drawings. I prefer Picasso myself, especially his nudes.'

'My God!' said Kirk, shaking his head. 'What next?'

'Leoni is very cultured ...'

'All Krauts love culture,' Kirk cut in. 'They have a positive thing about it. Only with the vast majority of them they see it from the outside in and not inside out.'

Eddy frowned. He wasn't quite sure he understood what Kirk meant by that.

'She'll have you going to the theatre next,' Kirk said.

'Oh we are, next week. A play by Bernard Shaw, which I won't understand a word of as it's all in German.'

'Then why bother going?'

'Because she wants to see it, that's why.'

'No hanky-panky, sitting through plays you can't understand, Picasso and Matisse! This is beginning to sound serious.'

'You're just jealous, that's your trouble,' Eddy replied, not realising just how true that actually was.

'Me? Jealous? Don't be ridiculous!' Kirk scoffed. But in truth he was greatly feeling the strain of not having sex. After his scare with Gottfried he'd decided that whores just weren't worth the risk and to date he hadn't found a decent and respectable German female to have an affair with.

There had been several who'd given him the come-on but he hadn't been sure that he could trust them not to be pox-ridden, the number of VD cases amongst the castle soldiers having risen steeply yet again.

'Anyway I like plays,' Eddy said, and went on to tell Kirk about the night he and Michelle had gone to see the famous actor knight as the knight's guest and of the meal the three of them had had afterwards at the Ivy Restaurant.

'That night gave me a taste for getting on in life,' Eddy said. 'If I can possibly get them I want the good things, the luxuries.'

'Now you're talking, Eddy. Getting on, getting ahead. That's where you and I are similar. And I'll tell you this, when you get back in civvy street, if you find you're not making as much selling used cars as you would like then think about a pub. They're little goldmines, all of them.'

Kirk patted the two-gallon jar he was holding. 'Anything to do with booze and you can't go wrong. There are an awful lot of people in Glasgow who'd give up eating before they'd give up drinking.'

'A pub, eh?' Eddy mused. Although he knew Kirk owned several of them it was a new idea that he go into that line of business.

'And by the time we've finished with Heather Dew and our friend Kolya Turushev, let's hope you'll have more than enough loot in your sky to be well able to afford one. I'll certainly be looking to add another, if not two to my string.'

That conversation stayed with Eddy and gave him much food for thought.

'"Circus Family, 1905",' Leoni Kruppermann said, then, turning the page, '"Friendship, 1908".'

The latter was a pen-and-ink sketch belonging to the early so-called Negro phase of Cubism. A note below the sketch said it had been inspired by Negro masks.

'It's amazing what that man Picasso sees in people,' Eddy said wonderingly. 'I'd hate to think how he might portray me.'

'Very romantic, I should think,' Leoni replied.

'How do you mean?'

'I don't mean in the sexual sense but rather in your overall attitude to life.'

They were sitting on Leoni's sofa with the art book spread on her lap. On the floor stood an empty bottle of wine that Eddy had brought along and which they'd drunk while talking and leafing through various art books.

'What's wrong with sex then?' he asked.

'Nothing. I never said there was.'

He found he couldn't stare her straight in the eyes that close together. Her gaze was too frank and penetrating for him. Not that he had anything to hide.

He wondered then about his reticence at making a pass at her. They'd been going out for some time now and he hadn't even as much as kissed her. He couldn't think why, except he'd got the impression that was the way she'd wanted it.

'I have a little tea. Would you like some?' she asked.

'No,' he replied quickly, taking hold of her by the arm. 'I'd much rather we just sat here for the moment.

She smiled, a faltering one that hovered round her lips.

'Leoni?'

'Yes?'

He drew her to him and stroked her hair. Her flesh against his was firm but springy, her breasts large and pressing. His right hand curled round her neck, gently pulling her head back and her face up to him. He laid his lips on hers and closed his eyes.

For the space of a few seconds she was rigid. Then with a sigh she surrendered herself. Her arms enfolded him, drawing him tightly to her. His fumbling fingers found the zip at the back of her dress. The dress split open as he pulled it down.

Still kissing her, he pulled the top of her dress over her arms so that her slip was revealed. He pulled the slip's straps and it, in turn, fell away. Shaking a little, he felt for the catch of her bra.

When her breasts were exposed he laid his face on them. It was like sinking into a deep pillow.

'*Mein liebe,*' she crooned, stroking his hair the way he had done hers.

He found a nipple and sucked.

'Have you a gummy?' she asked.

'A what?'

'A gummy?' She frowned trying to think of the English word. And when she couldn't remember it she touched him on the penis. 'A covering for that,' she said.

'Oh! Yes,' he replied.

She rose with his hand in hers so he was forced to rise also.

'Come,' she said.

The bedroom was as small and dingy as the rest of the flat but Eddy didn't notice that now. He was too busy taking his clothes off and watching while she did the same.

She had a magnificent body, he thought. And he trembled thinking he was going to make love to her.

'Are you cold?' she asked.

'No. It's just ...' He trailed off.

'I understand.'

She came to him and took the contraceptive he was holding. She knelt before him and rolled the sheath down his erection.

'Have you been to bed with a German woman yet?' she asked.

'No,' he lied.

'Then I will have to make your first an occasion to remember.'

She led him to the bed and sank down upon it with him on top of her.

Her breath was hot in his face. Her skin like warm silk. He hadn't felt like this since he'd last been with Annie Grimes.

'That's it then,' said Kirk, loading the last box of Heather Dew.

Eddy brought the lorry's back flaps into place and tied them off. He then joined Kirk in the lorry's cabin. Kirk was in the passenger seat.

'Ready?' Kirk asked. Eddy nodded. 'Then let's go.'

At the entrance to the castle they were stopped by the duty sentry. 'Rotten night you've got for it,' Kirk said with a smile, handing over the pass McQuarrie had written out for them. He was referring to the rain which was bucketing down.

'It always seems to piss down when I draw sentry duty,' the man grumbled, holding the pass under his cape and flicking his lighted torch over it. 'Taking some stuff to the station, eh?'

'That's right, mate. Sending some faulty stores back down the line and picking up a fresh consignment for the kitchens.'

'Everything seems in order, then.'

Kirk accepted back the pass. As far as he was concerned, getting past the sentry was the tricky part. The bloke might decide to have a good look in the back of the lorry, in which case they would have a hard time explaining away their load.

Eddy slipped the lorry into gear and the lorry trundled forward. He would have to drive all the way into town before turning off down a side road which would eventually lead them into open countryside.

The place chosen by Kirk and Turushev for the meet was a secluded spot rarely visited by British patrols. Kirk had reckoned this to be the safest spot, and also the most accessible for the lorry, for the exchange to take place.

They left Uelsberg behind and took a narrow dirt road in the direction of the Russian sector.

'Nervous?' Kirk asked.

'A little. You?'

Kirk thought back to the days when he'd been flogging Harry Hydelman's whisky round the Glasgow boozers. 'I've done this sort of thing before,' he replied. 'You don't get so twitched second time round.'

Eddy glanced sideways at Kirk. This was the first time Kirk had ever referred to previous nefarious activities and Eddy could only wonder what it was he had been up to. He hoped Kirk would go on to explain, but he didn't.

To take his mind off his nervousness, Eddy thought about Leoni as he drove. He'd been to bed with her on innumerable occasions now and each time was better than the last. He had the same sense of belonging with her that he'd had with Annie Grimes. As though together they formed a whole, a completely rounded human being.

He knew he was falling in love with her – if he hadn't already. At night he dreamed of her. The pair of them laughing together, making love, enjoying life and each other.

'Careful!' Kirk said as the lorry bounced and shook. One of its wheels had gone into a hole in the road. He added, 'We don't want to break that stuff back there.'

'I'm doing my best, but it isn't exactly Sauchiehall Street we're driving along,' Eddy retorted.

'Cow!' Kirk exclaimed.

Eddy swore as he braked to a halt. The cow turned to look at them before ambling on into a field.

'You don't get those in Sauchiehall Street either,' Eddy said, slipping the engine into gear and edging the lorry forward.

'Oh, I don't know. Have you seen some of the things that come out the Locarno Dance Hall on a Saturday night?'

Eddy couldn't help but laugh. 'Aye, you have a point,' he said.

'Moo-ve along there, ladies please!' Kirk giggled.

'How about, "Would you care for anudder dance, miss?"'

'To which she replied, "Aren't you the horny one!"'

It was silly and corny but it appealed to them. They both chuckled at the daftness of it.

A little later Eddy turned off the road to drive across a field. When he came to a dark, lowering wood he skirted it, heading north.

When they reached the agreed spot, Eddy flicked his lights twice. Men appeared as though out of the ground and moved towards the lorry. Eddy and Kirk climbed down from the lorry's cab, Eddy having left the engine running and the lights on.

'Good evening,' Turushev said. 'Everything go all right?'

'Hunky-dory,' Kirk replied. 'You know Eddy. He and I are going to be partners on this deal.'

Turushev nodded and shook hands with Eddy. 'Now, let's have a look at your load,' he said.

Eddy untied the flaps at the rear of the lorry and flipped them out of the way. Kirk produced a torch, as did Turushev, and all three of them clambered inside.

'You don't mind if I check, do you?' Turushev asked.

'I'd be surprised if you didn't,' Kirk replied.

Turushev selected a cardboard box at random and tore it open. Pulling out a bottle of Heather Dew, he unscrewed the top and took a swig.

'Mother's milk,' said Eddy, thinking of Meany, who had now served his time at Colchester and, reduced to the ranks, had been reposted to another battalion within the regiment.

'And labels too,' Turushev commented.

'A fresh consignment just over from Bonnie Scotland,' Kirk said.

Turushev then opened a carton of cigarettes and lit up. He smoked as he checked one of the large tins of coffee.

'Satisfied?' Kirk asked.

'Everything seems to be in order.'

'All right, get your blokes to unload while we settle up.'

The three of them climbed out of the lorry. Turushev barked an order in Russian and a number of his men moved forward. Without exception the men were all short and stocky. Their faces were flat and oriental looking. Eddy thought it must have been men like these who rode with Genghis Khan.

'Wait here a moment,' Turushev said and, striding away, vanished into the darkness.

Eddy was suddenly nervous again. He licked dry lips and glanced at Kirk who seemed quite unperturbed. All around them the yellow-faces worked silently.

A minute went by and then Turushev rematerialised holding a small, square tin. On joining them he handed the tin over to Kirk.

'You won't take offence if I check, will you?' Kirk said.

'I'd be surprised if you didn't,' Turushev replied, echoing Kirk's earlier words. They all grinned.

Kirk laid the tin on the ground and took its top off. The little yellow bars of gold inside gleamed in the light from his torch. He touched each bar to count it.

'I wonder why the Jerries cast it in such small bars,' Eddy said.

Turushev shrugged. 'There could be a number of reasons. My own theory is it was to be used as small payments for a great many people. But that's only a guess on my part.'

'Nazi gold,' said Eddy. 'It's like something out the *Wizard* or *Hotspur*.' When he saw Turushev was looking puzzled he went on to explain. 'Children's comics, *Boys' Own* sort of stuff.'

Kirk put the top back on the tin, which he then lifted to hold in the crook of his arm. 'Same time, same place next month?' he suggested.

Turushev opened a diary which he glanced at using his torch for light. 'That's the Tuesday?' he asked.

'Yes. I looked it up before we set off.'

'Then the Tuesday it is.'

Eddy glanced round and was surprised to find the three of them alone. The yellow-faces had all vanished.

'*Do sveedaneeya!*' Turushev said, having shaken Kirk and Eddy by the hand. Then he melted into the darkness after his men.

'Let's hit the road,' Kirk said.

The drive back to Uelsberg seemed to pass a lot more quickly. In the early hours of the morning they drove into Uelsberg and headed for the station, where they parked. Here they would wait for the first morning train through, from which they genuinely had to pick up supplies for Sergeant McQuarrie.

'Can I have a look?' Eddy asked.

Kirk took the top off the tin before placing it on Eddy's lap. Eddy reached down and ran a caressing hand over the gold.

'The first run of many, let's hope,' Kirk said.

'Amen,' Eddy replied.

★

311

Eddy was buffing his boots when Kirk stuck his head round the door.

'Eddy, can I see you for a minute?' he asked, then to the rest of the section, 'Everything all right?'

There were various comments, all of them rude, and then Napier said, 'How was Hamburg, Corp?' Kirk had been on a twenty-four-hour leave which he'd taken in Hamburg, that being the nearest big city only a few hours away by train.

'It's true,' said Kirk. 'They really do have them sitting in windows.'

'This whoor for rent,' Smart said, giggling.

'Did you, Corporal? Did you?' Rennie asked.

'You know I'm not like that.'

Everyone laughed.

'What are you like then?' Ogle demanded.

'Give me a kiss and I'll tell you.'

The section were still guffawing when he shut the door behind himself and Eddy.

'My room,' he said.

Kirk twisted the key in the lock, then went to sit on his bed. From an inside pocket he produced a large manila envelope absolutely bulging with Deutschmarks.

'I see it but I don't really believe it,' Eddy breathed.

'It's real, all right. And most of it's pure profit.'

Kirk dumped the money on the bed. 'First of all, we take out what we've had to invest so far. Bottles, labels, buying the hooch from McQuarrie and what we had to pay out to the black marketeers.'

This outlay they'd split fifty-fifty between them, both having had money transferred over from Glasgow, where their capital was.

Kirk counted out the correct amount and put it to one side. This would have to be reinvested to make up the second load due to be delivered to Turushev in a month's time. Kirk then started to divvy the profit. Sixty per cent to him and forty to Eddy as agreed.

'Did the bullion dealer ask any questions?' Eddy inquired,

for that had been the real reason behind Kirk's visit to Hamburg.

They could have sold the gold to one of the local Uelsberg jewellers but Kirk had been against that. If cashing in fairly large quantities of gold was to become a habit with them, he didn't want raised eyebrows, questions asked, and perhaps even word of the gold getting back to the castle, which would very soon result in an inquiry. Far better the anonymity of a large city and the professional retiscence of a bullion dealer used to such transactions.

'Not one,' Kirk replied. 'He took the gold, weighed it, told me to come back in a couple of hours and when I did told me the price he was willing to pay. He didn't even look curious as to where I'd got it from.'

Eddy lit a cigarette as Kirk continued counting. The money on the bed fascinated him.

'There we are then,' said Kirk finally. He picked up the smaller of the two piles and handed it to Eddy. 'Not bad, eh?'

Slowly Eddy counted his pile. He was absolutely stunned when he'd finished. 'It's unbelievable,' he whispered.

'Don't forget we're making two thousand per cent profit on Heather Dew alone,' Kirk replied. 'That's quite some mark-up.'

'And we're going to make this every month?'

'As long as Turushev wants and we can supply, then yes.'

Eddy whistled. 'Bloody hell!' he said.

'How does it feel being a capitalist?'

'Just lovely!'

Kirk laughed. 'Think big. That's what my mother always said. Think big!'

Eddy clutched the money to him. His mind was full of dreams. Dreams that all included Leoni Kruppermann.

Eddy and Leoni were lying in bed having finished making love only seconds before.

'Just what the doctor ordered,' he said languorously.

'But *I* am the doctor!' she replied, laughing.

'Then you've just had a taste of your own medicine.'

'And I liked it.'

'How about another dose?'

'Can I have a cigarette in between?'

'What a good idea!' he replied, and nipped her nipple with his teeth before jumping out of bed.

Leoni squealed and then smiled. She was a woman who occasionally liked a bit of rough handling.

Eddy padded to the table where his cigarettes and lighter were. As he was picking them up his eye was caught by an envelope lying beside them. The envelope was addressed to 'Gräfin von Kruppermann'.

'What does "von" mean?' he asked.

Leoni sat up and regarded him. She was a splendid fulsome sight with her golden-blonde hair cascading over her shoulders to partially hide her large coral-pink-tipped breasts.

'It means the person belongs to the upper classes. There isn't an English equivalent.'

'You're upper class?'

'Very much so. Although I tend not to use the "von" when practising as a doctor. It has an unsettling effect on patients.'

'And what about "Gräfin"?'

'That means "countess".'

His face dropped. 'You're joking?'

'No.'

'You? ... A countess?'

'I'm afraid so.'

'You mean I've just been ... with a countess?'

She laughed. 'You should see the expression on your face!' she exclaimed.

'You never said!'

'You never asked. Why is it important?'

'I don't know. I'm just ... stunned, that's all.'

'You are funny,' she said.

He lit two cigarettes and passed her one. To think that he, Eddy King, from the Glasgow slums, had been having it off with a countess. It was mind boggling.

'Your husband, who died on the Russian Front, was a count, then?' he asked.

'That's right. Graf von Kruppermann. He was also a general.'

Eddy whistled. 'And now here you are with a common-or-garden British private. Bit of a come-down for you, eh?'

'It's the man that interests me. Not his rank or position.'

'But a count and a general to boot!'

Her smile became wistful. 'Times change, Eddy. We in Germany have had to adapt or else go under. Before the war I was a countess and very grand with my diamonds and limousine, my great town house and our castle in the country.'

'You owned a castle?'

'Oh yes. And a drafty old place it was, too. It was picturesque though, and the view was breathtaking.'

'What happened to it?'

'It's still there but now American soldiers live in it. Just like you and the other Scottish soldiers live in Schloss Schwartzberg.'

He shook his head in wonder.

'But as I said, all that was before the war. Now ...? Now I am just a doctor trying to make my way, just like everyone else.'

'I take it, then, he left you stony?'

'Pardon?'

'The count didn't leave you any money?'

'He did, but everything we had was confiscated. The town house, the schloss, the business, land, jewels, everything.'

He stroked her cheek, thinking how sad she looked. He drew her to him when tears welled in her eyes.

'Love me, Eddy. Please?'

He took her cigarette and placed it along with his in the ashtray.

'Be tender,' she whispered.

And he was.

★

315

'A countess!' Kirk exclaimed. 'She was pulling your pudding. Having you on!'

'No she wasn't. It's straight up. I saw an envelope with her full name and title on it. Gräfin von Kruppermann. "Gräfin" means countess and "von" means she belongs to the upper classes.'

'Well, well, well,' said Kirk. 'Imagine you landing a countess!'

They were in the still-room putting labels on bottles that had previously been filled. Heather Dew dripped steadily from the still into a rapidly filling two-gallon jar.

'God, she's marvellous!' Eddy said, eyes gleaming.

Kirk slapped on another label and looked thoughtful. He was remembering how he'd felt when he'd first screwed Susan, how chuffed he'd been at doing it with someone of her class. But a countess! Now that really would be something.

'Put your backs into it, you vile chaps!' Kirk bellowed. It was an expression he'd heard one of the officers use and he knew it amused the section to hear him parrot the man.

'What are you?'

'Vile chaps sir, Corporal!' they chorused back.

'And don't you ever forget it!'

'No sir, Corporal!'

The section was removing large sandbags that had been used to shore up a crumbling wall. When all the bags were removed a team of civilian masons would move in to start repair work.

Eddy was working a two-man team with Ogle.

He grunted as he pulled another bag free and twisted it on to its end. The sack and sand inside it were wet through, which made the sandbag doubly heavy.

Gripping the bag firmly, Eddy began to drag it along the ground, while Ogle began pulling another bag free.

He'd only taken a few steps when he felt something in his groin go rip. It felt exactly as though a zip there had been opened quickly.

'Oh!' he grunted and let go of the bag. Bending over, he clutched himself.

'What's wrong, Eddy?' Kirk asked, coming striding up.

Eddy couldn't stand any more so he sank to the ground. Through his pants he could feel a large bulge of flesh. God, what have I done to myself? he thought.

He'd gone pasty white and there was sweat running down his face. The pain in his groin was like that of a large aching tooth.

'Let's have a look, my old son,' Kirk said. With Ogle helping him he unfastened Eddy's trouser's and pulled them down, after which they pulled down Eddy's underpants. What he saw caused him to wince.

'I think he must have ruptured himself,' said Ogle.

Eddy stared in fascination at the bulging flesh. It was as though a small balloon had somehow got under his skin.

'It's the medics for you,' Kirk said, and gently pulled Eddy's underpants and trousers back up again.

By this time the entire section were crowded round.

'Smart, you're the strongest. Help Ogle and myself to carry him,' Kirk said.

Eddy groaned as he was gently lifted from the ground.

'Easy there, lad,' Kirk said.

Those of the section remaining behind called out good luck and well wishes as Eddy was carted off.

At the castle hospital Eddy was laid on a stretcher and taken away. Kirk told Ogle to go back to the section and carry on. He would wait till there was news of Eddy.

Kirk was kept hanging around for well over an hour before being told he could go through and see Eddy.

Eddy was lying flat out on the bed wearing pyjamas and a grim expression.

'Well, what did they say?' Kirk demanded.

'It's a hernia, right enough. I've been examined by a surgeon called Major McDougall who told me I'll have to have an operation. He's setting it up for Monday next.'

Kirk pulled a face. 'Bad luck.'

317

'After that I'll be in for ten days. Then they'll give me a fortnight's leave.'

'Will you go home?'

Eddy thought of Leoni. 'No, I think I'll take it here,' he replied. 'That way I shall be on hand to help you with Turushev's next consignment.'

Kirk nodded. 'Good.'

'There's just one thing. I need a favour.'

'Name it.'

'I'm supposed to be meeting Leoni tonight, picking her up at her place at seven. Will you go and tell her what's happened? She doesn't have a phone so I can't contact her that way.'

'Consider it done,' Kirk replied.

'You're a pal, Kirk.'

They chatted for another ten minutes and then Kirk said it was time he got back to the section. They'd all be eager to know the doctor's verdict.

The last thing Eddy did before Kirk went was to write down Leoni's address and hand it to him.

She answered his knock almost at once, a frown crossing her face when she saw it wasn't Eddy.

'Dr von Kruppermann, I'm Kirk Murray, Eddy's friend. Do you remember I came with him to your surgery?'

'Oh, *ja!*' she replied, recognition flooding into her eyes.

'Eddy's asked me to call on you. May I come in?'

She ushered him into a dark and dingy hallway. He followed her into an equally dark and dingy room.

'Has something happened to Eddy?' she asked.

'I'm afraid it has.'

Cap in hand, Kirk explained in detail about the heavy sandbags and Eddy's rupturing himself. As he spoke he thought she was certainly good-looking if a little long in the tooth.

'Poor Eddy,' Leoni said, after Kirk had stopped speaking. 'Will I be able to go and visit him?'

318

'I doubt it, Doctor. It wouldn't be appreciated in certain quarters.'

'I understand.'

There was a small pause and then Kirk said, 'Well I suppose I'd better be on my way.'

'Oh! Excuse me for being so impolite. I was thinking. Would you care for a cup of tea? I'm afraid that's all I can offer you. I have no coffee or alcohol in the flat.'

'I'd love a cup of tea,' Kirk replied.

When she left the room he looked around. What a dump! he thought. High up one wall there was a damp patch, while further along some wallpaper was peeling away. The furniture was long overdue to be scrapped and the carpet underfoot was threadbare. One of the windows was cracked, through which, because there was a wind outside, came a low moaning noise. On a sort of stand there was a very old bell-mouthed phonograph beside which was a stack of records. On an impulse he crossed and picked up the first half-dozen records, which were all in faded cardboard covers. Wagner, Liszt, Beethoven. A quick flick through the remainder of the pile showed they were all classical pieces.

'I'm afraid I have no sugar,' Leoni said, entering the room carrying two cups. 'But I have milk, if you'd like?'

'No thanks. I prefer it without.'

He devoured her with his eyes as she moved away having handed him one of the cups. He'd had sex in Hamburg with a very high-class prostitute whom he'd been certain was clean. At the prices she'd charged she'd bloody well better be! But apart from her and the brass at the Blue Pig he'd been going without since his arrival in Germany. Highly sexed by nature, he was therefore continually randy as a rabbit in heat.

He sipped some tea and then said, 'I was wondering, as you're now at a loose end as I am, if you'd care to come out for a drink? I'm sure Eddy wouldn't mind. In fact he'd probably insist, not wanting you to be left here disappointed on your own.'

319

Leoni looked uncertain. 'I don't know ...' She trailed off.

'Or if you don't fancy a drink there's a Mozart concert on that I think I might be able to get tickets for.'

Her eyes opened wide. 'Could you really? I knew it was on, of course, and desperately wanted to attend. But when I tried I just couldn't get a ticket.'

'Maybe I can do better. I have certain connections, shall we say.' He glanced at his watch. 'But if we're going to try we'd better hurry.'

Tea was forgotten as he helped her into her coat. 'I just adore Mozart,' she said excitedly.

'Me too,' he replied. Truth was Mozart, like Wagner, Liszt and Beethoven, was just a name to him. He had no experience or knowledge whatever of classical music. He was a Glenn Miller man himself.

He took her to a small café where he left her sitting at a table while he sought out the proprietor, who lived upstairs.

Herr Goetz looked like a schoolteacher or clergyman with his freshly scrubbed, cherubic face topped by silvery white hair. He was the black marketeer Kirk dealt chiefly with.

Kirk told Goetz what he wanted. Goetz said he'd left it rather late, but Kirk said he expected to pay more for that. Goetz told him to go back downstairs and wait. He would see what he could do.

Fifteen minutes later Goetz appeared downstairs to beckon Kirk into the back of the café.

'Did you get them?' Kirk asked.

Goetz held up two tickets and then named his price. 'I don't charge too much because I expect to do a lot of business with you in the future,' Goetz said.

'You can count on it,' Kirk replied.

Money changed hands and then with the two tickets safely in his pocket Kirk hurried back to Leoni.

'Let's go,' he said.

'Did you ...?'

He nodded.

'How marvellous!' she exclaimed.

'Nothing's impossible when you know how,' he said as they made their way down the street in the direction of the hall where the concert was being performed by a touring company of German musicians.

'And if you've got the wherewithal,' she added.

He was correct when he thought he detected bitterness in her tone when she said that.

After the concert – which he found excruciatingly boring but which she thoroughly enjoyed – he walked her slowly home. At the door to her flat she thanked him but made no move to ask him inside.

'We'll be going on patrol tomorrow night,' he said. 'And the day after that I'll be going to see Eddy. If you like I could call by here in the evening to tell you how he's doing.'

'That would be kind of you. I'll look forward to that,' she replied.

He stepped back a pace and nodded. 'Till then.'

Turning, he strode rapidly off. Nor did he look round.

A countess, he thought. Yes he could see it now. She had breeding that shone like a beacon through her poverty. And if there was one thing attracted him, and always had, it was breeding.

Two nights later he was back. She led him through to the same dark and dingy room as before and asked him if he'd care for some tea.

'I hope you won't think me forward,' he said, smiling. 'But I took the liberty of bringing along a few things.' And having said that he handed her a bag he'd brought with him.

She laid the items out on the table. 'Butter!' she exclaimed excitedly. 'Coffee! Sugar! Cigarettes! A dozen eggs! Oh, how absolutely marvellous! I can't thank you enough.'

'It must be extremely difficult for you,' he said sympathetically. 'Eddy mentioned to me what it had been like for you before the war.'

'Yes,' she replied wistfully. 'There is so much I miss, in – what would you call it in English? – my reduced circumstances.'

'I hope you won't take this the wrong way but I was offered some and I was about to turn them down when suddenly I thought of you. I'm sure the good doctor could use a few pairs of these, I thought, and so I took them.'

He extricated an envelope from an inside pocket and handed it to Leoni, who regarded it quizzically. When she peered inside the envelope, an expression of sheer delight mixed with incredulity blossomed on her face.

'Nylon stockings!' she whispered.

'I had to guess your size so I hope they fit all right.'

'I must try them on right away.'

'Do you have a couple of glasses? I'll pour us both a drink while you're doing that.'

From another pocket he produced a bottle of Heather Dew.

'Scotch whisky?' she said, awed.

'And my favourite brand,' he replied, chuckling.

She handed him two glasses before hurrying off to the bedroom. He hummed as he poured.

When she returned her eyes were shining. 'They fit perfectly,' she said. 'I haven't had nylon stockings in ... well, more years than I care to remember. I can't even begin to thank you enough.'

He handed her a glass and they both drank.

'Whew!' she gasped. 'That's strong.'

'Malt whisky usually is. It's one of it's attractions. Do you like the flavour?'

'It's rather ... smoky?'

'That comes from the peat which the water runs through before it's taken up by the distillery.'

He wasn't sure whether that was right or not, with regard to real malt whisky that is, but it certainly sounded convincing.

He sat and watched her while she put a record on. She flashed him a smile as she wound up the ancient phonograph.

'Do you like Liszt?' she asked.

322

'There'll never be another like him,' he replied.

As the strains of the music curled round the room she sat across from him, her eyes taking on an introspective, sad look about them.

'Those records are all I have from before the war,' she said. 'There were times when they were all I had to hang on to. I think I might have died without them.'

'Can't you find better accommodation than this?' he asked.

She pulled a face. 'Dreadful rooms, aren't they? I am ashamed to ask anyone in. But better flats are ... very, very hard to come by. And expensive. Money must be given, you understand?'

'"Key money" we call it in Britain.'

'So, key money. And I am, eh ... not well off from what I earn as a doctor. I can only charge what people can pay. And believe me, they can't pay much.'

He nodded sympathetically.

'Still, things are getting better all the time. Already there is a great difference between now and just after the war. We are starting to build on the ashes.'

While she talked he imagined her in bed. He saw her naked with that splendid hair spread out on the pillow around her head. Eddy had mentioned she had fabulous breasts. His hands itched to get hold of them, straining as they were now beneath her dress.

'But here am I chattering on and I have forgotten to ask how poor Eddy is,' she said.

'He's painful round the rupture but apart from that in fine spirits. I think he's a little nervous of the operation,' adding with a laugh, 'I know I would be! I'd be having nightmares that the surgeon's knife might slip. I mean it's not exactly something you can sew back on again, is it?'

Leoni smiled. 'You laymen, what funny ideas you have of us doctors,' she said.

He poured more Heather Dew into their glasses. He could see she was already a little flushed from the first.

'It really is most kind of you to bring me the coffee,

cigarettes and other things. Especially the nylon stockings. I shall keep those for very special occasions.'

'I'll see what else I can do ...'

'No no, you mustn't. That would be too much,' she cut in.

'Nonsense! What else are friends for?'

'But they are so expensive!'

'I make a few bob.'

She frowned. 'I don't understand that.'

'I'm not exactly short of money,' he explained, thinking Eddy must have been a right fool not to get these things for Leoni himself. It was blatantly obvious she was desperate for them. But then, from the long talks he'd had in the past with Eddy on the subject, he'd already gleaned that Eddy was somewhat naïve about women.

Outside the wind blew causing the cracked window pane to rattle and moan.

And in that instant he had an idea.

Eddy came to, feeling as though someone had had a right go at his head with a hammer. His mouth was parched and there was a faint ringing in his ears.

His hand fumbled under the bedclothes to his groin, where it encountered a swathe of bandages. He pressed lightly and felt nothing. He pressed harder but still couldn't feel anything.

There was the patter of feet and a rustling sound. Then a Queen Alexandra nurse was bending over him.

'How do you feel?' she asked.

'Water,' he croaked.

She picked up a porcelain jug with a long spout from his bedside table and slipped the end of the spout into his mouth. Water ran over his swollen tongue and down his throat.

'I could drink ten of those,' he rasped.

'Well one's enough for the moment,' she replied crisply. She laid the jug back on his table and then proceeded to smooth down his bedclothes.

'Nurse?'

'Yes?'

'The operation. Did it go all right?'

'Of course,' she replied, looking surprised.

'It's just – I can't feel anything down there. Where the rupture was.'

'Ah!' she said. 'That's perfectly normal. The flesh has been cut, you see, which means the area surrounding it will feel dead for quite some time. But feeling will grow back there eventually.'

Eddy was suddenly panicky. No one had said anything about this to him beforehand.

'Will that affect my ... I mean, will I be able to ...?'

The nurse smiled. She considered teasing him and then decided not to. 'I don't think you'll have any trouble with the ladies, if that's what you're asking.'

Relief surged through him. 'I had myself worried there for a moment,' he said.

'It's best you try and get some sleep now. When you wake up I'll bring you something to eat and then the doctor will want to see you.'

Eddy closed his eyes and soon drifted off. He dreamed it was Leoni who would be taking care of him.

He slept for a number of hours, wakening when a voice said, 'How's the patient then?' Kirk held up a bunch of grapes and added, 'I'm told this is the thing to bring!'

Eddy managed a weak smile. 'How did you get in here?'

'It wasn't easy. But you know me. I'm irresistible. They've given me five minutes. Now, how do you feel?'

'Not too bad, I suppose. Tell you the truth, I'm not quite sure.'

Kirk leered. 'Still got it then? You have had a feel to make sure?'

'Oh aye, it's there all right. But my entire right groin feels dead as mutton. The nurse who was here earlier says it will take a while but the feeling will eventually come back there.'

Kirk laid the grapes on the bedside table, helping himself to some in the process.

'How's Leoni?' Eddy asked eagerly.

'Fine. She's asked me to drop by this evening to let her know how your op went.'

'You're a good pal, Kirk. I won't forget this.'

'Oh,' said Kirk, 'I nearly forgot.' He produced several packets of cigarettes which he slipped into the bedside locker. 'I know you're not supposed to smoke in here but I also know you'd go daft without your fags. Maybe you can get the chance of a puff when no one's looking. Now ...' he said, standing, 'I'd better get back to the section. We've got quite a bit on today.'

'Thanks again,' Eddy said.

'I'll be back when I can. And in the meantime keep your hands off those nurses.'

'That's the last thing I have in mind,' Eddy replied.

Kirk nodded, thinking Eddy meant he wasn't up to it.

But Leoni was the reason for what Eddy had said.

'What you ask is difficult,' Goetz said.

Kirk stared into the German's eyes and smiled.

'That's why I've come to you,' he replied.

'And when something is difficult it is also expensive.'

'Naturally.'

'Would this be for yourself? I ask because I have to know whether it will be a short or long let.'

'For a lady,' Kirk replied.

'Ah!' said Goetz. 'I understand.'

'How much do you charge for a bottle of Scotch whisky?' Kirk asked.

Goetz frowned, not seeing the connection. He stated a round figure in Deutschmarks.

'And malt?'

Goetz stated a higher figure.

Kirk said slowly. 'I have access to a limited supply of malt whisky. What I thought was we might agree your fee in cases. Not all payable at once, I'm afraid, but over a period of say ... six months?'

'Of course, I couldn't allow you the same figure as what I

would sell them for. I have to make a profit,' Goetz replied smoothly.

'Of course.'

Goetz folded his hands, put them under his chin and gazed into the distance. 'A dozen cases,' he said after a while.

'I'd want *Berchtesgarten* for that,' Kirk replied with a razor smile.

'That's my price. Take it or leave it.'

'You drive a hard bargain, Goetz.'

Goetz spread his hands. 'I have a living to make.'

'Tell you what. Because I'm going to put so much business your way, make it eight and it's a deal.'

'Twelve, Corporal Murray.'

Kirk groaned. 'I honestly doubt if I can do that many.'

Goetz went back to staring into space. A full minute went by before he spoke again. 'To maintain good feeling between us I'll settle for ten.'

Kirk extended his hand and they shook.

'A nice flat now,' Kirk said, as he was about to leave.

'Trust me,' Goetz replied.

Out in the street Kirk began to hum. He'd enjoyed that. He wasn't quite sure yet how he was going to squeeze out ten extra cases in the next six months but he'd do it somehow.

He hoped Goetz wouldn't take too long.

'You're joking!' Leoni exclaimed.

'No,' Kirk replied. 'It's all yours as from the first of next month.' And he named a rent which wasn't all that much higher than she was now paying.

'I just can't believe it,' she said.

'Come and let me show you around.'

'But you must have paid a fortune in key money for this place.'

'I happen to think you're worth it,' he replied.

The tone of his voice told her precisely what he had in mind. But then she'd known that since the first night he'd come calling with presents.

Eddy was sitting by the side of his bed reading a book. He looked up at the sound of approaching feet.

'And how are you today, King?' Major McDougall, the surgeon who'd done Eddy's operation, demanded.

'Dying to get out, sir,' Eddy replied.

'Hmm!' said McDougall thoughtfully, looking sideways at Sister Hardy who was accompanying him on his rounds.

'Stand up please, King,' Sister said. Eddy stood. 'Now walk over there and back.' Eddy did as he was told.

'Any pain or discomfort?' McDougall asked.

'A little stiff, sir, that's all.'

'All right then, lie on the bed and let me have a look at you.'

Sister Hardy pulled screens round the bed while Eddy clambered into a horizonal position. He unloosened his pyjama bottoms and slipped them down.

McDougall's fingers probed the long, angry-looking wound and the flesh surrounding it. 'Good . . . good,' he said, nodding to himself. 'How long have the stitches been out, Sister?'

Sister consulted the chart at the end of Eddy's bed. 'Two days, sir,' she replied.

McDougall snorted. 'Pull your pyjamas up again, King,' he instructed. He held out his hand for the chart which Sister Hardy handed to him.

Eddy retied his pyjamas and then swung his feet over the side of the bed while McDougall studied his chart.

'The thing is, King,' McDougall said, looking up, 'you're not really supposed to be discharged till tomorrow but I have a problem inasmuch as I need a bed. How do you feel about going out today?'

'That would be marvellous, sir!' Eddy grinned.

'I think he'll do, Sister,' McDougall said. Then turning back to Eddy. 'You'll be due a fortnight's recuperative leave. Will you be going home?'

'No sir. I have a friend in Uelsberg I thought I'd spend it with.'

Sister cleared her throat and looked away.

'Well, nothing too strenuous for a while, King. Do I make myself clear?'

'I understand, sir.'

'Right, well I think that's you, then. Good luck. And I hope I don't see you in here again.'

'Thank you for everything, sir.'

McDougall smiled and moved on.

Sister Hardy said, 'I'll have a nurse bring you your clothes after the doctor's rounds.' Then she hurried after Major McDougall.

An hour later Eddy walked out of the hospital area. Slowly he made his way to the billet, hoping to find the section there.

'Christ sake, look what the wind blew in!' Napier exclaimed.

'You look like death warmed up!' said Smart.

'No he doesn't. He looks great,' said Ogle, punching the large Norrie Smart on the shoulder.

'Well I'm hardly a hundred per cent but at least I'm back on my feet again,' Eddy said.

'We're all off to the Naafi for a beer. Want to come?' Kirkwood asked.

'No thanks. I've got other plans,' he replied, holding up the form Sister Hardy had signed and which entitled him to two weeks' leave.

'Jammy bugger!' said McKenzie.

'Where's the corp?' Eddy asked.

'Don't know. Around somewhere, I suppose. To tell you the truth we haven't seen all that much of him off-duty hours of late.'

Eddy nodded. Well it didn't matter. He'd catch up with Kirk later. The important thing for him now was to get into town to see Leoni.

He picked up one or two things from his locker which he added to what he'd brought from the hospital. Then he went in search of Lieutenant Gilzean whose signature was needed on the form Sister Hardy had given him. When added, the lieutenant's signature then made the form a two-week pass.

It was a long haul into town so he waited by the castle gates until he could hitch a lift, which he eventually did from a captain.

From where the captain dropped him off it wasn't very far to Leoni's. He prayed she was in. She wasn't expecting him till the following night.

Outside Leoni's flat he groped in his pocket for the key she'd given him. Quietly he slipped it into the lock and opened the door.

All the lights were out except in the bedroom whose door stood ajar.

She was singing, 'Lili of Marlene', the number Dietrich made famous during the war.

'*An der Kaserne vor dem grossen Tor,*
Stand eine Laterne und steht sie noch davor;
Da woll'n wir uns mal wiederseh'n,
Bei der Laterne woll'n wir steh'n,
Wie einst, Lili Marlene,
Wie einst, Lili Marlene . . .'

He made his way towards the bedroom door, imagining her to be sitting at her dressing table as she was fond of doing, combing her hair or otherwise attending to her toilet.

On reaching the open door he stopped to stare in. She wasn't at her dressing table but sitting naked on her bed. He couldn't think what she was doing as hands on hips she moved up and down.

And still it didn't dawn until suddenly there was another movement and for the first time he noticed two hairy legs projecting out from underneath her.

'Oh my God, but it's good!' Kirk voice sighed.

Eddy felt sick and for a moment or two he thought he was actually going to throw up. It seemed to him as though the blood in his veins had turned to iced water.

Leoni threw back her head and stroked her hair in a downward movement. The song had become a croon now which she husked from the back of her throat.

But I love her, Eddy thought. I *love* her!

330

'Yes!' she cried suddenly. 'Oh yes!'

Her body spasmed as did Kirk's and then with a groan she collapsed on top of him, her large breasts squashing against his chest.

Rage rose up in Eddy. Shaking with anger he stepped through the doorway and into the room. He stood beside a wooden standard lamp.

Still panting from her exertion Leoni looked up. When she saw him she exclaimed.

'What is it?' Kirk demanded, and pulled her head out of the way so he could see.

'You bastard!' hissed Eddy.

'You're not supposed to be out till tomorrow,' Kirk said reproachfully.

'I can see I surprised you.'

'We were going to tell you.'

'That's big of you.'

With a plopping sound Leoni pulled herself free and sliding from the bed made her way to a chair, over which her dressing gown was draped. Picking up the gown she hurriedly shrugged it on.

'I'm truly sorry you had to find out this way, Eddy,' she said.

'Why?' he asked simply.

She tried to look him straight in the face but couldn't. Her eyes dropped away to stare at the carpet.

'Whore,' Eddy said quietly.

'Now wait a minute pal ...' Kirk said, coming off the bed.

'Pal?' Eddy interjected, his voice dripping sarcasm.

'Leoni and I didn't mean this to happen. It just did somehow.'

Eddy nodded, but said nothing. His rage was getting more explosive with every passing second.

'You asked me to come round and then I kept returning to give her progress reports. And somewhere along the line we just fell for one another. I'm sorry too. I'd do anything rather than hurt you.'

Kirk might just have got away with it then if he hadn't allowed a patronising glint to show in his eyes. Eddy saw that glint and knew right away Kirk was lying. Kirk had intentionally set out to steal his woman.

A berserk rage burst within him as he reached for the nearest thing to hand, which turned out to be the standard lamp. The plug came ripping from the wall as, using the lamp like a huge club, he swung its heavy base at Kirk.

Kirk tried to dive to one side but didn't quite make it. The base of the lamp took him full in the ribcage, knocking the wind from him and sending him spinning to the floor.

Eddy twisted the lamp round and with a roar brought it scything down at the sprawling Kirk. Leoni screamed. She saw murder written all over Eddy's face. The dazed Kirk rolled to one side as the lamp smashed against the floor. The base and part of the stem broke off leaving Eddy clutching what now virtually amounted to a spear, the end of the stem being sharp and jagged.

Kirk was scared and being naked felt incredibly vulnerable. Desperately he tried to scramble away from that advancing point. Eddy lunged and the sharp end of the lamp stem lanced towards Kirk's face. A split second before it struck home, Kirk managed to twist his head out of the way.

Leoni, hysterical now, ran to Eddy and wrapped her arms round him. 'Stop it! Stop it! Stop it!' she screamed.

Eddy tried to shrug her free but somehow she managed to hang on. Her feet drummed against the back of his legs.

Eddy lunged with the lamp stem again but by this time Kirk had managed to grab hold of a wooden chair which he used to ward off the blow.

'*Eddy!*' Leoni screamed in his ear.

He heard her voice from a long way off, which caused him to pause. The mists of his awful rage thinned and began to disperse as he became his own man again.

Trembling, he dropped what remained of the standard lamp. He felt so weak he thought he must surely collapse to the floor.

Her scent was thick in his nostrils and he was only too painfully aware of her body wrapped round him.

'Get off!' he said quietly.

Her face was streaked and puffed. She looked ten years older than she had a few minutes before.

Kirk still held the chair in front of him. He too was trembling and weak, the latter in his case from shock and fear.

Leoni moved away from Eddy, tugging her dressing gown tightly round her as she went.

'You were going to kill me,' Kirk said.

Eddy remembered Gloag and the adjustable spanner he'd used to smash the man's skull in. 'Yes,' he said.

'I think you'd better go, Eddy,' Leoni said, her voice more thickly accented than usual.

Eddy staggered and nearly fell. His body was covered in a cold clammy sweat and his wound was paining him. But the pain was nothing like that in his heart.

Kirk stood the chair back on its legs. Then edging round the bed he picked up his trousers and hurriedly put them on. As he buttoned up his flies Eddy watched him balefully.

Eddy dragged a breath deep into his lungs. The reason he hadn't already gone was he wasn't sure his legs would carry him to the outside door and beyond.

'I could put you on a charge for this,' Kirk said.

'You could but you won't,' Eddy wheezed in reply.

Kirk's lips thinned. Eddy was right.

Eddy took a long last look at Leoni, his countess. He never wanted to see her again. 'Whoor,' he repeated, this time using the emphatic Scottish pronunciation.

Leoni flinched and turned her head away.

'The lady told you to go,' Kirk said.

'What lady's that? I don't see any lady.'

Leoni's head dropped in shame. Eddy ran his fingers through his hair and then did his best to pull himself together. If nothing else, he would make a dignified exit. Slowly, and with great effort, he walked from the bedroom into the darkness of the room beyond. He closed the main door silently behind him, leaving the key she'd given him in the lock.

Out in the street he hobbled to where he knew he would get a taxi.

In the back of the taxi heading for the castle he sang quietly, '*Underneath the lamplight, by the barrack gate* ...'

He managed to make it to the still room and the whisky there before the tears came.

'King, I want a word with you,' Kirk said.

The rest of the section looked up. They knew that for the past few days there had been bad blood between Eddy and Kirk. No one knew what it was about.

'I'm on leave, Corporal,' Eddy replied. He stretched out on his bed reading a book.

'I know that. I still want a word with you all the same.'

Eddy dropped his book a fraction so he could see over the top of it. His eyes met and locked with Kirk's.

'What about?'

'In private, if you don't mind.'

Eddy carefully marked his place and then put the book on top of his pillow. He winced a little as he came to his feet.

At the door Kirk said, 'My room.'

Eddy followed Kirk out into the hallway. Silently they walked in the direction of Kirk's billet.

Once there Kirk said, 'It's about Heather Dew and Turushev. Do you want to stay in or get out?'

Eddy stared at Kirk whom he now hated. The last thing he wanted was to continue in association with this man. But on the other hand it would be downright stupid to cut his nose off to spite his face. There was far too much money involved.

'I'm still in,' he replied.

Kirk nodded. 'All right. We continue as before.'

'Not quite,' said Eddy.

And left Kirk standing there.

Eight months passed, during which the Turushev run, as Eddy and Kirk had come to call it, went smoothly.

After every run, Kirk would arrange to go to Hamburg to convert the gold into cash at the bullion dealer's. And on his return he and Eddy would get together and divvy up.

It never failed to amaze Eddy how much money he made out of the run. After nine runs he considered himself a modestly wealthy man.

The relationship between Eddy and Kirk remained a stilted one, the pair of them only talking to one another when it was to do with either army business or the run. Kirk continued seeing Leoni, spending usually two or three evenings a week with her. Countess Leoni von Kruppermann was a name never mentioned between Eddy and Kirk.

Then one morning the section were roused from their beds by a new corporal called McPherson.

'Let's be having you then!' McPherson shouted, rubbing his hands briskly together. 'Lots to do today. Lots to do!'

Rennie asked the question everyone was wondering. 'Where's Corporal Murray?' he queried.

'Gone sick, lad. Don't ask me what's wrong with him because I don't know. All I was told was he was admitted to the hospital last night and is likely to be there for some time.'

'Will you be in charge till he gets back?' McKenzie asked.

'Don't know that either, lad. I've just been ordered to look after you lot until further instructed. So who knows what that could mean? It could be a day, a week, a month or until you've done your time and are sent home. Now come on jildy jai! Lots to do! Lots to do!'

The section were out on patrol that night so it wasn't till late the following morning after he'd caught up on his sleep that Eddy was able to get to the hospital.

He told a Q.A. nurse he was there on section business so she looked up Kirk's name and told Eddy where to find him.

There were six in the ward which comprised three beds on either side. Kirk was behind some screens awaiting further treatment which a nurse would shortly be giving him.

He looked up from the book he was reading as Eddy slipped between the screens.

'I've only got a minute,' Eddy said. 'What the hell's wrong with you? And is it true you're going to be laid up here for some time?'

'Nice of you to be worried about me,' Kirk replied.

'I'm thinking about the run, that's all.'

'I knew you'd come, so I've written it all out here,' said Kirk. And from his bedside locker he produced a sheet of paper on which he'd written various addresses and instructions.

'See Goetz and tell him you'll be handling the next shipment of coffee and fags. I've marked down the prices you've to pay. Watch him, he's a shark. He's bound to try for an additional mark-up. Now there's the run itself. Can you manage that on your own?'

'I think so. They're used to us making that monthly journey down to the railway station. I don't think they'll give me any trouble just because you're not there for once.'

'It may be more than once.'

'I can still manage it.'

Kirk pointed to another address on the sheet of paper. 'The bullion dealer. You'll have to do that as well. Slip McQuarrie a few quid and he'll see you get the necessary pass.' Kirk handed the sheet of paper to Eddy who folded it and put it away.

'Any problems, try and get to see me. Although that won't be easy. They don't exactly encourage visitors in this ward.'

'What's wrong with you then?'

A pink flush crept over Kirk's face. 'You may as well know now as you'll find out anyway. I've caught a dose.'

'VD?' Eddy said incredulously.

'What other sort of dose is there?'

'But I mean ... how? Who?'

'*Who* do you think?'

Eddy gaped. 'Leoni?'

'Right first time,' Kirk replied bitterly.

'But ... but that's impossible!'

'I can assure you, Eddy, there's been no one else.'

'Then why didn't I catch it?'

The two men stared at one another. Then Eddy's face broke into a grin. 'She's been two-timing you,' he whispered.

Kirk turned his face away. 'Looks like it. It's the only explanation as far as I can see.'

'Oh, that's rich. That's really rich!' Eddy said.

'I thought it would amuse you.'

'Does she know she's infected?'

'Presumably not. From what I gather it's far more difficult to detect in women than in us men. She'll have to be told, of course. I suppose I'll write.'

Eddy sat on the edge of the bed and chuckled to himself.

'Meany was right,' Kirk said. 'The treatment *is* bloody painful. The penicillin jabs they give you in the backside are like being stuck by a harpoon.'

'And how long does the treatment go on for?'

'Six weeks at least. And then I'm up on a charge for catching it. That'll probably be ten days in the guard house.'

'What about your stripes?'

'I've seen the end of them. It'll be plain Private Murray when I rejoin the section.'

'Well I never!' said Eddy, thinking there was a God after all.

'I mean, I thought I was safe with her. A doctor and a countess to boot!'

Eddy laughed at the expression on Kirk's face. 'A dose!' he exclaimed, the laugh becoming a guffaw.

'And it *is* just like peeing over broken glass,' Kirk said.

Eddy guffawed all the way back to the billet.

'Well well, if it isn't Romeo Murray himself,' said Smart, looking up from cleaning his gear.

'How's the old cock, then?' Ogle inquired politely.

'Hasn't fallen off, has it?' Rennie asked.

'Eff off, you horrible lot,' said Kirk.

'Now now, you can't speak like that to us any more, ex-Corporal Murray. You've lost your stripes don't forget,' said Kirkwood just a little maliciously.

Kirk dumped his gear on the one empty bed. 'And speaking

of corporals, what's the new one like?' he asked.

'We had a corporal McPherson for a couple of weeks,' replied Napier. 'But he moved on.'

Smart eagerly added, 'You're going to love the one who took his place.'

'Easy is he?'

'I wouldn't say so.'

'Do I know him?'

'Oh yes. You do that,' said Ogle.

'Don't tell me Meany's back with stripes up?' Kirk asked thinking how absolutely horrendous that would be.

Kirkwood smirked. 'Not Meany.'

Just then the door flew open and Eddy marched in.

'Speak of the devil,' said Napier.

Kirk stared at the two stripes on Eddy's arm. Then his gaze travelled up to Eddy's face.

'Back with us again, Murray?' said Eddy.

Kirk stood and saluted. 'Yes, Corporal,' he replied.

'There have been one or two changes while you've been away.'

'I can see that ... sir.'

'My billet, Murray. I want to have words with you in private.'

'Yes, sir.'

Eddy led the way.

Once in his room, the same one Kirk had inhabited as a corporal, he locked the door behind him. While Kirk watched, he removed a tin box from a secret hiding place. The box was crammed with Deutschmarks, most of them higher denominations.'

'What we've made from two runs,' Eddy said. 'Will you trust me or will I go through it all bit by bit.'

'I trust you. That's why I took you on as a partner in the first place,' Kirk replied.

'Pity I couldn't trust you the way you trusted me,' Eddy said.

'Money and women, Eddy. Two different things entirely,' Kirk replied.

Eddy grunted. Then he emptied the contents of the box on to his bed.

'The way I see it is this,' Eddy said. 'I've done two runs on my own on top of which the positions are now reversed. I'm the corporal and you're the private. Taking all that into account, I think we should switch the percentages. Namely forty per cent for you now and sixty for me.'

Kirk stared hard at Eddy. 'What if I say no?'

'Then I'll fix it so you end up with bugger all.'

'In which case I'll spill the beans and it'll be a long stay in Colchester for the pair of us.'

Eddy lit a cigarette and studied Kirk. 'I'm not going back to the way it was,' he stated flatly.

Kirk pursed his lips, looked at the money and then back again at Eddy. He stroked his scar.

'What if we both give a bit?' he suggested. 'Fifty-fifty, equal partners straight down the line.'

Eddy blew a perfect smoke ring. 'You count,' he said.

Having gone in on the same day they also came out on the same one.

At the Central Station they disembarked and side by side walked out into Gordon Street.

'Glasgow,' said Eddy. 'God bless her!'

Kirk glanced at his watch. Susan was supposed to be meeting him but hadn't arrived yet. The train had been early.

Kirk extended his hand. 'I know we had our differences but well . . .' He shrugged. 'I suppose that's life. Will you shake?'

Eddy took the proffered hand. 'Goodbye then.'

'We'll keep in touch.'

'Oh aye, sure.'

'I'll contact you when we've both had time to settle in. I have your address.'

'You do that,' Eddy replied. And lifting his case he headed for the nearby taxi rank.

He didn't look back nor did he wave.

Kirk had no intentions of seeing Eddy again. Their original friendship had been all right when they were in the Army, but it was different now they were home.

Eddy was a workie, a peasant, and spoke like one. A different class entirely to what he'd become.

Anyway what friendship they'd had had well and truly expired that night Eddy had walked in on him and Leoni.

A car squealed to a halt and Susan stuck her head out of the window. 'Kirk!' she called excitedly.

As he went to her he put Eddy King out of his mind. As far as he was concerned, Eddy now belonged to the past.

Having moved back into his house, which the neighbours had very kindly been looking after while he'd been away, Eddy decided a celebration pint would be in order. At opening time he therefore took himself down to the nearest pub which he'd been in the habit of frequenting during his last visit home.

'That the national service done, then?' John the publican asked, setting a frothing pint in front of Eddy. 'No no,' he added when Eddy went to lay some money on the counter. 'First one's on the house.'

Eddy sipped the pint of heavy appreciatively. 'It's rare to be back,' he said. 'You can keep abroad as far as I'm concerned.'

'I'm afraid the wife and I are off ourselves,' John said miserably. 'Not that we really want to go, mind you. It's a case of having to.'

'How so?' Eddy asked.

'It's the wife's chest. It's been playing her up something awful these last few years.' He shook his head. 'Bronchitis on top of asthma. Bad.'

Eddy nodded sympathetically.

'The doctor recommended we go and live in a dry climate, which he promises will help her condition a lot. So it's Arizona for us. I've got a brother out there, you see, and I'll be working with him.'

They talked for a few minutes more and then John moved away to serve an influx of customers.

Staring into his beer, Eddy suddenly remembered the advice Kirk had given him about getting into the pub business. All pubs were goldmines, Kirk had said. And whatever else he was, Kirk certainly had his nut screwed on the right way when it came to making money.

When John was again free, Eddy called him over. 'Does that mean you'll be selling this place?' he asked.

'Aye, just as soon as we can find a buyer,' John replied; then, seeing the gleam in Eddy's eye, 'Why, are you interested?'

'I might be. What sort of price do you have in mind?'

John stated a figure which Eddy thought quite reasonable.

'Is there somewhere we can have a natter?' Eddy asked.

'Come away through the back and we'll talk there.'

John lifted the flap and Eddy went behind the bar. He had to wait there for a moment or two while John checked the staff were able to cope. Then John was leading him into the rear of the pub.

'And maybe I could have a wee look at your books? Just to give me some sort of idea what kind of trade you do,' Eddy said.

'Books? Who the hell keeps those?' John replied.

And they both laughed.

'What you'll want to know is all up here,' said John, tapping his head. 'And I'll be only too happy to tell you.'

A fortnight later the pub was Eddy's.

SUSAN AND KIRK (2)

Lizzie Murray squealed with delight as Kirk popped the bottle of Dom Perignon and the cork bounced off the ceiling to fall slithering away out of sight under some chairs. Champagne frothed and foamed into two glasses, one of which Kirk handed to his mother before hoisting the other in a toast.

'To my twenty-first pub!' he said, and drank.

Lizzie's eyes shone. 'Twenty-one,' she breathed, shaking her head in amazement. 'Who would ever have imagined it?'

Kirk laughed. He was feeling marvellous, on top of the world. That afternoon he'd taken possession of his seventeenth pub since coming out of the Army only a few short years before.

'Who said you needed a university degree to be successful?' he said to Lizzie. 'It just goes to show if you've got it you've got it.'

'Aye, there's no keeping a good man down,' Lizzie added, the pride she felt for her son clearly written all over her face.

Kirk topped up their glasses and then sat down. He'd put on a considerable amount of weight since coming out of the Army. He was now very chubby, bordering on the rotund – this thanks to drink and lashings of good food, the latter always having been his weakness.

'So where do you go from here, son?' Lizzie asked.

'On and on, I suppose. Just keep buying more and more pubs.'

Lizzie sat facing Kirk, a shrewd, cunning look on her face. 'Maybe you should give things a wee bit more thought than that,' she said.

'How do you mean?'

'Well, there's been an awful lot in the papers of late about what's happening amongst the breweries down in England. And we all know that what happens down there tends to happen up here not all that long after.'

'Go on,' Kirk prompted softly, knowing that when his mother spoke like this it was wise to listen. He had long since come to respect her judgement and insight when it came to business matters.

Lizzie played with her double chin, she too having put on a great deal of weight during the past few years. 'There's an awful lot of buying going on,' she said. 'Where before there were five or six local breweries, one has bought the rest out and now services that entire area. Nor is it stopping locally. These big breweries are getting bigger all the time, either merging with or swallowing up their larger competitors. The way I see it the only logical end to all this will be a small number of huge breweries tending to the needs of the entire country, by which I mean Britain as a whole.'

Kirk pondered on that before replying. 'You could be right. But how do you see that affecting me?'

Lizzie reached out to take his hand. 'I always told you, son, think big. It might well be that in, say, ten years' time there will be only two breweries left in Scotland, and whoever owns these will have an awful lot of power. It doesn't matter how many pubs you own then; you'll be their lackey to jump when they say jump because if you don't they can stop supplying you and thereby put you out of business. If they don't, do so anyway, and why not? If they put you out of business they'd be able to buy up your pubs at rock-bottom prices.'

Kirk's champagne suddenly didn't taste so good any more. He swished the remains round his glass and looked at it sourly.

'You say think big? Just what do you mean by that?' he asked.

'Now's the time to be thinking ten years ahead. When the dust finally clears why shouldn't *you* be one of the two, possibly three, that are left?'

346

'You mean I should be making as well as selling?'

Lizzie's face cracked into a smile. 'Precisely.'

'Run my own brewery,' he said softly. It was a thought that had crossed his mind more than once but not for the reasons Lizzie had just put forward.

'The way I see it,' she went on, 'we'll end up with one brewery in Glasgow, one in Edinburgh and possibly, just possibly, one in the north, say Dundee or Aberdeen. But that third one will only be a small giant so to speak compared to the other two. And when it comes to Glasgow you know who the front runner must be at the moment, don't you?'

'Black Lion.'

'Aye, your friend and father-in-law, the high and mighty Major.'

Unconsciously Kirk reached up to touch the scar on his cheek. Over the years the scar had faded considerably but was still clearly discernible. From certain angles it gave his face a somewhat lopsided look. Slowly he traced the scar, anger burning in him as he remembered how he'd come by it. He and the Major were still bitter enemies although, for Susan's sake, they suffered one another's presence from time to time.

'What you're saying is I get him before he's in a position to get me?' Kirk said.

Lizzie nodded. 'That about sums it up.'

A wolfish grin lit up Kirk's face. He found the idea most appealing.

'You've got a mind on you that's sharp as a Blue Gillette,' he said admiringly.

'Maybe so. But you're the one can get things done. That's your talent.'

'Quite a team, eh Ma?'

'Quite a team, son,' she replied, squeezing his hand.

There was a loud yelling sound from the pub below. Lizzie cocked her head to listen, wondering if it was the portent of trouble. But the sound swiftly died away again. Walter had everything under control.

When she turned her attention back to Kirk he was already deep in thought.

Kirk sat in the back seat of his car gazing out at the passing scenery. Glasgow never changed, it seemed. Dirty houses, dirty streets with dirty children playing on them.

A wee boy wearing ragged clothes and wooden clogs came clattering along the pavement. He had an old rubber tyre which he was 'making go' with a stick. For a moment or two Kirk felt jealous. That was the sort of thing he'd always wanted desperately to do as a child but had never been allowed to.

As the wee boy clattered by out of sight he put the incident from his mind and concentrated on the meeting which he had requested and which he was now on his way to attend.

Turk McGhie brought the car into the brewery's forecourt and killed the engine. He turned to Kirk. 'Want me to come with you, Mr Murray?' he asked.

Kirk shook his head. Turk wasn't needed here. He climbed out of the car and made for the main entrance. Once inside, he announced who he was and whom he'd come to see. He was requested politely to sit. Mr McRae was on the phone and would see him directly.

The building Kirk was in was over a hundred and fifty years old and looked it, he thought. It had a geriatric air about it, as though at any moment it might just suddenly give up the ghost and come crashing down.

It was a month since Kirk had taken over his twenty-first pub and in that time he'd made extensive inquiries about the nine breweries currently functional in Glasgow. Thistle Brewery was the one he'd chosen, for the simple reason it was on the verge of bankruptcy and therefore it should be possible to buy it at the cheapest price.

'If you'll follow me, Mr McRae will see you now,' a pinch-faced man said, having appeared at Kirk's side. All the way along the passageway the man continually 'washed' his hands.

McRae was a bluff man in his early fifties, who rose as Kirk entered his office.

'Pleasure to meet you, Mr Murray,' he said, extending his hand. After they'd shaken and they'd both sat he added, 'I must say, you're a lot younger than I'd expected.'

Kirk nodded. That was a remark often made.

'Will you take a dram? Or perhaps you'd like a beer. I can recommend our 80/- ale. Smooth as silk.'

Kirk had already decided shock tactics were in order. He was already well known as someone who invariably came straight to the point – when it suited him, that was – and never pulled his punches.

'I never touch any of your beers,' he replied. 'I've tried all three of them. Your 70/- ale, your 80/- ale and your Scotch Ale. All three of them are dreadful, which is why I don't sell them in any of my pubs.'

McRae blinked and sat back in his chair. He'd never ever been spoken to like this before. Kirk stared at McRae, his eyes hard and unyielding. He wanted to dominate McRae, make the man buckle to his will.

McRae was completely thrown. 'I, eh ... I rather thought when you asked to see me today that you were considering putting Thistle beer into your pubs. I see now that isn't the case.' He waited expectantly but Kirk didn't reply. Finally he was forced to go on. 'What did you want to see me about, then?' he asked.

Kirk opened his briefcase, extracting a sheaf of papers which he laid on his lap. 'I've been doing a considerable amount of checking up on Thistle Brewery, Mr McRae. To put it in a nutshell, you're in one god-awful mess.'

McRae looked angry. 'You'd no right ...'

'I had every right,' Kirk cut in. 'I didn't do anything illegal.' McRae fumed. Kirk continued. 'For years now you've been lurching from one crisis to the next. During the past six years you've lost forty-four per cent of your business to Black Lion and several other brewers. On your current performance – and frankly if you haven't improved it by now, Mr McRae, you aren't going to – Thistle will go under next year or the following year at the latest.'

'That's pure conjecture!' McRae blustered.

'Like hell it is. You're mortgaged up to the hilt, you personally as well as the firm, with no other collateral or options up your sleeve to produce at the last minute. You've been running for years, McRae, and now you're on the point of running out of road.'

'How did you find out all this?'

'There are ways and means. Some of it was public knowledge; the other bits weren't too difficult to discover.'

McRae slumped at his desk and it was obvious most of the stuffing had been knocked out of him a long time since.

'What do you want?' he asked.

'To buy you out. I'll give you a fair price. Which won't be all that much, I warn you, considering the state the firm is in. But remember, it's a lot more than you'll get if you go into receivership.'

'Are you acting on your own or for someone else?'

'On my own.'

'Will ... will you continue brewing or have you something else in mind?'

'I plan to continue brewing.'

'I'm pleased about that,' McRae said, gazing off into space. 'There's been a brewery on this site for over three hundred years. Did you know that?' Kirk shook his head. 'This is the second building.' He sighed. 'It's a relief in a way. I've been at my wits' end a long time now worrying about keeping going. It's not just the firm, you see. It's the men. Some of them have been with us man and boy. If Thistle was to close down they'd be thrown out of work. And you know what unemployment's like in Glasgow. Some of them might get taken on by other breweries, the younger ones in particular. But for the majority, closure would be the finish of their working lives.'

'If they're good workmen who know their jobs they'll have nothing to fear from me,' Kirk said.

McRae crossed to a cupboard which he opened to reveal a row of bottles. 'How about a dram, then, if you don't like our beer?' he asked.

The man was a born loser, Kirk thought. It was stamped all over him.

'Fine. Then I suggest we arrange for our solicitors to get together. I'd like to get this thing sorted out as soon as possible.'

'If you'll come this way, Mr Murray,' said James Ogmore. 'Our entire creative department, including the team we hope will be eventually handling your account, are dying to meet you.'

Kirk strode along the deep-pile carpeted hallway. It was his first visit to Ogmore, McCall and Bird Ltd, Scotland's leading advertising agents, of whom James Ogmore was the chief partner.

The room he was ushered into was luxurious in an 'arty-crafty' way. The people in it, eighteen in all, rose smiling to their feet as he came through the doorway. While Kirk was being introduced around, wine was opened. When the gathering sat again everyone held a glass.

'This of course is just a preliminary meeting, a sort of "getting to know one another" occasion,' James Ogmore said. 'Now, have you anything particular in mind? Something that will at least give us a starting-off point?'

Kirk said slowly, 'What I want is the sort of advertising that will make people stop in their tracks and then go on to buy my beer. Something new and stunning. Something far better than the usual sort of beer adverts seen in Scotland today. What I want is something like the new S H Benson Guinness ad, "Down With Guinness ..." in giant letters, while in tiny totey ones underneath, "Then You'll Feel Better."'

'That is a particularly good ad,' Ogmore said wryly, raising a laugh when he added, 'I wish we'd thought of it first.'

'Will you continue calling the brewery Thistle Brewery?' an intense-looking bearded man asked.

'No. As far as I'm concerned Thistle is associated with a rotten pint. I want a brand new name, something completely fresh.'

351

'Speaking right off the top of my head, how about KM Brewery?' a female suggested.

Kirk stared at the woman while he considered that. She was a striking redhead in her early twenties with large green eyes.

'Your initials,' she added softly.

'Speaking as an out-and-out egotist, I rather like it,' Kirk replied.

The others laughed and the woman grinned.

Kirk wracked his memory trying to remember her name. It was a funny one, gaelic he thought. And then it came back to him. *Ciona. Ciona ... Campbell? No ... Cran ... Cram ... Crammond. Yes, that was it. Ciona Crammond.

'KM Brewery it will be then, Miss Crammond.' Kirk smiled.

James Ogmore signalled that Kirk's glass should be refilled. 'You mentioned something about brewing new beers?' he said. 'Perhaps you'd like to elaborate on that.'

Kirk sipped his wine before replying. 'I intend selling three draught beers,' he said. 'A good pint of heavy, stronger and more flavoursome than the one Thistle do now. That'll be for the ordinary working man who enjoys his pint of wallop. The second one I want to aim more at the middle classes. Not quite so strong and lighter on the palate. The sort of beer a woman might well appreciate.'

Several in the room nodded. All were intent, hanging on his every word. He found he rather liked that. He also found he was addressing most of what he was saying directly to Ciona Crammond.

He went on. 'The third beer will be for the younger side of the market. The sub-twenties, just-over-twenties. Students. That sort of clientele which, speaking now as a pub owner, I'm finding is increasing as a corner of the market all the time. Young people nowadays, it seems, have a great deal more money to spend than did their parents, and a lot of what they

*Pronounced Shona.

spend goes on drink. For them, I want a beer they can identify with, something they feel belongs to their age group. For that I want an ultra-modern name, completely different to any other beer name that's gone before.'

'A very exciting and original concept, if I may say so,' Ogmore commented.

'The last two beers will be keg. The first one traditional barrel,' Kirk added.

'What's keg?' Ciona asked.

'A fairly new idea that's come out. Basically it's pasteurised beer put into a metal container which, when it reaches the pub, is delivered to the pump by CO_2.'

'Doesn't that damage the beer?' a man asked.

Kirk smiled. 'It's a slightly new taste, you might say. And incidentally, it's also a lot cheaper from the brewery point of view.'

The man looked as though he was about to add something but a sharp glance from James Ogmore caused him to change his mind.

'Keg's easier to handle and lasts longer in the pub, has a longer pub life we say,' Kirk said.

'But your first pint of heavy will remain in traditional barrels?' Ogmore asked.

'Correct,' Kirk said.

Kirk spoke for a few more minutes about his plans and ideas after which he answered a number of questions from the floor.

When the meeting was concluded, Ogmore suggested lunch and Kirk accepted.

Ogmore was in his office putting on his coat and Kirk was idly staring at some plaques on the walls when Ciona Crammond knocked and entered.

'Ciona will be in charge of the team who'll be drawing up our proposed campaign for you,' Ogmore said.

'Then I think she should come to lunch as well,' Kirk said smoothly.

Ogmore's eyes flickered ever so fractionally between Kirk

and Ciona. 'Good idea,' he replied. 'The more you two speak with one another the more insight she'll have on how to give you satisfaction.'

Kirk thought of a reply to that which brought a smile to his lips.

After lunch Kirk returned to the brewery, where he found Bill Baxter, his head brewer, by the mash tuns. Bill was an old groutchedy sort of a man well known for his sour disposition.

'How are you doing, Bill?' Kirk asked.

Baxter curled his lower lip in contempt. 'This beer 3 is more pish water than beer,' he said scornfully. Beer 3 referred to the beer Kirk would be aiming at the younger market. Beer 2 was for the middle-class market. And beer 1 was the traditional heavy.

'Let's have a taste,' Kirk said.

They moved on past the coppers and hop backs to where several small kegs had been racked and fined. Kirk waited patiently while Baxter drew off a glass of bright amber liquid, which Baxter then grudgingly handed him.

'CO_2,' Baxter muttered under his breath. 'The whole damn thing's sacrilege.'

Kirk took a swallow and then another. 'What's the gravity?' he asked.

'1034,' Baxter grunted in reply.

Kirk finished off the glass. The beer was light on the tongue, middle bodied and went down very easily.

'Drop it another four points,' he said.

Baxter shook his head in bewilderment. 'It'll be hardly alcoholic at all, then. Who's going to drink the likes of that, man?'

'*Mr Murray* to you, Baxter,' Kirk snapped in reply. 'And it's not your job to worry about who buys it. All you have to think about is making the damn stuff.'

Baxter looked at the floor, grumbling under his breath.

'And what's more, if the job doesn't suit you you can pick up your cards right now.'

Baxter looked up, fear edging into his eyes. 'It's just so different to what I'm used to brewing, Mr Murray,' he replied.

'I'm well aware of that, Baxter.'

'And as for this keg business, sir. It's ... it's immoral!'

Despite himself Kirk had to smile at the man's outrage. 'You know Thistle was on the verge of closure when I took over?' he said.

Baxter nodded. 'Aye, it had been rumoured long enough.'

'Well, a lot of the reason Thistle wasn't doing well was because of the muck you were putting out.'

Baxter spluttered, his face flaming. 'Thistle 70/- and 80/- ales won prizes forty years ago!'

'Forty years is a long time, Baxter.'

'The quality never changed. Not in my time anyway!'

'I'm sure. But tastes do change and Thistle never moved with the times. There's going to be a revolution in this industry, mark my words, and I want to be at the head of it.'

'But you'd have to drink God knows how many pints of beer 3 to get drunk!' Baxter said.

Kirk smiled. 'Precisely. And the more beer drunk the bigger the profit.'

Light dawned in Baxter's eyes. 'I see,' he said slowly. 'I hadn't looked at it from that point of view before.' Then changing back, 'I don't approve, mind you. But at least I see what you're driving at now.'

'Now, how's beer 2 coming along?' Kirk asked.

'I'm just not getting a good wort so far,' Baxter replied, and then launched into a lengthy and detailed explanation, three-quarters of which was way over Kirk's head.

Kirk got home that night feeling tired but elated.

'How was your day?' Susan asked, bringing him a whisky and water while he kicked off his shoes and sank into a comfortable chair.

'I have a feeling these advertising agents are going to work out,' he replied.

'Good.'

'I'm going to call the brewery KM Brewery. Like it?'

'KM for Kirk Murray, I presume?'

He laughed. 'Right first time. Think it's too much?'

'Do you?' Kirk shook his head. 'Then there's your answer.'

He sipped his whisky as he thought back over the day's events.

'I've been having trouble with Baxter, the head brewer. But I think I've finally got him straightened out.'

'By that I take it you've got him round to your way of thinking.'

'When you work for me that is the *only* way to think,' Kirk replied.

'Poor Baxter,' Susan said sympathetically. 'I'll bet you really gave him a flea in his ear.'

'Nothing to what he'll get if he doesn't come up with the new beers I want soon.'

'How are they going?'

'Beer 3's almost there. But 2 still has a long way to go.'

'Speaking of beer,' Susan said slowly. 'I spoke to Father today. He rang up this afternoon.'

Kirk sat bolt upright. 'He didn't know anything about the new beers or any of my plans, did he?'

'He didn't mention anything.'

'And you were careful not to . . .'

'Yes I was,' Susan cut in angrily. 'You told me not to say anything to anyone and I haven't.'

Kirk grunted and sank back into his chair. 'So what did the Major want then?' he asked when he was once more in a comfortable position.

'The same old question. When are we going to give him a grandson?'

'Ah!' Kirk replied, and then his brow furrowed. 'It is peculiar how you've never got pregnant after all this time, isn't it?'

'I thought . . . Well I thought perhaps I should see a doctor and get myself checked over.'

'You think something might be wrong in that department?'

'Who knows!' she shrugged. 'It's certainly possible. And if there is, it might well be something simple which can be easily put right.'

'Then you'd better see a doc.'

All this was a ruse on Susan's part. She had been to the doctor about the problem of her continuing non-pregnancy the previous year. The doctor had confirmed there was absolutely no reason why she shouldn't have a baby.

She now came to what all this was really about.

'As long as I'm going to see the doctor, why don't you as well? It can't do any harm.'

Kirk wasn't too sure he liked that idea, feeling that in some way it questioned his masculinity.

'I don't know ...' he prevaricated.

But Susan was ready for this. She went on, 'Why I think it's a good idea you go is connected with something I read on the subject. It seems a high proportion of non-pregnancies, where both partners are fertile, is due to the woman being too acidy – the acid killing off the sperms – for her mate, in which case she's given pills to reduce her level of acidity. Now the doctor wouldn't be able to tell if I was too acid for you unless he was able to test you as well.'

That seemed a fair enough argument to Kirk, and one which let his manhood off the hook, so he capitulated.

'All right, you set up the appointment and I'll be there,' he said.

Susan came across and kissed him on the cheek. 'Thank you,' she whispered.

'Of course, maybe we haven't been trying hard enough to have one,' he replied.

'You must be joking! You're forever at it.'

'Nonetheless. Perhaps I need to try just that little bit harder.'

'Dinner's in the oven. It'll burn,' she said as he nibbled her neck.

357

'Let it,' he replied, slipping out of his chair and dragging them both to the floor.

And it did.

Kirk sat beside James Ogmore, both men with large whiskies in their hands. They were in Ciona Crammond's office and she was just about to explain her proposed campaign for the KM Brewery. Several of her team sat in the background ready to add their two cents' worth if asked.

Ciona held up a large sheet of cardboard on which a pint of beer had been painted. Below the pint was the new KM logo and a line of copy which said simply: KM HEAVY - A TRADITIONAL PINT FOR THE MAN WHO KNOWS AND APPRECIATES HIS BEER.

'Beer 1,' said Ciona. 'Straightforward, basic, aimed directly at the working man who doesn't like frills or fripperies. What I would call a no-nonsense ad.'

Kirk nodded. That sort of ad would go down well with working-class Glasgow.

'Beer 1 is obviously the easiest of the lot,' said Ciona.

'All this will be going out on hoardings, newspaper ads, cinema ads, what we call give-aways, that sort of thing,' Ogmore chipped in.

Ciona continued. 'Beer 2 I thought we might call Golden Brew ...'

'Golden Brew?' muttered Kirk. He liked it.

'I think Golden has such marvellous, and indeed middle-class, connotations. Happy, healthy, sun-drenched, goodness, that sort of thing.' She held up a second sheet of cardboard on which was depicted an obviously middle-class family enjoying themselves on a seaside outing. Overhead the sun was bursting through a powder-blue sky, the two children were rosy-cheeked and bonnie, while before Dad sat a brimming golden pint and before Mum a sparkling half-pint.

'This is just one setting of which there could be many appropriate ones,' Ciona said.

'Not bad,' said Kirk. In fact he thought it excellent. It

portrayed exactly the sort of image he was after.

Golden Brew, he thought to himself. It definitely had a ring about it and was very different to anything else currently on the Scottish market.

'Now beer 3,' said Ciona, 'and the one I'm sure we'd all agree was the hardest of the lot. Well I've personally thought to call it KM '60, the drink of tomorrow here today. The '60 stands for 1960.'

'Yes, I got that,' Kirk said.

Ciona held up another cardboard picture. This one portrayed a group of older teenagers dancing to what was very obviously a rock-and-roll band.

'Or,' said Ciona, 'KM '60, the drink of tomorrow in keg, the barrel of the future.'

There was a pause and then Kirk said, 'I like both slogans.'

'If you give us the go-ahead we can develop all these ideas,' Ciona said.

Excitement gripped Kirk as he stared at the cardboard picture Ciona was holding up. His gut reaction told him she was on the right track with all three beers. He could smell money here. And that particular sense of smell had never yet let him down.

'The idea behind KM '60 would be to identify it with the new wave of international singers, musicians, bands, screen idols –'

'And sport,' Kirk interrupted. 'Incorporate sport as well.'

Ciona nodded that she'd taken his point on board, then continued. 'We wouldn't use the actual names themselves but rather associate through look-alikes, inference, that sort of thing.'

Ciona spoke non-stop for another five minutes before finally coming to a halt. When she'd done so, several of the others present added a few comments. When they were finished silence reigned.

'What do you think, Mr Murray?' James Ogmore asked eventually.

Kirk allowed a smile to light up his face. 'I like very much what you've done so far. You've got my account for a year on trial. After that we'll see.'

James Ogmore extended his hand which Kirk shook. Then Kirk shook hands with Ciona Crammond.

'I think this calls for a drink,' said Ogmore.

'I think it calls for several,' said Kirk.

Everyone laughed. While some minions fetched the booze Kirk drew Ciona down beside him.

They had a great deal to talk about.

Kirk was stunned. 'But that's impossible!' he exclaimed. 'I've already impregnated a woman.'

Doctor Goldberg adjusted his spectacles before glancing back at the report spread before him. 'The results of your tests are quite definite,' he said. 'You have an extremely low sperm-count - nine thousand to be precise. Anything below ten is considered infertile.'

'Then how do you explain what happened before?'

Goldberg took off his glasses and stared at Kirk. 'It's not completely out of the question, of course, although highly improbable.'

'But it *did* happen.'

'Not to Mrs Murray, I take it?'

'No,' Kirk replied. 'The woman I was associated with previously.'

'And how long ago was this?'

'A handful of years.'

'Hmm!' said Goldberg, looking thoughtful. He picked up a pencil and tapped its butt end on his desk. Eventually he added, 'There is the possibility that in these intervening years something may have happened to you physically to render you infertile.'

'Like what?'

'Excessive stress and strain, far too much alcohol over a prolonged period, disease ...'

'What sort of disease?' Kirk cut in quickly.

'Venereal, Mr Murray.'

360

Goldberg knew from the stricken look on Kirk's face that he'd struck home. He sighed; these things were invariably very sad. The callow youth sowing wild oats only to reap a great deal more than ever dreamed of. It was a story he knew only too well having heard it so many times before.

'I was over in Germany doing my national service ...' Goldberg sighed again. 'And I caught a dose. The army medics treated me.'

'That would seem to be it then,' Goldberg said. 'The disease must have fouled things up in the tubes from your testes, hence the sperm drop.'

'Is there anything you can do?'

Goldberg shook his head.

'Then I'll never be a father?'

'As I said before, it's not totally impossible. But what we're talking about is the proverbial chance in a million.'

Kirk thought of Leoni von Kruppermann. 'That bitch!' he whispered, his hands knotting into fists.

'You're sure there's no treatment?' he demanded.

'Positive,' Goldberg replied. 'I'm sorry.'

'Not half as much as I am, doctor.'

Kirk rose and shook Dr Goldberg's hand. 'Just one thing. I'd like this kept confidential between the pair of us. I don't want my wife to find out, not yet anyway. And certainly *never* what I've just confided in you.'

'I understand perfectly,' said Goldberg.

Half-way home, Kirk started to laugh. In an ironical way what had happened was very, very funny.

Susan was waiting up for him. 'How did it go?' she asked anxiously, the moment he walked into the room.

He poured them both a drink before replying. As he handed her a glass, he said brightly, 'There's nothing wrong with me. A1, top of the bill. Everything functioning just as it should be.'

'Well, that's a relief!'

'So if there's nothing wrong with either of us, it's just one of these things. God's will, as they say. We'll just have to keep on trying and hope that one day something happens.'

She came to his side and put her arm round his waist. 'It's getting late. How about bed?' she suggested.

'If you don't mind I think I'll stay down here a while and have a few drinks. I've a lot on my mind at the moment, things to do with the brewery I want to work out.'

'Are you all right?'

'I'm fine! Fine! Just got a lot running around inside the old bonce, that's all.'

She kissed him on the cheek. 'Don't be too late up. And if I've fallen asleep you can wake me if you like.'

He pecked her back but didn't commit himself one way or the other.

At the door she turned to add something but didn't when she saw he was already lost in thought.

For a long time after Susan had gone to bed, Kirk sat drinking steadily, thinking about his German countess and the legacy she'd given him.

Then eventually he started thinking about Ciona Crammond, wondering, not for the first time, what she'd be like to have.

When he finally turned in, he was more than a little drunk and randy as hell.

It might have been his wife Kirk made love to, but it was another woman he had pictured in his mind.

Writing this letter was something Kirk had been looking forward to since the day he'd bought what was now KM Brewery. Of the twenty-six pubs he now owned – five more had come with the brewery – twenty-one sold Black Lion beer.

In his own handwriting he informed Major Keith Gibb that as from the first of the coming month he would no longer be selling the Black Lion product, replacing it with his own KM brews.

When the letter was finished he signed it with a flourish and then sat back in his chair to stare at it. His fingers came up to stroke the scar on his cheek. He'd sworn revenge the day the Major had given him that. Susan had been part of his revenge. The rest was about to follow.

The letter in front of him was the point of the knife going in. From now on, he'd be pressing on that knife, driving it deeper and deeper until one day ... Kirk smiled thinly to himself. Until one day the bastard was destroyed.

'Come in,' said Ciona Crammond. 'It was good of you to come over.'

Kirk shrugged himself out of his coat and, while she was disposing of it, had a quick look round the room.

At one time, the house had been one of Glasgow's grander ones, inhabited by a large well-to-do family and all the various servants needed to cater to their needs. Now it was subdivided into a number of flats of which Ciona's was on the ground floor.

The room was extremely high, with a great deal of fancy plaster-work on the ceiling. An absolutely enormous mirror was fastened to one wall, which cleverly made the room seem larger than it actually was. There were a great many books scattered around, together with a number of other miscellaneous items including articles of clothing. Whatever else Ciona Crammond was, she wasn't a tidy person.

'Drink?' she said on re-entering the room.

'Please.'

'Whisky, wine ...?'

'Whisky would be fine,' he said, smiling.

He watched her as she poured the drinks. He hadn't been all that surprised to receive her phone call at the brewery. It had been only a matter of time before one of them made the first move.

'Everything going to your satisfaction so far?' she asked, handing him a whisky and water, half and half, the way she knew he liked it.

'Anybody in Glasgow who hasn't heard about KM beers by now must be deaf, dumb and blind,' he grinned.

'Slainthe!' she toasted.

'Slainthe!'

Their eyes were on one another as they drank.

'I've been working from home today – I do from time to time – which is why I asked you here rather than the office,' she said.

He nodded.

'I've been thinking: launch day. What we need over and above what we've already planned is something physical to actually take place.'

He grinned inwardly at the choice of her words.

'Something to give the newspapers good photos and copy. But more than that, something the people can actually see. Now, launch day is a Saturday, right?'

'Right.'

'Which is the day most of Glasgow comes into the town to do their big shopping.'

'Right again,' he said.

'What about a pipe band then? You know we Scots are suckers for tartan and the sound of the pipes. To use a common expression nowadays, we just lap it up.'

It was true, he thought. Nothing went down better amongst the populace than a pipe band.

'How does advertising KM beers come into it?' he asked.

'Placards, sashes, that sort of thing.'

'If it went up Argyle Street from the Trongate, up Buchanan Street and along Sauchiehall Street to Charing Cross, and then came all the way back again, say round about mid-day, it would be seen by an awful lot of people.'

Ciona nodded eagerly. 'Precisely.'

'Can you get a band?'

'I've already made inquiries. I've got one which will happily do it providing you make a contribution to their instrument fund.'

'What sort of figure?'

Ciona mentioned one Kirk thought extremely reasonable.

'We'll have them then,' he said.

'I like a man who can make up his mind,' she replied, smiling. 'Now how about another drink?'

After their refills had been poured they sat facing one another across the room. 'You've done a very good job on my campaign,' he said.

Her eyes crinkled at the corners. 'Thank you.'

'Have you been with Ogmore, McCall and Bird long?'

'Eighteen months. Before that I was down in London working for one of the agencies there. J Walter Thompson.'

'I've heard of them,' Kirk said.

'Very big, very good. I learned a great deal.'

'So why come back here?'

'The parents are getting on a bit. I thought it best to be close by.'

'Do they live in Glasgow?'

'Helensburgh now. But they only moved there a few years ago.'

'So you were born and brought up in Glasgow?'

'For my sins,' she grinned.

'Tell me about your father. What does he do?'

'Did. He's retired. He was a judge.'

Kirk raised an eyebrow. 'I'm impressed.' Then suddenly, 'Not Justice Crammond, the one they called "Hanging Crammond"?'

'He's ever such a pet really,' Ciona said. 'He just seemed to get an awful lot of murderers at one point, that's all.'

'Most of whom went to the gallows at Barlinne, hence the name.'

Kirk was more than impressed now. Mr Justice Crammond had been one of Scotland's best-known figures for many years, not only famous but also part of the establishment and one of the leading lights in the highest strata of Scottish society.

'Laurel Bank or Park?' he asked, these being the names of two of Glasgow's very best private girls' schools.

'Craigholme, just to be different,' she replied.

Well she certainly belonged to the country's cream, he thought. There could be no denying that.

'What school did *you* go to?' she asked, a mischievous twinkle in her eye.

He knew from that twickle she was well aware he wasn't from the upper crust, as he sounded to a lot of people. The genuine article always recognises the masquerader.

'The school of hard knocks. About five million miles away from Craigholme,' he replied.

She nodded her approval. She would have been disappointed if he'd lied.

'And what about your wife?' she asked, the mischievous twinkle stronger than before.

'Ah! Of better stock than me. The rose to my thorn.'

'I've heard she's very nice.'

'She is.'

'A vet, isn't she?'

'Qualified but never practised.'

'You think a woman's place is in the home?'

His lips thinned wolfishly. 'I think a woman's place is in the bed. Whether she works or not doesn't bother me.'

'You're an extremely arrogant man, aren't you?'

'Yes.'

'And conceited.'

'Dreadfully.'

'I think I like you.'

'I *know* I like *you.*'

She laughed. 'Are you always so positive?'

'Only about women, money, business and life in general.'

'In that order?'

'Not necessarily.'

He rose and crossed to her, taking her hand and drawing her to her feet.

'Don't you think we've talked enough now?' he asked.

'What else did you have in mind?'

'The same thing you did when you asked me here.'

He kissed her hard, pulling her to him and squashing her against his chest.

366

'Have you a double-bed?' he asked, when their mouths finally broke apart.

'Yes.'

'Good. I hate being cramped.'

'Come on,' she said, her hand hot and sticky with expectation in his.

As she led him to the bedroom, he said, 'You aren't an Honourable, are you?'

'No. Why?'

'Pity. I would have liked that.'

'Are you a snob, Mr Murray?' she asked sweetly.

'Kirk, please. And yes I am. Through and through.'

The bedroom looked as though a bomb had struck it, the dressing table littered with make-up, powder – more of which seemed spilled than was actually in the box – cotton wool, toilet roll and a number of cups containing the remains of coffee. There was a table by the bed. The table-top was absolutely covered with rank upon rank of standing smoked-down cork-tipped cigarette butts.

Kirk stared at that little army in fascination. It was the first time he'd ever seen anything like it.

Ciona's hands went up behind her, and several seconds later her dress fell away. She kicked it to one side, then pulled her slip over her head. Crossing to the bed she sprawled across it. 'Well?' she demanded.

Ten minutes later the bed was rocking violently as Kirk and Ciona went at it hammer and tongs.

Suddenly she shrieked and threw her arms around his head. And as she did so the bed tilted and sort of slid away from beneath them.

'Jesus Christ!' said Kirk, as with Ciona clinging tightly to him the pair of them went rolling to one side, to end up dumped on the floor.

'I've heard of orgasms that made the earth move but that was bloody ridiculous!' he exclaimed.

Ciona giggled and buried her head in his shoulder. Her red

hair lay spread below them like a carpet of red gold.

'I forget to mention that one of the legs isn't there any more,' she said. 'That bit's held jacked up by a pile of books.'

Kirk looked and sure enough the bed only had three legs.

'We've knocked all your cigarette ends down,' he said.

'There's nothing down that I can't put up again,' she whispered in his ear.

And she was right.

The pipe band turned into Buchanan Street playing 'Scotland The Brave'. Behind the band came a dozen pretty lassies dressed up in the same tartan as the band, and all carrying placards and wearing sashes proclaiming the virtues of KM beer. Hordes of people in the middle of their shopping stopped and cheered. Wee boys ran up and down the gutter shouting various things, including, 'Kiltie kiltie cauld bum!'

'What do you think?' Kirk asked.

'Impressive. Certainly dear dull Glasgow hasn't seen anything like it since the end of the war,' Susan replied.

'I've got a great feeling about all this, you know. There'll be no stopping me now.'

'I believe you,' Susan said, and meant it.

They followed the pipe band up the street. A street which only minutes before had been grey and dreich but which was now magically transformed. The air was alive, thrumming with gaiety and excitement.

'Just listen to them,' Kirk said. KM Brewery, KM heavy, KM Golden Brew and KM '60 seemed on everyone's lips.

'Your advertising agency has certainly done you proud. No doubt about it,' Susan said.

And all thanks to Ciona Crammond, Kirk thought. She was the driving force as well as the really creative one behind this campaign.

'Come on, let's get round and ahead of them on to Sauchiehall Street,' he said, and, taking Susan's hand, pulled her off to one side and out of the throng.

On the other side of Buchanan Street, Eddy King stood in a

doorway, his gaze fixed on Kirk and Susan as they hurried away.

It was the first time he'd seen Kirk since the day they'd both come home from their national service. As he'd known at the time, Kirk had never contacted him nor he Kirk. He thought of Heather Dew and Kolya Turushev – 'the Russian run', they'd called it – and smiled. You've come a long way, Kirk my old china, he thought. A long way. But then so had he.

He waited till the press had subsided a little, before venturing out of the doorway. Making for his car, he presented a smart figure in his brand new camel coat, below which he wore a well-cut twenty-pound suit. He eased himself into a gleaming Jaguar and drove off, the very epitome of the self-made man: hard, ruthless and determined to keep getting ahead.

But at the back of his eyes, there was a sadness, the pain of memory. Annie Grimes, Leoni and Kirk had done that to him. They'd undermined the ruthlessness, given him a soft spot.

Some people would have said they'd made him more human.

George Penn and his Pennmen were in one corner blowing up a jazz storm. The room was packed with heaving bodies, all eating, drinking, smoking, enjoying themselves.

'Marvellous party,' said James Ogmore. Surrounded by a few acolytes and sycophants, he was talking to Susan.

Although she'd met him a number of times now, this was the first occasion she'd seen him really let his hair down. She hadn't realised before that he was queer.

'Kirk and I both thought it went extraordinarily well today. He was very pleased.'

'So were we at the agency, if I may say so. Mind you, most of the credit must go to Ciona. This campaign was mainly her baby.'

Susan smiled. Her throat was sore from having to shout so much in order to be heard above the din.

'And speaking of Ciona where is she?' Ogmore said, looking around.

A man from the brewery came up to Susan and said that the barrel of Golden Brew that had been laid on was now empty and should he open another.

'If they've gone through an entire barrel this quickly then I'd think you'd better,' Susan replied.

'I'll need the keys to the garage then,' the man said. That was where the various barrels and crates had been stored.

Susan pulled a face. 'We'll have to find Kirk for that. He's got them.'

'I saw him only a few minutes ago,' one of the acolytes said. 'He seemed to be heading for the rear of the house.'

'Will I go look for him?' the man from the brewery asked.

'No, you keep dishing out the KM '60 in the meantime, and I'll find and send him to you,' Susan replied.

The man nodded and moved off.

The reason Susan wanted to hunt for Kirk herself was that by going to the back of the house she could nip outside for a few moments and get a breath of fresh air. The noise and smoky atmosphere were beginning to give her a bit of a headache.

Excusing herself, she started to squirm through the mass of pressing flesh in the direction of the door, being stopped every few seconds to be congratulated on the success of the party and the launch of KM beers.

'Not here, dope!' Ciona whispered. 'What if someone walked in?'

'Bugger them!' said Kirk.

'Now, you don't mean that.'

'You're right,' he replied, removing his hand from her breast. 'Would be a bit embarrassing to be found groping my lady advertising agent in the back kitchen, wouldn't it?'

Ciona giggled. Both of them had had a fair amount to drink.

'There must be somewhere we can be alone,' he said, looking about.

'What about the rest of the house?'

He shook his head. 'People everywhere. Upstairs, downstairs, in my lady's chamber.'

'I like your lady, you know.'

'Susan? She's all right. Bit boring, mind you. Hadn't noticed that till recently.'

'Are you saying since you met me?'

'Yes ... Yes, I think I am.'

She smiled and buried her face in his chest. 'That's a lovely compliment. Thank you,' she whispered.

'Hold on a mo',' he said. 'Follow me.'

At the rear of the back kitchen was an old pantry now used as a storage room. He opened the door to this and bundled her inside.

The pantry was very narrow, and because of various sacks and boxes there was only about two feet of standing room.

'Rather cramped, don't you think?' she giggled in the darkness. 'And didn't you once tell me you hated being that?'

'I hate being randy and not being able to do anything about it even more,' he retorted.

Susan stumbled into the front kitchen, a veritable cavern of a place, to find several servants hired for the party busy making more sandwiches.

'Has anyone seen Mr Murray?' she asked.

'Sorry ma'am,' one said.

Another, a young girl, said, 'I think I might have seen him going into the back, Mrs Murray, but I couldn't be sure like. I mean it might well have been somebody else.'

Susan muttered thanks and moved on. She had intended going through to the back kitchen anyway as there was a door to the garden there.

All the lights in the back kitchen were on and there was an opened bottle of whisky on the table.

Well if he had been here he must've moved on, Susan thought. Crossing to the garden door she tugged it open and stepped outside. The air which washed around and over her

371

was cool and invigorating, like sparkling wine, she thought. She drank in a deep lungful and immediately felt better.

Wind rustled the trees and flowers in the garden. And what was that? An animal? After a few seconds it dawned on her it was somebody giggling, but where?

Her eyes and ears followed the sound until she traced it to the small projection at the back of the house which was the old pantry now used as a storeroom.

There was the murmur of a man's voice and then she understood. Some couple had wanted a little privacy and had found their way there. Probably a couple of young things after a bit of snogging, she thought. And why not? She'd enjoyed doing that sort of thing herself when she was their age.

She was about to turn and re-enter the back kitchen when suddenly, and quite clearly, the man's voice said, 'Oh that's lovely!'

The voice was unmistakable. It was Kirk's.

She closed her mouth, which she'd suddenly realised was hanging open, and swallowed hard. She felt numb all over. She considered briefly tearing the pantry door open and confronting him and whoever he was with. But second thoughts told her that would be a stupid thing to do. It was probably just some passing fancy, a young bird who'd thrown herself at him and whom he was having a couple of minutes' stolen passion with. A few kisses, a little petting. Nothing more.

She'd do herself more harm than good by making a mountain out of a molehill, she told herself. Let it go. Let it pass. And closing the garden door quietly behind her, she tiptoed back to the front kitchen, where she picked up two plates of sandwiches to take through to the party. She sought out James Ogmore and spoke to him, as he had an easy manner about him which was just what she needed then.

Twenty minutes later – she knew precisely how long it was because her eyes had kept straying to a wall clock – Kirk re-entered the room, and a few seconds after him, although apparently not with him, came Ciona Crammond.

'I don't know about anyone else but I'm thoroughly enjoying myself,' declared Kirk, his face flushed and his hair messed. He was carrying a glass containing a very large whisky.

Susan forced a smile on to her face and made herself act as though nothing had happened.

'Ciona! Come and join us!' Kirk called out.

'The lady wonder,' said James Ogmore, making a mock bow. One of his sycophants tittered.

Kirk took Ciona's hand in his and squeezed it. Susan saw the look which passed between them, and knew then that it had been no young thing that Kirk had been in the pantry with. It had been Ciona Crammond.

She raised her glass to her lips and it took all the willpower she possessed to stop it from trembling.

'A big, big day for you and Kirk,' said James Ogmore.

'Yes,' Susan replied. 'It is that.'

The last guest didn't leave till five in the morning, by which time Susan was absolutely worn out.

The house, a new one on the outskirts of Glasgow they'd moved into two years previously, was a shambles. But thank god she didn't have to worry about that. Several cleaners would be arriving later to put it all back in order again.

She poured herself a glass of cold milk which she took with her up to the bedroom. There she found Kirk had stripped off and gone through to the adjoining bathroom where she could hear he was having a shower.

She was about to strip off herself, when she suddenly noticed something peculiar about his underpants lying by the side of the bed. There was a streak of what looked like blood on the front of them. Frowning, she bent and picked up the underpants, wondering how he'd come to get blood there. She ran her finger along the mark, from which the colour transferred rather greasily on to her skin. A quick sniff confirmed her mistake.

Not blood but lipstick. And she knew then what it was Kirk

and Ciona had been doing in the pantry. Or to be more precise what Ciona had been doing.

Curling the underpants in her hand she angrily threw them from her. Sitting on the bed she hung her head. She desperately wanted to weep but wouldn't. At least not yet.

When Kirk came out of the bathroom shortly afterwards he found her in bed, apparently fast asleep. Humming, he got in beside her and within minutes had nodded off.

When he started to snore Susan opened her eyes and stared at the ceiling. Silently, so it wouldn't waken him, she allowed the tears to flow.

With a satisfied grunt, Kirk added the last name to the list it had taken him the best part of a week to compile. He pressed a button and a few seconds later Turk McGhie entered the office. Turk nodded and sat down facing Kirk across the desk.

'A list of every pub in Glasgow,' Kirk said, tapping the sheets of paper in front of him with his hand. 'With details of whether they're tied houses, free houses, and if the latter, which beer they sell. We'll start with north Glasgow where most of my pubs are and which is the area I wish to consolidate first. I've sectioned the north into half-mile squares so you can do a steady progression from square to square until every free house north of Sauchiehall Street is selling KM beers. Over and above your regular wages, there'll be a bonus for every pub you persuade to give its business to my brewery. Any questions?'

Turk McGhie shook his head.

'Well there's the list and a map with the sections clearly marked. Good luck.'.

McGhie accepted the map and sheets of paper, folding them and putting them into his pocket.

After Turk had gone Kirk shivered. Turk in one of his silent moods always had scared the living daylights out of him.

'Time gentlemen, please!' the publican of The Doch And Doris called. It was twenty past nine at night.

Several of those in the pub grumbled but nonetheless got on with the business of drinking up. The publican, whose name was McKevitt, came round the front of the bar to start collecting glasses. Behind the bar, his son Joe ran water into the basin in preparation for the washing up.

Fifteen minutes later McKevitt and Joe were the only ones left in the pub. Or so they thought. They both looked up in surprise when the door to the toilet opened and McGhie emerged.

'Time's been called, Jimmy,' McKevitt said. 'You're the last one.'

McGhie walked slowly to the bar where he gave McKevitt a cold, baleful, fish eye.

'I'm a representative from KM Brewery,' he said.

'Oh aye?'

'As you're a free house, we'd like you to give up the Black Lion muck you sell now and take our beers.'

McKevitt grinned as he hefted a bucketful of ullage on to the bar. 'And why should I do that?' he asked.

'Because ours is a better beer.'

'Keg?' McKevitt laughed. 'It'll never catch on. Anyway, I've been dealing with Black Lion for over twenty years now. Why should I change? I've always got on with them and they've always dealt fairly with me.'

Turk's eyes bored into McKevitt's. 'You'd find we're very competitive. In fact, it may well be we can give you a better deal than you're now getting from Black Lion,' he said.

McKevitt shook his head. 'You're wasting your time, Jim. Not interested.'

'You heard my dad. Now let's be having you,' said Joe.

'I haven't finished speaking yet,' said Turk quietly.

Irritation flashed across Joe's face. 'I think you have. My dad said we're not interested and that's that.' He then made the mistake of taking McGhie by the arm and trying to propel him towards the door.

McGhie shrugged himself free. And a second later the heel of his flattened palm scythed in a downward arc which ended

375

on the bridge of Joe's nose. There was a cracking sound followed by a spurt of bright red blood as Joe's nose broke where bone meets gristle. Joe's hands came up to his damaged face as he hastily back-pedalled. He never even saw the vicious rabbit punch which took him on the back of the neck to send him sprawling unconscious on the cigarette-end-strewn floor.

'What sort of bloody maniac are you?' screamed McKevitt, backing off as Turk advanced on him.

'Now, about changing your beer. I think you'll find it's going to be all the rage around here soon, so I advise you to get in at the very beginning when the terms are still good.'

'Get away from me!'

'I think traditional heavy and Golden Brew would be your best bests. I doubt if you'll have much call for KM '60, the beer of tomorrow in keg, the barrel of the future,' McGhie said. Grabbing hold of McKevitt's shirt front he drew the publican to him. 'Well? What do you say?'

'I'll ... I'll call the police. They know how to deal with the likes of you.'

McKevitt screamed, his feet trailing on the floor, as Turk dragged him across to where the bucket of ullage stood on the bar. Grabbing the back of McKevitt's head, Turk then swung himself round behind the man.

'If you like Black Lion beer so much then drink it,' Turk said and forced McKevitt's head down till his face was deep in slops from ear to ear. McKevitt struggled violently but found it impossible to break Turk McGhie's iron grip.

Turk counted thirty seconds before pulling McKevitt's face free.

'What's it taste like? Good, eh?' he asked.

McKevitt's eyes were popping and his face was puce. 'I ... I ...' he spluttered.

'Still thirsty, eh? Then be my guest!'

McKevitt shrieked as his face was forced back down, this time slowly, into the beer slops. When his mouth disappeared under, a stream of bubbles broke the surface.

Turk made the second immersion a short one, fifteen

seconds only, before yanking McKevitt's head back up again.

McKevitt made choking sounds and staggered away from Turk when the grip on his hair was released.

Turk took his time about lighting up a cigarette.

'There will be another representative from KM round to see you in the morning to take your order. Welcome to KM Brewery. It's a switch you'll never regret.'

Joe McKevitt had come to his feet where he stood panting.

'And don't either of you go to the polis,' said McGhie, moving to the door. 'It would be a very, very stupid thing to do.'

There was a blur of light as he produced an ivory-handled cut-throat razor, which he held in the cocked position. Slowly, and emphatically, he drew it down the door curtain, whch parted like sliced butter. 'If you get my meaning,' he added.

The razor vanished as quickly as it had appeared.

'Good night,' said Turk. 'It's been a pleasure doing business with you.'

'Your favourite, *coq au vin*,' said Susan, placing a plate piled high in front of Kirk.

Her own plateful was tiny by comparison, as she was on a diet. She wanted to have as trim a figure as possible in case it was that which had caused Kirk to stray.

Kirk attacked the meal with relish, washing every mouthful down with a gulp of red wine. 'Sure beats the mince and tatties my mother used to make,' he said at one point.

Sweet was jam roly-poly which he absolutely adored. He scoffed down the first helping in seconds, grinning when, without asking, he was immediately given another.

'Smashing!' he said when he was finished.

He was putting on weight again, Susan thought. But she didn't want to tell him that in case it made him angry with her. It had been a long long time since he'd last been to the sports club where they'd met.

'You sit comfy by the fire and finish that bottle of wine,' she said. 'I've just got something to do first, then I'll be with you.'

Rising from her chair she slipped out of the room to the bedroom where the special negligee she'd bought earlier on that day was laid out waiting for her. She stripped naked, looking at herself in a full-length mirror. Not too bad, she thought. But there was room for improvement which was why she was on the diet. Her flesh was firm, her bust still standing up with no hint yet of sag. Her bottom was a little droopy but then it had always been like that. Her tummy and thighs were where she needed to take off a few pounds and she was working on that.

She powdered herself down and then dabbed a brand new perfume on her neck and breasts. She then shrugged into the negligee after which she patted her hair back into place.

Kirk was in an extremely contented mood as he sat by the fire sipping wine. The brewery was going great guns and, thanks to Turk McGhie and his persuasive ways, production was having to be increased every week to keep up with demands. Since the grand launch, nearly all the Glasgow distilleries had been clamouring to see him, wanting him to sell their spirits in his pubs. In the end he'd decided to do a deal with his old pal Andy White at Carswell's. Not because of any sentimentality but for the simple reason Andy had come up with the best terms.

Kirk sighed and refilled his glass. Life was certainly good. He thought of Ciona whom he'd been with before coming home. He'd called at her flat and for an hour they'd tested the new bed he'd insisted on buying her. After several spills off the old three-legged one he'd decided a joke was a joke but to hell with nonsense.

By God, she was a demanding woman, that, who fair took it out of him! he thought. An early night he decided. As usual he had a busy day ahead of him tomorrow. He had a meeting with a man up from England who wanted to try and convince him to can more take-away beer rather than bottling it.

His heart sank the moment Susan re-entered the room. The seductive nightdress, the perfume he could smell even at this distance, all added up to one thing.

Damn! he swore inwardly. He just didn't fancy her after Ciona. And what was more Ciona had drained him so much he wasn't even sure he was capable.

Susan sat by the side of the fire and curled her legs up under her.

'I was out in the park today watching some children play,' she said quietly. 'They really are tremendous fun.'

He grunted.

'It would be such a marvellous thing for us if we could have one.'

'Yes,' he said reluctantly.

She looked into the fire, a coy expression on her face. 'Perhaps if we tried it at different times of the day. Mornings, afternoons, that sort of thing. And if we varied the positions, that might also help.'

'Six days of the week I'm at work mornings and afternoons . . .'

'We could wake up early.'

'I just don't feel like it nowadays at the crack of dawn.'

'There was a time when you did.'

'I didn't have the responsibilities and worry then that I do now,' he said.

'Well what about afternoons? You're the boss. If you want to come home for a little while there's no reason why you can't.'

He barked out a laugh. 'What do you think I do in my office all day? Sit playing with paper clips? There's work to be done, Susan. A great deal of it. There never seem to be enough hours in the working day now as it is, far less taking time off in the middle of it to come home for some hanky-panky.'

'I'm sorry. I was only trying to help,' Susan said miserably.

Kirk stared at his wife, thinking how pathetic she looked. Mind you, there had always been something of that in her but it had never been so pronounced before. Suddenly he found himself repulsed by it, and couldn't help comparing her to the bubbling, vivacious Ciona. It was a comparison Susan didn't come out of well.

'Perhaps we should think of adopting,' she said. 'I know it's not the same but it would be an awful lot better than having no children at all.'

There she was, harping on about bloody children yet again! He knew her father was ringing her during the day from time to time. All that old fart could think about was children too!

Christ! why couldn't they just let things be? There weren't going to be any bloody kids, thanks to that German sow of a countess and the pox she'd given him. But of course Susan didn't know about that, nor could he bring himself to tell her. He felt he would lose face somehow, that his masculinity would lose credit.

What a bloody mess! he thought. For the truth was that secretly he wanted a child as well. He thought bitterly of the baby Minnie had had aborted. It might well have been a boy. His son. That thought had been preying a great deal on his mind of late. If only he'd known what lay in store he could've encouraged Minnie to have the child. He wouldn't have married her, of course, that had never been on the cards. And later, when the child was older, especially if it had been a boy, perhaps some arrangement could've been made.

'I love you, Kirk,' Susan said.

He brought himself out of his reverie. 'Eh?'

'I said I love you.'

'And I love you too.'

Wistfully, 'Do you?'

'You know I do.'

'I sometimes wonder, Kirk.'

He sipped his wine to give him time to think. Did she know something? She couldn't. He and Ciona had been most discreet. And yet there was a knowing look in her eye. Or was that merely his conscience making him see something that wasn't really there?

Susan picked up the poker and stabbed the fire. Ever since discovering about Kirk's affair she'd been unhappy in the way she'd been unhappy as a child. She felt lost, terrifyingly alone again. Abandoned.

Kirk knew he was going to have to make the effort. She'd done herself up especially. Knowing him to be the randy sod he was, she'd twig there was something wrong if he didn't make love to her. Anything else would have been totally uncharacteristic of him.

He laid his empty glass by the empty bottle and came to his feet.

'Let's go on up,' he said.

Later, as he made love to her, she closed her eyes. It was a mechanical thing he was doing to her. His mind was elsewhere.

Inwardly she wept.

Major Keith Gibb frowned as he studied the report he held. Another six free houses, making fourteen this month in all, had served the brewery notice they no longer wished to be supplied with Black Lion beer.

This was getting serious. In fact, if the trend continued this way it would be downright disastrous. For a panicky moment, he felt everything he'd built up over the years since the war slipping away from him. Then his old army discipline reasserted itself and he brought himself back under control. This was only a trend, he told himself reassuringly. A new brewery making something of a hit because of all the razzmatazz surrounding its launch, not to mention the enormous amount of advertising that had gone before and after that launch.

KM '60, the drink of tomorrow here today, he thought scornfully. The beer itself was dreadful. He'd sampled it personally.

No, all this was a flash in the pan. A novelty that would soon lose impact. What he had to do was sit tight and weather the onslaught. The tide would turn back in his favour soon enough.

There were four burly barmen and the manager had been a

well-known boxer in his day. It was the biggest challenge Turk McGhie had faced so far.

'I'm happy enough with Donaldson's beers,' McKenna, the manager, said.

'Perhaps you should take time to think it over,' Turk suggested politely.

'I know your type,' McKenna said. 'You're a troublemaker. A hard man. Well I don't like people like that in this club. In fact I actively discourage them. Do I make myself clear?'

McGhie knew he hadn't a hope, even if he was to use his razors, against these five. They were too big and too many.

'Every other free house and licence in the area has switched over to KM beers,' he said.

'Well good for them. I'll just have to be the odd man out, won't I?'

'You're making a mistake,' Turk said softly.

McKenna's eyes blazed with anger. 'If you try threatening me, you'll be the one making a mistake,' he replied.

Turk shrugged. 'If that's the way you want it.'

'We'll see you out,' one of the barmen said.

When Turk walked to the door he had three escorts. Once outside, he sat on a low wall and lit a cigarette. He blew smoke at the gun-metal grey sky and thought.

The Labour Club was a wooden barn of a place containing a large bar and a hall where fund-raising dances and whist-drives were held. Every Friday and Saturday night, with the exception of the Glasgow Fair when everyone was on holiday, it was jam-packed to the gunwales, at which time it got through an awful lot of beer.

Donaldon's, who supplied their beer, was a small brewery which had already lost most of its few outlets to KM. If it were to lose the Labour Club, it was almost certain to go under.

Turk sat for a good hour on the wall smoking cigarette after cigarette but no solution to his problem came to him. He took a tramcar to his local boozer, finding himself an out-of-the-way seat, where he drank half after half.

The next day he returned to the Labour Club but didn't go

in. Instead he walked round it, viewed it from a distance, watching those who came in and went out, all the time cudgelling his brains for the idea he knew would eventually come.

On the afternoon of the second day, he was walking past a nearby row of tenements when something he saw chalked there caused him to come up short.

The Shamrock Are The Boys! the legend proclaimed. The Shamrock was the name of the local gang. A ferocious, violent lot of youngsters who had a terrible reputation ranking that of the legendary Tongs and Cumbie. The gang held sway over a small area which was a Catholic ghetto surrounded by Protestant neighbours. Relationships between the two groups, as was always the case in Glasgow, were uneasy. The Shamrock, in common with most of the gangs, was divided into two sections. The Wee Shamrock, consisting of boys aged between roughly eight and twelve, and The Big Shamrock, lads between twelve and eighteen.

The Labour Club, situated on some waste ground, bordered on to Shamrock territory but was used mainly by the Protestants, the Catholics having a Hibernian Club they frequented.

Turk moved on to a café where he sat mulling over a cup of tea. The Shamrock was the solution he'd been looking for, he was convinced of that.

Slowly the bits and pieces of a plan fell into place.

On the Friday night, the publican of the pub The Big Shamrock used looked up fearfully as Turk entered. He'd already experienced Turk a few weeks earlier when Turk had persuaded him to take KM beers in place of what he'd sold up until then.

A group of The Big Shamrock stood grouped round the bar. Only a handful of them were of drinking age but the publican would never have dreamed of chiselling them about it. It would have been worth his life to do that. Nor did he have to worry about being prosecuted for selling to minors. Police never came into the pub. They had more sense.

Turk ordered a pint and a half-gill. He was wearing a brand-new baby-blue suit with a white shirt and a thin red tie. He wore more sober clothes when with Kirk, Kirk demanding it, but when out and about on his own he wore the sort of paraffin he liked best.

Several of The Shamrock glanced suspiciously in his direction. They were obviously wondering if he was looking for trouble. For there was no mistaking he was a fighting man. An aura of danger and violence clung to him like a cloud.

He finished off his whisky and then picked up his pint. Hooking the thumb of his free hand in his waistcoat pocket he sauntered over to where The Shamrock stood.

Instantly muscles tensed and hands edged towards hidden weapons.

'You The Shamrock?' Turk demanded.

'What's it to *you*?' one of the bigger lads replied. He had thick, greasy, black hair and beetling eyebrows.

'Heard a lot about you. That's all,' Turk replied, sipping his pint.

'We're well known. And not only hereabouts, either,' the lad said.

Turk nodded. 'That's true enough.'

'So what do you want?'

'Nothing in particular. I don't know anyone in here and then I saw you and I thought I'd just have a wee dauner over. Just to be friendly, like.'

'I've never seen you around here before,' the lad said accusingly.

This was their leader, the kingpin, Turk thought. This was who he'd work on most.

'Naw, I don't come from this part of Glasgow myself. I'm around for a while on business.'

'What sort of business?' another lad demanded.

Turk fixed the lad with a glacial eye. 'That's my affair, sonny,' he replied.

The lad stiffened and took half a pace forward.

Turk gave a frozen smile. 'I'm not looking for trouble. But I was brought up to always mind the questions I asked a body. Never to pry into anything personal. Still, I'm sure it was a slip of the tongue and not meant, eh?' He laughed. 'Tell you what, as we seem to have got off on the wrong foot with one another a wee bit, what do you say I buy you a drink? In fact, I'll buy you all a drink. I had a big win on the dogs today. What do you say?'

'Aye, all right then,' the one he'd called sonny said. Then turning to the leader, 'That okay, Frankie?'

'Sure.'

Turk called the publican over, telling the man to set up pints and whiskies for his good friends here.

'Right away, Turk,' the man replied, busily getting on with it.

'An unusual name that,' said Frankie the leader. 'Should we know you?'

'I'm Turk McGhie.'

Several of the group glanced at one another, respect registering on their faces.

'I've heard of you all right,' said Frankie.

'Aye, well don't believe everything you hear. An awful lot of it's lies,' said Turk pretending mock humility.

'I'm sure,' replied Frankie.

Turk glanced at the bar clock, working out how much time he had.

'Do you fancy the Celts against Queen of the South tomorrow?' he asked.

'Och, the Celts will walk it,' a lad said.

'Do you support them yourself?' Frankie asked.

Turk patted hs left leg and winked. 'I do that.'

The fact he was a Catholic like themselves was an instant bond between The Shamrock lads and Turk.

Whisky and pint followed whisky and pint, all of them paid for by Turk out of his mythical win at the dogs. And the more drink disappeared down their throats, the more The Shamrock accepted him as one of their own.

'How many in your gang then?' Turk asked eventually.

'Sixty in The Big Shamrock, seventy-five in The Wee,' Frankie replied.

Turk whistled. 'That many, eh? I'm impressed.'

'We control this whole area,' Frankie boasted. 'Nothing goes on here but it has our say-so.'

'That a fact? I'm surprised then you let them paint slogans about you the way they do.'

'What slogans?' Frankie demanded.

'The ones on the … Och no, forget it. Let's have another round,' said Turk.

'No come on, what slogans?'

'The ones the prods have written over the walls of that Labour Club over by.'

Frankie glanced at his men who were already looking angry. 'What do these slogans say?' he asked Turk.

'Now I'm only repeating what I saw as you're asking me to do,' said Turk. 'There was one said, "The Shamrock are Fenian poofters", and another said, "The Shamrock are not fit to lick King Billy's boots".'

Frankie's face contorted with fury. Already flushed from drink, it became a beetroot colour.

'There must've been a dozen like that,' Turk added. 'All written in orange paint.'

'Prod bastards,' one of the gang said vehemently.

'More whiskies all round,' Turk called out to the barman. 'And make them big ones.'

'I say we go and kick their heads in,' the one Turk had called sonny said.

'Aye, give them what for!'

'Call all the boys together, Frankie. There's still time the night.'

'We'll murder the whores.'

'Any of them call me a poof to my face and I'll take my bayonet and ram it up his Khyber, so I will!' another of The Shamrock spat out. His mouth split open in a chilling leer, revealing a set of badly rotting teeth.

The last order started to arrive and Turk began passing the glasses round.

'*Could* you get all your lads together tonight?' Turk asked, pressing a glass into Frankie's hand.

'Oh aye.'

'Friday night, that Labour Club will be jumping round about now,' Turk said. 'Probably quite a few of them having a good laugh at your expense. It was the orange paint that got me. Orange! I ask you. They couldn't have got more insulting if they'd tried.'

'Right,' said Frankie, having arrived at a decision. 'We'll call the lads together and then we'll away over there and see what's to do.'

He started issuing orders and a number of those present peeled away to summon the rest of the gang.

'You'll be going in armed, of course?' said Turk.

'Too right and we will,' Frankie retorted.

'Well it looks like it's going to be a hot time in the Labour Club tonight,' said Turk. And ordered more whiskies.

McKenna, the manager of the Labour Club, sat staring into the fire roaring in the grate. His face was badly bruised and one cheek was bandaged and taped where it had been sliced open. It was six o'clock at night and he was home for his tea. He'd been at the club all day long and would be going back again after he'd eaten. The place was an absolute wreck, everything having been either smashed, ripped or broken.

Ding dong! the doorbell went.

'Can you get that, love? I'm busy with the chips,' Chrissie McKenna shouted out from the kitchen.

McKenna grimaced as he rose. He was stiff from the fight.

When he opened the front door, Turk McGhie was revealed standing there. Turk was clutching the hand of Agnes, McKenna's wee lassie of six.

'I had to ask some children playing in the street which was your house and one of them turned out to be your daughter,'

Turk said affably. 'Smashing wee girl she is too.'

McKenna's heart did a flip seeing Agnes with McGhie. 'Away through,' he said to her. 'Tea's almost on the table.'

Agnes ran past her father, calling out to her mother about the nice man who'd given her sixpence for showing him where Daddy lived.

'What do you want?' McKenna asked.

'I heard today about what happened last night. I'm awful sorry.'

McKenna nodded.

'The inside of the club's a complete write-off, I'm told?'

'That's right.'

Turk tut-tutted. 'Could I come in? I have an idea or two that might interest you.'

'We're about to have our tea.'

'It would be to your - and the club's - advantage, Mr McKenna.'

McKenna was shaken by Turk's appearing with his daughter. He didn't like that idea at all. Grimly he thought it might be best to hear Turk out.

McKenna ushered Turk inside to the living room and offered him a seat.

'At least we can be thankful no one was killed,' Turk said.

'I'm surprised no one was,' McKenna replied. 'They came in with swords, bayonets, chains, razors, you name it and they had it. It was sheer bloody pandemonium I can tell you.'

Turk shook his head in sympathy.

'Most of the men were too busy looking after their wives and trying to get them out the hall to get themselves organised properly. In a way that was the worst part of it, having all those women there.'

Turk shook his head again.

'In five minutes they just demolished everything inside that place. It's taken the club members years to get the club the way it was and now they're going to have to start all over again from scratch. It'll cost a fortune.'

'That's one of the reasons I'm here, Mr McKenna. I spoke

to my boss Mr Murray this morning, and he was appalled to hear what had happened. He has to make his offer a business one, of course, you'll appreciate that I'm sure, but he says he's willing to scratch the club's back if they'll scratch his. He'll rebuild the entire bar and kit it out if the club will take his beer as opposed to Donaldson's. That's a handsome offer that'll save the club an awful lot of money. I doubt if you'll find a wee brewery like Donaldson's are willing to do the same. What do you say?'

It *was* a handsome offer. There was no denying that. 'I'll have to put it to the club secretary. That's a decision that isn't up to me alone.'

'I'll tell you what else I'll do, Mr McKenna. I happen to know some of The Shamrock. I'll have a wee drink with Frankie their leader and tell him those daubings were all a mistake and that it wasn't any of your club members who put them there. I'll tell him it was some outsiders, mischief-makers who did it.'

McKenna was no fool. He knew then that McGhie had been instrumental in daubing the club walls. The man was almost admitting as much.

'I mean it would be terrible if the club was to be all done up again only for The Shamrock to pay it another visit. Wouldn't you agree?'

'I would,' McKenna said softly.

'That's settled then. I'll have a word with The Shamrock and you'll speak to your club secretary about KM beer. When the club's made up its mind if you just let us know the decision we'll go ahead with getting the bar rebuilt.' Turk stood. 'I think that's that, then. And I must say that's a grand wee lassie you've got there. A wee charmer if ever there was. Going to grow up to be really pretty too. You must be proud of her?'

'We are.'

'Heard a story recently about a wee lassie over in Partick who was out playing one night, just like your Agnes was now, when some animal got hold of her and took a razor to her. They say it's just awful to see her now.'

A cold sweat had formed on McKenna's brow. He wasn't scared in the least of McGhie, not for himself that is. But he was for his wife and daughter. They were his Achilles' heel.

'Now what sort of mind does a thing like that?' Turk demanded.

'God alone knows.'

At the door McGhie said affably. 'We'll look forward to hearing from you. And I hope it isn't too long before the club's back on its feet again. We at KM Brewery will certainly give it every support we can. Goodbye now.' And with a cheery wave he set off down the street.

McKenna closed the door and stood stock-still for a moment. He didn't have any doubts at all that McGhie would carry out the threat against Agnes should KM not get the club business. A man like McGhie didn't make idle threats.

'Tea's on the kitchen table,' Chrissie McKenna said, appearing in the hallway. 'What was all that about?'

'Just a little bit of business, that's all,' McKenna replied.

All through tea he couldn't keep his eyes off Agnes's face, thinking about what McGhie had said about the wee lassie – imaginary or otherwise, it didn't matter – over in Partick.

As McGhie passed the Labour Club he glanced up at the various daubings that had caused so much trouble. It was amazing what you could accomplish with some whisky and a can of orange paint, he thought.

And, grinning, he continued on his way.

Kirk entered Ciona's flat holding an already chilled jeroboam of champagne. 'It's celebration time!' he announced.

'What's the occasion, then?' Ciona asked, producing glasses.

'Today Donaldson's Brewery packed it in. That's one less competitor for yours truly and the first of the many who're going to go to the wall in the next couple of years.'

Champagne frothed and gurgled as he poured. 'The day's not all that far away when there will only be one beer made and sold in Glasgow. Mine!'

'You sound pretty certain of that.'

'I am.'

'So you're aiming for a monopoly in Glasgow?'

'Ah!' said Kirk, drinking. 'There's nothing quite like champagne.' Then turning his attention back to Ciona. 'That's right. That's the trend in the beer industry. Bigger, larger, all encompassing.'

He sat and beckoned her to his side. He kissed her, lingering on her lips which he'd often told her were the softest he'd ever known.

'I could eat you,' he whispered.

'You say the nicest things.'

'Especially when I'm randy.'

'When aren't you randy?'

'With you? Never,' he replied.

Ciona laughed softly and sipped her champagne. 'So when did you get this monopoly idea?' she asked.

'Had it for some time now. The way I see it, chances are high there will only be two or three breweries functioning in Scotland at the end of this decade or the middle of the next. It's already happening in England, and what happens there happens up here soon after.'

'But two or three? Surely there will be more than that?'

'It's possible, of course. It may slim down to half a dozen big breweries and stop there, if left to its own devices, that is. But I'll tell you this: having seen the possibility of there being one and one only brewery in Glasgow, I intend making absolutely sure that situation comes about, and furthermore that the brewery to whom the prize falls is mine.'

His eyes suddenly took on a faraway look. 'Why not?' he said to himself.

'Why not what?'

'Well, I saw it as two or three breweries left. But what if they were all owned by the same person?'

'Like you?'

'It's a mind-boggling thought, isn't it?'

'Don't they have laws against that sort of thing?'

391

Kirk snorted. 'There are always ways and means round laws. Especially where that sort of money would be involved.'

He lay back in the couch and gazed off into space. 'It would be a lifetime's work, but what an achievement to pull it off.'

'Well no one could certainly ever accuse you of lack of ambition,' Ciona said.

Kirk brought himself back to reality. 'But first there's Glasgow to contend with. And Black Lion Brewery in particular. They're my main competitors. I've got them on the slide but I'm still a long way from delivering the coup de grâce. But it'll come, oh yes, it'll come.'

He fingered his scar. 'And I can't tell you how much I'm looking forward to that day.'

Ciona tried to smile but the smile died on her face. There was something in Kirk's tone which made the hairs on her arms stir and rise.

Susan lay in the darkness listening to Kirk stumbling up the stairs. When he entered the bedroom the lights snapped on, causing her to blink.

He stood swaying, staring down at her. He wore a foolish grin on his face.

'You're drunk,' Susan said.

'Get away! How clever of you to figure that one out,' he slurred.

'Who were you with?'

'That's my business. But if you must know, one of my pub managers.'

Susan swung herself out of bed. 'Let me give you a hand to get undressed. You'll never manage on your own.'

The moment she came close to him she knew he'd lied to her. He'd been, as she'd suspected, with Ciona Crammond. The perfume clinging to him was one she'd come to know.

Suddenly something snapped in her. She wasn't going to take any more of this. She'd had enough. The guilt she felt at failing to conceive was swamped by anger and humiliation.

'How dare you come home reeking of another woman and

expect to get into bed with me? How *dare* you!'

Kirk blinked, the same foolish grin still plastered all over his face.

'Don't think I don't know what's been going on. You've been sleeping with that slut Ciona Crammond ever since your beers were launched, maybe before, for all I know. Do you think I'm stupid or something? That I haven't got two eyes in my head or a nose to smell with? You stink of her!'

'Now hold on a minute, Susan –' Kirk said.

'And don't try and soft soap me. I want it to stop, here and now, understand?'

'You've got it all wrong ...'

'Like heck I have,' she interrupted.

'Ciona and I are just good friends.'

Susan barked out a laugh. 'You *are* drunk if that's the best you can come up with.'

'No honestly, I've never touched her.'

'Don't lie to me, Kirk.'

Kirk's good humour began to evaporate; the beginnings of violence bubbled in his stomach.

Susan went on, her voice thinning and becoming shrill. 'It's finished after tonight. I want your word on that.'

'Aw, go to hell.'

'Kirk!'

'Stop moaning, woman. You're becoming a pain in the backside.'

'If I am moaning it's because I've got plenty to moan about. I'm sorry I can't give you a baby ...'

'Don't bring *that* up again, for God's sake!' He stopped as a thought came to him. 'Has the old fart been on the phone again to you? Has that been what's triggered all this off?'

'Daddy didn't ring ...'

'Babies! The old bugger's absolutely demented by them. Or should I say *boy* babies. There's a difference as far as he's concerned, isn't there?'

Kirk took his jacket off and threw it across a chair. He then tore his tie from round his neck and hurled it into a corner.

'That bloody man! Well I'll get him yet. You just see if I don't.

'Babies, babies,' Kirk muttered a few seconds later, holding his head in his hands. 'Why do you and he always have to be going on about them?'

'I won't let our marriage be wrecked by this affair,' said Susan.

'Shut up!' growled Kirk.

'If you haven't the guts to end it with her then I'll do it for you.'

Crossing to the bedside table Susan picked up the telephone there. She flicked open a small directory, knowing Ciona's number to be in it. There had been a number of times during the ad campaign when Kirk had had to ring her legitimately on business.

'Get away from there!' Kirk slurred.

Susan, a look of determination on her face, started to dial.

'I said get away from there, Susan!'

Susan completed dialling and waited for the rings to start. She should have done this before now, she told herself. But she'd hoped Kirk's affair with Ciona a thing that would soon blow over. Only it hadn't.

Kirk stumbled across the room. The inside of his head was numb and everything was beginning to go hazy at the edges.

'Give that phone to me!' he snarled.

Susan gasped as his hand clamped on her wrist. 'Let me go!' she exclaimed.

'Give it to me!'

'Hello?' Ciona's voice said.

Kirk desperately tugged on the phone, trying to jerk it from Susan's grasp, but she hung on doggedly, determined not to let it go.

'Hello who is this, please?' Ciona's voice asked.

With a roar Kirk backhanded Susan across the face, she screamed as her head snapped back.

'What's going on there?' Ciona's voice demanded.

Kirk hit Susan again and again till at last she fell backwards off the chair to collapse on the floor in a heap.

Chest heaving Kirk replaced the phone on its cradle, while at his feet Susan cried into the carpet.

'Teach you to do as you're told,' he said, adding after a few seconds, 'Stupid cow.' He lurched over to the bed and sat down. Everything was turning round and round, and he felt decidedly sick. Groaning, he fell sideways, where he curled into a foetal ball. The picture and sensation in his head was of himself falling from a towering skyscraper. He whimpered as the ground rushed up to meet him.

Just before he hit the ground he lapsed into unconsciousness.

'Oh my God!' Kirk said, coming awake. He'd never felt so dreadful.

He rolled onto his back and then ran a hand over his stubbled face. Dehydration had made his tongue feel twice its normal size.

Something had happened the night before, but what? Minnie kept popping into his mind. He'd had a go at her, or hit her or ... But Minnie was years ago. So what? ... who? ...

'Christalmighty!' he husked as it came back to him. He'd hit Susan. Yes that was it. The memory was jumbled but he had most of it now. A glance told him her side of the bed hadn't been slept in. So where was she?

He gasped with pain as he came to his feet. Clutching his head he staggered to the bathroom where he swallowed a couple of tablets and a number of glasses of water.

He found her in the kitchen where she was already dressed and eating her breakfast. He came up short when he saw her face.

One eye had a hideous purply-black swelling underneath it. And what had been the white part of the eye was now blood red. Her nose was swollen and there was a scratch on one cheek.

He sat facing her, noting his hands were trembling from the after-effects of the alcohol when he laid them on the table.

'Where did you sleep?' he asked.

'The lounge settee.'

'I, eh ...' He licked his lips. 'I'm sorry, Susan. Truly I am. I don't know what came over me.'

Susan crunched toast and regarded him steadily.

'What can I do to make it up?'

'Get rid of Ciona Crammond.'

He lowered his gaze, staring at the tablecloth and running his fingers over it.

Susan said very quietly, 'The only reason I haven't gone back to Mummy and Daddy this morning is I can't bear the thought of proving them right about you. That you're the peasant they always claimed you to be.'

He cringed when she said that, as she'd known he would.

He reached out to take her hand but she snatched hers away. 'Don't touch me!' she hissed, fury and indignation in her voice.

He was genuinely appalled at what he'd done. Another look at her face caused him to grimace. Poor bitch, he thought.

'Well?' Susan demanded.

'All right. I'll end it today,' he said reluctantly.

'You swear?'

He nodded.

'And there will be no more ... tarts?'

'No more,' he whispered.

Susan pursed her lips. She didn't know whether to believe him or not. But time would tell.

'You'd better hurry up. You're already late for work,' she said.

As was usually the case with him after a heavy drinking bout he was starving. 'I could eat a horse,' he said.

Susan rose to her feet. 'Then you'd better cook one,' she replied. And swept from the room.

Two months later, Susan knew Kirk was back seeing Ciona Crammond again. There were so many things gave it away. The odd trace of perfume. The occasional guilty look in his eye when he thought she wasn't watching him. The over-elaborate explanations of where he'd been and what he'd been doing there. And then the most significant of all. The many nights that passed without him trying to approach her sexually. With his sex drive, that was a dead give-away.

She thought of leaving him, taking a flat on her own. But somehow that idea didn't really appeal. Probably because her parents would then know her marriage had broken down, and she didn't want that.

The idea came to her when she was standing at a window watching a horse and cart trundle by. The horse was old and bowed from a lifetime's hard work. Her heart went out to the beast, making her think of the animals she'd had as a child.

That was it, she thought. She needed something to take her mind off things. And she was a qualified vet, after all, so why didn't she set up practice? It would occupy her days and she would be accomplishing something worthwhile in the process.

The idea excited her and she couldn't wait to get cracking.

The first thing was to find premises and then ... She wondered briefly if she should ask Kirk if he minded. Why should I? she thought. Why the hell should I!

When she had occasion to mention it she'd *tell* him what she was going to do.

Eddy King was doing the rounds of his pubs one night when he saw an old familiar face sitting dejectedly in a corner hunched over a pint.

He bought two large whiskies and strolled over. 'Hello Norrie, how are tricks?' he said, placing one of the whiskies beside the pint.

Norrie Smart looked up at Eddy, and on recognising him his face broke into a grin. 'Help my bob! Where did you spring from?'

Eddy laughed and sat. 'It's good to see you again. What about the others? Do you ever see them?'

'Naw. Although I did hear from somebody that Ogle

emigrated to Canada. You know about Kirk Murray, of course? I keep reading about him in the paper. He's big-time now. Owns this new KM Brewery.'

'Yes, I know about him,' Eddy replied.

'You two used to be pals when we were first in Germany. But something happened between you. The others in the section never found out what.'

'We stopped being pals and that's the way it remained.'

Smart suddenly laughed. 'Remember Meany and that drinking contest you two had? And him so pished at the end of it he started bashing up officers.'

'Mean by name and mean by nature!' said Eddy, doing his best to imitate Meany.

Smart laughed. 'Then Kirk became corporal, and when he lost his stripes because of catching a dose they made you one.'

Eddy swallowed his whisky. 'Seeing you fairly takes me back.'

Looking embarrassed, Smart pushed his glass around the table. 'Listen, I'm helluva sorry but I can't buy you one back,' he said, adding, 'I'm out of work.'

'Don't worry about it,' Eddy replied quickly. 'I've got more than enough for the two of us.'

Eddy went back to the bar and bought two more large whiskies and a brace of pints.

'You're a toff, so you are,' said Smart when the fresh drinks were placed in front of him.

'So how come you're not grafting?' Eddy asked.

'I keep getting the sack because of my headaches.'

'What headaches are these?'

'I wasn't home long from Germany when one Saturday morning I was out playing football with the boys. A real good kick-around, that sort of thing. Anyway I go charging into the goalmouth and the next thing I know I'm flat on my back having whacked my head against the post. A few weeks after that the headaches started, migraine, the doctor calls it. They're really hellish Eddy. When I have one, all I can do is lie in bed with the blankets pulled up over my head waiting for it to stop. Two days, three sometimes before it goes away. As you can imagine, employers aren't very keen when you start having that sort of time off at least once a month. I'm sure most of them think I'm skiving but it's just not true.'

'I'm awful sorry to hear that, Norrie.'

'Makes life difficult, I can tell you. Especially now I'm married with a wean.'

'Congratulations!'

Smart looked pleased with himself. 'Aye, she's a real nice woman. You'd like her.'

'I'm sure.'

'And the wee fella's a right humdinger. A chip off the old block.'

Eddy thought for a few seconds before asking, 'What is it you do, Norrie?'

'Plastering.'

'I see.'

'Why? Do you know someplace I might get a start?'

'I do. But not as a plasterer. How do you fancy being a bar cellarman?'

'You mean in a pub?'

'That's right. One down the road called The Bowlers' Tavern.'

'That would be grand,' replied Smart. 'Why, do you know the owner or something?'

Eddy grinned. 'I *am* the owner. Just as I'm the owner of this place we're drinking in now.'

'You're not pulling my leg now, are you?'

'Not only The Bowlers' Tavern and this pub but thirteen others as well. All of them round about here.'

Smart whistled. 'Christ, you have got on, haven't you! You're almost as big a success story as Murray.'

'Not quite,' said Eddy. 'But I'm working at it. So – what about the job then, eh? I'll make allowances for your migraines and keep you covered at all times.'

'If you'll lend me a pound in advance I'd like to buy you a drink on that,' Norrie Smart said.

Eddy handed over a fiver. 'Get them in and then we'll away down to The Bowlers' and I'll introduce you around. You can start Monday.'

'This is my lucky day. You won't regret taking me on, honest, Eddy.'

Eddy laughed. 'I believe you.'

Smart made his way across to the bar to get another round in.

It was late that night after the pubs had closed that Eddy got a phone call from Willie Crerar who managed The Exchange Bar for him.

'Aye, what is it, Willie?' Eddy asked.

'There was a geezer in here from KM Brewery wanting me to change over to their beer. I told him it was nothing to do with me and that he should speak to you. He said he would do that and asked for your address, which I gave him. Maybe I shouldn't have done that, Mr King, but quite frankly he scared the bejeesus out of me.'

'Did you get his name, Willie?'

'No. Sorry.'

'All right Willie. Thanks for letting me know.'

'You just be careful, Mr King. Yon's the queerest brewery representative I've ever come across. He's got bad news written all over him.'

'I'll be careful Willie. 'Bye now.'

Eddy cradled the phone and stared thoughtfully at the wall. All his pubs sold Black Lion beer and he had no intention of changing breweries. And if he had he certainly wouldn't have gone to KM. It was the principle of the thing, Black Lion belonging to Kirk.

Not that he would have had all that much choice of breweries to change to anyway, he thought grimly. The number of breweries in the city was decreasing every year, with one after the other going to the wall, all of them forced out of business by KM, which was expanding at a phenomenal rate.

'Eddy, are you coming through?' a female voice called from the bedroom. Eddy grinned. Maisie was a new barmaid who'd come to work for him recently.

Pulling pints wasn't the only thing she was good at.

The following mid-morning, Eddy was sitting at the table doing some paper work when there was a knock at the front door. Some sixth sense told him the man from KM Brewery had come calling. And he was right.

'Mr King?' Turk McGhie inquired.

Eddy nodded.

'I wonder if I could come in and talk to you?'

Eddy ushered McGhie through to the front room. Willie Crerar had been right. This one positively exuded violence and mayhem.

'My name's McGhie and I represent KM Brewery,' Turk said, having declined the offer of a seat.

The man's eyes were mesmeric, Eddy thought. They reminded him of those belonging to an eagle he'd once seen at Calderpark Zoo.

'I called at one of your pubs last night and your manager was good enough to give me your address,' McGhie said. 'Neither myself nor the brewery realised that many of the pubs round about there were owned by the one man. You, Mr King.'

'Fifteen, to be precise,' said Eddy.

'Yes, that checks with the list I made up,' Turk replied.

'Did you now?'

Turk's pale blue eyes bored into Eddy. 'As you probably know we've been operational in the north, west and east of Glasgow up until now –'

'And now you want to move into central Glasgow. The town itself,' Eddy cut in.

'That's correct.'

Eddy stuck a cigarette in his mouth and lit up. He regarded Turk McGhie through a streamer of cloud. He'd wondered a number of times in the past why so many independents had changed seemingly *en masse* to KM Brewery. The reason was now becoming obvious.

Eddy said slowly, 'The town pubs being the juiciest plums of all, catering as they do not only to the town itself's needs but also the entire south side, which, of course, is dry.'

'And with more and more people being moved out to south-side housing schemes, the town pubs are going to be doing even better still in future,' Turk added.

'Which is why you want them to sell your beer and not Black Lion, as most of them do now.'

'The people aren't very happy with Black Lion beer of late,' Turk said. 'It's said they put out a bad batch as a result of which two men are supposed to have died and another gone insane.'

'I've heard that rumour myself. But nobody seems to know who these men were or are. No names, just anonymous hearsay.'

'It's said that there's no smoke without fire.'

Eddy stared at Turk for a few seconds in silence. Finally he said, 'And what happens if I decline your offer to switch my business from Black Lion to KM?'

McGhie raised an eyebrow. That simple gesture spoke volumes.

'I think I'm beginning to see.'

'We can be very persuasive when we put our minds to it,' Turk said. 'I haven't yet met anyone I've failed to convert to KM.'

'There's always a first time.'

McGhie's thin smile was truly frightening. A tremor of fear ran up Eddy's back to play for a few seconds across his shoulder-blades.

'What's the brewery's number?' Eddy asked.

McGhie frowned. He hadn't been expecting that question. He spoke the number after which Eddy crossed to the phone and dialled. When through to the brewery, Eddy asked to speak to Mr Murray. And when the girl said Mr Murray might well be tied up Eddy told her to tell him it was Eddy King on the line.

Turk watched Eddy through slitted eyes that seemed never to blink.

'Eddy! How are you?' Kirk's voice said.

'Fine. Never better. And you?'

'In the pink.'

'Well, certainly in the money since you took over the old Thistle Brewery.'

Kirk chuckled. 'And how are the used cars getting on?'

'I wouldn't know. I never went back to selling them.'

'Oh?'

'I decided to take an old pal's advice and go into booze. Can't fail with booze in Glasgow he used to tell me. And what's more, he was right.'

'Well, well, well,' said Kirk, a new tone in his voice.

'I own some pubs in the town ...'

'Pubs! You mean two or three? You have done well for yourself.'

'Fifteen, Kirk. All bought, paid for and doing nicely, thank you.'

'Whose beer do you sell then? Mine, I hope. I won't forgive you if you don't.'

'Well, that's why I'm ringing you actually. I've got a representative of yours here who's trying to persuade me to ditch Black Lion and come over to you. His name's McGhie.'

There was a pause and then Kirk said. 'I'll tell you what, why don't you and I get together for lunch and talk over old times? I'd enjoy that, what about you?'

'Fine. As long as you pay.'

'It'll be my pleasure to. And listen, I am sorry I never contacted you after we got back from Germany but you know how things are? I just never seemed to have the time.'

'Same with me,' Eddy lied.

They talked for a few more minutes, making a time and date for when the lunch would take place.

Eddy hung up and turned to find those ice-cold eagle eyes boring into him. 'All right?' he asked.

McGhie nodded his head fractionally, the expression on his face telling Eddy he'd made himself an enemy.

'You know the way out,' Eddy said.

Turk McGhie left the house without saying another word. And when he was gone Eddy had the intense urge to get a duster and polish out and clean everywhere McGhie had either touched or stood.

Instead he made himself a cup of very strong tea but even the four sugars he heaped into it didn't take away the sourness McGhie's visit had left in his mouth.

He thought of Leoni and the hand gripping the cup tightened. 'Not twice, my old son,' he said aloud. 'Not bloody twice!'

'You've got fat,' said Eddy, shaking Kirk's hand.

'I wouldn't exactly say that.'

'I would. Look at your belly, it's like a rubber tyre.'

Kirk smiled daggers. It always irked him to have his ever-increasing weight referred to.

They sat and the wine-waiter appeared. Kirk ordered, without consulting Eddy, choosing a particularly heavy Bordeaux.

Eddy hated Bordeaux, always finding it sat like lead on his stomach. He decided to let it go. He'd have a few token sips and leave it at that.

'Fifteen pubs, eh?' Kirk said. 'You *have* come up in the world.'

'Not as much as some I could name not a million miles from here,' Eddy replied.

Kirk laughed. 'I've been lucky.'

'Where you're concerned, Kirk, luck rarely has anything to do with it. You were always the man to make your own opportunties.'

'Like Heather Dew and the Russian run?'

'Certainly gave me enough money to get started,' Eddy acknowledged.

Kirk nodded, his eyes twinkling. He seemed to find that amusing.

'Did you get married?' Kirk asked.

'Nope. Haven't found the right girl yet.'

'And you still haven't forgiven me for Leoni. I can read it in your face.'

'I was never an easy forgiver. Especially about the important things.'

'We are what we are, Eddy. There's no changing that.'

'Sounds like an excuse to me.'

Kirk smiled suddenly, but there was the hint of something far deeper than the present conversation behind the smile. 'Anyway I paid for my indiscretion. Remember?'

'How could I forget?'

'There but for the grace of God, eh?'

'I don't know. She might not have felt the need to cheat on me.'

Anger flashed in Kirk's eyes and then was gone.

'So, now you're moving into the town pubs,' Eddy said.

'That's right.'

'All my pubs are supplied by Black Lion, with whom I have no complaint whatsoever.'

'They're getting an awful bad name of late.'

'Your man McGhie mentioned that. But, as I told him, it's only wild rumour. Anonymous hearsay, Kirk. Nothing more.'

'You can say what you like. I wouldn't be too happy swallowing a pint of theirs. I care about what I put down my throat.'

Eddy shook his head. 'You're right. The leopard doesn't change its spots. Especially when it's called Kirk Murray.'

The wine arrived and while it was being poured they placed their order.

'So you don't want to switch over to KM then?' Kirk said, when they were once more alone.

'Correct.'

There was a pause before Kirk went on. 'I like you, Eddy. Always have done. And what's more I still feel a little guilty over the Leoni thing. That's why I asked you to lunch today. So I can personally make you see sense. To make amends for what I did to you in the past.'

Eddy smiled thinly. 'You persuade me rather than let your hard man try to do it. Is that what you mean?'

'Let me tell you why I bought the old Thistle Brewery,' Kirk said. And went on to tell Eddy what his mother had originally pointed out to him and how this had formed itself as a plan in his mind for KM Brewery to end up with a Glasgow monopoly.

When Kirk had finished talking, Eddy sat back in his chair and stared at Kirk in astonishment. 'Can you do it?' he asked.

'I believe so. It'll perhaps take a few more years yet, but it'll come. Once I control the majority of town pubs, on top of those already selling my beer, I will have cut the feet from under my main rival – Black Lion. By that time, they'll be in such reduced circumstances it will be relatively easy for me to buy them out, take them over, or whatever. And with Black Lion gone, there will be nothing to stop me. KM Brewery will be number one in Glasgow and the surrounding districts. There will be no number two.'

Kirk paused before continuing. 'By that time, of course, anyone who doesn't want to sell my beer will have no beer at all to sell. With no alternative, they either change their mind or close. I'd hate to see that happen to you, Eddy.'

'There's always Edinburgh beer. Or Belhaven down in Dunbar. What's to stop an enterprising publican selling them?'

'It's a possibility I've already considered. The short-term answer is Turk McGhie. It's amazing the amount of accidents there are on the Edinburgh road, for example. That stretch is a veritable death trap. Particularly with heavy waggons.'

'And the long-term?'

'With Glasgow under my belt, who's to say I won't be

casting my eye over the country as a whole? If a certain brewery was trying to ship into Glasgow then I might turn my attention in its direction. I think you would find that would deter most of them.'

'You really have this all figured out, haven't you?'

'If you're going to do something, then do it well. My mother used to always say that.'

'Along with: if you're going to bother to think at all, then think big.'

Kirk grinned. 'I see you remember.'

All this had given Eddy an enormous amount of food for thought. The flat refusal he'd come ready to give couldn't possibly be his answer now. This needed a great deal more thinking on.

Kirk went on. 'As KM gets bigger and bigger I'll need to delegate authority. Manager in control of this, manager in control of that. High heid bummers, as they say.'

'Are you offering me a job?' Eddy asked.

'Sell me your pubs and I'll make you one of the top men in the organisation.'

'And if I don't?'

'Then at least stock KM. The alternative is to end up with fifteen pubs and no beer to sell in them. Or spirits come to that. For by then, not one local distillery would dare cross me. I'll be their largest, and only, local bulk buyer then, you see.'

'I'll have to think about this,' Eddy replied slowly. 'I mean you've hit me with an awful lot today.'

'Take as long as you need. A month say, you should be able to make up your mind in that, surely?'

The meal arrived and Kirk tucked in with relish.

Eddy merely toyed with his. He'd been hungry on arrival, but he wasn't any more.

'Wh... wh...!' Major Keith Gibb mumbled, as the telephone by his bedside clamoured into life.

Switching on the bedside lamp he glanced at the alarm clock, frowning when he saw it was only a few minutes past five A.M. Who in God's teeth could be ringing him at this unholy hour?

'Yes?' he snapped into the phone.

'Major Gibb?'

'Speaking.'

'Detective Inspector Hamilton, sir. I thought you'd want to be contacted personally. Your pub The Black Lion is on fire.'

Keith was instantly wide awake. 'How bad is it?'

'Pretty bad, sir. The firemen are doing everything they can, but the flames had already taken a firm grip before any of us got here.'

'Thank you for ringing and I'll be there as soon as possible,' Keith said and hung up.

'What is it?' Jean asked, raising herself on to one elbow.

In a few terse sentences he told her.

Jean's face hardened. This on top of all the other worries. Was there no end to it?

Keith swung himself out of bed and started to dress. His face was drawn and haggard. What had once been a well-fleshed robust body was now thin and spindly, the belly projecting as though gas had been pumped into it. Keith had to stop when he started to cough. Groping for his handkerchief, he brought it to his mouth and spluttered into it.

'Perhaps you shouldn't go?' Jean suggested tentatively.

He shook his head and then coughed again before replying. 'I have to,' he said. 'It's not just any pub. It's The Black Lion itself.'

Jean nodded. She understood.

When he was gone she too rose from her bed and got dressed. Any further sleep would have been impossible.

Twenty minutes later Keith arrived at the scene of the fire. Leaving his car he crossed to where a small knot of policemen stood, one of whom quickly identified himself as Detective Inspector Hamilton.

Keith stared at the roaring flames shooting high into the early-morning sky. Other flames shot from windows while yet others licked round the building.

408

'Everybody out?' he asked.

'Yes,' Hamilton replied.

The intense heat hammered at Keith's face. In a well-organised fashion, fireman ran hither and yon, playing out even more hoses, redirecting those already operational, shouting instructions to one another.

The pub was a write-off. There was no doubt about that. All that was left for the firemen to do was try and contain the blaze and stop it spreading to the neighbouring buildings.

'Any idea yet how it started?' Keith asked.

'Not so far,' Hamilton replied. 'There will be a full inquiry of course.'

Keith turned his attention back to the flames and the building they were intent on consuming.

The Black Lion was the biggest and best, the showpiece, of the pubs the brewery owned. For years, it had been a shining gem in the brewery's crown, an early Victorian masterpiece that had been lovingly preserved and cared for.

It was insured, of course, but money couldn't replace that Victorian interior or façade. Aesthetically, they were irreplaceable. The pub could be rebuilt. Not in its old form but a new one. But that would take time, the entire building being gutted even as he watched. And while it remained closed, yet another outlet, and the one most previous to it, had been lost to the brewery.

The heart and fight went out of Keith then. He was beaten and knew it.

The trouble was, he thought, he was an admin man. And a damn good one too! But this sort of business, and what had been happening ever since KM came into existence, was beyond him.

Gerald might have known how to cope, he thought bitterly. But then, he wasn't his brother. And that admission to himself caused his bony shoulders to slump even further.

He looked quickly up as with a great roar one of the walls caved in. Some onlookers screamed, as sparks and flaming debris burst around the holocaust like a roman candle going

409

off. Those windows remaining started to pop, sending shards of glass flying everywhere.

'I think we'd better move back, sir,' Hamilton said.

Keith was lost in his thoughts.

'I said I think we'd better move back, sir!'

'Yes ... yes I think you're probably right,' Keith replied.

For the next four hours he and the policeman stood side by side, occasionally talking but mainly saying nothing, until, at long last, the fire was extinguished.

The Black Lion pub was no more, the three-storey building having been reduced to a one-storey blackened shell, from which the occasional wisp of smoke still rose.

Keith thanked Hamilton for calling him and then thanked the chief fireman for the job his men had done. Wearily, he walked to his car and drove to the brewery. He'd never taken a day off from his work yet and, no matter that he felt wretched as could be, he certainly wasn't going to start now.

Once in his office he sent out for a razor. And after he'd washed and shaved he felt somewhat better.

'You've a Mr King to see you, sir. He made the appointment yesterday but in light of what's happened I'm sure he'd understand if you said you preferred to see him another day.'

Keith opened his diary and glanced at the small notation he'd made regarding the appointment. This refreshed his memory as to who King was.

'No. I'll see him now,' Keith said. 'Send him through.'

Eddy had never met the Major before, always having dealt with subordinates. But this time he wanted the top man himself.

'Now, what can I do for you, Mr King?' Keith asked, as Eddy entered the room.

'First of all, let me say how sorry I was to hear this morning's news. The Black Lion was a grand old pub, one of Glasgow's finest.'

'Yes,' replied Keith looking sad. 'It'll be a great loss. Not only to the brewery but the community as a whole, I'd say.

They just don't build public houses like that any more, nor do I think they ever will again.'

'Have they any idea what started the blaze?'

'Not yet, but I'm assured there will be an inquiry. I suspect however the verdict is going to be cause or causes unknown.'

Eddy detected the bitterness in the Major's voice, and he guessed the Major was thinking of Turk McGhie, as indeed had he after hearing about the fire.

Keith's lips thinned as a sudden pain spasmed through him. His fingers sought out his stomach which he held until the spasm had passed.

'Sorry about that,' he said, seeing the look of concern on Eddy's face. Pulling open a drawer, he groped for the pills he kept there, two of which he washed down with a glass of water.

Eddy waited till the Major had regained his composure before saying, 'I had lunch with Kirk Murray of KM Brewery a few days back. He wants me to leave Black Lion and transfer my business to him.'

'Lunch, eh?' mused the Major. 'Not like him to give the personal touch for that sort of thing.'

'We used to be friends once upon a time.'

Keith raised an eyebrow. 'Used to be?'

'We did our national service together. We ... eh ... sort of fell out. I don't wish to elaborate.'

'I understand. So if you're not friends, are you enemies?'

'Not quite to the point of hostility ... yet,' Eddy said.

'Well, he's *my* enemy,' Keith replied. This was a conversation he would previously have been unlikely to indulge in. But with the burning of The Black Lion, he just didn't care any more. He tapped his cheek. 'You know the scar he has there?'

Eddy nodded.

'Well I gave it to him.'

Eddy gawped, so unexpected had that been. '*You* did?'

'For impertinence. You do know he's married to my daughter, don't you?'

Eddy shook his head. This again was news.

411

'Married her for the brewery, I always maintained. Only he didn't get it. I made sure of that.' Then as an afterthought, 'At least I have so far.'

'That's what I've come to talk to you about, sir. Kirk is convinced he'll either buy you out or else close you down. He intends KM beer to be the only one bought and sold in Glasgow.'

'Yes. I already guessed that to be what he had in mind.'

'He wants me to sell my pubs to him. Or, failing that, at least to sell his beer. If I don't comply with either, and he gets total control of Glasgow, as he says he will, he'll eventually cut off my supply. No beer and no spirits.'

'And what do you think of that?'

'I was hoping for your assurance that Black Lion won't go under.'

Keith closed his eyes and sighed. 'Believe me there's nothing would please me more than to give you that assurance. Unfortunately I can't. You see, he's got me every way.'

'How so, Major?'

'Well to start with he's been taking away my outlets right, left and centre. I'm now down to a third of what I had when KM opened. And every week there are new outlets to add to the casualty list.'

Keith stood and crossed to a window through which he stared out over Glasgow. 'Eventually I suppose the situation will get to me having only the brewery pubs as outlets, and unless he burns *those* down, I could hang on, a rump situation of what the brewery had formerly been. Unfortunately I'm an extremely sick man, Mr King. The same sort of cancer that killed my brother Gerald. And when I go, the brewery will go to my wife and after her, our only child and daughter, Mrs Kirk Murray. I'd imagine the Black Lion label will disappear about a week after that happens, and the brewery itself will become a subsidiary of KM, the old Thistle that was.'

'I see,' replied Eddy, adding in a softer tone, 'and I'm sorry to hear about your illness.'

'I would sell,' went on Keith. 'But who would buy, given the

412

present situation? A few years ago, if I'd put Black Lion on the market, there would have been a dozen takers. Today I'd be surprised if I even got an inquiry.'

Keith sighed and knotted his fists. 'If only I was twenty years younger. If only I had more of my brother Gerald in me. I would fight that man to hell and back. I disliked Murray vehemently the moment I clapped eyes on him. He's a scoundrel through and through, and it breaks my heart to know that one day he'll get what he was after, all those years ago when he married our Susan: to own this place.'

Eddy thought of Leoni. 'He's ruthless, all right. He'll stop at nothing to get what he wants. I found that out to my cost. He knows damn well I won't work for him and be his toady so I suppose I'll have to opt for the alternative and sell his beer,' said Eddy, adding with great feeling, 'but by Christ, it's going to hurt! The very thought brings bile to my throat!'

'If only I could find a buyer for this place. Someone really strong, with the guts to defy him! I tell you, Mr King, I'd die a happy man.'

Keith was half-way back to his desk when he stopped as though he had run into a brick wall. A curious glint came into his eyes as he fastened his gaze on Eddy.

'Perhaps there is such a man after all,' he said softly. 'A man who hates Murray almost as much as me.'

'Who?' said Eddy, frowning. When the Major didn't reply but merely continued to stare at him, the penny suddenly dropped.

'*I* couldn't afford the Black Lion Brewery!' he exclaimed. 'It's way outside my pocket.'

'Maybe not. I could sell it to you at a token price.'

'But you'd be losing a fortune!'

Keith shrugged. 'You can't take it with you. And once I'm gone, my wife's got more than enough to see her through the rest of her life comfortably. And don't forget, as Susan is our heir, what we leave goes to her which is just the same as handing it on a plate to Murray. This way I not only give the brewery another fighting chance, I also deprive Murray of the money it would've raised had I been able to sell it at its proper value.'

Eddy sat back in his chair, quite overcome by the prospect of what the Major was offering. He'd come to see the man to make a simple inquiry and here he was being handed Black Lion Brewery, gift-wrapped.

'Surely there's someone else in your family could take up the fight?' Eddy asked.

Keith shook his head. 'No one. Only Susan and she's married to Murray.'

Eddy couldn't contain himself. Rising, he paced up and down while he tried to put his racing thoughts in order. It was an incredible opportunity. And one he'd be a fool not to grab. This way, rather than being at Kirk's mercy, he'd be in direct competition to the bastard, which was a sweet, sweet thought.

Keith leaned forward on his desk, his eyes gleaming. He'd lost some of his sickly pallor, there being the hint of a flush in his cheeks. 'Well?' he demanded.

'What sort of token price did you have in mind?'

Keith considered that. 'Five thousand?' he suggested.

'That's ridiculous!'

'All right then, two and a half.'

'I didn't mean it that way ... I meant ...'

'I know what you meant, Mr King,' Keith said with a grin.

Eddy extended his hand. 'Done, Major. You've just sold yourself a brewery.'

They shook hands.

'I'll get on to my lawyers and have the necessary papers drawn up right away. I suggest you work alongside me until such times as they're completed, and that way I can teach you what I can about running a brewery. Now, I know it's early yet but how about a dram? I think we both need one.'

'I'd love to see Kirk's face when he finds out,' said Eddy as the Major poured out stiff ones.

Laughing together, they drank.

Kirk's secretary looked up in alarm as he went striding by her.

Missing was the customary "good morning" or "how are you?" She thought she'd never seen him so angry looking.

'Get me McGhie,' Kirk snapped at her, before slamming his office door shut.

He threw the morning *Herald* on to his desk, then sat glaring at it. He'd read the article on page two a dozen times or more. He almost knew it by heart.

'Eddy King!' he said through clenched teeth. Eddy, of all people, to buy Black Lion Brewery!

He sat fuming, staring into space, until he was roused from his reverie by a knock on the door.

'Come in!' he snapped.

Turk McGhie entered the room.

'Have you read this?' said Kirk pushing the *Herald* to the front of his desk. 'The article about Black Lion.'

Turk picked the paper up and read, mouthing words as he did so. Reading wasn't exactly his forte. Finally, he replaced the paper on the desk and stared at Kirk.

'No more arsing around cutting the brewery down piecemeal. I want the bloody place finished in one fell stroke. Understand?'

Turk nodded.

Kirk's fist banged the desk. 'Down and out for the count. Kaput!'

'Leave it to me, Mr Murray,' said Turk, and turned to the door.

'Turk?'

'Yes, Mr Murray?'

Kirk ran a hand over his face. He musn't let his anger warp his judgement. To make a move so soon would be too obvious. It was best to allow some time to pass first.

'Not yet though, Turk. Think about it. Plan it. Give it three or more months. Then do it.'

'Will there be extra in this for me, Mr Murray?'

'There certainly will.'

Turk grinned, then strode silently from the room. Not even the door made a sound as he closed it behind him.

It was ten o'clock at night and Susan sat with a large drink in her hand. She was more than just a little drunk.

As usual Kirk was out on what he called business, but which actually meant he was with Ciona Crammond. It had got to the stage where he spent five nights out of seven with her.

Susan gazed morosely into her glass. She knew she was hitting the bottle far too much of late but when night fell, and that terrible loneliness settled on her, she needed solace from somewhere. And far too often it was the bottle which provided it.

She had no problem with the daytime. Then, she had her practice and beloved animals to occupy her and keep her busy. But the nights were something else entirely.

If only they'd had a child, things might have been different. But their marriage continued to be barren. In fact there was now no chance of her getting pregnant as for some time she'd cut Kirk off from having sex with her.

The first time she'd done it, he'd asked her why and she'd replied he knew damn well why. He'd never broached the subject again. Nor her in bed.

She listened to the clock ticking forlornly, thinking how unhappy she was and how she'd been unhappy for most of her life. Reaching for the bottle she poured herself another drink.

And when she went up to the bedroom a little later, she took the bottle with her.

Eddy was working at his desk when the secretary buzzed through to say there was a Mr Smart to see him. No appointment had been made. When Eddy didn't reply at once, the secretary added, 'A Mr Norrie Smart, sir. He said you'd know who he was.'

'Send him in,' said Eddy.

He rose when Norrie came into the room and they shook hands.

'Sorry to bother you when you're at work but I wanted to see you before the other applications came in,' Smart said.

Eddy waved him to a seat. 'What applications are these?' he asked.

'For the job of night security officer that the brewery advertised in last night's *Citizen*. I know it's a cheek on my part, considering you gave me the job I've got now, but you see we've had another wean ...'

'Congratulations!' Eddy cut in.

Smart smiled and looked generally pleased with himself. 'A wee lassie this time. We're calling her Isobil after the wife's mother.'

Eddy desperately envied Smart at that moment. He would have loved to have had a wife and child of his own. But since Leoni he hadn't met anyone he cared enough for to marry.

Smart went on, 'And, you see, the night security job offers quite a bit more than I'm making now. That extra would be an awful big help.'

'How are the headaches?'

'A lot better of late. The doctor's put me on a special diet which seems to be helping.'

'Hmm!' said Eddy thoughtfully.

'I also think working nights would help as well. It's quiet then, less noise and hassle to set the headaches off.'

Eddy could see how badly Smart wanted the job. Well – why not? The least he could do was give him a chance. And he was a big strapping fellow after all. Just the sort to deal with any intruders.

'I'll give you a month's trial and we'll see how you get on,' Eddy said. 'And if it doesn't work out you can always go back to the Bowlers' Tavern.'

'You're a right toff, Eddy. I won't let you down. And listen, congratulations to you on taking over Black Lion. Who would have thought back in the days of the section you and Kirk would end up owning rival breweries?'

'Yes, who would have thought,' mused Eddy.

'Intimidation? That's quite a charge, Mr King,' Super-intendent McIlwham said.

417

'It's been going on ever since KM opened,' Eddy went on. 'A thug called Turk McGhie does the actual nasty work, and from all accounts he's brilliant at it.'

'In a case like this we're powerless unless someone will come forward and testify. Can you provide such a person?'

'I can.'

McIlwham took out a pencil and scratch pad. 'What's the person's name?'

'Danny Porteous. He owns a pub in Hillhead, The Byres Arms in Byres Road. He used to sell our beer till he had a visit from Turk McGhie. To begin with, he told McGhie to take a running jump, but he changed his mind after having a pint-pot smashed in his face. He came damn close to losing an eye.'

'Why didn't he come forward before?'

'Because he was scared to. Why else?'

'And now he isn't?'

'Oh, he still is, but now he's willing to take the chance. He's been brooding about the incident ever since it happened, finding it difficult to live with himself because of backing down. It didn't take too much persuasion on my part to make him agree. To use his own words, he wants to be able to live with himself again. He's that sort of person.'

'I see,' said McIlwham.

'Can you give him protection till this is all over?'

McIlwham laughed, causing Eddy to frown. 'Isn't that a bit melodramatic, Mr King? I think you've been watching too many American movies.'

'I'd call getting a glass in the face fairly melodramatic, wouldn't you?' replied Eddy quietly.

'I doubt if protection will really be needed. But I'll have a word with this Porteous myself and decide whether it is or not.'

'Murray and McGhie musn't find out his identity until there's a trial. McGhie would be bound to go after him then.'

'I don't need you to tell me my job, Mr King,' McIlwham stated coldly.

'I wasn't trying to –'

'You just leave the police side of things to me. I'll do what has to be done, I can assure you.'

'All right then.'

'Fine,' said McIlwham, nodding.

'You'll be in touch,' said Eddy rising.

'I will.'

Eddy left the Superintendent's office confident that Black Lion's fortunes would soon be on the turn. The Major had once gone to the police about McGhie's intimidation but nothing had come of it, due to lack of witnesses. Well, now he had Porteous willing to testify. The whole rotten can of beans that was KM Brewery was going to be split wide open.

'Very interesting indeed,' said Kirk thoughtfully. And after a few minutes' more conversation, hung up the phone.

So, Eddy was on the move, he thought. Well, he'd soon put a stop to that little ploy.

A glance at his watch told him it was three-thirty p.m. Turk would be reporting in the back of five. He'd give Turk his instructions then.

'Mr King?'

'Speaking.'

'Superintendent McIlwham here.'

'Oh good morning, Superintendent.'

'I'm afraid I've got some bad news for you, sir. Mr Porteous, who was gong to testify? Well, I'm afraid he had a fatal accident last night.'

Eddy went cold all over. 'What sort of fatal accident?'

'He fell down the pub cellar steps and broke his neck. Death apparently was instantaneous.'

'You're sure it was an accident?'

'No doubt about it, sir. Mr Porteous was serving in the bar and left some customers to whom he'd been chatting to go down and change a keg. When he didn't reappear a barman went looking for him and found him at the bottom of the cellar steps. Very bad steps those, I've since seen them myself. He must've tripped.'

'Convenient for some people, wouldn't you say?'

There was no reply.

'Thank you for ringing, Superintendent.'

'Have you anyone else will testify, Mr King?'

Eddy gave a grim smile. 'No. And if anyone was considering it, I'm sure Danny Porteous's death will convince them it's best to keep their mouths shut.'

'But that was an accident, sir.'

'Thank you again for calling, Superintendent. Goodbye.'

Eddy hung up. 'Accident, my backside!' he said. Somehow Kirk and McGhie had found out about Danny. But who could've tipped them the wink? Danny sure as hell wouldn't have mentioned to anyone that he was going to testify. And he certainly hadn't. The only person he'd spoken to about it being ...

Acting on a hunch he picked up the phone and dialled the Major at home.

'Major Gibb?'

'Yes?'

'Eddy King here. Point of information, if you don't mind. When you approached the police previously about bringing intimidation charges against KM, who did you speak to?'

'Let me see now,' replied the Major. A few seconds elapsed before he said, 'A Superintendent McIlwham, I think his name was.'

'I thought it might be,' said Eddy, and went on to tell the Major about Porteous and Porteous' 'accidental' demise.

After his call to the Major he made another to a different police station.

There he said he had a complaint to make about the KM Brewery. The sergeant he spoke to said he would take his number and have someone ring him back.

'Who will that be?' Eddy asked.

'A Superintendent McIlwham,' replied the sergeant.

'He personally handles all complaints about KM Brewery, then?'

'That's correct, sir.'

Eddy hung up.

Very neat, he thought. Very neat indeed, and typically Kirk. It gave credence to the old joke that used to be bandied about that the Glasgow police were the finest money could buy.

The moment he'd given McIlwham Danny Porteous' name, he'd signed Danny's death warrant.

When Turk McGhie strolled into the Tam O' Shanter Inn he was noted instantly by the two men sitting with an eye on the door.

As Turk vanished into the toilet one of the men glanced up at the bar clock. Ten minutes to closing time. Turk was working to his usual pattern of staying behind in the toilet till the rest of the customers had gone.

Mike Jardine and Sandy Pettigrew were two ex-commandos, both unemployed until Eddy had sought them out and put them on the payroll. Their job was to negate Turk.

Pettigrew came across to the bar, and in a whisper told the publican Turk had arrived. The publican was to carry on in his usual fashion and leave to them what had to be done.

Jardine and Pettigrew had been sitting in the pub for two days now, waiting for McGhie to appear. It was Eddy who'd worked out that Turk was acting according to a preconceived plan, advancing from pub to pub within a given area. Once that had been established it had been easy to spot that the Tam O'Shanter was one of the next in line of independent pubs to be 'converted' to KM beers.

Last orders were called and slowly the customers started to drift off. Jardine and Pettigrew positioned themselves in a darkish corner, from where they could watch the length of the bar as well as the door to the toilet.

Grumbling, the last of the customers went off into the night, leaving the publican, a barman and the two ex-commandos. The doors were shut and locked, the glasses piled by the sink.

Turk appeared right on cue. He was gliding quietly towards the bar when he suddenly became aware of the two figures sitting watching him. He frowned in their direction, thinking they might be police.

The publican was so nervous he dropped a glass, which went crashing to the floor. He tried to smile it off but the smile somehow got twisted on his face, turning it into what can only be described as a demented leer.

'Polis?' Turk asked softly.

Jardine and Pettigrew rose and crossed to within half a dozen feet of Turk. They positioned themselves so that they formed a triangle with Turk at its apex.

There was nothing particularly startling looking about either of the two ex-commandos. Neither was over average height or more muscled or broad in the shoulder than was normal for Glasgow. In fact they looked just what they were. Two lower-middle-class family men.

But Turk had been too long a fighting man to be fooled by appearances. He knew he was being confronted by men as deadly as himself.

'Landlord!' called out Jardine. 'I think this gentleman has something to say to you.'

The publican was now in such a state a tic had started to jump at the corner of his left eye. The result was to make him appear to be constantly winking. In other circumstances it could have been very funny.

'Are you the police?' Turk asked again, thinking that if they were, Kirk would soon sort all this out through his police contact.

'No,' replied Pettigrew.

'Then who?'

'We work for Black Lion Brewery just like you work for KM.'

Turk nodded. Everything was now crystal clear.

The publican hovered behind the bar.

'Say your piece,' instructed Jardine to Turk.

For a brief few seconds Turk considered trying to take these two. But in the end he decided against it. He felt the possibility was quite high that the two together outmatched him, razors and all. No, his best policy was to back off and discuss this new turn of events with Kirk.

'I'm a representative from KM Brewery,' he said to the publican. 'And I'm here to see if you'd be interested in changing from Black Lion to us.'

'No, I wouldn't,' the publican stammered.

'You're sure?' Jardine asked.

The publican nodded.

'So there you are, McGhie,' Jardine said.

'Do you get the point?' Pettigrew asked.

'You've made it quite clear.'

'I hope we have. Because we're going to be around from now on in, protecting our brewery's interests. There's going to be no more of the nonsense that's been going on up till now.'

'Because if you try it we'll jump on you from a great height,' Jardine added.

Turk bit back the anger that flared in him. He wasn't used to being talked to this way. His hands twitched involuntarily as though they had a life of their own.

When Jardine saw that, a lazy smile settled on his face. There was a number of dead Germans in the war for whom the last thing seen in this life had been that smile.

'Well?' Pettigrew asked.

'If the man doesn't want our beer, then he doesn't want it,' Turk said. And it almost choked him to do so.

Again he considered making a play here and now and again told himself not to. If these two did manage to take him he'd lose all credibility. And the job he had with Kirk was far too soft - and lucrative - a number for that to happen. There would be other ways and means.

'Goodbye, Mr McGhie,' said Jardine, making the 'Mr' part sound like an obscenity.

'I'll let you out,' said the publican, hurrying round the bar to the door.

Turk, Jardine and Pettigrew stared at one another as bolts

423

rattled and the key was turned in the lock.

Silent as usual, Turk strode from the pub.

'What you did was right,' said Kirk the next day.

'I thought I might find out where they live and take them individually, one after the other,' Turk suggested. He was still smarting under the previous night's humiliation and wanted this new situation resolved as soon as possible.

Kirk's mouth thinned in thought. He also wanted this resolved at the earliest opportunity.

'How long now since King took over Black Lion?' he asked.

'Eight or nine weeks.'

'All right then,' said Kirk, making up his mind. It was earlier than he'd planned but he was going to give the go-ahead just the same.

'I told you to think about finishing off Black Lion Brewery in one fell swoop. Have you done so?'

Turk nodded.

'Then do it as soon as you can. And we'll see what side of his face Eddy King smiles on then!'

It was the opening night of a new season at the Citizens' Theatre. Five minutes before curtain-up, an eager throng had gathered in the foyer. The atmosphere was one of heady excitement and expectation.

It was the first time Eddy had gone out with Jane Miller, a long leggy blonde who worked as a beauty consultant in Pettigrew & Stephens of Sauchiehall Street. He'd met her the previous week through a radio scriptwriter friend of his who held lunchtime court every Monday to Friday in a cheapish Sauchiehall Street restaurant. Eddy found the scriptwriter amusing, and not for the man's supposed witty conversation either. The scriptwriter's idea of chic and sophistication was to drink beaujolais with his cod and chips.

Jane was done up to the nines and drew many admiring glances. Beautiful she might be, but she was decidedly short of chat as Eddy was rapidly finding out.

424

Eddy bought them a programme and then led her to their seats in the stalls. The play they were about to see was *Dandy Dick* by Sir Arthur Wing Pinero.

'Ever been to the Citizens' before?' he asked with a smile.

She shook her head.

'How about the variety theatres then?'

'No,' she said.

'I hope you'll like the play. It's a comedy.'

She smiled back at him.

This would be their first and last date, he decided. As far as he was concerned, the lovely Jane Miller was proving to be a complete washout. She had about as much personality as a stale loaf.

After Jane had quickly glanced through the programme he took it, always liking to familiarise himself with the names of the actors he was about to watch.

He'd actually read the name and gone on before it struck him just whose name it was he'd read. His eyes crawled back up the list and there it was, Toby Grimes.

Annie had said she'd travel round the reps with Toby. If she was still doing so that meant she was in Glasgow. Perhaps even in the theatre!

It was if he'd been shot through by a bolt of pure energy. He tingled from head to foot.

Then the house lights dimmed and the curtains opened. The play had begun.

When the curtain came down at the end of the first act, Eddy couldn't have said what he'd just seen and heard. All he'd been able to think about was Annie.

'Like a drink?' he asked.

'Mmm!'

Side by side, he and Jane moved up the aisle to the bar.

Like most theatre bars in the interval, it was pandemonium trying to get served. But eventually Eddy succeeded, and clutching two glasses made his way back to where Jane was standing by a large mirror.

'Cheers!' he said and raised his glass to his mouth. But it

425

never got there for what he saw reflected in the mirror caused him to pause in mid-action.

The same willowy figure. The same brown hair he remembered so well. She looked as though she hadn't aged, but the distance between them might have been deceiving.

Slowly he turned to stare at her, devouring her with his eyes. She was with a young man who, judging from his clothes and manner, would seem to be an actor. They were deep in conversation, the man gesturing floridly to make some point or other.

She must have become aware of Eddy's gaze on her for she frowned and glanced around her.

When their eyes met Eddy smiled.

For a second or two he was just another stranger, and then suddenly recognition flooded her face, manifesting itself in high colour which stained her cheeks.

He wanted to go to her. Talk to her. Just look at her. And indeed, he was about to excuse himself from Jane, when with great deliberation Annie turned her back on him.

It was like being punched or kicked. Or something equally physical.

It was quite obvious she didn't want to speak to him. Nor would he force the issue. She must have her reasons, which he would respect.

The bell rang, announcing that the second act would shortly begin. Seeing little and hearing less, Eddy escorted Jane back to their seats.

Norrie Smart hummed as he made his way along the gangway. With this hourly walkaround over, it was time to get the kettle on and the sandwiches out.

He never even saw the blow to the back of his head which sent him sprawling unconscious.

The play was over and Eddy was fitting the key in the car door when suddenly the night erupted with the clamour of a fire engine with all sirens going.

426

'Somebody's chimney's probably gone up,' said Jane when the din had receded a little.

Eddy had just moved the car out into the street when he had to draw back into the kerb to let a second fire engine past.

'If there's two of them it's more than a chimney,' he remarked.

A little further along the street he had to stop yet again to let a third by.

As they drove in the direction of Jane's house he knew from her manner he'd proved as big a disaster to her as she had to him. Pity, he thought. She'd seemed such a bright prospect when he'd met her at the scriptwriter's table.

'Thanks for the evening,' she said when he parked outside her house, already fumbling with the door handle. Opening the door she slid out. 'You stay where you are. I'm fine from here by myself,' she said quickly.

'I'll ring,' he lied.

''Bye!' she called out. Then her feet were scrunching up the gravel path as she beat a retreat.

Eddy sighed as he engaged the gears. All the way home his mind was on Annie, remembering, as he'd done so often in the past, the time they'd spent together in Fulham.

As he let himself in the telephone started to ring.

'Mr King, is that you?'

'Yes.'

'It's Tam McFadyen here. I manage the ...'

'I know who you are, Tam.'

'You'd better get to the brewery right away, Mr King. The whole bloody shebang is going up in smoke!'

'What are you talking about, Tam?'

'Fire, Mr King. The place is on fire.'

Eddy caught his breath. In his mind all he could see was the blackened shell The Black Lion pub had been reduced to.

'Thanks, Tam, I'll be right there,' he said and slammed down the phone.

He was turning away when the phone rang again.

'Yes?' he snapped.

'Is that Mr King?'

'Speaking.'

'This is the police, sir ...'

'If it's about the brewery, I already know and I'm on my way.'

At the outside door the phone started to ring yet again but this time he left it. He hurtled down the stairs and into his car, which he drove like a maniac, jumping four red lights and not giving a damn. Crouched over the wheel it came to him that the fire engines he'd heard in the Gorbals must have been going to the brewery. He muttered a string of obscenities to himself as he dodged in and out of the traffic.

The sky was lit up where it hadn't been before. When he got closer he saw yellow flames and sparks. It was just like bonfire night. Only in this case the bonfire was his brewery.

He slammed the car to a halt and climbed out. A cordon of police were holding back onlookers, while firemen did their best to contain the blaze. A figure waved to him, which he recognised as Tam McFadyen. He waved back.

'You can't go any closer now, sir,' said a big Highland policeman.

'Like hell I can't! That's my brewery that's on fire!'

'You own the premises?'

'I just said that, didn't I!'

'Through you go, sir.'

He went as near to the fire as he dared, hand to face to ward off the intense heat that battered him. The building was a write-off, that was blatantly obvious.

'Who are you, sir?'

'Eddy King. You police?'

'Detective Inspector Ireland of the CID.'

'My God!' Eddy exclaimed, as there was an explosion inside the building, which sent huge shafts of flame shooting skywards.

'We've been trying to ring you at home ever since the 999 came through, sir.'

'I was at the theatre and ...' A sudden thought struck Eddy,

428

causing him to glance around. 'Did you get the security guard out?' he demanded.

Ireland glanced from Eddy back to the building and the raging inferno consuming it. His grim expression was reply enough.

'Oh!' Eddy sighed.

'Just the one guard was there, sir?'

Eddy nodded.

'Must have been overcome by the smoke. Some of the first firemen here did get in on the ground level but there was no one there. He must've been higher up.'

Beyond the cordon a group of youths capered and cavorted, thinking the fire great sport. For two pins Eddy would have gone across and smashed their teeth down their throats.

A woman in the crowd screamed and pointed up at the building.

'Yon's a man!' somebody else shouted.

Norrie Smart stood framed in a blown-out window, his head, arms, torso, everything, burning fiercely. He was a flaming human torch.

'Oh Christ!' said Eddy, a lump suddenly clogging his throat.

Smart seemed to dance and wave to the crowd. Then he pitched forward, turning end over end, to fall to the ground below. Eddy found himself running toward the still burning figure. All he could think of was Norrie's new wee wean.

As he ran he tore his coat off and, arriving at Norrie's side, threw the coat over his body. He ripped off his jacket, which he used as a flail to try and beat the flames out.

Underneath the flames Norrie's face was a nightmare. The hair was gone as were the eyes, the latter melted. The lips had been burned away to reveal the teeth. Norrie moaned, the most pitiful sound Eddy had ever heard.

Then suddenly Eddy wasn't alone with Smart. A dozen uniforms surrounded them both as the firemen took over.

Foam spurted and other articles were brought into play. Within seconds the fire enveloping Norrie was extinguished.

Eddy and the firemen reeled under the heat from the building. Later Eddy would discover that a lot of his skin had been scalded. A stetcher appeared and Norrie was gently lifted on to it. He was covered by a blanket before being taken to an ambulance which was standing by.

'I'll follow on behind,' said Eddy to the ambulance driver. But as he was turning to spring to his car the other ambulanceman said, 'He's gone, mate. Too late for hospitals now.'

Feeling sick to the very depths of his being, Eddy stared down at the body of Norrie Smart. Big dumb Norrie who'd always seemed two mental paces behind everyone else but who'd always stand by you and do you a good turn if he could. And now, ridiculously young, he was dead, leaving a wife and two wee ones behind.

'It was best he died now rather than lingered on,' the driver said. 'With those burns they'd never have saved him. This is by far the best way for him, believe me.'

Tears rolled down Eddy's cheeks as the ambulance, with siren howling, took the burnt remains of Norrie Smart to the morgue.

Poor Norrie who'd never done anyone any harm. Who'd only wanted a wife and family and the opportunity to support them.

In the flames Eddy saw Turk McGhie's face laughing at him and behind Turk was Kirk, also laughing. His hands knotted at his side as a terrible anger was birthed in him, an anger that within seconds had blossomed into an awesome rage. He was dimly aware that Ireland was talking to him but he heard nothing. There was a roaring in his ears and a fire, as intense as that he was watching, in his belly.

Suddenly he knew what he must do. Turning abruptly he strode for the police cordon, beyond which he had to fight to get through the milling onlookers.

Once in his car he opened his wallet and extracted the card Kirk had given him the day they'd had lunch together. He memorised Kirk's address before starting the car and moving off.

Glass in hand, Susan sat staring into the fire. She heard the front door open and then close again, followed by the sound of Kirk hanging up his coat.

He would have been with Ciona Crammond again, she thought bitterly. How she'd come to hate that name!

'I'm home, Susan!' he called out.

'I'm in here,' she slurred. 'Having a nightcap.' Nightcap, my foot! She'd been having nightcaps since arriving in from work hours previously.

On entering the room, Kirk saw immediately that she'd been hitting the bottle again. That disturbed him but he didn't comment on the fact. After all, those who lived in glass houses . . .

'Pour me another, will you?' said Susan, holding out her empty glass.

'Think I'll join you,' he replied, hoisting a smile on to his face.

'Another busy day?' she said sarcastically, adding a second later, 'And evening?'

Kirk ignored the taunt. He handed her the refill and said he was going down to the basement for a bottle of wine. That was what he fancied and the claret jug was empty.

She watched him swagger away, a swagger that was becoming more and more pronounced as the years went by. His bottom really was getting far too big, she thought dimly. Then she shrugged. Why should she bother? Let Ciona Crammond try and get him to stick to a diet. After all, if Ciona was getting the pleasures of the front then it was only fair she get the worries of the rear. Susan laughed aloud at the vulgarity and absurdity of that thought.

She frowned as the doorbell rang. Who on earth could that be at this time of night? She'd have to answer it herself. The servants were off duty now. Sighing, she came to her feet and lurched for the door.

'Is Kirk home?' Eddy asked, his face contorted into a thundercloud of anger.

'Who are you?'

'Eddy King.'

Susan's eyes narrowed. 'Oh yes! Kirk's spoken of you. The pair of you were in the Army together.'

'Is he home, Mrs Murray?'

'Come in. He's downstairs getting some wine.'

The inside of the house was opulent and in very good taste, but Eddy noticed none of that as he followed Susan through to a drawing room.

'Kirk will be back in a moment,' Susan slurred. 'Can I get you a drink?'

Eddy shook his head.

'Then please sit down.'

'I prefer to stand.'

'Suit yourself, Mr King,' she replied, and sat herself.

Kirk entered with an opened bottle of wine. 'Susan, I . . ' He came up short when he saw Eddy.

The anger Eddy had somehow managed to bring under control threatened to break its banks. He started to shake as though he had the ague.

'To what do we owe this pleasure?' Kirk asked, a hint of mockery in his voice.

'Black Lion brewery was burned down tonight.'

Kirk expressed mock concern. 'I am sorry to hear that. What a blow for you. But surely you mean it burned down?'

'*Was* burned.'

'Can you prove that?'

Eddy gritted his teeth. 'I doubt it. Same as we couldn't prove The Black Lion pub was deliberately burned down. As an arsonist your man McGhie is excellent.'

'Careful, Eddy. There's a witness present.'

Eddy took a step forward and his shaking got worse. 'Intimidation, arson, and now murder, Kirk.'

'What are you talking about? Who's been murdered?'

'Remember Norrie Smart?'

'From the section? Yes, of course I do. What's he got to do with this?'

432

'Norrie was my night security guard at the brewery. Tonight he was burned to death. He came out of a top window, a human torch, and was still alive as he fell to the ground. When I got to him it looked like every inch of his flesh was on fire, his hair was gone and his eyes – oh his eyes, Kirk.. they'd melted.'

Susan gagged and turned away.

Kirk had gone pale.

'Well?'

'Well what?'

'Nothing to say?'

'I, eh.. I'm sorry about Norrie, naturally. But it had nothing to do with me.'

'Liar!'

'I swear!'

'Lying bastard!'

Fear appeared in Kirk's eyes as Eddy advanced on him. Slowly he began backing away.

'You told McGhie to burn me out, so as far as I'm concerned you're as guilty for what happened as he is.'

'You've got it all wrong, Eddy!'

'Like hell I have!' Eddy roared and threw himself at Kirk, his anger breaking its banks and enveloping him.

Kirk smashed the bottle against the side of Eddy's head causing him to stagger. Suddenly the two of them, and the carpet beneath their feet, were covered in claret, the colour of blood.

Eddy wrapped his arms around Kirk and started to punch, his fist pile-driving time and time again into Kirk's flabby middle.

Kirk brought his head down, trying to break Eddy's nose, but he missed and hit Eddy's shoulder instead. Thrown off balance, he stumbled and then fell, dragging Eddy to the ground with him as he went. They rolled over and over on the carpet a few times, then Eddy was sitting astride Kirk with Kirk's throat between his hands.

Kirk's eyes bulged as Eddy began to squeeze.

'Stop it! Stop it!' Susan screamed, tugging frantically at Eddy's shoulder. 'You'll kill him!'

Kirk's face turned plum coloured. His legs kicked as he struggled valiantly to heave Eddy off. But Eddy hung on grimly, intent on finishing what he'd come to do.

Hysterically Susan hit Eddy again and again round the head and ears but he felt nothing. His entire world was focused on his two hands and Kirk's throat.

Kirk was convinced the next few seconds were to be his last, when suddenly the vice round his neck was relaxed. Coughing and spluttering, he sucked in life-giving breath.

With a peculiar expression on his face, Eddy rose to his feet. 'I can't do it,' he mumbled. 'I just can't do it.'

Kirk rolled over on to his side, bringing his legs up into an embryonic position, which made his breathing easier.

Eddy shook his head. When it came to the bit he was a lot different from the boy who'd killed Gloag all those years ago. Life, Annie Grimes and Leoni von Kruppermann had done that to him.

'Get out of here!' Kirk husked.

Eddy's fury was gone now, leaving him strangely tranquil inside. He stared down at Kirk, a mixture of hate and contempt on his face.

Kirk glared back.

Susan sobbed. She seemed to be trying to eat the hand stuffed in her mouth.

'I'm going to see Norrie's widow now,' Eddy said. 'Want to come along?'

Kirk dropped his gaze.

Eddy strode from the room.

The next morning Eddy woke early. He washed and shaved but couldn't face food. Getting into his car he drove out to the brewery – or what was left of it.

The building was cordoned off by ropes and two policemen were on duty to see no unauthorised person tried to go inside.

A solitary figure stood apart, staring at the still smoking ruin. Eddy recognised the Major.

Eddy joined Keith, who shook his head sadly.

'So, there we are then,' Eddy said.

'A man dead, I believe?'

'Aye. The night security guard. A bloke who was in the Army with me.'

'Married?'

'Wife and two kids. I saw her last night. You can imagine the state she was in. I only hope no idiot lets her see the body.'

'So,' Keith said squaring his shoulders. 'What now?'

Eddy laughed hollowly.

'You're not thinking of quitting, are you?'

'I don't see what else I can do. Salvage what I can out of this mess, which probably means putting KM beer into my pubs.'

'I expected more of you than that, King.'

'What else can I do? Look at the brewery, for God's sake! You know how long insurance takes to come through and then I'd have to knock down what's left and rebuild from scratch. And in the meantime every pub I have would have to be closed due to lack of beer. The whole thing would take years, by which time Murray would have the rest of the Glasgow market sewn up anyway.'

'I know of a way in which you could have Black Lion beer back in your pubs within a month,' Keith said softly.

'How?'

'Thanks to Murray, there's half a dozen breweries have closed down within the last few years, one of which was Donaldson's. And Fergus Donaldson is a friend of mine. I'm sure he'd be only too happy to sell.'

Eddy frowned. He hadn't thought of that. But then since the fire he hadn't really had a chance to think things through.

'You still have the workforce and the outlets,' Keith said. 'Your only problems are premises and equipment. Solve those and you're back in business again.'

'But I couldn't raise that sort of capital,' Eddy replied. 'At least not until the insurance money came through.'

'Why don't we talk to Fergus and see what he thinks?' Keith suggested.'

'I've nothing to lose.'

'And everything to gain,' Keith added, smiling.

They used Eddy's car to drive to the outskirts of Glasgow, where they found Fergus Donaldson just about to sit down to breakfast. Eddy and Keith took coffee while Fergus ate. And while he did so, they took it in turns to speak.

At the end of the meal Fergus poured them more coffee and then sipped his, looking thoughtful.

'Well, the way I see it is this,' he said. 'There's nobody else going to want to buy it as a brewery and frankly I've had difficulty selling it at all. It's been on the market as light industrial premises since we closed down, but I've had no nibbles, far less takers.'

'Everything's still there as it was, isn't it?' Eddy asked, suddenly thinking Donaldson might have had the guts ripped out the place.

'Oh aye. Exactly as the day we stopped production,' Donaldson replied.

'Then there's no reason why Eddy couldn't have Black Lion beer back in the pumps within a matter of weeks?'

'None at all.'

'There is the money problem,' Eddy said, and went on to explain about his lack of capital.

'That's no real problem at all,' said Donaldson. 'Let's agree a price that's fair to both of us and I'll wait till your insurance money comes through to collect. You're doing me a favour taking the brewery off my hands so the least I can do is a favour in return. Tit for tat, so to speak.'

'What sort of price did you have in mind?' Eddy asked.

Donaldson named a sum that Eddy thought was more than reasonable.

'Agreed,' Eddy said, and they shook hands on it.

'I'll get my solicitors on to the matter right away,' said Donaldson. 'But as their office won't be open for a good hour yet would you like to go and have a look at the place? I'd be only too happy to show you around.'

'I'd love that,' replied Eddy, full of enthusiasm. 'And before we go, do you think I could have a piece of that toast? I've suddenly got very hungry.'

The Donaldson Brewery was a lot smaller than Black Lion had been. But then with the loss of trade Black Lion had suffered since KM came into existence, the new premises were more than adequate for the amount of beer needed to supply their outlets.

On the second day after the fire the workforce reported to the new premises, where they set about getting the brewery producing again.

That first week was the most hectic Eddy had ever known but gradually things began to sort themselves out. He estimated another fortnight and then the first of the beer would be in the pumps. In the meantime all Black Lion pubs were closed down.

A few nights later Eddy came home dog-tired and after washing and having a dram, tumbled into bed. Within seconds he was fast asleep.

In his dream he was back at the scene of the fire and Norrie Smart was standing framed in the window. He seemed to close in on Norrie's face where he saw the eyes slowly turn into a horrible gooey gel which ran down Norrie's burning face.

He woke screaming and covered in sweat, gulping in breath after breath when he realised it had only been a nightmare.

But the fact remained; Norrie was dead. Murdered by that bastard Turk McGhie. Of course there would be no police action. No doubt when the results of the inquiry into the fire came through, the cause, or causes, of the blaze would, as in the case of The Black Lion pub, be found to be unknown. Superintendent McIlwham would undoubtedly see to that.

Rising from his bed, Eddy poured himself another dram. Turk McGhie was the key to all this, he thought. Remove Turk and the reign of terror would be over. Kirk would then have to fight fair and square for his business same as everyone else.

There was no use going to the police about Turk. Both he and the Major had tried that to no avail. So if the law wouldn't help then it would have to be the other way.

McGhie was a rabid animal and the kindest thing for them was to be put down. And Turk's case, if for no other reason than Norrie Smart's horrible death, demanded it.

But how? And who?

He couldn't ask Jardine and Pettigrew. Although well capable, he had no doubt they would baulk at civilian murder. Protecting his business interests was one thing, cold-blooded assassination quite another. Anyway it would be stupid of him to ask them. That would have been putting his own neck out on a limb in a way he had no intention of doing.

The drink was sour in his stomach so he made himself a cup of tea. And while he was doing so his mind drifted back to the theatre visit and Annie Grimes.

Thinking of Annie brought a half-remembered conversation percolating up into his mind.

'Can you do me a dozen rollers by tomorrow lunchtime?' Eddy asked in a loud voice. He was standing just inside the showroom door.

Gil Crabtree blinked and turned to face the man who'd just uttered the sort of request every used-car dealer dreams about.

'A dozen Rolls Royces, sir?' Gil repeated, just to make sure he'd heard correctly.

'Assorted colours will be fine,' said Eddy.

Gil's forehead suddenly puckered into a frown which cleared again just as suddenly in an explosion of recognition.

'Eddy! Eddy King!'

'The one and only,' said Eddy.

Gil threw his arms round Eddy and hugged him tight. 'It's great to see you again!' he laughed. 'But what brings you down here from darkest Scotland?'

'To see you and buy you a pint.'

438

'Gin and tonic, if you don't mind. Nothing so vulgar as a common pint. But come on now, why have you returned to civilisation?'

'I told you. To see you.'

'You're after a special car?'

'I'm after something. But not that.'

'If it's to do with Annie, she's..'

'She's in Glasgow,' Eddy cut in. 'I bumped into her recently but we didn't speak. She made it quite obvious she didn't want to so I didn't even try.'

'Are you married yet?'

'No. And I'm not carrying a torch either, if that's what you're getting at.' The latter was a lie of course.

Gil called out and a man emerged from the back of the showroom. 'Harry, my partner,' he said in explanation.

A few minutes later Eddy and Gil left for the local pub, where they ensconced themselves in an out-of-the-way corner where they wouldn't be overheard. Eddy brought Gil up to date on his career. The first pub that had started it all, leading up to his now owing the Black Lion Brewery.

'I always knew you were a winner, Eddy,' Gil said. 'And it couldn't have happened to a nicer bloke.'

Eddy came to the nitty-gritty: why he'd travelled down from Glasgow to see his old employer. Lowering his voice a little, he said, 'You once mentioned to me you had high friends in nasty places.'

Gil's eyes narrowed. 'Yes,' he said slowly.

'To put it bluntly, I want someone killed. Do you have a contact?'

'Christ Almighty, Eddy, you're joking! What would you want to get mixed up in a thing like that for?'

'So you don't have a contact?'

'I didn't say that.'

'Then you do?'

Gil sipped his large G and T. 'Are you certain about this?'

'Yes.'

'Absolutely?'

'Absolutely.'

'He's expensive. But the best there is.'

'Then he's the one I want.'

Gil shook his head. 'Times change right enough. Who'd ever have thought you'd come asking me something like that.'

'Life's full of surprises,' Eddy said. 'I found that out early on. Now look, I want to make my visit to London as brief as possible, so can you put me on to this person this morning?'

'I can try. There's no guaranteeing he'll be there, though. He might be out on a job or tied up in some other way.' Gil finished his drink and stood up. 'I'm going out to make a phone call. You wait here.' He paused before leaving. 'I ask again, are you certain about this?'

'Make the call, Gil.'

While Gil was gone Eddy sat staring into his drink. He was seeing Norrie Smart at the high window and hearing Norrie's moan after he had come crashing to the ground. He also thought of Danny Porteous, whom he'd liked.

Ten minutes later Gil was back. 'You're in luck. He's available,' Gil said.

'What do I do? Do I meet him?'

'No. You speak to him on the telephone.'

Gil took Eddy round the corner to a public telephone box. There was somebody using it so they had to hang on for a few minutes. When the box was free Gil went inside and dialled, Eddy having to stay outside while he did so. When he made his connection he spoke briefly, then beckoned Eddy in. After Eddy had taken the phone Gil left the box to go back outside.

'Hello?' said Eddy.

'I don't know your name nor do I want to. Nor will you ask me mine. Okay?'

'Yes.'

'Now tell me all you know about the party in question.'

When Eddy had given all the information he had on Turk McGhie there was a fairly long pause.

Finally the man asked, 'Is there a time limit?'

'I'd prefer sooner rather than later.'

440

'Okay then. My fee is five hundred quid. Half in cash now, the other half when the job is done. Money to Crabtree on both occasions. He'll get it to me.'

'Fine,' said Eddy.

The man hung up.

Eddy stared into his now dead receiver. It had all been so cut and dried, formal almost. The man had been well spoken. He might well have been discussing some minor problem with his bank manager.

Ten days after Eddy's trip to London, two patrolling Glasgow policemen came across a figure slumped in a tenement close. As the pubs weren't long out they thought it must be a drunk.

They discovered their mistake when they saw what remained of where the man's face had been. There was a small, neat hole at the back of the neck where the bullet had gone in. On emerging, the bullet had taken the face with it.

The policeman searched the corpse's pockets but there was no identification.

Neither of the policemen were particularly disturbed about what they'd found. They'd seen it all before. Murders were an everyday occurrence in Glasgow. The only unusual thing about this one was that a gun had been used. Shooters were a bit uncommon.

'Whoever he was, he carried nice razors,' one of the policemen remarked.

'Ivory handled. Expensive,' his mate replied.

One stayed behind while the other went to call up the meat waggon.

It was a great day for Eddy. Black Lion beer was back on flow and this time there would be no Turk McGhie to play with matches or otherwise put a spanner in the works.

It was eight o'clock at night and he'd been at work since eight that morning. A twelve-hour day and he was shattered. He decided a drink was in order so he stopped outside the Renfrew Hotel and went into the back bar where he ordered up a large whisky and half-pint chaser. The hotel was one of the few outlets for his beer that he hadn't previously been to in person. He was in the process of lighting a cigarette when he saw her in the corner. He knew the face but for a moment or two couldn't place her.

Then he did. The woman drinking on her own was Susan, Kirk's wife. He wondered whether to ignore her or not. Then he thought about how upset she'd been the night of the big fire when he'd had the fight with Kirk. He felt he should at least attempt to apologise. After all, he had no quarrel with her. It was her man who was his enemy.

'Mrs Murray, isn't it?' he said, having walked over to her table.

She glanced up at him, her face puffed and swollen from crying. 'Yes, that's right. Who are you?'

She'd had a fair amount to drink, that was obvious. And Eddy recalled she'd been the same way last time he'd seen her.

'I'm Eddy King. I own Black Lion.'

'Oh yes,' she said.

'I thought I should apologise to you for the other night. It must have been very distressing for you.'

'Was it true? What you accused Kirk of?'

'Yes. But I can't prove it.'

An expression of indescribable sadness came into her eyes, eyes which seemed to be sunk like deep holes into her face.

Eddy was about to walk away again when on a sudden impulse he said, 'Can I join you?'

'Why?'

'No reason other than you're alone as am I.'

She regarded him thoughtfully. 'Why not?' she replied, and nodded to a vacant chair.

Once he'd sat he said, 'Look, I hope you don't think I'm sticking my nose in, but is there anything I can do to help?'

'In what way?'

'You, eh.. appear to have been crying.'

She ran a hand over her face. 'That noticeable? I hadn't realised. Well no, there isn't anything you can do, Mr King..'

'Call me Eddy.'

'All right, Eddy, there's nothing you can do. Unless you can tell me how to make my husband get rid of his mistress and start paying attention to me again?'

Another woman, Eddy thought. The same old Kirk.

'That stuff's never a solution,' he said, indicating her glass.

She smiled bitterly. 'Can't face the nights without it.' Then, 'I must be crazy. The first stranger to talk to me and here I am laying all my problems at his feet!'

'I'm hardly a stranger,' replied Eddy. 'Don't forget Kirk and I spent two years together in Germany. And I also sold the pair of you a used car once. You can't call a man a stranger who's sold you a used car.'

'I suppose not,' she grinned.

'And I was the one who was forward in asking if I could help.'

There was silence between them for a few seconds and then she said, 'You must have got to know him pretty well in Germany.'

'We were inseparable for a while but we fell out.'

'Over what?'

He thought of telling her and decided against it. 'It's not important now. Let's just say it was at the time.'

'He hates you for taking over Black Lion.'

'I'm sure.'

'You do know the Major's my father, don't you?'

'Yes. He mentioned.'

'He and I never got on all that well. He and my mother were abroad a lot when I was a child.'

'I like him,' said Eddy.

'He always wanted a boy. I was a disappointment to him.'

'I'm sure it wasn't as bad as that.'

'I'm still a disappointment to him because I haven't given him a grandchild. I guess I'm just a disappointment all round.'

Eddy finished his drink. 'Would you like another?'

'Please.'

443

He went to the bar and ordered for them both. In the mirror he watched her staring into space.

Not particularly a looker, he thought. But she wasn't unattractive.

An hour later they emerged together out into the night. He was a lot drunker than he'd intended, having forgotten he hadn't eaten all day. The alcohol was going straight to his head as a consequence.

Susan stumbled and might well have fallen had he not grabbed her. 'Whoops!' she exclaimed.

'I think we could both do with a cup of coffee to sober up,' he said.

She hiccuped in reply.

He racked his brains trying to think of somewhere that would be open but nothing came to mind. When it came to restaurants and coffee bars, not to mention pubs, Glasgow was notorious for its early closing hours.

'Look, I live not all that far away,' he said. 'Why don't I drive us there and then when we've had coffee I'll run you back to your car.'

'All right.'

He drove slowly and carefully, desperately concentrating on the road. He was lucky inasmuch as there wasn't much traffic about.

He shivered as he got out of the car. The cold night air was further compounding the effects of the alcohol on him.

'Lots of coffee, and black,' he said, leading her up the close stairs. Despite his ever-increasing affluence over the past few years he'd continued to live in the same house.

Once inside Susan gazed curiously around. What she saw was a typical bachelor's place. Mess and muddle everywhere.

'You live here alone?' she asked.

'That's right,' Eddy replied as he filled the kettle.

Susan collapsed into a chair. She'd been all right for the past half-hour but now she was suddenly morose and dejected again.

'He still loves me,' she said. 'It's just he's been sidetracked by that bitch.'

'I'm sure he does.'

'I know he does because I can feel it here.' And she placed her hand over her left breast.

Eddy concentrated on trying to spoon coffee into cups.

'Do you think I'm attractive?'

'Pardon?'

She repeated her question, a furrow in her brow as she spoke.

'Yes I do.'

'You wouldn't lie?'

He turned to stare at her. He'd found her attractive in the hotel and he still did. More so. 'No,' he replied.

He was pouring the milk when the idea presented itself to him. I'm more drunk than I'd thought, he told himself. He had to be to even consider it. To seduce Kirk's wife. God, what a blow that would be to him! And the ideal revenge for what had happened with Leoni. He knew how lonely she was. Her conversation had been full of it.

He almost laughed out loud. Seduce Kirk's wife and then make sure the bastard found out! It was the perfect riposte and would knock a hole as big as a fist in Kirk's ego.

Christ, he was pissed! he thought, holding his head. He should've eaten something.

She came to him, swaying across the room. 'Are you all right?'

He turned into her and took her in his arms. She gasped but that was stifled as his mouth joined with hers.

Her mind was numb with alcohol and awash with emotion. She so desperately wanted to be loved, to be cherished. Her body was crying out for release, after all this while. And if Kirk could have his damned Ciona Crammond, why couldn't she have someone?

Tears streamed down her face as she pressed herself close to Eddy.

Disentangling himself, he took her hand and led her through to the bedroom.

She walked with head bowed.

EDDY, SUSAN AND RACHEL

Kirk was in Ciona's flat mixing some Black Velvet, which had become their favourite drink, when the telephone rang. Both of them were naked underneath their robes, having just made love.

'Ciona Crammond speaking,' Ciona said into the receiver, at the same time winking and pouting a kiss at Kirk.

Kirk blew a kiss back. Then poured himself a glass of Black Velvet which he eagerly sampled. Smooth as a maiden's thigh, he thought. He chuckled, pleased with himself at having conjured up such a phrase.

'Oh!' said Ciona, sagging where she stood. Her hand clutched the wall for support.

Her face lost colour and became pinched, the rosy afterglow of love fading completely from her cheeks. It might have been an illusion but it seemed her very hair lost its sheen.

'Thank you for ringing. I'll be home as soon as I can get there,' she said, and hung up.

'What's happened?' Kirk asked. Obviously it was something dreadful.

Disregarding the Black Velvet, Ciona made her way across to where the drinks stood and poured herself a huge brandy. She shuddered after she'd taken a swallow. Her shoulders hunched and started to shake. Tears splashed from her eyes.

'Ciona?' Kirk said, putting his arms round her.

'Mummy and Daddy,' she sobbed. 'They were killed an hour ago in a road accident. Some drunk ran into their car killing them instantly.'

'Oh my angel,' said Kirk, pulling her to him and holding her close.

For a little while she cried and he made soothing noises, stroking her as she gave vent to her grief.

Finally she said through her sobs, 'I've got to drive down to Helensburgh.'

'I'll drive. You're not in a fit state to.'

'But you can't. It's Susan's birthday. She's expecting you home in an hour.'

'Then she'll just have to wait.'

Ciona broke away to light a cigarette with trembling hands. 'At least there was no pain,' she said.

'And they were both a good age with their lives behind them.'

'And they went together. They would have liked that,' Ciona said softly. 'They were very much in love you know. From the day they met neither looked at another person.' She paused before adding, 'I'm going to miss them dreadfully.'

He took her in his arms and kissed her. 'I love you,' he said.

She looked up at him through eyes still brimming with moisture. 'You ring Susan while I wash my face. Then we'd both better get dressed.'

'I'm ever so sorry. Truly I am,' he said.

She gave him a brave smile before heading for the bathroom.

Damn! he swore to himself when she was gone. Of all the days for this to happen. Susan's birthday! And he'd promised faithfully to be home early for the special supper she was laying on for the occasion.

He glanced at the clock and worked out how long it would take him to get to Helensburgh and back. He was going to be dreadfully late, probably past midnight.

But what else could he do? He couldn't allow Ciona to drive in the state she was in. Nor could he explain the real reason to Susan why he was going to let her down on this day of days.

Sighing, he picked up the telephone. There was going to have to be yet another invented crisis at KM.

'I understand, Kirk,' Susan said into the phone. 'There's no need to go on. You do what you have to and I'll see you when you get in. Yes.. yes all right.. 'Bye now.'

She hung up. Then exhaled, long and slowly.

'You chromium-plated, died-in-the-wool bastard,' she said.

She refreshed her drink and then carried it to the fire where she stood gazing into the flames. She was wearing a special dress she'd bought for the occasion and that morning she'd had her hair especially done. And all for what? Nothing. He didn't even care enough about her to leave his mistress for an hour or two on her birthday.

She felt wretched and lonely standing there. Abandoned. The way she'd done as a child of four when her parents had gone off leaving her at Miss Buchan's School For Young Ladies.

She swallowed her drink, enjoying the warmth it spread through her insides. She contemplated pouring herself another, but decided against it. She would make a phone call first.

Eddy was at home studying some papers when the phone rang.

'Hello?'

'It's me.'

'Happy birthday. I've got a present for you. When are you coming over to collect it?'

Susan smiled. She'd mentioned briefly some months back that today was her birthday. It was just like Eddy to take it in and not forget.

'How about now?' she suggested.

'What about Kirk?'

'He's off with his fancy woman somewhere. He won't be back for hours yet.'

'I'll be expecting you then.'

'I'm on my way,' she said and hung up.

Eddy returned to his papers. It was a Tuesday night.

Normally he saw her on Thursday nights and occasionally Mondays.

He never had told Kirk about their affair, as his alcohol-muddled brain had suggested that night they'd first gone to bed together all those months ago. It had been a stupid idea. The sort of thing Kirk might well do. But not him.

Anyway, he'd come to discover he actually liked Susan. Apart from the sex aspect, which they both enjoyed, he found her relaxing and an enormous pleasure to be with. If asked to describe their relationship, he'd have said they'd become good friends who were having an affair.

Kirk sat at his desk rereading the article in the paper spread before him.

Five police officers had been suspended from duty pending inquiries of corruption. The new Chief Constable had stated on his appointment some six weeks previously that he would scourge all corruption from his force. It would seem the scourging had begun.

Kirk dialled and asked to be put through to Superintendent McIlwham.

'It's Murray. Can we speak?' he asked, when McIlwham came on the line.

'Hold on a moment and I'll have this transferred through to my private office.'

A few seconds later McIlwham announced, 'It's safe now.'

'I've been reading about the suspensions.'

'Got a lot of people in a flap, that has. It would seem that bastard means what he says.'

'What about you?'

'I'll have to be doubly careful from now on in.'

'So they're not on to you yet?'

'Not as far as I know. But should they start asking questions I'm going to have a lot of trouble explaining away the house I live in and the car I drive. Both are way outside what I should be able to afford.'

Kirk chewed a nail. He didn't like this at all.

'Are you worried?' McIlwham asked.

'Frankly, yes.'

'To be truthful so am I.'

'So what happens if you get your collar felt?'

'From your point of view?'

'Precisely.'

McIlwham said slowly, 'I've been thinking about that. You see my problem is if I go down what happens to the wife and kids? What'll they live on? There won't be any money coming in apart from what she can get out of the parish. I'd certainly be a lot happier knowing they were being looked after.'

Kirk got the message loud and clear. 'Just supposing you do go down. What sort of amount would you have in mind?'

'Say fifteen a week arriving by post. That would make life an awful lot easier for them.'

'And what would I get in return?'

'My word that I'll keep my mouth shut. Your name will never ever be mentioned.'

Kirk sat back in his chair and thought about that. Fifteen pounds a week was nothing. McIlwham was being clever by not asking too much. As insurance went it was a small price to pay for the man's guaranteed silence.

'Consider that an agreement, should the worst come to the worst,' Kirk said.

'Let's just hope it doesn't,' replied McIlwham.

Eddy followed Mike Jardine into a pub called The Neuk. With Turk McGhie dead, and no other trouble of that sort having reared its ugly head in the meantime, Mike Jardine and Sandy Pettigrew had been upgraded to representatives with the special brief of trying to win back some of Black Lion's lost outlets.

The Neuk was one such outlet which had gone over to KM but which had now returned to the Black Lion fold.

Since McGhie's death KM's momentum had stopped and indeed was now beginning to fall back. Without the Damoclean threat of McGhie hanging over their heads, free houses were leaving KM, some returning to Black Lion while others were giving their business to the other surviving breweries.

Eddy was a pleased man as he strode up to The Neuk's bar. KM was on the retreat while Black Lion was expanding again. Expanding slowly, mind you, but expanding nonetheless. And that was the main thing.

It had been Eddy's own idea he visit every outlet that returned to Black Lion. It was the sort of gesture that went down big in Glasgow that he, the boss man, thought enough of the pub or outlet to put in a personal appearance.

'Mr King, I'd like you to meet Mr Hannigan, the publican,' Mike Jardine said.

'I'm Eddy and you're .. ?'

'Rab.'

'Welcome back to Black Lion, Rab. I know it's going to be a pleasure doing business with you again.'

Hannigan pumped Eddy's hand and then beamed round the pub.

'Anyone who'd like a drink on Mr King of Black Lion just step up to the bar,' announced Mike Jardine.

A grinning Eddy was nearly bowled over in the stampede.

Kirk was at home, sitting sunk in thought. Ever since Turk's death things had started to go wrong. The straight sweep to a Glasgow monopoly had been halted and there was nothing he could think to do about it. He had considered hiring another nard man but with the police situation the way it was at the moment he thought it best to lay off those sort of tactics for a while.

Another four police officers had been suspended and three of the originals had been committed to Barlinne Prison pending trial. So far McIlwham was safe, but according to him he had the feeling the net was closing in. From one or two hints McIlwham had dropped, it seemed he'd been up to a great deal more than merely looking after KM's interests.

Anyway, Kirk thought, no matter what happened to

McIlwham, he was in the clear. He had his arrangement with McIlwham to thank for that.

But the prime source of his moroseness was Eddy King and Black Lion Brewery. They were his main competitors and under Eddy's guidance regaining ground they'd lost when that old fart the Major had been running the place.

And thinking of the Major .. that was one thorn in his flesh who wasn't long for this world. According to Susan the old fart was so gone with cancer he'd have to be admitted to hospital as soon as he was proving too much for his wife Jean to look after at home.

Good riddance to bad rubbish, Kirk thought; then, fingering the scar on his cheek, and if you're in as much pain as Susan says you are don't go quickly, but rather linger on, drawing it out.

Susan entered the room to say she'd just had an emergency call. A horse in nearby stables had come down with some mysterious fever and her presence was required right away.

After she'd gone, Kirk thought of how she'd picked up of late. She wasn't drinking nearly as much and there was a new spring to her step and gleam to her eye. Opening up a practice had certainly made a world of difference to her, he thought. It had given her a new zest, a new sort of life about her. There were times when he definitely regretted not being able to have sexual relations with her. Of late she had been extremely fanciable.

Putting Susan from his mind, he went back to thinking about Eddy and Black Lion. If only he could get rid of them somehow the other smaller breweries, the few left that is, would soon fall to him.

But how? That was the question. How?

Hours passed and Kirk sank lower and lower in his chair as he cudgelled his brains to no avail.

'I don't understand why you don't move out of this place,' Susan said. She and Eddy were in Eddy's front room.

455

'I don't see any reason to, that's why,' he replied.

'But it's a slum!'

'Only outside these four walls, not inside,' he grinned.

And it was true. Inside his house he had the very best money could buy. He'd never forgotten his night at London's Ivy Restaurant with the actor knight. Since having started to make a great deal of money he hadn't stinted himself when it came to the luxuries in life. And always he insisted on the very best. Top quality.

'That's true,' Susan admitted grudgingly.

On her first visit to his house all she'd seen was bachelor muddle. But on subsequent visits when sober it had surprised her to see what was beneath that muddle, and it had surprised her even further to discover what unerring good taste Eddy had. Whether it was silver for the table, pictures for the wall or even material for curtains, Eddy had the knack of choosing whatever was just right. To begin with she'd thought there had to be another woman somewhere in the background. Even if only in an advisorial capacity. But no. Eddy chose and selected everything himself.

Eddy looked up from the novel he was reading – a Thomas Mann story he'd only recently come across – to say, 'Maybe someday, should I ever get married. But until then what's the point? I know and like the people roundabout, and what's more they know and like me. I feel at home in this area. If a wife and children come along sometime then I'm only too willing to review the situation. But until then I'm staying put.'

There was a basic honesty about Eddy which attracted Susan. So different to Kirk, who was completely the opposite – and yet Kirk had his qualities too. She sighed. Why was it women always fell for the bastards? It was a question she couldn't answer.

Eddy placed his book on his lap and put his clasped hands behind his head. He always felt so contented when he was with Susan, he reflected, her presence being enough to satisfy him.

'Do you mind us not going out and about more?' he asked.
'No.'

'We could if you wanted to. It's just . . . well I prefer being home, cosy with you.' Susan smiled as he went on. 'Listening to the radio, reading a book, even sitting doing nothing makes me feel so contented when you're there. Does that sound soft?'

'Terribly,' she mocked.

'No, be serious.'

'I enjoy just being with you too.'

'Do you, eh. . feel that way with Kirk?'

Her smile became wistful. 'Perhaps once. But that was before he met Ciona Crammon. Now he can be there but we're not together, if you know what I mean.'

'I know.'

She sat lost in her thoughts for a while and when she looked again in his direction it was to find he'd fallen asleep.

She took that as a compliment.

Kirk was aghast. 'What?' he exclaimed.

'I'm going to America. New York to be precise,' Ciona replied.

'But why?'

'You haven't been listening. I've been offered a job there in the office of one of London's top agencies. It's an enormous step up and an opportunity I'd be crazy to let slip by.'

'But I thought you wanted to stay in Glasgow?'

'Only when my parents were alive. But with them gone there's nothing to keep me here.' It was now four months since she'd buried her parents in the cemetery at Craigendoran, a small village just outside Helensburgh.

'Nothing to keep you here?' Kirk echoed. 'What about me?'

'We've had good times together . . .'

'I'd thought we'd get married one day.'

A look of feminine interest expressed itself on Ciona's face. 'You never mentioned it,' she replied. 'Anyway you already are married.'

457

'I could get a divorce. Scottish law being what it is, it would take a while mind you, but there's nothing to stop it happening and then you and I could wed.'

'I don't think so, Kirk,' Ciona said gently. 'You're a lovely man and we've had great times together. But I wouldn't marry you for all the tea in China.'

'Why not?'

'Various reasons, one being I could never trust you not to do to me what you've been doing to Susan. You're a born marital cheat. I doubt you could stay faithful if you tried.'

'That's just not true. It wouldn't be at all like that if you and I were married.'

'No?' she queried mockingly.

'For Heaven's sake Ciona, I love you!' he said imploringly.

'I think you probably do. For the time being, anyway. But how long would it last? Till the next piece of skirt came along that you fancied, I suspect.'

'You've got me all wrong!'

Ciona laughed. 'I doubt it.'

'Listen, I'll start divorce proceedings right away . . .'

'Do what you like. I'm still off to America. This is a chance in a lifetime and I'm grabbing it with both hands.'

'I just don't believe this!' Kirk said despairingly, running a hand through his hair. 'I thought you and I had something special going together. That we understood one another.'

'I understand you, all right. I always have.'

He pulled her into his arms. 'Please?' he pleaded. 'At least think it over. Consider marriage.'

'I already have and the answer is still that I'm going.'

Kirk sighed. 'God, I never realised how hard you are. I can see it now all right, though.'

Ciona laughed again. 'Me, hard? Isn't that a touch of the pot calling the kettle black?'

'Only in business. I've had to be.'

She shook her head. 'If you really believe that, then you've been kidding yourself all these years. Look at the way you've treated Susan. Well I'm certainly not going to put myself in the position where you could treat me that way.'

'It would be different with you. I swear!'

'I don't believe you, Kirk. Oh, you might be faithful and loving for a little while but soon the old eye would begin to wander and before I knew where I was I'd be sitting home on my birthday while you were out gallivanting elsewhere with God knows who.'

'That's not fair. It was your parents that had died that night. You were in no fit state to drive yourself.'

'Yes, that was a little bit uncalled for,' Ciona admitted. 'Nonetheless, it's still true. But thank you all the same; I did need you desperately that night. You were a tower of strength.'

Kirk ground his teeth in frustration. He was going round and round in circles here and getting nowhere.

'Is it because I'm working-class and you're, well you're what you are?'

'That's got absolutely nothing to do with it.'

'You never introduced me to your parents when they were alive, nor have I ever met any of your friends from that background.'

'Kirk, you're a married man! What was I supposed to say? "Mummy and Daddy, I'd like you to meet Kirk, he's a married bloke I'm having an affair with"?'

'Well you wouldn't have had to put it like that.'

'What other way would I have put it? One minute after being introduced they would have started asking questions of you and me. And I was never in the habit of lying to my parents. By omission, yes. But not face to face. Besides, my father would have seen right through it. He would have known you were married. Don't ask me how. He would just have known. And as for my friends, the same thing applies. It never figured in my scheme of things that you and I would get married. You were just a nice man whom it was fun to be with, and that was that.'

'I see,' he said slowly.

'I'm genuinely sorry if you read more into it than that. I certainly never intended you to.'

They were in Ciona's flat. Kirk crossed to where the drinks were and poured himself a large one.

'Don't make it any more difficult than it has to be,' Ciona said.

'Is there someone else?'

'No.'

That mollified him a little.

'When do you go?' he asked.

'That hasn't been settled yet. But probably next month.'

'So soon?'

'They have a new campaign coming up they want me to work on.'

'Is it a permanent position or temporary?'

She shrugged. 'If things work out it could be permanent, should I want it that way. Then again I may decide after a while that I want to come back to Britain.'

'I'm going to miss you,' he said into his drink.

'You'll meet someone else. Or you could even start up again with your wife.'

'Do we continue seeing one another till you go?'

'Of course.'

'Are you sure I wouldn't be boring you?'

'You will do if you come out with nonsense like that.' Adding a few seconds later, 'Now how about some dinner? I'm starved.'

It was a cold bitter day with the wind howling off the sea.

Kirk shivered and pulled the collar of his coat up even higher. He wished he'd thought to wear a hat; he could certainly have used one.

A group of passengers emerged from the terminal to walk across to where a plane stood ready for flight. Even at this distance Ciona was easily discernible because of the distinctive fur coat she wore.

The coat had been his going-away present, albeit there was a side of him said she didn't deserve one.

The coat had cost him a small fortune. Perhaps he'd spent

that amount of money hoping it would cause her to change her mind and stay. But it hadn't and now she was on her way.

At the bottom of the steps leading up to the plane she stopped and turned to stare at the visitors' platform. She waved once. Then she mounted the steps and disappeared from view. And out of his life.

A few minutes later, the plane's propellers burst into life and shortly after that the plane itself was taxying down the runway. Once in the air it made a wide sweep round and over Prestwick. Then it headed out to sea, beyond which lay America.

Kirk stuffed his hands deep in his pockets and headed for the exit.

He felt terribly alone. And for some reason second-rate.

It was ten days since Ciona's departure and Kirk was randy in the extreme.

He let himself in through the front door and, having hung up his coat, went through to the drawing room where he found Susan reading a magazine.

Susan looked up in surprise. 'You're early again,' she said.

His reply was an indistinct mumble as he poured himself a drink.

'Like one?' he asked.

'Please. But make it small.'

Susan regarded him thoughtfully as he sank into his chair. He'd been positively melancholic for the past week, which was most unlike him. And that coupled with the fact he was coming home early night after night could only mean something was up. Ciona must be away on holiday, she thought. Or perhaps a business trip.

As though reading Susan's mind Kirk said suddenly, 'We've broken up, in case you've been wondering.'

'Pardon?'

'Ciona and I. I gave her the elbow.'

Susan didn't reply to that. Instead she dropped her gaze back to her magazine.

461

'Don't you want to know why?' he asked.

Susan didn't reply.

'Susan?'

'All right, why?'

'Because I'd come to realise what a bloody stupid fool I've been. She was an infatuation, that's all. In reality she meant nothing to me. Nothing at all.'

'It took you a long time to discover that.'

He pulled a face. 'So who's perfect? I certainly never claimed to be.'

'What's this leading up to, Kirk?'

'I want us . . . to be man and wife again.'

Susan smiled thinly. 'Do you think you can come to me and with one snap of your fingers have me running back to you again? God! What a low opinion you must have of me.'

'I have nothing but the highest opinion of you. Always had.'

'Well that wasn't the way it came over . . .'

'If you mean Ciona then I've explained that. It was an infatuation. It could've happened to anyone. But as I've just told you that's over now, for good. It's finished.'

'Bully for you.'

'If you're going to be unreasonable . . .'

'How do you expect me to be, after what I've been through? The lies, the deception, the degradation. Have you any idea at all what I felt like, knowing you were off sleeping with that . . . that woman? Night after night, sitting here with only the fire and a drink for company, knowing you were out with her, wining and dining her, taking her here, there and every bloody where, from all accounts? The laughter, the sniggers behind my back. That's Susan Murray, her husband Kirk is knocking off Ciona Crammond, you know, the beautiful advertising lady. Poor bitch. Yes, poor bloody bitch! And after all that, I'm supposed to forgive and forget all within the space of a few short seconds. Well I've got news for you. It isn't going to be like that. Now if you'll excuse me, good night.'

And throwing her magazine to one side she swept from the room.

Kirk gave her ten minutes and then followed her up to the bedroom where he found her sitting at her vanity table brushing her hair. She had already changed into her nightdress.

'I think I'll have a shower,' he said.

He stripped and went through to the shower where he spent a leisurely quarter of an hour under steaming hot water. When he finally towelled himself dry his entire body shone a healthy pink. He splashed talcum powder over himself and then liberally doused his face with after-shave, choosing a brand from amongst a number which he knew Susan was particularly fond of.

Returning to the bedroom he found her pretending to be asleep. Crossing to her side of the bed he sat. 'Susan?'

There was no reply.

'Susan?'

Again no reply.

He pulled the bedclothes down, then slipped his hand down the length of her back.

He smiled to himself when he heard her breathing change. He found her bottom and stroked it. Something she'd always liked in the past.

'Go away,' she hissed.

Languorously, he continued stroking, deeply sensual strokes that became wider and more probing.

'No Kirk,' she said, eyes still closed.

'Can't a man be allowed one mistake? It'll never happen again, I swear.'

'Go away.'

'I love you, Susan. Always have done. Always will do.'

'You're annoying me. And get your fingers out of there. That's private.'

'But I'm your husband.'

'You should have remembered that before you started screwing that tart.'

'Being with that tart, as you call her, has made me come to appreciate just how lucky I am to be married to you. She's fish and chips compared to your *filet mignon*.'

Fish and chips! he thought. Ciona would have loved that!

'Please Kirk. You're annoying me.'

'You still love me. I know you do.'

'Talk about ego! When it comes to that, you certainly take the cake.'

He brought his free hand down, through the covers she was clutching to her front, to a breast. He kneaded it gently, occasionally flicking her nipple with his pinky.

'I'm not going to tell you again to stop it,' said Susan.

'Come on, love.'

With an exclamation of annoyance she opened her eyes to stare at him. 'Take your hands off me this instant,' she said through gritted teeth.

His finger slipped inside causing her to suck in her breath. He lowered his mouth to kiss her neck.

He grunted with pain and astonishment as her nails raked his cheek. Her hooked hand flailed again but this time missed.

He pulled both hands free to hold his damaged face. Blood oozed through his fingers to fall to the covers.

'I mean what I say,' Susan hissed.

'Why you . . .'

Breath whooshed out of her as he forced her hands back into the bed. She brought her knee up but probably caused herself more pain than she inflicted on him when she came into contact with his thigh. Her eyes blazed with anger.

Letting go her hands he tore off the covers. Blood from his cheek splashed over her nightdress and one exposed breast.

'You won't . . . you won't . . .' she gasped as he tried to heave himself on top of her.

Her fists drummed against his chest. And when that proved to be no deterrent she lashed out again to rake his other cheek. Passion mingled with anger enveloped him then. Grasping her nightdress he ripped it, needing three goes before her naked length lay exposed beneath him.

She clawed his back, his neck, his sides, but it was no use. He was far too strong for her.

'You're my wife, damn you, and I love you,' he said, and,

forcing her arms back yet again, manoeuvred himself into such a position that he could go into her. This he did in a pile-driving, thrusting motion which instantly filled her to capacity.

For the first few seconds he was urgent, brutal, and then he got hold of himself and played her the way he had the very first time he'd made love to her. The fight melted from Susan in an overwhelming welter of sensations. For the truth was she still loved Kirk and had desperately wanted this to happen ever since he'd taken up again with Ciona Crammond.

Kirk was a master at lovemaking and he employed every nuance of technique and trick in his repertoire as he brought Susan thrilling to orgasm after orgasm after orgasm.

When, at long last, they finally fell into an exhausted sleep there was no doubt they were man and wife again.

'I see,' said Eddy.

Susan twisted her handbag in her hand as she stood facing him. 'I'm sorry, but that's the way it is.'

'And when did you two get back together then?'

'Last night.'

'Well, I suppose you know what you're doing.'

'I don't regret what happened between us. I'll always think of you kindly.'

'And I you. He's a lucky man. But then from what you've just told me it seems he's come to realise that.'

'I always knew that Ciona Crammond wasn't really for him. But he had to find that out for himself, I suppose.'

'And he gave her the push?'

'Yes,' smiled Susan.

I wonder? thought Eddy. I wonder?

'It was good of you to come and tell me like this. I appreciate that,' he said.

'What else could I do? Send you a note? That would have been absurd.'

Eddy came to her and took her in his arms. 'I'm pleased for you, Susan. I won't even pretend to like your husband. But if

465

his being back with you makes you happy then I'm pleased that's the case.'

'I'll miss our evenings together. I enjoyed them.'

'Even if we didn't do all that much?'

'I seem to remember there were times we did quite a lot,' she teased.

Eddy laughed. 'If you put it that way, then yes we did.'

Suddenly he was excited and wanting her. He knew from the sudden startled look in her eyes she could tell.

'No, Eddy,' she said putting pressure on to break away.

'One last time, Susan?'

'It wouldn't be right.'

'One last time to remember you by. You won't deny me that, will you?'

One part of her was surprised that, under the circumstances, she wanted to go to bed with him. Another part wasn't.

Eddy's lovemaking was a completely different experience to Kirk's. Kirk's was mountains and troughs of wild, abandoned, ecstatic passion. Eddy's was cosy like the many nights they'd spent together.

'Come on, Susan, where's the harm?' he urged.

She was going to miss his safeness, she thought. The utter dependability that was him.

He saw she was weakening so drew her back close. Placing his mouth against hers he kissed her tenderly.

'All right,' she whispered. 'One last time.'

Hand in hand they made their way through to the bedroom.

'There's no doubt about it,' said Doctor Goldberg. 'You're thirteen weeks gone.'

There it was, the confirmation she'd so desperately been praying for.

Smiling, she nodded, a glint of moisture in her eyes. At long last, after all this time, they'd finally gone and done it.

Goldberg took out a stubby fountain pen and wrote on the

scrap pad in front of him. Tearing off the top sheet of paper he handed it across to her.

'Accordingly to the tests and the information you gave me, these are your dates.'

'Thank you,' she replied in an emotion-charged voice, accepting the sheet of paper.

'My receptionist will give you details of my ante-natal clinic and I shall expect to see you there regularly. In the meantime, if anything at all worries you, contact me and I shall be only too happy to answer any questions you might have.'

'You've been most kind, doctor.'

He smiled. 'That's what I'm here for.'

She rose, gathered herself together, thanked him again and then left the surgery.

After she was gone Goldberg's smile faded to become a hard look of speculation.

'Hmm!' he said, staring at the door. Then, 'Hmm!' again.

'No!' exclaimed Kirk.

'Yes!' she said.

'My God!' he roared, and catching her in his arms birled her round and round.

Suddenly he stopped, thinking what he was doing. This was stupid of him, dangerous. He set her down immediately.

'It's definite now?' he demanded.

'Thirteen weeks, according to Doctor Goldberg.'

'Which is more or less how long we've been back sleeping together. This calls for a drink! A celebration!' And capering on the spot, 'We're going to have a baby! We're going to have a baby!'

Susan stood rooted at the thought which had just struck her. Kirk was right. It was thirteen weeks since they'd been back together as man and wife. Thirteen weeks back, thirteen weeks pregnant. Could it possibly be that...? No, she told herself. No. And yet...

'A toast!' said Kirk, thrusting a glass into her hand and

disturbing her train of thought. 'To our child! My child!'

Smiling in a rather lopsided way, she drank.

A little later she made her excuses, saying she wanted a bath. Once upstairs she stripped and then sat on the bed in her dressing gown.

She racked her brains trying to remember the precise day she and Kirk had made up. And it had been the next one she'd slept with Eddy for the last time. So there was an overlap there. Then she recalled an engagement she'd had two days after Eddy, which meant she could be precise about both days in question. Hurrying to her vanity table, she opened a drawer and extracted the diary she kept there. Swiftly she leafed through its pages.

Her heart crowded into her mouth when she finally saw what she hadn't wanted to. According to her dates, the baby she was expecting could be either Kirk's or Eddy's.

'God!' she whispered, closing her eyes and hunching forward.

It was eleven o'clock that night and Susan had been asleep for well over an hour.

Kirk sat in his favourite chair with a bottle of whisky by his side. Three-quarters empty, the bottle had been full when he'd opened it.

His eyes were screwed up in concentration as he sipped his drink. Since Susan had gone to bed he'd had time to think properly, the initial euphoria having passed away.

A million to one chance, Goldberg had said. And now that one chance had come up. Or had it?

Of course the baby had to be his, he told himself. Susan just wasn't the type to have an affair. It wasn't in her. At least, so he'd always believed. But on the other hand, how well did he really know her? He would have said through and through, but was that really the case?

He shook his head. This endless speculation was getting him nowhere. He was looking a gift horse in the mouth. Against all odds he'd been given one more chance. He was going to have a family after all. And of course the child was his. Any other idea was ridiculous.

But no matter how hard he tried to convince himself there was still that worm of doubt wriggling at the back of his mind.

A million to one chance was awful long odds to come up. Awful long.

Keith beamed when Jean told him the news. 'A grandchild, a *grandson* at long last!' he said.

'There's no guarantee it'll be a boy,' said Jean hurriedly.

'Of course it'll be a boy. What else would it be? Boys run in the family, you know that. Our having Susan was a sheer fluke, the sort of thing that probably only happens every ten generations or so.'

Jean stared at her husband, thinking how ill he looked. He'd lost a great deal of weight and was now only a shadow of his former self. Bones showed clearly through his skin while his face had become so sunken it was like looking at a talking skull. She knew from having spoken to the doctor that he was being given whisky laced with morphine and cocaine twice daily. That was to deaden a little the terrible pain he was having to endure.

Keith's skeletal hand reached out to clasp hers. 'Six months to go, you say?'

She nodded.

'Then I'll have to see I hang on that length of time.' He gave a weak grin. 'For I'll be damned if I'll be pipped at the post now. I waited long enough for a son and then a grandson to be beaten by a few measly months.'

'That's the spirit, Keith.'

'A wee boy!' he said, his eyes lighting up. 'A wee boy at long last.'

Then suddenly, his grip digging into Jean's arm, he said, 'They wouldn't deny me seeing him, would they?'

'Not Susan. She'll bring him, I'm sure of it.'

'That's all right then,' Keith said, relaxing his head back on to his pillow.

Minutes later he was asleep, his mouth curled upwards in a smile. Jean knew he was dreaming about the grandchild that was on its way.

She left him to his slumber.

'The A.C.C. Crime wants to see you right away,' the voice on the phone said.

'Okay,' replied McIlwham and hung up.

He sat there for a moment or two staring straight ahead. There it was, the phone call he'd been dreading all this while. He'd been rumbled.

There was a leaden feeling in his stomach as he rose and made his way upstairs to the office of the Assistant Chief Constable, Crime. He took a deep breath before knocking.

'Come in,' the A.C.C.'s voice rapped out.

'You sent for me, sir?'

The A.C.C.'s face was a stone mask betraying not one flicker of emotion.

'Know what this about, Superintendent?' he asked.

'No sir,' McIlwham lied.

'You've been under investigation for some time now. And as a result of that investigation you are hereby suspended.' He paused. 'Any comment?'

'What am I supposed to have done, sir?'

'Accepting bribes from various parties.'

'May I know the names of these parties, sir?'

The A.C.C. rattled off three names and McIlwham knew he was sunk.

'I see, sir,' McIlwham replied.

'I'll need your warrant card, McIlwham, and have you any court appearances coming up?'

'Several, sir.'

'I'll arrange a replacement officer for those.'

McIlwham laid his warrant card on the desk in front of the A.C.C. 'Can I go now, sir?' he asked.

The A.C.C., his eyes never wavering from McIlwham's, nodded.

Without a further word McIlwham left the room.

The A.C.C.'s stone face cracked to display disgust and anger. Contemptuously he threw McIlwham's warrant card into a drawer.

On leaving the station, McIlwham went straight to a pub where he ordered himself a drink.

His thoughts were in a turmoil as he stared into his whisky. The good thing was the three names the A.C.C. had thrown at him were tiddlers. Sure, he'd accepted money from them but the amounts involved had been minimal. If he was charged on these three offences alone he couldn't possibly draw a heavy sentence. A year, eighteen months at the most, he figured. So it was to his advantage to keep his mouth shut about his dealings with Murray and the others he'd been helping. But they weren't to know that.

He'd already made an arrangement with Murray and one other. Now was the time to inform the remainder what was expected of them.

And who knew? Perhaps when he came out again one of them might be grateful enough to give him a job. Murray was his best bet there, he reckoned. He'd fancied running a pub on retirement, anyway.

Kirk threw the report he'd been studying down in anger. Another five outlets lost in the past month, three of them to Black Lion.

God damn you, Eddy King! he raged.

Rising abruptly, he strode to his window where he stood gazing out over Glasgow. Why in hell's teeth had McGhie gone and got himself killed? What a gut blow that had been to him. The mystery of Turk's death had never been solved. The police put it down to a revenge-motive gang killing.

Not that the police had tried all that hard to solve the mystery anyway, the truth being they didn't care who killed Turk. If they'd found the murderer they'd probably have given him a medal rather than charge him.

And, thinking of the police, he'd lost his contact there when McIlwham had been suspended. That was another bad loss; McIlwham had been useful in so many ways.

Well at least he didn't have anything to fear there. McIlwham was going to be charged on the three original counts, which meant, McIlwham having agreed to keep his trap shut, that Kirk's involvement with the bent Superintendent would be kept secret.

Eddy King, he thought bitterly. Everything had been going forward smoothly until that bastard had appeared to throw a spanner in the works. Staring out over Glasgow he saw nothing but Eddy's face. Despair and frustration welled in him. With the use of force currently ruled out, McIlwham's suspension being one of the main contributory factors to that, there just had to be another way to knock out Eddy and Black Lion. There just had to be.

Patience, he told himself. Patience, lad. The answer would come in time. Of that he had no doubt.

'Stop fussing!' exclaimed Susan. 'Honest to God, you're like an old mother hen.'

Kirk grinned. 'I just don't want you to be doing anything you shouldn't, that's all.'

'I'm pregnant, not an invalid, you know.'

'I just don't want you to take any chances.'

'I promise you, Kirk, I have absolutely no intention of doing anything that would cause harm to either myself or the baby. Give me credit for some sense.'

'I do.'

'You could have fooled me the way you've been carrying on these past few months. Honestly, you'd think I was the first woman ever to have a baby.'

He looked down at his hands and cleared his throat. The thing was he couldn't tell her just how precious this child was, not without explaining about Leoni von Kruppermann and the dose that bitch had given him, which he had no intention of doing.

472

This was his last chance to have a child. There would be no repeats.

'Just take it easy, that's all I ask,' he said.

Susan sighed and rolled her eyes to Heaven.

'How about a drink?' she asked a little later.

'Do you think that's a good idea so early in the evening?' he replied.

She sighed again.

'What I want is your confirmation this baby will be all right. That it won't be deformed in any way,' Kirk said.

'I take it you're worried because of what you contracted in the Army?' Doctor Goldberg asked.

Kirk nodded.

Goldberg made a pyramid with his hands and stared at Kirk. 'Providing you were cured out in Germany, as you say you were, then you've nothing to worry about. Damage to the baby can only come about if the male partner infects the female, who in turn passes it on to the unborn child.'

'Well that's a relief,' said Kirk smiling.

Goldberg went on, 'And as you're both still young the possibility of mongolism is extremely remote. So if I was you I'd put my mind at rest.'

At the door Kirk said, 'A chance in a million. Incredible that it came off, eh?'

'Yes, quite incredible,' replied Goldberg, smiling with his mouth, but not his eyes.

'Come on, Mr King, cheer up!' said Maisie, handing Eddy a drink. She was the barmaid he'd had a fling with before taking up with Susan. This was the first time he'd seen her since then.

The Christmas party was in full swing and it was obvious from the flushed faces and goings-on that the brewery employees were enjoying themselves. Eddy had decided to treat the staff, and some of the people from his pubs as well, because of all the hard work they'd put in over the year. He

473

considered them a good, hard-working bunch and the party was a token of his appreciation.

'Here, put this on,' said Maisie. And before Eddy knew what was happening he was wearing a green pointed hat which had a gold star on its front.

'He looks like Noddy,' someone said, causing a roar of laughter to go up.

'Just you lot wait till Monday. I'll show you then who's Noddy!' Eddy said.

They all laughed again, knowing he didn't mean a word of it.

Patting his pockets, Eddy discovered he was out of cigarettes. Muttering excuses he made his way to his office where he knew he had a spare packet in his desk drawer.

He was about to light up when the door opened and Maisie slipped inside.

'It's getting a bit too much through there,' she said with a smile.

He lit two cigarettes and handed her one.

'Thank you,' she said throatily.

'Enjoying yourself?'

She nodded.

He suddenly felt ridiculous wearing the pointed hat so he removed it and sat it on the desk.

Maisie regarded him quizzically. 'Why did you stop seeing me, Eddy?' she asked, and when he didn't reply right away, 'Another woman?'

'Yes.'

'Serious?'

'We've broken up.'

'That doesn't answer the question.'

He blew smoke into the air, watching it spiral to the ceiling. 'I was very fond of her, if that's what you mean,' he replied.

Maisie came to him and put her arms round his neck. Drawing his head down to her she kissed him. The female in her didn't fail to note that part of him was holding back. It hadn't been like that the last time they'd kissed. But that had been before he'd met this other woman.

474

Breaking away, she made for the door, where she stopped. 'I think you should try and see her again,' she said. And smiling enigmatically, she left the room to rejoin the party.

After Maisie had gone, Eddy poured himself a whisky and then sat at his desk to drink it. He'd never imagined he'd miss Susan so much. But he did.

His relationship with her had been nothing like that with either Annie or Leoni. He'd loved both of them whereas with Susan he ... he ... he what?

As though a curtain in his mind had been suddenly drawn back the truth dawned on him. He'd come to *love* Susan. Perhaps he hadn't realised that was so because unlike the others, which had more or less hit him instantly, this had sort of sneaked up on him to catch him unawares.

He examined his feelings again. There was no doubt, and it only amazed him he hadn't realised before, he loved Susan Murray, Kirk's wife.

The biter bit, he thought ruefully. That drunken night he'd first slept with Susan, he'd intended using her as a card against Kirk. Instead of which the involvement had backfired in his face.

'What a balls-up!' he said into his drink. 'What a bloody balls-up!'

Every weekday afternoon a copy of the *Evening Times* was laid on Eddy's desk, which he'd glance through, providing he had the time, with his afternoon coffee.

That particular afternoon he had the time.

The news was unspectacular and sport was virtually non-existent. He read through the gossip section, called The Chit-Chat Column, which he rarely did.

The piece about Susan and Kirk was the fourth article. It stated that Mrs Susan Murray was expecting and that Mr Kirk Murray was overjoyed. There followed a brief story about Kirk and KM Brewery's meteoric rise and how Susan was the daughter of Major Keith Gibb, until recently the owner of Black Lion Brewery, KM's chief rival.

475

Eddy laid the paper down and pushed it away from him. Any thoughts he'd entertained, and he had given it quite a bit of consideration, of trying to win Susan back had just been blasted by that article. Now she was pregnant by Kirk she would want to stay with him. The baby would be the cement that would render whole again the cracks that had previously divided them.

Eddy shook his head. When it came to women it seemed the very Fates conspired against him. He wondered idly what he should do that night. He didn't want to go home to the house all on his own. Somehow since Susan had gone back to Kirk it had seemed a terribly lonely place to be. Prior to her coming into his life he hadn't minded being there on his own. Now he did.

He considered going to the pictures but there was nothing on he really fancied seeing. Nor did he want to go to a pub. He didn't want to fall into the same trap as Susan had for a while.

He would go to the theatre he decided, the Citizens'. It was a new season and Annie and Toby had gone, he'd previously checked on that.

He'd never seen Annie again after the night of the brewery fire. And he had the feeling he never would again.

He hoped she was happy. He just wished he could be.

'Mr Murray?'

Kirk looked up at the staff nurse who'd entered the waiting room where he'd been passing the time doing some paper work.

He came to his feet, papers clutched in his hand. 'Yes?' he demanded eagerly.

'You've got a wee girl.'

For a split second he was disappointed but he brushed that aside. 'Is she healthy? I mean, is everything as it should be?'

The staff nurse smiled. 'She's absolutely perfect, Mr Murray,' she replied.

Relief flashed through Kirk. Despite Goldberg's assurances

it had preyed at the back of his mind that something would be wrong with the baby.

'Your wife's also fine,' the staff nurse went on. 'Tired, of course, but that's only to be expected.'

'When can I see them?'

'They're cleaning the baby up now and also sorting your wife out. Fresh nightie, a bit of a wash, that sort of thing. I should think they'll let you in in about fifteen minutes.'

Kirk gave a combination nod and smile and sat. A wee girl. Well as long as she was healthy, that was the main thing.

In fact in a way he'd been hoping it would be a lassie. He knew via Susan just how much the Major was longing for a grandson.

Well, even at the last the old fart would be denied.

'A girl,' said Keith hollowly. He just couldn't believe it. He'd been so positive it would be a boy.

'A bonnie wee lassie,' said Jean encouragingly. 'I've seen her. And you know I think she's the spitting image of you.' That last was a lie, dreamed up as a consolation prize to try and take the edge off his disappointment. But it didn't work.

'Gerald had two boys and so had my father,' Keith said, his voice sounding as though it came from a long distance away. 'Boys run in the family.'

'Maybe they'll have a boy next time.'

'I won't be here to see it though.'

'Of course you will, Keith. You're tough as old boots. You've a lot of life left in you yet.'

He closed his eyes and sighed. The spark that had been keeping him going since learning of Susan's pregnancy died within him. Already shrivelled, he seemed to shrivel even more.

'I'd like to sleep now,' he said. 'So tired.'

Jean leant across to kiss him on the cheek. 'I'll be back tomorrow morning,' she said.

'Aye,' he breathed, the sound like a wind going out of him.

When she was gone he turned his head to the wall. In his mind he was young and back in India. Such good days, such marvellous times, he thought. And there was Jean just as he'd first seen her. Velvet nights, twinkling stars overhead, warm scented smells that belonged to India and India alone.

His one regret was he'd never had a son. If only . . . if only . . .

In the early pre-dawn hours of the morning when all human life is at its lowest ebb, he passed away.

The instant before he went he muttered one word. 'Gerald,' he whispered. Then he was gone.

Susan sat nursing the baby at her breast. Rachel, she'd decided to call the wee thing. It wasn't a name that had connections with either Kirk's family or her own. It was merely one she liked and which she thought suited her daughter.

Her daughter, yes – but certainly not Kirk's. For Rachel was the spitting image of Eddy.

She'd known the instant she'd clapped eyes on Rachel who her father was. The resemblance was remarkable. The same eyes, the same look about the face, the same shape of the head.

Rachel bawled lustily as Susan removed her from the now empty breast, and continued bawling while she did up the front of that bra cup and undid the other. The bawling only ceased when the tiny mouth fastened like a leach on to her other nipple.

Susan crooned as the baby fed. For the umpteenth time she told herself there was no reason for Kirk ever to find out he wasn't Rachel's father. After all it was quite common for children not to look like either parent. Her mother's side she would say, should it ever come up.

Yes, her mother's side of the family. That was the answer.

McIlwham felt as though he'd been struck by a sledge-hammer. He sagged a little as the judge's words echoed in his ears.

'. . . this terrible corruption in our police force . . . must be stamped out . . . intend to impose the maximum sentence I am allowed under the circumstances... officers must realise they are not above the law... betrayal of trust... of colleagues and the community at large... hereby sentence you... Ronald Alan Forbes McIlwham to five years... five years... five years...

The number repeated itself over and over again in McIlwham's head. Five years! When he'd been expecting no more than a year, eighteen months at the very most.

In a daze, the court swimming before him, he was led away, downstairs to the cells, from where he would be taken by Black Maria to start his sentence.

'Strip!' shouted the warder. 'Put your clothes in the basket provided and then queue up by the door here. And hurry up, get a move on. I haven't got all day!'

There were six of them that had come in the Black Maria to Barlinne Prison. From what McIlwham had gleaned during the journey, he was the only first-time offender. He shivered as he took off his clothes. It was freezing in the room. When he was naked he walked to the door indicated, where he stood clutching his basket.

When all six were ready, the warder opened the door and shouted at them to go on through. They found themselves in another room, this one divided by a counter behind which stood several trusty prisoners. There were also two other warders present to keep an eye on things.

'Baskets on the counter!' shouted the original warder.

The trusties went along the line, going through each basket and writing what it contained on an official form. When each item had been detailed the new prisoner was asked if he agreed with the itemisation, and on saying he did the new prisoner was asked to sign the form, after which the basket was taken away.

The next part of the procedure was their being issued with their prison outfits, moleskins as they were referred to. McIlwham was handed a well-worn corduroy jacket and trousers which didn't match in colour, being different shades of brown. After these he was given a singlet, underpants and boots with no laces. There were no socks.

One of the new prisoners started to put the underpants on, which proved to be a mistake as he soon found out.

'*Not yet*, you stupid man!' a warder screamed. 'We don't want your filthy bodies in our clean clothes. Wait until you've had your bath.'

The prisoner hastily removed the underpants, wilting under the warder's fierce gaze.

Christ, what have I let myself in for? McIlwham thought. He'd have given his eye-teeth to be back in his comfy home with his equally comfy wife... Get a grip of yourself, he chided himself. You'll soon settle in and get used to it. But it was a grim prospect.

'This way!' shouted the original warder, when the six new prisoners had collected their new clothes. The trusties looked on unsympathetically.

McIlwham and his five companions were herded along a corridor into a bathroom comprising many stalls. The water had already been run in six of the baths. In each case it was no more than six inches in depth and smelled strongly of disinfectant. The soap they were issued was carbolic. They were allowed ten minutes in the bath and then they were ordered to get out and dry themselves. The towels were like sandpaper.

McIlwham climbed into his moleskins and then, sitting on the edge of the bath, tugged on his laceless boots. When the order came he shuffled off with the rest of them down to the cell block where he was put in a cell with two other men.

In the days to come he reached the conclusion that the worst thing of all about being inside was, when he and his cell mates were locked away for the night, the utter degradation of having to use the toilet situated in one corner of the cell in full view of the others.

The second worst thing was the smell. A fetid combination of stale sweat, urine, excrement, unhealthy bodies – and perhaps even unhealthy minds – mingled with the sauce of fear and hopelessness. The stink was everywhere and indeed seemed to be impregnated into the very brickwork itself.

McIlwham was put to work sewing heavy canvas mailbags for the Royal Mail.

On her second day out of hospital Susan went to her father's funeral, which had been delayed so she could attend.

Kirk hadn't come, of course. Nor had she expected him to. Instead he'd taken a few hours off his work to stay at home and look after the baby. She had suggested getting someone in for the short babysitting session but he'd insisted he do it personally. She'd been touched by that.

It was a small funeral, the Major not having had many friends. Susan stood with her mother, who right at the very beginning of the ceremony broke down and cried. In her heart she didn't think her mother would be long behind her father. They'd been that sort of couple.

While the minister droned on about the resurrection to come, Eddy kept his eyes fastened on Susan. He knew she was aware he was watching her. She looked good, he thought. She was carrying a bit more weight than normal but that was only natural under the circumstances. Her face still held the bloom of motherhood. He guessed correctly it had been a happy pregnancy for her.

Jean Gibb threw a handful of earth on to the coffin, followed by Susan as second mourner.

The ceremony over, everyone started trooping towards their cars parked outside the cemetery walls. Jean and Susan were with several other people so Eddy didn't feel too guilty about taking her away from her mother for a moment or two.

'Susan? Can you speak for a second?'

'It was good of you to come, Eddy,' she said, joining him.

'Not at all. I owed your father a lot, as you know.'

'You look well.'

'I was just thinking the same about you back there. And congratulations, I believe they're in order. Rachel, isn't it?'

'That's right.'

481

'I read about the birth in the paper. I'm happy for you. Is Kirk pleased?'

She thought that might be some sort of dig or insinuation, but searching his face she saw it wasn't so. It hadn't occurred to him Rachel might be his. That was a relief.

'Very. He thinks the world of her.'

'And what about you? Happy?' he asked softly.

'Extremely.'

'No regrets?'

'About what?'

He smiled. 'No regrets,' he said, answering his own question.

'Are *you* happy?' she asked.

'Oh yes,' he lied.

'That's good, then.'

Suddenly it was awkward between them. He smiled falsely while she played with her hands. Overhead, crows cawed forlornly.

'I'd better get back to Mother,' she said.

Eddy nodded. 'Good luck then.'

'And you.'

On a sudden impulse she kissed him on the cheek. 'Take care.'

He strode away from her in the direction of his car. A three-time loser, he thought bitterly. It seemed he would never win where women were concerned.

Kirk had had very good reasons for volunteering to babysit while Susan went to her father's funeral.

The baby had been fed and was fast asleep in her crib. He sat reading a newspaper, patiently waiting. He rose the instant the doorbell went.

'Come in Doctor Aitken,' he said. 'You're nice and prompt.'

Aitken looked around, blinking. He carried a small black bag in his right hand.

'The child's upstairs,' said Kirk, and led the way to the baby's bedroom.

482

Aitken didn't ask questions. He just got on with what he'd come to do. From his black bag he extracted a syringe. 'Could you bare her arm, please?' he said.

Kirk gingerly picked up Rachel, who immediately awoke. She smiled up at him, eyes wide, trusting. He didn't find it easy but eventually he managed to roll up her sleeve. He though how tiny her arm looked. No bigger than a doll's. He grimaced as the needle slid in. The moment it did, Rachel started squawling and trying to pull away. On Aitken's instruction he held her more tightly.

'There we are,' said Aitken, when the syringe was about half-full. He pulled the needle out and rubbed the spot with some impregnated cotton wool.

Rachel was really bawling now, so Kirk held her close and crooned a lullaby he remembered from his mother's knee.

'When can you let me know the results?' he asked.

'Usually takes about a week. But if you're in a hurry I can have it rushed through. That'll cost you a few pounds extra, though. Not for me but for the hospital.'

'Hurry it through.'

'Right. I'll probably have the results tomorrow afternoon then.'

'You know my number at work. Ring me there.'

While Kirk tried to settle Rachel again, Aitken let himself out.

True to his word, Aitken rang Kirk the following afternoon at KM Brewery.

'Your baby has B-type blood,' Aitken said.

'Thank you, doctor,' Kirk replied and hung up.

He stared at the phone for a few seconds before taking a book from his desk drawer which he opened at a marked place. He'd got the book from the library and had already read the relevant sections. He didn't have to read the page again to know what he'd feared was in fact reality. He read it nonetheless.

When he'd finished he ran his fingers through his hair and

stared off into space. His normally good complexion had gone pale and there was a small red anger spot on either cheek.

His intercom buzzed but he ignored it. His secretary popped her head round the door. When she saw the expression on his face she hurriedly closed it again.

Finally Kirk rose and crossed to the drinks cabinet where he poured himself a stiff whisky. He drank it neat, then poured himself another.

'Oh, you bitch!' he muttered.

Susan looked up as the outside door closed. Kirk was later than usual. An infrequent occurrence now that Ciona Crammond was out of his life.

He stumbled into the room. His face was flushed and hair awry. There was a terrible expression on his face and his eyes positively glittered with a combination of anger and other emotions. He made straight for the drinks and poured himself a whisky. He'd been drinking steadily since the afternoon, when Aitken had rung.

'What's all this about?' Susan asked.

He turned to face her, a vicious slash of a smile twisting his mouth upwards as he swayed on the spot.

'Look at the state of you,' she said.

'Who's the brat's father?' he demanded harshly, coming straight to the point.

Susan was taken aback. 'I beg your pardon?'

He lurched across to her and leered in her face. 'Who's the brat's father?' he repeated.

'Which brat?'

'The one, I presume, who's upstairs in bed.'

A cold wind washed over Susan. She decided to try and bluff it out. 'If you mean Rachel, you're her father,' she replied.

Kirk shook his head. 'No I'm not.'

'Of course you are. What makes you think otherwise?'

He slurped whisky into his mouth, spilling some of it in the process, which stained his shirt front.

484

'You see there's something you don't know about me,' he slurred. 'Something I only found out when I went to see, at your suggestion, Doctor Goldberg. Remember?'

Susan nodded.

'He took what's known as a sperm-count and it was found that my count was nine thousand which is one thousand less than fertility level. In his own words, it would be a chance in a million for me to father a child.'

'Why didn't you tell me this before?' Susan asked quietly.

'I had my reasons. Not least of which was pride, the pride of masculinity. After all, what man wouldn't find shame in the fact he was sterile?'

'But you said there was a million to one chance? That means you're not completely sterile, surely?'

'Precisely what I clung to. Especially when you announced you were pregnant. The long shot has come off, I thought. The one in a million chance has come up. Aren't I the lucky man!'

'So what's made you change your mind?'

He poured himself another drink. Everything was getting very fuzzy around the edges now. And although he didn't realise it he was swaying even more than he had been.

'I wanted that baby to be mine. I desperately wanted it. But being the naturally suspicious bugger I am, I decided to make absolutely certain I was the father. Well, not absolutely certain, I couldn't do that, but what I could establish was I *could* be the father.'

This was a nightmare, Susan thought. 'Go on,' she said.

'So I had a blood test done on Rachel and guess what?'

'What?'

'Well let me put it this way. I'm an A blood-group, I know that from the Army. And you're also A, I know that from looking at your chart at the hospital. There it was, quite distinct, A blood-group. Which brings us to Rachel, your daughter but certainly not mine. She's B, you see. And according to the medical books A plus A can never equal B. Therefore I cannot be her father.'

Susan bit her lip and lowered her gaze. Her heart was pumping nineteen to the dozen.

'So,' said Kirk, 'that brings me back to my original question. Who *is* the brat's father?'

Susan shook her head.

He grabbed her by the shoulder and shook her. 'Tell me, woman! I want to know.'

'It's unimportant.'

'Not to me it's not!'

She decided attack might be her best form of defence. 'Anyway, what right have you to go on like this? You, who had an affair with that advertising tart.'

'Shut up about her,' he snarled.

She continued vehemently, 'I'm supposed to turn a blind eye and keep my mouth shut while you go out whoring night after night, but let me give you back a little of your own medicine and look at you! Nearly beside yourself with righteous indignation.'

'You were trying to pass the brat off as mine. Can't you see that's different?'

'If you're as sterile as you say you are, then we'd probably never have had a child. Be thankful that we've got this one.'

'Thankful!' he barked. 'You just don't understand, do you!'

'I understand that we both wanted a baby and now we've got one.'

'But she isn't *mine*! What good's a child to me who isn't mine?'

'She *is* mine. Doesn't that mean anything to you?'

He dismissed that with a drunken wave of his hand. 'Are you still seeing the father?' he asked.

'No.'

'I don't believe you.'

'Don't judge others by yourself. I don't lie.'

'You did about her upstairs.'

Susan had no answer to that.

'A bloody cuckoo in the nest. Who would ever have thought

486

that would happen to me?' he slurred. Then suddenly, like a volcano erupting, *'Fuck!'*

Susan rocked back in her chair. And for the first time fear took hold of her. She stared mesmerised at his contorted face which seemed as though it must surely explode from within.

'Who?' he choked, stumbling to her and taking hold of her dress. 'Who?'

She shook her head.

'Who was it, damn you?'

Thank God Rachel's safe upstairs, she thought, a second later crying out as his hand cracked against her cheek.

A berserk rage swamped him then. His hand flashed again and again knocking her head left and right, left and right. Her lip burst and blood spurted over her chin and his hand. His watch caught her cheek, ripping it open.

'Tell me!' he screamed.

And when he still got no reply he threw her to the ground where he started putting the boot in.

Susan retched and was sick as his foot thudded into her stomach. The pain exploding inside her was unbelievable in its intensity. On her hands and knees she tried to crawl away through the sick but she collapsed again when his foot smashed into her ribcage, causing a cracking sound.

Falling to the floor Kirk grabbed her by the front of her dress and pulling her into a half-sitting position proceeded to shake her as a dog would a rat.

'Who? ... who? ... who? ...' he repeated over and over again.

He's going to kill me, she thought. And her only regret was Rachel. For the wee one's sake she must somehow survive this terrible beating. Please God! Please! she prayed. For the baby's sake.

She was still praying when unconsciousness suddenly took her into its bosom.

Kirk came to his senses kneeling over her prostrate figure. For a stunned moment or two he thought he'd killed her, but a quick feel in the appropriate place told him her heart was still

487

beating. Although a long way from being sober the events of the past few minutes had burned a great deal of the alcohol from his system. Coming to his feet, he staggered to the telephone. Susan had to have medical treatment. That was obvious. And as he dialled 999 he made up his story. After being told the ambulance was on its way he stumbled upstairs to their bedroom from where he got a quilt which he used to cover her.

She looked dreadful, both eyes already discolouring and her cheeks puffing up like pastry. Her lip was still seeping blood but the blood on the torn cheek had coagulated to form a long lumpy maroon line.

Going through to the downstairs bathroom he doused his face with cold water after which he combed his hair. He was getting more sober and regaining his composure by the second.

Susan started to moan. Her hands clutching her stomach while she slowly writhed.

'Help's on its way,' he said, kneeling beside her. He was appalled at what he'd done. He'd intended giving her a beating but nothing like this.

'Can you hear me, Susan?' he asked. And when he got no reply he repeated himself. 'Can you hear me?'

When he still failed to get a reply he put his hand on her arm and shook her very gently. 'Susan?'

She stopped writhing and blinked her eyes open. They were like two currants sunk deep in still swelling blue-black dough.

'I'm sorry,' he said. 'Truly I am.'

She opened her mouth but no words came. Only some pink spittle which slowly meandered down to her chin.

'I didn't mean it. I didn't know what I was doing. Please, please believe that,' he pleaded.

'So sore,' she whispered.

'They'll give you something for the pain and then everything will be all right. But listen, love, you mustn't tell them I did this to you. They could put me inside for assault and battery. Do you understand?'

'Yes,' she croaked.

'I'll say you were upstairs with the baby and came downstairs to disturb an intruder. He panicked and beat you up before fleeing. When I came home I found you like this. Now is that clear?' And he went over it all again.

As he spoke her eyes were on him, probing him, staring at him as though she'd never really seen him before. He wilted under her gaze, unable to look her in the eye. It was a relief when the doorbell rang and he was able to come to his feet.

'Now don't forget the story,' he said, before hurrying to the door.

There were two ambulancemen, one of whom carried a stretcher. Kirk showed them straight through. One man prodded Susan gently all over and while he did Kirk told the lie about having come home and found her this way and how she'd muttered to him about coming down and surprising an intruder.

'A couple of broken ribs, I think,' said the ambulanceman who'd carried out the examination.

'If I ever catch the swine who did this to her, so help me God I'll murder him,' Kirk said.

Despite being as careful and gentle as they could, Susan cried out in pain as she was being lifted on to the stretcher.

'My baby,' she husked. 'I won't go without my baby. She mustn't stay here.'

The second ambulanceman looked strangely at Kirk then. 'Where is the baby, missus?' he asked.

'She's upstairs,' Kirk replied before Susan could. 'I'll get her.'

'Best wrap her up well. It's cold outside,' the first ambulanceman said.

'Won't go without her. Won't,' Susan repeated.

'Don't you worry, lass. We'll take the wean along,' the second ambulanceman said.

At the top of the stairs Kirk started shaking. He hurried through to the baby's room, picking Rachel up and wrapping her in the warm blankets that had been covering her. Rachel awoke and started to cry. A thin, tremulous wailing sound that, to Kirk's ears anyway, seemed to say she was aware all wasn't well with her mother. Clutching Rachel to him he hurried back downstairs.

Susan insisted on taking the baby, whom she hugged tightly to her bosom. Tears oozed from her eyes to fall coursing down swollen cheeks.

The ambulancemen covered mother and daughter with a red blanket before lifting them and taking them outside to the ambulance.

'I'll follow in my car,' shouted Kirk, locking the front door.

He winced and his stomach turned over when the ambulance's siren started up.

Kirk sat with his head in his hands. He'd been in the hospital waiting room over an hour and a half now. All he'd been told so far was that Susan was being attended to and that a policeman was interviewing her about what had happened.

There were about twenty in the Accident and Emergency waiting room and nurses and doctors came and went constantly.

'Mr Murray?'

Kirk looked up to find a very young nurse smiling at him.

'If you'd like to come with me you can see your wife now.'

He followed her down a corridor and into a lift.

They rode the lift up to the private wing where, on his instructions, Susan had been installed in a room with bathroom attached. He found her alone staring at the ceiling. The colour surrounding her eyes had deepened to a rich purple. The rips on her cheek and lip had been neatly sutured. She was a ghastly sight.

'How are you?' he asked when the nurse had gone.

There was no reply.

Licking his lips he moved closer to the bed. 'I, eh ... was told a policeman had been to see you.'

Still no reply.

He'd started to sweat under the arms and down his back.

'Did you say anything?' he asked.

'They've taken Rachel away to check her over. I told them she was all right but they wanted to make sure.'

He nodded.

'She cried all the time they were stitching me up. It was just the strangeness of the place, I think.'

'How long before you ... you get home?'

'A week at least they say. Maybe ten days.'

'I really am truly sorry, Susan. But finding out about Rachel was such a shock. You see I've come to love her since you brought her home. And then to find out she wasn't mine at all ... it was one helluva blow. I just went out my mind.'

He paused before continuing. 'I've always thought of you as a far better, more worthwhile person than myself. I never ever conceived of you having an affair. You were too good a person for that in my mind. For you to cheat would be like finding out there was no God after all or something equally as shattering. I'm not denying I was initially attracted to Ciona Crammond but the fact I did something about it was because I'd just learned I was sterile. Can you imagine what it was like to be told that?'

'You should have confided in me.'

'I should have done but I didn't. What I did do was go out and prove to myself that I was still a man. Because that's all going to bed with Ciona was. A reaction against my sterility. And then when you told me you were pregnant I was over the moon. We were to have a family after all and that meant so much to me. The shock of learning Rachel wasn't mine was traumatic, to say the least. To be truthful, I came home intending to hurt you because you'd hurt me. But I never meant it to be as bad as this. Please ... please forgive me? Please?'

The hardness she felt towards him melted. She'd sinned as much as being sinned against. There was fault on both sides. Her hand crept out from beneath the covers to lie on top of them. She extended her hand palm upwards in a gesture of invitation. He sat on her bed and took her hand in his. There

491

was moisture in his eyes when he said, 'We'll start again.'

'The three of us?'

'As you said, Rachel's part you and I'll continue loving her for that part.'

'Thank you,' Susan whispered.

'I have to ask, what did you tell the policeman?'

She smiled. 'What you told me to say. That I came downstairs and disturbed an intruder. He panicked and beat me up. I was asked for a description but I said it was all very hazy. All I remembered was there had been a man. Short, fat, tall or whatever I couldn't say. The next thing I really knew was waking up and finding you kneeling by my side.'

'You're marvellous,' Kirk said. And kissed her on the cheek that wasn't stitched.

'You'd better go now. I'm awfully tired.'

'I'll be back tomorrow morning,' he said, rising. 'And if there's anything you want, ask them to get it for you. Or if they can't, get word to me at the brewery and I'll get hold of it.'

'I feel a lot better already,' she said.

He blew her a kiss at the door.

Eddy had taken to frequenting a Black Lion pub just round the corner from Albion Street, where he was fond of talking to many of the journalists who used it as a watering hole cum second office.

He found the company of these men stimulating, learning a great deal about the world at large from what they had to say. In a way the journalists reminded him of the actor knight who'd impressed him so much when he'd been in London. They had the same spirit of adventure and excitement about them. The same surging life force.

Eddy was just ordering up a pint when a journalist called Dougie Mitchell, whom he'd become particularly friendly with, came through the door.

'Better make that two pints,' said Eddy to the barman as Mitchell joined him.

'So what's happening amongst Mungo's children tonight?'
he asked.

Mitchell shook his head. 'Very quiet. A stabbing in Jamaica
Street, a bird giving her boyfriend a sherricking outside the
Dennistoun Palais, a couple of half-cut eejits trying to break
into a bonded warehouse just off St Enoch Square, none of
which is likely to make page two, far less page one.'

The pints came up and Eddy paid.

They talked for a few more minutes about this and that, then
Mitchell said, 'Your big rival's wife got a right duffing-up the
other night. She surprised an intruder, who gave her a proper
going-over.'

Eddy frowned. 'You mean Kirk Murray's wife?'

'Aye, the same.'

'Is she badly hurt?'

'A couple of broken ribs. A face like she's just gone twelve
rounds with Rocky Marciano. Myself and a few of the boys
went to see her, thinking there might be a story in it, but
according to her, her mind's a blank about what actually
happened. The *Express* and the *Herald* gave it a couple of lines;
my paper didn't.'

'When did you say this happened?'

'Three nights ago. We saw her the following day.'

Three nights ago meant it had happened the day after her
father's funeral, Eddy thought. The day after he'd last seen
her.

'Have they kept her in hospital, do you know?'

'Oh, I'd think so. She was in a pretty bad way.'

Eddy tried not to let too much interest show in either his
face or voice. 'Poor woman,' he said. 'Knowing where Murray
lives, I suppose they took her to the Western Infirmary?'

Mitchell nodded as he drank his pint.

'She'll be all right there. It's a good hospital that,' said
Eddy. And promptly changed the subject.

Eddy sat on one of the several chairs provided with a
newspaper held in front of him. He'd been there for half an

hour waiting for Kirk to leave. He knew Kirk was with Susan, having seen him when he'd briefly glanced through the small glass panel on Susan's door.

Visiting time was almost up and he was beginning to think he'd have to go away and try again another time, when suddenly the door to Susan's room opened and Kirk emerged.

Immediately Eddy buried his head in the paper from which place of concealment he listened to Kirk's approaching footsteps. Stopping at the lift Kirk pressed the down button. When he glanced in Eddy's direction all he saw were feet and legs projecting from underneath a newspaper. When the lift arrived he stepped inside and seconds later was plunging downwards.

Eddy waited till the floor numbers above the lift confirmed that it had reached the ground floor before turning and making his way to Susan's room.

He tapped the door and entered.

'I hope you don't mind, Susan, but I ...' The rest of the sentence died in his mouth when she turned to face him. 'Jesus Christ!' he exclaimed.

She grinned ruefully. 'Not a pretty sight.'

'You can say that again.'

Susan was feeding Rachel, who was twisting both hands in the air while sucking lustily.

'Kirk's just gone,' she said.

'I know. I was lurking outside waiting for him to go. I wanted to see you but I didn't want to cause any friction. That's why I didn't bring you anything. I thought you might have trouble explaining away a bunch of flowers or a bowl of grapes that hadn't come from him.'

Eddy glanced around but there were no flowers in the room. Evidently Kirk wasn't the flower-buying type. At least not as far as his wife was concerned.

'An intruder, I was told,' he said.

'That's right.'

Eddy shook his head. 'Bastard to do that to you.'

Susan dropped her gaze to stare at the baby.

494

'So this is the young lady,' Eddy said, coming closer and peering at the suckling Rachel.

A few seconds later, Susan removed Rachel from her breast and adjusted her nightdress. She then put Rachel to her shoulder in order to wind her.

'I find this bit difficult because of my broken ribs,' she said.

'Here let me,' said Eddy and took the baby into his arms.

Rachel stuck out her tongue and smiled at him. She smelled very strongly of milk and powder. Eddy gathered her to his shoulder and gently patted her back.

'You look like you've been doing that all your life,' said Susan.

'Hidden talents,' he smiled back.

The smile died when the door opened and Kirk marched in.

'Forgot my brief-case ...' said Kirk, the last two words hanging suspended in the air when he caught sight of Eddy.

'What are *you* doing here?' he demanded.

Eddy's mind raced, trying to think up an explanation. Susan sat speechless.

'I think I know,' Kirk said slowly.

'Kirk ...' Susan started to say.

'Shut up!' he hissed.

Kirk looked at Rachel's face, then at Eddy's, then back again at Rachel's.

'So it was *you*,' he said in a choked tone of voice.

'What are you talking about?' Eddy said.

'You're the baby's father.'

Eddy was thunderstruck. That possibility had never even entered his head.

'It's obvious,' said Kirk. 'I don't know why I didn't see it before. Rachel's the spitting image of you.'

Eddy held the baby from him and stared hard at her face. Kirk was right. She did look like him. And in fact, now he'd been told, the more he looked at her the more he saw the resemblance.

'No wonder you wouldn't tell me who the father was,' Kirk

said to Susan. 'Of all people to choose, it had to be him. You bitch!'

Susan cowered away from his anger. 'Don't hit me again, please,' she pleaded.

Eddy sucked in a breath. 'What does that mean?' he demanded.

'No,' said Susan, shaking her head.

Eddy swung round on Kirk. 'Did you . . . was it *you* did that to her?'

Kirk glared at Eddy.

'Oh, you bastard.'

'Give me that child,' said Kirk, a vicious smile on his face.

'You just said she's mine.'

'She is. But she carries my name and as such is my daughter.'

Eddy's grip on Rachel tightened. His mind was whirling. The revelations of the last few minutes had left him not knowing whether he was coming or going.

'Is the baby mine?' Eddy asked Susan.

'Yes,' she whispered.

There it was. Confirmation of the obvious.

'But you'll never have her,' taunted Kirk. 'I will. And by God, that's something that's going to eat your guts out for the rest of your life.'

Eddy wanted to put the baby down and go for Kirk. To hammer him. To do what he should have done years ago. But somehow, and the effort plainly showed on his face, he brought himself under control.

'Please go, Eddy, before matters get worse,' said Susan.

'Give me the baby,' said Kirk, extending his hands.

Eddy couldn't bear the thought of Kirk bringing up his child. If he could beat Susan up the way he had then what might he do to Rachel? The very thought caused Eddy to shudder.

'I'm waiting,' said Kirk.

Eddy felt then that his entire life had been in preparation for this moment. Annie Grimes, Leoni von Kruppermann, even Gloag.

'Divorce Susan so I can marry her,' he said.

Kirk's smile was that of the shark. 'Get stuffed,' he leered.

'You don't love Susan. The only person you've ever cared about in your entire life is yourself. And perhaps your mother, although she'd rank a poor second.'

'Watch your mouth, King.'

'I should have sorted you out in Germany.'

'Just because you couldn't hold your woman that's no reason to start whining now.'

'What woman?' asked Susan quietly.

'The Countess von Kruppermann,' said Eddy. 'She was my girlfriend until your husband took her away from me. He found the thought of screwing a title irresistible.'

'Kirk?'

Kirk swallowed, at the same time glaring hate at Eddy. 'She meant nothing to me,' he said.

'But you slept with her?'

'Yes.'

Susan sagged a little. 'And us only newly married. But knowing you now as I do I suppose I shouldn't be surprised..I was a fool to think you'd remain faithful for two years. Two weeks would be stretching it.'

Rachel pawed at Eddy's lapel. His heart went out to the wee lassie, this extension of himself. That thought brought a lump to his throat.

'Tell me,' said Susan to Kirk, 'how many other women are there that I don't know about?'

'None. I swear.'

She regarded him steadily, obviously thinking he was lying.

'There's only been Leoni and Ciona ...'

'Leoni?'

'The countess. No one else. You have my word on that.'

Susan lay back on her pillow, her expression still disbelieving. She'd had Kirk's word too many times before.

'And why did you choose my wife to have an affair with, King? Pure coincidence?'

'Are you thinking I was trying to get back at you because of Leoni?'

'The thought had crossed my mind.'

'Eddy?' said Susan when Eddy didn't reply straight away. The word came out a pitying plea.

Eddy knew he'd have to tell the truth. 'When I first . . . when we first . . . the night Susan and I . . .'

'Oh my God!' she said, burying her face in the pillow.

Eddy moved close beside her, the baby between them. 'Susan, that was in my mind that first night. I was going to sleep with you and then see Kirk got to hear about it. But I couldn't do it. I liked you too much, and then later it became more than that.' He paused before adding, 'I fell in love with you.'

Kirk barked out a laugh. 'You're breaking my heart,' he said scornfully.

Susan cried into the pillow.

'Now give me that child and get out of here,' said Kirk.

It came to Eddy then what he must do. 'I'll make a deal with you,' he said.

Kirk frowned. 'What sort of deal?'

'Divorce Susan and relinquish all claims on Rachel and I'll sell you Black Lion.'

Kirk's eyes narrowed. 'You mean that?'

'I've never been more serious in my life.'

Susan looked up from her pillow, her expression one of incredulity. She couldn't believe that Kirk was even considering the offer.

Kirk was ice-cold inside. After all these years and a number of aborted attempts, Black Lion could be his for the taking. At long last. At long bloody last!

'We could have lawyers start to draw up the papers today,' Eddy went on, 'Black Lion becoming officially yours the day Susan is free and your hold over Rachel relinquished.'

'Kirk?' said Susan.

Kirk took a deep breath and then another. With Black Lion finally under his control it would only be a short time before he'd come to realise his dream and have a Glasgow monopoly. And after that major hurdle, surely nothing would be able to stop him extending his empire to include all Scotland.

And what was Susan to him after all? Not very much, if he was truthful. There were plenty more fish in the sea. And as for the brat? The sooner he saw the back of her the better.

'Kirk?' Susan said again.

He disregarded her. '*Give* me Black Lion and it's a deal,' he said.

'You mean for nothing?'

'Exactly.'

Eddy looked at Susan and then down at Rachel gurgling away, blissfully unaware of the drama going on around her.

'And that includes the pubs you used to own before you bought the brewery,' added Kirk.

'Eddy, you can't,' said Susan.

Kirk retorted quickly, 'If he doesn't I'll make sure you never get a divorce. I'll have my lawyers tie any attempt you make for one in so many knots, it'll take a lifetime to unravel. And in the meantime Rachel will be my daughter, subject to my wishes, under my jurisdiction.'

'You've got yourself a deal,' said Eddy. 'Providing it takes place from now. By that I mean you don't see Susan or the baby again.'

'And Black Lion?'

'Officially yours the day the divorce is absolute. I'll appoint you manager in the meantime.' Then Eddy went on to name a few more provisos to guard himself against a double-cross.

Somewhere during the last few minutes all the love Susan had felt for Kirk had melted like so much snow in a hot desert sun. She felt nothing for him now, except perhaps to despise him. How could she ever have loved a man like that? And yet despite all the pain and heartbreak he'd caused her in the past, she had done up until a few minutes previously. Somehow in her muddled, love-starved mind, she'd mistaken sex for love.

499

A mistake she saw, with hindsight, quite clearly now. What a gullible fool she'd been! But ever since her days at Miss Buchan's School For Young Ladies her need for love had been a desperate one.

She knew then Kirk had been using her all along. Why he'd married her, when it had been made quite clear to him he wouldn't get the brewery because of it, she didn't know. But he hadn't loved her, nor had he ever. Of that she was certain.

Eddy and Kirk had stopped talking, their arrangements complete.

Eddy, still holding Rachel tightly to him, gestured with his head towards the door. 'Now *you* get out of here,' he said.

Kirk flushed at being spoken to like that. He was about to make an angry retort when Susan said softly, 'If you don't go right now I'll change my statement to the police.'

Kirk's flush deepened. 'I'll expect your lawyer to be in touch with mine this afternoon,' he said to Eddy.

He then left the room without saying another word or looking back.

When he was gone Susan mutely held out her arms for her baby.

'You're well rid of him,' Eddy said, handing Rachel over.

Susan wept copiously.

McIlwham was humming to himself as he turned away from the urinal, his fingers fumbling with the buttons of his flies. His fingers froze when he saw the man confronting him.

'Hello Superintendent' said 'Baa Baa' Lamb.

McIlwham's frightened gaze dropped to the home-made knife 'Baa Baa' was holding pointed at him. The knife was a sharpened nail set in a piece of bamboo, lashed into place by mail-bag twine.

'Ten years you got me for a fit-up. You knew bloody well I never did yon burglary. Somebody planted evidence and that somebody was you,' hissed 'Baa Baa'.

McIlwham backed away as 'Baa Baa' advanced. 'You've got it all wrong,' he said.

500

'Like hell I have.'

'If there was a fit-up I had nothing to do with it.'

'Pull the other one, Superintendent. You were in charge of the case. It couldn't have been anyone else but you.'

'Baa Baa' was a small rat-faced man with bandy legs, the latter a legacy of childhood rickets. He had a name as a ferocious fighting man. The type who only stopped when they'd either won or were dead.

McIlwham decided on a change of tactics. 'If you weren't guilty of that job then you were of a dozen others. Caley Motors and Yoker Leather, to name but two. They screamed your handiwork.'

'But you couldn't prove anything otherwise you would have nicked me for them.'

'You were guilty as sin.'

'Aye, but you couldn't prove it so you fitted me up. You, Superintendent. You.'

McIlwham knew that if he didn't do something now he'd be a dead man within the minute. 'Baa Baa' couldn't allow this conversation to go on too long in case someone else came into the toilet.

'I couldn't believe my luck when I saw you in the cell block,' 'Baa Baa' went on. 'And talking about luck, yours just ran out, pal.'

'Baa Baa' tensed himself for a lunge. As he did so McIlwham threw himself at him, one hand going round 'Baa Baa's' neck, the other grabbing hold of the fist which grasped the knife.

'You would, would you!' 'Baa Baa' exclaimed as they struggled.

Fear lent McIlwham strength he didn't normally have. The hand clamped round the knife fist was a vice of iron.

'Help!' McIlwham shouted. 'Help!'

'Baa Baa's' foot snaked round McIlwham's leg. 'Baa Baa' pushed and then pulled, knocking McIlwham off balance. They both went tumbling to the toilet floor where they rolled over and over.

McIlwham screeched like a banshee. 'Help! Help!'

Suddenly he was on his back with the point of the knife edging towards his left eye. Sobbing, he exerted every ounce of his strength to push it away.

'Baa Baa's' rancid breath washed over McIlwham's face as the point of the makeshift knife inched closer to his eye. Even his superhuman strength lent him by fear wasn't enough to match that of 'Baa Baa', who was a man possessed.

McIlwham screeched again, a long drawn-out yodelling sound that sawed the eardrums. He was convinced a hideous death was only seconds away.

And then suddenly it was all over. Warders appeared as though out of the woodwork to disarm 'Baa Baa' and haul him off the prostrate McIlwham.

'Baa Baa' lashed out to send one of the warders hurtling back against a washstand. Retribution was instantaneous. Fist and boot went in, time after time. 'Baa Baa' writhed and choked but wouldn't give in. Snarling, he was hauled from the toilet face down and at waist level, a warder on each leg and arm.

'If I don't get you someone else will!' he shouted as he disappeared through the doorway. 'You can count on that!'

'You all right?' a warder asked McIlwham.

'Shaken, that's all.'

'Then get back to work.'

Trembling all over like a leaf in an autumn wind McIlwham returned to his mail-bags. Nor was he unaware that every eye he passed was on him.

Right on the dot the door clanged shut for the night. More than ever, McIlwham felt like a man who's just been buried alive.

There were three of them in the cell, one and three being the customary numbers – this an attempt to prevent homosexual pairing off.

'Well, well, well,' said Cooper. 'Imagine our friend McIlwham here turning out to be a bluebottle. You could have knocked me over with a feather when I heard that.'

'Aren't you the sly one?' added McNaughton, the third member. 'You sure kept quiet about that.'

McIlwham lay on his bunk, staring at the bottom of the bunk above him. He was still very much shaken from the incident in the toilet.

'I wondered when you never said what you were in for,' smiled Cooper. 'Now we know why.'

'What was it then?' asked McNaughton.

'Still not telling?' smirked Cooper.

McIlwham pulled out his makings and rolled himself a snout. The tobacco helped to calm him a little.

'Come on McIlwham you can tell us,' urged McNaughton.

McIlwham didn't reply. He wasn't afraid of these two. Neither of them were the physical type. Who he was afraid of were the others in the prison whom he'd either sent down himself or else helped send down. At a conservative estimate there must be at least a dozen in the various cell blocks, a number of whom, like 'Baa Baa' had been fit-ups.

Without warning the cell lights went out, plunging the small, curved-ceilinged cell into darkness. The only thing relieving the Stygian gloom was the cheery glow from McIlwham's cigarette.

'A bloody bluebottle!' said Cooper and laughed.

The previous night they had been a threesome in the cell. Now they were two and McIlwham, a fact McIlwham was only too painfully aware of.

At least a dozen other bastards out there, he thought. How many of them might take it into their heads to try for revenge as 'Baa Baa' had done? Fear encompassed him like an ice-cold blanket. If he behaved himself, as he had every intention of doing, he would get full remission for good behaviour, which would mean he'd be out in three and a half years. But would he be alive then? That was the big question. He'd just never considered this turn of events. And how stupid of him not to have foreseen it would happen.

For the rest of the night he gazed into the darkness,

rethinking his position. When morning came he'd worked out what he'd do to try and protect himself.

When the door was unlocked, he was the first out heading for the sinks. En route he fell into step alongside one of the warders. 'I want an interview with the Assistant Governor in charge of the wing,' he whispered.

The screw's eyes flicked sideways and he gave the slightest of nods.

McIlwham strode ahead to turn off to where the sinks were situated. As he washed he felt incredibly vulnerable. Every few seconds his back rippled with gooseflesh.

Later, when breakfast came he couldn't eat it. He would've thrown up if he'd tried.

Eddy parked the car and then leapt out to help Susan who was holding Rachel. When she was safely on the pavement he took her case out of the boot.

The area around Susan's eyes was still discoloured but the swelling had gone. Her stitches had been taken out, leaving an angry red line on her cheek and another small one on her lip. The doctor had assured her she wouldn't retain a scar in either case.

The street was filthy, tin cans, garbage and other debris littered everywhere. Several women were hanging out of windows talking and calling to one another. The air was so thick with chimney smoke you could taste it on your tongue.

Eddy smiled reassuringly as they made for the close. Going up the stairs he said, 'We can move later on when I've got myself sorted out. I'll find somewhere nice, I promise you.'

Susan thought of her mother, whom she was convinced wouldn't be long behind her father. When Jean went that house would be hers. She'd mention it to Eddy later and see what he thought.

Neighbours had washed down the stairs which smelled strongly of disinfectant. Eddy had told them he was bringing his future wife home. Sometime during the following week most of them would call by to be introduced and say hello.

Once inside the house Susan put Rachel to bed in the cot Eddy had bought. While she was doing this Eddy put the kettle on. He was making the tea when she came through to stand by his side. Through the kitchen window she could see more wee boys playing 'guns' on top of the brick and concrete air-raid shelters. The guns consisted mainly of walking sticks and carved pieces of wood.

'Any regrets?' he asked, handing her a cup.

'No, nor will I have.'

Eddy stared up at the bleak sky. En route from the hospital she'd asked him if he'd decided yet what he was going to do and he'd replied that he'd go back into selling used cars. After all, that and pubs – he included running Black Lion in the latter – were the only things he knew.

'I love you and the baby,' he said awkwardly.

'I know. I'm only sorry you had to give up everything to get us.'

Eddy smiled. 'You and Rachel are worth a hundred Black Lion's. Kirk was the one who lost out on our deal. Not me.'

Susan's eyes brimmed over with tears when he said that.

'Welcome home,' he said, kissing her on the top of her nose.

She laid down her cup and came into his arms. Neither had ever felt so much at peace as they did at that moment.

The rightness of their being together was indisputable. They were a couple.

It was Kirk's first morning as manager of Black Lion Brewery. Until such time as the divorce came through and Black Lion became officially his, he'd be splitting his working day between it and KM. When it was his, as Keith Gibb had forecast, he intended ending production of Black Lion beers and turning its brewery into a subsidiary of KM.

At the moment his lawyers were working full out to push the divorce through, but the Scottish divorce laws being what they were it was going to take a little while for that to happen. A year minimum, possibly even two.

In the meantime with Black Lion now under his control he

could turn his full attention to those other breweries still surviving. Well, survive they might have done but not for long. He would see to that. And when they were gone, the Glasgow monopoly he'd dreamed about for so long would be his.

Smiling, he leaned back in his chair and put his feet up on what had been Eddy's desk.

Nothing could stop him now.

Nothing.

McIlwham sat in the interview room drumming his fingers on the wooden table in front of him. He was waiting for Chief Superintendent Cairney, the Officer In Charge of his case.

The warder standing in front of the door opened it when there was a knock. Cairney entered.

'Well?' asked McIlwham eagerly, the moment Cairney had sat down.

Before replying, Cairney pushed a packet of cigarettes and a box of matches across to McIlwham, who muttered his thanks. Tobacco was like gold inside. He lit up, savouring the luxury of a tailor-made.

'I've spoken with the Deputy Chief Constable and he takes your point about there not being a prison in Scotland in which you'd be safe. He's therefore authorised me to do a deal with you providing you come totally clean, names, dates, the full thing, about everything you were up to and connected with before being sent down.'

'Reduction in sentence?' McIlwham asked.

Cairney shook his head. 'That's out. But you will be transferred to an English open prison where no one will know you and where life should be an awful lot easier than in here.'

Relief surged through McIlwham. He was going to come out alive, after all.

'When does the transfer take place?' he asked.

'As soon as you've given us everything you know. And McIlwham ... it had better be good.'

McIlwham thought of his wife and the money she was

receiving every week. It was going to be tough on her when that stopped. But it would be tougher on him unless he got that transfer.

'I'm ready when you are,' he said.

Cairney nodded to the warder who left the room, returning less than a minute later with a stenographer. McIlwham puffed on his cigarette while sorting out his thoughts. He started to speak when he saw the stenographer was ready.

'I'll begin with a man named Kirk Murray who owns KM Brewery...'

And as the minutes rolled by, McIlwham spoke at length and in detail about Turk McGhie, Danny Porteous, the burning of the Black Lion pub, the burning of the Black Lion Brewery, intimidation, bribery... The list went on and on.

The Princess of Poor Street

Contents

Part One

A Strong Wind Blowing
1934–35

'Yes, A strong wind blowing, and carrying us all
with it.'

MARY STEWART, *The Last Enchantment*

One

Later, folks were to say that there was a different sound to the knocking-off hooter that evening, a sad, mournful note quite in contrast to its usual stridency. If there was such a difference, Vicky didn't notice it; the hooter sounded just the same to her as it had always done, since her first recollected awareness of it as a tiny wee lass.

The date was Friday, 7 September 1934, and Vicky Devine was washing her hair at the kitchen sink, preparing for the party that night to celebrate her Ken's seventeenth birthday.

'You'd better hurry up, girl. Your dad will be home in a minute and you know he'll disapprove of you doing that at the sink just before tea's put on the table.' Recently turned forty, Vicky's mother remained as handsome in middle age as she'd been in her salad days. Mary Devine was still a looker, was what the neighbours said.

Vicky gave her hair a final rinse, then wrapped it in a towel. She gazed into her dad's shaving mirror hanging from a nail at the window. The face staring back was bright, full of life, with the mark of determination upon it and, aye, mischief as well.

'What's for tea?' John demanded from a chair by the fireplace where he was reading the *Wizard* comic. He was thirteen years old, two years younger than Vicky.

'Stew, cabbage and boiled tats,' Mary replied, standing at the cooker and thinking that the tats had been a bad buy.

Mary sighed to herself. George would complain about them, no doubt about it. He was a good man, one of the best. If he had a fault however, he was faddy about his food.

She made a mental note to tell off Mr Emslie the green-

3

grocer for selling her potatoes like these. It just wasn't on.

'Are you going to have bevy at this "do" tonight?' John asked wickedly, knowing he was putting his sis on the spot, for if their dad thought there would be strong drink at the party he would refuse to let her go.

Vicky whirled on her brother. Little bugger! she thought. 'Mainly soft drinks with a few screwtops of beer for the older boys.'

'Oh aye!' John replied, giving her a fly wink.

Vicky narrowed her eyes, her look plainly saying: keep this up and you'll be sorry, I promise you.

John smirked. He thoroughly enjoyed stirring it for his sis, though it was best, as he had learned from long experience, not to go too far. For Vicky, if roused sufficiently, would inevitably exact some awful revenge. Like when she had dropped his lovingly-made matchstick and glue model of the Leaning Tower of Pisa out the front window so that it smashed to smithereens on the pavement below. Two whole months it had taken him to make that model! At the time she couldn't have thought of anything that would have hurt him more.

'I hope there isn't going to be hard drink at this party?' Mary said to Vicky.

'I just said there wasn't.'

'Are you certain?'

'Cross my heart and hope to die,' Vicky lied.

Mary heard the clatter of feet on the stairs outside. That would be George and the other men up the close now. She took the pan of tats off the cooker and crossed to the sink to drain them.

John watched Vicky rubbing her hair with the towel, and wished he was going to Ken Blacklaws's party. He'd have given his eye teeth to have been invited, but he was too young to run with that set. He thought the sun shone out Ken's backside, as did an awful lot of people, Ken being a natural leader with real charisma. Why, even lads much older than Ken deferred to him, hanging on his every word, anxious for acknowledgement and approval.

John continued to watch Vicky, amazed to think that

4

the great Ken Blacklaws was winching his sis, and had been for six months now. Ken Blacklaws, who could've had the pick of any bird in Townhead! Och well, he told himself, she was his sister after all, he probably wasn't seeing her the way other boys did. But still, her and Ken Blacklaws, he couldn't help considering it a marvel, right enough.

Vicky was the first to see her dad's face when he came in, and the sight of it made her stop what she was doing. It was a dirty-grey colour, and there were deep lines etched under his eyes that had not been there that morning. But it was his expression that was the most startling; it was grim with a capital G.

'Dad?' she queried.

Vicky's tone made Mary turn round from the sink, where she was still draining the tats. George's eyes, hard with despair, locked onto hers.

'It's bad news, Mary,' he said quietly.

Mary went cold inside and her lips thinned. Filled with a sense of impending doom, she waited for George to explain.

'I've been laid off.'

She reeled mentally on hearing what every wife she knew lived in dread of being told. 'Short-time lay-off?' she asked hopefully.

'The factory's gone broke. Everyone has been laid off permanently as from tonight.'

As if in a dream, Mary laid the steaming pan of tats on the side of the sink, wiped her hands on her pinny, then went over to the chair facing John's and sat.

'What happened?'

Vicky was equally stunned by this completely unexpected bombshell. Ken worked at Agnew's, so he too had been laid off.

'We were all called to a meeting this afternoon and addressed by Mr Robertson, the high heid one himself. He said he was sorry but the factory had been in deep financial trouble for some while. According to him, the banks have called in various loans. I didn't understand all of it, but the upshot was the factory had to close down, and right away.'

5

'Just like that!' Mary whispered.

'Just like that,' George echoed.

George thought of the paint factory which had employed him all his working life. He'd gone there as a lad when old man Agnew still owned the place, and had soon learned what the word graft meant. But it had been a better job than many – better than going down the pits, for example, or than the extra-heavy physical toil that his pal Danny Blues had to contend with in the chain-making factory over in Cambuslang.

He pulled out a packet of Capstan and frowned on discovering it was empty. There was a spare packet on the mantelpiece behind one of the wally dugs: Vicky picked it up and handed it to him.

Vicky noted that her dad's hands were trembling as he lit a cigarette. She had never seen her dad's hands tremble before. She asked the question Mary couldn't bring herself to utter.

'What now, Dad?'

George sucked smoke into his lungs and felt nothing. His entire body might have been shot full of anaesthetic.

'I don't know, I just don't know,' he replied hollowly.

Mary wanted to scream at the top of her voice and smash every breakable thing in the house. 'We'd better have the tea before it spoils,' she said instead.

Vicky picked at her meal. Never a big eater at the best of times, she had completely lost what little appetite she might have had. A glance round the table confirmed that she was not the only one in this state. Her dad was gazing into space, while her mum stared fixedly at a boiled tat as though it were a crystal ball. John was the only person doing justice to what had been set before him.

George turned his attention to Mary. 'Do you know there are only three men living in Parr Street who didn't work for Agnew's?' he said softly.

Mary nodded. 'Aye, I know. It had already crossed my mind.'

Parr was a fairly short street, with Black Street running parallel to it on the one side, Glebe Street on the other – the same Glebe Street where Scotland's most famous fictional family were supposed to stay: the Broons, who were featured weekly in the *Sunday Post*, and were known, and followed, by Scots from Tallahassee to Timbuctoo. Black Street also had a minor claim to fame in that it was where the area VD clinic was sited – or perhaps, in Black Street's case, the word should be infamy.

George pushed his plate away with a muttered apology for the waste and, rising, went to sit by the fireplace. It wouldn't be long before winter came on, he thought, and the amount of money the Labour gave out wouldn't run to coal, not by a long chalk. Mary would be doing well if she could provide a half-decent meal a day on it, let alone anything else. Then he remembered the rent: a half-decent meal every two days, he corrected himself. By half-decent he meant porage and dry bread, that sort of thing.

'I won't go to the party tonight if you don't want me to, Dad,' Vicky offered.

'No, lass, you go and enjoy yourself while you can. After today parties are going to be in short supply around here for some time to come, I'm thinking,' he replied, giving her a soft smile that tore at her heart, for she loved her dad.

'We mustn't be over-gloomy, something might come up. You might land yourself another job no trouble at all,' Mary said, trying to inject a cheery note into her voice.

Another job no trouble at all! George knew that this was highly unlikely. Unemployment was rife in the city, with thousands and thousands laid off, in the same boat he now found himself in. For any vacancy that did occur there was always a long line of applicants, willing to take any pay, work any hours.

'Maybe so,' he replied, trying to appear positive for Mary's sake.

Vicky glanced from her mother's face to her father's, and saw that they were both pretending, making a bold show of it.

'I suppose this means I have to stop my comics,' John said. He was used to getting the *Wizard* and *Adventure* every week.

'There's a lot more besides your comics will have to be stopped,' Mary told him.

John coloured. 'I didn't mean that to sound the way it came out,' he mumbled.

Mary leaned across the table and patted his left wrist. He was a good boy, if a wee bit unthinking at times. But then that was his age. 'We know that, son.'

'I have six bob saved, from pocket money and that. You'd better have it, Mum,' John replied.

Mary's eyes shone.

'And I have two pounds seven and a kick. I did have more, but I spent it on Ken's present,' Vicky added.

Mary wished that she could have told them to keep their savings, but the lad was dead right: now was a time for everyone to muck in; from here on, every farthing would count.

George took his pay packet from his hip pocket and tossed it onto the table, where it landed in front of Mary's plate. 'I'll sign on first thing Monday morning, and as soon as I've done that I'll start making the rounds looking for work.'

Mary reached out gently to touch the buff-coloured pay packet. She did not have to open it to know how much it contained: three pounds exactly.

'What's the dole nowadays?' she asked lightly.

It was a subject Mary had always shied clear of. Her subconscious hope had been that, by not knowing about it, the evil would never befall her.

'Fifteen and threepence per week for a man,' George replied.

Mary blanched. Dear God!

'Plus eight bob for an adult dependant and two bob for each child,' George went on.

Mary did a rapid mental sum. Twenty-seven and three-pence a week, less than half of what George had been bringing home, and it had been a struggle to make ends meet on that! 'We'll get by somehow. We'll just have to,' she whispered.

George lit another cigarette. 'I stop when this lot are

finished,' he said. He had been a smoker all his adult life, but stop he would. There was nothing else for it.

Mary fought to control her tears. She would cry later when she was in bed, and George asleep. To let him see her cry would only make it the worse for him.

After helping Mary wash and dry the tea dishes, Vicky dolled herself up for the party, putting on her best dress, silk stockings and the make-up she was allowed. Normally this was something she derived great pleasure from, but not that night.

That night, it gave her no pleasure at all.

The party was due to begin at about half past seven but Vicky went early, wanting to talk to Ken before any of the others arrived.

Ken lived further down on the other side of Parr Street. When he let her in, in answer to her chap, he said that his parents had already gone out visiting, which meant they were alone.

Mr and Mrs Blacklaws had promised Ken that they would visit his Aunt Bell over in Carntyne so that he could have his party without them being present. Despite the day's happenings – Mr Blacklaws had also been employed at Agnew's – they'd kept their word, though visiting, and being away from their own home, was the last thing they wanted in the circumstances.

Once she was inside the hallway, and with the door shut, Ken encompassed Vicky in his arms and kissed her.

'Oh, Ken, what dreadful news,' she whispered when the kiss was over.

He cupped her left breast and gently squeezed. 'Aye, you can say that again,' he replied.

'And there was never any hint of what was to come?'

'None whatever.'

He kissed her again, thinking how gorgeous she was. He drank in the smell of her scent: heavy, and musk, and mouth-watering.

'I could eat you,' she whispered.

He gave a throaty laugh and adjusted his glasses. He was

9

very short-sighted. Without glasses, his clear vision was limited to half a dozen feet. Beyond that everything became hazy and jumbled.

Ken had long since got used to wearing glasses, having had them since a child, but he had never stopped hating them. His bad eyesight was the one defect in an otherwise excellent and muscular body.

'My parents are worried sick about what's happened. The atmosphere at home's awful. It's as if there's been a death in the family,' Vicky said.

'Let's have a half together before the mob get here,' Ken proposed and, taking her by the hand, led her through to what Mrs Blacklaws somewhat grandly referred to as the front parlour, and which most other people in the street just called the big room. Most of the furniture usually in there had been moved to other parts of the house and the carpet rolled back. To one side stood an opened-out gateleg table with a clean cloth over it. On the cloth were various soft drinks and a number of screwtops.

'I've got a bottle of whisky, but I'm keeping that planked,' Ken explained, producing the bottle from a built-in press.

He poured them both good-size halves, then went into the kitchen to get water for Vicky, for she insisted her glass be topped up with that.

'Happy birthday, Ken,' she toasted and, having taken a sip of her drink, handed him his present.

'Och, you shouldn't have,' he said, smiling in delight as he accepted the gift. He opened the small brown-paper parcel to find a box, inside of which, cradled in satiny material, was a Ronson lighter.

'It was the best in the shop,' she said proudly.

'It's really smashing, Vicky. I'll treasure it always,' he told her, giving her a peck on the cheek.

The lighter was silver-coloured, with a firm igniting action. His initials had been engraved on one side in fancy script.

'The only trouble is, you won't have a use for it now you'll be giving up smoking,' she said.

Ken frowned, not understanding. 'Why should I do that?'

'Being on the dole, you won't be able to afford to smoke. My dad's stopping after he's finished those he's got at home.'

Deliberately, in a gesture of defiance, Ken, using his brand-new lighter, lit a cigarette and blew a perfect smoke ring at the ceiling.

'I won't be signing on for long, damn right and I won't. They're not going to chuck Ken Blacklaws on the scrapheap,' he declared vehemently.

His tone, and intense belief in himself, caused the fine hairs on the back of Vicky's neck to rise and a shudder to ripple through her.

'I've got my whole future ahead of me. That future isn't going to be the Broo and the semi-starvation that goes with the Labour handout. I've always had plans, ambitions, to be somebody. I view this as a minor setback, no more. In fact, maybe it's even a blessing in disguise, for I was getting far too settled at Agnew's. It was high time I made a move to something with real prospects.'

He was unbelievable, she thought. Here he was, in the teeth of adversity, not only insisting he would soon land himself another job, but one with prospects, a proper career even! Who else but her Ken would have reacted like that?

His eyes became partially hooded and brooding. 'The world's full of nobodies, those content to be picked up and dropped at the whim of the big boys, those at the top, with power. Well, I tell you, Vicky, someday, I swear, I'll be one of the stringpullers. Completely my own master, and the master of many.'

Vicky opened her mouth and her breath came slowly streaming out. If Ken said it would happen, then it would. If he'd said he was going to fly to the moon, she'd have believed that too. With Ken, anything was possible.

As Ken threw the remainder of his whisky down his throat, there was a knock on the outside door. With that, the spell his words had cast over the room was broken. He started to leave the room, halted, came back to Vicky and kissed her once more. 'Just to keep me going.' He smiled, and lightly ran a hand over the swell of her buttocks.

'I might have known it would be you,' Ken said when he

opened the door to discover Neil Seton there. Neil lived in the next close, and the pair of them had been good pals since the infants' class at school, where they had shared a desk. Prior to that they had already known each other from playing out on the street.

Neil had a name for being brainy and had stayed on at school when Ken left to go to Agnew's. It was Neil's intention to take his Highers, and if they were good enough – which they would undoubtedly be – and he could win a grant or bursary, go to university after that.

Neil had brought a bag of screwtops with him which he took through to the front parlour and placed beside the ones already there. He tapped his inside jacket pocket. 'I've got a wee half-bottle here, but that's not for general consumption,' he said.

'Talk about great minds thinking alike!' Vicky exclaimed.

'She means I've got one planked too. Only in my case it's a full bottle,' Ken explained.

Neil gave a thin smile. No matter what he did, Ken always seemed to go one better. It had been that way as long as he could remember.

'How's your dad taking the layoff?' Ken asked, pouring himself and Neil a dram, Vicky having shaken her head when he had raised an eyebrow in her direction.

'He could be a shell-shocked soldier straight out of the last war. He's walking about the house in a complete daze, hearing nothing and seeing nothing,' Neil replied.

Ken shook his head in sympathy.

'As he's well over fifty, he hasn't a snowball in hell's chance of finding something else, and he knows it. It's the end of the line for him,' Neil went on.

'Does that mean you'll have to leave school?' Vicky asked.

'What would be the point of that? I'd just be adding to the unemployed. No, I'll be staying on.'

It suddenly struck Vicky that there was a selfish streak in Neil, something she'd never noticed before. From his stubborn expression she guessed he would have refused to leave school even if a job had been handed him on a plate.

'Black Friday, that's what today will become known as in Parr Street,' Ken mused.

Neil swallowed some of his drink. He was not all that keen on alcohol, but pretended that he was so as to be the same as the other lads who couldn't get enough of it.

'You're all alone then, Neil, no lassie with you?' Vicky teased, and watched Neil mentally squirm.

'Neil's never been a great one for the girls, have you, Neil?' Ken grinned.

'I wouldn't say that,' Neil replied softly.

'Well, you're hardly a Don Juan.'

'Like some we know have been in the past,' Vicky jibed at Ken.

'It's hardly my fault if they've thrown themselves at me,' Ken retorted and, half in fun, half serious, inflated his chest.

There was a lot of truth in that, Neil thought jealously. Maybe lassies didn't exactly throw themselves at Ken, but they did contrive to make themselves awfully available.

'Well, they'd better not throw themselves when I'm around, or they might get more than they bargained for,' Vicky said, eyes glittering.

'What would you do to them, hen, eh?' Ken prompted, lapping this up.

'I'd mollicate them,' Vicky replied, and making a hissing sound clawed the air as if she were a cat.

Neil stared at her in admiration. Gosh, but wasn't she something! Then he altered his expression before either Vicky or Ken noticed it.

Vicky turned again to Neil. 'Honestly, though, you'd better be careful. I've heard it said that men who don't have girlfriends turn funny after a while.'

Neil was appalled. 'That'll never happen to me, I assure you,' he replied quickly.

'I'd be careful just the same,' Vicky persisted.

'Och, leave the poor lad alone, Vicky. You're embarrassing him,' Ken said.

Filled with devilment, Vicky slunk over to Neil and sensuously rubbed herself against one of his arms. 'Is that right, Neil? Am I making you embarrassed?'

13

Neil cursed inwardly when his face flamed scarlet; that made him feel even more foolish.

'You've given him a reddie now,' Ken admonished Vicky.

'Are you shy, Neil? Is that it?' Vicky purred.

He wished that the floor would open and swallow him up. He wished he was anywhere else but there. He wished . . . Oh God, how he wished!

She thought of teasing Neil about the scattering of plooks he had on his cheeks and forehead, and decided against it. That would be going too far. In fact, she'd gone too far already. It wasn't that she didn't like Neil; she did: he had many admirable qualities, and Ken thought the world of him. It was just that, in some ways, he was such a natural victim. If you were going to pick on someone, and he was present, there would be no question: he'd be the one.

There was another knock on the front door, which let Neil off the hook. 'I'll get it for you,' he said to Ken, and fled the room.

'You're cruel, so you are.' Ken smiled at Vicky.

'Do you think he's still a virgin?' Vicky whispered back.

Ken smothered his laugh so that Neil didn't hear, for Neil was indeed a virgin, as Vicky well knew, Ken having told her.

Despite Ken's and Vicky's attempts to liven it up, the evening was a muted affair, more like a wake than a party. But, as Ken said afterwards, that was hardly surprising as there hadn't been a single person present not directly affected by the closure of Agnew's.

On Monday morning Mary called Vicky and John at the usual time to get ready for school. Vicky found it strange to see her father still at home, as in the past he'd always already left for work by the time she and John put in their appearance. It was then that it truly sank in that her dad was unemployed.

'It's a change for us all to have breakfast together during the week. Rather nice really,' Mary said, placing a plate of margarined bread beside the teapot.

Vicky stared at the empty plate in front of her father.

14

She knew it was his habit to have a boiled egg before going to the factory, and bacon and egg at the weekend. There was no egg that day; eggs had gone by the board, as had weekend bacon.

Mary poured out cups of tea for them all. Vicky could tell from its colour that the tea wasn't as strong as usual. There was a bowl of sugar out, but no milk. No one asked for the milk they normally had in their tea, not even John.

George ate and drank in silence. He felt guilty, as though it was his fault he was idle. It was silly, he told himself, but he continued to feel guilty all the same. Mary kept up a steady stream of chatter, which Vicky found disconcerting. In the normal course of events it was rare for her mother to waste words at this time of the morning.

'And you'll start looking directly you've signed on?' Mary said eventually to George, who nodded.

'Will the Broo give you some leads?' John asked.

George glanced over at his son. He seemed about to make a caustic reply, but didn't. 'If they have any. But I'd be most surprised if they did,' he answered.

'Not directly round here, that's for sure. Everyone laid off from Agnew's will be doing that. I'll try further afield, though where I haven't decided yet. I'll go where my feet lead me,' George said.

Mary rose from the table and went to the cooker, where she boiled more water. This she poured into the teapot to make a second brew from the already used leaves. When the tea was masked, she poured it into a vacuum flask, which she handed to George along with a paper poke containing two slices of margarined bread.

'Your dinnertime piece, as you're going to be away all day,' she explained.

George got his jacket from the hallway and put it on. 'We'll walk down the stairs together,' he said to Vicky and John, who were now ready to leave for school.

'I'll see you when you get back then,' Mary said to George, her voice artificially bright.

Going down the stairs, Vicky did something she had not done in years; she slipped her hand into her dad's, just as though she was a wee girl again and he was taking her out. He shot her a quick sideways look, but did not comment. On reaching the closemouth, she detached her hand again.

There was a group of men standing on the corner, all of whom lived in Parr Street, and who had worked at Agnew's. Nothing had been arranged but, as if it had, they were all waiting on one another. They would go to the Labour en masse. The men of Parr Street.

Vicky spotted Ken and waved. He waved in return and gave her the thumbs-up sign. He was the only one in the entire group who appeared cheerful. Although she passed directly by the men, she did not stop to talk to Ken. It would have embarrassed her to do so in front of the others, particularly as she was wearing school uniform and carrying her school-bag.

However, Ken had no such inhibitions. 'Do you think they'll accept an X where I'm supposed to put my John Hancock?' he cried after her, making out as if he couldn't write.

Vicky laughed. Idiot! she thought. She gave him another wave, but without turning round.

Ken would brook no argument. Friday night had come round again and he was insisting on taking Vicky to the flicks. He had a few quids' worth of savings put by, and was damned if he was going to eke it out in halfpennies and farthings. Besides, it would not be long before he was back in work, earning once more.

They went to the Trocadero, or the Troc as it was known, the local fleapit. He was not particularly keen on the picture that was showing, a silent called *City Lights* starring Charlie Chaplin and Virginia Merrill. The fact that it was silent, and therefore seemed dated although it was only three years old, did not deter Vicky, who adored Chaplin. As she told Ken, the wee clown never failed to make her laugh.

On arriving at the Troc, Vicky and Ken were surprised to discover the manager standing beside the ticket kiosk.

He pumped her hand while Ken paid for the tickets. Then he pumped Ken's, all the while blethering on about how good it was to see them, and how he hoped they'd enjoy the picture and that they'd come back again soon.

'What was all that in aid of?' Vicky whispered to Ken after they had made their escape.

Ken's mouth twisted cynically downwards. 'A lot of the folk who come here worked for Agnew's, and now the factory's shut I imagine that man sees nothing but trouble for his cinema. I would say he was panicking myself, for a personal welcome won't make any difference. The only thing that'll do that is for those now unemployed to find jobs again.'

Vicky giggled. 'His smile looked as though it had been set in starch.'

Ken nodded in agreement.

Going through swing doors, they plunged into the darkness of the auditorium. They stood for several seconds, waiting for their eyesight to adjust.

'I've never known it so empty on a Friday night,' Vicky whispered. At a rough count there couldn't have been more than a couple of dozen folk present, whereas usually the place was packed.

Vicky glanced round, looking for the girl with the torch to show them to their seats. There was no girl. At that moment it came home to Vicky that Agnew's closing-down was going to affect many more people than just those who had worked there.

'It seems we find our own way down,' she whispered.

When the interval arrived, a lassie appeared with a tray of ices. Another cutback, Vicky thought. There had always been two lassies before. Ken wanted to buy her an ice, but she put her foot down at that extravagance. She told him firmly that if he bought it she wouldn't eat it, so there. As the lights were up, Vicky took the opportunity to have a good gander about her. She saw a boy she knew from school, and asked Ken if he could see anyone else from Agnew's. There was no one.

'It's spooky it being so quiet on a Friday,' Vicky said.

Finally the lights dimmed and, as the plush red velvet curtains swished open, she brought her attention back to the silver screen.

On leaving the pictures, Vicky hooked an arm in Ken's. 'That was smashing, thanks.' She smiled.

'I'd have enjoyed it more if it had been a talkie,' he replied.

Vicky said talkies might be the thing, but good old Chaplin hadn't failed her. She'd had a right laugh.

They were passing an alleyway running behind a line of shops when a movement caught her eye. There it was again, and it had something furtive about it.

'Somebody's along there,' she whispered to Ken, her grip on his arm tightening. God, she prayed it wasn't a razorman, a headcase out looking for someone to carve up.

Glass tinkled, followed by a scuffling sound. 'There's several of them, and they're breaking into one of the shops, probably the tobacconist's,' Ken whispered back.

'Move away, quickly,' Vicky urged, and forced Ken to resume walking. Her heart was hammering. 'We'd better contact the police.'

Ken pulled her to a halt. 'No, we won't. We'll mind our own business.'

'But those men were burgling that shop. They're thieves.'

'Don't get involved, that's the best policy. Do you want to go to court and have them find out who you are? Help put them away and you'd likely get a visit from their friends intent on evening the score.'

Vicky thought again of razors and shuddered. It would not be the first time a woman had been marked, and the result was not a pretty sight. 'I suppose you're right,' she said reluctantly.

They started walking again, Vicky's heels click-clacking on the pavement.

'As you wouldn't let me buy you an ice cream, how about a bag of chips?' Ken suggested.

They began arguing about that, and soon the incident of the burglars was forgotten.

Neil Seton was in a study class sitting by a large window below which lay a large section of the playground. He was thinking about a trigonometry problem when suddenly Vicky appeared at the far end of the playground where a gate led into the street beyond. The breath caught in his throat at the sight of her. Jesus, but she was lovely!

It was seven months since he had noticed her in another part of the playground and realised that the wee lassie he'd seen over the years playing peever, skipping ropes and the other games lassies played in the street and back courts wasn't a wee lassie any more. She had been transformed into a young woman – and, in his opinion, a proper stunner. When the penny had finally dropped that the girl he was ogling was Vicky Devine, his mouth had literally fallen open in amazement. From then on he'd been stricken. Cupid's bow had twanged and the arrow of love had lodged firmly in his heart.

Neil had wangled his way into Vicky's company, and in his own tongue-tied, stammering fashion began chatting her up – though, to be honest, he'd been so oblique about it that she'd never apparently been aware of what he'd been attempting to do.

Then he had made his fatal mistake: he had spoken about her to Ken. A double mistake: first, to discuss her with Ken at all; second, not to make his feelings clear. He ground his teeth in frustration at the memory. Why hadn't he kept his big mouth shut! Hell mend him for being so stupid.

Ken had taken a fresh look at Vicky, seeing her anew as Neil had done. And swooped. There had been no beating about the outer periphery of the bush with Ken. Oh no, that wasn't Ken's way. It had been straight in there, bang! 'Hello, how are you? Fancy going out one night?' Of course she'd accepted like a shot. Ken never needed to ask twice. Out they'd gone and that had been that, the pair of them had started winching.

Jealousy flamed in Neil. Being jealous of Ken was nothing new; he had been jealous of his pal as long as he could remember. But until now he had never wished Ken ill because of it. The trouble in this instance was that Ken had

19

bested him in something he really cared about. Vicky was not just another bird; she had bowled him over. And no bird had ever done that before. Oh sure, there had been a few he'd liked, could tolerate, so to speak. But Vicky was different. He . . . Yes, there was no other word for it. He *loved* her.

He picked a pimple and wondered how long it would be before Ken tired of Vicky and gave her the elbow, for that was what must inevitably happen; it was the fate that had befallen every single one of Ken's women in the past. They never got rid of Ken; he got rid of them. When that happened, he must try and step into Ken's place, take over where Ken had left off.

Apprehension and uncertainty gnawed his insides. How easy it was to imagine. Take over where Ken left off. But could he? He wasn't a patch on Ken physically; Ken had the sort of shoulders women swooned over, whereas he had hardly any at all. More than once, to his bitter chagrin, he'd been described as weedy. Then there was Ken's strong and vibrant personality, where his was – well, not exactly as forceful or appealing.

If he could match Ken in any field, it was brainpower; there they were equals, with, Neil liked to think, himself having the edge. It had amazed him that Ken had left school when he had and gone into Agnew's, where the position of foreman was as high as he could ever rise. He had thought Ken mad at the time, especially as there was no domestic pressure on Ken to leave school and start grafting.

Neil, on the other hand, was going places in life, oh yes! – providing he could get a grant or bursary to the university, and when the time came no one in Glasgow, or in Scotland come to that, would try harder for one. His goal was to become a lawyer, but not just any old lawyer – one who devoted his energies to helping the poor and needy, the underprivileged, of which, God knew, there was an abundance in the city. A lawyer! He conjured up an image of himself in wig and gown. What an exciting prospect that was. He intended being the best lawyer Glasgow had ever produced.

His gaze refocused on Vicky. The best lawyer Glasgow had ever produced – and Vicky as his wife.

Now there was a dream indeed.

It had been cold for some while, but the grates in the Devine household remained empty, for, although it was now November, George had not yet been able to find another job. Neither had any of the other men, including Ken, who had been laid off from Agnew's.

Vicky chittered as she drank her morning tea; it had grown not only cold but damp, which made matters even worse. Her underclothes were clammy against her skin. Usually they were aired before the fire, but with no fire this was of course impossible.

George, lacing up his boots, was sunk in black, black despair. The streets he daily walked were endless; the phrase 'Nae work here, Jim', which he'd swear he'd heard a million times, rang constantly in his ears. His belly was taut and griping with hunger, his trousers baggy at the waist because of the weight he'd lost. And he'd lost not only weight but strength as well. Since the layoff and subsequent reduction in food, his strength had slowly drained till now he had no more strength than a gawky adolescent.

'Fuck it!' he swore when a bootlace broke and, hunching back in his chair, he covered his face with his hands.

Mary stared at him in shock and consternation. It was unheard of for George to swear in front of the children. She opened her mouth to make a comment, then bit it back.

John looked at Vicky, who, thinking he was about to make some silly remark to alleviate the situation, shook her head.

'Sorry,' George muttered and, addressing himself again to his boot, fixed the broken lace with a reef knot, then tied the boot.

'So where are you going to try today then, George?' Mary asked, a hint of tremulousness in her voice.

If George had ranted or raved, it wouldn't have been so bad. The fact that he spoke calmly and rationally made it terrifying.

21

'I don't think I'll bother. As far as I can see, what it boils down to is a waste of boot leather. I've tried and tried, but there simply isn't any work out there to be had.'

Vicky went prickly all over. The atmosphere was charged. It seemed as if at any moment the room and all its contents might explode like some gigantic bomb.

'You have to go, George. None of us can afford to just give up,' Mary said quietly.

'It's a waste of time, woman, I'm telling you.'

'But we have to keep trying.'

'Why?'

'Because we have to.'

'But *why?*' George demanded softly.

Mary wished she was clever, could voice what she knew and felt. 'There has to be work, some place there must be. Stay at home and it'll never be yours. Nobody's going to come chapping the door offering it on a plate.'

'I haven't been looking for the past two days. I've been going to the Monkland Canal instead, sitting there on the bank, watching the water. I've found it's very soothing to watch water. It melts away the worry and heartache and, aye, the fear.'

'You never told me this.' Mary frowned. She had never known there to be a secret between them before.

'I'm telling you now.'

Vicky knew that this was a crisis, and a deep one. Her dad had lost hope. 'Dad, can I say something? Something I think might make sense in the circumstances?'

George glanced over at her. It was on the tip of his tongue to say: mind your own business, this is strictly an adult concern. Then he reminded himself that, though she was only fifteen, Vicky was grown up and, as such, entitled to speak her piece. Also, it wasn't simply an adult concern, it was a family one.

'Remember King Robert the Bruce and the spider?' Vicky asked.

George shook his head. He might have known the story once, but if he had he'd forgotten it.

'It happened when Robert the Bruce was fighting the

English for the Scottish throne. The English had beaten him repeatedly till he'd come to believe he'd never win against them. As the story goes, he was hiding in a cave from the English one day when he noticed a spider dangling on a thread of web, trying to swing from one bit of rock to another. Six times the spider tried, and failed. But it didn't give up. Then on the seventh it succeeded, and got where it wanted to go.

'Robert the Bruce was filled with admiration, for the distance the spider had been trying to cover had seemed far too great. Yet it had tried again and again and eventually succeeded. Sheer bloody-mindedness, you could say.

'Then he realised he'd fought the English six times, and failed, and swore to himself he' d make a seventh attempt as the spider had done. And like the spider he succeeded on the seventh attempt, and because of this victory he eventually became King of Scotland.'

She was a clever lassie, Mary thought. You had to give her credit.

Vicky was right, as was Mary, George told himself. He had to keep trying. It might well be that he wouldn't find another job, that he'd be idle for the rest of his life. But for the sake of his own self-respect, and because something might just come up, he had to keep on tramping the streets.

'Bloody-mindedness, eh?' he said to Vicky and smiled. Vicky smiled back.

George took a deep breath and straightened his shoulders. Rising, he went out into the hallway, where he put on his jacket, coat and cap.

'Where's my dinnertime piece then?' he asked Mary.

When the door was shut behind George, Mary crossed to Vicky and, eyes brimming with tears, swept Vicky into her embrace and hugged her tight. 'He's a good man, you know, one of the best,' she said huskily.

'I know,' Vicky agreed.

That evening Vicky went across the road to Ken's, where the pair of them had the house to themselves, as Mr and Mrs Blacklaws had gone out visiting. They talked for a wee while, then started kissing. Vicky had come expecting to be made love to. She had first slept with Ken after they had been going out together for a month, and had been doing so ever since when the chance presented itself. Vicky had had various sexual encounters before Ken, but he was the first she had allowed to go all the way. She found him irresistible.

He opened her blouse beneath her cardy, undid her bra and began caressing her. He had such beautiful hair, she thought, running her fingers through his thick chestnut mop. She gave a little grunt, half of pleasure, half of pain, when he nipped a nipple with his teeth.

'Let's go to your bedroom,' she said, her voice breathy with passion.

Taking her by the hand, he led her there, switching on the bedside light before they both collapsed onto his quilt.

'There's no chance of them coming back early, is there?' Vicky asked, as she always did before they made love when his parents were out. It would be a nightmare, and so shaming, if Mr and Mrs Blacklaws were to walk in on them.

'They're expected where they're going; they won't be home for another hour at least,' Ken assured her as he pulled off her skirt.

When he had stripped her naked, she lay back and watched him take off his own clothes. He had a gorgeous body, she thought. His waist was trim, his shoulders wide, his buttocks firm and muscly. His skin was the colour of ivory and seemed to shine as though polished.

Lying beside Vicky, Ken fastened his hot mouth onto her shoulder nearest him and proceeded to lick. Vicky squirmed with delight. Her hands became busy, touching, fondling, caressing. It was not long before they were both roused to fever pitch. He pulled himself on top of her and prepared to enter her.

She held him off, thinking he had got carried away. 'You've forgotten something, darling.' She smiled.

'I haven't. I haven't got any,' he replied.

Her slitted eyes jerked wide open. 'You must have! You're teasing me!'

24

'I'm not. I couldn't buy any because I'm flat broke.'

For Vicky it was like being doused with cold water. 'Then we can't do it.'

'It'll be all right. I promise. I'll jump off at Charing Cross.'

She thrust him off her and back onto the bed. 'No, I don't trust you. I know what you're like once you get going.'

'I swear I'll jump off. My word of honour.'

For a moment or two she was tempted by the beseeching look on his face. Then her resolve hardened. 'No, I'm not doing it without a french letter,' she insisted.

'Vicky?' he pleaded. She had never refused him before. But then this was the first occasion he had been without a condom.

'What if I was to get pregnant?' she argued.

'You won't. I'll jump off. Cross my heart and hope to die if I don't.'

'Even if you did, it's a known fact that isn't a hundred per cent safe. There can be leakage before you get there,' she said.

He swore with frustration.

'It would be awful to get pregnant. Apart from anything else, I just couldn't present my father with another mouth to feed when he hasn't got a job,' she went on.

'I'd take care of any baby you had.'

'How in hell would you do that? You haven't got a job either, although you boasted to me you'd get another one quick as a wink. And not only any old job but one with real prospects, a proper career!' she said scathingly.

As soon as the words were out, Vicky wished she had never uttered them. She watched his face flame with embarrassment and shame. 'I'm sorry, I shouldn't have said that,' she whispered.

It was true, that was the trouble. He had boasted that he would pull a job with real prospects out of the hat. How hollow that boast sounded now. And not only hollow, downright stupid.

She put a hand on what for him was aching flesh. 'Ken, I can . . .'

He shrugged her away. 'Forget it,' he spat.

She stared at the back he presented to her. 'I said I'm sorry.'

Bouncing off the bed, he snatched up his underpants. His embarrassment and shame had given way to fury – fury at himself for failing to accomplish what he'd said he would. What he'd *boasted* he would. Vicky knew that she had hurt him deeply. She would have given anything to be able to retract those withering words.

She was rehooking her bra when Ken flounced from the room, and left the house, slamming the outside door loudly behind him.

After half an hour, when he had not returned, she put out the lights and went home.

Ken walked and walked, up this street, down that. When it began pelting cats and dogs, he hardly noticed. Finally his fury subsided. He knew he should not have gone off and left Vicky as he had, that it was childish. But he had felt so humiliated! He suddenly realised that his right foot was wet. Stopping, he lifted the foot to have a look at the sole. 'Buggeration!' he swore when he saw the hole there – this was the only pair of shoes he owned.

He noticed then he was standing beside the alleyway where he and Vicky had seen the burglars that night shortly after he had been laid off. In that instant an idea was born to him.

Vicky lay in bed gazing up into the darkness. The wall clock in the front room had just chimed midnight, but she was not in the least bit sleepy. It was worrying her sick that Ken had walked out on her that evening. Why hadn't she kept her big yap shut! She should never have said what she had.

As for refusing to make love, she was right about that. She just could not take the risk. As things stood, it would be disastrous for her to get in the pudding club. But if only she hadn't taunted him about his boast. If ifs and ands were pots and pans, she thought grimly.

But the situation had hardly been easy for her; she also had been worked up, and then let down. And she had been

26

the one having to force herself to say no when she really desperately wanted to say yes. If it had been difficult for him, it had been even more so for her. Why couldn't the silly sod have understood that!

What did his storming off like that mean? Would he be round tomorrow sheepishly to make up? Or did it mean he didn't want to know any more, that she had lost him? Fear gripped her at the thought of losing Ken. She could not imagine life without him. He was the man for her, no other would ever do. Her fear was a leaden lump in her breast. He would come chapping her door tomorrow, or wait for her in the street, she tried to reassure herself. Of course he would, it would be daft of him not to. Surely some hastily spoken words would not break them up? Except that Ken was fiercely proud and she had badly dented that pride. When that happened to a man, he could react very foolishly indeed. React in a way that didn't really make sense.

Oh, please God he would continue seeing her. Please God!

Mary had made a sort of soup containing cut-up chunks of tripe, in the Glasgow manner. Vicky loathed the stuff. The sight alone of that spongy so-called delicacy was enough to make her want to throw up. She stared in horror at the evil-smelling bowlful that Mary had placed in front of her for tea. Mary, knowing full well her daughter's feelings about tripe, apologised for serving it, but said it was the only thing at the butcher's shop they could afford and, when possible, the family had to have something substantial to eat to supplement their now more or less standard diet of bread, porage and tats.

'Oh lovely!' teased John, and sucked a large piece of tripe off his spoon.

Vicky shuddered to think how slimy and slithery it would have felt as it slipped down the throat.

'That's enough, boy,' George growled, which stopped John's teasing. George was not very keen on tripe either, but had nothing like his daughter's aversion to it.

Vicky was ravenously hungry. She could've, as the

Glasgow expression went, ate a scabby-heided wean. But tripe? She doubted it.

'There's nothing else. That's it,' Mary said.

Vicky's belly heaved, and heaved again. Her skin had become hot and cold at the same time, and there was a sheen of perspiration on her forehead. She moved her spoon in the bowl and attempted to lift it. Her hand refused to obey the command her cringing brain was sending it.

Rat a tat tat went the front door.

'You get that, son,' Mary said to John, who immediately got down from the table and left the room.

'It's Ken Blacklaws,' John announced on his return.

Vicky glanced up and there, behind her brother, stood a smiling Ken.

Relief surged through her. It was four days since Ken had gone off, leaving her in his house, and this was the first she had seen or heard of him since.

'Hello,' she said shyly.

'As it's Friday night, I thought we might go out. The pictures, or dancing, or whatever you fancy?'

Vicky frowned. How was that to be possible with him skint? 'What about money?' she queried.

Ken's face broke into a broad smile. 'I'm grafting again. Nothing great, and it's only casual, but it pays, which is the main thing.'

George came to his feet. 'Congratulations, Ken. That's smashing news. It's fair bucked me up to hear it,' he said, shaking Ken by the hand.

'You're the first of all those laid off by Agnew's to find something else,' Mary said.

'Aye, well, I told Vicky I'd be – and having said that, I had to live up to it,' Ken replied.

Vicky pushed aside the bowl of tripe. 'I'll need a few minutes to get my glad rags on,' she said to Ken, eyes shining with happiness. She wanted to take him into her arms and kiss him there and then, but would contain herself until they were going down the close stairs and didn't have any onlookers. Her Ken was back! He hadn't given her the chop after all! And he was in work! Excitement bubbled in her as she went through to the bedroom to change and put on some make-up.

'So what kind of a job is it then?' George asked Ken.

'Labouring, real donkey work. But, as I said, it pays – and that's all that matters.'

George nodded his agreement. In hard times like these a pay packet at the end of the week *was* all that mattered; beggars couldn't afford to be choosers.

'Whereabouts?' Mary asked.

'I'll be moving about from site to site, all over the city, I believe. The firm itself is based in the town.'

'And what's the firm called?' Mary went on, continuing her probing.

Ken had expected to be asked these questions, so he'd prepared the answers to them at home, before making his announcement.

'McGilvray's.' There were all sorts of companies by that name listed in the phone book.

'And you say it's only casual?' Mary went on.

'For the moment anyway,' Ken answered, his smile never wavering.

When Vicky was ready, she and Ken said their goodbyes and left the house. As she had planned, she stopped him halfway down the stairs and kissed him. When his tongue jabbed into her mouth, she went tingly all over and her skin broke out in goose flesh. The warm smell of him made her feel weak at the knees.

'So where's it to be? Anywhere at all that you fancy. Tonight, money's no object,' he said when the kiss was finally over.

The kiss had left Vicky panting. 'I don't mind. Where would you like to go?'

He thought for a moment. 'How about St Andrew's Halls? The dancing's usually good there.'

'Then St Andrew's Halls it'll be,' she agreed.

As they reached the street Ken said, 'As I took you away from your tea, how about some fish suppers before we go into town?'

'Are you sure you can . . . ?'

29

He placed a finger across her lips. 'I'm sure I can afford it. As I said, money's no object.'

Fish and chips! Her mouth watered at the prospect. 'Yes please then,' she said.

They went to a fish shop in Parliamentary Road, where he ordered an extra fish each for them. 'Last of the big-time spenders!' he said to a delighted Vicky.

Oh, but that fish supper was rare! The fish were succulent, the chips gorgeous. She declared she'd never tasted anything better. Adding, of course, that hunger was the best sauce.

'Better now?' Ken asked when she had consumed the last chip and crumb of batter in her poke.

Vicky nodded. She was a new woman after that.

'I love you,' he said lightly and, taking her now empty poke from her, he scrunched it up with his own and tossed them into a waste basket.

She stared at him, those words that he had uttered so lightly booming in her mind. 'I love you too.'

This was the first time he'd said he loved her, and the first she'd admitted it to him, having been waiting for him to declare himself before she did.

He crooked his arm and she hooked hers round it. 'St Andrew's Halls and the jigging,' he said, and they started for the nearest tramstop.

He loved her, Vicky thought. *He loved her!*

She loved him so much it positively hurt.

Two

'One pound dead, that's the best I can do for you, hen,' the pawnbroker said.

Vicky stared at her mother's wedding ring which Mr Levi had placed back on the counter in front of her. 'How about making it a guinea?'

'A pound dead, take it or leave it,' Mr Levi replied firmly.

Vicky nodded, knowing it was useless to argue further, and Mr Levi moved to the till. Mary had been expecting more for the ring, but had instructed her to take whatever offered.

It was three days before Christmas and Mary had decided to pop her wedding ring in order to be able to buy a chicken for their Christmas dinner. Unemployment or not, she was determined that they would have a decent traditional meal that day. Apart from the chicken, boiled so soup could also be made from it, there would be roast tats, brussels, carrots, mashed turnip and, if there was any money left over, a screwtop, or several, for George, who hadn't tasted drink since Agnew's closed down.

Mary had said she would pop her ring, but could not face going to the shop herself. George had refused point-blank to do so. Therefore the task had fallen to Vicky.

Vicky took the pound note and ticket, then watched Mr Levi place the ring in a display tray underneath the counter. When Mary had given her the ring to take to Mr Levi's, it was the first time ever she had seen it off her mother's finger. George's face had turned pasty and he had left the room. He would have given anything to have owned something of value that could have been pawned so that the ring could stay where it belonged. But he had nothing.

On leaving the shop, Vicky discovered that it had started

to snow; large flakes were swirling all around, falling out of a leaden grey sky. She shivered, thankful that she had a good thick coat to wear, bought new for her the previous winter.

'Vicky? I thought it was you,' said a woman coming up to her. It was Sylvia Binnie, her cousin, who was four years older than her.

The Binnies lived just off the Alexandra Parade but, although it was not far from Parr Street, Vicky rarely saw her cousin, or aunt and uncle. There had been a time when she had, but her mother and Aunt Lena, Mary's sister, had fallen out a number of years back and, so far anyway, had never made up.

'I was sorry to hear about Agnew's. How are things at home?' Sylvia asked.

Sylvia was a plain girl, with a squint in her right eye. Despite these drawbacks, she was never without a boyfriend, and usually a good-looking one at that. When asked how she managed this – as she was occasionally, by other women – she answered that it was a chemical thing; men were just attracted to her.

'Pretty bad. I've just been in the pawnshop popping Mum's wedding ring,' Vicky replied.

Sylvia pulled a sympathetic face. She was employed by Copland and Lye, a big shop in Sauchiehall Street, as she had been since leaving school. Her father was a cabinet maker for a firm which made quality goods that were mainly sold in London. 'The whole unemployment situation seems to be getting worse. I heard yesterday that a large factory over in Provanmill is to shut down in the New Year. Apparently they've gone bust, same as Agnew's.'

'But your dad's all right?'

Sylvia crossed two fingers. 'So far anyway.'

'And you?'

'Still selling lots of lingerie. Thousands of folk might be starving in the city, but there are still plenty with money. I've no fears for my job.'

Vicky showed her the pound note she was holding. 'For a Christmas bird and some of the trimmings. Mum's

32

determined it won't be porage and dry bread that day,' Vicky said, voice tinged with bitterness.

'How's your dad taking being laid off?' Sylvia asked.

'Well, he's doing his best to keep his pecker up, but between you, me and the gatepost he's the lowest he's ever been in his life.'

Sylvia groped in her bag to produce two half-crowns. 'Here, take this dollar. It's not much, but it's all I can spare for the moment. Add it to the pound for your Christmas dinner.'

'I couldn't,' Vicky said, pushing her hand away.

Sylvia's hand darted down, and the five bob was dropped into Vicky's coat pocket. 'I insist. We're family after all.' She paused, then added, 'I know your mum wouldn't like getting money from me, so tell her you got twenty-five bob for the ring.'

'It's very good of you, so it is,' Vicky mumbled.

'Och, away with you. I only wish it had been earlier on in the week and I'd have been able to give you more.'

Vicky kissed her cousin on the cheek. 'I'd better be getting on then,' she said.

'Aye, all right. I'll be seeing you about.'

Sylvia stared at Vicky's retreating back. She looked so pinched and drawn, Sylvia thought. And her hair, usually a cap of shiny curls, had been dull and lifeless. Then she remembered Bess Dickson, and what Bess had told her during the dinner break.

'Vicky!'

Vicky turned to see Sylvia hurrying after her. Stopping, she waited for her to catch up.

'Look, this might not come to anything at all, but I've just had an idea. There's a china of mine at Copland and Lye's called Bess Dickson who's decided to emigrate to New Zealand with her husband. She kept it hush-hush from everyone at work, including me, till today, when she handed in her notice. She'll be leaving Copland and Lye at the end of January, a couple of days before she and her hubby are due to sail.'

Vicky could not understand why Sylvia was telling her

this. What did it have to do with her? 'Uh-huh?' she prompted.

'Don't you see? If Bess has handed in her notice, then she'll have to be replaced.'

The penny dropped. 'You mean, by me?'

'You're old enough to leave school and start work, so why not? There certainly wouldn't be any harm in putting yourself up for the job. And it's a fair lassie's wage. Two pounds a week isn't to be sniffed at.'

Indeed it wasn't. 'How do I go about applying?' Vicky asked eagerly.

A little later, when she finally parted from Sylvia, Vicky had all the details, and would be presenting herself at Copland and Lye's first thing the next morning. She was bursting to tell her mum and dad about this chance which had so unexpectedly come her way.

The house was detached, made of grey stone blocks, and very, very large. Six or seven bedrooms, maybe even more, Ken thought. The driveway was red-chip gravel, and empty of cars. Although it was dark out, not a single light showed at the front of the house. Ken made his way round to the rear, which was also in darkness.

He had developed a system, and now he put the next phase into action. Returning to the front, he took a package from one of his pockets and, walking up to the door, rang the bell. If he was wrong, and someone was at home, he would ask for Mr Ivory, saying he had a package for the gentleman. Of course there wouldn't be a Mr Ivory living there, so he'd apologise, say he must have the wrong address, and leave. In the unlikely event that there was a Mr Ivory on the premises, he would hand over the package, then leave. All the package contained was screwed-up tissue paper and a stone to give it weight.

He did his best to appear relaxed and casual, but apprehension was knotting his insides. He knew from experience that the apprehension would stay with him until it was all over. No one answered his ring, so he rang a second time. When there was still no answer, he strolled round to the

34

back of the house and chapped the door he had seen there.

The door was locked, but that did not present much of a problem. It took only a handful of seconds to jemmy it open. Heart thundering, he stepped into the house to find himself in the kitchen. Using a small torch, he located a study, closed the curtains, and switched on the lights.

There was a desk, button-down-leather chesterfield, chair to match, and two of the walls were lined with books. A third wall had a number of prints on it, the fourth a painting of a man dressed in the clothes of the previous century.

Ken went to the desk and began rifling through it. His luck was in; he found thirty pounds in fivers. His hands were shaking as he slipped the money into his wallet. Thirty quid! A bloody fortune. He wondered if he should go through the whole house. There might be more money elsewhere, and there was bound to be jewellery.

He almost jumped out of his skin when there was a sudden sound behind him. He whirled in fright, ready to lash out at the person he thought must be there. Lash out, push the person aside, and make his escape. A tortoiseshell cat with a cheeky, impish face stared up at him. It licked its chops, then wagged its tail. It was clearly a friendly animal.

Ken sagged in on himself with relief. 'Jesus!' he swore softly, and took a deep breath. That made up his mind. To hell with looking through the rest of the house. He was off.

When he was well clear of the house, and leaving the neighbourhood, he saw the funny side and began to laugh. That damned cat had given him the fright of his life!

Miss Elvin was having a period and was consequently in a filthy mood. Periods gave her a great deal of pain, and blackened her outlook. Normally a pleasant female, she became quite the opposite at this time of the month.

She glowered at Sue, her secretary, who had come into her office to say there was some wretched lassie outside asking to see her. Her official title was head of personnel.

'What's the name?' she asked grumpily.

'Victoria Devine.'

'Send her in then.'

Sue did not pay any attention to Miss Elvin's ill humour; she knew the cause of it, and that it would pass in a few days' time. She had been Miss Elvin's secretary for a number of years, and they were fairly good friends.

Vicky was sitting with hands folded in her lap. She was extremely nervous, and hoping she wasn't going to stammer or fall over her words when she spoke to Miss Elvin. She was wearing a black skirt of her mum's that Mary had been up half the night altering to fit her. The cream blouse, a sober affair, was also her mum's. She had had nothing suitable in her own wardrobe.

Vicky had walked past Sylvia on her way in and given her a conspiratorial wink. They had not spoken, as Sylvia had been busy serving.

'Miss Elvin will see you now,' Sue said to Vicky and gestured at the door leading to Miss Elvin's office.

'Come in!' Miss Elvin called out when Vicky knocked tentatively.

Miss Elvin saw a tallish girl with a good figure and intelligent eyes. Beautiful? She wouldn't have gone that far, but certainly extremely pretty.

For her part, Vicky saw a woman in her early thirties, very smartly dressed in a navy-blue suit, wearing a querulous expression and a heavenly perfume that filled the office. A strong-willed woman used to getting her own way, Vicky thought as she smiled.

'Sit down, Miss Devine,' Miss Elvin said, pointing to a hard-backed wooden chair strategically placed in front of her desk.

Vicky sat as instructed. 'It's good of you to see me without an appointment, but I wanted to come straight away and forego the delay of writing when I heard there was a job going,' she said in a rush.

Miss Elvin frowned. Vicky's words had rubbed her up the wrong way. 'And how did you know that?' she asked softly, but with the ring of steel and irritation underneath the softness.

Alarm flashed in Vicky; she'd said the wrong thing. 'I eh . . . I have a friend who works here,' she replied.

'Who?'

'A cousin.'

Miss Elvin's annoyance increased. She gave a thin, chilling smile. 'Don't prevaricate with me, girl. I asked a straightforward question and expect a straightforward answer.'

Vicky hesitated, then made a decision. Badly as she wanted this job, she dare not name Sylvia, for it was obvious that by doing so she would get Sylvia into trouble, perhaps even get her the sack.

'I'm sorry if my cousin has done wrong in telling me there was a job going. She certainly didn't realise she was doing so.'

'And which job was that?' Miss Elvin demanded, knowing full well which one it had to be, as there had been only one job fall vacant in the last six weeks.

'In the toiletries department,' Vicky replied.

Miss Elvin took a cigarette from a mother-of-pearl box and lit it with a Ronson lighter which Vicky recognised as being identical to the lighter she had given Ken for his birthday. 'Mrs Dickson's position was filled an hour after she handed in her notice.'

Vicky's face fell.

'The new person, a Miss Ireland, starts the Monday after the Friday that Mrs Dickson leaves,' Miss Elvin added.

Vicky became aware of a strange noise, then realised it was her own laboured breathing. She was disappointed, cruelly so.

Cow! Miss Elvin thought, referring to herself. She was being totally unreasonable, and knew it.

Vicky rose. 'I'm sorry for wasting your time. Thank you again for seeing me without an appointment,' she said with all the dignity she could muster.

She fought to control her emotions. Why had the woman been so nasty with her! Surely what Sylvia had done hadn't been a breach of the firm's rules? Sylvia would have known if it had.

Sue glanced up at Vicky's face as she went past. What she saw there made her own expression turn grim.

'Can I do anything for you?' she called after her.

Vicky halted. 'Is there a toilet please?' she replied, voice quavering.

Sue personally took her down a side corridor and showed her where the toilet was. Vicky muttered her appreciation and slipped inside.

Vicky felt sick. Sick, angry and humiliated. At least she had kept Sylvia's identity secret from Miss Elvin. It would have been a tragedy if Sylvia had got the sack on her account.

She thought of her father, who had been so excited earlier on when she had left the house. Now this: not only a let-down, but a terrible one. Then the tears she had been fighting back for the past few minutes came, a flood of them that washed the make-up from her face and created pale shadows under her eyes.

Miss Elvin opened the door to the toilet and stared in surprise at the distraught Vicky. She was instantly filled with guilt, knowing that the girl's state was as a result of the interview with her. Vicky, hand over mouth, shoulders heaving, saw Miss Elvin through a rain of tears and turned away.

The goodness and sweetness that was Miss Elvin's normal nature reasserted itself. Contrition was added to guilt as, coming forward, she fumbled for the clean hanky she knew to be at the bottom of her bag. 'Use this,' she said, pressing it on Vicky.

Vicky accepted the hanky, and bubbled into it. 'I feel so ashamed,' she sobbed.

Miss Elvin swallowed hard. 'It's hardly you who should feel ashamed, but me. I was absolutely rotten to you in my office,' she confessed in a small voice, and immediately felt the better for doing so.

Miss Elvin crossed to the sink and ran some water into a tumbler that had been standing there. 'Have a drink of this.'

Vicky took a sip, then another.

'You really did need that job, didn't you?' Miss Elvin probed gently.

Vicky nodded, and wiped her nose with the hanky.

'Your father out of work, is that it?'

Still sobbing, but not crying any more, Vicky told Miss Elvin the story of Agnew's going bust, and all its employees, including her dad, being laid off. She spoke of her father tramping the streets day after unsuccessful day looking for work, and how cold it was at home with no coal for the fire, and how desperately hungry they all were.

Miss Elvin listened in silence, the shame of how she had treated Vicky deepening with every passing second. She thought of her own good job, the excellent money it paid, and how she wanted for nothing. She resolved to make it up to the girl. It meant breaking one of her own cardinal rules about queue-jumping, but there was always the exception to every rule, and she considered this to be such.

'The job in toiletries has been filled, but one of our female packers and dispatchers is pregnant and close to the time where she'll have to leave to have the baby. The pay, at thirty shillings a week, is less than on the floor, but if you did well we could promote you to a floor at a later date when a suitable vacancy there comes up,' Miss Elvin said.

'If that's an offer, I'll take it,' Vicky replied quickly.

'We have a combination of male and female packers and dispatchers. The females unpack the more delicate merchandise and repack and dispatch the same.'

'It sounds wonderful, the very dab,' Vicky enthused, hardly able to believe this sudden turn around in her fortunes. One moment she had been in the pit of despair, the next it was as if a bright golden sun had suddenly burst from behind a cloud.

'Then consider the position yours.'

Vicky clapped her hands in glee.

Miss Elvin gave a broad smile. What a relief to have made amends for her earlier shocking behaviour! 'I'll tell you what, why don't you rinse your face at the sink while I'm in the cubicle here, then we'll go back to my office and have a nice cup of coffee while I take down your details.'

'That would be smashing.'

As she rinsed her face, Vicky thought of her father. She just knew he would whoop with joy when she told him the news.

And so he did.

It was Hogmanay, the Scottish night of nights. Bairns and the English celebrated Christmas, but the working Scot grafted right through that – those in work, that is – till the arrival of Hogmanay, then they downed tools at five or six p.m., went on holiday, and had themselves a four-day-and-night binge.

Vicky was hurrying home, having been over in Lister Street sitting with Eunace, a pal of hers who was down with a dose of the flu. They had had a good old natter together, and the pair of them had thoroughly enjoyed it. Ken was coming over later with a bottle, the plan being that she and he would see the New Year in with her family, then go over and first-foot his.

She had decided to go via the back courts, it was quicker that way, so she plunged into a yellow-tinted close, the yellow light coming from the hissing gas mantle three quarters of the way up the left-hand close wall. Once out in the back court, she paused for a moment to regain her night sight and became aware of two figures standing swaying in the darkness. The splattering sound was unmistakable: they were peeing against the tenement wall. It didn't bother Vicky to come across such a thing; it was common enough. Probably a couple of chaps caught short returning from the pub, she thought, as she hurried past.

At least she tried to hurry past, but she didn't make it. A hand shot out to grab her by the shoulder.

'Why hello there, darling,' the chap who'd caught hold of her said. He had finished urinating but made no attempt to put himself away.

She peered into their faces but did not recognise either of them. They weren't locals. She attempted to wrench herself free, but the hand on her shoulder tightened, gripping her fast. The man pulled her to him. He was nineteen or twenty, Vicky judged. The other a little older.

'She's a proper cracker, isn't she, Mick?' the one holding Vicky said.

'She is that, Tommy.'

Vicky's mouth curled downwards in distaste. Tommy's breath was stale with beer and had overtones of halitosis. His eyes were hard and vicious from drink.

Mick buttoned up his trousers, but Tommy made no attempt to do the same.

'How about a wee kiss? It's Hogmanay after all, time for celebration, making new friends and all that guff,' Tommy leered.

She started to scream, but her scream was swiftly stifled by Tommy clamping a hand over her mouth. 'Och, don't take it that way,' Tommy whispered and, removing his hand, fastened his mouth onto hers.

She struggled, but he was too strong for her. Her stomach contracted as he roughly fondled first one breast then the other. A hardness nudged her crotch.

Mick came up behind to press himself against her rear. He groped her bottom while Tommy continued fondling her breasts, then the hand which had been doing that came up under her skirt.

'Leave her go,' a new voice said.

Cursing, Tommy twisted round to face the direction from which the voice had come.

It was Neil Seton, his slim frame tight with fury.

'Bugger off,' Mick said.

Neil knew they weren't carrying weapons. If they had been, those would have been out by now. 'On you go, get walking,' he hissed.

Tommy gave a scornful laugh. It was two against one, and the one was hardly the most robust of specimens. 'Away and raffle your doughnut, pal,' he said and, provocatively replacing a hand on Vicky's right breast, proceeded to knead it.

Neil saw red. How dare they do that to Vicky, these bloody animals, how dare they!

If only it had been Ken who had happened by, Vicky thought desperately. She could see him taking on Tommy

41

and Mick and beating them. But Neil! The idea was absurd.

What Vicky didn't know was that Neil was madly in love with her, and love can do many things, including making a normally cowardly man brave.

'Let's have a bit then, hen,' Tommy said and, thrusting Vicky back against the wall, reached once more under her skirt and began tugging down her knickers.

Neil spied a brick at his feet. Snatching it up, he hefted it. 'Stop that and go, or, so help me God, I'll brain you bastards.'

Tommy paused and looked at Neil afresh. There was something in Neil's tone told him Neil wasn't bluffing.

'Now sod off the pair of you!' Neil shouted and, lowering himself into a semi-crouch, moved forward several paces.

Mick also realised that Neil meant what he threatened, and it was he who broke first. A bloke could get killed being bashed over the head with a brick. 'It was only a wee bit fun, that's all, it being Hogmanay and that. We'll move along just as you want, Jim.'

Neil's lips were wolfishly drawn back to show his teeth. He brought his concentration to bear fully on Tommy, though still aware of Mick, should his capitulation turn out to be a trick.

Tommy had been drunk to start with but was sobering rapidly now. For a moment he considered rushing Neil, then decided against it. 'It was only a bit of fun, as my china says,' he mumbled. Releasing Vicky, he put himself away and started doing up his fly.

Vicky stumbled away behind Neil, where she spat on the ground, trying to get the sour, revolting taste of Tommy out of her mouth.

Side by side, Tommy and Mick slunk off into the darkness and were soon lost to sight behind some middens.

'Oh, Neil!' Vicky choked, and fell into his arms. He dropped the brick so he could hold her properly.

How lucky it was he had happened by, Neil thought. If he hadn't the consequences were just too awful to contemplate. He gently stroked Vicky's hair to try and soothe her down. She was shaking like a leaf, and no wonder after the events of the past few minutes.

'I'm all right now,' she declared eventually, and took a deep breath. 'Thank the Lord you came along,' she said, marvelling that he'd stood up to those two. She would never have guessed he had it in him.

'They were both pissed as newts, but that hardly excuses what they attempted to do,' Neil said lightly.

'You would have used that brick too, wouldn't you?'

'Oh, aye. It was you they had, Vicky, I couldn't let them hurt you.'

Vicky frowned. There was something in his voice that she didn't understand. 'I'll need a minute or two to collect myself before I go in. I don't want to tell Mum and Dad about this. It would only cause them anxiety and worry, and they've had more than enough of that of late.'

She eased herself out of his embrace. 'I've just come from visiting Eunace Walker. She's down with the flu.'

'I was doing a stint of studying myself, and went out to try and clear a headache that had come on with a breath of fresh air.'

Trust Neil Seton to be swotting during the school holidays, she thought. He was a right keenie. 'And did it?'

He regarded her blankly. 'Did it what?'

'Clear your headache?'

He had to think for a couple of seconds. 'Well, it was still there when I came upon you and them, but it's gone now. My anger must have burned it away.'

'And you certainly were angry. I've never seen you like that before.'

He gave a self-conscious smile. 'There's a first time for everything, I suppose.'

She would rinse her mouth out with hot salty water when she got home, she thought. She could still taste Tommy.

'Do you mind turning round so I can pull myself together?' she asked.

He wondered what she was on about, then it dawned she was referring to her underclothes. 'Aye, certainly,' he replied, and did as requested.

He gazed up at the tenements lowering all around. How sad they looked, and forlorn. He couldn't see, but he knew that only a few of their chimneys would be making smoke. Normally at this time of year they would all be belching.

'There will be little Black Bun and Shortie in Parr Street tonight, and it'll be a cold welcome to the New Year for those who do stay up to greet it,' he said.

Vicky tugged her knickers into place; they'd been halfway down her thighs. 'Parr Street is a poor street tonight right enough. In fact it should be cried Poor Street instead of Parr,' she replied.

What he said next just popped into his mouth and was out before he knew it. 'If this is Poor Street, then you're the Princess of it. There's not a lassie in the street to touch you, Vicky.' He paused, then added, his voice crackling with emotion, 'Not only Parr Street, but all of Townhead.'

She stared at him in astonishment. He *did* fancy her, and rotten too from the sound of it. That was something else she wouldn't have guessed about him for, before tonight, he had never let on by even an inkling.

Well, well, this was a turn-up for the book. Swotty Seton an admirer of hers!

Neil was amazed at his own forthrightness. He could only think that some of the courage he had conjured up earlier had remained.

Vicky decided to change the subject. She did not want to embarrass him, not after what he had just done for her. 'You can turn round again,' she said.

He did, and made to speak, but before he could do so she cut in. 'I must tell you my big news. I'm not going back to school, I've got a job.'

She wasn't going back to school! That meant he wouldn't be seeing her around nearly as much as he had. 'Where's the job?' he asked, shocked.

'Copland and Lye's. I'm to be a female packer and dispatcher.'

'That's great. When did you land the job?'

'I actually knew the week before last but I didn't want to tell anyone outside the family, and of course Ken, until

44

official confirmation came in. The letter giving me a starting date arrived this morning.'

He was pleased for her, of course he was that, there was no question her family needed the money. But to lose her from school! That was a blow, and a hard one. 'I'm happy for you,' he mumbled.

She gave a low tinkling laugh. 'You certainly don't sound it!'

She was so gorgeous, he thought. He would have given his right arm for her to be his and not bloody Ken Blacklaws's. Ken could have virtually any bird, after all, whereas Vicky was the only one he wanted. 'I'd better be getting along,' he said huskily.

'I'd ask you up for a drink, but we haven't any till later when Ken comes.'

'I understand. We've no drink in either.'

She touched his arm. 'Thanks again for what you did tonight, Neil. I'll never forget it.' She paused for emphasis, then added, 'I'd be obliged if you didn't mention the incident to anyone. I know it's daft, but I don't want word of it getting round. I'd prefer if it was kept strictly between you and me.'

'I'll never mention it, you have my word,' he replied softly.

'Not to a soul, not even Ken,' she insisted.

'Stum's the word, Vicky.'

She swithered about what seemed the natural thing to do next – she didn't want him getting any wrong ideas – then kissed him on the cheek, he starting as she did.

'Happy New Year when it comes,' she said.

'Happy New Year to you too when it comes.'

When she'd gone, he gently touched the spot she'd kissed, and drank in the lingering smell of her.

He was euphoric, till he remembered he would not be seeing her during schoolhours any more. Then his heart sank.

Oh, but it was a glorious, glorious day, the best she could remember for a long time.

Vicky's shoes clattered on the pavement as she hurried along Parr Street. It was the end of her first week at Copland and Lye, and her pay packet was burning a hole in her pocket. She could not wait to hand it over to her mum.

She passed a couple of youngsters playing peerie, the home-made wooden top whirling as it was struck again and again by the home-made leather-thonged whip. Her pay packet coming into the house was going to make all the difference. The coal bunker would be full once more and meat would make a reappearance on the table. Mince and tatties, how she craved a plateful of that, her favourite, not having tasted it since Agnew's went bust. Her mouth watered at the thought.

She and Ken were going out later on. He had promised to take her to pictures in the town. The next night, Saturday, they would be staying in at his house while his parents went visiting. She smiled to herself. It was nearly three weeks now since they had last had the opportunity to make love; it would be so good to do so again.

As she turned into the close, she met Mr Smith the lamplighter coming out. They exchanged words, for they knew each other well. Mr Smith had been the lamplighter for Parr Street and the streets directly round about since she had been a baby.

She found her mum, dad and brother John in the kitchen. Right away she could see something was up, for her father was grinning from ear to ear, his eyes twinkling like blue stars.

'You look pleased with yourself,' she said to him.

'First things first,' George replied, indicating the buff-coloured envelope she was holding. He did not want to spoil her moment.

Vicky handed the envelope to Mary. 'My pay packet, Mum,' she said.

Mary proudly accepted the envelope and clutched it to her bosom. She was remembering Vicky as a wean in nappies. It seemed like only yesterday, how time had flown!

'Thank you, lass,' she replied softly.

'No more tripe,' Vicky pleaded.

Everyone laughed. 'No more tripe,' Mary promised.

George produced a ten packet of Capstan and lit one with a match from a box of Swan Vestas. He drew the smoke gratefully into his lungs. How he'd missed his fags! It had been sheer purgatory going without them. Not a day had passed when he hadn't craved nicotine. But he had never given in to that craving, not even a solitary fly one. He was proud of that.

'Remember Robert the Bruce and the spider?' He smiled.

Vicky squealed with delight. She could see what was coming. 'Oh, Dad!' she exclaimed, and throwing her arms round him gave him a big smacker on the side of the mouth.

'Aye, you've guessed it. All yon endless tramping the streets finally paid off. I start Monday as a conductor on the trams,' he said.

Two of them working. The family were going to be in clover indeed.

'Only the fourth man from Agnew's to find work,' Mary said and thought sadly of those still idle.

Vicky sniffed and wiped tears from her eyes. Oh, but this was rare.

'And I've you to thank, girl. I'm sure I'd have given up that time if it hadn't been for you and your wee story,' George said to Vicky.

'Now let's have our tea. It's mince and tatties,' Mary announced.

What a day! Her cup really was flowing over, Vicky thought.

She made a right pig of herself and had two heaped platefuls. As far as she was concerned, a French chef couldn't have cooked anything that would have tasted better.

Mince and tatties. Food of the gods!

The blood pounded in Vicky's head. All she could feel was Ken's maleness splitting her down there. Jesus, it was gorgeous! Suddenly he locked deep into her. In response, she thrust herself onto him, fully impaling herself. She gasped as the most exquisite sensation blossomed within her. A sensation belonging more to heaven than earth. Ken

47

collapsed onto her to lay a cheek in the hollow of her neck. He was panting and streaming with sweat.

'That was incredible,' she whispered, thinking it had never been better. It was so natural with them somehow, everything fitted perfectly.

When he finally tried to withdraw, she protested, and told him to stay where he was. If she could, she would have kept him – and herself, as she was, totally happy and complete – in the same place for all eternity.

Eventually nature took its course and the joining broke of its own accord. Vicky watched the muscles briefly play on his arm when he flicked his Ronson alight. She kissed a shoulder, tasting the saltiness of his sweat, and adoring it. 'We don't get a chance to do this nearly often enough,' she complained.

'We will when we get married.'

She sat up straight to stare at him. 'Say that again?'

Icing on a cake, that was what she always reminded him of, sweet icing on a cake, he thought.

'We will when we get married,' he repeated.

Those were words she had been longing to hear, that she had dreamt of hearing. 'Is that a proposal?' she asked, suddenly coy.

'Yes and no. If you want, we will get married, but not just yet. Maybe next year.'

She threw herself at him, and hugged him. 'If I want! Of course I want. I love you,' she exclaimed.

'And I love you, which is why I wish to marry you when the time's right.'

She lay back and pulled the quilt up over her nakedness, not because she was shy but because she was cooling down and becoming aware that it was chilly in his bedroom.

'Will we live round here?' She already saw herself and Ken in a wee house of their own.

'We can, to start with, till I really get on my feet. For don't forget I've got ambitions to be somebody and "somebodies" don't live in Townhead, or in tenements even.'

'A stringpuller. Your own master and master of many,'

she said, echoing his words from the night of his birthday party.

He gave a deep laugh, and kissed her on the mouth, delighted that she had remembered what he'd said, and furthermore was even able to quote him on it.

'When we get officially engaged, I'll give you a diamond ring, you have my promise on that,' he told her.

'People don't give diamond rings any more, Ken, they haven't the money.'

'Some people do, and I'll be one of them. I swear.'

She was frowning. 'I wouldn't want to have to wait longer because you were saving up for that.'

'You won't have to wait longer.'

'You really are doing well in this job, aren't you?'

'I've no complaints. Though it's still only a temporary job, mind you, something to see me through these hard times that folk are having to contend with.'

'You say you've got ambitions, but to be what?' she probed.

'I don't know yet. Some day an opportunity will present itself. I've no idea what sort of opportunity or in which direction it'll take me, but when it does come I'll grab it with both hands, and from there on in there will be no stopping me.'

She gave a teasing smile. 'You sound as though you consider yourself a man of destiny?'

'Men of destiny are those who *make* things happen, who control life and don't just let life control them. And I'm certainly one of those,' he replied.

She reached for him and squeezed very gently, causing him to breathe in sharply. 'You're not the only one who can make things happen,' she said.

And she was very quickly proved right.

A keen March wind was gusting as Vicky left Copland and Lye by the staff entrance, having just completed her day's work. She walked round to the front of the shop on the way to her nearest tramstop.

She stopped in front of a window whose display had been

49

changed since she'd gone in that morning. The new display was a wedding scene, the bride in a white organza and satin dress with flowing train, the groom in top hat and morning dress. There were two boy pages, each wearing a Royal Stewart kilt, and two bridesmaids, same young age as the boys, wearing frilly pink dresses.

Marriage, Vicky thought. It had hardly been out of her mind since the night Ken proposed. 'Mrs Ken Blacklaws,' she whispered, savouring the words in her mouth. 'Mrs Ken Blacklaws,' she repeated, and a shiver ran through her.

Staring at the display, she imagined herself as the bride, Ken as the groom. She saw herself walking down the aisle on her dad's arm, a smiling Ken waiting for her in front of the minister.

'Do you take this man . . . ?'

'I do . . . I do!'

'Do you take this woman . . . ?'

'I do.'

She shivered again, feeling a fluttery, scary coldness that left her all of a tingle and slightly breathless. Their wedding would be nowhere as fancy as that depicted in the display of course and, because of financial saving, might even be in the registry office. Just as long as she and Ken were married, that was all that mattered to her.

Next year: he'd said they'd get married then. Why, that was hardly any time away at all. And with Ken a foreman now – he had been promoted recently – they might be able to get married sooner rather than later, which was to say fairly early on in the year as opposed to the middle or end. Early on in the year . . . yes, she thought excitedly, she must somehow bring that about. But she must be careful. The last thing she wanted was for him to think he was being hurried into it. She must make it appear that the idea was his, not hers.

Mrs Ken Blacklaws! She wanted that so much she could taste it. Humming 'Here Comes The Bride', she left the window display and continued on to her tramstop.

•

50

Ken was in the St George's Cross billiard hall, a favourite haunt of his since 'going to work for McGilvray's'. Initially his days had been long and tedious, for he could only spend so much time reconnoitring possible break-ins, and then he had hit on the idea of going into various pubs for a bevy. He had soon learned that that was not such a good idea after all. A couple of pints at dinner time had quickly developed into five or six, which wasn't only costly but meant that his afternoons and evenings were lost to him, for he certainly couldn't go reconnoitring, or breaking in, when he was bevied to the gills.

So the dinnertime visits to the pubs had gone by the board, and he had taken up going to the pictures instead. But after a while he had got fed up with going to the pictures on a more or less daily basis, so eventually he had found this billiard hall where he could either just sit and watch, as he was doing now, or play the occasional game of snooker, which he preferred to billiards.

It was quite some time now since he had to start going to work every weekday in order to explain the amount of money he was 'earning'. His so-called promotion to foreman was a ruse on his part to explain further why those earnings were so high.

Ken was sitting watching a game of snooker in progress. At least he'd started out watching it, but was now deep in his own thoughts. It was a Tuesday afternoon and, that morning, to waste an hour or two, he had gone to the Motor Market, where he'd seen a motor that had fair bowled him over. It was a big Armstrong Siddeley, bluey grey in colour, and beautifully kept. It was obvious that whoever had previously owned that motor had loved it. The moment he clapped eyes on the machine he had known he wanted it, had to have it. Forget that he couldn't drive – that was a minor detail. Once he had the motor, he'd soon learn. What a booster it would be in Townhead, not only to own a car, but to own a beauty like that! He'd be cock of the walk right enough. Not that he particularly cared about Townhead. Oh sure, it had been good to him, and the folks who lived there were nice enough, but whichever way you looked at it it remained a slum, and slums had no place in *his* future.

Today was viewing day at the Motor Market; tomorrow was the auction itself, and the Armstrong Siddeley was due to come under the hammer some time early morning. He'd inquired about that. He had also inquired about what it was likely to go for. The sum mentioned had been fifty pounds. That was an excellent price for a car such as yon. The only trouble was that at present he had only eight pounds ten shillings, plus some coppers, to his name. He was just over forty nicker short.

If he had had a week, he could have come up with the difference, but to raise that amount overnight! Almost impossible. There was no one he could borrow from. The chap to whom he sold the bits and pieces he picked up would only laugh in his face if he tried. And he didn't know anyone else with access to such a sum. Dammit to hell! he raged, and worried a nail.

He was hoping to do a break-in that night. He had three possibles lined up and would choose whichever one was empty. If none was, he would have to leave it to the following night, or even the night after that. If he did pull off a job that night, it still wouldn't help; even in the richest houses, that sort of cash was never left lying around. Why, there had only ever been one house where he'd . . .

A smile slowly lit up his face. If there was an answer to his problem, that was it. The house with the cat who'd scared the living daylights out of him. Of course the odds were against that house being empty on that particular evening, but it just *might* be. And why shouldn't there be another wad of fivers in that study desk? Having already been burgled, the owner would hardly think that lightning would strike in the same place twice. At least not in such a short space of time.

He brought his attention back to the game going on in front of him, and watched Jacky Mulhearn pot an almost impossible shot.

Almost impossible, he thought, and smiled again.

'Nice one, Jacky,' he called out, and clapped his hands. It was an omen for tonight, he told himself. Had to be.

Neil Seton stared at his open maths textbook. It wasn't figures and formulae he saw but Vicky's face, surrounded by its cap of shining curls, gazing enticingly back at him. Uttering a soft groan, he snapped the book shut, then ran a trembling hand over his forehead. Vicky – she haunted him, and how he positively ached for her.

Three months left to go till he sat his Highers and tried for the Carnegie bursary. He was also to be considered, he'd been told at school, for several Corporation grants that would be awarded after the results of the exams were known.

He was certain that he would pass all the Highers he was sitting, unless he had a total mental block that is, and such things had been known to happen, but if he performed as he was capable he should pass and pass well. The big question was, would he pass well enough to get either the Carnegie bursary or one of the Corporation grants? Competition for these awards would be stiff, he was under no illusions about that. He had been warned by his teachers that there were some very bright sparks indeed sitting the Highers next time round.

Panic welled in him, which he fought to control. He had to go to university, he told himself, he just *had to*! There was no viable alternative as far as he was concerned.

He took a deep breath, and thought again of Vicky. Oh, the dreams he had! Dreams that were really nightmares, because he could not have what he saw, and imagined, in them. This was not the first occasion that thoughts of Vicky had disturbed his studying. But tonight it was even worse than usual, tonight she was like a fever in him. Her face, her tantalising flesh; there, but at the same time out of reach.

It amazed him that Ken was still going out with her. It had to be a record for Ken, who normally ditched his birds after a month or two at the most. But ditch her Ken eventually would, and when that happened he would be there waiting to pounce. Neil allowed himself a small grin.

53

Pounce was a rather strong word to use in connection with himself and a female. Insidiously move in and take over was far more appropriate.

He thought jealously of how flashy Ken had become of late since starting to earn such a good screw. Foreman now, he'd been told, which meant even more mazoola per week. He, on the other hand, didn't have two brass farthings to rub together. With his dad out of work, and likely to remain so, he didn't get the pocket money he once had, and so was skint as could be. Mind you, pocket money hardly rated against what Ken must be coining a week, but it would have been better than sod all.

Rising from the spot where he did his studying, he went to the kitchen, where his mum and dad were sitting in front of an empty fireplace. Like him, both were wearing several woollies to combat the cold – cold that might not be as bitter as the past three months, but bitter all the same.

His mum had fallen asleep, his dad was gazing off into space, seeing God alone knew what. His dad was withdrawing more and more into himself, which was a great worry.

'Hello, Dad.' He smiled.

There was no answer. His dad hadn't heard.

Neil shrugged, and left it. He did not want to bellow with his mum asleep. A glance at the ticking clock on the mantelpiece told him that it was just after half past seven, early yet. What to do; more studying or something else? He thought about it, and knew he was in no fit state to do any more studying.

Then he knew what he would do. There was a meeting down at the Cooperative Hall. James Maxton, chairman of the Independent Labour Party – and fieriest of the Glasgow socialists, was scheduled to speak. It would be a treat to hear Maxton, whom he'd heard several times in the past, and whose oratory never failed to rouse his socialism and humanitarian feelings to fever pitch. Maxton would be bound to pull out all the stops with an election looming on the horizon, an election that could just restore the ILP to its former glory, when it had been a force to be reckoned with in British politics, before what many considered to be its disastrous split from its parent Labour Party.

He remembered three years previously, October 1932, when the ILP and the Communists had jointly organised the first hunger march. Now yon had been a sight: thousands and thousands of hungry and despairing men marching off to London to make their protest. To be truthful, not a lot of good had come of those marches, but they'd been an awesome and inspiring sight all the same. There was another reason to go to the Cooperative Hall, one that brought a smile to his face, and made him rub his hands at the thought. The hall would be heated. While there, he'd be warm as toast.

Neil crossed to the shaving mirror hanging above the sink and peered into it. His hair badly needed cutting; he'd get Mum to do it for him, probably over the weekend. When he was wee, his hair had been very blond and a great source of pride to his mother, who'd been forever declaring it made him look like a little prince straight out of a fairy story. However, it had long since dulled to an unexceptional fair colour, the colour of dirty straw.

He gave a soft groan to see his complexion. Those bloody pimples were the bane of his life. He'd have given anything to be rid of them. Well, *nearly* everything, he qualified, being a cautious man, and knowing there was always a price that was unacceptably high. He groaned again when he spotted a cluster of blackheads in the crease of his left nostril. He'd thought he'd got rid of those for good. Now the buggers were back!

Why did he get so many plooks and blackheads, and Ken Blacklaws never a single one! Nor boils – something else he suffered from occasionally. He shuddered at the memory of the last one, a veritable monster that had sat like a small egg on his neck. The boil itself had been agony, the treatment of it sheer hell. He touched the small scar on his neck where the boil had been.

Filling the basin from the tap, he splashed water over his face to waken him up a bit after his abortive study session and to clear his skin of surface grease. He washed his face at least half a dozen times a day to try and keep the nasties away. A doctor had once advised him to do this and he had followed the advice assiduously ever since.

Vicky marched her brother down the street. It was their parents' wedding anniversary, and Vicky had decided that she and John should leave them alone together for a couple of hours. They might be her mother and father, she'd reasoned with herself, but that didn't mean they were 'past it'. On that special night they might well fancy a wee bit of romancing, and if they did she would make certain that neither she nor John were about to spoil their fun.

She tried to imagine her parents in bed doing what she and Ken did, but somehow couldn't. She knew they must, but to imagine them at it was beyond her. Why, in her entire sixteen years she had never seen her dad without his clothes on, and her mum only once, and that when she had walked in on her by mistake.

'Where are we going?' John whined. He hadn't wanted to come out, and only some quiet and fairly deadly threats by Vicky had persuaded him to do so.

'Your father has always told us we should use our minds, and you're going to start tonight. I'm taking you to hear Scotland's greatest politician. A great man right enough, though there are those who describe him as an anarchist,' she replied.

Vicky's statement that James Maxton was Scotland's greatest politician was a contentious one. There were many in the country who would have wholeheartedly agreed with her, many would have argued that such an honour belonged to the Prime Minister, Ramsay MacDonald. A third group might have plumped for Emanuel Shinwell, known to all and sundry as Manny.

'I can already use my mind. I've been using it for years now,' John retorted sharply. He hated it when Vicky pulled age on him, as she was doing now.

Vicky sniffed. 'If that's true, you've a queer way of showing it sometimes.'

'No queerer than you.'

'Don't be cheeky!' she snapped.

'I'm not being any more cheeky to you than you are to me,' he replied, grinning, for he knew he had her there.

Vicky thought about that, determined to have the last word. 'I was being acerbic, you were being cheeky, that's the difference,' she said airily.

John's grin vanished. What the hell did acerbic mean! He certainly wasn't going to ask her, as she well knew. He ground his teeth in frustration. She always won, even when he was right!

They arrived at the Cooperative Hall to find a crowd milling round the entrance. They were passing inside when Vicky was hailed.

'Vicky, over here!'

She glanced across to see Neil Seton frantically waving at her, and boring through the crowd in her direction. He couldn't believe his luck. Vicky without Ken: his night was made.

'So you've come to hear Maxton speak. It should be quite a treat,' he said enthusiastically on reaching her side.

'My dad raves about him, but this is the first time I'll have heard him myself,' she replied.

'Well, take my word for it, you're in for something special. He's the best orator since Cicero.'

They were into the hall itself now and standing at the top of an aisle.

'Follow me,' Neil commanded, leading the way down.

That had been said with authority, Vicky thought. It was a side of Neil's character that was new to her, and pleasing. She liked authoritative men, as Ken was.

When they sat, Neil contrived it so that he was between Vicky and John. The scent of her, strong in his nostrils, made his head spin. He and Vicky talked and talked, all about politics, and Glasgow politics in particular, till finally it was time for Maxton to appear.

Maxton came on to roars and shouts, and a standing ovation. Normally Neil would have sat entranced while Maxton spoke, but not that night. In fact he hardly took in a word of what Maxton said. All he could think of, and be aware of, was Vicky next to him. Every few minutes he used his handkerchief to dab sweat from his brow. His discomfort had nothing whatever to do with the heat in the hall.

Elation surged through Ken. He could hardly credit it: the house *was* empty. Although it was pitch dark out, not a light was showing either front or back.

He had to make dead certain though, and went into the next phase of his system. Carrying the package for Mr Ivory, he walked up the gravel path to the front door and rang the bell. When there was no reply, he rang a second time.· When there was still no reply, that confirmed there was no one at home.

Nonetheless, the usual apprehension knotted his insides as he made his way round to the rear of the house and the door he'd jemmied previously, which he now jemmied afresh. It was a new lock, but no stronger than the last one, he noted to himself, as he slipped into what he knew to be the kitchen.

Heart thudding, he put the jemmy away, and pulled out his small torch. The narrow beam pierced the blackness, lighting his way to the study. Inside the study he closed the door and the heavy curtains and switched on the overhead lights.

It was just as he recalled. The button-down-leather chesterfield, chair to match, and two of the walls lined with books. The man in the painting in nineteenth-century clothes seemed like an old friend.

Moving towards the desk, he went straight to the place in one of the drawers where he'd found the wad of fivers and, sure enough – he felt like letting out a whoop of joy – there was another wad, and this one even thicker than the other. Quickly he counted this new wad of fivers to discover that, in all, there were fourteen of the large white beauties. Why, that was seventy pounds! Tons more than he needed for the Armstrong Siddeley.

Seventy pounds – half a year's wages for a working man, he thought gleefully as he stuffed the notes into his wallet. He had really fallen on his feet tonight.

Should he have a rifle through the rest of the house or leave now? he wondered. Then he remembered that he had promised Vicky an engagement ring; he would have a look upstairs to see if he could find her one.

He switched off the study's overhead lights and his small torch back on. He padded along a hallway till he came to a staircase leading to the upper floors. There was nothing of interest to him on the first level, so he went up another flight, which brought him to the bedrooms.

He closed the hall curtains, returned to what was clearly the master bedroom, and closed the curtains there. He then switched on twin bedside lights. The decor was sumptuous, with a lot of velvet and gilt and deep-pile carpet. The sheets on the bed were baby-blue silk, he noted enviously. Whoever owned this place, they certainly didn't stint themselves, Ken thought, crossing to a vanity table laden with bottles, phials, boxes and make-up accoutrements of all sorts.

The box was covered in blood-red leather and bound with silver filigree. He opened it and gasped at what was inside. There was an eight-row string of pearls, pearls that just couldn't be anything other than the genuine article. It was all real: the ruby bracelet, sapphire pendant, two ruby rings in gold settings, a number of gold chains of varying lengths, an amethyst brooch in what he thought might be a platinum setting, a silver ring with a green stone in it – which, he decided, was jade – an eternity ring encrusted with diamonds, and a diamond engagement ring that was made up of a very large central diamond surrounded by rubies.

'Jesus Christ!' he whispered. It was mind-boggling to think how much all this must be worth.

The jewels mesmerised him. How they glittered and sparkled and shone. How fabulous they were! He twisted the engagement ring between thumb and forefinger. He couldn't possibly give this to Vicky. She would know he'd have to have come by it dishonestly.

There was a sudden sound behind him, coming from the direction of the door. Ken froze.

That cat again! he thought, and smiled with relief. It

59

must be the tortoiseshell cat with the cheeky impish face who'd put the fear of God into him during his last visit. Still smiling, and holding the engagement ring, he turned to the door intent on whispering, hello kit-ee-kit-ee-kit-ee.

His smile vanished abruptly, and the intended words stuck in his throat. It wasn't the cat, but a stark-naked middle-aged man glaring at him out of puffy eyes.

The man hadn't been asleep on this level – Ken had already checked it out. So he must have been sleeping on one of the higher ones. Why hadn't he answered the doorbell!

Ken shot to his feet and the jewels went scattering in all directions, the red-leather box coming to rest on its side so that it gave the impression of an open, mocking mouth.

The stark-naked man was liberally covered in body hair and reminded Ken of a gorilla he'd once seen in a travelling circus menagerie. This gorilla took a deep breath, and the barrel chest seemed to go on expanding for ever. Though strong, Ken was completely outclassed here. The gorilla was quite capable of tearing his head off – and probably would, given half a chance, judging from the expression it was wearing.

'Caught you, thief!' the man hissed in a heavy foreign accent, and formed his hands into enormous fists.

'You wouldn't hit a chap wearing glasses, would you?' Ken said, his mind racing, trying to think of a way out of this, and failing to do so.

The gorilla charged.

There was a standard lamp between Ken and his adversary, and the flex from this, snaking across the floor, caught the gorilla's right foot, to send it, with a surprised yell, sprawling.

Ken reacted instantly. He leaped round the gorilla, flew to the staircase and took the stairs down four at a time. If only he could get out of the house and onto the street he'd be safe, for a naked man wouldn't follow him there, he told himself.

He shot through the kitchen and threw open the rear door so hard that it smashed into the wall on his left.

Gulping for air, he whirled round the side of the house and headed for the gravel path and the street beyond. The chips scrunched beneath his flying feet as he pumped both arms in an effort to increase speed further. He swiftly glanced behind to see the gorilla still chasing him. Then he was into the street. The gorilla would give up now, he assured himself.

But the gorilla kept coming on.

A naked man doesn't run along a public street! Ken thought in amazement, but this one did. This one didn't seem to care who saw him in his birthday suit.

Ken whizzed past a driveway as a woman came out. Seconds later she screamed, a shrill shredding sound that tore at the eardrums. He went round a corner into another street, better lit than the last. 'Shite!' he muttered, and put a hand in front of his face to try and mask it.

About a hundred yards further on, he glanced back again, just in time to see the gorilla come up short, clutching his heaving chest. The gorilla bent over double and was sick onto the pavement.

Round another corner, and yet another, went Ken, entering a main road where there was a tram just ahead of him drawing to a stop. He was almost spent himself by now, and was thankful on reaching the tram to climb aboard and sink into one of the downstairs seats.

Oh Christ, that had been close! If the gorilla hadn't tripped over that flex, it would have been all over with him. It would have been a right doing from the gorilla, followed by a spell in Barlinnie Prison.

'A fourpenny please,' Ken said to the conductor, asking for the first fare to come into his head. He had no idea where the tram was going, nor did he care – as long as it took him away from the gorilla and that house.

Reaction set in. He went chill all over and began to shake. Control yourself, his brain commanded his body, but his body wasn't paying heed, and he continued to shake. The engagement ring! He had been holding it when he'd made his dash for freedom. He wasn't still holding it, so he searched his pockets in vain. Somewhere along the line he had dropped it, probably even before he had left the house. It didn't matter about the ring, or the other jewels. He had got safely away, that was all-important. And he still had the money, the seventy pounds. He patted his wallet, revelling in how bulky the sheaf of fivers made it feel.

The next thing Ken knew he was somewhere down by the docks and, spotting a pub, he jumped off the tram and went inside. He desperately needed a drink to try and calm himself.

'A large whisky and a pint of heavy,' he instructed the bartender. His hands were still shaking when he lit a cigarette, though not as badly as they had been. The rest of his body, with the exception of his thighs, was now still.

He swallowed the dram in a single gulp, closed his eyes and shuddered. Oh, but that was good! He ordered another large one, and had a mouthful of his pint.

He was on his third large whisky, and second pint, when he became aware of the lassie staring at him from the other side of the pub.

She was a ginger-haired girl about his own age, and attractive in a gallus sort of fashion. Even at that distance he could make out that she was freckly, and that her eyes were green – the same colour green as that jade ring back in the house he'd fled from. She was with a group of men, all a lot older than her, two of whom were in suits and wearing bowler hats. The men were talking animatedly amongst themselves.

Ken glanced away, drank more beer, then looked back again. She was still staring at him, her expression deadpan. Somewhat flummoxed by the situation, and still all of a jangle from what he'd just been through, he gave her a nervous smile.

The deadpan expression slowly melted into a warm reciprocal smile, then she turned her back to Ken and began speaking with one of the bowler-hatted men.

Ken ordered another pint and fell to dreaming about the Armstrong Siddeley he was going to buy in the morning, for, with seventy quid to his name, he sure as hell wasn't going to be outbid!

A little later he went to the cludgie; and when he returned the girl and the men with her had gone.

By the time he got home to Parr Street he had forgotten all about her.

Vicky gazed at Ken in admiration. What a clever, marvellous man he was. She had nearly died when, coming out of work, he had hailed her from behind the wheel of this beautiful car. How the other girls had chattered and nudged one another, envying her, as she had climbed inside to sit beside him. Then, with a blast on the horn, and a wave from him to the goggling, giggling girls, they had been off.

Questions had immediately tumbled from her lips. Whose car was it? Since when could he drive? Did he have a licence? Where were they going?

The car was his; he'd owned it for six weeks now, he told her, and during that time he had learned to drive, taking and passing his test that very morning.

If he had owned the car for six weeks, why hadn't he mentioned it before? she demanded. And he replied with a grin that he hadn't wanted just to show it to her, but to take her for a spin in it. What did she think? Wasn't it a humdinger?

It was that indeed, she confirmed, but where had he got the money to buy such a car? Something like this must have cost a pretty penny indeed.

He replied that it hadn't cost nearly as much as she might think – quite cheap really, considering. He had paid for it out of the money he had saved since going to work at McGilvray's. And she wasn't to worry about the engagement ring, that would be the next big item on his list.

He drove her right round the central area of the town, Argyle Street, Buchanan Street, Sauchiehall Street. Up and down and round about they went, till finally he announced that he was taking her back to Parr Street and the biggest kick of all: parking the Armstrong Siddeley in front of his close and the pair of them getting out of it with all the neighbours watching on.

He explained that, so far, he had been keeping it in a

wee garage over in the Cowcaddens, but from now on it was going to be parked in front of his close, the first car the street had ever boasted.

When Parr Street hove into sight, Vicky sat up straight and bounced up her curls. How thrilling this was! She had never felt so grand, or spoiled, or cherished.

As they entered Parr Street, Ken gave a couple of toots on the horn, knowing that the noise would bring everyone to their windows out of curiosity and nosiness. Until now the only cars to turn into Parr Street had been the doctor's, those belonging to the local undertaker, and taxis when folk were getting wed.

'I love you,' Vicky whispered, and in an intimate gesture touched the swell of his left buttock.

'And I love you too,' he answered.

Mary heard the tooting and hurried through to the front room to find out what was going on. 'George! Come right away!' she called out excitedly.

George and John went ben to join her at the window. 'Well, I'll be a monkey's uncle!' George exclaimed to see it was his Vicky getting out of the car, and that it was Ken who'd been driving it.

'Do you think it's his?' Mary asked.

'Oh aye, look at the way he's behaving,' George answered.

'The jammy beggar,' John said, green with envy.

Mary shook her head in amazement. Someone from Parr Street owning a private car, and when so many of the men were out of work! Who would have credited it?

Down in the street Ken was thoroughly enjoying himself, adoring every minute of this. 'Look around,' he whispered to Vicky as he locked her door.

Vicky glanced about. There wasn't a single window in the street without a face pressed to it. She saw her parents and John, and waved. In response, Mary's hand flashed like semaphore.

Then Vicky noticed Neil in his window, and waved to him. While she was doing this, Ken was waving to his astonished parents, whom he'd also kept in the dark about the car.

Neil returned Vicky's greetings. A car! Trust Ken Blacklaws to pull a stroke like that, he thought bitterly. Vicky really was the Princess of Poor Street now, no one could dispute it. A princess whose prince had supplied her with a bright shining chariot. He stared down at Ken, hating Ken, *hating him*.

'I'll see you to your door,' Ken said to Vicky and, in sight of the watching street, kissed her.

'This is just the start of what it's going to be like,' Ken told her as they made their way to her close.

Vicky believed him. At the moment she would have believed him if he had said he was the Archangel Gabriel himself. 'And the engagement ring is the next big thing you buy?'

'On my word of honour,' he promised.

As she mounted the stairs, Vicky felt every inch the princess that Neil had termed her.

Three

Vicky was thoroughly enjoying the task she had been assigned by Mr Ferrier, her supervisor. A consignment of crystal chandeliers had arrived from Murano, Italy, and it was her job to unpack them and reassemble each one – they had been dismantled into individual pieces for greater safety during transit.

It was delicate and responsible work: enormous care had to be taken, for if any section was chipped or broken it meant that the entire chandelier was useless and would have to be scrapped at the loss of a considerable amount of money.

Vicky, brow furrowed in concentration, glanced up to find Miss Elvin gazing at her. 'It's just like doing a jigsaw,' she said, which caused Miss Elvin to smile.

'Let's go to Mr Ferrier's office. I want a word with you,' Miss Elvin replied.

What was all this about? Vicky wondered, as she laid the chain of crystal teardrops she'd been holding onto a cradle of tissue paper. Sudden panic flared in her.

'My work's all right, isn't it?' she stammered.

'Your work's very good indeed, we're all pleased with you. You don't think you'd have been trusted with those chandeliers if we hadn't been,' Miss Elvin answered.

That was a relief, Vicky thought. For a moment there she'd been worried. She had thought she was doing well, but then, you never really knew.

On entering Mr Ferrier's office, empty by arrangement between Miss Elvin and Mr Ferrier, Miss Elvin told Vicky to sit. She remained standing.

'So how are you enjoying being with Copland and Lye's?' Miss Elvin opened.

'I'm enjoying it very much. What I do is interesting, and the folk are all nice,' Vicky replied truthfully.

That was what Miss Elvin had expected to hear. She had been keeping close tabs on Vicky, and knew that Vicky was happy in Packing and Dispatch, and that she was well liked by her fellow workers. Mr Ferrier had nothing but praise for her.

'The reason I've come to have a chat with you is that – and this is in strictest confidence for the time being – Miss Cobb in the Furs department has informed me she's getting married in September to a businessman who has said she's to cease work at that time. Consequently, her position will be coming available and I've earmarked you for it.

'The Furs department, because of the large amounts of money involved per item, is one of the most important departments in the shop, and only specially selected people work in it. We consider the positions there among the plums that Copland and Lye have to offer,' Miss Elvin said.

Vicky had been holding her breath, which now came out in a whoof. 'Let me say how grateful I am, Miss Elvin, and deeply honoured.'

'Don't think I'm doing you a favour. I'm not. It's my responsibility to select the best available for that department, and in my opinion you're the one for the job. Your wages will rise accordingly, of course, and you'll also be on commission, two per cent of the retail value of all you sell, settled on a six-monthly basis.'

Commission into the bargain, better and better! Vicky thought jubilantly.

'Mr Ferrier will sorely miss you here, but he has told me he'll do nothing to stand in your way of promotion, which he and I agree you richly deserve. We only hope we can get someone as good to replace you,' Miss Elvin went on.

'So I'll continue here till September, then I'll move up to the Furs department, is that right?' Vicky queried, wanting it all spelled out clearly.

'Not quite. You'll move up at the beginning of the third week in August. Miss McKissock, who's in charge of Furs, will give you a fortnight's training prior to you being allowed to deal with the public.'

'I understand,' Vicky said. She was so excited that she wanted to shout and yell and do a little dance on the spot. She couldn't wait to tell Ken and her parents.

Miss Elvin was thinking how much she enjoyed being the bearer of good news. Her interview with Vicky had quite made her day. What wasn't enjoyable, indeed was often loathsome, was the other side of the coin, the reprimands and sackings. They had to be done however, being part and parcel of her duties.

'Pleased?' she asked.

'You know I am.'

'And I know I can count on you. You're not the sort of girl to let me down, which is one of the main reasons I'm giving you a position on Furs. Mistakes on that department can be very costly indeed.'

The Furs department! Sable, beaver lamb, red fox, mink, blue mink, chinchilla. Vicky could hardly wait.

Vicky slipped into the front passenger seat of the Armstrong Siddeley. Ken had come to pick her up from work as he had promised.

'You'll never guess what,' she said breathlessly, eyes blazing with excitement.

Ken put the car into gear, and they moved away from the kerb. 'You lost a tanner and found a pound?' he joked.

In a cascade of words she told him about her promotion, explaining that it was not just onto the floor, but into one of the best and most important positions that Copland and Lye had to offer.

'That's terrific, Vicky, I'm really pleased,' he enthused when she had finally finished.

She wriggled in her seat, unable to keep still. She had been like that since speaking with Miss Elvin earlier on.

'This calls for a celebration, something special. What do you say?' Ken demanded.

Vicky clapped her hands in glee. 'That would be great.'

'I'll tell you what. We'll go into town this Friday night

and have a drink at someplace really posh. Or, better still, we'll have a meal and a drink. How about that?'

Doubt creased Vicky's face. 'The meal's fine, but I don't know about the drink. I'm still only sixteen, don't forget.'

Ken considered that. There were pubs he could take her to where her age wouldn't be questioned, but they weren't at all the sort of places he had in mind. A little further on they had to stop at traffic lights, and Ken pulled out his wallet and extracted a five-pound note, which he handed to Vicky. 'Get yourself a really grown-up dress, a sophisticated number that'll make you look older. And while you're at it have your hair done in a more mature style. The combination will be bound to fool them when Friday comes round.'

Vicky fingered the fiver. 'You're awful good to me, Ken,' she whispered.

He reached across and patted her thigh. 'Nothing's too good for my future wife,' he replied.

Future wife. To hear him say that sent prickles coursing up and down her spine.

'I'll go up to Dresses during my dinner break tomorrow,' she said and then fell to thinking about how she could have her hair done.

It had been arranged between Vicky and Ken that he would pick her up at seven p.m. that Friday. He arrived promptly at one minute to and chapped the door. He was let in by John and ushered through to the kitchen, where he found George and Mary enjoying a dram in front of a roaring fire.

'Will you have a touch of the cratur?' George asked, indicating the bottle on the table.

'I will indeed, that's kind of you,' Ken replied.

This was a ritual in which both George and Ken were playing their parts. As drink was in evidence, it was deemed polite for George to offer his guest some – just as it was deemed polite for Ken, as a known imbiber, to accept that offer. Anything else would have been an insult.

George made it a large one, topping up the glass with lemonade at Ken's request.

'Slainthe!' toasted Ken.

'Slainthe!' George and Mary responded.

Mary took in the neat blue suit, shining white shirt and fancy tie. 'You look like you've just stepped out of a bandbox, so you do,' she said approvingly.

'You're doing well right enough. I'm proud of you,' George smiled.

Ken's suit had come from the Thirty Shilling tailors and was the first suit he had ever had made for himself. 'You're doing not badly yourself now, Mr Devine,' Ken replied.

George didn't even try to hide his pleasure and gratification to be told that. 'It's true, I can't deny it. Getting the job with the Corporation was a godsend, and now Vicky's about to be promoted, which will mean even more money coming into the house.'

'To Vicky's new job,' Ken toasted, and the three drank in unison.

Vicky entered the kitchen, having been putting the finishing touches to her make-up when Ken arrived. 'What's the verdict then?' she asked, and slowly twirled so that Ken could get an all-round view of her new dress.

This was the first Ken had seen of the dress he had paid for. When Vicky had brought it home in the car, she had kept it in its box, saying that he would see it on her and not before.

He whistled in appreciation. 'It's a knockout,' he said.

'And the hair-do?'

'If you told me you were a London model, I'd believe you,' he replied.

Vicky laughed. She liked that.

George, on the other hand, was frowning. This was a woman standing in front of him. Where was his wee lassie?

'Don't you think the overall effect is a bit old?' George queried hesitantly.

Vicky glanced at Ken: that was the whole object of the exercise.

'Older, but not too much so. I'd say it's just perfect,' Ken replied.

George was not at all sure he agreed with that. Then

again, maybe he was just being a typical anxious parent, he thought.

'Where are you off to?' Mary asked.

'Ferrari's,' Ken answered.

George gaped. 'You mean, yon restaurant at the end of Sauchiehall Street, the one facing the Empire Theatre?' he spluttered.

'The same.'

'But that's real grand, not at all for the likes of us.'

Ken's face went cold and a hard smile came to his lips. 'There's no rule says that, Mr Devine. Ferrari's is open to those who can pay its prices, which I can, and who are suitably dressed, which we are. As long as we conduct ourselves in an appropriate manner, which we will, there is no reason on earth why Vicky and I shouldn't spend an evening there.'

'Argue as you like, Ferrari's is for the nobs, those with big houses in Kelvinside, Whitecraigs, Thornton Hall and such, not workies from Parr Street,' George countered.

Ken's smile became thin and stretched, while his eyes glittered in such a way as to make Mary shiver. 'Some day I fully intend to have one of those big houses in Kelvinside or Whitecraigs or Thornton Hall, so the folks at Ferrari's better get used to seeing me around, for if I get my way this is only the start of my joining the ranks at that level.'

It was a revelation to George that Ken had such high aspirations. Nor had he previously realised just how ruthless Ken was, for in Ken's present mood that ruthlessness stuck out a mile.

'Then good luck to you, son,' George said and finished off his dram.

Mary hadn't liked at all what she had just heard, and foresaw nothing but trouble for Ken. She had been brought up to believe that everyone had their place and should know it and stay in it. This was for the general social good.

'We'd better be going,' Vicky said quietly to Ken.

They were a sombre couple as they left the house, but Ken soon had Vicky laughing. And he kept her laughing all the way into town.

•

71

Vicky was in Ferrari's ladies' toilet touching up her make-up, Ken was paying the bill. Soon they would be leaving.

The evening had been a huge success, Ferrari's quite out of this world. As for the meal, it had been simply the best Vicky had ever tasted. To begin she had had melon, followed by sirloin steak, sauté potatoes and diced baby carrots, while Ken had ordered veal and spaghetti to follow his prawns. For sweet she had chosen the most scrumptious chocolate cake with a cherry on top, Ken the fresh-fruit salad. They had drunk red wine – she couldn't recall the name of the wine, but it had been French – and, after the sweet, coffee and liqueur. They had both gone for Drambuie, she the one glass, Ken spoiling himself by having three.

Vicky dreaded to think what it had all cost, but Ken had said money was no object that night and insisted that she ordered whatever she fancied from the menu regardless of price. Feeling very daring, and for some reason ultra-feminine, she had taken him at his word. The sirloin steak had been one of the more expensive dishes on the card. There had been no question asked about her age, which was a huge relief. The wine waiter had not even glanced in her direction when Ken ordered the wine and Drambuie.

She sucked on her lips and put her lipstick away. Normally she would have plumped up her curls next, but couldn't because of her hair-do. She was not particularly pleased with the hair-do, but it had served its purpose. She decided to give her hair a thorough wash next morning in the hope of restoring its usual style.

As she left the toilet, Vicky became aware of a commotion in the lounge where she was to meet Ken. As she entered the lounge, she saw two men struggling together, and with horror realised that one of them was Ken. The other was middle-aged and wearing a red and white checked Arab headdress.

'Got you you thief, you thief!' the Arab screeched hysterically.

Ken's face was ashen as he fought to break free. He had been caught completely unawares when the gorilla pounced.

The shock of meeting up with the gorilla again, and in such circumstances, had made him go all weak inside, and filled him with blind panic. All he wanted was to be out of there, to flee into the night.

People in the lounge were looking on in consternation as the two men heaved to and fro.

'Call the manager,' someone shouted.

'Thief! Thief!' the Arab repeated and, getting his hands round Ken's throat, started to squeeze.

Vicky dashed forward. She did not know what this was all about, but the Arab had to stop choking Ken before he killed him, which he seemed intent on doing. She carved a passage through the tables and chairs, and came at the Arab from behind. On reaching him, she pummelled his broad back, to no avail, then scratched and gouged his left cheek – again to no avail. Ken, glasses skewwiff, had turned puce. His eyes were bulging in their sockets.

A desperate Vicky spied a marble ashtray on a nearby table, and snatching it up crowned the Arab, smashing the ashtray ferociously down on the man's headdress.

The Arab buckled at the knees, and released Ken, who, clutching his throat, staggered backwards, at the same time gulping breath after breath into lungs that felt as though they had been set afire.

Vicky dropped the ashtray and made to go to Ken, only to be grabbed by the Arab.

'Let me go, you brute!' she squealed, and clawed again at the already damaged cheek which was bleeding profusely.

The Arab struck her, sending her reeling off to one side and into a small alcove. Someone who was clearly the manager came running up to the Arab and grasped hold of his jacket, trying to restrain him. 'What's going on?'

'He is the thief who broke into and robbed my house,' the Arab answered, pointing at Ken.

Vicky frowned. What was the man yabbering on about? Thief? Robbed his house? The Arab had to be mistaken.

Ken bolted. Elbowing his way through several gawpers, none of whom made any attempt to stop him, he ran to the main door and out into the night.

As Ken went through the door, the Arab howled, broke free of the manager and gave chase. The manager followed the Arab and the pair of them, the Arab in the lead, disappeared after Ken.

A babble of conversation broke out in the lounge. Everyone, in a high state of excitement, began to remark on the events that had just taken place. Vicky was bewildered and confused. Of course it was a case of mistaken identity, had to be. Only – if he'd been innocent, why had Ken run as he had?

The alcove she was in was darkish and, glancing about, she realised that her part in the proceedings seemed to have been temporarily forgotten. But not for long. Once the Arab and the manager returned, she would be bound to be questioned.

If Ken was innocent, *why had he run?* The question throbbed in her brain.

The Arab and manager reappeared outside the glass main door and angry words were exchanged between them. Then the Arab threw a punch which sent the manager sprawling onto the pavement. Everyone in the lounge, with the exception of Vicky, surged to the door for a better view.

This was her chance to get away, she thought, hurrying to the rear of the lounge and out into the vestibule beyond. There had to be a back exit somewhere, she would make her escape that way. Luckily, she already had on her coat. There was a passage off the vestibule that seemed to be heading for the rear of the building, so she plunged into this, walking quickly. She should have stayed, she told herself, her behaviour was ridiculous. There had to be a rational explanation for what had occurred. Only, *Ken had run!*

To her disappointment, the passage eventually became a dead end, as did the second one she tried. In desperation she mounted a short flight of stairs, wondering if she could find a route to the back of the building that way. When she heard the approaching clamour of a police siren, she swallowed hard. As it came closer and closer, she had no doubt that its destination was Ferrari's. With relief she happened upon a window which, on testing, slid smoothly open. There was a drop of about a dozen feet to a narrow alley below. She hiked up her coat and new dress, and swung first one leg over the sill, then the other. Turning round, and holding the sill tightly, she slowly dropped her body down. When she was at arms' length, and could go no further, she took a deep breath and released her grip, falling the rest of the distance.

She broke a heel on landing, and counted herself fortunate that she'd broken nothing more. Breathing heavily, her heart going *thump thump thump*, she hobbled the length of the alley, squeezed past some dustbins and found herself in a dingy street. She paused to get her bearings, then headed in the direction of where Ken had parked the Armstrong Siddeley.

When she reached the spot where the car should have been, she found it gone. She bit her lip. Ken had run, and kept on running, abandoning her. At that moment the suspicions she had been nurturing during the past few minutes began to solidify. She worked out where her nearest tramstop would be and set off in the direction of it.

The Armstrong Siddeley was parked outside Ken's close when she arrived back in Parr Street, a figure huddled in the driver's seat. As she reached the front passenger door, he opened it for her and the pungent smell of whisky wafted out.

'Did you tell them who I was?' he demanded.

'No, while they were fighting amongst themselves, you obviously having given them the slip, I made myself scarce. I talked to no one,' she replied.

Ken was completely still for a second or two, then shook himself the way a dog does. 'We'd better talk,' he said cheerfully, but his cheerfulness had a false ring to it.

She got inside the car and closed the door behind her. He had managed to buy a half-bottle somewhere, she saw. She shook her head when he offered her a swig.

'Why did you run, Ken?' she asked quietly, steel below velvet.

75

'Wouldn't you have, if some madman had been trying to strangle you! All I could think of was to get the hell out of there, and fast.'

'He called you a thief, said you robbed his house.'

Ken gave an unconvincing laugh. 'Oh sure, Burglar Bill, that's me. I'm a dab hand at breaking and entry, didn't you know?'

'I thought it must be a case of mistaken identity.'

He seized on that. 'Had to be, what else?'

'And yet you ran when the manager appeared, leaving me in the lurch, the girl you say you love and are going to marry.'

The latter was a key speech she had prepared, one she wanted his reaction to. Her worst fears were justified when he went a deep shade of red and the guilt he had been trying to hide crept unmistakably into his eyes.

She took the half-bottle from him and had a swig after all. She had not planned to do what she did next, it just sort of happened. She slapped him across the face as hard as she was able, then choked back a sob.

'You bloody fool,' she said.

Ken hung his head in shame.

She had another swig of whisky and pulled herself together. She felt as if she were in the middle of some nightmare. 'You'd better tell me all about it.'

Deep down he had known he wouldn't be able to lie to her, that she would see through his charade. Still, he had hoped he was wrong, that somehow he could pull it off.

'Tonight scared me, I've never been so scared before,' he admitted.

'Start at the beginning,' she whispered.

He did, taking her back to the time when they had heard, and vaguely seen, the burglars when they were coming home from the pictures, and explaining how, later, when he was desperate for a job and money, he had remembered the incident and got the idea of doing a spot of burgling himself.

Vicky listened in silence, her hands clasped, fingers con-

76

tinually twisting upon each other. At last, he finished his tale.

Vicky was numb all over, her brain might have been turned to solid ice. She got out the car, closed the door and waited while he rolled down the window.

'Vicky I . . .'

She cut him short. 'No more, Ken, not tonight. I have to sleep on this.'

He stared up at her with an expression of wretchedness. 'How about I pick you up in the morning and we go for a run in the car down the coast?'

'No. I'll come to you when I've thought this thing through. Until then leave me alone. Please?'

'If that's how you want it.'

She left him gazing after her, crossed the street and entered her close. She found the flickering yellow gaslight comforting, as she did the familiar smell of the close. She climbed several of the well-worn grey stone stairs, then stopped and leaned against the wall as the tears came.

A burglar! Her Ken was a burglar, a thief. There was no job at McGilvray's, never had been. There wasn't even a McGilvray's – that was all part and parcel of the lie he had concocted to explain away the money he'd been stealing. Bile churned in her stomach as the tears rained down her cheeks. This was a nightmare right enough, a nightmare to end all nightmares. Only she wasn't going to wake up next morning to find it was all a dream. What she had been told that night was horrible reality.

She started up the stairs again, but managed only a couple more before she felt scalding bile and nausea flood her throat. She fled to the back court, where she was violently sick, throwing up the meal she had so enjoyed, and which was now poison to her stomach and mouth.

Vicky was still awake when dawn crept over the slate rooftops of Parr Street. There had been no sleep for her since getting into bed, not a wink. Her mind had been in turmoil, as she went over and over what Ken had told her and tried to decide what she might do about it.

Give him up? She had rejected that early on. She loved him, and would continue to do so no matter what he'd done. But she could not allow matters to continue as they were, this pretence of his that he was out grafting, when in fact he was housebreaking.

The housebreaking was going to have to stop. The trouble was, though she could make Ken promise, swear even, that he was finished, how could she be sure he would keep that promise when the money petered out and things got rough again? She worried a nail as the pale morning light gradually seeped into every nook and cranny in the room. *How to ensure he kept his word?*

Sex? She could threaten to deny him if he backslid. But that might only drive him into another female's arms, the last thing she wanted. Why, only the other day, she had seen Helen Morrison from Kennedy Street giving him the come-on – that cow wouldn't have to be asked twice to go on her back for him. No, denial of sex was a bad idea, for it would deprive her of control.

Then the answer came to her. Simplicity itself. And that way she would maintain complete control. She was smiling grimly, and with satisfaction, when sleep finally claimed her. Ken would do as she instructed. He would have no choice.

As for Helen Morrison, she could go and boil her can.

Vicky let Ken stew all day Saturday. Then, on Sunday, after dinner, she went over and knocked on his door. His father answered, and cried out that Vicky wanted him. He was there like a shot.

'Let's go for a walk,' she said.

'I'll get my jacket.'

He invited her in to wait. She replied that she would wait in the street, and he joined her there a minute later.

It was a braw May day, the wind fresh off the Clyde, and with the tang of salt to it. Smoke from several chimneys gusted hither and yon, while the sky was a duck-egg blue liberally dotted with fluffy white clouds. The blue sky made Vicky think of summer, which was not far off.

78

She knew where she wanted to go and led the way, he quietly following her, not even bothering to question her about their destination.

The banks of the Monkland Canal had long been a favourite haunt of Vicky's, ever since her dad had first taken her there as a wee lassie not yet at school. It was a place she escaped to when she wanted to be alone or to think, or in this instance have the sort of conversation she intended having with Ken.

When they were facing the White Horse Distillery, she stopped. 'You've been lucky so far, but that luck's running out, as Friday night proved. Keep on burgling and it's only a matter of time, probably sooner rather than later, before you end up in Barlinnie.'

Ken winced and lit a cigarette. 'Bumping into that bloke was a chance in a million,' he retorted.

'Chance in a million or not, it came within a whisker of doing for you. If I hadn't been there to intervene, you'd be in jail the day, and up before the sheriff tomorrow morning. By tomorrow afternoon you'd have been ensconced in Barlinnie, the only question being how long for. One year, two years or three.'

Ken took a deep drag on his cigarette. His face had turned a muddy colour.

'I've heard tell of what conditions are like in Barlinnie, grim in the extreme. And you'd be living, if that's the right word, amongst the worst scum in Glasgow,' she went on relentlessly.

Ken knew that Vicky was not exaggerating, Barlinnie was a right hellhole, that was common knowledge. 'I was only burgling till I found myself a job,' he said.

'You haven't been looking for one! You told me yourself on Friday night that, when you haven't been housebreaking or sizing up prospective houses to burgle, you've been spending all your time in billiard halls and picture houses,' she snapped back.

No wonder he had shied away from seeing so many of the flicks she'd suggested of late, she thought. The sod had already seen them all!

'I fully intended . . .'

'Fully intended, my Aunt Fanny! You considered yourself to be on a soft number, and had every intention of sticking with it. You may have kidded yourself on that you were eventually going to look for a job, but that's all it was, kidding yourself on.'

'Not to start with!' he protested.

'Maybe so, but that's how it became. Come on, admit it. Admit it, Ken!'

He shrugged.

'And I always gave you credit for being intelligent, for having a good brain in your head.'

'I *do* have a good brain.'

'Aye, a criminal one, it seems,' she said scathingly.

'Och, Vicky,' he whispered, and tried to take her in his arms.

'Don't attempt to soft soap me. We're going to get this mess sorted out here and now, and until we do you can keep your mitts to yourself,' she told him, wagging a finger under his nose.

She broke away from him, picked up a chuckie and threw it into the still brown water. She loved doing that, listening to the plop the chuckie made as it entered the water. She must have thrown a million chuckies into the Monkland Canal since she'd been coming there. She gave a sudden grin – maybe not a million, it just seemed that many.

'And the same man chased you stark naked down the street?' she asked.

Ken nodded.

'And he was covered all over in hair?'

'More or less. He reminded me of a gorilla I once saw in a circus menagerie.'

'*Stark* naked, nothing on at all?'

'Not a stitch.'

Vicky laughed. 'That must have been a sight!'

'I could hardly believe it at the time. I mean, nobody, but nobody, runs starkers down the street. But that Arab did.'

'Tell me again about the jewels.'

Ken had only mentioned the jewels in passing on Friday night. Now he described them in detail. Vicky's eyes grew huge as she listened. Imagine having such an engagement ring as he was talking about! she thought in wonder and envy. It was a ring fit for a queen. She threw in another chuckie, but this one went chink, not plop. It had hit something metal just below the surface.

'How much were you averaging a week as a burglar?' she asked, curious.

Ken did some mental arithmetic. 'Weeks varied tremendously, but on average I'd say between ten and fifteen quid.'

Vicky whistled. Burglary was a profitable business. 'That's all over and done with now. You've burgled your last house, understand?'

Ken had been expecting this. She was hardly likely to condone what he had been up to, after all. He would keep her sweet. 'Completely over and done with,' he agreed.

Vicky glanced sideways at him. His reply had been too glib, his agreement too easy by far. 'I'm serious,' she said.

'So am I.'

'You'd better be, because if after today I ever find out that you've burgled another house I'll personally turn you in to the police.'

He grinned. 'You wouldn't, Vicky. You love me.'

'And it's precisely because I do love you that I'll turn you in, to save you from yourself.'

His grin wavered. Jesus, did she really mean this!

'I promise you, Ken, on everything I hold holy, one more burglary and you're for the high jump. I'll hate doing it, I'll have to drag myself down to the police station, but drag myself I will, and I'll put the finger on you.'

That business on Friday night had put the wind up him, and he had decided to lay off for a while. A fortnight say, maybe even a month. By then Vicky would have accepted that thieving was how he came by his money. Oh sure, she might not like it, and bend his ear about it upon occasion, but she would have come to accept the situation.

'You'd put me in Barlinnie?'

'The way I see it, if you continue burgling, you'll

inevitably end up there anyway, so all I'll be doing is bringing matters forward. So you've a straight choice, Ken, and I guarantee I'm not bluffing. You either stop burgling or it's prison.'

He was still grinning, but his grin now had a sickly quality. She *meant* what she said, she'd convinced him.

He tossed his dog-end into the canal and lit another cigarette. There was a crazy logic about it, after all, he told himself. She would do what she threatened because she loved him, to save him from himself, as she put it. And because he knew she'd do it, he would comply with her wishes and stop burgling.

'I'll be skint again before long,' he said.

'At least you'll be free. And this time round I'll be working, so it won't be like it was when you got laid off from Agnew's.'

'You mean, you'll buy the french letters,' he jibed, bitterness in his voice.

She ignored that.

'Of course I do have an alternative. I could stop seeing you,' he said casually.

She went cold inside. She had not foreseen this possibility. She was stricken at the thought of losing him, but remained resolute nonetheless. 'That would mean you don't love me, as you've said you do. But it wouldn't make me change my mind. If I saw you continue to have money, I'd know where it had to be coming from, and I'd be down to the police station,' she said quietly.

He was beaten. She had him. 'If only there was work available,' he sighed.

'It's hard to come by, granted, but not impossible. My dad proved that. You just have to keep on looking, and never give up.' Heart hammering nineteen to the dozen, she threw another chuckie into the water. 'Are you going to keep on seeing me?' she asked.

His reply was to take one of her hands in one of his, clasp it tightly, then kiss her. 'Let's walk further on.'

Her anxiety drained away, to be replaced by a sense of achievement and contentment. She had saved him from prison and what might have ended up as a life of crime. He might not thank her now, but he would some day. She prayed to God that he would find a job – it didn't matter what, just as long as it kept him occupied and paid a reasonable amount.

'Tell me about those jewels again,' she requested.

And she listened, riveted, as he once more described them in detail.

'You're hurting me,' Vicky complained as Ken's fingers dug into her bare flesh.

They were nude, making love on the rug in front of the kitchen fender. She gave a soft whimper when a gouging nail drew blood.

Ken didn't have to be told he was hurting her, he'd been aware of the fact and enjoying it. From behind half-closed eyelids he watched her face contort in pain as he gathered a fistful of buttock and squeezed.

Vicky writhed, her heels drumming on the rug. She could not understand why he was doing this to her. It was so unlike him, and so unlike his usual lovemaking, which was tender and considerate, if selfish at times.

It was a Wednesday night, the day of George and Mary's wedding anniversary. To celebrate, George had booked tickets for the Alhambra theatre, second performance, where he and Mary now were, having taken John with them.

Vicky had also been invited, but had declined, saying, truthfully, that she had already seen the show the previous month with Ken. She would not have wanted to go anyway, for with the family safely out of the way it gave her and Ken a chance to be alone together, and to make love.

When it was over for Ken, she pushed him from her. She had not enjoyed that one little bit. In fact she'd hated it.

A quick examination on her part revealed that, luckily, the blood he'd drawn had not stained the rug they'd been lying on. A large patch of her right buttock was red and tender to the touch. She knew that by morning that area would be black and blue.

'Why?' she demanded angrily.

He shrugged, refusing to meet her eyes.

'You wanted to hurt me, I could tell.'

He lit a cigarette from a packet of five Woodbine. That's what he was reduced to, he thought bitterly, a rotten lousy packet of five.

'I suppose I was getting my own back,' he said quietly.

'For what?'

'The fact that I have to take the Armstrong Siddeley into the motor market tomorrow.'

Her furrowed brow cleared. Now she understood. He blamed her for losing the car, his pride and joy.

'So it's come to that, eh?' she commiserated.

'I'm down to my last half-dollar, I need the cash.'

'It's a pity you haven't been able to land a job before the car had to go. It would have been nice for you to hold onto it.'

'Aye, it would have been.'

'Look on the bright side. At least you're free. You might not have been if I hadn't found out about your burgling,' she said.

That was true, but it did not make his having to sell the car any easier.

'There'll be other cars, you'll see,' she went on, trying to give him a sense of perspective.

He had a sudden desire to hit her hard, clenched fist, right in the mouth. There were times, like now, when she got under his skin so much that that was what he wanted to do to her. What he didn't want was bloody sympathy, or to be told about other cars. He wanted the Armstrong Siddeley, and he wanted it here and now, in 1935, not 1945 or whatever!

Men: they all had an unreasonable streak in them, Vicky was thinking. Why, look at Ken. He was like a big wean about to have his favourite toy taken away from him, a toy he had no right to in the first place, because he'd acquired it through dishonest, and therefore as far as she was concerned invalid, means.

'I'll tell you what. Why don't we go for a sail this weekend?

84

We could go down the Clyde?' she suggested, trying to dispel his brooding gloom.

Then, remembering her recent talk with Ken on the banks of the Monkland Canal, she had a better idea. 'Or how about a wee cruise on the Firth and Forth Canal? You know how much I like canals, and I've heard so much about that one, yet never been on it.'

'Why not, I'll have the car money by then.'

'My treat,' she insisted.

He closed his eyes and thought of prison. It gave him the creeps to imagine himself locked away for umpteen hours of the day, *every* day. That would be purgatory right enough.

She was correct in forcing him to give up burgling, he told himself. And yet . . . Christ! but it was so awful and humiliating having to scrimp and scrape, to look after every ha'penny.

He recalled the seventy pounds he had taken out of the Arab's house on his second visit there, and the jewels that could so easily have been his if he hadn't been so damnably unlucky. A few more minutes and he'd have been clear with a pocketful of sparklers that would have set him up for years to come. He would not have got anything like their real value for them, but he would still have realised hundreds and hundreds of pounds, maybe even as much as a thousand. A thousand pounds! What he could do with that, the life of Riley wouldn't be in it.

'I said *my* treat,' Vicky repeated.

'Aye, all right, fine,' he replied.

'Well, don't sound so enthusiastic!'

'Sorry, my mind was elsewhere.'

She gently rubbed the area of her right buttock that he had squeezed in his fist and which had begun to throb. 'I appreciate how you feel about losing the car, but if it has to be it has to be,' she said.

'It's just that . . . I truly thought I was on my way, Vicky, that a new door had opened for me, a door through which lay the future I've dreamed of.'

'It was a door for fools, Ken, a door leading to prison. You must realise that.'

85

He didn't answer. He knew she was right, but deep down was unwilling to accept it.

He started to get dressed. 'I'll drive you to work in the morning, it's on my route to the motor market,' he told her, changing the subject.

He didn't wait for her parents to return from the Alhambra but left early, pleading tiredness.

After he had gone, Vicky applied cold compresses to her sore buttock. He had never been cruel to her before; she hoped he never would be again.

But she understood, and forgave him.

That Saturday Vicky and Ken went to Port Dundas, there they embarked upon the *Fairy Queen* for Craigmarloch, where, according to the man who'd sold them their tickets, there would be amusements for the passengers.

The *Fairy Queen* was a grand wee boat with a single stack that belched black smoke into the sky. It was a slowish journey along the Forth and Clyde Canal but, as Vicky said to Ken, there was no rush, they were out to enjoy themselves.

An awning had been erected at the rear of the boat for folk who wanted to be in the shade. It was a sunny day, and a dense knot of people had gathered there. Vicky and Ken elected to go to the boat's prow because it was less crowded.

'I bumped into Neil Seton last night, he's gey worried about his dad,' Vicky said.

'Oh aye?'

'He's taking to mooching round the house in his semmit and longjohns, refusing to get dressed.'

Ken knew old man Seton well and liked him. Often on a paynight Malkie Seton had slipped him a Saturday penny for no other reason than he was pals with Neil.

'Why's he doing that?' Ken asked.

'Depression at being idle. Neil says it's really getting through to him now.'

'I know how he feels,' Ken grumbled.

'Och, away with you. You're a young man, you'll find

work eventually. You have hope. The trouble with Mr Seton is that at his age no one's going to take him on again, and he knows it. He might have gone out looking like everyone else, but in his case he was only going through the motions,' Vicky said.

Fifty-odd and on the scrapheap. It was a terrible indictment of the society they lived in, Ken thought. 'Why isn't MacDonald doing something about it all!' he said tightly, referring to the Prime Minister.

'It's not just Glasgow, or Britain even, it's all over, so you can't blame him. Look at America, they're in just as bad a state as we are, and they're supposedly one of the richest nations on earth,' Vicky replied.

Ken glanced down the left-hand side of the boat and a vaguely familiar face caught his attention. It belonged to a ginger-haired lassie standing beside an older man, whom she appeared to be with. Now where did he know her from? It was the freckles and green eyes that reminded him: she was the lassie in the pub down by the docks the night he'd been chased by the gorilla. And the older man with her was one of the two who had been there wearing bowler hats. Now he was wearing a flat cloth cap, or doolander as they were often cried.

The girl, becoming aware that she was being stared at, turned and looked in his direction. The deadpan expression dissolved as she recognised him. He smiled, and she returned the smile.

Imagine their paths crossing again! he thought, and wondered what her name was.

A woman joined the lassie and older man – her mother, he reasoned, for there was a likeness there. That meant that the older man must be her father. Right enough, he could now see the resemblance there as well.

'So what do you think will be the outcome of the next election, which must surely be just round the corner?' Vicky demanded, and she and Ken fell to discussing and speculating upon that.

When the cruise was over – and thoroughly enjoyable it had been too – they disembarked at Port Dundas. There

Ken watched the ginger-haired lassie and her parents climb into a chauffeur-driven Riley.

Whoever she was, she was well off, Ken thought as the Riley disappeared round a corner. He and the lassie had exchanged smiles several times during the cruise and stop-over at Craigmarloch, but hadn't spoken; that wouldn't have been at all appropriate in the circumstances.

When Vicky and Ken arrived back in Parr Street they were greeted with the awful news that Malkie Seton had hung himself from the kitchen pulley. Mrs Seton was in hospital in a state of total collapse. Neil, attended by a number of neighbours, was under sedation administered by the doctor. As a mark of respect, condolence and profound sorrow, every set of curtains had been drawn, every blind lowered. The normal cries and shouts of the children at play in the street and back courts had been stilled, the children taken indoors.

Everything was quiet, as quiet as the grave.

Four

Vicky was darning her father's and brother's socks. John's were in by far the worse condition, for he was heavy on socks, and not a week went by but he went through one heel, often the entire heel, if not two. George was reading an evening paper, John his comic, the *Wizard*, and Mary was baking.

George stopped his reading to sniff the air. 'That smells rare,' he said, looking forward to a good tuck-in later on. He had regained all the weight he'd lost when idle, and even, as though in compensation or defiance, added a few extra pounds.

Mary opened the oven door and took out a steaming applecake, followed by a fruitcake, which she laid on the table. She then popped an identical couple of cakes and a tray of jam turnovers into the oven to be baked. She wiped a sweaty brow, for it was hot work baking in this June heat. The kitchen window was wide open to let in any breeze.

'Get your shoes on. I want you to take these to Mrs Seton over the street. I'm sure the poor soul would appreciate a wee tasty bite,' Mary said to John.

'Aw, Mum, I'm just settled here,' John complained.

'Do as your mother says, and less lip, boy,' George growled.

Muttering under his breath, John stood up, made to throw his comic angrily onto the chair where he'd been sitting, then thought better of it. That might earn him a clout from George.

'I'll tell you what, I'll go over. I haven't seen Neil since the funeral and would like to know how he's bearing up,' Vicky said, laying aside her darning. Malkie Seton's funeral had been ten days previously, and the entire street, with the exception of Mrs Rae, who was bedridden as a result of a stroke, had turned out for it.

'Fair enough.' John beamed, and within seconds had his nose buried once more in his comic.

While Vicky got herself ready, Mary wrapped the applecake and fruitcake in clean teacloths and told Vicky to be sure she brought the cloths back with her. Mary then carefully placed the baking in a wicker basket she used when shopping.

As Vicky went down the stairs, she thought of the funeral. It had been a long trudge up the Springburn Road to Sighthill Cemetery, nearly too long for some of the older mourners, but the old ones had stuck it out, and they all arrived together as they'd begun. There had been few flowers, for the simple reason money was too tight to buy them, and nearly all those there were had come, one way or another, from gardens and allotments.

Mrs Seton, though clearly riven with grief, had borne herself bravely throughout the proceedings. As for Neil, he had looked like a wee boy again, lost and very scared. After the coffin had been lowered and the minister had spoken, they sang 'Abide With Me' and 'There Is A Green Hill Far Away', the latter because it had been Malkie Seton's favourite hymn.

Only relatives had returned to the Seton house afterwards, the boiled-ham meal and whisky being paid for by Malkie's younger brother from Edinburgh – he'd apparently flitted through there years previously – who was in work.

Arriving at Neil's door, Vicky chapped and waited. She heard the scuffling sound of slippers on linoleum. It was Mrs Seton who answered.

'From my mum. She thought you probably hadn't got round to baking again yet,' Vicky said, proffering the basket.

Mrs Seton's eyes were watery. Vicky guessed correctly that she was still having weeping jags, and that she had had one recently.

'Oh, that's kind of Mary. Come away in, girl,' Mrs Seton replied, and led the way through to the kitchen, where she unpacked the applecake and fruitcake.

'Will you have a cup of tea while you're here?' she asked.

'I won't if you don't mind, I'm not long after a couple,' Vicky replied.

Mrs Seton put the baking on plates, then neatly folded the teacloths and placed them back in the basket.

'Folk have been so good since . . . since what happened. We couldn't have wanted for better neighbours,' Mrs Seton said.

'And you're getting by all right?'

'Oh aye. The parish are seeing to that. It's hardly a life of luxury, mind, but no worse than others in the same situation.'

'And Neil, how's he? I haven't seen him for a while.'

'It hit him hard, you know. He and his dad were very close. Would you like to speak to him? He's been studying.'

'I would, please,' Vicky replied.

Mrs Seton took Vicky through to Neil's bedroom, where they found him hunched over a mound of papers and textbooks. Other pieces of paper, some screwed up, a few ripped and torn, lay scattered around.

Vicky was alarmed at the sight of Neil. He looked absolutely dreadful. He was gaunt and hollow-eyed, and gave the impression of being feverish. His cheeks had sunken in and, beneath the unshaven wisps on his chin, he had a fresh attack of plooks, the most virulent yet.

Neil rose to greet Vicky effusively, saying she was a welcome break from the maths problem he was trying to puzzle out.

'Her mum's sent over an applecake and fruitcake for us,' Mrs Seton said to Neil.

'Smashing.'

'Malkie aye liked a freshly . . .' Mrs Seton broke off and gulped.

'I'll be in the kitchen, give me a shout when you leave, Vicky,' she said in a husky voice, and fled.

'Do you want to go after her?' Vicky asked quietly.

Neil shook his head and pushed hair away from his forehead where it had fallen in a tangle almost to his nose.

'She'd prefer to be left alone,' he replied, equally quietly, as though they were sharing a secret.

Vicky glanced at the mound of papers and textbooks. 'I'm surprised you're still able to carry on studying.'

Neil frowned. What was she havering about? 'Why shouldn't I be?'

'Because of your dad. I would have thought you'd have left the exams till next time round.'

Neil's face contorted into an almost savage grimace. 'I'll sit my Highers this session, and what's more I'm determined to get the best results I'm capable of, the *very* best, so that I'm assured of winning that bursary or one of the grants. I have to do that, for my father's sake. It's something I've promised myself, do you understand?'

Vicky had never before seen Neil so intense, and she found it just a little frightening. 'We'll all be keeping our fingers crossed that you get to the university. You know that, Neil.'

His eyes gleamed fanatically. 'I'm going to go, Vicky. Nothing will stop me. I'm going to get qualified, and you know why?'

She shook her head.

His voice became bitter. 'Because some day . . . some day there *must* be a better world than that we're living in now, a world where a man isn't driven to hang himself because of his frustration and shame and complete inability to influence his circumstances. And I want to be part of that new world, Vicky. In fact, I want – no, *intend* – to be more than merely a part of it. I intend to be a driving force, one of those responsible for shaping it.'

Vicky had been caught up by his excitement. The way he had just spoken reminded her of James Maxton; he had the same qualities of fire and total belief. She realised then that the Neil she had known had gone for ever, that his father's death had turned him into a man.

'I want to give the people back their freedom, and self-respect. And I shall accomplish this, to honour my dad's memory,' Neil added.

Emotion clogged her throat. She could imagine what

torment Neil had been through since Malkie had hung himself. Well, if this new commitment of purpose was the result, Malkie's death had not been in vain.

'Give them work, Neil, that's what they need above all else. Give them work and the rest will fall into place, including, if they're honest and hard-grafting, self-respect.'

Her words were music to his ears. 'My God, you're a woman and a half, Vicky. Why, with you behind him there's nothing a man couldn't do, nowhere he couldn't go. He could move mountains, fly to the moon . . .'

'Or create a new world?' she chipped in.

'Exactly!' Neil thundered back.

Vicky laughed. 'I don't know if that's what Ken has in mind.'

'What do you mean?' Neil asked, his face creasing into a frown.

'We've been keeping it quiet, but I've been bursting to tell someone and, because you and he are such great pals, I'm going to tell you. Ken and I are unofficially engaged to be married.'

'How unofficial?' was all Neil could think to reply. Her statement had stunned him, made him feel sick inside.

'He wants to find his feet first before buying the ring, which has hardly been helped by him losing his job. Still, it's only a temporary setback. When he finds another job, we'll make it official just as soon as we can.'

'Congratulations,' Neil said, trying to keep his voice from betraying the shock and turmoil he felt. Ken and Vicky getting married! He had never dreamed it would go this far. He had been convinced that Ken would eventually give her the bullet, leaving the field free for him to step in. Damn Ken! Damn damn *damn* him!

Vicky touched Neil on the wrist. 'I'm sure when the time comes he'll want you to be best man,' she said.

Neil gave a weak, pained smile.

It was only then that she remembered that Neil fancied her, as she had found out on Hogmanay when he'd saved her from the two would-be rapists. She had hardly thought about it since.

You're a stupid, insensitive bitch, she told herself. But she had been so enthralled by Neil's words and vision that confiding to him about her and Ken's unofficial engagement had happened naturally as part and parcel of their conversation. She could see she had hurt him, the last thing she had wanted to do, particularly now, when he was still in mourning for his father.

'I'd better get along,' she mumbled.

'Aye, and I'd better get back to studying.'

'How long till the Highers?'

'I start next week.'

She had not realised, though she should have, that they were so soon. Since going to work at Copland and Lye, she had lost all track of school timetables and events.

'Good luck.' She smiled. She considered adding a kiss to the cheek, but decided against it, just in case he misinterpreted the gesture – though it was hard to see how he could after what she had just told him. Anyway, she hated kissing plooky faces. It aye scunnered her.

When Vicky was gone, having cried her goodbyes to Mrs Seton in the kitchen, Neil returned to his bedroom and sat again before his papers and textbooks. He gazed darkly at them. Jesus! He'd have given his eye teeth for Vicky to be his. More, he'd have given an arm and a leg.

Then he had a thought. The engagement was still unofficial. Could it possibly be that Ken was playing Vicky along, never intending the engagement to become official? It would be quite like Ken to pull a rotten trick like that. Even if Ken was serious about her, it would be ages yet before they could get married – years perhaps, for who knew how long it would take Ken to find another job! And where there was time, there was hope, hope for *his* cause with her. For the fact remained: Ken was a ladies' man, and Neil couldn't believe that that particular leopard was going to change its spots. Certainly not when he was still of a fairly young age.

Neil smiled, a thin razored smile that appeared to slice his face in two, and would have been chilling to a beholder. He had not lost Vicky yet, not by a long chalk. Not by a mile.

He focused his attention on the book he had been immersed in when disturbed, and forced himself to concentrate on what was written there and, temporarily, to forget about Vicky.

George took six screwtops of beer out of a paper bag and laid them on the sideboard. 'Do you think six will be enough?' he asked Vicky.

'Oh aye, plenty, I'm sure. Mum and I won't have more than half a one each.'

'And what about me?' John demanded, trying to sound indignant and hard done by.

'You'll get a thick ear if you're not careful,' Vicky replied.

'And are you going to give it to me? You and whose army?' John snorted.

'Enough! You can have a glassful and that'll be your lot, understand?' George said.

John nodded. That was acceptable, and the best deal he was going to worm out of George. He adored having a wee taste with his parents: it made him feel so grown up.

The wall clock in the front room chimed eight times. The alarm clock standing on the mantelpiece tinged in unison.

'Ken will be here any moment,' Vicky said unnecessarily. They all knew that he had been invited for eight. The four adults were going to while away a couple of hours playing rummy and having a good old natter. Mary was the card fanatic in the family and often attended the whist drives put on at the local Labour Hall.

'How is he anyway? I've seen him round and about, but haven't spoken to him for nearly a week now,' George asked.

'Fine.'

'I take it, as you haven't said anything, that he hasn't found another job yet?'

'He's trying hard, but so far it's the same old story, nothing doing,' Vicky replied, pulling a face.

'He should never have tempted fate the way he did. He was just asking for what happened to him,' Mary said.

The story Ken had put round the street, and which George and Mary believed, was that McGilvray's had been forced, due to a short order book, to contract their labour force, and he had been one of the unfortunates laid off. Vicky was the only person other than himself to know the truth of the matter.

'How do you mean "tempted fate"?' Vicky queried, puzzled.

Mary hesitated before replying, then shrugged. 'What he said about some day owning a house out in Whitecraigs, Thornton Hall or Kelvinside, and that the nobs had better get used to seeing his face around for he fully intended joining the ranks at that level,' Mary said disapprovingly.

'I fail to see how that's "tempting fate"?' Vicky replied.

Mary glanced over at George, then went on. 'And that big car he bought which he swanked around in like nobody's business, that turned a lot of folk against him, I can tell you.'

'They were just jealous that's all.'

'Well, they weren't jealous for long, for the car's gone by the board now, as has his job,' Mary retorted, becoming fairly heated.

'You sound pleased about that,' Vicky snapped back.

'Maybe losing his job and car will teach him a lesson. We all have our God-given place and should stick to it. It doesn't do to try and be what you're not.'

'With all due respect, I've never heard such nonsense,' Vicky said.

'Vicky!' George growled in warning.

'I don't mean to be cheeky, Dad, but if everyone believed as Mum seems to then no one would ever move up in the world.'

George did not entirely agree with his wife, but he did in some respects. 'You have to admit he was getting gey big for his boots. I've nothing against Ken. On the contrary, I've always liked the lad. But he did seem to be getting real flashy Dan above himself. And as for taking you to the likes of Ferrari's, that was really sticking his nose in where it wouldn't be welcome.'

96

Mention of Ferrari's alarmed Vicky. Did they know something and not let on? 'Why did you bring up Ferrari's?' she asked quietly.

'Because I was astounded he had the bare-faced cheek to take you to a place such as that,' George replied, now embroiled in the argument.

They *hadn't* heard anything about the business at Ferrari's and Ken's flight from there, Vicky thought with relief. For a moment she had been scared that he had been seen by someone who knew him and word had got back to the street.

'Are you saying your own daughter isn't good enough for Ferrari's?' she riposted.

'What we are trying to say is that we don't want you getting hurt, which you will be if you attempt to swim out of your depth,' Mary answered.

'So you *are* saying I'm not good enough, and that neither is Ken?'

Mary sighed. 'You have to recognise that you're both working-class keelies. Get ideas above your station, you or him, and it'll only bring unhappiness.'

'Ken is ambitious. I see absolutely nothing wrong in that,' Vicky retorted, glowering at her mother.

'And there is nothing, as long as that ambition is within reason,' George said.

'And what do you call within reason?'

'Well, I'd certainly call thinking of living at the three places Ken mentioned outside of it.'

'Why?' Vicky demanded.

'Because only grand folk live there,' George explained.

'And who's to say Ken couldn't become grand, or me?'

Mary laughed, a high shrill laugh filled with scorn and derision. 'Neither of you have the education, for one thing. And you both talk common, for another.'

'There's nothing wrong with good plain Glasgow speech,' Vicky said, infuriated.

'Nothing at all, I agree. Unless you live in Kelvinside, Whitecraigs or Thornton Hall, in which case, because they all talk with jorries in their mouths, you'd stick out like a

97

couple of sore thumbs. You'd be different from the rest and, by being different, alienated.'

'You listen to your dad, he knows what he's speaking about,' Mary said.

'Anyway, there's no hope of Ken living in any of those posh places, he hasn't even got a job,' John chipped in, smiling.

'You be seen and not heard!' Vicky shouted at her brother.

John's smile turned into a supercilious smirk. He did not often score against Vicky, but he considered that he had there.

'Ken will go far, you just wait and see if he doesn't,' Vicky declared defensively.

'Maybe as far as Australia, you can't go much further than that,' John instantly replied.

Vicky glared at him. If her parents had not been present she would have slapped the cheeky bugger. She would soon have wiped that infuriating smirk off his face.

'That's enough, boy,' George admonished.

'I think we should drop this now, it's gone far enough,' Mary said, taking the heavily embroidered velvet tablecover off the table in preparation for playing cards.

'I've never heard you criticise Neil Seton. He's another determined to go places,' Vicky protested.

'Neil's attending to his education, that's the difference between him and Ken,' Mary answered.

'He still talks common, like the rest of Parr Street.'

'Neil might be determined to go places, but I doubt he has delusions of grandeur, as Ken seems to have developed. I have no worries about Neil, as I do about Ken,' Mary said.

There was a knocking on the outside door.

'I'll get it,' John said, and vanished from the kitchen.

Vicky was fuming. They were being unfair about Ken. He *wasn't* flashy, nor was he a swanker.

The outside door banged shut, and Ken, followed by John, strolled into the room.

'Come away in, son, it's lovely to see you.' Mary smiled, and gestured that he take one of the good seats by the fireplace.

Hypocrite, Vicky thought.

'I brought a bottle of whisky. If we're going to stay in, we might as well do it in style,' Ken said, and produced a bottle of whisky from behind his back, which he placed on the sideboard beside the screwtops. He then sat down.

Vicky stared at the bottle in dismay. That was quite unnecessary when he was out of work, and would have used up even further the rapidly dwindling cash he had got from the sale of the Armstrong Siddeley.

Mary glanced at Vicky, a glance that spoke volumes, and made Vicky writhe inside.

'You shouldn't have,' Mary said to Ken, her rebuke ever so gentle, the type usually given, and expected, when such a generous gesture had been made.

Vicky looked again at the bottle. She could have hit Ken with the bloody thing.

Vicky sat alone, toying with the tomato, cucumber and lettuce salad she had chosen for her midday break, in Copland and Lye's canteen. She was deep in thought, worrying about Ken and the fact that he still had not found a job. She was pushing a slice of tomato round her plate when she became aware there was someone standing beside her. She glanced up to find that it was Miss Elvin.

Miss Elvin was holding a cup of coffee. 'Do you mind if I join you?'

Vicky did not really want company, which was why she had sat apart from the others, including her cousin Sylvia whom she often lunched with, but she did not feel she could say no. Miss Elvin was one of the shop's VIPs, after all.

'Please do,' she replied.

Miss Elvin sat, and spooned sugar into her cup. She had a weakness for sugar and was forever fighting a losing battle against it. 'Why so glum? Is it something to do with the work?'

'No, work's fine. I've no complaints there,' Vicky answered quickly.

'So what's the problem? There obviously is one.'

Using the edge of her fork, Vicky cut the slice of tomato

99

she'd been pushing round her plate into halves, then quarters, then eighths.

'It's . . . Well, it's my boyfriend. He's been laid off for the second time and, this is in confidence, we were supposed to be getting engaged and married next year.'

'And now, because of lack of money, that's all off?'

Vicky nodded.

'What rotten luck. And I suppose you're very much in love?'

'Oh yes,' Vicky breathed in reply, her eyes suddenly shining where before they had been dull and listless.

Miss Elvin sipped her coffee. She had been in love once, now a long time ago. It had not worked out, and there had been no one important since. Men in her life yes, but no one she could truly say she loved. Which was why she had remained a spinster, married to her job. 'Had you planned a church wedding?' she asked.

'I don't mind, church or registry, just as long as we get married.'

Miss Elvin approved of that. The trappings, though very nice, were only superficial. It was the ceremony, and joining, that was important. 'I hope he gets something soon then,' she said.

'Thank you.'

'What's his name?'

'Ken. Kenneth Blacklaws,' Vicky replied.

Her young man had been called Pharic. He'd been a Highlander from Inverness, working in the whisky business. He was doing very well, she believed, and had three bonny children by the woman he had chosen over her to marry. Miss Elvin drank more coffee and put all thoughts of Pharic McCrone out of her mind. It usually made her weepy to dwell on what might have been.

'I came to the canteen especially, hoping to find you here,' Miss Elvin stated.

There was that about Miss Elvin's tone which made Vicky's heart sink. 'Is it about my being promoted to Furs?' she asked.

'I'm afraid I've got some bad news.'

Vicky stared at Miss Elvin in consternation.

'Oh, you're still being promoted. Only I'm sorry to say there's going to be a delay.'

Vicky relaxed a little. Her promotion was still on. For a horrible few seconds there she'd thought it had gone out the window. 'Am I allowed to ask why there's been a delay?'

'Of course. Miss Cobb has just been up to my office to tell me that her fiancé was hurt two days ago in a climbing accident in the Cairngorms. Fairly seriously too, according to her – the man he was with was killed.'

'How awful,' Vicky said.

'So the wedding has had to be postponed, and they're now thinking about December rather than September. And if not December then January, the final date depending on the progress he makes. He broke both legs and damaged his pelvis.'

'I take it, then, that Miss Cobb will be continuing in Furs till close to the new wedding date?'

'That's what she wants to do, and has every right to do, not having yet handed in her notice.'

It was a setback, but only a temporary one, Vicky told herself. And the position, when it did fall vacant, was still hers, that was the main thing. She would just have to bide her patience a while longer than she had expected.

Her big worry, the one she had been brooding about when Miss Elvin appeared, remained Ken's spending. He could not seem to hold onto cash; if he had it, he spent it. He had almost completely gone through the money he had got for the Armstrong Siddeley; she had winkled that out of him the previous night. And when that lot went, he would be reduced to what he received from the public assistance, and which would have to be handed over to his mum anyway towards the upkeep of the house.

She had reminded him forcibly that she'd meant what she had threatened: if he returned to burglary, she would inform the police, and it would be prison for him. He reacted by growing tight-lipped, then changed the subject. But before he had been able to do the latter she had seen in his face that he believed her.

Miss Elvin had been well aware of how much Vicky had been looking forward to moving to Furs, and had not at all enjoyed being the bearer of ill tidings. She hated disappointing people once she had promised them something, and even though the cause of this disappointment had nothing to do with her she still felt somehow responsible.

Vicky stared at what had been a slice of tomato. The eighths had become squashy sixteenths. She looked up. Miss Elvin had started speaking again.

'I'll tell you what. I'll put it to the powers that be, to see if they're agreeable, that your wage is put up to the two pounds you would have got in Furs from the date you were supposed to go there. I'm sure that would be some compensation for having to wait to move until December or January.'

'That would be marvellous!' Vicky exclaimed. How kind of Miss Elvin to think of that.

'I'm not promising anything, mind, but I'll have a word in the proper place and hope to twist an arm or two.'

Shortly afterwards Miss Elvin left the canteen feeling better than when she had entered. She was pleased she had had that idea; it salved her conscience a little.

The trick would be to pull it off.

It was early Monday morning and Vicky was making for work. Clattering down the stairs she turned into the street, heading for her nearest tramstop. She was almost at the end of the street when Neil appeared, clutching to his chest a white paper bag. When they came alongside one another, she stopped, as did he.

The delicious smell emanating from the paper bag was mouth-watering and unmistakable. 'Hot rolls, nothing better first thing.' Vicky smiled.

'Not only rolls, but baps as well.' He smiled back.

'Special treat, is it?' she asked, knowing how hard up the Setons were, and how every farthing counted.

Neil nodded. 'My exams start the day. Mum said I could have whatever I fancied for my breakfast, and I chose these,' he replied.

'I'm pleased I bumped into you then. All the best. I'm sure you'll do well.'

A strange gleam crept into his eyes. His expression became set and intense. He seemed to burn from within, reminding Vicky of the night she had taken the applecake and fruitcake round to his house – he'd been like that then. He was a man with a mission, she suddenly thought. Yes, that was it, that described him exactly.

'If I don't, it won't be because of lack of preparation,' he answered, voice quiet but hard with determination.

He had lost even more weight, she thought. He was nothing but skin and bone, whether from lack of food or studying, or a combination of both, she could not say.

'Do you feel all right? You don't look too well,' she asked, and then bit her lip. That wasn't at all the right thing to say to him just before his exams.

But the voicing of her concern did not worry Neil, not in the least. As far as he was concerned, he couldn't have been better. As athletes reach a peak in their pre-race training, so had he reached a peak in his pre-exam studying. His entire world – and even Vicky had become excluded – was narrowed down to the exams he was to sit over the next few days. Nothing, but nothing, else mattered.

'I'm fine, I assure you,' he replied, giving a thin, wolfish grin.

The grin startled Vicky. She had always thought of Neil as being the victim, not the predator. She considered this another sign of how much he had changed since his father's death.

'You'd better hurry on home before those rolls and baps get cold,' she told him.

They exchanged goodbyes, after which he hastened off down the street, hunched over the paper bag he was clutching. Vicky stared thoughtfully after Neil, till she was roused from her reverie by the rattle of a tram in the distance. She slowly crossed two fingers, the sign of good luck. Then continued on her way.

•

That afternoon Vicky was packing a china tea set bound for America when her supervisor came up.

'Go and see Miss Elvin, she wants to speak to you,' he said.

That will be about my pay increase, she thought triumphantly. 'Thank you, Mr Ferrier.'

He grunted and moved away. When, only several seconds later, he glanced back to where Vicky had been, she was already gone.

Vicky went straight to the ladies' room. She had no intention of going to see the always immaculate Miss Elvin without first making sure that she was looking her best. She repaired her make-up, ran fingers through her cap of curls, straightened her seams and sighed in despair at the dowdiness of her overall, which she could do absolutely nothing about. Then she was ready.

Sue, Miss Elvin's secretary, told Vicky to have a seat while she informed Miss Elvin that she was here. When Sue returned it was to tell her to go right in.

'I'm afraid your wages won't be going up until you actually do start work on Furs. I did what I could, but it just wasn't on. I'm sorry,' Miss Elvin said, coming directly to the point.

Vicky's shoulders slumped, and her perky, expectant manner evaporated.

'Still, December or January isn't all that far off. It'll soon roll round,' Miss Elvin added.

'I suppose so,' Vicky replied, trying not to sound too disappointed, for she had convinced herself the pay rise would happen in August, her original date for moving up to Furs.

Miss Elvin, however, had an ace up her sleeve which she hoped would rectify the situation, and also neutralise her own guilty feelings towards Vicky. 'Is your boyfriend – Ken, wasn't it – still out of work?' she asked.

Vicky nodded.

'How do you think he would feel about coming to work for Copland and Lye? Alistair Gillies, in your current department, Packing and Dispatch, is also being promoted upstairs, which means his job will be falling available,' Miss Elvin said.

A job for Ken! Her disappointment vanished, to be replaced by elation. She jumped for joy.

'Of course I must interview him first, make sure he's suitable,' Miss Elvin added.

'Ken's very hard-working and conscientious. You won't find anyone better,' Vicky blurted out.

Miss Elvin smiled at Vicky's enthusiasm. 'If he's anywhere near as good a worker as you, we won't have any complaints. So you're saying he *would* be interested?'

'Definitely.'

Miss Elvin glanced at an open diary in front of her. 'Then ask him to come and see me tomorrow morning. Ten o'clock be all right for him?'

'He'll be here,' Vicky stated emphatically.

'I'll look forward to meeting him.'

Vicky left Miss Elvin's office feeling as though she were walking on air. To hell with her own disappointment about not getting her pay rise until December or January. This more than made up for it. If the job came off, and Miss Elvin had more or less indicated it was certain that it would, she and Ken would be working in the same department for the next four or five months, seeing each other every week day. And afterwards, when she moved to Furs, they would still be able to come to work together, and go home the same way.

And . . . She stopped dead in her tracks. With him employed again, they could set a date for their engagement, and eventual wedding. She was so excited! She was bursting to tell Ken about this stroke of good fortune.

That evening, when she returned from Copland and Lye, instead of going directly to her house, as she normally did, she went instead to Ken's. His mother informed her he was down in the back court.

There she found Ken helping a couple of lads from the street mend their bogey that had been broken in a crash. The bogey consisted of an old stout orange box fixed on a plank of wood. At the front and rear of the plank were single crossbars below which had been attached pram wheels. The front crossbar, for guiding purposes, was able to swivel left and right, tugged in either direction by a loop of rope that ran back to the orange box, the latter being the cockpit. The rear crossbar was immobile.

Ken, having nothing to do all day, had been feeling bored, when, looking out the kitchen window, he had spied the boys trying to mend their broken bogey. He had come down to offer assistance, because he had nearly always kept a bogey himself as a young lad, and was a dab hand at their construction and repair.

'Hello, pet,' Ken said to Vicky, waving a hammer at her in greeting.

She did not want to break the news to Ken with the two boys squatting beside him, earwigging in. 'Come over here a minute, I've got something to tell you,' she said excitedly.

'I'll be right back, lads,' Ken muttered to the boys, and tossed the hammer to the nearest one. Now what was this all about? he wondered as, rising, he followed Vicky to another part of the back court.

'I've got you a job at Copland and Lye's. You've to go for an interview at ten tomorrow morning,' she said in a rush of words.

This was so out of the blue it rendered Ken temporarily speechless.

'Well?' Vicky queried with a broad smile.

He automatically groped in a pocket for his cigarettes. All he had was a fag end, which he lit using the Ronson Vicky had given him.

'What sort of a job? And how have you managed to get it for me?' he asked at last.

She recounted her chat with Miss Elvin, saying that Miss Elvin had more or less promised him the job. All he had to do was turn up on time, looking smart, and the job was his. Now how about that?

'What does it pay?' he asked.

'The other men in the department get thirty-seven and six.'

Ken scratched his chin. That was seven and six more than Vicky was getting as a female packer and dispatcher, but half a crown less than the counter assistants were getting, which meant that Vicky would be earning more than him when she moved to Furs. Quite a bit more once her two per cent commission was taken into account.

She stared at his face. She had been expecting jubilation, not this expression of dour introspection. 'What's wrong?'

He shrugged. 'I know they say you shouldn't look a gift horse in the mouth and all that, but thirty-seven and a kick a week! It's pocket money beside what I was earning before.'

She knew he was referring to the proceeds of his burgling rather than what he'd been bringing home from Agnew's. 'It's an *honest* thirty-seven and six, Ken, that's the difference,' she retorted.

'I still won't get fat on it.'

She blew up. Of all the ungrateful sods! 'If that's how you feel, then hell mend you!' she spat, and stormed away.

She had just reached his back close when he caught up with her, stopping her by grabbing her arm. 'Here, don't take it like that. I was only passing comment.'

She turned to stare coldly at him, and did not reply.

'I'll be pleased, no grateful, to take the job if it's offered. And, presuming it is, thank you for getting it for me, Vicky, it's a life saver.' He smiled.

Her anger died as quickly as it had flared up. This was more like it.

'Packing and Dispatch needs only be a beginning for you at Copland and Lye, Ken. There's no reason why you shouldn't become a supervisor or counter assistant in time or, who's to say, even a buyer! Now they earn really good money.'

'That's how I'll look at it then,' he replied.

'You've got the brains to go up the ladder. We've just got to get you back on the first rung,' she said.

He hooked his arm in hers. 'Let's away to your house and discuss it further. Tell me all about Miss Elvin. And what do you think I should wear tomorrow?' he asked, knowing full well that she would adore talking about what he should wear and say and how he should conduct himself. But it continued to niggle him nonetheless. Grafting again was one thing, earning less than his lassie soon would be quite another. It was hardly manly, and if there was anything he prided himself on it was being that.

For her part Vicky soon forgot about his initial reluctance, ingratitude almost. Providing everything went all right tomorrow, and it surely would, then Ken would be working again, earning an honest wage. Och, but life could be lovely right enough, she thought. And it was the dark patches that made the bright ones seem even brighter.

It was Ken's first day in Packing and Dispatch, and Vicky had connived it so that it was she who showed him around. As of yet, the rest of the department, including Mr Ferrier, did not know Ken was her boy-friend but, as they had no intention of keeping it a secret, the others soon would.

The overall Ken was wearing had belonged to Alistair Gillies and was several sizes too small for him. Vicky had not been able to stop herself giggling when she'd seen him in it, thinking he looked ridiculous. He was getting a new one, he'd told her huffily when her giggling had subsided, Mr Ferrier had promised him.

Vicky indicated a squat stack of boxes. 'This is another consignment of chandeliers that has just arrived from Italy. I put the last lot together,' she said. She selected a box from several standing by the main stack, and opened it to show Ken the dismantled pieces within. The many-faceted pieces of crystal caught the light from the bulb above their head, and sparkled. Golden rays shot out in all directions.

'It's beautiful, don't you think?' she asked.

'Oh aye, but nowhere near as beautiful as you.' He smiled back.

'Patter merchant!' she accused.

'Not at all, just telling the truth.'

It was patter, but she loved it nonetheless.

'How much would a chandelier like that cost in the shop?' Ken asked.

She told him and, eyes opening in surprise, he whistled.

He glanced again at the contents of the open box, and a sudden thought made him laugh. 'Here, can you imagine one of these chandeliers hanging in a house in Parr Street?'

Vicky also laughed. 'Not on your Nellie Duff!'

Still laughing, they moved along the aisle they were in, to stop before an already opened, and partially unpacked container. Inside the container were rank upon rank of items each individually wrapped in blue tissue paper. Curious, Ken unwrapped one to reveal a large glass.

'This is heavy,' he said, amazed at its weight.

'It's a whisky glass, also crystal.'

He twisted it one way, then the other, so that it sparkled as the pieces of chandelier had done. 'You'd have to be gey rich to be able to fill this right up to the brim every time,' he said, being used to thimble glasses, or small tumblers, when drinking whisky.

'Och, you don't fill it up to the brim, daftie. Even with a mix it should never be more than a third to a half full.'

He made a mental note of that, in case he was ever – *when* he was, he corrected himself – in company where such glasses were used.

'Well, well, you live and learn,' he murmured.

Vicky then showed him other crystal articles that the shop stocked, all of which were in that particular section. There were candle holders, bowls, ornaments, vases, various types of dishes and a whole range of glassware, ranging from champagne flutes to brandy goblets.

'I'm impressed, I have to admit it,' Ken said when they reached the end of the crystal ware.

'And the crystal is only a tiny part of what's down here,' Vicky told him.

He thought back to the whisky glass. The price of that alone was more than he was being paid in a week.

'It's just like Aladdin's Cave,' Vicky added.

He glanced around, confirmed they were out of sight of the others in the department and swept Vicky into his arms. He kissed her, and as he did so his right hand strayed down to grasp her crotch.

'And what if like Aladdin I should say open sesame?' he

whispered in her ear nearest him when the kiss was over.

She wriggled free. 'Open sesame or not, that cave stays shut, at least while we're at work.'

'Spoilsport!' he hissed.

'Do you want to get us both fired on your first day here!' she chided, but only half-heartedly, for despite her protestations, she had rather enjoyed that.

'I love you,' he whispered.

'And I love you too,' she whispered in return. Then, on a sudden impulse, she took his head between her hands and kissed him deeply, her tongue darting in and out and entwining with his. 'You don't know what you do to me,' she groaned, pulling herself away from him again.

'I do, for you do the same to me.'

She shivered to hear that. 'We'd better get on. I've thousands of things to show you yet.'

He was already impressed, but became more and more so. Vicky was right, it was Aladdin's Cave, stuffed to overflowing with gorgeous and often costly items. He was left wondering how all these many and varied objects were accounted for.

It was a Tuesday night, and Ken had promised to take Vicky to the pictures. It had been arranged between them that he would pick her up at half past six, which was when he duly presented himself. He found her ready, waiting and anxious to be on their way.

He did not say anything till they reached the close mouth, and there he stopped her with a sheepish look on his face. 'I'm afraid the flicks are out tonight.'

She stared at him in consternation. She had been looking forward to this. 'Why?'

Embarrassed, he cleared his throat. 'I've only got enough money left for my tram fares to and from work for the rest of the week. Other than that I'm skint,' he confessed.

'But it's only Tuesday! How can you be skint already?'

He stuffed his fists into his trouser pockets. He felt guilty, like a wee boy caught with a hand in the sweetie jar. He mumbled incomprehensibly.

'I didn't hear that?' Vicky snapped.

He mumbled a second time.

'And I didn't hear that either!' she snapped again, more loudly than before.

'I said I played a couple of games of snooker last night, and lost,' he retorted.

Vicky took a deep breath. She could have sloshed the silly bugger. 'How *much* did you lose?' she demanded.

'Half a sheet.'

'Ten shillings! But that's most of what your mum gives you back from your wages.'

'I thought I could win,' he said angrily and, noticing an empty tin can within tempting range, he kicked it, to send it rattling right across the street onto the opposite pavement.

'You must be soft in the head to gamble when money's so hard to come by nowadays,' she admonished.

'I'll remind you it wasn't always like that with me. It's not so very long ago I was used to spending what I wanted without having to think twice about it. And when you've grown accustomed to having money to burn it's a difficult habit to break,' he replied bitterly.

He had a point there, it *must* be difficult for him, she thought. Nonetheless, he would just have to get a grip on himself and live within his means.

'Well, we're still going to the flicks, because I want to go. It'll just have to be my treat that's all,' she said.

He refused to meet her gaze. 'Aye, all right then. As you're determined to go.'

'I am.'

She crooked her arm for him to take, which he did. And they started along the street.

'I'm sorry for letting you down,' he told her after a while.

'It's not me you let down, Ken, but yourself. You've just got to stop chucking your money about as if it's going out of fashion. You might have got used to having money to burn, but that was only for a relatively short period. A period which is now over, a fact you're going to have to accept.'

Ken sighed. That was easy enough for her to say. She

hadn't been in the position he had. Fags, booze, virtually anything – if he had wanted it, he got it. That was hard to put by for ever, to go back to worrying about tuppences and thruppences.

Vicky enjoyed the main feature, as she had known she would – a love story that soon had her groping for her hanky. Ken preferred the B picture, a thriller with lots of action and rather gory in places.

When they came out again the upset of Ken's losing ten bob at snooker had been forgotten. Vicky, having enjoyed a good cry, was in a marvellous mood.

'Now you're in work once more, don't you think it's time we set a date?' she said to Ken about halfway home.

'Set a date for what?' he asked, turning to stare blankly at her.

'Us getting married.'

'I can't afford to get married, not on what I'm earning!' he exclaimed.

'*We* can afford to be married, if we take my wages into account.'

'No wife of mine is going out to work, it's not right for a wife to do that,' he said adamantly.

'Oh, Ken, that's the old-fashioned view. It's well accepted nowadays for the wife to work. At least till kiddies come along, and we can ensure they don't until we decide we're ready for them.'

He adjusted his glasses, a gesture he made when angry or upset. 'I am not old-fashioned,' he replied tightly, clearly miffed.

'Times are changing, Ken, and we've got to change with them to survive. We don't want to end up like the poor dinosaur, do we? Look what happened to them – they didn't move with the times, didn't adapt, and became extinct as a result.'

He turned to stare at her. Vicky never ceased to amaze him. She could come out with the damnedest things!

'I hadn't exactly seen myself as a dinosaur,' he admitted.

'So you'll set a date then?'

He considered the question. 'I can't until I know what

the housing situation is like. I'll tell you what. Next Saturday, after work, I'll pop into various factors' offices and find out,' he prevaricated.

'That's a good idea, put us on their waiting lists. But of course we can go ahead and still get married without having our own house.'

'How do you mean?'

'There's no reason the pair of us can't stay with your parents. For the time being anyway. Until a house of our own comes along. I'm sure they wouldn't mind, and would appreciate the extra cash coming in.'

He could see that Vicky had thought this through. 'It's a possibility I suppose,' he admitted reluctantly.

'So what date would you fancy?'

'Hold your horses. We have to get engaged first.'

'Then let's get engaged now, tonight,' she said.

'No, not until I have a diamond ring to put on your finger.'

'It's not necessary, Ken. I've said that to you before, and meant it.'

'It's maybe not necessary to you, but it is to me. When we get engaged, it'll be with a diamond ring and a bit of a party,' he said stubbornly.

He had a blinking fixation about this diamond ring, she told herself. And they *cost*. The daft thing was this was the wrong way round. It was usually the woman who insisted on the niceties. 'It doesn't have to be a big diamond does it?'

'Not at all, just as long as it's real.'

'And when we get the ring, you'll set the date then?' she prompted.

'I'll set the date for the wedding the day we get engaged,' he promised.

'All right. But swear to me that from here on in there will be no more stupid wasting of money on snooker and the like? What money we can save goes towards that diamond ring?'

'I swear.'

She hugged his arm. 'We can get it from the jewellery

department at work, we'll get staff discount,' she said.

He thought of the jewellery department at Copland and Lye. Outside opening hours everything was kept in a vault, every piece checked in and out. Security was as tight as a midge's bum.

She would inquire about the price of suitable rings during her tea break next morning, Vicky thought. She wanted to know just how much they needed, so she could try and work out how long it was going to take them to save up for one. She would have been happy to settle for a plain nine-carat gold wedding band, but if he had his mind set on giving her an engagement ring, then that was how it would have to be.

Vicky lay with the hot sun beating on her face and exposed arms and legs. She and Ken were having a wee day out, picnicking on the banks of Loch Lomond, and had just made love. Her nicks were off, and in her handbag, which meant she was naked underneath her skirt. She felt marvellously wanton and very, very satisfied.

The brae they were on was called Conic Hill. Below them was the loch and, out into the loch, Inchfad Island. Ken, naked to the waist, sat smoking, staring into space.

They were in a dip carved into the brae, with trees behind and around them. They had walked there from the bus stop several miles away, deliberately searching out a secluded place where they could be quite alone together and make love.

Vicky blinked open an eye, to stare at Ken. He was lost in a dwam. 'What are you thinking about?' she asked lazily.

'The overtime rota at work.'

'Why that?'

'I was considering asking Mr Ferrier to put me onto it,' he replied.

Vicky gave a low laugh and pulled herself up onto an elbow. 'Don't bother, he'll only turn you down. Overtime is reserved for the long-serving members of the department, it's a sort of perk.'

Ken grunted, as if this was news to him. But it wasn't;

he had already inquired about the overtime situation.

'Pity about that, for I was thinking if I could get on the overtime rota it would mean more money coming in, and the more money coming in the sooner I can get your diamond ring, and we can become engaged and set a date for the wedding,' he replied, and blew a perfect smoke ring at the island.

Vicky chewed her lip, then shook her head. 'It's a good idea, Ken, and certainly one I'd be all for, but Mr Ferrier just wouldn't entertain putting you on the rota when you've hardly been there five minutes.'

A swallow dived and zoomed and skimmed the placid surface of the loch. Out beyond the island a rowing boat with what appeared to be some anglers in it had appeared.

Vicky stared at Ken, wanting him to make love to her again. She watched, fascinated, as a trickle of perspiration ran down his left shoulderblade. If she'd been closer, she would have licked it off with her tongue.

'He might not give me overtime if I ask him, but what about if you do? Now there's a thought,' Ken said. This was what he'd been leading up to all along.

'You mean give me overtime?'

'No, *you* ask him to give it to *me*. He thinks the world of you, Vicky, and it was only the other morning you boasted you could twist him round your little finger when you had a mind.'

It was true. She had said that. Just as it was true that Mr Ferrier had a soft spot for her. Nothing dirty – he wasn't at all like that – but because she was such an excellent worker.

'Well?' Ken asked.

'I could explain the overtime was to help us get engaged and married. It's possible he might make an exception because of that,' Vicky replied.

Ken threw away the remains of his cigarette and crawled over the few feet separating them. He glanced round at the anglers, but they were so far off as to be no more than dots. 'Two nights a week would be ideal. See what you can do,' he said, and removed his glasses.

Smiling, he took her in his arms.

'All right lads, time to pack it in and go home,' Mr Ferrier called out from the door of his office.

Ken finished off the knot he was tying and snipped the string. The parcel he'd just made contained curtain material and was to go to an address in Fife. He would stencil the address on when he returned next morning.

There was an eerie atmosphere in the department when the rest of the shop was closed, a hushed stillness that made Ken feel he should be tiptoeing through it. There were four of them working late, including Mr Ferrier. The only other person in the building was Mr Broadley, the night-watchman.

Ken took off his new overall, and put on his jacket. The next few minutes would tell him what he wanted to know.

'So how did you enjoy your first dose of overtime?' Larry Elder asked. Larry was in his fifties, and had been with Copland and Lye man and boy.

'Makes it a long day,' Ken replied.

Larry grinned. 'It does indeed, but you'll soon forget that when you get your wages on Friday, eh?'

'Wait till you've been married a couple of years, you'll be thankful of the break away from the wife,' Iain Coats called out, and all those within hearing burst out laughing. Iain was married to a big fat woman who, according to him, was an awful nag. He'd have worked late every night given the chance.

Ken glanced over to where Vicky's overall was hanging. He hadn't been wrong in thinking that she would get Ferrier to put him on the overtime rota, God bless her cotton socks! But it could still be all for nothing.

Ken, Iain Coats, Larry Elder and Maurice Webster collected together, chatting amongst themselves, till Mr Ferrier joined them. The supervisor led them in the direction of the staff exit.

At the exit they found Mr Broadley waiting. 'It's pelting down outside,' he said.

Iain Coats swore.

'Is it just a shower, do you think?' Mr Ferrier asked.

'If it's a shower, it's a gey long one, it started more than an hour ago,' Mr Broadley replied.

'No use waiting then. Goodnight, Mr Broadley.'

'Goodnight, Mr Ferrier. Goodnight all,' Mr Broadley said.

The rest of the goodbyes were said, and Ken stepped out into the teeming rain. There was no check, he thought jubilantly. *There was no check!*

During normal working hours there were spot checks at the staff door on all those leaving, and during the hours of work there were always so many folk to-ing and fro-ing that it was rare to be alone and unobserved for even the shortest length of time. And sometimes when you thought you weren't being observed, you actually were. In short, it wasn't impossible, but highly dangerous, to attempt to steal.

But on overtime, as he had now proved, stealing would not only be possible but downright bloody easy. A real dawdle. As long as he kept it small, pocket-sized, there should not be any trouble.

Ken decided that he would do a second night without taking anything, just to make sure that the non-check at the staff door hadn't been an aberration on Broadley's part because it was raining. But he doubted that it had been an aberration. Ferrier was such a thorough person that he would probably, almost certainly, have reminded Broadley.

He had briefly toyed with the idea of sending himself parcels through the firm, and stealing that way. But he had quickly abandoned the plan when he'd learned of the in-built tally system with the post office. If he had sent himself parcels, his name would have continually popped up on the postal payments sheets, and it would have been bound eventually to have been seen by someone. If that happened, two and two would swiftly have been put together.

From now on he could stop the penny pinching. Jesus, the argument he'd had with Vicky to get her to agree to that picnic at Loch Lomond – you'd have thought it was going to cost pounds, rather than a couple of bob, the way she'd carried on. And she mustn't find out about his stealing during overtime shifts. She'd stop him if she did, which was the last thing he wanted.

He cursed as some water ran down his neck. What an awful night! he thought. Then, smiling, he corrected himself. It might be belting cats and dogs, but as far as he was concerned it was a lovely night. A really smashing one.

Vicky, Neil and Ken were having a rip-roaring celebration. A letter had arrived at Neil's house that morning, informing him he'd won a Corporation grant. It was definite; he'd be going to Glasgow University in the autumn to start reading Law.

They were in the Argyle Arms, the nearest pub to Parr Street. Quinn, the landlord, was a ferret-faced Irishman reputed to have connections with the IRA.

Ken lurched to his feet, and stood swaying. 'Another round, eh?' he slurred.

Vicky was thoroughly enjoying herself but considered that they had had enough to drink. 'I think we've had sufficient,' she said.

'Sufficient, is it!' Ken replied, imitating Vicky's tone, and winking at Neil. 'Sufficient my bumbaleeree,' he added.

Neil hiccupped. His head was swimming and he was beginning to feel queasy. But he didn't want this to end. Or, to put it another way, he didn't want to lose Vicky's company. 'I'll have another pint,' he said.

'Stout lad,' Ken beamed, and staggered across to the bar.

It was a celebration after all, Vicky reminded herself. She just hoped Ken wasn't going to be sick. Mr Quinn would take a dim view of that, and he had been good to let her in, knowing she was under age.

Reaching over, she placed a hand on one of Neil's. 'All of Townhead is fair bursting with pride at what you've achieved, I hope you know that,' she told him.

'I had to go to uni, for my dad's sake,' he replied.

'He would have thought the world of you, Neil. Winning a Corporation grant is a huge achievement.'

Neil lowered his eyes, thinking about his dad, remembering. 'I only wish he could have hung on, to share today with me, to know that I'd be going to university.'

Vicky squeezed his hand. 'They say that God moves in mysterious ways. Perhaps he took your dad to give you that added motivation to win a grant,' she murmured.

Neil glanced up at her in surprise. He had never thought of it that way before.

'You know something, Neil, you're a fine young man who's going to make some lassie a grand husband one day,' Vicky said.

'Pimples and all?' he replied ruefully.

'Och, you'll grow out of those. A couple of years from now you'll have forgotten you ever had them.'

He prayed that she was right about that. Dear, lovely, darling Vicky. He worshipped the ground she walked on.

Ken returned with a trayful of pints *and* whiskies. 'May as well be hung for a sheep as a lamb,' he said, getting a dig in at Vicky. He laid the tray down, slopping beer from the pints onto the tray and table.

Vicky was about to make a caustic retort when suddenly, as a result of the pints she'd already consumed, she had the overwhelming urge to be elsewhere. She hurriedly excused herself, and left the two men, weaving her way through tables and chairs, heading for the ladies' toilet at the far end of the pub.

'Here, these are *large* whiskies!' Neil exclaimed.

'And why not? It isn't every day you win a grant to the university,' Ken replied.

'But the *expense*, Ken!'

Ken glanced after Vicky, saw her disappear through the toilet door, then turned again to Neil. 'Money's no object with me, my old son,' he said.

Neil frowned. 'What do you mean?'

Normally Ken wouldn't have let Neil into his secret, he wouldn't have let anyone into it. But the alcohol had loosened his tongue, making him want to boast. He beckoned Neil closer. 'I'll tell you something if you promise not to mention it to another soul, particularly Vicky – she'd have a canary if she found out,' he whispered.

'I promise,' Neil replied, puzzled.

'Word of honour?'

'Cross my heart and hope to die if I don't.'

That was good enough for Ken. It was the vow they'd aye taken as children; to break it meant the breaker would die a horrible death, eaten slowly alive by thousands of man-eating spiders, or some such.

He produced his wallet and from it took a wad of notes. 'What do you think of that lot?' he demanded.

Neil gaped. He could see that there were only a few single notes in the wad; the rest were all fivers. 'What did you do, rob a bank?' he replied.

'Closer than you think,' Ken answered and, sniggering and smirking, he told Neil about the stuff he was taking from Copland and Lye's and flogging elsewhere.

'Careful you don't get caught,' was all Neil could think of to say when Ken had finished.

Ken tapped his nose. 'Not me, I'm far too fly.'

Ken nicking stuff! He wouldn't have believed it if he hadn't heard it from the horse's mouth, Neil thought in wonder.

Everything had become hazy for Ken, he was in a rosy land, floating along on a comfy white cloud.

'Vicky wouldn't understand, not at all,' he said, and belched.

Neil thought of Vicky's touching his hand only a few moments since, and her talk about his making some lassie a grand husband. If only that lassie could be her.

'You and Vicky have been going a while now, I must say. Knowing you, I'm surprised it's lasted so long. I thought you would have moved on to pastures new,' Neil said.

'The grass isn't always greener, Neil. I'll tell you this, I've had some good fucks in my time, some really tremendous ones. But Vicky? She's the best of them all,' Ken slurred.

Cold anger erupted in Neil. How dare Ken discuss Vicky in that way! It just wasn't done, not when you supposedly had feelings for the girl.

'You get inside her and, well, it's even better than drink,' Ken said, and laughed.

Neil's face had gone stony. He wanted to punch Ken, to lay the bastard out flat.

'You did me a great turn when you put me onto her, I'll never forget that,' Ken went on.

Ken ran fingers through his hair, leaving it sticking up in places. Whew! but he was pissed. When he peered at Neil through his glasses, he saw two Neils.

'She's got a gorgeous body, tits like melons, thighs you could cry over. And her arse, Christ! I could die for that arse.'

Neil's fists were so tightly clenched they were milk white right up to their wrists. It made him sick to hear Ken talk about Vicky as though she was just so much flesh. Why, she might have been a whore the way he was going on.

'But then you don't know a lot about women, do you, Neil?' Ken leered.

Neil shook his head.

'No doubt you'll learn at university, there'll be lots of willing crumpet there. Crumpet that laps up the intellectual type. Why, there'll probably be so many open legs on offer you won't know which pair to stick it up first.'

'I doubt if I'll ever be promiscuous,' Neil answered, voice trembling.

'Don't knock it until you've tried it, son,' Ken said, and laughed raucously, thinking that awfully funny.

'So are you going to go ahead and get engaged then?' Neil asked.

'Oh aye, no buts about it,' Ken replied.

He didn't deserve her, he *didn't*! Neil thought in despair, and self-pity, and outrage.

At the far end of the pub Vicky reappeared. Ken saw her, and peeled one of the single notes off his wad. 'Listen, I'd better not buy any more bevy or she might get suspicious. You buy the next couple of rounds, tell her it was a wee something you'd put by for a rainy day, or extra-special occasion,' he said, and thrust the pound note into Neil's hand.

Neil didn't argue. A couple more rounds meant even longer in Vicky's company.

*

Vicky heard the commotion and made in the direction it was coming from. She found Mr Scott, the general manager of the shop, Miss Elvin and Mr Ferrier grouped round an ashen-faced Ken. Other members of Packing and Dispatch were forming an outer ring, which she quickly joined.

Mr Scott, a small tubby man with a florid complexion, stabbed an accusing finger at Ken. 'Come on, Blacklaws, admit it. We know you've been stealing. We've had a stock check and a number of items are unaccounted for,' he said in a squeaky voice that had long since earned him the nickname 'Mouse'.

Ken took a step backward and came up against a pillar. 'I'm not admitting to anything. You can't prove it was me who stole these things,' he replied, half paralysed with fear.

Stealing . . . items unaccounted for . . . Vicky had given an involuntary gasp on hearing those words. She could not believe that he had been so stupid as to have done what he stood accused of. Surely this was a mistake, a coincidence?

'We've received information that you've been stealing. The stock check confirmed that information to be correct,' Mr Scott went on.

Mr Ferrier glanced sympathetically at Vicky. It was he who had received the phone call and taken its message to Mr Scott. Poor lass, he thought to himself.

'I don't know what information you got, but it's all lies, lies!' Ken replied, almost screaming.

'The missing items have all walked from this department since you joined it, that has already been proven. And there was no stealing going on in this department prior to your arrival, which has also been proven. It all adds up to one answer, and one only. You're the thief,' Mr Scott said.

'Admit it, Ken, it's the best way,' Mr Ferrier urged.

'I'm telling you, I'm innocent,' Ken gabbled desperately.

Vicky was looking directly at Ken, but he steadfastly refused to meet her gaze. It was that which told her that this was no mistake, no coincidence – that he was guilty.

'Mr Ferrier, ring the police,' Mr Scott instructed.

The police! Vicky thought in alarm. Once they became involved, the business of the burglaries was bound to come out, for Ken was sure to have left fingerprints in at least several of the houses he had broken into. And then there was that Arab, the one they had run into the night at Ferrari's. He'd clearly been a VIP, a diplomat even. If Ken was connected with that burglary, the authorities would throw the book at him. Why, he could be facing ten to fifteen years in prison.

She staggered where she stood. Ten to fifteen years – a lifetime! She couldn't let that happen to him, there had to be some way out of this.

That same way was obvious. To save him, she would take the blame on herself. They would not go hard on her. Why, the shop might not even prosecute, she being a girl and such a hard worker. She'd lose her job of course, but that was a small price to pay to keep Ken out of prison for such a horrendous length of time.

Ken was about to lunge past Mr Scott and attempt to make a run for it when Vicky spoke. 'He *is* innocent, Mr Scott, I'm the person you want,' she said.

Mr Ferrier, almost at his office door, stopped to turn and stare at Vicky, as did everyone present.

'You!' Mr Scott queried in amazement.

'I've no idea where your information came from, but it's incorrect. Maybe they've got mixed up between Ken and me because we're a lot together, but I'm the one who's been stealing from the department,' she went on.

'I don't believe that!' Miss Elvin exclaimed.

'It's true. Just as it's true that I've only been stealing since Ken started work here. It was all to help with our engagement and wedding, you see.'

That was the moment when Ken knew he should have confessed, said that Vicky was only trying to protect him. But he kept his mouth shut.

'Miss Devine, and you Miss Elvin, I think we'd better

123

proceed with this matter in Mr Ferrier's office,' Mr Scott said, quite thrown by this turn of events.

Vicky started for Mr Ferrier's office, with Miss Elvin and Mr Scott following behind.

'Do you want me to come also?' Ken croaked, but his voice was so quiet that nobody heard.

Once they were inside his office, Mr Ferrier shut the door, thinking to himself that he had never been so mistaken about someone's character. He would never have dreamed in a million years that Vicky was a thief.

Vicky stood with head bowed, hands clasped in front of her.

'Well, I don't know what to make of this at all,' Mr Scott said. He was well acquainted with Miss Elvin's report, and Mr Ferrier's report, on Vicky, and that she was scheduled to be promoted to Furs.

'I suppose the question is, do we prosecute?' Mr Scott asked Miss Elvin.

Miss Elvin was suddenly furious with Vicky as it sank in on her how badly Vicky had let her down. She had broken one of her own cardinal rules about queue jumping to give Vicky the job in Packing and Dispatch, and it was on her *personal* recommendation that Vicky had been accepted for Furs. And it was she who had got Blacklaws his job, entirely on account of Vicky. Why, she had bent over backwards at every turn for Vicky, and this was the result. Vicky had more or less spat in her face. How dare the little baggage, *how dare she!*

'I think dismissal would be punishment enough. Give her the sack, and let that be that,' Mr Ferrier said.

'Oh no! She's a thief, and therefore has to be tried by the law as such. That's only right and proper,' Miss Elvin hissed vehemently, determined on revenge.

Vicky's hopes, which had momentarily risen when Mr Ferrier had spoken, now plummeted.

'I don't know, she is a girl after all, and a young one too,' Mr Scott prevaricated, rubbing a hand over his pink and shining chin.

'Her sex and age have nothing to do with it. That she's a thief and has stolen from this shop are what's important.

You must give her over to the police, and prosecute,' Miss Elvin insisted.

Still Mr Scott hesitated. He had a daughter at home the same age as Vicky.

'Fail to prosecute and you'll only encourage others to try it on,' Miss Elvin said.

Mr Scott sighed. She was right of course. If he didn't prosecute, he would be failing in his duty. Crossing to Mr Ferrier's desk, he picked up the telephone. 'Put me through to the police,' he told the operator when she answered.

Miss Elvin flashed Vicky a venomous look of triumph. That'll teach you to make a fool of me, the look clearly said.

Vicky thought of her mum and dad – this was going to cut the feet right out from underneath the pair of them.

That night Neil turned into his close to discover that the gas light had gone out. And the one on the first landing too, he saw, glancing up at the half-landing, which was also in total darkness. He groped his way forward.

He had just reached the bottom stair, and was about to ascend, when he was suddenly grasped tightly by the arm.

'Hello, Neil, I'd like a word,' Ken's voice, hard and grating, said out of the darkness.

Fear clutched Neil's insides. Ken was here when he shouldn't have been, and he *knew*!

Neil tried to wrench himself free, but failed to do so. Ken literally dragged him into the dunny, a secluded section of the back close just before it opens out onto the back court, and a great favourite of courting couples because of that seclusion.

Neil gasped as Ken thrust him hard against a paint-flaking wall. 'Information received was what they said at Copland and Lye. Information fucking received,' Ken spat into Neil's face.

'I don't know what you're talking about,' Neil whimpered.

'Only one person in this world knew I was nicking from

the shop, and that was you. You're the only one I let on to,' Ken said.

'I'm still not with you, Ken?'

Ken hit Neil with the flat of a hand, knocking Neil's head first one way, then the other.

'Why?' he demanded.

Neil's fear dissolved, and his feelings all boiled up to come gushing out. 'Because I love Vicky and want her, and because she can't really mean anything to you. How can she when you talk about her as you did that time in the Argyle Arms? Why she could have been a slut and a whore the way you were going on.'

Ken took that in, then laughed, a low-pitched rasping sound that had a wild, skin-tingling quality about it.

'Oh, you stupid bastard, Neil, you stupid stupid bastard. Instead of getting me the jail, you've got her it instead,' he replied.

'Eh?'

'There's a lot more to this than you're aware of, so when I was accused Vicky stepped in and said it was her, that she'd been doing the stealing, so as to protect me.'

Neil closed his eyes. 'Oh my God!' he whispered.

'She'll be up before the sheriff and sentenced, tomorrow,' Ken added.

'Oh, my God,' Neil repeated.

Ken thought of Vicky in a jail cell with no knowing what sort of scum, and the fury that had been in him since he had realised that it had to be Neil who'd been in touch with Copland and Lye now erupted, filling him with awesome violence. He released Neil, then hit him as hard as he could. And hit him again.

Neil tried to defend himself, even to fight back, but, weakened by guilt, he was no match for the raging Ken, who, in a flurry of blows, overwhelmed him. Sobbing, Neil sank to the stone floor, thinking that, by doing so, Ken, considering he'd had enough, would surely stop.

But Ken didn't stop, he merely changed to using his feet rather than his fists. Neil's sobbing changed to a shrill scream as Ken's lashing foot caught him full in the genitals.

126

Pain such as he would not have believed possible, and which made what had gone before pale into insignificance, scalded through him.

He tried to turn over, but even as he did Ken let go with the other foot which, in turning, he went straight into. This also took him in the genitals, throwing him backwards to go banging into the wall behind.

Neil's fluttering hands tried to protect his crotch, to no avail. When the toe of Ken's shoe seemed to flatten his testicles, the shriek he gave was blood-curdling to hear.

When the red haze finally lifted from Ken, it was to find that he had kicked Neil unconscious. He was panting from exertion and wringing with sweat. He steadied himself against the closest wall while he regained breath.

Then he heard the sound of inquiring voices, and footsteps, on the stairs above, neighbours coming to investigate. Stumbling out into the back court, he ran to his own back close and disappeared inside.

Part Two

The Fallen God
1935–37

'. . . We make Gods of men and they leave us.'
OSCAR WILDE, *Lady Windermere's Fan*

Five

Vicky stared numbly out into the black night. She was still stunned by the sentence the sheriff had given her earlier. She had been hoping that the sentence would be suspended or, failing that, if she did go down, that she would get three months, six at the maximum. Sheriff Dunlop had had other ideas. The sentence had been three years, to be reviewed in two years' time, on her eighteenth birthday.

Vicky had managed to hold back the tears until she was out of the courtroom; then they'd come, in torrents. She had been escorted to the same cell in which she had previously been held while waiting to go before the sheriff, and there a hatchet-faced policewoman had told her that she would be taken to a borstal later that day. It had been nine p.m., and her tears had long since dried, when they finally came for her.

There were two of them, Detective Inspector Copelaw, a tall, prematurely bald man, and WPC Lundie. They had walked her out to the police car, where she had been instructed to sit in the rear with the WPC. The detective inspector drove.

Three years! The figure hammered in Vicky's brain and, although it was only mildly cold, she shivered all over.

Her mum and dad had been in court, as had Ken and Miss Elvin. Miss Elvin had gloated as Vicky was marched away; her mum and dad had been just as stunned as she was. Ken had been so shaken that he had had to sit down. He had watched her, his eyes never leaving hers, till she disappeared through the side entrance leading to the cells.

Vicky eventually roused herself when she smelled the unmistakable tang of the sea. 'Where are you taking me?' she asked in a dull, dispirited voice.

WPC Lundie glanced at her superior, who nodded. 'It's down the coast this side of Port Glasgow. It's a borstal institution called Duncliffe,' she replied.

Vicky ran a hand through her hair. She felt manky after her night in jail, and wondered if she would be able to get a bath and hair wash where she was going. 'Is it going to be awfully hard there?' she asked.

WPC Lundie's lips thinned. 'It won't be a Sunday school picnic, you can bank on that.'

Three years *without* Ken! How would she survive? Vicky thought in desperation and abject misery. She groaned and turned away from the WPC, burying her face in leather upholstery and imagining that the leather was Ken's cheek against her own.

Eventually the police car, having come cross country via Houston, joined the coast road and, as it did so, the moon broke through the heavy cloud layer above. Vicky listened to the muttering of the sea and soft sighing of the wind. Her mind was filled with images of Ken and the pair of them together.

'We're almost there,' Detective Inspector Copelaw said a little later.

Vicky sat upright in her seat. The brooding, forbidding pile she saw ahead appeared to be a small castle. Only two lights showed, like a pair of yellow eyes staring unblinkingly out into the night. Malevolent eyes, on watch.

Copelaw stopped the car in front of a set of heavy iron gates and gave a short sharp toot of the horn. A figure materialised out of the darkness; there was the rattle of a key being inserted into a lock and the gates swung open. As Copelaw took the car past the figure, Vicky saw that it was an old man stooped from either age or rheumatism, or perhaps both.

Detective Inspector Copelaw brought the car to a halt before some steps leading up to a door. 'All out,' he said.

Vicky found herself in a large courtyard, but just how large it was she could not quite make out. The old man appeared beside the car and politely asked them to follow him.

Inside the building he guided them by means of a torch, explaining as they went – for neither the detective inspector nor the WPC had previously been at Duncliffe during the hours of darkness – that this was how he made his rounds. The Head did not approve of wasting electricity. The old man wove his way through a maze of corridors. Eventually he paused at an oaken door and knocked respectfully.

'Come in, Strachan,' a female voice called out.

Vicky's initial impression of the room was of austerity. There was a bed in one of the corners, a desk, chair, a bookcase crammed with books, a standard lamp, desk lamp, and a rug on the stone floor. The walls were whitewashed brick. The ceiling had been plastered, and also whitewashed.

The female sitting at the desk bordered on middle age; she was slim, with a finely chiselled face and hair cut in a pageboy style. Her eyes were the palest blue Vicky had ever seen.

Strachan knuckled his forehead. 'I've brought along the new arrival and her escort, as you told me to, Miss Ganch.'

'Wait in the corridor. This will only take a few moments,' Miss Ganch replied, voice crisp with authority. It was a voice used to being obeyed instantly, without question.

Strachan hurriedly left the room, quietly closing the door behind him. Miss Ganch waited till he was gone before extracting a printed form, with attached copy, from an already opened drawer in her desk.

'Name?' she demanded, looking directly at Vicky.

'Victoria Devine.'

'Victoria Devine, *miss*.'

Vicky swallowed hard. There was something about Miss Ganch that terrified her. 'Victoria Devine, miss,' she repeated.

Miss Ganch wrote Vicky's name onto the form and copy, then pushed them across her desk, glancing up at Detective Inspector Copelaw as she did so. Copelaw came to the desk and countersigned the form. He tore off the original, folded it and placed it in an inside pocket.

'Goodnight, safe return journey to Glasgow,' Miss Ganch said, dismissing the police.

Their business concluded, Copelaw and WPC Lundie left, and Vicky found herself alone with Miss Ganch, who was studying her in the most disconcerting manner.

'How old, girl?' Miss Ganch asked, after what must have been a full minute had slowly passed.

'Sixteen, miss.'

'Hmmh!' Miss Ganch murmured thoughtfully. She again reached into the open desk drawer and took out a second printed form and attached copy, which she spread in front of her, smoothing it flat with her hand.

'I am Miss Ganch. You are to be in my section. That means that from now on you belong to me. Understand?'

Belong! Vicky did not like the sound of that at all. 'Yes, miss,' she replied.

'This room, my room, is at the head of the dormitory where my girls sleep, where you will be sleeping from now on. Understand?'

'Yes, miss.'

'Have you eaten?'

'I had a corned-beef sandwich at around five o'clock, but nothing since.'

'Pity, for I'm afraid the kitchens here are closed. However, I do have a tin of digestives. You can have some of those.' Miss Ganch opened another desk drawer to produce the tin. She rose and, coming round to Vicky, handed it to her. Her stern features suddenly relaxed into a smile. 'Help yourself while I go and get your bits and pieces. I couldn't have them ready waiting for you as I didn't know what size you were. Thirty-six bra, I'd say?'

'Yes, miss.'

'I'm usually spot on about that,' Miss Ganch said, and walked from the room, leaving the door open behind her.

Vicky slumped where she stood. Miss Ganch might have been smiling latterly, but she did not trust that smile, not one little bit. Miss Ganch reminded her of a garden snake her brother John had briefly kept when a wee lad. The woman gave her the horrors just as that snake had done.

Mum, Dad and John – she hoped they were bearing up. They would all be worried sick about her, as would Ken. Three years! Her spirits sank again. But it probably would not be that long, she argued with herself. Her sentence was to be reviewed on her eighteenth birthday. If she kept her nose clean, which she had every intention of doing, she would surely be released then. That realisation brightened her a little.

She was surprised to find herself not only hungry but ravenously so. The digestives were delicious. She wolfed down half a dozen and had just started on yet another when Miss Ganch, still smiling, returned. She laid the pile of clothes she was carrying on her desk and placed the form she had previously put on the desk beside them.

'That form contains a list of what you've been issued. Check each item off by ticking it. If you agree you've got everything, sign the form in the first space provided. The second space is to agree the list I will now draw up of those clothes you're handing in and will be given back to you on your eventual release. Understand?'

'Yes, Miss Ganch.'

Miss Ganch took the tin of digestives from Vicky and replaced it in her desk. Sitting again, she made a pyramid with her hands, watching Vicky over the top of it while Vicky checked what she had been issued against the list.

'It's all here,' Vicky acknowledged and signed the form and copy.

'Now strip, and get into one of the nightdresses provided. I'll itemise what you take off once you've done so.'

There was a hiatus while Vicky glanced round, but the glance only confirmed what she already knew from her earlier scrutiny of the room: there was no screen, or anything else, to hide behind while she changed.

'Strip *here*, miss?'

'To the buff, everything,' Miss Ganch spelled out.

Vicky took off her jacket, then the maroon cardy that was a great favourite of hers and which her mum had knitted. Heart thumping, she started to unbutton her blouse. Miss Ganch did not even pretend to be doing something else.

135

Leaning back in her chair, she watched unashamedly. When Vicky reached her bra and knickers, she felt that she could not go on. It was so humiliating!

'Well?' Miss Ganch prompted, and the word was a threat, promising Vicky that something awful would happen to her if she didn't continue.

Vicky undid her bra and her breasts fell free. When it came to her knickers, she turned sideways on to Miss Ganch. As she pulled her knickers down and off, her face, neck and breasts flamed with embarrassment. She hurriedly put on the grey flannelette nightdress she'd been issued, thankful that the degradation was over.

Coming forward in her chair, Miss Ganch took the form Vicky had signed and separated it from its copy. She itemised what Vicky had taken off/first on one sheet, then on the other.

After Vicky had signed in the second space, agreeing that the itemised list was correct, Miss Ganch handed her the copy. 'Yours. Hang on to it.'

Miss Ganch reached into the drawer containing the tin of digestives and brought out a thin pair of cotton gloves, which she slipped on. 'This next bit is usually done by the nurse, but as she's off duty, and it has to be done as part of the admittance procedure, I'm afraid it's up to me. Please bend over my desk and lift your nightdress up over your buttocks.'

Vicky was aghast. 'What are you going to do to me?'

'I have to examine your rear passage for haemorrhoids – piles, that is – and also to make sure you're not trying to smuggle in anything you shouldn't that way. I also have to examine your vagina for signs of disease, and the smuggling reason as well.'

Vicky gagged.

'It's standard procedure. Every girl arriving at Duncliffe has to undergo it.' Rising, Miss Ganch came round to stand beside Vicky. 'Bend over and lift your nightdress.'

Slowly, Vicky bent over the desk and, even more slowly, rucked up her nightdress to expose her buttocks. She closed her eyes, and shuddered inwardly when Miss Ganch's hands spread her buttocks. She choked back a sob when a probing finger entered her anus.

The finger stayed a lot longer than necessary, Vicky thought. And what a strange sensation it was, extremely uncomfortable and painful. She gave a sigh of relief when the finger was finally removed. Then she remembered that her vagina was also to be examined.

'Put your bottom against my desk, spread your legs, lift the front of your nightdress and lean backwards,' Miss Ganch said matter-of-factly.

When she was in that position, Vicky thought to herself that, if it had been degrading to be naked before Miss Ganch, how much more so it was to be as she now was. She shrank against the desk when her sex lips were prised apart. Feeling completely defiled, she wanted to wail in anguish. From behind what had been shut eyelids, she peeked out to see that Miss Ganch was on her knees peering up and into her. She groaned when a finger forced its way into her dryness. Please God, let this be over! she screamed inside her head.

Miss Ganch stood and removed her gloves, which she tossed onto the desk. 'Sorry about that,' she said.

Vicky didn't think she sounded sorry at all. The bitch had enjoyed it. She looked into Miss Ganch's eyes and saw an amused glitter there, and the glitter itself, a reflected sheen, again reminded her of John's garden snake.

Vicky had already dropped the front of her nightdress and now tugged it down as far as it would go, wishing it reached all the way to the floor instead of merely to her knees.

'Pick up your new issue clothes and follow me.'

When Vicky had the clothes cradled in her arms, she turned to discover Miss Ganch holding a torch similar to the one Strachan had used. Out in the corridor she went in the opposite direction to that from which Vicky had been brought and almost immediately they were into a dormitory.

The light from Miss Ganch's torch revealed the room to be narrow and fairly long. There were heavy curtains at the windows, all drawn. One of the sleepers, a girl on the left-hand side, was snoring loudly and rhythmically. It reminded Vicky of her dad. They came to the sole bed in the dormitory not occupied. 'Put your issue in there and be quiet about it,' Miss Ganch whispered, pointing to an empty wooden locker standing beside the bed.

Vicky worked by the light of the torch, bundling everything in as neatly as she was able.

'Into bed and asleep. Reveille's at five.'

Vicky climbed into the hard bed; it was so unyielding that she might have been lying on solid rock. The sheets were the roughest she'd ever come across. Miss Ganch, without uttering further, vanished from the dormitory and Vicky was plunged into Stygian darkness. Her skin was still crawling from what she had been through, the feeling of having been defiled still strong within her.

What terrible place was this? Would all the people in charge be like Miss Ganch? She prayed not. Oh Ken! she howled silently. Why had he been so stupid to steal from Copland and Lye! Why why *why*!!!

If it hadn't been for Miss Elvin, Mr Scott would not have prosecuted. But she could understand Miss Elvin reacting as she had; Miss Elvin had been made to look a right mug after all.

Gradually her heaving, jangled emotions quietened. She found solace in the snoring coming from the opposite line of beds. She pretended she was at home, listening to her dad. Finally, exhausted after the day's events, and thinking of Ken, she fell asleep to dream of him.

The shrill blast of the whistle pierced Vicky's brain, causing her to come awake with an exclamation and sit up straight in bed. The lights were on, and Miss Ganch was standing in the centre of the dormitory. She had a riding crop in one hand, the whistle in the other. She blew a second blast, at the end of which Vicky was the only one still in bed. All the other girls had been galvanised into action.

'Hurry! Hurry! Hurry!' Miss Ganch bellowed, and striding to the nearest window ripped its curtains wide open.

It was freezing at that time of the morning, and Vicky

saw that it was still dark out. She gaped to see that all around her girls were whipping off their nightdresses to reveal themselves nude and dressing in a flurry where they stood.

'Sweater and slacks, you'd better be quick about it,' the girl from the bed on Vicky's left whispered to her.

'Hurry! Hurry! Hurry!' Miss Ganch screamed, and ripped open more curtains.

By the time Vicky reached her plimsolls, nearly everyone else was ready and that included having made their beds and straightening their lockers. As each girl finished, she came to attention at the foot of her bed.

Vicky was acutely aware of Miss Ganch, again standing in the centre of the dormitory, glaring at her. She was the last to finish. Then she too came to the foot of her bed and took up a position of attention.

'You're allowed one day's grace, Devine, and one only. Starting tomorrow you'll be expected to have learned what's what. Understand?'

'Yes, Miss Ganch,' Vicky replied.

The riding crop shot out to point at a dark-haired girl whom Vicky judged to be fourteen or fifteen. 'You, McCrimmond, you were last. Prepare to receive punishment.'

McCrimmond gulped. Turning round, she bent over the end of her bed, presenting her bottom. Miss Ganch crossed to McCrimmond and the riding crop whistled through the air. The blow, when it landed, was a sharp crack. Vicky winced, thinking how painful it must have been.

'McCrimmond leads. Now go! Go! Go!' Miss Ganch shouted.

McCrimmond ran off through the dormitory door at the speed of a startled gazelle, the rest of the girls in pursuit. Vicky found herself in the middle of the pack as they jostled along corridors and down several flights of stairs. Eventually they left the building by a different entrance from the one she'd arrived at the previous night.

Dawn was breaking and she could spot several other packs of girls, heading in various directions. They descended steep stone steps onto a beach of golden sand. The sea was rough, crashing ashore to go hissing out again. The wind was gusting, sometimes drenching the runners in spume, other times whirling and eddying about them.

Vicky gritted her teeth. Already her lungs and legs were sore and she was having to struggle for breath. She was not used to sustained running – running for a tramcar had been her limit up until now. She dropped to the back of the pack, a glance over her shoulder confirming that Miss Ganch was bringing up the rear.

Miss Ganch suddenly darted forward to slash with the riding crop. A plump girl, who had been last in the pack, yelped, and spurted forward. After another two girls had been struck across the backside, Vicky got the message: to be last meant a stroke from Miss Ganch's riding crop.

They came to a clump of dunes dotted with marram grass, which they struggled up and over. Beyond the dunes was more beach, and then a formation of rock. At its highest the rock was about sixty feet off the ground, and it had to be climbed. Vicky was coughing and choking as she went up hand over hand.

Coming down the other side, she realised with alarm that she was now last and Miss Ganch was directly behind her. When the riding crop wasn't used on her bottom, she remembered what Miss Ganch had said in the dormitory: this was to be a day of grace for her *and her only one.* The run became a nightmare, but Vicky forced herself to complete it, knowing that she was going to have to do so the next day. She dreaded to think what the punishment for not doing so was.

The finishing point was the castle courtyard, and there the pack halted. Vicky collapsed to the ground, where she lay, chest afire, feeling as though she was about to die. Other packs arrived in the courtyard, six in all, a full complement being a hundred and twenty girls.

The sensation of impending death passed as Vicky's breath returned. She got back onto her feet, thinking that they would all be going off to breakfast now. She was wrong.

One of the women in charge barked out that they were to get in their lines, and the girls formed six lines, each line a section. Then began thirty minutes of gruelling physical jerks. The conclusion of the physical jerks found Vicky devastated. She swayed on the spot, a limp rag that had been squeezed and squeezed again.

'Dismissed!' the woman who'd conducted the physical jerks shouted, and instantly the lines broke up.

It *had* to be breakfast now, Vicky thought, for, despite her condition, she was ravenous. Again she was wrong. Her section returned to the dormitory, where they collected towels from their lockers. From there they trudged to an adjacent shower room, where they started stripping off.

Vicky caught sight of Miss Ganch watching her, and knew she was expected to follow suit. She stripped naked and joined the others in the showers. The water made her gasp – it was ice cold! The steam she'd seen rising didn't come from the water but the bodies it was battering against. Within seconds she was so cold that her teeth were chittering. She lathered herself with the poor soap provided; it had the feel and texture of candle wax. The water ceased abruptly and, thankfully, the showering ordeal was over.

Vicky scampered across to her towel and began briskly rubbing herself dry. Some of the girls were talking, and even laughing amongst themselves – so silence was not obligatory.

The last girl dressed got a swipe across the buttocks from Miss Ganch's riding crop, then they were marched off down the corridor, arms swinging, military fashion.

This time it *was* breakfast. The dining hall was domed and had a wooden floor. Trestles had been laid out in six lines, each line for a section. The meal was served from a seventh line of trestles at the top of the hall, set square on to the others. Off to one side, and quite apart, was a circular table. Vicky guessed correctly that this was where Miss Ganch and the others in charge sat.

Whatever else she thought of Duncliffe, she could not accuse them of being stingy with their food, or 'scoff' as she heard it referred to by several of the girls. There was juice, cereal, boiled and fried eggs, bacon, sausages, kidneys, toast, plain bread, jam, marmalade, tea and cocoa. And you could help yourself to as much as you wished. Vicky devoured her heaped plate, then sat back, over her tea, to study the faces around her. It was her first proper chance to do so.

Some of the girls looked downright nasty, and she made a mental note to keep away from them. Others appeared pleasant enough, and she wondered what they'd done to end up in Duncliffe. Several were beauties, real crackers, a handful plain in the extreme, with one poor lassie so ugly that she made Vicky thank God that she hadn't been born like that. The remainder were middling, not too good-looking, not too plain.

Most of the girls chatted as they ate but, although a few curious glances were cast in Vicky's direction, no one started up a conversation with her. Nor did she with them, thinking that the wisest course for the moment.

When she went up for another cup of tea, Miss Ganch came over to her. 'Directly after breakfast you've to go to the Head's office. She wants to meet and assign you.'

Assign? 'Yes, Miss Ganch.'

Miss Ganch then gave Vicky directions on how to find the Head's office, after which she returned to her table.

Vicky was halfway through her second cup of tea when a bell rang. Immediately everyone rose and began filing from the hall.

Miss Ganch's directions had been explicit. Consequently Vicky had no trouble in finding the Head's office, which was in a small turret on the seaward side of the castle. The brass plate on the door said HEAD OFFICER. Vicky knocked and waited.

'Enter!' a voice cried out from within.

Vicky judged the woman behind the desk to be in her late fifties, possibly just turned sixty. She wore black-framed spectacles, and her pepper and salt hair was tied severely back in a bun. She had a wedding band on, but no engagement or eternity ring.

'I'm Mrs Meehan, you call me Head. Understand?'

'Yes, Head,' Vicky replied.

The Head picked up a manilla folder, opened it and carefully scrutinised the contents.

'Stealing eh?' she said, glancing up at Vicky.

'Yes, Head.'

The Head laid the folder, still opened, down in front of her. She studied Vicky, her eyes bright and penetrating. 'Steal anything, anything at all, while at Duncliffe and you'll rue it. Understand?' she said softly.

Soft, but deadly, and meaning every word, Vicky thought. 'Yes, Head.'

'Do *anything* you shouldn't while at Duncliffe, and you'll rue it. Tough nuts don't stay tough here for very long, we have tried and tested ways of dealing with them. Understand, Devine?'

'Yes, Head.'

'I hope you do, for your sake.'

Vicky shivered and went prickly all over.

The Head gazed at the top sheet in the opened folder. 'Three-year sentence, to be reviewed on your eighteenth birthday. You're going to be with us quite a while then.'

'Yes, Head.'

'Plenty of time to learn a useful skill, something to earn your living by when you're released. We have a number of courses on offer. Book-keeping for example.'

The Head paused and a small, cynical smile twisted the corners of her mouth upwards. 'But perhaps not that for a thief. Too tempting, eh?'

Giving no reply, Vicky lowered her eyes. How galling to be considered a thief, but that was what she'd branded herself, and what she now had to live with.

'We also train girls to be tailoresses, a popular course that, hairdressers, cooks, shorthand typists . . .' The Head broke off, her brow creasing in thought. 'Yes, shorthand and typing, we have a vacancy there. How would that suit you?'

'Just fine, Head,' Vicky replied. She would really have preferred to learn hairdressing, but considered it best to agree to the Head's suggestion.

The Head nodded her approval: Vicky learned quickly. 'Mrs Gardener is in charge of that course. I'll take you along and personally introduce you. Besides, there's something I want you to see on the way.' She closed the folder.

The Head walked with a limp, and Vicky saw that one leg was shorter than the other. She wondered if the woman had been born like that or if it was the result of accident or disease.

The Head did not speak again until they had reached a black-painted door. Here she stopped and selected a key from a bunch dangling from a chain at her belt. 'This is the Black Room. Offenders who've spent time in it are rarely keen to repeat the experience.' She unlocked the door, which swung silently open, and a shaft of light knifed into the small room. The stench of defecation hit Vicky, causing her to take an involuntary step backwards. The smell was so strong that it threatened to make her gag.

The room was square, with no windows. There was no lightbulb, or gas mantle, or any other form of illumination. When the door was shut, and it had been especially fitted to exclude all light from the corridor, there was total darkness inside. The only form of ventilation was a grille set into the skirting board, just big enough to ensure there was some airflow.

A girl sat on an army-style cot staring at them. Her eyes were wide, her mouth trembling. Beside the cot was a brimming chamber pot.

'Hello, Kathy, how are you today?' the Head asked.

Kathy slid from the cot onto her knees, her hands coming together in supplication. 'Please, Head, let me out. I'll be a good girl, I swear. On my life I swear.'

'No more brawling?'

'No more, Head.'

There was a pause. Seconds ticked past. 'Maybe another twenty-four hours, just to make absolutely sure the lesson has been driven home.'

Tears burst from Kathy's eyes. 'Please, Head, please?' she whimpered.

'Tomorrow,' the Head decided and, slamming the door shut, locked it once more.

From inside the room came the muffled sound of crying.

'As I told you, we have tried and tested ways of dealing with troublemakers. Be warned,' the Head said and started off down the corridor. Vicky, appalled and thoroughly frightened by what she had just seen, hurried after her.

Vicky was out on her feet when she left the dining hall at the finish of tea, a meal as splendid and generous as the two preceding it. All she wanted to do was topple into bed and dream of Ken.

She thought about what a revelation the day had been, the most enjoyable part being the shorthand/typing class under Mrs Gardener, who was a gem of a person and a natural teacher. After shorthand typing it had been dinner, and then outside again, where she had learned that there was far more to Duncliffe than the castle building.

Miss Ganch had explained to her that it was the Head's policy for Duncliffe to be as self-sufficient as possible. Vicky was shown fields where potatoes and all manner of vegetables, root and otherwise, were grown, and fields where cattle and sheep were grazing. The girls did everything themselves – with the exception of slaughtering, which was done at a Port Glasgow abattoir – right down to making the jam and conserves from the soft fruit from the many berry bushes. They were allotted chores and, because some chores were harder than others, the sections took them in turn. Miss Ganch's section was currently in charge of the livestock, which included, apart from the cows and sheep, horses, pigs, ducks and chickens. Vicky's task had been to assist in mucking out the cow byre, and, pitchfork in hand, she'd been engaged in this all afternoon.

On entering the dormitory, Vicky was instantly aware of an atmosphere. She came up short when she saw a lassie rifling her locker – one of those whom at breakfast time she'd classed as a beauty. In a quandary as to what to do, she went slowly forward. 'Excuse me, that's my locker you're going through,' she said on reaching the end of her bed.

The lassie turned to face Vicky. She was clutching the second of the sweaters Vicky had been issued, the as yet unworn one, which she now held up against herself. 'You're the first newcomer into this dormitory for ages who's my size. One of my sweaters is threadbare, so I'm swopping it for yours. Hope you don't mind.' The girl smiled sweetly.

Vicky was flabbergasted. What barefaced cheek! 'I do mind,' she snapped.

The lassie raised an eyebrow, then twirled the sweater round her shoulders, tying it at its front by its sleeves. 'Tough tittie,' she replied.

Vicky was no pushover. Being brought up in Townhead, she had learned to fight for what was hers. In other circumstances she would have forced the matter, but all she could think of was the Black Room and Kathy, who had been incarcerated there for brawling. 'I'll complain to Miss Ganch,' she said.

The lassie threw back her head and laughed. A loud, gutsy, pealing laugh. 'You do that, dearie,' she said, and swaggered past Vicky out of the dormitory.

Fists clenched, Vicky watched her go.

'Don't even think about it. It wouldn't be worth it,' a voice said behind Vicky.

The speaker was the same girl who had spoken to Vicky that morning, advising her what to wear, and whom Vicky had subsequently spotted as being another member of Mrs Gardener's shorthand and typing class. The girl now came over and sat on Vicky's bed, while a muted hum of conversation began round the dormitory, the dorm having fallen silent during the confrontation.

'Her name's Muriel Mitchell, and that's her way of telling you she rules the roost round here,' the girl explained in a whisper.

Vicky sat across the bed from the girl. 'How do you mean?' she asked, also whispering.

'She has, shall we say, special privileges. If Muriel tells you to jump, it's best you do just that.'

Vicky frowned. 'I don't understand. How does she get away with it?'

'She's Miss Ganch's friend. *Special* friend, get my meaning?'

Vicky had to think about that, then the penny dropped. 'Are you saying they actually . . . together?'

The girl nodded.

Vicky remembered Miss Ganch's examination of her the previous night, and how much Miss Ganch had enjoyed it. At the time she had thought it pure sadism on Miss Ganch's part, causing her hurt and humiliation; now she knew there had been more to the woman's enjoyment than she'd imagined. Her skin crawled at the memory of that probing, exploring finger.

'By the by, I'm Tina Mathieson,' the girl said and extended a hand.

They shook. 'And I'm Vicky Devine, pleased to meet you.'

'How do you feel?'

'A total wreck.'

Tina smiled grimly, recalling her own first day at Duncliffe. 'It's hard going to begin with, but if you're healthy you'll soon get used to it, feel the better for it even,' she said.

Tina was considerably shorter than Vicky, and plumpish, with auburn hair. There was a warmness about her, and something more, something engaging, the combination of which Vicky took to right away. Vicky wondered what crime Tina had committed to be sent to Duncliffe; she looked as if butter wouldn't melt in her mouth.

'What about the others, are they friendly enough?' Vicky asked.

'Most of them, once they get to know you. But there are a few like Muriel about the place whom it's best, whenever possible, to keep well clear of.'

'And what's the situation with mail and visitors?'

Tina gave a sudden grin. 'There's a boyfriend then?'

'Yes. His name's Ken.'

Tina's grin turned to a sigh. 'Mine was called Robin, a real handsome lad, and a collier from Bellshill. But he's mine no more, he met someone else,' she said wistfully.

'Ken will wait for me, we're in love,' Vicky told Tina, and gave a little nod of the head as if to underscore that both points were so.

How many times had she heard that said! Tina thought cynically. Still, some chaps did wait, that couldn't be denied. She hoped Vicky's would be one of those who did.

'Visiting day is the last Sunday in every month, but as you're new you have to wait till the second visiting day comes round, and then it's only one visitor at a time. You're allowed to send a single letter out before that, but not to receive any. After your first visitor you can send one out every week, and receive as many as arrive. Incoming mail is handed round by Miss Ganch after tea on Saturdays, and only then,' Tina explained.

'I see,' said Vicky, working out how long it would be before she was due her first visitor. She groaned inwardly with the realisation that it was six and a half weeks away. And no mail before then either!

'What about days off, any of those?'

'Sunday, after obligatory church service, is your own to do with as you like. Saturday is different still; you don't attend your course on that day, but spend the entire working day, after the morning run and PT, doing chores.'

'Is there a run and PT on Sundays?'

Tina smiled and nodded.

'Well, when I leave here, I'm certainly going to be fit,' Vicky commented ruefully.

Muriel Mitchell, wearing Vicky's sweater, came back into the dormitory.

'If she's Miss Ganch's special friend, why didn't she just ask Miss Ganch for a new sweater?' Vicky asked in a whisper.

'She can't have been very bothered or she'd have had a new one long before now. She was probably only using the sweater business to show you she's top of the pecking order in this section,' Tina whispered back.

They talked for a while longer, Tina telling Vicky all the things she should know, and Vicky grateful for the information. She was also grateful for the tips Tina gave her, tips to make life at Duncliffe a little easier. But Vicky was most grateful of all for the fact that she had found a friend and ally.

Lights out in the evening was at eight forty-five. Vicky was already tucked up reading a book that Saturday night when

Miss Ganch strode into the dormitory to stand by the light switch.

'One . . . two . . . three . . .' Miss Ganch began counting.

There was a great scurrying as those not already in bed hastily dived into them. To have still been out on Miss Ganch's reaching the count of ten meant a trip to the bottom of the bed, bending over it and receiving a slash from the riding crop.

'Ten,' said Miss Ganch and the lights flicked off. The curtains were already drawn, McCrimmond having done this after tea. It was a task allotted to a different girl every week.

Vicky settled down. As Tina had said, she was beginning to get used to the strenuous life at Duncliffe. She still ached all over from the hitherto unaccustomed exercise and manual graft, but the aches were beginning to fade and should soon be gone altogether. She was amazed at her appetite; she would never have believed she would eat as much as she was now doing. She was putting it away at every meal as if she were a starving Irish navvy. She was certainly looking a lot better in the short time she'd been at Duncliffe. Thanks to the sea air, her city pallor was quickly replaced by a rosiness in the cheeks and general freshness of the skin.

It was about half an hour later, and Vicky was on the point of dozing off, having been thinking about Ken and remembering various times they'd had together, when she dimly heard the soft pitter-patter of feet. Someone off to the toilet, she thought.

'Vicky, are you still awake?' Tina whispered a few moments later.

'Yes.'

Vicky stiffened in alarm when her bedclothes were pulled aside and a body got in beside her.

'It's only me.'

'What are you doing in my bed?'

Tina chuckled softly. 'Don't worry, I'm not one of *them*. It's just easier to talk and be together this way.'

'We're not supposed to talk after lights out, you know that,' Vicky said, thinking of the Black Room.

'It's Saturday night, "pash" night, we can chat for hours if we want to, as long as we keep it fairly quiet, that is. And do other things too, like having a drink. Do you fancy one?'

'Wait a minute, what's this "pash" night?" Vicky asked.

'Pash, short for passion. That was Muriel leaving the dormitory. She's away, as she goes every Saturday night after lights out, to Miss Ganch's room. There the pair of them have a fine old time, culminating in sex. Now do you want that drink or not?'

'Yes, please. What have you got?'

Tina gave a soft chuckle. 'Ever heard of Fowler's Wee Heavy Ale? It'll blast your head off. Well, I've·managed to get hold of three, that's one each and one to share.'

Tina had brought the small bottles into Vicky's bed with her and an opener. She de-capped two, and gave Vicky one. 'As I said, it's right powerful stuff that, so don't gulp, just sip,' Tina instructed.

Vicky pulled a face. The Wee Heavy was bitter, and Tina wasn't joking, it was strong. It was a bit like drinking runny bitter treacle.

'Hardly my first choice for a Saturday night boozing session but all I could get. And lucky to do so,' Tina whispered.

'How did you get it?'

'We all have our secrets in Duncliffe, Vicky, and where I lay my mitts on the occasional bevy is one of mine. As they say, ask no questions, get no lies . . .'

'Shut your mouth, and you'll catch no flies!' Vicky chipped in, finishing off the well-known children's doggerel.

They both laughed softly and had another sip of Wee Heavy.

Vicky could hear now that they weren't the only people to be having an after-lights-out natter. Quite a few of the girls were paying a 'visit' to their pals.

'Tell me something, do you know if Muriel has always preferred women to men?' Vicky asked.

'Don't be soft, she's as normal as you or I. She does it for the perks.'

'And what are those?'

'The biggest I would say is that she does hellish little in the way of hard work. She's forever being allowed to skive off, and spends most of the time sitting on her backside smoking like a lum, ciggies that Miss Ganch provides.'

'And what else?'

'While she's in Miss Ganch's room on "pash" night, Miss Ganch spoils her rotten. Miss Ganch keeps beautiful clothes there that she's allowed to dress up in, silk négligé and stockings, embroidered housecoat, velvet slippers, that sort of thing. Then there's sherry, wine and chocs, boxes of those, Muriel can stuff herself to the gills with them if she wants to.'

Vicky cocked an ear. 'Is that music?' She could just hear faint strains.

'Oh aye. Miss Ganch has a gramophone she brings out for the occasion. They play records and dance together.'

'And does Miss Ganch get all dressed up as well?'

'To the nines, Muriel says. And over and above the clothes and other goodies I've mentioned, Muriel also gets to use Miss Ganch's perfume and powder, both of which are the very best money can buy, according to Muriel.'

Vicky had another sip of Wee Heavy; she could already feel the effect and she'd hardly dented the contents of the bottle yet. 'What I can't understand is why the Head puts up with such goings on. I mean, she must surely know about Miss Ganch?'

'She knows all right. She knows everything that goes on in Duncliffe. I've wondered about that myself, and I can only suppose she tolerates it because she must have trouble getting staff to come and work here. It's a foul job really, living out in the wilds, cut off from family and social life. Who would want that? Very few. And Miss Ganch is good at the job, you have to give her that. Our section is one of the best, and most efficiently run, at Duncliffe.'

'Thanks to that riding crop,' Vicky said.

'Have you had a taste of it yet?'

Vicky shook her head. 'I've been lucky so far.'

'Well, it's only a matter of time before you do. The only person who doesn't get hit is Muriel, another of her perks.'

'Is it awful sore?'

Tina gave a thin smile at the memory of the countless times she'd been at the receiving end of that detested riding crop. 'It hurts like buggeration. I thought, to begin with, that you'd get used to it after a while. But you don't.'

'Have you been here long then?'

'Eleven months. I've got another thirteen to serve.'

'Can I ask what you did, or isn't that polite?' Vicky queried.

'I stabbed a lassie for trying to get off with that ex-boyfriend of mine I was telling you about,' Tina replied sombrely.

'Stabbed her?'

'I didn't mean to. It just sort of happened in the heat of the moment. But the polis picked me up, and the next thing I knew I was at Duncliffe. I've always thought the sentence harsh as I was a first-time offender. I'd never been in trouble before, not even as a wean for ring-bang-scoosh.'

'I'm a first offender also, and I too thought I might be shown leniency, and wasn't,' Vicky said.

'And what did you do?'

'I stole from the big shop where I was working, and eventually got caught,' Vicky replied, giving Tina the official version of events. Then she changed her mind, deciding that she would tell her new friend the truth.

Tina listened wide-eyed to Vicky's tale of how it had been Ken who'd been nicking from Copland and Lye, and of the burglaries he'd committed previous to that, and how Vicky had sacrificed herself in order to save him from a heavy sentence – only to be landed with a sentence far heftier than anything she had envisaged.

'That's dead romantic, so it is,' Tina whispered when Vicky finally stopped speaking.

'I'm going to write and ask him to be my first visitor. I can't wait to see him again,' Vicky said.

'Is he handsome?'

'A Greek god, with specs that can make him look ever so distinguished.'

'He sounds just rare.' Tina was envious and jealous of Vicky, but in the nicest way, wishing that she had a Ken of her own.

'Oh, he is, he is,' Vicky answered.

Tina spent an hour in Vicky's bed before returning to her own. Vicky considered it the best hour she had had so far at Duncliffe. She fell asleep thinking about the letter she would write Ken on Sunday, the one letter she was permitted to send prior to her first visitor, inviting him to be that visitor.

It was a bitter November morning, with the temperature below freezing and a cruel biting wind blowing in off the sea. Vicky stood chafing her hands, waiting impatiently for the bus that would be bringing Ken and the other visitors to Duncliffe, a chartered bus organised by the Head which picked visitors up from an assembly point in Port Glasgow, and returned them there afterwards.

The previous night had been a bad one for Vicky. She had had little sleep; it had mostly been spent tossing and turning in a fever of impatience for the coming morning – and Ken. Now the morning was here, and any minute now she would be in his arms again, have his lips on hers. The prospect made her all of a quiver.

She glanced across the courtyard to where Tina was standing chatting to a knot of girls. Tina wasn't expecting anyone, but had come outside to have a gander at Ken. Tina saw her, and waved. Then gestured into the distance. When Vicky looked in the direction Tina was pointing she saw that the bus was at long last in sight.

The double decker meandered along the coast road. The damn driver couldn't have gone more slowly! Vicky thought, and mentally raged at the man. Eventually the bus stopped before the heavy iron gates at the entrance to Duncliffe. Strachan unlocked the gates – taking his time about it too! – and ponderously swung them open. The bus crawled forward to halt in the courtyard, and its passengers

153

started getting off. The next one would be Ken, Vicky told herself and, when it wasn't, the next, and the next. She could not help the squeal that burst from her when he finally did appear.

'Ken!' she cried, and ran to him, arms flung wide.

It was the moment she had waited for, the anticipated moment which had borne her through pain, exhaustion and downright despair. He hugged her tight, then in front of everyone kissed her deeply, tongue in mouth.

When they broke off they both had to gasp for air. 'You look terrific! You're positively gleaming with health,' he said.

There was something different about him, something she couldn't quite put her finger on. And then she had it.

'You've grown a moustache!' she exclaimed.

'Do you like it? Everyone says it suits me.'

'It makes you seem older.'

'And even *more* handsome?'

'Don't be so vain!' she scolded, and they both laughed.

She hooked an arm in one of his. She intended being alone with him, and had already decided where they would go. She took him across the courtyard, then round to the steep stone steps that brought them onto the beach. From there she headed for the dunes.

'This is the first chance I've had to thank you for what you did,' he said.

She glanced into his face, then away again, staring out to sea where whitecaps were dancing, preparing to come surging ashore. 'You were stupid to steal from the shop. You should have known you'd be caught.'

It was on the tip of his tongue to say that he wouldn't have been if Neil hadn't informed on him, but he bit that back. Well, he'd had his revenge on Neil, and sweet revenge it had been too. The bastard hadn't walked for a week after the kicking he'd given him. And Neil had kept stum about the identity of his assailant, so no one in Parr Street knew. That had been a wise move on Neil's part, for to say anything would have meant divulging that he'd informed

154

on a pal and was directly responsible for Vicky ending up in Duncliffe.

'I'm only sorry you're the one who's having to pay for that stupidity,' Ken said contritely.

They reached the dunes, and there they sat facing the sea. 'How are my folks, and John?' she asked.

'They're all fine, and send their love. I'm sure they were disappointed that you wanted me to come today and not either of them, but I'm equally certain they understood.'

'Are they awfully ashamed of me?'

Ken lit a cigarette. 'I don't have to answer that. You know how they must feel,' he mumbled in reply.

Her parents must be mortified, Vicky thought for the hundredth time. Her poor mum would find it difficult keeping her head held up in the street.

'The neighbours have all been right decent about it. It's just simply never referred to,' Ken said.

She made a fist and chewed one of her knuckles. 'I had to do what I did. If they'd found out about your burgling, and they were bound to, they would have sent you away for anything up to ten years,' she whispered.

His throat was suddenly dry at the thought of that. And he felt uneasy to be with Vicky, because she had been his saviour. 'Ferrier at Copland and Lye sends his regards, the old goat,' Ken said, thinking, Jesus! it's cold out here: I'd much prefer to be indoors.

'I liked him. He was a nice man who must believe I let him down.'

'No, he doesn't. He knows it was me who was stealing, and not you.' Ken blew a stream of smoke seawards.

Vicky looked sharply at Ken. '*How* does he know?'

Ken shrugged. 'I've no idea, but he does. He told me, in a round-about way, that I could forget about any advancement at Copland and Lye. I'll stay put in the job I'm in.'

Panic welled within her. 'You haven't been stealing more things have you?' she demanded shrilly.

'Of course not. That wouldn't just be stupid, it would be suicidal. Anyway, I couldn't even if I wanted to. Since your confession, there's been no more overtime for me, and Ferrier watches me like a bloody hawk.'

Vicky swore, using a word she'd never have spoken before coming to Duncliffe. Ken glanced at her in surprise. 'Is it rough here?'

She wanted to tell him exactly how rough it was, to pour out her heart to him, which was what she'd intended. Only now, somehow, that didn't seem right. Why hadn't he inquired straight off how she was! Now that he had come to ask, it had been almost as an afterthought, as if he didn't really care.

'Rough enough,' she answered vaguely.

'So it's not bad then?'

She didn't reply.

'I must say it seems all right, big castle and all that. How's the food?'

'Very good, and plenty of it.'

'Bit like a holiday, eh? Like going camping with the Girl Guides.'

She could've sloshed him. How could he be·so dense and unfeeling! She might appear healthy enough, but couldn't he sense some of what she'd been through! Now she was confused. She had been looking forward so much to his visit, and it wasn't turning out at all as she'd hoped. He could have at least restated that he loved her: there had been no mention of that either.

'It's gey chilly down here. Couldn't we go inside?' He shivered.

Vicky led the way to the castle building, her expression as chilly as the weather he was complaining about.

Vicky sat on a wide inside window ledge staring out to sea. It had started to rain about an hour since and was now teeming down. It would have been a dismal journey home to Glasgow for Ken, she thought, and remembered how they'd parted at the bus, she trying to hide her anger and dismay, he saying that he'd enjoyed himself – *enjoyed*! what sort of word was that to use – and that he'd come again after her parents had both been. Right up until the last moment, she had waited for him to utter the magic phrase. But it hadn't been forthcoming.

She sighed, and her brooding mind took on a new course. She was being daft, she told herself. She'd been expecting too much of the visit, so of course it had been an anti-climax. As for his offhand manner, couldn't that be a result of the terrible guilt he felt? Guilt at her being in an institution of correction when it should have been him? That had to be it, and it was her fault for not realising sooner what the problem was. She had been selfish, completely self-centred, wallowing in self-pity. After all, think how hard it must have been for him to come and face her, to see her in a borstal as a direct result of his actions and dishonesty.

Vicky cheered up. It all made sense now; she understood why he'd acted as he had. Squirming from the ledge, she strode in the direction of her dormitory. There was time for her to write a letter to him before tea. Time to write, and apologise. For it was entirely because of her lack of insight and understanding that the visit had been a failure.

It was June 1936, a month that had come in as a scorcher and remained one. Vicky and Tina had recently been delegated responsibility for one of the chicken coops, of which there were three, and that afternoon found Vicky feeding their charges, with Tina inside the coop collecting eggs. The chickens were clucking noisily as Vicky moved amongst them scattering corn left and right. The big rooster called Sandy, comb blood-red and standing up straight, was strutting to and fro as if he personally had arranged these proceedings.

Vicky was halfway through what she was doing when she suddenly caught sight of Miss Ganch at the side of the coop gazing over at the castle. She followed her gaze and realised that it wasn't the building itself Miss Ganch was staring at but a car just leaving the courtyard.

The car stopped at the iron gates, waiting for Strachan to open them. As it went through the open gates, Miss Ganch raised an arm, and gave a small salute.

Vicky remembered then that Muriel Mitchell was due to

leave Duncliffe that day, it must be her being taken to Glasgow for her official release. The car sped off and vanished from view, leaving Miss Ganch with arm still upraised. She turned abruptly, exclaiming in surprise to find Vicky there. Her eyes were moist, her face drawn and haggard. Vicky glanced away and continued feeding the chickens. Miss Ganch hurried off.

Vicky finished feeding the chickens, then went into the coop to help Tina. Tina had already gathered two baskets of eggs and said that plenty more remained to be picked up. Vicky said that she would make a pile of those while Tina took the filled baskets to the kitchens and returned with empty ones.

Vicky was at the far end of the coop, by the door there, when she became aware of a strange noise outside which she couldn't place. She opened the door and stepped out into a secluded part of the chicken run.

Miss Ganch, slumped against a wall, was dry-heaving into a handkerchief. Her cheeks and chin were awash with tears. Here, temporarily, was no longer a formidable woman, but a very sad and lonely one, Vicky thought. A woman who had just lost, so it would appear, someone she cared a great deal about.

'I'm sorry,' Vicky commiserated quietly.

'She was so beautiful,' Miss Ganch choked.

'Yes, she was.'

Miss Ganch tried to say something further but was too overcome to do so. A huge spasm wracked her body and she threw up.

Vicky went back into the coop, closing the door gently behind her.

Ken had a swallow of his pint and glared balefully round the pub. Saturday night and he was on his tod again, the fourth Saturday night on the trot. All the mates were winching, leaving him spare. He wondered whether he should bother with another pint or head back to Parr Street. It was no fun drinking alone, being miserable, when everyone else was having so much fun.

It was ten months since Vicky had been committed to Duncliffe, ten long lonely months. Even if she did get out on her eighteenth birthday, and she was convinced she would, that was still an eternity away. He had played the white man so far, dead true and all that, never straying, not even the once. But it hadn't been easy. Where he had looked forward in the past to Friday and Saturday nights, he now dreaded them.

He drank more heavy and watched a lassie and her bloke leave. Probably off to the jigging, he thought. It was getting a bit late for them to be aiming for the flicks. He spied a lad he'd been to school with – what was the bugger's name again? – and gave him a nod. If the chap had been alone, he'd have strolled over, but Ronnie – aye, that was the name, Ronnie – was with a bint. And a pretty bint too. He stared jealously at the bint – not in Vicky's class, nowhere near, but at that moment looking very attractive indeed.

Dougie Steele from the Parli Road came into the pub, and Ken's spirits briefly brightened, only to plummet again when he saw Dougie was 'with'. Dougie saw Ken, gave him a wink of greeting, and steered his bird in the opposite direction to Ken. He was much enamoured by this wee bird whom he'd only met the night before, so why take chances? Best to keep clear of any possible competition while he got on with his chatting up, consolidating his position.

Ken finished his pint. He was off home, he decided. If he hurried, he could still buy a half-bottle to share with his dad. Out in the street he paused to rift and, as he did so, changed his mind. To hell with home and a half-bottle; he was going dancing.

He walked into Sauchiehall Street and paid his entrance money at the first dance hall he came to. Inside it was jam-packed, but it would have been unusual for a town dance hall not to be at the weekend. He began eyeing up the available talent.

She was standing by a pillar with another lassie, and this time he recognised her straight off. It was the ginger-haired girl from the *Fairy Queen*, the one who'd been in the pub down at the docks before that. The one he'd thought

159

attractive in a gallus sort of way. He made his way across.

'Well, hello there,' he said to her, and smiled.

The green eyes came round to fasten onto him and he was surveyed from behind a deadpan expression.

'Hello there,' she replied.

'Taken any boat trips lately?' he asked.

The hint of a frown creased her freckly forehead. She glanced at her pal, then back again at Ken. 'Do I know you?'

'We've never spoken up until now, but seem to have the habit of bumping into one another. Remember the trip on the Forth and Clyde Canal to Craigmarloch and back?'

The green eyes twinkled with memory. 'You had a female with you then,' she replied.

'That's long finished,' he lied.

'And the time before that was . . .'

'In a boozer down by the docks. You were with your father and some other men,' he finished for her.

He was even more handsome than she recalled, she thought.

'It's funny, but I always felt we'd cross paths again,' he said.

'Excuse me, I must powder my nose,' the lassie's pal said diplomatically, seeing how things were going, and moved off.

'My name's Lyn Fyfer,' the ginger-haired lassie told Ken.

He stuck out a hand, and they shook. 'I'm Ken Blacklaws. Are you for up?'

'I'd love to dance, thanks,' she replied and, taking him by the arm, led him onto the floor.

A thrill ran through him as they came together. She was gorgeously soft and smelled delicious. As for her green eyes, he could have stared into them till the cows came home.

'I take it you're on your own?' she inquired as they started to waltz.

He nodded. 'And what about you? Are you here with that china of yours?' he replied, making sure she was there with a female friend and not a male one.

Lyn also nodded.

A few minutes later the music stopped and everyone applauded. 'Will you stay up?' he asked her.

She looked him directly in the face and saw that he was as enamoured as she was. 'I will.'

They both knew then that it was a click.

'All right, what's up? Your face has been tripping you ever since we met,' Lyn asked Ken, who had been in a mood when they'd rendezvoused quarter of an hour previously, a mood that had since worsened. They were sitting in an Argyle Street pub where they had come for a mid-week drink.

Ken scowled into his pint. 'It'll just have to be a single bevy the night, I'm afraid. I can't afford more than that.'

So that was the source of his ill humour, *embarrassment*, Lyn thought with relief. She had been worried sick he was going to say he wanted to stop seeing her, that would have been a catastrophe as far as she was concerned. For, in the three months they had been going out together, she had taken a big shine to Ken Blacklaws. A very big shine.

'It's not a problem. I've money,' she told him.

'Och, I couldn't take money off you, it wouldn't be right,' he said, for it was considered extremely bad form for a Glasgow man to accept money from a bird he was only winching, and neither engaged or married to. It was a matter of pride.

'I'm not short, I assure you. And we've just arrived. I don't want to be rushing off again right away,' she argued.

He hadn't wanted to come out that night, not when he was verging on being skint. But the arrangement had already been made, and he had no way of contacting her to break it and make a new one.

The frustration and resentment he had been trying to keep a lid on for so long now boiled over. 'It's that effing job of mine. The pay's diabolical and for some reason the bastarding supervisor hates my guts. The bugger's made it known to me that I'll never get promotion, thereby blocking me from earning a larger pay packet.'

'So why not leave?'

'You think I'm not trying to! But you know what the work situation's like, jobs aren't exactly ten a penny.'

It was news to Lyn that he felt this way about his present job. He had never talked about it before other than to tell her what he did when she'd inquired.

'You say your pay's diabolical. I know one isn't supposed to ask this question, that it's rude, but how much is it exactly?'

'Thirty-seven and six a week,' he mumbled in reply.

That was diabolical right enough, not a man's wages at all, she thought. 'And I suppose you give some of that to your mum for your keep?'

'Twenty-five bob of it.'

She took a cigarette from her packet and offered the packet to him. He couldn't disguise his eagerness to light up, a dead giveaway that he'd been gasping.

Ken exhaled smoke and gave a bitter laugh. 'It's not all that long ago that I was boasting to someone about how ambitious I was, how I intended getting on, that nothing would stop me. I said I'd be one of those who achieved power, a stringpuller who made others dance to his tune. I said I would completely be my own master, and the master of many. Somebody really important. What hollow words they sound now that I'm stuck with no prospects, in the Packing and Dispatch department of Copland and Lye.'

'Something's bound to come along,' she sympathised.

'Oh aye, sure, and pigs will sprout wings and fly,' he retorted and had a savage pull at his pint.

The idea came to her then of how she could help him, and herself into the bargain. For if he earned more money, he would be able to see her more often – and he'd be obliged to her.

'Are you strong?' she asked.

He blinked. What had that to do with it? 'Fairly,' he replied.

'And are you a grafter, not afraid of getting stuck in?'

'I am,' he said softly, wondering what this was leading up to.

Lyn glanced at her watch, had a think, and nodded.

'Finish that pint and let's go. We should just catch him.'

'Catch who?'

'You'll find out,' she said mysteriously and swallowed what remained of her whisky and lemonade.

Lyn rose from the table as the last drop of heavy vanished down Ken's throat. She led the way out into the street to where her car was parked. It was a brand new Austin 7, with a deep-blue body, black mudguards, running boards and roof. The wheel spokes, originally black, were now the same colour as the body – she had painted these herself. The overall effect was, in her own words, 'to make the car look really eye-catching'.

Ken was much taken with the Austin; its distinctive colouring appealed to him. Of course it wasn't a patch on the Armstrong Siddeley he'd so briefly owned, but it was a wee smasher nonetheless.

They got in and started off. Before long they had left Argyle Street and turned down into Finnieston. The river came into view, dark and brooding at this time of night. For a short while it was lost to sight, then it reappeared as they entered Queen's Dock. The rest of the river had been quiet, ominously so, but not here. Queen's Dock outer basin was abustle with activity; a large ship was being unloaded.

Lyn parked the car just beyond the perimeter of the pool of light that flooded the ship and the warehouse into which the ship's cargo was being unloaded.

'The *Star of India*. It was three days late berthing because of bad weather. As its entire cargo consisted of fruit, it's being unloaded as quickly as possible to get the fruit into the market and shops before it spoils,' Lyn explained.

'How come you know so much about it?'

'Ever heard of the Honourable Society of Dock Workers?'

He shook his head.

'Well, it's one of the four unions that control the docks in Glasgow, and my father is its president. It's his men who are unloading that ship tonight, and I happen to know he negotiated a special rate for the job which will give each and every one of them a fiver for his night's work,' she said.

Ken whistled. Five pounds for a night's work! Earned

honestly, that was very good going indeed. In fact it was spectacular.

He had known that her father was connected with the docks, but had presumed – remembering that flashy chauffeur-driven Riley at Port Dundas – that Mr Fyfer was on the management side.

'I can't promise you power to be able to make others dance to your tune, or even to be your own master, but the basic rate is one pound ten a day, which adds up to nine pounds, before stoppages, for a six-day week. On top of that you'll have overtime and special jobs such as the *Star of India* there, hoisting your take-home pay to between twelve and fifteen pounds a week, some weeks even more.'

He stared in astonishment at the outline of her face in the darkness. 'Are you offering me a job as a dockie?'

'If you're agreeable, let's go over and see my dad. I'll put it to him,' she replied.

If he was *agreeable*! He reached out and drew her close. 'I think you're smashing,' he whispered.

'You're a bit of all right yourself,' she told him, also in a whisper.

He kissed her, their tongues flickering together. She broke away when he squeezed her right breast and was swiftly out the car. Laughing, she strode towards the warehouse where she knew her father would be.

Ken, straightening the tie he was suddenly glad to be wearing, hurried after her.

Vicky and Tina were leaving tea together when Miss Ganch came up to them and addressed Vicky. 'Follow me, Devine,' she snapped, and walked quickly away.

Vicky's stomach contracted with fear. Had she done something wrong, been remiss in one of her duties? She glanced at Tina, shrugged to say she hadn't a clue what this was all about, and ran to catch up on Miss Ganch.

Miss Ganch, expression stern to the point of being fierce, made for her room. Once inside, she stood with hands on hips, and gazed about. 'This place is filthy. I want it cleaned from top to bottom, *thoroughly*. Understand?'

'Yes, miss.'

'Then hop to it,' Miss Ganch said, and sat at her desk.

Vicky muttered a quiet excuse and left the room to get the cleaning things from the corridor cupboard. She lugged them back to the room and, with Miss Ganch apparently immersed in paperwork, started in.

Miss Ganch was right: the room was manky and couldn't have been touched for months. Before long the sweat was lashing off her as she swept and scrubbed, dusted and polished.

'I'm finished, Miss Ganch,' she proclaimed at last, having been at it for several hours.

Miss Ganch laid down the pen she had been using and regarded Vicky thoughtfully. Vicky was again reminded of John's garden snake.

'There's no need for me to check. I've been watching you and know you've done a good job.'

'Thank you,' Vicky said, and made to gather the cleaning things together, to return them to the cupboard.

'Wait. There's no need to do that just yet,' Miss Ganch told Vicky, and smiled.

Vicky immediately halted what she was doing. It had only been a suggestion, but from Miss Ganch that amounted to a command.

Miss Ganch rose and crossed to her bed. Kneeling, she pulled out a sliding drawer that had been concealed beneath it. There were a number of bottles and sweetie boxes in the drawer, and various types of glasses. 'How about a sherry as a reward?'

Oh God! Vicky thought and quailed inside. 'I'm under age, miss.'

'Then we'll just have to keep this to ourselves, our little secret between you and me.' She poured out two hefty sherries.

Vicky accepted hers, mumbling her thanks.

'You've settled in well at Duncliffe, we're all pleased with you,' Miss Ganch said, regarding Vicky over the rim of her glass.

'I'm trying to do my best, Miss Ganch,' Vicky replied,

thinking she didn't know much about sherry, but this tasted like an expensive one.

'How do you find that?'

'Lovely, miss.'

Miss Ganch snapped her fingers. 'Tell you what, you must try one of the new chocolates I've bought. They're Swiss.' She opened a box from the underbed drawer, and proffered it to Vicky. Vicky chose a chocolate in the shape of a unicorn. It melted in her mouth – it was simply exquisite.

'Very nice, miss,' she said, not wanting to show too much enthusiasm.

'Have you ever mentioned to the others about the day Muriel left?' Miss Ganch asked softly.

'No, miss.'

'Are you certain? Not even to Tina Mathieson? You and she appear to be great chums.'

'Not even to Tina, miss, I swear. That was a moment of private grief for you. I wouldn't blab about something so intimate and personal.' Vicky lied, for she had told Tina. But it had stopped there; neither had thought it politic for the story of what she had witnessed to go further.

'In which case you've earned a further reward, and I know just the very dab. Come with me.'

Miss Ganch, with Vicky tagging along behind, left the room and crossed to a door on the other side of the corridor, which she unlocked with a brass key. Vicky knew what lay beyond, but had never seen inside. It was Miss Ganch's private bathroom. The woman went in and beckoned Vicky to join her. In trepidation, Vicky did so.

Miss Ganch closed the door. 'How about a hot bath? And you can use any of my crystals and powders that take your fancy.'

A hot bath! It had been nothing but ice-cold showers since she had come to Duncliffe. Vicky could not think of anything she desired more – with the exception of Ken, that was.

Miss Ganch put the plug in the huge white enamelled tub and twisted a tap. Steaming water gushed forth to splatter on the bottom of the bath. Her eyes glinted. 'Take your time, enjoy yourself. Just don't fall asleep, that tub's big enough to drown in.' She left Vicky, reshutting the door as she went.

Vicky slumped her body with relief. She had had the horrible suspicion that Miss Ganch might want to stay with her while she had the bath – or, worse still, join her. There was a snib on the door, which she snecked. She felt a great deal better for that.

There was a jar of pink crystals and another of blue. She chose the pink, which had a flowery smell to them, and tipped in a fair amount. The flowery smell filled the bathroom. She found towels in a cupboard, half a dozen in all, each one thick and soft as down. When the bath was ready she undressed. Slowly she slipped into the water, groaning with the sheer pleasure of the experience. She sank up to her neck and closed her eyes.

After a while she poured in a little of the oil standing on the side of the bath. Its odour was musk and mingled fragrantly with that of the crystals. She had forgotten how stupefyingly luxurious a hot bath could be; aches and pains that had become part and parcel of her everyday living gradually seeped from her body as it relaxed, unwound and was revitalised.

Eventually, reluctantly, she climbed out of the bath and towelled herself dry, after which she liberally doused herself with talcum powder. She ran a comb through her hair which she'd washed when in the bath. It had not felt so clean since she'd last washed it at home – why, it actually squeaked when she rubbed it with the towel!

She had been reluctant to get out of the bath; she was even more so to leave the bathroom itself. But finally she did so, sighing as she shut the door on that place of heavenly delight.

She found Tina in the dormitory waiting for her. 'Well?'

Before Vicky could reply, Tina's nose twitched and she took a deep sniff. 'Is that powder or perfume?'

'Both,' Vicky answered, and went on to relate what had happened.

Tina, chewing a thumbnail, listened in silence. 'You

know what this means, don't you? Ganch wants you as a replacement to Muriel,' she said when Vicky was finally finished.

'I'd already arrived at the same conclusion myself.'

'So?'

Vicky shook her head, appalled at the idea. 'I'm in love with Ken. Why, I couldn't go to bed with another man, no matter how attractive, far less a woman.'

'It might not be that bad, and consider how easy life would become for you.'

'I find the thought of it quite repulsive. Even if there wasn't Ken, I couldn't go through with it. That sort of thing revolts me. Doesn't it you?'

Tina shrugged. 'Before I came here I'd have said yes. But now? I'm more broadminded than I used to be, and certainly less dogmatic. If Ganch propositioned me, I'd certainly give it serious consideration on account of the perks involved.'

'You really would!' Vicky exclaimed, amazed.

'What she did to you wouldn't be that hard to endure. Surely you've learned to take yourself off inside your head by now? Detach yourself, float away in the mind. I soon learned that was the only way to survive bloody Duncliffe at times.'

Vicky knew exactly what Tina was talking about; it was a trick she also employed when it all got too much. 'But you'd have to live with yourself afterwards, and that's the bit I wouldn't be able to stomach.'

'Maybe it won't go any further. If she sees you're not keen, she might settle for one of the other girls, one who'd jump at the chance as Muriel did.'

'Aye maybe,' Vicky said, fervently hoping that would be the case.

Vicky awoke with a start to find a hand clamped over her mouth. Miss Ganch, torch in other hand, was staring down at her. Terrified, she swallowed hard and waited for the hand to be removed.

After a few moments it was, and Miss Ganch crooked a beckoning finger. She then padded off down the dormitory, pausing at the entrance, waiting for Vicky to catch up.

It had come at last, the summons Vicky had been dreading. Why else would Miss Ganch wake her in the middle of the night, and with such secrecy? Shaking, she followed her to her room, where Miss Ganch shut the door and switched off the torch. 'I was sitting here all alone and thought I'd like to talk to somebody. Hope you don't mind?' Miss Ganch declared, giving a thin slash of a smile.

'No, miss,' Vicky replied, wondering what else she could possibly have said!

Miss Ganch dropped her gaze to stare – hungrily, it seemed to the apprehensive Vicky – at Vicky's body. 'Why, you're shivering, my dear, but it is midnight, and this is December.'

Going to her wardrobe, a fairly new acquisition, she took out a beautiful cream quilted robe, which she brought to Vicky. 'Slip this on, it'll soon warm you up.'

Miss Ganch helped Vicky with the robe, tying it at the waist for her, and smoothing the material down at the shoulders where it had become momentarily bunched. Vicky wanted desperately to scream for help, but knew that would have been futile. She might have brought people running, but what then?

'Would you care for a drink? I'm on whisky myself.'

'Perhaps a small one,' Vicky replied, forcing a smile.

Miss Ganch poured the whiskies, and handed Vicky hers, which was anything but small. 'When we're alone together, you can call me Jo,' she said.

She didn't look at all like a Jo, Vicky thought. Jo was a nice name; hers should have been something horrid, such as Gertrude or Senga. Vicky had always considered Senga a particularly horrid name, associating it with a girl she had once known who'd been a proper nasty piece of work.

'Yes, Jo,' Vicky replied unenthusiastically.

'How did you enjoy your hot bath the other day?'

'It was tremendous.'

'Those crystals make all the difference, don't you think? So relaxing.'

'Yes, Jo.'

Miss Ganch drank some whisky, then slowly licked her lips in an overtly sensuous and vulgar manner. Laying her glass aside, she picked up the riding crop and began running a hand up and down it, stroking it as if it was a male sexual organ.

Vicky stared, fascinated and repulsed at the same time.

'There are lots of little treats I could put your way if I had a mind to,' Miss Ganch purred.

Vicky wondered if she should say straight out that she wasn't interested, that she didn't want to know. She held back, hoping that she would be able to refuse in a more oblique fashion.

'Treats that could make your stay at Duncliffe far less harsh than it's been up until now,' Miss Ganch continued, hand still moving up and down the riding crop.

Vicky gazed into those palest of blue eyes, which had taken on a hypnotic quality. They made her think of the sea in summer, still and enticing.

'All you have to do to earn my gratitude is show a wee bit of affection,' Miss Ganch murmured, voice now low and husky.

There was a charisma about the woman that Vicky had not before been aware of, and which was now reaching out to envelop her. Nor had she realised that Miss Ganch had such lovely skin, skin that would be smooth and silken to touch.

Miss Ganch's bosoms started to rise and fall. Staring at Vicky, she imagined her naked; the vision was so exciting that it made her belly twist inside. She glided over to her. The breath caught in Vicky's throat when Miss Ganch kissed it. Then a hand delved inside her robe first to touch, then caress, a thigh.

That broke the spell. For the past few moments she had been the rabbit mesmerised by the snake, the prey transfixed by the predator, all set to be devoured.

'No, please,' she pleaded, and pushed down on the hand, trying to thrust it away.

But Miss Ganch was not to be so easily put off, and in the tussle that followed Vicky lost her balance, and went tumbling to the floor, Miss Ganch falling on top of her. With a quick and strong yank, Miss Ganch tore open Vicky's robe and nightdress so that her breasts were exposed.

Vicky knew she was no match physically for Miss Ganch; the bitch was just far too strong for her. There was only one thing she could think of that would possibly stop this. Her nails sank into Miss Ganch's cheeks and ripped downwards, gouging furrows in the flesh as they went.

Vicky's legs were leaden. She was sickeningly tired, not having slept a wink after fleeing Miss Ganch's room. She had lain in bed waiting for the wrath she had been certain was about to descend. So far, it hadn't.

At reveille Miss Ganch had behaved as normal, blasting on the whistle, flinging the curtains open, causing the section to go like the clappers to avoid being last dressed.

Her cheeks did not look as bad as Vicky had feared they would; the gouge marks were obvious, and would later be a matter of intense discussion and speculation amongst the section, but they were not the horrendous wounds that had grown in Vicky's imagination during the early hours of the morning.

Vicky's feet pounded sand. The section was halfway through the morning run, and she was third from last. So far Miss Ganch had said nothing to her, and Vicky had avoided her gaze when it swept her way.

'Jenny Connors, move your arse!' Miss Ganch suddenly shouted, and the riding crop cracked home on the named girl's backside.

Vicky winced. From the sound of it, that had been a particularly vicious swipe – even harder than the sort Miss Ganch normally ladled out.

The castle courtyard, and end of the run, was in sight when Vicky stumbled and measured her length on the ground. Winded, she lay there, unable to move until she had caught her breath. Those girls who had been behind her flashed past, leaving her last. She was gulping in air and attempting to struggle onto her knees when Miss Ganch came up to her. She was for it now, she thought. She had given Miss Ganch the opportunity she must have been praying for.

Out of the corner of her eye Vicky saw the riding crop begin to descend and gritted her teeth in anticipation of the blow. The first of many, she was convinced.

Wonder of wonders, the blow turned out to be a mere tap, a tickle on the rump.

'Come along, Devine, come along,' Miss Ganch said sweetly.

Vicky couldn't believe it; there was to be no thrashing after all. Had she been forgiven? It seemed so. Hardly able to credit her luck, she staggered back to her feet and finished the run.

Vicky was in Mrs Gardener's class, busy on a shorthand exercise, when the crunch came. A girl arrived to tell Mrs Gardener that the Head wanted to see Vicky straight away in her office.

It had to be about what she'd done to Miss Ganch, Vicky thought grimly as she left the class. There had been no reprieve after all; it had no doubt amused Miss Ganch to let her think that there had.

'Enter!' the Head called out when she knocked the office door.

The Head was seated behind her desk, with Miss Ganch standing to one side. There was no expression on Miss Ganch's face but her eyes were as cold as charity.

The Head adjusted her spectacles, a gesture that reminded Vicky of Ken, then leaned forward and fixed Vicky with a baleful glare. 'I warned you the day after you arrived at Duncliffe that if you stole anything while here you'd rue it,' she said softly.

'But I haven't stolen anything!' Vicky exclaimed, thrown by the accusation. It wasn't at all what she had expected to have to defend herself against.

'You attempted to,' the Head went on.

Vicky glanced at Miss Ganch, then back at the Head. 'I swear on my word of honour that I did no such thing.'

Miss Ganch snickered. 'Word of honour, indeed!'

'Are you attempting to deny that, while Miss Ganch was out of her room late last night, you entered it and were about to steal a bottle of her perfume when she returned and caught you in the act?' the Head elaborated.

'I never touched her perfume last night. I was in her room, but at her invitation,' Vicky replied.

The Head's gaze slid sideways. 'Miss Ganch?' she prompted.

'I was having trouble getting to sleep and decided to have a bath. I was about to get into the bath when I realised I'd left my book behind. I put on my dressing gown and returned to my room, where I surprised Devine in the act of leaving it. She was holding a bottle of my perfume which she was clearly in the process of stealing.

'When I challenged Devine about this, she pleaded with me not to report her, but I said I had to, the offence was far too serious for me not to do so. When she saw I meant that, she flew into a berserk rage and attacked me, the results of which are all too evident. That is a true account of what happened,' Miss Ganch said.

'It's not true at all. It's a complete lie, coming from a dirty lesbian who tried to seduce me last night!' Vicky burst out.

'So you admit you did attack Miss Ganch?' the Head said.

'I didn't attack her. I was defending myself. She was sexually assaulting me, and digging my nails into her cheeks was the only way I could think of to make her stop, and get off me.'

'Lesbian, sexual assault! What utter nonsense and total fabrication,' Miss Ganch hissed.

'You were trying to bribe me. You said that, if I slept with you, you'd make life at Duncliffe easier for me, that you'd give me lots of little treats, as you put it,' Vicky retorted.

'The girl's not only a thief but an accomplished liar as well it seems,' Miss Ganch said to the Head.

'I'm not the liar. *You* are!' Vicky yelled.

'Then it's her word against mine as to what happened,' Miss Ganch said, continuing to look at the Head.

173

Seconds ticked by. The Head exhaled, long and slowly, then rose. 'Follow me, Devine,' she said, and went to the door, where she paused, waiting for Miss Ganch to open it.

Vicky knew what was going to happen to her, what her punishment would be. She had known it when the girl arrived in Miss Gardener's class to say she was to report to the Head.

The Head went first, Vicky behind her, and Miss Ganch behind Vicky. They walked like that, in a straight line, one behind the other, till they arrived at the black-painted door which was the entrance to the Black Room. The Head unlocked the door and it swung open.

The room was as Vicky remembered it: square, with no windows. There was no lightbulb, nor gas mantle, nor any other form of illumination. There was the same army-style cot, but in a different position. On the cot, at one end, were two neatly folded blankets and a pillow. At the other end of the cot, and underneath it, was the chamber pot, now empty and clean. The smell of disinfectant impregnated the air.

'Go in,' the Head commanded.

Vicky, heart hammering, the small of her back prickly with goosebumps, stepped inside.

The Head stared at Vicky, then turned to Miss Ganch. 'How long for?'

Miss Ganch pondered that. Then a malicious, evil smile twitched the corners of her mouth upwards. 'Till my face is completely healed,' she pronounced.

The black door was then closed, leaving Vicky in total and profound darkness. She knotted a hand into a fist and stuffed the fist into her mouth. It wasn't fair, it just wasn't fair! Damn Ganch, damn the bloody cow to hell! With that, Vicky crawled onto the cot and wept.

Day and night ceased to have meaning for her. There was only darkness, punctuated at intervals by the brief coming of light and the food that went with the light. Seconds of precious blinding light. One second, two, three, four, five, six . . . Bang! The door was shut again, and she was plunged once more into darkness.

Then, out of the void, and smiling, Ken came. He had a surprise for her, he said, handing her the most enormous bunch of red roses. No, not the flowers, he laughed, and from behind his back produced a small box of the type one gets from a jeweller's shop.

She opened the box and gasped. It was an engagement ring boasting a solitary diamond, but what a diamond. It was the size of a pullet's egg! He'd promised her a diamond ring, he said, and he wasn't a man to fall down on his promise. No, sir!

She told him the ring was gorgeous, and hugged him close. He replied that that wasn't all; he had something else to show her.

The next thing she knew they were in a house in Parr Street – *their* house, he proclaimed, just waiting for them when they were married. Literally dancing with joy, she went from room to room, saying that the bed would go there, her dressing table over there, and here would be the sofa, while there would stand the table and chairs they would have to buy.

Then, out of that same void from where Ken had emerged, slithered Miss Ganch, human above the waist, a snake below, hissing that she would destroy Ken and the house, and all Vicky's dreams. As she cackled horribly, Miss Ganch's tail whipped through the air to encoil Ken and, with him firmly trapped, she began to squeeze, intending to squeeze him to death.

But Ken, screaming to Vicky that she wasn't to fear, that she could always depend on him, made a titanic effort and burst free of his entrapment. Somehow he gathered the writhing and screeching snaky Miss Ganch above his head and bore her to the window. He tossed her out the window, where, hissing and cackling horribly, and screeching all at once, she fell from view. Quick as a wink Vicky was in his arms. There she was safe and secure, and with him would be so for ever.

After that Ken came often, and with each visit stayed longer and longer.

The door opened and light flooded the Black Room. This time it did not bang shut again almost immediately. Vicky forced herself to concentrate. She saw a hazy figure, then another. She blinked. The light was hurting her eyes.

'Enjoyed yourself?' Miss Ganch asked, and gave a low, cruel laugh.

Vicky sat up on the cot and tried to focus. But everything remained blurred. Why was Ganch here? Was this to be a taunting session? She tried to make out who the other figure was, but couldn't.

'Punishment's over. My face is healed,' Miss Ganch stated.

It could be another lie, with the door to be slammed shut on her when she attempted to leave, Vicky warned herself.

'Nothing to say, Devine?'

Vicky did not reply. Was that other figure Tina? She thought it might be.

'Take her to the showers. She stinks like a pig, a pig who's been wallowing in shit,' Miss Ganch said and walked away.

It *was* Tina who was now beside her, embracing her. 'I can't see very well,' she whispered.

'That'll soon clear.'

'Do I really smell that bad? I've grown used to it, I suppose.'

Tina glanced down at the brimming chamber pot, which had only been slopped out twice since Vicky's incarceration. 'You smell worse,' she replied.

Vicky laughed tremulously. Good old Tina! 'How long?' she asked.

'You may be interested to know you hold the record. You've been in here for twenty-four days,' Tina answered.

'It seemed like twenty-four years.'

What a state Vicky was in, Tina thought. She was nothing but skin and bone. She had a sickly, haunted pallor, with dark bags under her eyes. What the poor darling must have been through, she shuddered to think!

She helped Vicky to her feet, then put an arm round her. 'You'll feel a lot better after you've had that shower,' she said sympathetically.

Vicky found that she was terribly weak, and was thankful for Tina's support. Initially anyway, she wouldn't have got far without it.

'We all knew you were in the Black Room, but not what for,' Tina said as they made their way, Vicky staggering, down the corridor.

In a few terse sentences Vicky told Tina what had happened in Miss Ganch's room that fateful night, and the false charges brought against her the following day.

'I thought your disappearance into the Black Room and those rip marks on Ganch's face had to be somehow connected,' Tina remarked.

Vicky halted by a partially open window and gulped in some chill January air. Oh, but it was good! A gust of wind swirled round them, and that was even better.

They resumed their journey to the showers, where Tina left Vicky while she dashed off for a towel. Vicky slowly stripped, the first time she had had her clothes off since going into the Black Room. The buffeting water was ice cold as always, but she welcomed it as it dashed away the stench of the Black Room. Using soap, Vicky scraped and scoured her skin till it tingled and glowed.

When she was done, Tina wrapped a towel round her, and they sat. Vicky, her sight rapidly improving, though her eyes remained sore, saw that Tina, without being told, had brought her a fresh set of underwear and clothes.

'I wouldn't have survived that hole if it hadn't been for Ken's visits,' Vicky said, her voice strangely hollow.

Tina stared at Vicky in astonishment. 'What visits?'

'He came to see me a great deal. We'd talk and laugh and do things together. It was his love that kept me sane, in an insane sort of way.'

'You mean you *imagined* he came to see you?'

Vicky gave a wry smile. 'In that room reality and

imagination become mixed. There were times when, try as I might, I wasn't able to tell whether I was awake or asleep. The two states, like reality and imagination, had become indistinguishable.'

'You're saying he seemed real to you when you imagined him there?'

'As real to me as you are now,' Vicky replied, and smiled, her smile both wan and ethereal, for she had not yet fully returned to the world.

'Love, his for me and mine for him, that was my saviour,' Vicky added after a while.

Tina then got Vicky dried and dressed and took her off to the dining hall for tea.

After tea, it being a Sunday evening, Vicky and Tina went for a stroll, and Tina brought Vicky up to date on all the gossip.

Hannah McCrimmond was Miss Ganch's new special friend, who went along to Miss Ganch's room on 'pash' night. And, for no reason the section could figure out, Miss Ganch had changed the route of the morning run to what was generally thought by the section to be an easier one . . .

Tina was still waffling on when they returned to the dormitory, where another bit of fuss was made of Vicky by those who had not yet spoken to her since she had come out of the Black Room. Holding the Black Room record as she now did, she was something of a heroine.

'Oh, by the by, there's some mail under your pillow that came when you were locked away. I put it there waiting your release,' Tina said.

Vicky's eagerly groping hands quickly found the letters. The writing on the envelopes told her that two were from her mum, the third from Ken. She tore that open first.

Her body froze as sharply as it had under the shower. Then she felt numb in mind and body alike.

'What is it?' Tina asked.

Vicky attempted to reply, and found she couldn't. She salivated and tried again. The words came out in a dry crackle. 'It's all off between Ken and me. He's found someone else. He's going to marry her. The date's been set for next month.'

'Oh shit!' Tina swore softly.

Vicky knew she had to get out of there, she had to be alone. 'I'm going for another walk . . .'

'Let me come with you?' Tina interrupted, suddenly scared stiff by Vicky's expression.

'No. I want to be by myself.'

'All right, but you won't do anything silly will you? Swear to me you won't.'

Vicky rubbed her forehead. She could not think. Then it dawned on her what Tina meant. 'I won't do anything silly,' she promised, her voice so low that it was barely audible.

Tina did not believe her. 'You can go on your own, but I'm tagging along behind to keep an eye on you.'

It didn't matter to Vicky what Tina did; it didn't matter to her what anyone did. In fact nothing at all mattered to her any more. In a stunned daze, totally unaware of what was going on around her, she left the dormitory.

But Ken loved her. *Loved her!*

Covering her ears with her hands, she ran, shrieking at the top of her lungs, along the beach.

Shortly after lights-out someone slipped into bed beside her. She stiffened, but only slightly.

'Don't take this the wrong way. I just thought . . . well, I thought you might appreciate a cuddle,' Tina whispered.

'Oh, Tina!' Vicky choked in reply.

Tina took her friend in her arms and rocked her as she would a baby.

They were clinging together when Vicky, riven with grief and pain but finding comfort and succour in Tina's embrace, eventually drifted into a fitful sleep.

Vicky stared at the infamous Duke Street jail for women offenders. It was made of grey sandstone punctuated by small barred windows. It was the bleakest, and grimmest building she had ever seen. It was 25 March 1937, the day after her eighteenth birthday, and the day after her sentence had been reviewed.

Miss Ganch had had her final revenge. She had submitted an adverse report on her, a report that had made the review board decide that she had to serve her sentence in full. As she was now too old for borstal, it meant that she had to serve the remaining seventeen months of her sentence in an adult prison – the dreadful place now in front of her.

Lines from an old Glasgow street song crowded into her mind, a song she recalled singing often as a wee lassie:

> There is a happy land
> Down in Duke Street Jail
> There all the prisoners stand
> Tied tae a nail
> Ham and eggs you never see
> Dirty water for your tea
> There you live in misery
> *God save the King!*

Prodded from behind, she stepped through an opened door set in one of the huge pair of iron-studded wooden gates.

The door crashed shut behind her.

Part Three

A Night Full of Mystery
1940–41

'The night is full of mystery,
whose understanding is
In trying no more to understand.'

WILLIAM MONTGOMERIE, *Estuary*

Six

A lump clogging her throat, Vicky gazed down Parr Street, thinking that it was far smaller than she remembered – smaller, meaner and dirtier. It was the first time she had been back since that awful day four and a half years ago when she had been arrested at Copland and Lye. High above the Parr Street roofs floated a barrage balloon, one of the many tethered thereabouts. They had been there since shortly after the declaration of war four months previously.

A man walked by, giving her a curious glance as he passed. His name was Waddell and he lived in number 22. He had not recognised her.

Picking up her suitcase, she headed for her close. On reaching it she paused to look over and up at what had been Ken's window. She wondered how he was and where he was living. Another house in Parr Street perhaps? If he was, she would take digs elsewhere.

The smell rekindled a thousand memories. The Glasgow tenement close has a unique smell – though, as with fingerprints, no two are exactly the same.

She stopped outside the family door and put down her case. What if she wasn't welcome? What if the family didn't want her any more? There was only one way to find out. She chapped.

Mary answered the knock. 'Aye, can I help you?'

Vicky didn't reply, but waited.

Mary gave a sudden exclamation, took a step backward and clutched at her throat.

'Vicky? Is it really you?'

'It's me right enough, Mum.' Vicky was so overcome with emotion that she could hardly get out the words.

'I wouldn't have known you. You're so . . . changed,' Mary said.

'It's the suntan and Yankee clothes that do it.' Vicky smiled. Through misty eyes Vicky noted that Mary had aged a great deal. Her mum had grown old and, like the street, somehow smaller.

With a sob Mary threw herself at Vicky and clutched her daughter to her bosom. 'Oh, lass, it's so good to see you,' she whispered, tears cascading down her face.

'And it's good to see you, Mum.'

They finally, reluctantly, broke apart and Mary, tears continuing to flow freely, wiped her nose with a hanky she had luckily had in her pinny pocket. 'Let's away in then,' she said, and attempted to lift Vicky's case.

'Don't you dare. It's far too heavy for you,' Vicky admonished, and took the case from her.

Vicky's heart seemed to turn over as she entered the house she'd been born into, and brought up in. If going into the close had rekindled a thousand memories, going into the house rekindled a million.

'I'll put the kettle on,' Mary said and began filling it at the sink.

There were a few new bits and bobs in the kitchen, but not many. On the whole the room was as it was when Vicky had left. Lovingly she caressed one of the wally dugs sitting atop the fireplace mantelpiece. These had been treasured possessions of her mum's as long as her mother and father had bided in Parr Street.

'So where have you been and what have you been up to, and why did you do a vanishing act when you got out of Duke Street?' Mary demanded.

Vicky laughed. 'One question at a time, eh?'

'As you asked in your letter just before you got out of Duke Street, we never came to meet you on your release. We waited here for you, at home. But you never came.'

Vicky sat in a chair by the fireplace. A fire had been laid but not lit. It was ready for her dad when he returned from work. It was a well-stacked fire, which would give a cheery, welcoming blaze when it got going. Her dad hated a green fire.

'When I wrote that letter, I still thought I might be able to come back here, but when I was actually faced with it, I just couldn't. That was why I didn't want you there: I might have felt obliged.'

'Was it because of Ken Blacklaws?'

Vicky nodded.

'Aye, we thought it must have been that. But nonetheless, you might have had the decency to tell us where you'd gone, and what you were doing. You must have known how worried and anxious we were, and have been ever since.'

As Vicky had been expecting, there was anger in Mary's voice.

'I should have at least written, I can't deny that, but . . . Every time I sat down to do so, something stopped me and I couldn't write a damn thing. I think, at the back of my mind, and purely because of Ken, I wanted to sever all connections with my past – with Glasgow, Scotland, and even Britain as a whole,' Vicky said quietly.

Mary stared at her daughter, beginning to understand just how deeply she had felt for Ken. *Had?* she wondered.

'As you're here the day, do I take it you're now over him?' Mary asked.

'I think I am. In fact I'm certain of it,' Vicky replied with as much conviction as she could.

'Is there anyone else now?'

Vicky gave a tight smile. 'No.'

Mary set out two of her best cups and saucers, the service she used for special occasions. 'So what did you do after Duke Street?' she queried.

'I landed a position with the Ellison Line as assistant to the purser,' Vicky answered.

'You went to sea! Help ma bob, I'd never have thought of that,' Mary exclaimed.

'The *Atlantic Star*, that was the ship I was on. We did the South American run,' Vicky explained.

Without saying anything, Mary got out the tea caddy.

Then she demanded, 'So now you finally have returned to Glasgow, is it for good, or what?'

'For good, and I'd like to stay here again, if you'll have me, and depending,' Vicky replied.

'Of course we'll have you lass. But what do you mean "depending"?'

'Do Ken and his wife live in the street? I couldn't bear staying here if they did.'

Mary could well understand that. 'They don't. Ken moved away when he got married. I couldn't say where, but certainly not locally. His folks have moved as well. They flitted to Largs shortly after the marriage. Mr Blacklaws found a job there, so they packed up and went off down the coast.'

'In that case I'll have my old bed back again,' Vicky said.

The kettle was now singing, so Mary turned off the gas and made the tea, putting the pot in a nice cosy she'd knitted herself.

'When war was declared, I thought I'd stay on at sea, at least for a while, but then our sister ship, the *Atlantic Sun*, was torpedoed off the Azores, and that was that. Because the war had made it too dangerous, the company decided to stop employing female personnel. All of us were to be paid off when the ship reached a home port. In the circumstances, it seemed to me right and proper to come home to Glasgow,' Vicky said.

Mary poured the tea and handed Vicky a cup. 'Were there many killed on this *Atlantic Sun*?'

'All on board,' Vicky answered softly.

Mary sighed. She had been Vicky's age when the Great War was fought – the war to end all wars, as it had been called at the time. What terrible destruction had been wrought then, and now it was starting all over again.

'Talking of ships being sunk, do you remember Ian Holt? Him that lived in Glebe Street and whose father worked at Agnew's?'

Ian had been very swarthy, Vicky recalled. But his disposition had belied his looks. He'd had a right sunny personality. 'I remember him well.'

'He joined the navy eighteen months or so ago, and was

186

on the *Royal Oak* when it was sunk in Scapa Flow last October. He was one of the eight hundred and ten that were lost,' Mary said.

Ian had kissed her once, long before she had met Ken. Vicky offered up a silent prayer for his soul.

'And what about my dad, how's he?'

'Just fine, never better. He was made a driver last year, which he much prefers to conductoring. And it pays more too.'

'And John?'

Mary's face clouded over. 'He got a grand job as an apprentice monumental sculptor with J. & G. Mossman in Cathedral Street after he left school, but as soon as war was declared the silly bugger broke his apprenticeship and went for a soldier. He's with the HLI.'

John a soldier! Who'd have believed it? Vicky still thought of him as the wee lad he'd been last time she'd seen him, the day of her arrest. For John had never been allowed by George and Mary to visit her at Duncliffe. With something of a shock she recalled that there was only two years between her and John, which made him eighteen now. It was just that he had always *seemed* so young beside herself.

'He's over in France with his regiment,' Mary added, a catch in her voice.

Vicky pondered that. 'Has he seen action yet?'

'Not so far, but he's bound to before long. You know the reputation of the HLI. If there's fighting, the Glasgow boys will eventually be in the thick of it. During the last war their casualties were horrendous.'

Vicky sipped her tea. It was fairly weak tea and tasted best without milk. Her mum had always made it like that.

'When will Dad get in?'

'In about an hour. Is he going to be chuffed!'

Vicky gave a smile as weak as the tea. 'Do you think it'll come round to him having to go?'

Mary's eyes filled with fear, fear that had already caused her endless sleepless nights of late. 'He's not all that far off fifty, which of course is in his favour. I suppose it all depends on how this thing works out. If the war's a short one, then he should be all right. But if it drags on, and casualties mount, then it might well be he'd have to go into uniform.'

Vicky and Mary continued to talk, catching up with one another, till there was the sound of a key turning in the front-door lock.

Mary had already lit the fire, which now glowed brightly, giving out an intense heat. Just the fire for a man to come home to after a hard day's work in bitter January. Vicky stood up, smoothed down her dress and folded her hands in front of her.

'Hello, Dad, how's yourself?' she said when George walked into the kitchen.

George came to an abrupt halt to stare at her in astonishment. 'You're back then, girl,' he said slowly.

'Aye, Dad, I'm back.'

'For good too,' Mary added, beaming.

He took off his hat and laid it aside. Then he went over to Vicky and embraced her.

He'd grown old too, Vicky thought. But not as much as her mother had. 'You're a driver now, I'm told. Congratulations,' she said.

He held her at arm's length, studying her, drinking her in. Tears crept into his eyes. Vicky could not remember ever having seen her father weep before. Glasgow men just didn't.

'Here's me greeting like some big wean,' George said and crossed to the fire, ostensibly to warm his hands but really to give himself a few moments to pull himself together.

'That was quite a shock,' he said huskily.

'She chapped the door right out of the blue, no word of warning or anything,' Mary said.

'I wanted to surprise you both.' Vicky smiled.

'Well, you certainly succeeded with me,' George said, keeping his back to her while he struggled to regain his composure. How he'd dreamed about this! There had been dark times when he had almost come to believe that he would never clap eyes on his daughter again, that she had gone out of their lives for ever.

'She's been at sea, as a purser,' Mary said to George.

'*Assistant* to the purser,' Vicky corrected.

George rubbed his hands and sat. 'You can tell me your story, young lady, while your mother gets the meal.'

Mary frowned. 'I should have thought, but forgot in the excitement. I haven't got enough in to include Vicky. I'll have to hurry round to the shops.'

'Tell you what, I'd love a fish supper, fish supper with black pudding. How about us getting three of those, my treat?' Vicky proposed.

'Are you sure?' Mary queried, thinking that she would prefer to cook something herself for Vicky, something special for her homecoming.

'As far as I'm concerned, a fish and black pudding supper would be perfect. Followed by some French cakes. You wouldn't have any of those, have you?'

Mary laughed. Vicky had always had a soft spot for French cakes. As a young lassie, given half the chance, she would have eaten them by the barrowload. 'The City Bakeries will still be open. I'll pop in and get a box.'

As her mother was getting ready, Vicky delved into her case to produce a bottle of bourbon, which she gave to George. 'That's Yankee whisky, I thought you might like to try it.'

'You two have a dram while I nip out and get the doings,' Mary said. When she left the house a few minutes later, she had a ten-shilling note of Vicky's in her purse, Vicky insisted it was to be her treat.

'You'll be going after a job then?' George said when Mary was gone.

Vicky watched her father pour the bourbon into thimble glasses, filling the glasses to the brim in Glasgow style.

'Aye, I'll sign on the Labour this Monday.'

'What sort of job will you go for, or will you settle for anything?'

'I'm an experienced shorthand typist and secretary. I'll go after a position as either of those.'

He'd forgotten that she had been taught shorthand typing at Duncliffe. 'You'll find there's a deal more work available in Glasgow than there used to be, and no doubt the war will create even more,' he said.

'So you don't think I'll have much trouble in finding something?'

He shook his head. 'Not in the least. As I say, it's changed days here.'

George swallowed the remainder of his bourbon and poured himself another. The taste was strange, alien to him. Not really to his liking, he decided. He wished she had brought a bottle of ordinary whisky – preferably Red Hackle, that was his favourite.

'How do you think the street will react to me?' she asked.

'Curious more than anything, would be my guess. Other than that, I would imagine their attitude to you will be as it's always been. After all, you're hardly the first jailbird we've had round here, you know. Townhead is fairly hoaching with them. Though, I must admit, you're the only female one that springs to mind,' he replied.

Vicky winced to hear herself described as such. But it was true: she was an ex-jailbird. She had not intended to tell her parents the truth of the matter, but now she decided she would. Why should she keep faith with Ken when he hadn't with her!

She knew that her father was deliberately being light-hearted about her having been in borstal and prison, but at the time, and probably even yet, he had been mortified by her supposed stealing – and undoubtedly, though he had never said it, had considered that she'd brought dis-honour on the family, dishonour and black disgrace. And the lightheartedness, the attempt to make it easy for her? Because her dad still loved her dearly. Despite everything, neither he nor her mum had stopped loving her.

Later, when Mary had returned, and the meal had been consumed, she requested that they all sit round the fire. When they were settled she proceeded to tell them what had really happened at Copland and Lye, and why she had done as she had. When she was finished, it was just as well for Ken Blacklaws that he had moved away from Parr Street.

For, if he hadn't, and George had been able to lay hands on him, George would probably have murdered him.

'Vicky! Vicky Devine!'

Vicky was hurrying along Parliamentary Road, having just been to sign on at the Labour. Halting, she turned in the direction of the voice that was hailing her.

He came charging across the Parli Road, nearly running slap bang into a coalman's horse and cart.

He stumbled at the kerb, almost sprawling his length on the pavement, which made her laugh. My God, he hadn't changed! Then she had a closer look at his face and saw she was wrong: he had.

'Hello Neil,' she said.

Neil Seton smiled hesitantly. When he'd spied her across the road, his calling out had been spontaneous. 'I heard you were back, the street's buzzing with it,' he told her.

They stood gazing at one another, sizing each other up.

'Your plooks and blackheads have disappeared. I promised you they would eventually,' she said.

'You did that, I remember. They've been gone a couple of years now. It was just like magic. One week they were there, virulent as ever, the next gone, never to return.'

He paused, then tapped his head. 'Touch wood,' he added.

It wasn't only that his skin was now clear as a bell: his face itself had altered somehow, sort of filled out, she thought. The effect was to make him quite handsome. And his hands – she'd noticed those when he'd tapped his head, those too were different. They had become long, slim and elegant; the type of hands she would have imagined belonging to a concert pianist.

'You look absolutely terrific,' he said. He was on edge, apprehensive inside, waiting for the tirade.

'You don't look so bad yourself, a big improvement on what you were.'

Neil blushed.

'Does it embarrass you, me saying that?'

'Not really, I know I was very much the ugly duckling

191

when younger. Mind you, it was those damn spots that were to blame, they were the bane of my life.'

Vicky resumed walking, and Neil fell in beside her.

'You're back to stay I hear?' he said.

'That's right.'

'I'm pleased about that. You were sorely missed.'

'Was I?'

'Oh aye, very much so.'

'If you include yourself in that, how is it you never came to visit me? I appreciate Duncliffe was a fair bit away, but not Duke Street.'

Neil glanced sideways at her. Still no signs of anger, no tirade. Had Ken kept his mouth shut after all?

'I always meant to visit you, but somehow never did,' he replied weakly, lying.

'I suppose your studies and new grand friends at university kept you busy,' she jibed.

He cleared his throat. He didn't want to pursue this. What he did want was to find out whether or not she *knew*. 'Did Ken ever mention me when you were at Duncliffe?' he asked, trying to make the question sound casual.

Vicky had to think about that. 'Not that I remember. Why?'

Relief surged through him. She *didn't* know. 'Nothing important, just wondering,' he replied vaguely.

He had become something of a dish, Vicky thought. It was he who had mentioned the ugly duckling, but hadn't the ugly duckling turned into a swan!

'Are you still studying?'

'I finish in June, five years' hard labour!' he replied with a laugh, which died when he saw her expression.

'Sorry, that was hardly the right thing to say in the circumstances . . . eh . . .' He shut up.

'And then what? Will it be straight into the forces?' she asked, initially put out by his tactlessness, then finding it rather funny, but not showing that she had. She recalled that Neil had aye had a talent for sticking his foot in it, a talent that he apparently retained.

Neil's lips set into a thin, stubborn line. 'This bloody war is a proper nuisance. My next step should be to work in a junior capacity for a law firm, but whether that will come about or not I don't know. After I leave uni, my call-up papers could come at any time,' he said bitterly.

'The war is going to interrupt a lot of lives, Neil. Yours will only be one of many. And it's going to do more than interrupt some, it's going to terminate them,' she admonished.

'Aye, you're right,' he conceded, but his lips remained thin and stubborn.

They walked a little way in silence. 'Speaking of Ken, do you still see him since he moved?' Vicky asked.

Neil thought back to that hellish night when Ken had given him such a terrible kicking in the rear-close dunny. He had thought that he would never walk again, and for a whole week his testicles had been swollen to the size of golfballs. If it hadn't been for the neighbours investigating his screams, the bastard might well have gone on to kill him. They had never spoken after that night, the night of the day Vicky had been arrested.

'No,' he replied tightly.

'What, did you fall out then?'

'I went to university and he got married. You know how these things are,' Neil prevaricated, and shrugged.

'And what about you? Have you married?' Vicky asked, thinking that, looking as he now did, the lassies at the university must be falling over themselves to get their claws into him.

Neil shook his head.

'Winching surely?'

'Oh aye, but no one special. They come and go, whole strings of them,' he said airily.

She wasn't sure whether that was true or not. It certainly *could* be.

'You were at sea, I'm told,' he went on, changing the subject away from himself.

'That got round quick enough!'

'Aye well, you know what it's like,' he replied, giving her a lopsided grin.

She talked about the *Atlantic Star*, about some of the people she had met and known and the exotic ports she'd visited, and recounted various anecdotes, till they arrived outside her close in Parr Street.

'It's been great seeing you again, Neil,' she said, offering her hand to be shaken.

He ignored the hand. 'There's a dance on at the uni this Saturday night. They're usually quite wild and fun. Do you fancy going?' he asked, trying to be nonchalant about the invitation yet sincere at the same time.

That caught Vicky on the hop. 'Are you certain you want to take me? You being a budding lawyer and me with my shady past?'

He hadn't thought of it that way. All he'd thought was that he'd be taking out Vicky, the same Vicky he had fallen for years ago, and for whom his feelings had never changed.

'I'll knock your door at seven sharp,' he said and, without waiting for a reply, he wheeled about and strode off across the street to vanish into his close.

Well well well! Vicky thought. And she fell to wondering what it would be suitable to wear for a university dance.

THE HONOURABLE SOCIETY OF DOCK WORKERS, the brass plate proclaimed. Vicky had found the address she had been seeking. She climbed the broad stone steps and went inside. Returning to the Labour Exchange that morning, she had been told that they had fixed her up with six interviews, three for that day, three for the next.

The place could do with a good cleaning, she thought, eyeing the grimy walls and ceiling. She doubted that it had seen a fresh lick of paint in twenty years or more.

'Can I help you?' a friendly-faced lassie asked, emerging from a doorway.

Vicky explained who she was and why she was there. The lassie took her through to an ante-room, told her to have a seat, and left.

Five minutes later a different girl poked her head round the door. 'Will you come with me please, Miss Devine. Mr Fyfer will see you now.' The girl smiled.

Vicky went back out into the carpeted corridor, which they started along. 'Is Mr Fyfer your personnel manager?' Vicky asked.

'We don't have a personnel manager. All personnel matters are handled personally by Mr Fyfer, the union president,' the girl replied.

She was to be interviewed by the union's president! Vicky was impressed.

The girl misinterpreted Vicky's expression. 'Don't worry, he'll not eat you, he's awful nice.'

They left the corridor to go up a twisting, carpeted stairway. The building might be a bit run down, seedy almost, but it had an atmosphere which Vicky decided she liked. She could tell that the folk who worked here were happy to do so.

Vicky judged Mr Fyfer to be in his late fifties. He had an honest, couthy face which she took to straight away. He was of middle height, and powerfully built, and he radiated energy. His office was in a right clutter. There were papers, diagrams, maps and all sorts strewn everywhere.

'Pleased to meet you, Miss Devine,' he said in a strong working-class accent, and ushered her to a seat that had already been placed in front of his desk.

He made a gesture that encompassed his office. 'Excuse the mess, but I can't function properly when everything's neat and tidy. Find it too constraining,' he apologised.

Mr Fyfer sat behind his desk and contemplated Vicky from underneath shaggy eyebrows. 'The Labour Exchange sent me a letter that said you'd been to sea. That could be useful to you and us if you came to work here.'

'The same thing crossed my mind as well,' Vicky replied, quite relaxed in Mr Fyfer's company.

'You've come ashore because of the war, is that it?'

'The company decided to discontinue employing women after we lost a ship,' Vicky explained, and went on to give Mr Fyfer all the details of her engagement with the Ellison Line.

Before the Ellison Line, she said, she had been at college, learning shorthand and typing, and before that unemployed since leaving school. She passed over her reference from the captain of the *Atlantic Star*, and her shorthand typing diploma, which Mrs Gardener had arranged, as Mrs Gardener did with all the girls at Duncliffe who passed the course, to be in the name of a well-known and established college.

After that Mr Fyfer asked her to take dictation, a short letter of six paragraphs only, which he rattled off at speed. When he had completed his dictation, he asked her to read back what she had taken down.

She clearly passed that test, so he took her to the typing pool, where she was introduced to three girls, then given a typewriter and told to type the letter. On finishing, she removed the letter and copy and gave them to Mr Fyfer, who studied them closely.

They returned to the corridor outside the typing-pool room, and there Mr Fyfer extended a hand. 'Thank you for coming in, Miss Devine,' he said.

Vicky shook the proffered hand. He wasn't going to say one way or the other, but that was normal practice.

'Can you find your own way? Or shall I have someone take you?' he asked.

She guessed correctly that the question was a trick, and another test. He was trying to find out if she had any initiative.

'I can find my own way no bother, thank you.' She smiled.

He gave the slightest nod of approval and left her. Going back to his office, she presumed. She quickly located the twisting stairway and went down to the ground floor. Her interviews for that day now completed, as she headed for the front door she began thinking about her first interview of the next morning, at William McPhail & Co.'s Violet Grove foundry in Grovepark Street.

Hearing voices, one of them raised in anger, she came up short in sudden shock as it dawned on her whose the angry voice was. No – it couldn't be, she was imagining things! she told herself. Hesitantly, heart thudding in her chest, she slowly walked in the direction of the noise. At a corner she stopped, took a deep breath and looked round it.

The two men were about a dozen feet down the passageway, and both were in working clothes. The one in half profile facing away from her, and now shouting loudly, was Ken Blacklaws.

'No ifs and buts. You'll do as your shop steward tells you, and that's the finish of it!' Ken ranted.

Some girls appeared at the far end of the passageway to stare anxiously at the two men.

The angry exchange continued, the other man having begun to shout as well. Vicky stood transfixed, her emotions churning within her. She was hot and cold at the same time, and there was a strange whistling in her ears. Ken! *Her* Ken!

Then she reminded herself that he wasn't her Ken any more, but another woman's, his wife's. She forced her legs to uproot themselves and move. Once past the passageway she broke into a run. In the street she collapsed against some iron railings. The inside of her head was whirling, and it seemed to her that at any moment she could faint clean away. She could still hear his voice, bellowing from inside the building.

The man at the Labour gazed at the sheet of yellow paper he was holding. He was thin and very pale, and made Vicky think of a fish that was more dead than alive.

'Congratulations. Of the six jobs you went up for, four have offered you a position,' he said without smiling.

'Which four?' Vicky asked.

The man told her. The Honourable Society of Dock Workers was third on the list.

'And I'm at liberty to choose between them?' Vicky thought this was a far cry from the days when she had first gone looking for a job.

'Of course. The usual thing is to go for the firm paying the highest wages,' the man said, not even a hint of smile or expression on his face.

'And which firm is that?' Vicky queried. Dreading to hear the answer, whatever it was.

'The union. The Honourable Society of Dock Workers. They'll pay a full pound more than the others.'

Vicky closed her eyes. There it was on a silver platter: the chance to see Ken again. But did she want to see him? She just did not know.

What she did know by now was the reason he had been at the union headquarters. From inquiries she had learned that he was now a dockie, having left Copland and Lye some time back. So he would have been at union headquarters on union business – a dispute of some sort that he'd been involved in, from what she had overheard.

Just because she had seen him there once didn't mean he went often, she argued with herself. It was entirely possible that, working there, she would never run into him again.

Then there was the money to consider. An extra pound a week was not to be turned down casually. Why the hell should she lose out because of sentiment? Because of an affair she had once had with a union member?

The truth was, she further argued with herself, she would be plain daft to turn this job down. For, of the six jobs she had been up for, this was the job that, because of the people involved – forgetting Ken – and the atmosphere, had attracted her most.

Then a niggle of anger asserted itself. She had lost so much already on account of Ken flaming Blacklaws, why should she lose this opportunity also! So what if she did bump into him occasionally! For a big city, Glasgow could be an awfully small one. No doubt she would have bumped into him from time to time in the normal course of events anyway. Sod him. An extra quid a week was an extra quid, after all!

Vicky's eyes snapped open. 'I'll take the job. When do I begin?' she said.

Later, having thought over her argument with herself, Vicky knew that it was not fully convincing. Partially so, but not fully.

She really did not know whether or not she wanted to see Ken again.

She did.

Then again she didn't.

She was due to start work at the Honourable Society of Dock Workers that coming Monday morning.

The sweat was running off Vicky, a combination of the exertion of dancing and the heat of the hall. Neil, sweating also, suggested they sit down and have a drink. He found an empty bench and parked her there. He left her staring round when he went off for the drinks.

Vicky was thoroughly enjoying herself: the band was good, and Neil had turned out to be a fine dancer. She smiled at him when he returned carrying two pint glasses. Nor was she the only female who had smiled at him that night: he was popular with the girls, as she had thought he would be.

'I hope you like scrumpy,' he said, handing her a pint.

She knew scrumpy to be extremely strong cider, but this was the first time she had ever had any. She took a swallow, decided she liked its slightly sour taste, and took a deeper swallow.

'Don't down it too quickly. That stuff bites back,' Neil warned her.

'Sometimes I enjoy being bitten,' she replied, eyes glinting with amusement.

He stared at her in open admiration. Jesus, but she was gorgeous! – if anything, even more so than she'd been when younger. But there was now a sad, haunting quality about her that hadn't been there before. It made him ache inside when he noticed it.

He tore his gaze away from her and glanced out over the dance floor, which was filled with hundreds of heaving bodies.

'The middle class at play, God bless their cotton socks,' he said.

'Aren't you one of them now?' she teased, keeping a straight face.

'No, I am not! I'm working-class through and through, and proud of it,' he retorted softly.

'That pleases me,' she told him. And it did.

He knotted a hand into a fist. 'There's so much wrong with Glasgow, and it just seems to get worse. Take the housing, for example. A lot of it isn't fit to keep pigs in, far less human beings. Parr Street is bad, but nothing compared to many of the tenements I've been in, as I'm sure you have. Some day they will all have to be swept away and decent housing constructed in their place.

'And employment, that's another thing. Oh sure, it's all right at the moment, as there's a war on. But what about after, when peace comes again? I'll bet you a pound to sixpence it'll be back to how we were before: a hundred men after one job, and ready to kill one another to get it.

'I'm telling you, Vicky, the ILP may be a spent force, but they had the right ideas. Their brand of socialism is what Glasgow needs, is crying out for. The old order must be dismantled and swept away for all time,' Neil said vehemently.

He took a quick gulp of cider, then hurried on. 'It breaks my heart to see what's become of this city. Even in our lifetime the decay has been enormous. It's horrible; it's like watching someone you love die slowly, and in great agony, of some terrible disease.'

Neil gestured at the dance floor and dancers. 'That's why that lot annoy me so much. Most of them were born with silver spoons in their mouths, and haven't the foggiest what poverty's like, the sheer degradation and humiliation of it. All they can think about is their silly selves, and their careers, and getting on and making money. Probably the latter more than anything.

'They're here tonight, surrounded by squalor, and I doubt if one in a hundred, even that, is aware of it. They . . . they disgust me. They disgust me and make me want to throw up.'

'You're a revolutionary, that's what you are!' Vicky declared when he finished.

'If I am, so what? There are times when revolutionaries are needed!'

'I'm not criticising, Neil, not in the least. As you say, the world needs men like James Maxton and Neil Seton. To voice its conscience, if nothing else.'

He laid down his glass. 'Let's go back up. If I keep on like this, I'll just get angry, and possibly boring, and ruin your evening.'

'I don't find politics boring, Neil. They fascinate me, and always have. I'd prefer to keep on talking if you don't mind.'

So they talked politics. Maxton, Brockway, Cripps, Churchill, Harry Pollitt, Baldwin, Morrison, Bevan, Attlee were only some of the names that were mentioned – and argued over, for Vicky didn't believe in everything Neil did. Though, she had to admit, they did see eye to eye on an awful lot of things.

They had the last dance together, the traditional slow waltz, then went home.

They stopped outside Vicky's close, with rain drizzling down, and Neil was suddenly nervous. He hoped it didn't show.

'Thanks for a marvellous evening,' Vicky said.

'How about us going to the pictures one night next week? Something local,' he asked hesitantly.

'Shouldn't you be studying?'

'Don't worry. I won't fall behind on that, not with my finals looming on the horizon.'

She decided that she would like to go out with him again. He had been excellent company, stimulating too. 'All right then.'

They made the arrangements. He would chap her door just after six on Wednesday night.

He took her hand. 'Can I kiss you?' he asked softly.

She pulled him inside the close and along to the dunny. There she offered up her lips.

Bliss! he thought as his lips touched hers. Absolute bliss!

On the Tuesday morning, Vicky's second day with the Honourable Society of Dock Workers, she was emerging from the ladies' toilet, when Ken Blacklaws walked by. He gave her a smile in passing. It was almost as big a shock for her as it was for him, but the difference was that she had known that the possibility of their meeting existed; he hadn't.

He was about to enter a doorway when he suddenly stood stock still. He whirled round to gape at her.

She had been watching him, waiting for his reaction. Now she crossed the corridor and went into the typing pool.

She sat down, put her hands on her typewriter, then hurriedly stuffed them into her lap, for they were quite visibly shaking. For a moment there she almost hadn't recognised him because of the elegant suit he was wearing. But why was he wearing a suit, and looking every inch an executive rather than the dockie she knew him to be?

Vicky rubbed her forehead. It hadn't been a daydream, had it? No, of course not, she assured herself. It had been him all right, in the flesh.

'Tea's up!' Madge Gallacher, one of the other three typists in the pool, said, and plonked a cuppa on Vicky's desk. As it was morning tea there was a plain biscuit on the saucer; in the afternoon it was a digestive. Vicky was halfway through her tea when the door opened and Ken entered. His gaze went straight to her and their eyes locked.

It was a titanic struggle for Ken, but somehow he managed to look away from Vicky. 'I've signed my letters, so this lot is now ready for the post,' he said to Madge, and laid a sheaf of envelopes in front of her.

His letters! *His* post! Vicky thought in alarm.

'You'd better meet our new typist,' Madge replied, and drew Ken over to where Vicky was sitting.

'This is Vicky Devine. Vicky, this is Mr Blacklaws,' Madge said.

What would he say? Vicky wondered. She would take her cue from him. She rose, but didn't utter. Ken licked his lips in apprehension. The eyes boring into his were far more mature than he remembered. And they seemed so accusing!

'How do you do, Miss Devine,' he croaked.

So that was how it was to be. They were going to pretend that they hadn't known each other previously. 'Pleased to meet you, Mr Blacklaws,' she replied in a neutral tone.

They shook hands; she was thankful that hers had stopped shaking. He had put on a bit of weight round the belly, and his hair had started to thin, she noted. He had kept his moustache, which was now thicker. And the horn-rimmed glasses were new.

They made the customary small talk for the circumstances, then he excused himself, saying he had to get on.

When he was gone, she picked up her cup and drained what remained in it. She was quite stunned by the happenings of the past few minutes.

'What does Mr Blacklaws do here?' she asked.

'He's the union's vice-president, and son-in-law to Mr Fyfer,' Doreen, the girl whose desk was nearest to Vicky's, replied.

Oh my God, what had she done! Vicky thought. How could she have been so incredibly stupid to land herself in such a situation! But how was she to have known what the set-up was? No one she'd spoken to about Ken had said he had anything to do with the union, so how could she have possibly known!

She went icy to think she might have to meet his wife. No, she just couldn't bear such a thing. She had made a horrendous mistake in accepting this job, and was now going to have to correct that mistake in the only way possible. She would give in her notice this Friday.

She started to copy-type a loading agreement but made such a hash of it that she had to abandon that effort and begin again. In the end she had six tries at the agreement before she managed a passable result.

Somewhere in the middle of this her hands resumed shaking.

She emerged from work to find it snowing heavily. Bowing her head against the flickering white wall, she hurried on her way. She had not gone far when she was suddenly grabbed by the arm. She gave an exclamation of fright, thinking she was being either attacked or molested. But it was Ken.

'We have to talk,' he said urgently.

She stared at him and didn't reply.

'There's a nice wee pub close by, we could go there,' he went on.

'Why should I?'

'Why shouldn't you? I was the one who let you down, after all.'

Oh you did indeed, you bastard, she thought, but didn't say so. Then she thought, why not! Wasn't that what she had wanted all along, and the real reason she had taken the job? Deep down she had wanted to see and speak to him again. It was the first time she had actually admitted that to herself.

'Lead on, MacDuff,' she replied.

They walked side by side, in silence.

She found the pub a disappointment. There was nothing particularly nice about it at all. It was no more than a very ordinary Glasgow boozer. She strongly suspected that this wasn't the pub he normally frequented in the area, but one where they were unlikely to be spotted together.

He brought the drinks over from the bar, a large whisky and lemonade each, and sat facing her.

'You've put on the beef, and I see the hair isn't what it was,' Vicky said, and smiled.

Her directness took Ken aback. Automatically he reached up and touched his hair. He was extremely sensitive and self-conscious about the fact that it was thinning. 'My hair's not that bad!'

Vicky arched an eyebrow.

'But I will admit to putting on a few pounds round the middle,' he said reluctantly.

She had him on the defensive, which had been her intention. It was a trick she had learned from Tina Mathieson.

'Did you know I worked for the union?'

She shook her head, for she hadn't. She had seen him in the building, but had not been aware that he actually worked in it. She would never have accepted the job if she had.

'So how did you come to be with us?' he probed.

'Through the Labour Exchange. I had an interview with Mr Fyfer, was offered the position, and that was that,' she replied.

Ken relaxed a little. It wasn't as he had feared. He had thought that she had deliberately come to work for the union in order to make trouble for him.

'Don't worry. Now that I know you work there as well, I'm going to give in my notice. I'll find another job,' she said.

That was a relief. Or was it? 'Probably for the best,' he muttered.

Remembering how she had clawed Miss Ganch's face. she had an intense desire to do the same to him, to inflict physical pain on him in revenge for the mind-bending mental anguish he had once inflicted on her. She saw him glancing surreptitiously at her left hand.

'No, I'm not married,' she said.

The hint of a blush stained his cheeks. 'I just wondered, that's all. I've often wondered . . .' He trailed off in confusion.

'How about you? Children?'

'A wee boy, five months old.'

'So your wife wasn't pregnant when you married her?'

That verbal stiletto thrust made Ken wince. 'No, she wasn't. Vicky . . .' He searched for words. Jesus, but this wasn't easy! It was because of him that she had gone to borstal and jail and, while she was there, he had ditched her.

'You were away for an awful long time. I suppose you might say I just couldn't last it out,' he said, the words stumbling from his mouth.

'You could have found yourself a fuck without having to marry her, surely?' Vicky retorted, being intentionally crude, and smiled again.

What remained of his blush vanished, and his face went stark white. 'It wasn't like that,' he mumbled.

'Oh? What was it like then?'

Vicky was not making this easy for him, but then he could hardly have expected she would. 'It wasn't merely sex, there was more to it than that.'

'You fell in love with her. Out of love with me, and in with her. Is that it?'

'Yes,' he lied, for he had never been in love with Lyn. He had married her for the career advantages that it brought him. Love had had nothing whatever to do with it.

Vicky fought back her bitterness and anger. 'What's your wee boy's name?'

'Kenny, after me.'

'Original,' she said scathingly.

'Aye, well. It wasn't my choice. It was Lyn's.'

Lyn, so that was his wife's name, now she knew. He had never mentioned it in the letter he had sent to Duncliffe, the letter breaking it off between them.

She downed her whisky. She'd needed that. And she'd have a repeat. She took her purse from her handbag and extracted a ten-shilling note, which she placed in front of Ken, 'Get another round in, will you.'

'That's all right, I'll do it,' he replied, pushing the ten-bob note back at her.

Her eyes snapped fury – fury caused not only by the dispute over who paid for the drinks. 'I said I'll pay for this round. Now will you please go up and get it in, or do you want me to go up to the bar myself?'

He saw her insistence on paying as an insult to him. For, as a man who was neither her fiancé nor her husband, it was his place to pay, his male place. Vicky saw it as a gesture of independence. He picked up the note and glasses, and left her.

When he returned with their refills, she sent him back again to the bar with hers to have more lemonade added to it. There was enough really; she was just cracking the whip a little.

206

'Are you staying in Parr Street with your folks?' he asked when he came back the second time.

'Aye, I am.'

'As you'll know, I moved out when I got married, and right pleased I was to leave the dump.'

Dump! How dare he! 'There might be a lot wrong with Parr Street, but there are some good folk live there don't forget,' she retorted.

'I wouldn't deny it, but then neither can you deny it's a slum. A place to get the hell out of when you've got the chance.'

'I suppose you live in a Bearsden mansion since you became vice-president of the union!' she replied sarcastically.

'Not yet, but one day, one day,' he mused.

'Still as ambitious as ever, eh?'

He couldn't help boasting, for he was proud of the fact: 'I've got letters after my name now. I'm an ACIBS.'

'Oh aye, and what's that, when it's at home?'

'It means I'm an Associate of the Cambridge Institute of Business Studies,' he explained.

Vicky was impressed, but didn't let him see that.

'It's a correspondence course that usually takes three years to complete. I did it in under two.'

Even if he had left school early, he had never lacked grey matter, she thought.

'I'm now studying for my Fellowship. Another eighteen months, maybe less, and I'll have that under my belt as well.'

'My, you have been busy,' she acknowledged in a voice that was ever so slightly mocking.

Vicky glanced down at her glass. She wanted to know more about the wife, was dying to know more. 'Where did you meet . . . Lyn, is it?' she asked, trying to make her question sound casual, as if the answer was of no consequence to her.

He told Vicky that they had met in a dance hall, which was true, if only part of the truth. He then went on to give Vicky a potted history of his life since that last letter he had sent to Duncliffe.

207

He had certainly fallen on his feet marrying this Lyn Fyfer, Vicky thought. It was on the tip of her tongue to ask him where he would be if she hadn't taken the blame for his thieving, but she restrained herself.

'And what about you? What became of you after Duke Street?' Ken inquired.

'So you knew I was sent there to complete my sentence.'

'I heard. But what happened? You always thought you'd get out, be set free, when you reached eighteen.'

How could she tell him about Ganch and 'pash' night? And particularly her incarceration in the Black Room, which she still had nightmares about? Or how could she tell him that for a long time after her release from the Black Room, and the time when he had broken it off between them, Tina had feared for her sanity? How could she tell a man who had spurned her these things? A man who had been the direct cause of her suffering?

'I got myself into a spot of bother, and having to complete my full sentence was the result,' she replied evasively.

'Bad luck.'

She closed her eyes and remembered Duke Street. Duncliffe had been awful. Duke Street, in a different way, ten times worse. She had had to endure things there that now made her shudder just to think of them. But one point in Duke Street's favour was that it didn't have a Black Room. She doubted whether she would have mentally survived another dose of that horror.

Ken glanced at his watch. 'I'll have to make a move. Can I give you a lift? I've got a car parked a few streets away.'

'I'll take the tram,' she replied, and pulled her coat back on.

Outside the pub he stopped to say goodnight, but she walked straight past him into the flurrying snow.

The tram rattled along, swaying and shoogling as it went. Vicky sat hunched against the cold, thinking about her conversation with Ken.

Then it came to her. Fallen on his feet marrying Lyn Fyfer, her Aunt Fanny! He had fallen on his feet all right, but not by chance. He had met this Lyn, seen the opportunity there was for him with her, and grabbed it.

Dockie to vice-president of the union: it all fell neatly into place. His next step would be the presidency itself. And how did she know this? Because she knew Ken Blacklaws, knew him for the opportunist he had always been. Did he love his wife as he claimed? Maybe he did, maybe he had even talked himself into believing he did. With Ken, that was entirely possible. So, the fact was he'd thrown her over for his ambition, not for another woman. The woman had been, and presumably continued to be, a means to an end.

Vicky took some consolation out of this knowledge. But only some.

Ken sat holding a large whisky, watching Lyn nurse wee Kenny as he suckled noisily and greedily at the breast. How contented she was since having had the child, how positively cowlike. Cowlike, passive and obsessed with the wean, obsessed to the point of ignoring all else.

He and she still had a sex life together – just. When he did get it, it was only after interminable pleading and cajoling, for she had lost all interest in lovemaking. Shortly after she had fallen pregnant, her voracious sexual appetite had, almost overnight, died right away.

He had hoped it would pass as she progressed in pregnancy. Then he had hoped it would pass with the birth of the baby. But here they were, five months after the birth, and still no signs of any sexual reawakening.

It wasn't only the sex – though Christ! that was bad enough – it was her whole attitude. Prior to her pregnancy, when she had been fun to be with, they had gone places together, done all sorts as a couple. Now she had hardly any time for him. The wean had become her entire world.

Ken lurched from his chair and crossed to the window. Pulling the curtain aside, he peered out. The snow had stopped, leaving the night crisp and clear. From his vantage point – the house was on a hill – he could see a good two-mile stretch of the docks. Over to the right was Merklands Quay, and he could just make out the floodlit stack of a cargo boat that his lads were in the process of unloading. They were doing it in conjunction with members of the Glasgow Wharf Workers' Association, one of the three rival unions.

When he had spoken to Jack Fyfer about amalgamating all four unions, Jack had said that the idea had merit but, unfortunately, was impracticable, as the other unions would never agree to it, not in a month of Sundays.

Make them agree! he'd said. When Jack had asked how, he'd replied: by any means it took. Jack had torn a strip off him then. There was enough violence in the world, he had admonished – this before the advent of war, though it had been brewing – without their adding to it.

Well, Ken didn't believe in such high-falutin moral principles. He *did* believe in taking what you wanted, by whatever methods were needed.

Jack pretended to be hard, but underneath it he was saft as shite. If only the old bugger would pop his clogs, he could step into the presidency and then . . . Oh, and then it would be a different kettle of fish altogether. He wouldn't just be president of a union; before long he would be master of the river and, as such, King of Clydeside. But Jack remained healthy and, by the union rules, Jack was president for life. Frustration welled in Ken, he wanted that presidency so much he could almost taste it. But while the old man lived, all he could do was drum his heels in impatience.

Vicky: his thoughts turned to her. And he began to cast his mind back, to remember.

He had started thinking about Vicky, and now he could not stop. Switching on the bedside light, he glanced at the alarm clock: three fourteen a.m., and sleep as far away as it had been when he had first come to bed. Beside him Lyn groaned, muttered something he couldn't make out and pulled the bedclothes up over her face. He switched off the light again.

He had so many memories of himself and Vicky, of the happy, magic times they had had together. And how marvellous she had been at lovemaking, far better than Lyn.

Even at her best, Lyn had never been a patch on Vicky. He thought back to the pub, to the exciting smell of Vicky. Her smell had always excited him. That cap of curls – he'd wanted to trickle his fingers through it, as he'd used to, and nibble an ear. She had always laughed when he did that.

He recalled the texture of her body skin, smooth as velvet, covered in soft, fine down. The skin itself had a sheen. He had adored stroking her all over; while he stroked, she'd lie with her eyes closed, sighing occasionally, loving every moment of the prolonged single caress.

A scene flashed into his mind: he and Vicky on a brae overlooking Loch Lomond. He remembered something he had done to her, and broke out in a cold sweat at the memory. That was something he'd never done to Lyn; she'd always forbidden it when he'd tried, saying it was disgusting.

Reaching under the bedclothes, he placed a tentative hand on Lyn's thigh. When she didn't object, he reached down, took hold of her nightdress, and rucked it up. Lyn grunted and made a sort of twisting motion. She tried to push his hand away.

'You'll enjoy it,' he whispered.

'Not tonight, perhaps tomorrow night,' she replied, annoyed.

'What's wrong with tonight?'

'I don't feel like it, that's why,' she said, and repeated the twisting motion.

'But I *do!*'

'Well, that's hard cheese,' she answered, her tone now one of irritation as well as annoyance.

'But it'll only take a minute, and I know you'll enjoy it,' he wheedled.

She sat up to glare at him in the darkness. 'Can't you take a telling, Ken? I said no, and I mean no. Now, will you leave it!'

With that she threw herself flat again, and within seconds was once more asleep. Ken knew she was asleep, for she had started snoring. She never did that when she was pretending.

Getting out of bed, he went to the toilet.

The next morning Vicky had hardly got her coat off when Ken breezed into the typing pool. He made a crack to Madge, making her laugh, then turned to Vicky.

'Right, Miss Devine. I'll give you a try out and see if you can do your stuff. Come to my office when you're ready. I have some dictation to give,' he said, and breezed out again.

'I certainly know what I could do with him given half the chance,' Madge commented to Joan, the fourth girl in the typing pool, and winked salaciously.

'You and me both,' Joan agreed.

It was clear that Ken had not lost his sex appeal, Vicky thought. He was still knocking the birds for six, just as he'd always done.

'What about you, Vicky, do you fancy him?' Doreen queried.

If only you lot knew! Vicky thought, and laughed inwardly. 'Doesn't do anything whatever for me, I'm afraid.'

'What sort do you like then?' Madge asked.

'*Unmarried* ones,' Vicky jibed, and left the room to the sound of laughter.

When she entered Ken's office, she could see right away how nervous he was. He had completely hidden that while in the typing pool.

'I really do have some dictation, but I wanted a word with you as well,' he said.

There was a chair set for her in front of his desk. She sat down and laid her notepad and pencil on the desk. 'I'm listening.'

'I've been thinking about you handing in your notice, and it seems so bloody unfair somehow. You've landed a tremendous job here, for old man Fyfer is terrific to his staff. He's a real joy to work for, the ideal employer . . . You get more holidays than other jobs, and a shorter working day, and it's double time if you have to work overtime or come in on a Saturday . . . Then again, there's the pay. He always pays more than anyone else, and usually by a fair whack at that.

'So, I was wondering, is it possible we could be friends?

We did mean a great deal to one another when we were together, and it seems to me that it would be criminal if all that went by the board.'

'Are you saying you don't want me to give in my notice?'

'I'm saying it would be a rotten shame on you if you did, for you'd lose financially as well as an ideal job,' he replied quickly.

He stared at her expectantly, but she didn't answer.

'If it would be any help, an inducement, so to speak, I could arrange it so that you get paid even more than you are now. Whatever your wage is, I could add another pound a week to it, and the other girls needn't know if you didn't want them to.'

That would mean two pounds a week more than she'd get anywhere else; it was certainly tempting, Vicky thought. But did she want to be in a position where she was seeing Ken day in and day out?

Ken hung his head. 'If you did stay on, it would make me feel a little less guilty about what happened. I can tell you, you've no idea *how* guilty I have felt about it.'

She was being plain stupid even to consider staying, Vicky thought. She should give in her fortnight's notice on Friday as she'd said she would.

'The last thing I want is for you to be done down yet again because of me, so please stay?' Ken pleaded.

'What about your wife. Does she ever visit here?' Vicky asked.

'She used to pop in occasionally, but hasn't since the baby was born. With the baby keeping her so busy at home, I expect it'll be quite some while before she does so again.'

Vicky studied the fingernails of her left hand. She had had beautiful fingernails when younger, but they had never been the same since Duncliffe and Duke Street.

'Does Lyn know about us?' she asked softly.

'She can hardly think I came to her unsullied and un-touched! But no names have been mentioned, ever,' Ken answered, making a bit of a joke out of it.

'And there would be no problem about the pay increase?'

'None at all, I promise you.'

She had heard his promises before, she thought grimly. She should turn him down out of hand, get the hell out as soon as possible. And yet . . . she'd lose at least a pound a week if she left, gain another if she stayed. And did it really bother her seeing Ken on a daily work-week basis? After the initial shock and panic, it wasn't that unnerving.

'So what's the verdict? Can we be friends and let bygones be bygones?' he urged hopefully.

'I'll think about it,' she prevaricated, and took up her notepad and pencil again.

The matter was closed for now, that was clear. Best not to try and push it any further, Ken decided. He switched his mind over to business and, after a short pensive pause, began to dictate.

Seven

Vicky and Neil were in her back-close dunny, having just returned from a local café. Neil had been able to snatch only an hour away from studying as his finals were now less than seven weeks off. They were kissing and cuddling to the accompaniment of a fearsome domestic row in a house close by. Smash, bang, wallop, scream! It wouldn't be long before the police arrived.

One of his hands slid onto her bottom, another sought a breast.

She pushed him away. 'If we don't stop now, you'll be in no fit state to go back to your books,' she said, laughter in her voice.

'Oh, Vicky, I enjoy nothing more than being with you. When I'm not with you, I can't wait to see you again.'

'I enjoy being with you too,' she replied.

He caught her nearest hand, raised it to his mouth and kissed it.

'Gallant,' she murmured.

'These Froggies and Eyeties aren't the only ones who can be that. We Scotsmen can be as gallant as the best of them.'

Neil was very caring, she suddenly thought. Caring, sensitive and considerate. Fine and admirable qualities all, and ones she much appreciated.

'I was hoping to take you to the pics on Saturday night, but I doubt I can: money's just too tight at the moment.'

She could have paid, but he would have been offended if she'd offered. 'It must be right rough for you and your mum at times.'

'Aye, it can be that, but up until now, thanks to my grant and a few other wee things, we've managed to get by, if only just.'

She had an idea that neatly solved the problem. 'Listen, my dad got hold of a slide lantern recently. Why don't you come to our house for tea on Saturday, and we can watch some slides afterwards, have our own picture show, like?'

'That would be great, Vicky.'

She would lay in a bottle of whisky for the occasion, she thought. Neil was not much of a drinker, but her dad never said no to a dram, and she and her mother appreciated a tipple as well.

'Till then,' she said, and kissed him lightly on the lips. They made their way to the front close, where the gas mantle was sputtering out soft yellow light, and there they had another quick kiss before Vicky ran up the stairs and he went across the road to his own close, and home.

Vicky found her parents in the kitchen. Mary was just finishing off the ironing, while George was mending a pair of his shoes with some good stout leather he'd managed to come by.

'So how was Neil?' Mary inquired.

'Looking washed out from all that studying he's doing, but it has to be done,' Vicky answered.

'Brainy lad Neil, always was,' George muttered.

'I've invited him to tea this Saturday, and I thought we might have the slides after,' Vicky said.

'Oh, so that's the way of it, is it? Getting his feet under the table now!' George exclaimed, tongue in cheek.

'No harm in that. Vicky could do an awful lot worse than Neil Seton,' Mary said primly.

George hefted his hammer. '*Is* it serious, lass?'

Vicky shrugged. 'I'm not sure.'

'Then it isn't?' Mary prompted.

'I didn't say that! I said, I'm not sure.'

George hammered in a nail, then another four in rapid succession. 'What about work? Any likely candidates for your affections there?' he asked.

'Why do you ask that?' Vicky replied sharply, alarmed.

George glanced up at her, wondering at the sudden rise in pitch of her voice. 'No reason other than you never speak of the place, or those who work there with you.'

Vicky had not told her parents about Ken being vice-president of the union and had no intention of doing so. She judged it better that way, for George held a bitter grudge against Ken because of all that she had gone through on account of him.

As for her continuing on at the union, the subject of giving in her notice had never been raised again between her and Ken since that meeting in his office three months back when he'd pleaded with her to stay. She had seen out the first week, then the next, and after that the matter had drifted. She had got the extra pound a week Ken had promised; he had kept his word there.

'I didn't realise I never spoke about work. Must be because everything there is fairly routine and boring,' she lied.

Her ironing finished, Mary put the iron by the sink to cool and wiped her sweaty hands on her pinny. 'Where's John's letter? I think I'll have a read of it again.'

The letter had arrived by the second post the previous day, the first word they had had of John for weeks.

'It's on the mantelpiece behind one of the wally dugs. Why don't you read it out loud? You wouldn't mind that, would you, Vicky?' George answered.

'No, in fact I'd like it,' Vicky said.

Mary found the letter and took it from its envelope. She read slowly, haltingly, her voice crackling with emotion.

John did not actually say that he had been in action, but it was clear from some of the things he mentioned that he must have been. He and a pal called Ginger had found a cache of French brandy, and John described how their squad had had a right old hooley on that before having to move on, taking a bottle each of what remained with them. The weather was not too bad where they were, and most nights they managed to sleep under a roof, which certainly made life a great deal easier than it might have been. The rations were dull but, so far anyway, in plentiful supply. From time to time they managed to buy, and in some cases 'liberate', local grub that augmented, and made an awful lot tastier, the aforesaid rations. He was in good heart, and missing them all. He couldn't wait to be back in Sauchiehall Street on a Saturday night – that, and to have a pint of real Scots heavy.

Mary finished the letter and dashed away a tear. George, face set hard yet somehow soft underneath, returned to his shoe mending.

'I'll put the kettle on,' Vicky said quietly.

Vicky and Neil were walking in Alexandra Park, the pair of them licking raspberry-topped ice creams in cones bought from a barrow run by a very worried-looking Tally, or Italian. The man had a right to look worried, for if Italy entered the war on the German side, as seemed likely, he'd be for internment.

They paused in front of the bandstand to stare at the empty stage area. Vicky could remember George and Mary bringing her here as a wee girl to listen to concerts and watch variety shows.

'Vicky?'

She turned to him, a smile on her face.

'Will you marry me?'

The smile wavered and slowly vanished. This was no horse-play; she could tell from his expression that he meant it.

She resumed walking, and he fell in beside her. When they came to a litter bin she tossed her cone into it; she had suddenly lost her notion for ice cream.

'You're not replying?' he asked anxiously.

'Neil, your finals are imminent. This isn't the time to propose to somebody.'

'I'm not proposing to just somebody. I'm proposing to the woman I love, and with whom I've been in love for the past six years,' he retorted.

She stopped to stare at him. 'You have?'

He nodded.

'I didn't know that,' she said, and resumed walking again. She had been aware that he fancied her ever since the Hogmanay night when he'd saved her from rape and called her the Princess of Poor Street. But to fancy someone was one thing; love was quite another.

'I didn't press my suit in those days because you were going out with Ken. I'd never have stood a chance against him with all those pimples and blackheads I had then. But it's different now, and we do get on so well together.'

That was true enough. And, as Mary had said, she could do a lot worse than marry Neil Seton.

'I'll be a good and faithful husband to you, Vicky, I promise that.'

Her mind was churning. She had thought that he was falling in love with her, not realising that he'd been in love with her all this while.

'What about the war?' she asked.

His face clouded over. 'I have to admit that's the one big drawback. Once I'm qualified they could pull me in at any time, but I doubt very much if I'll be seeing any of the fighting. With my training, they're bound to put me behind a desk – and who's to say that desk might not be in Glasgow or not far away?' he replied.

She was twenty-one now, and not getting any younger, she thought. Common sense told her to accept. Then again, she shouldn't be rash and rush into anything. Of course it had occurred to her to marry Neil but – because of the war, she supposed – she'd seen any possible marriage as some distance in the future, not here and now.

Oh dammit! She didn't know what to do. He had quite caught her on the hop. 'Look, I have to think about this. Will you give me a breathing space?'

His mouth drooped. 'That means you're going to say no.'

'It does nothing of the sort. Your proposal has come straight out of the blue. I just wasn't expecting it, that's all.'

They walked a little way in silence. 'All right, a breathing space,' he agreed grudgingly.

She slipped a hand into one of his. 'You're lovely,' she told him.

'You're not so bad yourself.'

She put his arm round her waist, and hers round his. They started talking about the National Government that

Winston Churchill had formed the previous month. Neither of them ever tired of discussing politics.

It was just before her lunch break the next day when the telephone call came.

'Vicky, it's your dad,' Madge told her.

Her stomach muscles instantly contracted: something had happened – it had to have done for George to ring her at work.

'What is it?' she asked him in a tight whisper.

'I was just about to leave for my shift when an army padre chapped the door. The 51st Highland Division took an awful pasting heading for Dunkirk apparently. The HLI were in a big fight at a place called St Valery. John and a lot of his mates were killed there.'

Her wee brother dead! She had gone cold and numb all over. 'Oh, Dad!' she whispered.

'Do you think you could come home? Your mother needs you.'

There was a choking sound. Vicky could not be sure, but she thought her father was crying. 'I'll be there as soon as I can,' she said, and hung up.

Madge, Doreen and Joan were banging away at their typewriters, engrossed in what they were doing. None of them had overheard her telephone conversation.

She could not just leave without asking permission. Mr Fyfer was out, but Ken was in. She would have to ask him.

He was in his office poring over a contract when she entered. He glanced up, readjusting his glasses as he did so. 'What can I do for you, Vicky?'

She swallowed back the hot bile that had seeped into her mouth. Everything seemed to have taken on a grainy quality, and why did Ken sound so far away, as if he were in another room?

'My brother John was killed trying to get to Dunkirk for the evacuation,' she said, and fainted.

When she came to she was sitting on a chair with Ken peering anxiously at her. 'Here, swallow some of this,' he said, and placed a glass to her lips.

The undiluted whisky made her cough.

'And again,' he said when her coughing had subsided, and held the glass once more to her lips.

The pungent alcohol helped revive her; it also started to reheat her cold body.

'I'm so sorry about John, Vicky. Really I am.'

Tears crept into her eyes. 'An army padre came to tell my parents. I've got to get back to them right away.'

'Aye, of course. But just take a minute to get yourself together again. Then I'll drive you to Parr Street.'

'That's kind of you, Ken.'

'Nonsense, it's the least I can do.'

'During the entire evacuation my mum went to church every day to pray. Not only for John, but for all our boys.'

'The papers say it was a miracle as many were saved as there were,' Ken commented softly.

She struggled to her feet, but it was too soon and her legs buckled under her. Ken caught her, holding her close to him.

'Oh, Ken!' she wailed, grief overwhelming her. She sobbed into his shoulder while he muttered words of comfort and stroked her hair.

It was as if the years had rolled back and Duncliffe and Duke Street had never been. She was in Ken's arms again; the feeling was the same, only more intense, as when she had stood at the head of Parr Street the previous January staring down it. She was home, back where she belonged.

Finally – and how she hated doing it – she broke from his embrace. 'I'll go to the cloakroom and wash my face and put my coat on.'

As she left his office, she was forced to admit to herself what she had been trying to deny and hide from this long long while. She was still head over heels in love with Ken Blacklaws.

Mary was the churchgoer, but it was Vicky who had organised the service, Mary being far too distraught to do so. All of Parr Street were present, and many from round about, for the family was a popular one, and John had been well liked. The Reverend Alan Chatto, who had baptised John, as he had Vicky, led the prayers for John's soul.

Vicky glanced over at Neil. She wasn't going to marry him. How could she, feeling the way she did about Ken? She had told Neil that, because of John's death, which she was using as an excuse, she would wait until after his finals to give him her decision. After all, she didn't want to upset him before his finals – she thought she owed him that much.

She raised her gaze to the gallery. Above Neil, and to her right, was Ken. There was a woman on either side of him, but she knew that neither of these was his wife, for she had seen him arriving alone.

Ken stared impassively back at Vicky, wondering how and when he was going to make his move for her. That day in his office when she had fainted after hearing about John's death had told him all he wanted to know. He was going to seduce Vicky again, and make her his mistress. He was determined about that, as determined as he had ever been about anything.

It was after the next hymn that George, quite by chance, caught sight of Ken. For a moment he did not recognise the face, then it clicked. Anger spurted in George: to think that his Vicky had gone to borstal and prison because of that bastard, and while she was there, saving his skin from long-term imprisonment, the bastard had gone and ditched her to marry another! This wasn't the time or place, but some day, George promised himself, he would see that fancy dan Ken Blacklaws again, and when he did he would have it out with him. And he wasn't thinking just about an exchange of words either.

George looked to the pulpit and bowed his head when the Reverend Chatto started to intone.

'Our Father, which art in Heaven . . .'

Vicky returned to work on the Monday following the service. The next afternoon Ken came into the typing pool.

'Vicky, I have to go to John Brown's and I'll need someone to take shorthand for me while I'm there. Be ready to leave in half an hour, will you?'

It was a fairly common occurrence for the girls of the typing pool to accompany Mr Fyfer, Ken and other union executives to meetings at the docks and elsewhere, so none of them thought this instruction odd in any way.

Ken drove the Riley himself. The union had a chauffeur, but Ken preferred to do his own driving. He always used the chauffeur, however, if he was attending an official function, for appearances' sake.

'How are your mum and dad?' he asked when they were under way.

'As well as can be expected in the circumstances. Mum in particular took it very badly, you know.'

'Yes, that was obvious in the church.'

She touched his left arm. 'Thank you for going to the service. I appreciated that.'

They headed for Clydebank, where the world-famous John Brown Shipbuilding yard was situated. 'By the way, I've got a surprise for you,' Ken said.

Vicky was instantly intrigued. 'What sort of surprise?'

'A nice one,' he teased.

'Does that mean you're not going to tell me what it is?'

He chuckled. 'It wouldn't be a surprise if I did now, would it?'

'Beast!' she murmured, wondering what on earth the surprise could be. As it turned out, she would never have guessed in a million years.

At John Brown's they went into the management offices, where Ken and a chap by the name of Dougie Glennie had a drink together. Vicky was offered one but refused, saying it was far too early in the day for her.

'Right then, where is she?' Ken asked when his drink was finished, standing as he did.

'Over at drydock four, that's the one by the east gate. Do you want me to take you there?' Dougie Glennie answered.

Ken shook his head. 'I know where the east gate is. We won't get lost.'

Ken and Vicky took their leave of Dougie. Outside the offices the yard was abustle with activity, the din tremendous. As she walked beside Ken, Vicky watched in fascination as a gang of riveters went about their work.

'Who's this woman you're meeting?' she asked.

'An old friend of yours. I've never met her before in my life.'

'A friend of mine! Is that the surprise?'

'That's it.'

Her mind raced. What friend could it possibly be? A school chum? Somebody she'd known at Copland and Lye? No, unless it was her cousin Sylvia.

Vicky recognised the ship the moment it came into view. It was the *Atlantic Star*, of which she had so many fond memories.

Ken laughed. 'I told you she was an old friend!'

'You remembered the name even though I only ever mentioned it to you once.'

'I did, and when I learned she was here for a refit I thought you'd like to come along and say hello.'

Men were swarming over the superstructure, which was not quite as she recalled it. She then realised that part of it had been removed. 'Why is she here?'

'Total refit. She's being turned into a troop ship, including having a number of guns fitted. Want to go aboard?'

'Can we!' Vicky exclaimed in delight.

'Everything's possible, when you know the right people. I'd already phoned Dougie Glennie before we came, and he's fixed it.' Ken smiled.

A gangplank which appeared a lot more rickety than it actually was brought them onto what had been the main passenger deck. Vicky pointed out to Ken where the swimming pool and the aft sun bar had been, both of which had now gone.

When they had had a good tour round the outside, Vicky marvelling at all the changes that had taken place, they went inside. She showed Ken what had been the ballroom, dining rooms and lounges, now all completely transformed. The purser's office remained as it had been, however, so Ken was able to see where she had worked.

'How about your cabin? Why don't you show me that?' he asked.

They plunged deep into the bowels of the ship to where the crew's quarters had been located, to discover that that area was still relatively untouched.

The cabin was tiny, eight feet by six, and without a porthole. 'It's nothing now, but I had it fine and cosy when I was here,' Vicky said wistfully.

It was funny, she thought, she had been in this cabin countless times thinking about Ken, remembering how it had been between them. And now here he was. Here they both were.

'Vicky,' he murmured, his voice husky, and swept her into his arms. They kissed, and kissed again. Then he nibbled her ear, which made her laugh, as he had known it would.

She read in his eyes what he wanted, and it was what she wanted too. But not like this, and not yet.

They kissed a third time, and this time it was she who kissed him, taking his head in her hands and pulling him to her.

'Did you plan this?' she asked.

'I planned to bring you to the ship when I found out it was here, I told you that,' he replied, playing dumb.

'That's not what I mean.'

He grinned. 'I must admit it did cross my mind, but how was I to know the cabin would still be here, and intact, with no workmen nearby?'

'I wouldn't put it past you to have arranged that.'

'I'm innocent, judge, I swear!' he exclaimed, and placed his open palms against her breasts.

Her insides went all soft while her nipples hardened into studs because it was Ken who was touching them – Ken, who had touched them and caressed them and loved them so often in the past.

'I can't, not for another fortnight,' she told him.

'Why a fortnight?' he queried, frowning.

With a sigh she turned away from him and took a moment to catch her breath. 'Because that's when Neil Seton's finals are.'

Ken's frown deepened. 'What has Neil and his finals got to do with it?'

'Neil has asked me to marry him, and I've told him I'll give him my decision directly after he's sat his exams. I'll be saying no, but it wouldn't be fair on him for me to get involved with you until I've done so.'

Ken sat on the bed and lit a cigarette. 'I'd forgotten he loved you. When I think about him, which is rarely now-adays, I only ever remember the other thing.'

'You knew that he loved me?'

'Oh aye. He told me the last time we spoke to one another, the night of the day you were arrested. I was chiselling him about what he'd done when he came out with it.'

'Done what?' Vicky queried.

'That's the "other thing' I just referred to. I don't suppose he's mentioned the telephone call he made to Copland and Lye?'

Vicky shook her head.

'He loved you and wanted me out the way. I stupidly, being drunk out my skull at the time, told him about my nicking while working overtime. He then rang Copland and Lye and put the finger on me. Only it backfired when you claimed it was you doing the nicking. So you've Neil to thank for your three years in borstal and jail!'

Vicky was dumbfounded. 'He's never breathed a word of any of this.'

'I'd be amazed if he had. I presume he's not aware that you and I work alongside each other?'

'No, I've never said. Not to him, or anyone.'

'So why should he mention it, then? As long as he believes I'm not about, how are you to find out otherwise?'

Now Vicky knew why Neil had never visited her in either Duncliffe or Duke Street. He had been afraid to in case she knew about his phone call.

She recalled how, when she had first met up again with Neil on her return to Parr Street, he had asked if Ken had spoken about him while she was at Duncliffe, and how relieved he had been when she'd replied in the negative.

Ken took a drag on his cigarette. 'Still feel you have to wait a fortnight?' He smiled.

She was sorely tempted. Then a pneumatic drill began clamouring nearby and blew temptation away.

'Forgetting Neil, when I make love to you again after all this while, I'd like it to be somewhere nice, where we can be romantic together. We certainly can't be that here, now can we?'

She was right, Ken thought. It would be a lot better in what she called somewhere nice. 'So you agree to us becoming lovers again?'

'I agree,' she whispered.

He threw what remained of his cigarette onto the floor and ground it underfoot. 'And the fortnight?'

'We've waited so long. What's another fortnight here or there? And in truth I'd be far happier if we did hold off till I can tell Neil. No matter what he's done, it would be on my conscience if we didn't.'

'All right, you're the boss,' Ken said, and stood.

Vicky unsnecked the door.

The evening after the last of Neil's exams Vicky arranged for him to come to her house. She also arranged for George and Mary to go out visiting.

'How do you think you did?' she asked, ushering him into the kitchen.

'Pretty well, but just how well I'll have to wait and see,' he replied, and tried to take her in his arms. But she wriggled free and went over to the sink, to put distance between them.

'What's wrong? Have I suddenly developed bad breath or something?' he joked.

'You'll never guess who I ran into the other day?' she said.

He raised an eyebrow, but did not reply.

'Ken Blacklaws.'

His face sort of crumpled in on itself and his body drooped. 'And?' he croaked, knowing what he was going to hear next and praying to God he was wrong.

'He told me what you did,' she stated, voice now chill.

Neil jerked like a gaffed fish. 'Fuck!' he swore softly.

'Neil, I can't possibly marry you now. You must be able to see that.'

She had been going to explain that, much as she liked him and his company, she just didn't love him. The telephone-call business made her refusal easier.

'No, I don't,' he mumbled, wishing he could think clearly, argue his case. But his brain had gone numb, refusing to function as he wished it to. Like sand running through his fingers, he could feel her slipping away from him.

'Have you any idea what I went through because of you? Three years of hell, Neil, three years of unmitigated bloody hell.'

He cringed. 'I never meant you to be arrested, that was all a horrible mistake,' he mumbled.

'I know. You wanted Ken to be arrested. Well, if he had been, I'd never have forgiven you for that either.'

'How can you say that about a man who had no respect for you? Who ditched you when you were inside?'

'I'm not going to defend Ken. What he did is between him and me. Now I think you'd better go, Neil. Goodnight and goodbye,' she said and turned away from him.

He launched himself at her, but she shrugged him off. 'I said goodbye, Neil,' she repeated, her voice a steel whiplash.

'Vicky?' he pleaded in a whisper.

Her lips thinned and set hard. She folded her arms in a gesture of finality.

When Neil was gone, Vicky burst out crying. She had hated doing that. Would she have married Neil if Ken hadn't happened along again, and despite the fact she didn't love him? She didn't know. She just did not know.

Vicky told Ken the next day that she had broken it off with Neil and he immediately asked her, winking as he did so, if she would work overtime that night. She replied that of course she would.

He came to the typing pool when everyone else in the building had left.

'I want to show you something,' he said, taking her by the hand.

Arriving at Jack Fyfer's office, they went inside. In one wall was a door which Vicky had always presumed belonged to a cupboard or suchlike. She could not have been more wrong. Ken opened the door and switched on a light. Vicky gasped. In front of her eyes was a beautifully fitted-out small apartment, including single bed.

'What's all this?' she asked.

Ken's eyes twinkled. 'How about "somewhere nice"?'

Vicky laughed and clapped her hands in glee. It was *very* nice. The fixtures, fittings and furniture were all of the highest quality and must have cost a mint.

Ken crossed to the window and closed the curtains, then he switched on the gas fire that replaced the original coal one.

'It's not such a mystery as it might seem. When Jack first became union president, he bought a grand house out in the village of Balfron, which is quite some distance from Glasgow.

'To begin with, Jack didn't find the drive home at night difficult, for he was leaving here at a fairly reasonable time. But then he started having to work late a great deal, and sometimes past midnight, and that was when the problems arose.

'It was a good hour and a half's drive home, and then the same back here again in the morning, which meant he was getting next to no sleep at all, and suffering from it.

'In the end it was Wendy, my mother-in-law, who suggested he have this room, which was a file room then, gutted out and done up so that if he felt it was too late for him to go home he could stay here.'

'And does he still?' Vicky queried.

'Aye, occasionally, but nothing like he used to. With the staff now being far larger than it was, and having a full-time vice president to help, his workload has been reduced considerably to what it once was,' Ken explained.

'But won't he know we've been in here?'

'We'll tidy up before we go, which should do the trick. My father-in-law is many things, but not one of your more observant men round the house, or apartment in this case. So what do you think? Perfect eh?'

'Couldn't be more so.' She smiled, and shivered in anticipation.

Ken poured them both drinks and, when she was sipping hers, switched off the light. The glow from the fire became their sole illumination.

They kissed lightly, butterfly kisses, and touched one another, she as eager to touch him as he her. She didn't say it, but she had had no one since the last time she and Ken had made love together. Nor had that been from lack of offers. She had had plenty of those while aboard the *Atlantic Star*, from crew and passengers alike. But she had remained celibate because she had not desired anyone that way – until Ken had come back into her life again, that was.

He slowly stripped her till she was standing naked before him. He nuzzled her left nipple, then the right. She stripped him, occasionally pausing to stroke and caress his skin as she did so. She laughed when he bent and gently bit her ear.

They sank to the floor and stretched out in front of the gas fire, its warmth washing over their bodies. It had been a long long time, she thought languidly as he moved within her. But it had been worth the wait.

Oh yes.

Neil, shoulders hunched, hands thrust deeply into his trouser pockets, walked through the night. All around him tenements loomed, foreboding and somehow sinister. He inadvertently kicked a can to send it clattering noisily along the pavement. A black moggie, which had been half asleep in a close mouth, jumped in fright.

He felt wretched, filled with despair. He wanted to shout and scream and knock down walls. He wanted Vicky, how he wanted her.

But he wasn't going to have her, not now, not ever. She had found out from sodding Ken Blacklaws about that damned telephone call, and that had been the end of her and him. If only he'd never made that telephone call! If only it had been Ken who had been put away, as he'd intended, and not Vicky! If only . . . If only . . . *If only!*

He'd have to get away from Parr Street, he decided. He wouldn't be able to bear bumping into Vicky from time to time. That would be sheer torture.

Suddenly he knew what he was going to do. It was inevitable anyway, so why not sooner rather than later?

Early the following Sunday evening Vicky turned into Parr Street having just returned from Springboig, where she had gone to try and re-establish contact with Tina Mathieson, something she had been meaning to do for a while.

She had found the address Tina had given her in Duncliffe all right, but the Mathiesons no longer lived there. According to a neighbour, they had flitted to Coventry eighteen months since, Mr Mathieson having landed himself a good job down there. Tina had gone with her family, the neighbour had been certain about that.

Vicky was lost in reverie, thinking about Tina, when Neil's mother materialised before her. Mrs Seton was in a state. She looked terrible. Her eyes were red and puffed from crying, and her face had a greyish pallor. She wagged an accusing finger. 'It's all your fault he's done what he has, Vicky Devine. You broke his heart, smashed it to smithereens, when you refused to marry him,' she said in a strident tone.

Remembering Mr Seton, Vicky was gripped by fear. Neil hadn't done anything stupid, had he?

'What's happened?'

'He's joined the army, volunteered. He left for Stirling yesterday morning,' Mrs Seton replied, sobbing.

Well, it wasn't what she'd dreaded there for a moment or two, Vicky thought with relief. 'He'd have had to go anyway,' she said.

'But not just yet, not yet a while!' Mrs Seton retorted, the beginnings of fresh tears glistening in her eyes.

'I'm sorry,' Vicky whispered.

'And so you should be.'

Neil clearly hadn't told his mother about the telephone call to Copland and Lye. Neither would she.

'He'll be killed. I know it. I know it! And I'll be left all alone in the world, no one to care for me, no one to think about me even,' she went on.

Vicky was not sure what Mrs Seton was grieving about most: Neil going into the forces or herself being left alone. She listened patiently while Mrs Seton ranted on. But finally, patience exhausted, she repeated that she was sorry about Neil but would have to away home now or her tea would be ruined.

Neil joined the army! That was a surprise, she thought, as she hurried down the street. Secretly she was pleased, though. It would have been uncomfortable having him about. She just hoped that he would be safe, for, despite what he'd done, she did not wish him any harm.

At least she had one thing to be thankful for: Ken wouldn't be going into the forces. He might work full time for the union, but that was strictly unofficial. Officially he was still a dockie, and as such in a reserved occupation. There would be no call-up for him.

She wondered which regiment Neil had joined. He should look very handsome in his uniform – he had the sort of male body that suited a uniform. He would probably be given desk work, some basic training and then desk work for the duration.

Summer gave way to autumn, and autumn to winter. During that time the Battle of Britain had been fought and won. But elsewhere the war was not going well for Britain and her Allies. At the end of September the Japanese had entered Indo-China, while a week previously, on 7 October, the Germans had entered Rumania. The outlook was bleak, but the national spirit remained strong.

The cold October winds were rattling the windowpanes when Ken visited Jack Fyfer in his office and told him what he had in mind.

Jack couldn't believe his ears. 'Strike! How can you talk about a strike when there's a war on and we've all got our backs to the wall!' he roared. Jack was a patriot through and through.

'It's precisely because there's a war on that we've got them by the short and curlies. Now is the time, when we can't be refused, to use our muscle to screw up our members' wages.'

Jack glowered at his son-in-law. 'None of the other unions would wear such a preposterous – and I may say, in my opinion, treasonable – notion. We'd be on our own.'

'I'm counting on that.' Ken smiled.

An infuriating smile, Jack thought. Old man or not, if Ken hadn't been married to his Lyn, he'd have wiped the smile off the bugger's face. 'How so?' he queried.

'When we win a large pay increase that'll mean our members are earning considerably more than the members of the other three dock unions. So what'll happen then? I'll tell you: an awful lot of members from the other unions are going to terminate their membership and apply to join us, which will boost our numbers at the expense of the other three.'

Jack shook his head. 'The other three would never allow that to happen.'

Ken and Jack fell to a furious row about the whys, wherefores and consequences of calling a strike; and, because of their diametrically opposed views, both men completely lost their tempers.

Jack Fyfer's stomach was killing him. He had already had three lots of antacid mixture but his indigestion remained as fierce as ever. He blamed Ken for the attack: what a ding-dong battle they'd had! He had felt totally drained afterwards, and a short while later the burning sensation had begun.

Jack let himself into the union building by the main entrance, carefully locking the doors behind him. Groping his way to the nearest light switch, he flicked it on.

He had just come from an after-work business meeting, and it was just as well he had had that meeting, for otherwise he would have gone home without his anniversary present for Wendy, who'd have been none too pleased. The row with Ken had driven the present clean from his mind.

However, he would retrieve it now from his desk, be driven home to Balfron, and that would be that. He wondered what Wendy had bought him. She had the knack of always getting something he really appreciated. It had been a watercolour last year, a rare volume of Robert Burns the year before that.

When he came in sight of his office, he stopped short. The door was open, the light blazing. He walked silently forward. Naked as the day she was born, and satiated with lovemaking, Vicky was lying in front of the gas fire. Her eyes were closed and there was a soft, satisfied smile on her lips. Ken had left her a few seconds previously to go to the toilet down the corridor.

She sensed, rather than heard, what she presumed was Ken's return. 'Hmmh!' she murmured, and jiggled her hips.

Jack stared at Vicky in shock and amazement. In his own little apartment, how dare she! How dare whoever she was!

Still smiling, Vicky opened her eyes. The smile turned sickly when she saw who was staring down at her. She sprang to her feet and threw herself at the place where her clothes lay neatly folded. Snatching up her blouse and skirt, she held them in front of her.

Ken, also stark naked, came striding into the apartment, to halt abruptly when he caught sight of Jack. His face drained to a milky-white.

'You!' Jack breathed.

'I . . . I . . .' Ken began, then trailed off, unable to think of a single thing to say in his defence.

Vicky dropped her gaze. How humiliating this must be for Jack, as Ken's father-in-law. She could well imagine what he thought of her.

Ken's usual glibness had completely deserted him. He might have been a naughty, tongue-tied schoolboy up before the headmaster.

'Tomorrow morning, eight o'clock sharp, the pair of you come and see me,' Jack said huskily, and walked stiff-legged from the apartment. He was to be halfway home before realising he'd forgotten Wendy's present for the second time that day.

Vicky took a deep breath, then another. 'I could use a very large drink.'

When Ken poured for them both his hands were shaking so much that he got more on the carpet than he did in their glasses.

Next morning, as instructed, they presented themselves in Jack's office dead on the stroke of eight. It had not been a good night for Vicky, but it had been an even worse one for Ken, who had seen the one big chance in his life disappearing down the plughole.

Jack fixed Vicky with a baleful look. 'You'll understand I can't possibly allow you to remain working here, Miss Devine. You're fired,' he stated.

Vicky bit the inside of her lip. It was what she had expected.

As had been agreed between Vicky and Ken, he didn't even attempt to speak up for her – that would have been stupid.

'Collect your bits and pieces and be out of this building as soon as you can. What wages and holiday pay you are due will be sent to you in the post. Now leave,' Jack said to Vicky.

She did as bid, without looking at Ken. They had already arranged to meet briefly that evening when he left work.

Jack pulled out his pipe and slowly packed it from an old, well-worn leather pouch. If it hadn't been for Lyn and wee Kenny, he would have sacked Ken as well, and been pleased about it, for he thought Ken far too ruthlessly ambitious.

'I won't have my daughter cheated on. Is that clear?' he said.

Ken nodded.

'You'll never see that Devine woman again or communicate with her in any way.' He paused and raised an eyebrow.

Ken nodded a second time.

'For, if you do, I'll tell Lyn what I saw last night: and, knowing my daughter, you'd then find yourself out on the street and cited for divorce.'

Jack used a finger to tamp down the tobacco in the

pipebowl. 'And if she throws you out, which I can assure you she will, you're finished with the union. Don't think you'd get a job as a dockie either. I'd make it my business to have you blacked along the entire length of Clydeside.'

Ken was sweating now. There was sweat running down his neck, under his arms and down the cleft of his buttocks.

'It was an aberration, Jack. It won't happen again, I promise you,' Ken pleaded. He didn't really give a damn about losing Lyn, or even the child come to that; but to lose his eventual ascendency to the union presidency – that was something else entirely.

'Not only will it not happen with Miss Devine, but it won't happen with any other female either. I'm going to watch you very closely, Ken, and from time to time, which you'll never know about, I'm going to call in some professional help to watch also.'

Having played his trump card, Jack lit his pipe and sat back in his chair to stare coldly at Ken. He was not bluffing about the professional help, and Ken knew it. He would instruct a company of private investigators within the week.

'Have you mentioned last night to Wendy?' Ken asked.

'No, it would only have distressed her.'

'So this matter is strictly between you and me and Miss Devine?'

'That's right.'

He was off the hook, but he had lost Vicky, for it was impossible for him to continue seeing and sleeping with her now. The price was quite unacceptable.

Jack was thinking, with grim satisfaction, that he now had a hold over Ken, an unspoken hold that would always be there in future dealings between the two of them. From now on he should have no trouble in remaining the dominant one in their relationship – and that domination had been under threat of late.

'Can I go now?' Ken asked meekly.

Jack made a chopping sideways motion with his right hand. Ken was dismissed.

*

Vicky glanced at her watch. It was just past knocking-off time. Ken should be appearing any minute.

Leaving the union building that morning, she had gone straight to the Labour Exchange to sign on and inquire about other work. The man who had interviewed her had not been at all happy to hear that she had been dismissed, and without a reference. He asked her the reason for her dismissal and, because she couldn't think of anything else that sounded plausible, she said that she had slapped one of the union executives for groping her. He had softened a little towards her then and promised that, even though she didn't have a reference, he would find her something. There was a war on, after all: workers were in demand.

After the Labour she had gone home and given Mary the same story. Mary had been furious, saying that she had done the right thing in slapping the dirty sod; if it had been her, she would have done more than slap him.

Vicky looked at her watch again. It was ten past now. Where was Ken? At half past it started to sleet. The sleet had a wind behind it that cut to the bone. Vicky shivered and continued to wait. Quarter to came and went. When a nearby church bell bonged the hour, she knew that he wasn't going to show.

He would get in touch, write to her, she told herself, as she headed for her nearest tramstop.

The entire advance was pinned down by murderous machine-gun fire that had already, in a very short time, inflicted a great many casualties. Under the command of General Wavell, they were attempting to take Sidi Barrani, a small town on the Egyptian coast roughly halfway between Alexandria and Tobruk. It was Wavell's intention that the capture of Sidi Barrani would start the annihilation of the Italian forces in Cyrenaica.

Corporal Neil Seton lay in a shallow depression in the sand while bullets whistled overhead and all around. To his left and right were the rest of his section, crumpled and sprawled where they had fallen. Most of them had to be dead, he thought, for they had been almost on top of the concealed machine gun before it had opened fire. Without medical attention, and in this unbelievable blasting heat, those who weren't soon would be.

Neil rasped a hand over an unshaven cheek. He was filled with fear and a terrible desperation. The spaghetti munchers would get him before nightfall: he knew that as sure as the Clyde flowed down to the sea. Fear, desperation and anger – anger that blossomed and grew.

The closing of Agnew's and his falling for Vicky Devine: the two disastrous watersheds in his life.

The closing of Agnew's, his father Malkie committing suicide, and the grinding poverty that followed. Poverty which at times had made him go off on his own and weep with frustration.

And Vicky – never a moment's peace since he'd fallen in love with her. To get to the point where he'd almost had her as his wife – and then Blacklaws, bloody Ken Blacklaws, had reappeared to blow the whole thing sky high by telling her about that accursed telephone call.

It was all so bloody unfair! What had he done to deserve such curses? He had suffered and been denied all down the line. From plooks and blackheads to a woman he was destined never to have.

His anger turned to fury. The only thing that had ever gone right for him was his going to university, but even his career had been snatched from him right at the very last, thanks to this war and Adolf bastarding Hitler.

Neil sobbed. Oh Vicky, I love you, I hate you, I love you.

Well, if he was going to die, he would do so in style. God owed him that, at least.

Private John Sullivan, shot through the pelvis and now lying doggo about twenty feet away, gaped when he saw Neil slowly come to his feet, heft his rifle and fixed bayonet into position, then move forward all by himself.

Tears ran down Neil's face as he went. He was only half there; the other half was back in Parr Street with the lassie he loved, his princess. He started to sing in a voice that was cracked and raw. 'I belong to Glasgow . . .'

•

Vicky came awake to discover that she was feeling nauseous again. This had been happening regularly since she had started work at the munitions factory. Mercifully it was Sunday, which meant a long lie-in. She twisted onto her back. Mary would bring her a cup of tea and the newspaper shortly. George was always up before his daughter on a Sunday, and read the paper first. She got it when he was finished.

She realised then that her breasts were sore. She felt a sort of tight, tugging sensation which, now she was aware of it, was really quite painful. She cupped her breasts and winced; the undersides were tender in the extreme. Now what had caused that? Was it another result of her breathing in daily doses of sulphur?

Perhaps it was best to look for another job. Her health had been acting up ever since she had started work at the factory. Why, she had even missed a period, her last, something that had never happened to her before. She had thought that her health would settle down after she had been at the factory a while, but it didn't appear to be doing so. Missed period, morning nausea, sore breasts, whatever next?

Suddenly she went very still inside and ran through those symptoms again. Could it be that she was pregnant and that what she'd seen as ill health had nothing whatever to do with the sulphur?

'Jesus!' she whispered, shocked.

Don't panic, she told herself. Could it be?

She thought of Ken. Why hadn't she heard from him! It was seven weeks since Jack Fyfer had sacked her. Surely he could at least have written – even if it was only to say that he couldn't see her for a while? She could not believe that he had abandoned her. After all, she hadn't asked him to leave his wife or precious union. She was resigned to being his mistress, and had told him so. She would give him more time to get in touch with her, but if he didn't she would contact him, she decided. There had to be a logical expla-nation for his silence.

Mary came bustling into the bedroom. 'You'll never guess

what!' she exclaimed, waving the newspaper in front of Vicky.

'Not until you tell me,' Vicky replied with a grin.

'There's a photograph of Neil Seton on the front page. He's won the Victoria Cross,' Mary announced.

'You mean our Neil, from across the road?' Vicky queried, dumbfounded at this news.

'The very same. He won it fighting the Eyeties in Egypt. There's a full account here of what happened.'

Neil had singlehandedly attacked a machine-gun post, bayoneting seven men to reach the post and shooting dead the two Italians manning it. Then, without waiting for help, he had made his way along a trench for several hundred yards, attacked a dugout and forced thirty-seven enemy soldiers to surrender.

In doing what he had, Neil had turned the tide of the battle in favour of the British by allowing them to break through what until then had been an impenetrable wall of bullets. The British had gone on to take their objective: the town of Sidi Barrani.

'Well, I'll be blowed. Our Neil. Who'd have thought he had it in him?' Vicky said, laying down the paper.

Then she remembered the Hogmanay night when he had faced up to the lads who'd had a mind to rape her. Maybe it wasn't so surprising after all.

'And apparently he came through it without even so much as a scratch,' Mary said in amazement.

He had bayoneted seven, shot two dead and gone on to capture thirty-seven others. Some desk job! Vicky thought.

There was a public phone box at the factory which Vicky was now making for, it being her morning tea break. She was going to ring Ken to tell him she was pregnant. She had missed a second period, her breasts had got larger and she had had to let out all her skirts. Thankfully the morning nausea had stopped.

Her heart was pounding as she lifted the receiver and put her money in. Nine weeks since she had last spoken to him – not that long really, but it seemed an eternity. She pressed

Button A when connected. Doing her best to disguise her voice so that the telephonist wouldn't know it was her, she asked to be put through to Mr Blacklaws. When the telephonist inquired who was speaking, she replied that it was confidential union business.

'Hello. Ken Blacklaws speaking.'

'Ken, it's Vicky. I . . .'

There was a click and the line went dead.

She took the receiver away from her ear and stared at it. She hadn't been accidentally disconnected by the telephonist – that had happened to her several times when she'd worked at the union, so she knew what it sounded like. No. The click was the giveaway. Ken had hung up on her. *Hung up on her!*

'Oh, you bastard!' she whispered as hot scalding tears crowded into her eyes.

She had been wrong. He had abandoned her.

Eight

Gibson Street had seen better and more prosperous days. These tenements had never housed working folk; it was not that sort of area. Shabby, down at heel, Vicky thought; that was how she would have described it. This wasn't a part of Glasgow she knew well, being as it was on the west side. Students lived here and arty-crafty types, and at least one struck-off doctor, the one she was going to see.

She had been told that Dr Sampson was the best abortionist in the city – a proper doctor, not some back-street wifey with a bottle of gin and a knitting needle. The last thing she'd wanted was one of those. He was pricey but, as far as she was concerned, it was worth it. She would have paid double what he asked to know that the person who aborted her had been properly trained. She had been recommended Sampson by a lassie whom she worked alongside at the factory. Elsie herself had used him, and swore by him.

Vicky crossed the street and entered the close of number 17. Today was only the examination. He would inform her when she was to return for the abortion itself.

Vicky, dog tired, was dozing in front of the fire when Mary, who had gone out to get three fish suppers for their tea, came bursting into the kitchen. George, sitting slumped across from Vicky, was also dozing.

'I've just heard. Neil Seton's in London being decorated by the King. He's coming home to Glasgow on leave. His mother says he's taking the night train and will be here the morn's morn,' Mary exclaimed excitedly.

Vicky yawned. Of late, thanks to her pregnancy, she couldn't get enough sleep. She would have slept morning, noon and night, given the chance. 'Decorated by the King himself. That's quite an honour,' she acknowledged.

George had also been wakened by his wife's return. 'And so the lad should be. He's a hero, after all,' he said.

'Mrs Seton says he was brought back so that the newspapers could photograph the King presenting him with his medal. He's to be in Glasgow for a month. That's the length of his leave,' Mary went on.

'I shall shake him by the hand when I see him. What he did was glorious, sheer glorious,' George said.

All the way through tea Neil was the main topic of conversation.

Vicky bumped into Neil two days later. Returning home from work, she was passing the Argyle Arms when he came out. 'Hello, hero.' She smiled.

Neil blushed to hear her call him that. He thought that she looked sensational. She seemed to be glowing with inner well-being.

'Have you lost your tongue? Or does a vc not talk to the likes of me, common as muck?' she teased.

'Don't be daft. You just caught me by surprise, that's all,' he stammered in reply.

She frowned. There was something wrong with his uniform. Then she realised what was bothering her. When she had read about him in the paper he had been described as a corporal; now he was wearing an officer's uniform.

'Congratulations on your promotion. What are you now?' she asked.

'A captain. General Wavell promoted me at Sidi Barrani to replace the man who'd been my captain, and who was killed in the battle.'

She had been right about him in uniform: he looked dead handsome. Really scrumptious.

Neil glanced at the door of the pub, then back at Vicky. 'How about a drink before you go home? To celebrate my promotion, if you need an excuse.'

She didn't see how she could refuse. 'All right,' she agreed, and with him smiling they went inside.

The idea came to her while he was up at the bar. She was going to Sampson's that Tuesday at eleven o'clock, and he had strongly advised that she have someone with her to take her home again. He had said that she would be weak and shaken after the operation. She had seen the sense in that, but her problem had been who to ask. Certainly neither George nor Mary; they didn't know she was pregnant, nor did she want them to find out.

There were pals in the street she could have approached but they would all be working, and she could hardly expect them to take a day off. Besides, pals or not, she wasn't exactly sure that she could trust them to keep their mouths shut afterwards.

Neil was the perfect solution. He was on leave, so there was no bother about time off, and being a man he wouldn't have the same compulsion to gossip as a woman would have. The only question was: would he do it?

When he returned she asked him about his visit to Buckingham Palace and what it was like meeting the King and Queen. She hung on his every word as he described the palace, the ceremony and what had been said by himself and the royals, both of whom he had found absolutely charming. She fired some questions at him. What had the Queen been wearing? Did she have much make-up on? Was the King really as shy as everyone said?

When they finished talking about that, Neil said he wanted to hear about her. The laughter vanished from his face when she told him she had had an affair with a man at her previous work, that she was pregnant by him and was going to have an abortion. She didn't say that the man was Ken Blacklaws.

Neil sat silent, plainly shocked, when she came to the end of her story.

'So, will you help me on Tuesday?' she asked.

Neil took a deep swallow of his pint, then another. 'What does the father say about you having an abortion?' he queried in a strained voice.

'He doesn't know. We'd already broken up before I found out I was pregnant.'

'Was it . . . you and he . . . was it serious?'

Vicky gave a grim, bitter smile. 'You don't break up when it's that,' she answered ambiguously, and Neil presumed that it was she who had done the breaking.

An abortion! Neil was appalled at the thought. It wasn't – well, it just wasn't right. 'It's murder, Vicky, you must know that,' he said softly.

Her smile widened. 'How can you talk about murder? You, who killed at least two men out in Egypt?' she mocked.

'That was different. They were the enemy, and we were at war. If I hadn't killed them, they'd have killed me.'

'What you did was still murder. The only difference between us is that your murdering was legal, whereas mine won't be.'

He swallowed more of his black and tan, and as he did so it dawned on him that Vicky's pregnancy explained the glow of inner well-being he'd noticed earlier. It was the radiance of expectant motherhood.

'You could have the baby,' he muttered.

'And bring further terrible disgrace down on my family? No, Neil, I couldn't do that to them. I just couldn't.

'And then there's me. I'd be branded a slut, a tart, easy game. You know what Glasgow's like. When it comes to that sort of thing, it's either black or white; there are no shades of grey. You're either a "respectable" lassie – in my case still respectable even though I've been to borstal and prison – or else a FALLEN WOMAN, and when they say those words they do so in capital letters. I don't think I could bear the sniggers, the sideways glances, the whispering behind my back. The laugh of course is that many of those who would be doing the sniggering, whispering and suchlike are at it themselves. They've just been lucky not to get caught out.

'Then there's the child to consider. He or she would be a bastard, literally. Remember Rossie Mair who went to school with us, and the hell he went through because he was a bastard? I can assure you I've no intention of allowing any child of mine to go through such purgatory.'

Neil minded Rossie well. He had aye liked Rossie, and would have chummed up with him if it hadn't been for his being a bastard, and therefore supposedly tainted. A particular incident was for ever etched in his memory. Poor Rossie being hounded round the playground by a great gang of lads all chanting, 'Rossie Mair's a bastard! Rossie Mair's a bastard! Rossie Mair's a bastard!' It had been horrible.

'How about flitting away from Glasgow to have it?' he suggested.

'And go where? I don't know anyone anywhere else. But, say I did move to another city to stay, how would I live? Who would look after the baby when I went to work?' She shook her head. 'No, I've thought this through, an abortion is the only way,' she whispered.

'It's such a hard decision,' he said.

'Don't you think I don't know that!'

'You want the baby then?'

'Of course I do, idiot. But it's impossible, a fact I've had to face up to.'

'And the father, there's no chance of the pair of you getting back together, and getting married? If only for the baby's sake.'

Her grim, bitter smile returned. 'I couldn't marry him even if I wanted to. You see, he already has a wife.'

Vicky finished her whisky and lemonade, and shuddered. She wasn't sure whether it was the drink that made her do that, or the conversation.

'So, will you help me on Tuesday?' she asked for a second time.

The chance was there, begging to be taken. He would be a fool to let it slip by, he told himself. She could only say no.

'You tell me there's no alternative to your having an abortion. Well, I'm going to give you one. I asked you once to marry me; now I'm asking you again.'

That stunned her.

'I love you, Vicky, and have done for years. You'd make me the happiest man in the world if you'd marry me.'

246

She found her voice. 'You'd still have me even though I'm carrying someone else's child?'

'Yes. And if I survive the war, I'll bring that child up as my own flesh and blood. You have my word of honour on that.' Neil took a deep breath. 'Let me put it this way. If I can save you from committing murder, and thereby allow you to have the child you want, I'd feel I'd gone some way to making up for the telephone call to Copland and Lye. And as I've just said, I do love you very very much.'

She thought of Ken. He was lost to her for ever now, no doubt about it. A whip had been cracked, and he'd jumped. She'd worked that out after he had hung up on her. If he did love her, as he had often sworn he did, he loved his ambition more.

'Get another drink in please,' she said huskily, and pushed her now empty glass at Neil, who, without uttering, rose and went to the bar.

It was a funny old world at times, she thought. Handsome, brave, a professional career ahead of him – if, as he said, he survived the war. What more could she ask for? The relief that surged through her was overwhelming in its intensity. She didn't have to go to Sampson's on Tuesday after all. Her baby was going to live. Closing her eyes, she thanked God for his mercy and compassion. Neil was a good man. She would never let him down, she swore to herself.

He returned to their table with fresh drinks and sat down to stare at her, awaiting her verdict.

'We'll have to get a special licence,' she said.

It was Neil's idea that they elope to Gretna Green – a suggestion he put forward for two reasons. First, it was more romantic to be married there than in a dreich Glasgow registry office; and second, it ensured that there wouldn't be any newspaper fuss, which, because of his vc, there might have been in Glasgow. He thought that journalists and photographers and, who knew, maybe even city dignitaries – he'd had lunch with the Lord Provost on his first day home – might have spoiled it for them, and Vicky agreed.

The only person Vicky let into the secret beforehand was

her supervisor at work. When Vicky and Neil left Parr Street for the station, they left behind notes, one for George and Mary, another for Mrs Seton.

When they reached Gretna they had a bite to eat, both being famished, then went in search of the smithy where the marriages took place and the blacksmith who performed the ceremony. They soon found both, only to be greatly disappointed when the blacksmith informed them that they had to live in the village for an establishing period before he could marry them.

'Neil here is on active duty and has to return to Egypt in a very short while. Delay means we'll be losing that time as a married couple,' Vicky argued.

Mr Yoole, the blacksmith, scratched his chin and wondered where he'd seen Neil's face before. It seemed gey familiar.

'There's a war on, you know. Couldn't you make an exception?' Vicky persisted.

Then Mr Yoole had it. It was Vicky's mentioning Egypt that placed Neil for him.

'Aren't you the chap who got awarded the vc?' he asked.

Neil nodded. 'That's me.'

Mr Yoole carefully wiped his huge mitts on a none too clean cloth, then stuck out his right hand. 'It's a real pleasure to meet you, son, an honour.'

Mr Yoole scratched his chin again and regarded Vicky and Neil thoughtfully. The lassie was right, there *was* a war on, and in wartime all sorts of rules and regulations got bent a little. And as she had pointed out, Neil had only so much leave.

'Och, tae hell with it. Have you got the ring?' he queried.

Neil's face lit up. 'Right here,' he replied and hastily produced the gold band.

They were wed over the anvil by Mr Yoole, with Mrs Yoole and a Mr Sawyers acting as witnesses.

'You may kiss the bride,' Mr Yoole told Neil when it was all over, and they were man and wife.

Neil took Vicky into his arms. As their lips met, the three other people present broke into applause.

'Have you booked a room yet?' Mr Sawyers asked when they had finished kissing.

Neil shook his head.

'Well, as it so happens, I'm the landlord of the pub over by. I'd be delighted to look after you while you're here.' He beamed. It was of course no accident that he had been called in to act as a witness for them – he was a witness whenever possible. It was excellent for business.

Neil took care of the financial arrangements, then he and Vicky, hand in hand, strolled over to the pub behind Mr Sawyers, who was leading the way. Mr Sawyers carried the two small cases they had brought with them.

'It was a brainwave for us to come here. Thank you for thinking of it,' Vicky said.

He squeezed her hand. He couldn't believe he was in Gretna Green with Vicky, and that she was his wife. It was a dream come true.

They had a drink while their room was made ready, then were taken up by Mrs Sawyers.

The room was delightful, a proper little love nest, Vicky thought. It had a view towards the English border.

'Would you like me to run you a bath? The water's piping hot,' Mrs Sawyers asked Vicky.

'That would be smashing.'

Mrs Sawyers gave an understanding smile. 'There are lots of young couples have their meals sent up. You only have to say.'

Vicky glanced at Neil, who nodded. 'We'll have tea in our room then,' she answered.

Mrs Sawyers explained where the bathroom and toilet were, then went off to run Vicky's bath.

Neil kissed Vicky again, a deep kiss that went on and on. 'I could eat you,' he whispered when the kiss was finally over, and she had laid a cheek against his breast.

A little later Mrs Sawyers returned to announce that the bath was ready. When she and Neil were once more alone, Vicky closed the curtains, laid out her dressing gown and best nightdress, and began to strip. Neil watched in fascination, unable to take his eyes off her. As she stood naked before him, his throat went dry and his heart began thumping.

She put on her dressing gown and gathered up the night-dress and a toilet bag. 'I won't be long. Why don't you get into bed and wait for me there?' she said. As she left the room, she blew him a kiss.

The bath was Victorian and massive. She put a little aromatic oil into the steaming water, a trick she'd learned while on the *Atlantic Star*, then clambered in.

When she emerged she felt dreamy and hazy – exactly how a girl should feel on going to bed with her new husband for the first time, she thought. She dabbed some powder under her arms, then placed a spot of perfume in several strategic places. When she had put on her nightdress and dressing gown, and run a comb through her thick cap of curls, she was ready.

He was in bed waiting for her, as she had suggested. She made sure to lock the door before joining him. Within seconds her nightdress was off again, tossed to the floor.

'Oh, my angel,' he whispered.

Half an hour later he was still touching and stroking – that was all.

'What's wrong?' she asked softly.

'I don't know,' came back the tight reply.

'You must be too tense. Try and relax a bit,' she said. She was pretty certain by now that she was his first woman for, if his caresses were gentle, they were also totally inexperienced. She did her best to help him, to no avail. A little later she decided it best that they halt, for they were getting absolutely nowhere.

'First night nerves. Don't worry about it. It's a common occurrence, I'm told,' she said lightly, and kissed him on the tip of the nose.

'I feel such a fool,' he muttered wretchedly.

'It'll be all right, it's just a case of us being at ease and getting used to one another.'

'Must be nerves,' he agreed.

'Listen. Instead of us having tea here, why don't we go downstairs and have it, and spend the time until it's served in the bar?' She knew that, as residents, they could use the pub's bar whenever they wanted.

'All right, fine.'

He needed his mind taken off his failure, she thought. And, although Neil had never been a heavy drinker, she would see to it that he had a good few between now and bedtime.

A good few, but not too many.

Before they left the bedroom, she had jollied him up to the point where he was guffawing at an outrageously funny story of hers which she had initially heard from the captain of the *Atlantic Star*.

'Oh Christ!' exclaimed Neil and threw himself away from Vicky. It was the fifth day of their honeymoon – and still the marriage remained unconsummated.

Outside bed everything had been wonderful. They had tramped the nearby countryside, borrowed bicycles and ridden into England and back, hired rods and fished – or at least attempted to fish, neither of them ever having used a rod before. That morning, following a heavy fall of snow the previous night, they had even built a snowman and had a snowball fight. Everything was as it should have been, with the exception of Neil's inability to make love.

He was sitting on the edge of the bed, shoulders bowed, head in hands. His posture was one of wretched despair. Vicky was at a loss. She had done everything she could think of to arouse him, even goading him into a fight to see if that would work.

'Is it me, Neil?' she asked softly, a frown creasing her forehead.

'No. I find you desperately attractive. I want you. I've never wanted any other girl but you. It's just that . . . nothing happens.'

'I am your first, aren't I?'

'Yes,' came the strangled reply.

On the one hand Vicky was not surprised to have that confirmed; it wasn't unusual for men to remain virgins until the marriage bed. Many might boast among themselves to the contrary, but that was the truth of the matter. On the other hand she had presumed from the way the girls at the university had given him the glad eye that he was bound to have had a tumble or two.

Was it because he loved her so much that his mind was stopping him? Having put her on a pedestal, was he now finding the realities of the physical side of love a debasement of her? In other words, even though he knew she had slept with Ken in the past, was he subconsciously resisting a physical relationship between them because it would defile the 'pure' image he had of her? Or was he just downright impotent? If so, she had read or heard somewhere that doctors could treat such a condition.

'I'm sorry, I'm so sorry,' he said in a cracked voice.

She went over to him and put an arm round his bowed shoulders. 'There's nothing to be sorry about. We'll sort this thing out together,' she told him.

'Shall we go back to Glasgow tomorrow?'

'Let's stay the week. Despite what you might think, I'm thoroughly enjoying myself here.'

When eventually he fell asleep, she remained wide awake, staring into the darkness.

The train rattled along, heading for Glasgow. Neil was gazing out a window, his expression bleak. Vicky was pretending to read a book.

The previous night she had managed to winkle some very private and personal details out of Neil – details which had further increased her concern for him.

She looked up from her book and over at him. Apart from themselves, the carriage was empty.

'Neil, I think you should go and see Mr Rose, the GP. Perhaps there's something he can do.'

He turned to stare at her with tortured eyes.

She went on. 'Rather than let this problem drag on, it seems only common sense to me that you go for professional advice, and right away. It could well be that by consulting him now you can have the problem sorted out before you have to return to Egypt.'

He continued to stare at her in silence.

'Would you like me to come with you or to go on your own?'

He considered that. 'I'd prefer to go on my own,' he mumbled.

'I'll make the appointment directly we get home,' she said firmly.

Was it only prolonged nerves or was it this purity theory she had dreamed up? She hoped that Mr Rose, as damned fine a GP as there had ever been, would find out.

Then she had another thought. When making the appointment for Neil, she would go in and see Mr Rose herself. She would prime him fully about why Neil was coming to consult him.

Vicky clattered up the stairs, returning from her shift at the factory. Neil had been to see a consultant at the Royal Infirmary that afternoon, his third visit to the man. He had been promised the results of the many tests that had been made during his previous visits.

She fumbled with her key in the doorlock, then was inside the house. She knew that Neil would be alone. They had arranged for Mrs Seton to go off to the early house at the pictures. He was sitting gazing into the fire, which he had nearly allowed to go out. That told her that the news was bad.

She took off her coat and laid it aside. She went over and squatted beside him, clasping one of his chill hands between hers. He looked at her for the first time; there were tears in his eyes.

'Well?' she prompted softly.

'The consultant says I have deep-seated prostatic damage caused years ago by a fractured pelvis. He pointed out the now healed fracture on one of the X-rays.'

'What does that mean?'

'It means that I'm impotent for life. It's impossible for them to cure or correct the damage,' he whispered.

She was appalled. 'Is he absolutely certain nothing can be done?'

'Absolutely.'

It was a nightmare, the worst news they could have had. So much for her stupid theory.

'When did you have a fractured pelvis?' she queried.

'I never knew I did have until the consultant told me, but then I never went to the doctor at the time, not having the money to be able to do so. I just stayed in bed till the worst of the pain was over, and then got back on my feet again,' he said, and made a sort of whimpering sound filled with such anguish that it wrenched Vicky's heart.

'When was this?'

'Remember the day you were arrested?'

'How could I ever forget it?'

'That night Ken was waiting for me in the close. He got me into the back dunny, where he told me what had happened – that you'd been arrested instead of him, and that it had to be me who'd telephoned Copland and Lye because I was the only one who knew he'd been stealing while working overtime. It must have been during that kicking that my pelvis was fractured, which in turn caused the damage to the prostate gland.'

Vicky's mouth was open, a hand covering it. Ken had done this to Neil! Ken had robbed Neil of his virility and ability to have children. And she was carrying Ken's child!

Anger crept into Neil's face. 'God damn that man. God damn him to hell! May he fry, screaming, in everlasting hellfire!' Neil choked.

She held him tight while he completely broke down.

She got the day off work to see Neil leave for Egypt. They went to the Central Station by taxi. The journey was mostly silent, with Neil sunk deep in gloom. There had been a lot of silence between them since his final visit to the Royal Infirmary. He refused point-blank to discuss anything to do with his impotence or its effect on their lives. The subject had become taboo.

On reaching the station, he paid the cabbie and they went inside. They were walking towards the arrival and departure board when he suddenly stopped and grasped Vicky by the arm.

'I'll perfectly understand it if you go off and leave me. I can't really expect you to continue on as my wife, not with me the way I am,' he said quietly.

'Don't talk nonsense. Lovemaking isn't all of marriage. It's only a small percentage of it,' she replied, equally quietly.

'I wish that was true.'

'It is. And it's not as though we'll have to do without a family. As for me, there are things I can teach you to do that will more than keep me happy that way, I assure you.'

He gazed at her, desperately wishing to believe that she would be there when and if he came home again, that their marriage could have a semblance of normality about it.

'You're still in a state of shock, Neil, and very very depressed. But I promise you, given time and thought on the matter, you'll come to see it isn't the total disaster you now imagine.'

'Whatever happens, I love you, and always will,' he stated simply.

'I know,' she whispered.

When the train left, she waved frantically till it had turned the bend and he was lost to sight. He was gone at last, for which she was thankful; the strain of the past few weeks had been awful.

She had said that she would wait for him, and she would. She had sworn to herself that she would never let him down, and she would keep that oath. The one thing he must never find out was that Ken was the father of her as yet unborn child.

Never ever.

Ken Blacklaws was in number 3 hold of the TSS *Lydia*, which was tied up in Plantation Quay having its cargo of copra, steel and powdered egg unloaded.

The *Lydia* had hit a ferocious gale en route to Glasgow, and during the gale had shipped a considerable amount of water in number 3 and 4 holds. This had only come to light when the dockies doing the unloading had discovered that a good third, the remainder, of the copra in number 3 hold and the same amount of powdered egg in number 4 hold were ruined. The water hadn't been detected by the ship's crew because the copra and egg had absorbed it. As a result, unloading was going to take longer than had been anticipated and would run well over normal knocking-off time.

The men would have to work through until the unloading had been completed, for it was imperative that the ship be away on the morning tide. It was scheduled for a run down to Southampton, where it would be quickly reloaded for a link-up with an Atlantic convoy.

Ken and Jack Fyfer had come aboard to inspect the remaining ruined cargo personally, and Jack had just gone off to hammer out an overtime deal for their members with a representative of the ship's owners. Ken had remained behind to listen to a complaint from a chap called Hyslop about a different matter entirely.

When Ken had taken down all the details of Hyslop's complaint in the notebook he always carried with him and told Hyslop he'd be in touch, he left Hyslop to climb back onto the deck, which was deserted. Ken guessed correctly that the men who had been working there had taken the opportunity to nip off for a fly smoke and cup of char.

He lit a cigarette and yawned. It had been a long hard day. He promised himself a hot bath when he got home and a few stiff whiskies.

Then he thought of Lyn and frowned. Sexually it was still bad between them. What might laughingly be called their sex life was almost non-existent, with no signs of improvement on the way. Wee Kenny remained her be-all and end-all. How he missed those sessions he'd had with Vicky in Jack's small apartment! He ached with longing and desire every time he thought of them.

Blast Jack Fyfer, and blast that private investigator who followed him from time to time. He had never actually been able to spot the man, but every so often he got a strange tingly sensation at the back of his neck which told him the man was about, spying on him.

There had been that strawberry blonde he had met only the other week. She was a real cracker, and available – she had made that clear enough. But he hadn't dared.

As for Jack, the old man was really getting on his nerves. There was no steamrollering Jack any more. Whenever he tried, Jack would stop and give an infuriating smile, and the sword of Damocles would sway above his head. Drawing viciously, he went to the ship's rail and leant on it. Down below, standing on the quayside, were Jack and the owner's representative, the pair of them engrossed in conversation.

'Sod you, you old bastard!' he thought darkly, glowering at Jack.

Apart from Jack and the owner's representative, the quayside was deserted – that smoke and cup of char again.

He glanced over to where one of the ship's derricks had been halted in mid-action. It had been transferring a crate of powdered egg from a hold to the quayside when the operator had stopped it at the moment the lads had downed tools.

Ken was turning away from the rail and about to make for the gangplank when in a flash the idea exploded in his brain. Very slowly he turned back to stare at the motionless crate of powdered egg that was dangling roughly forty feet in the air, *directly* over Jack and the owner's representative. A crate weighing – what? – two to three tons.

Ken went very still inside, cold sweat breaking on his forehead. Accidents happened round the docks every day of the week. Why not one that would be ever so convenient, and advantageous, to him?

He walked along beside the rail till he was adjacent with the derrick. The operator's cab was empty. There wasn't another soul to be seen.

He strolled over to the cab and glanced inside. The controls were of a type well known to him. He had often operated similar derricks when he had worked as a dockie himself. His eyes zeroed in on the emergency-release button.

All he had to do was press that – and ensure that no one saw him doing so, of course.

The inside of his left thigh was fluttering as he returned to the rail. The two men below had not moved an inch. He wiped cold sweat from his brow and noted that his palms had begun to leak. Did he have the guts to press that button? To kill for what he so desperately wanted?

He returned to the operator's cab, transfixed by the red button. If he was going to do it, he had to do it *now*, he told himself. Another handful of seconds and it could be too late.

A final glance round confirmed that he was still quite alone on deck, and unobserved. Leaning into the cab, he thumbed the red button.

There was a snap, followed by a crash. Even as the crash came, he was throwing himself down a companionway, hurtling back to the ship's lower levels.

When the alarm was raised, he made sure that he was seen to be well below decks. When he clambered up on deck again, he was in the company of Hyslop and five others.

'I wonder what's happened?' he said to Hyslop as they emerged into the March sunshine.

Ken stood outside what had been Jack's office, and which was now his, and stared at the door. A smile of satisfaction curled his mouth upwards as he grasped the handle and opened the door. The smile widened as he went inside. It was his first official day as union president.

At last, at long last, he was president of the Honourable Society of Dock Workers! By God, it was a glorious feeling.

The inquest into Jack's 'accident' had been held at the coroner's court. There had been no eyewitnesses, nor had any malfunction been found in the derrick when it was examined by experts. But it was known that such derricks did act up from time to time, and were far from being a hundred per cent reliable. No foul play had been suspected. The verdict was death by misadventure.

The remark had been made afterwards that it was a

dangerous life working on the docks: Jack and the owner's representative weren't the first to die there, and certainly wouldn't be the last.

Ken crossed to the drinks cabinet, took out a bottle of best Highland malt and poured himself a generous tot. He then selected one of Jack's Havana cigars, clipped the end with Jack's silver clipper and lit it. Malt in hand, trailing cigar smoke, he sat behind Jack's desk. Puffing on the cigar, he pushed back the chair and placed his feet on the desktop.

Power, that's what he had now, and what he'd always craved. Power. The next step was to enlarge that power.

Vicky gave a little exclamation of fright when she was grasped by the shoulder. She had just come off the tram, having been in town. Her mind had been elsewhere.

'Hello, Vicky.' Ken smiled.

She stared at him for several seconds, then wrenched herself from his grasp and walked away. He ran after her.

'I hung up on you, Vicky, because I panicked. I'd have lost my job at the union if Jack had found out that I'd even so much as spoken to you again.'

'And how would he have known you'd done that?'

'The telephonist might have been listening in on Jack's orders. I couldn't take the chance,' he explained.

'I hardly think she would have done that.'

'You don't understand. If he could go to the extent of having a private investigator follow me about, then he was well capable of ordering the telephonist to listen in on my telephone conversations.'

Vicky stopped and faced Ken. 'He had a private investigator follow you about?'

'He did. I was forbidden to communicate with you in any way. To have done so would have meant me out on my ear.'

'Surely you could have written? He'd never have found that out.'

Ken shrugged. 'I couldn't take the chance.'

She stared at Ken, then nodded, very slowly. 'I understand,' she said. And she did, perfectly.

Then Vicky realised that they were talking in the past tense. 'What do you mean "would have meant you out on your ear"? Doesn't it still?'

'Jack's dead. There was an accident on Plantation Quay and he was killed. I'm president of the union now.'

'I'm sorry to hear about Mr Fyfer. He was always kindness itself to me, until he caught us together, that is. So now you're the big boss, number one in command.'

'That's it.' He grinned.

'And without having Mr Fyfer to worry about, you've decided to look me up to ask me to become your mistress again?' she said sourly.

'If it was, what would your answer be?'

'To tell you to take a running jump! My God, Ken Blacklaws, you do have some brass nerve. So you think all you have to do is snap your fingers and I'll come bounding back like some well-trained mutt. Well, I've got news for you, I'm bloody not!' she hissed and strode off, fuming.

He ran after her again, caught up with her and forced her to stop.

'Will you take your hands off me, or so help me I'll shout for a policeman!'

'Vicky, I didn't come here to ask you to be my mistress. I came to ask you to be my wife.'

She thought she hadn't heard correctly. 'Say that again?'

'I want you to be my wife.'

'And what about the wife you already have?'

'I'll get rid of her. She can go and live with her mother in Balfron. You can move in as soon as she's moved out.'

'And you'll divorce her?'

'I swear it. And as soon as I'm free, you and I will marry.'

She gave a low laugh. Oh God, but this was funny. You had to laugh – it was either that or cry. For despite all that he'd done to her, she still loved Ken desperately.

'I'm afraid I can't move in with you or marry you,' she said, voice crackling with emotion.

'Of course you can. But I do understand if you need time to think about it.'

'Time won't alter matters. I can't and that's that.' She

held up her left hand so that he could see the gold band there.

He stared at the ring in amazement. It had never entered his head that she would go off and marry someone else, not so soon anyway.

She had said that she would wait for Neil. She had sworn to herself that she would never let him down, and she would keep that oath. But, sweet heaven, when she had said and sworn those things, she had never envisaged that this would happen, that Ken would re-materialise so quickly into her life and propose to her.

'And I'll give you another reason,' she said and opened her raglan coat, which effectively hid her pregnancy when buttoned. She pointed to her small but very clearly visible bump.

Ken swallowed hard, his normally agile brain now leaden with disappointment. 'Do you love whoever it is you've married?'

'Yes,' she lied instantly.

'Well, that's that then – between you and me, that is.'

She nodded her agreement and rebuttoned her coat.

There was nothing left for him to say. He didn't want to ask her any of the details of her marriage, he just didn't want to know.

'Congratulations and good luck then,' he said, giving a lopsided smile, and stuck out his hand. Vicky wanted to wish him good luck also, but couldn't. Her throat was clogged.

Tears were stinging her eyes as she made to turn a corner. She glanced back to where she had left him standing, but he was already gone. She made it to her close before collapsing against an inside-close wall. She sobbed as tears washed her cheeks. What a mess, what an awful bloody mess! It just wasn't fair. *It just wasn't!*

The doctor had told her to scream as loudly as she wished – they were used to that. She had taken him at his word, shrieking at the top of her lungs as unbelievable pain after pain seemed to be ripping her apart.

261

'And again, Mrs Seton, push!' the doctor's voice commanded.

Gritting her teeth, she pushed and pushed and . . .

'Aaaaaahhhhhh!'

Then it was all over. The tiny feet, legs and buttocks slipped from her body. The baby was born.

There was the sound of a smack and a lusty cry rent the air.

A few moments later the doctor said, 'It's a wee girl, and she's absolutely perfect.'

One of the nurses placed the baby, wrapped in a length of soft sheeting, into her arms.

Martha – that was what she would call her daughter, she decided. It was a name she'd aye liked. Totally exhausted, she fell asleep, and they took Martha from her.

Part Four

You're My Wee Gallus Bloke Nae Mair 1946–56

'Oh you're my wee gallus bloke nae mair,
you're my wee gallus bloke nae mair.
With your bell blue strides,
and your bunnet tae the side,
you're my wee gallus bloke nae mair.'

Glasgow street song (Trad.)

Nine

What a marvellous feeling to have so much time to myself, Vicky thought with glowing satisfaction, for this was Martha's first day at school.

She had expected the worst – tears, tantrums, the lot – but had been pleasantly surprised when Martha had gone into the classroom meek as a lamb. When she took her home that afternoon, she would make the wee mite some Melting Moments, which she adored.

Vicky was en route now to Neil's office in Renfrew Street. The pair of them were going out for lunch together, and to celebrate Martha's starting school Neil had promised that they would have a bottle of good wine as a special treat. A leisurely lunch, perhaps a bit of window shopping afterwards. Life was certainly going to be very different now that she didn't have Martha, seemingly forever demanding, tied round her neck all day long. Not that she didn't love the lassie; she loved her to distraction and so did Neil. It was just that for a while now she had craved some time off for herself, a breathing space. A little respite from Mummy . . . Mummy . . . Mummy . . .

Mary had told her that it was quite natural; she had felt positively claustrophobic when she had had Vicky and John at home together prior to their attending school – the same school Martha was now going to.

Neil worked in a junior capacity at a firm of solicitors named MacDonald, Lindsay and Hogg. They were very grand solicitors with sumptuous offices, not at all the sort of people Neil wanted to work for – but when he had been demobbed there was such a deluge of men applying for positions that he had grabbed the first offered him. The fact he was a vc had got him the job, and in particular because his vc had been won in Egypt. Michael Lindsay's son had been a desert rat who had been killed at El Alamein, the turning point of the war.

Neil's plan was to stay at the firm for a few years, then open up his own office in the Townhead area. He still wanted to help the poor and deprived. Wealth and possessions held no attraction for him.

Vicky was thinking about Neil and their forthcoming lunch – she was calling it lunch only because Neil had said she should if she spoke to anyone about it while at MacDonald, Lindsay and Hogg; to have called it dinner would have been a social clanger in those august surroundings – when a vaguely familiar face rushed by. Several strides further on it struck her who the face belonged to.

She whirled round. 'Tina! Tina!' she cried, and ran back to where Tina had stopped.

Recognition came to Tina Mathieson, and the pair of them fell into one another's arms.

'Vicky Devine, Christ but it's good to see you. You're a sight for sore eyes, right enough,' Tina enthused.

Vicky held up her left hand and tapped the gold band there. 'Not Devine any more, Seton. I'm married, with a wee girl. And you?'

Tina shook her head. 'No such luck. I'm beginning to think I'm going to end up an old maid.'

Tina was still as plump as she had been at Duncliffe, maybe even more so. Her auburny hair had faded somewhat, and had streaks of grey in it, and there were a number of lines round her eyes, several of them quite deep. One thing that hadn't changed was the warmth she exuded, and which Vicky remembered so fondly. Vicky could have shouted with delight at having run into her great pal again.

'I went to the address you'd given me, but you and your family had flitted to Coventry,' Vicky said.

Tina grasped her by the arm. 'Listen, I honestly can't stop. I'm ten minutes late with something that's desperately important. Let's name a time and place and we'll meet up for a good old chinwag,' she suggested.

'How about this Friday? Come to tea and meet the family?'

266

'It's a date.'

Tina opened her handbag and started rummaging amongst its contents. 'Give me your address and I'll write it down.'

'No need to do that,' Vicky answered and snapped open her own handbag. She presented Tina with one of Neil's business cards, of which she always carried a supply.

'Posh,' Tina said, visibly impressed.

'Half past six?'

'I'll be there, with knobs on.'

They kissed each other on the cheek, then Tina hurried off down the street, walking so fast that she was on the verge of breaking into a run.

'Oh, this is rare!' Vicky said to herself. She couldn't wait to tell Neil.

Vicky was waiting impatiently for Tina to arrive. The table was set, the meal in the oven. Martha was wearing her party dress with a ribbon in her hair. Neil had on his new cardigan, knitted by Vicky herself, and a pair of new cavalry twills. Vicky had wanted him to put on his business suit and tie, but he had said blow that. It was his home – theirs, since Mrs Seton had passed on two years previously – and he wanted to feel relaxed in it, so if this Tina didn't like it she could lump it.

Vicky had been miffed by his refusal but had soon got over it. She had only wanted to show him off. She supposed she could do that just as well in cardy and cavalry twills.

'I hope she's not going to be late. I'm hungry,' Neil said.

'Could you eat a scabby-heided wean?' Martha asked, repeating the old Glasgow saying (a scabby-heided wean being a baby with scabs on its head).

'Not quite, but I might if I had to wait for ages and ages.' Neil smiled. How he doted on that child; she was sweetness itself.

'Have you noticed her squinting the way she does?' Neil asked Vicky.

'Who?'

'Martha. Sometimes when she's looking at things she sort of squints. Do you think she needs glasses?'

'I've never seen her squinting,' Vicky replied hotly.

'All right, keep your hair on. I'm not implying criticism. It's just that if she does need glasses we should see to it sooner rather than later.'

Vicky hadn't noticed Martha squinting, or if she had she hadn't taken it in. 'It wouldn't do any harm for the optician to have a look at her, just to be on the safe side,' she conceded.

'I don't want glasses. They'll call me speccy at school,' Martha complained, alarmed at the prospect.

'If you have to have them, then you'll have to have them, and that'll be that. But just because you might squint occasionally doesn't mean you do,' Vicky said, placating her daughter.

'If I get specs, will I get false teeth as well? A boy in my class says his mummy and daddy both have specs and false teeth.' Martha asked anxiously.

Vicky and Neil laughed. It was amazing what the wee one could come out with at times.

'No false teeth, I promise you,' Vicky replied.

The doorbell rang. 'That'll be her,' Vicky said and rushed from the room.

Neil stood and straightened himself down. He took Martha by the hand as Vicky's voice erupted excitedly in the hallway. Another female voice spoke, as excited as Vicky's. He wasn't sure whether or not he was looking forward to meeting Tina. One thing was certain: he could not have objected to her coming over even if he'd wanted to; Vicky would have gone daft if he'd tried. All he had heard from her since she had bumped into Tina last Monday was: Tina this, Tina that and Tina the next blinking thing.

Vicky and Tina, each with an arm round the other's waist, entered the kitchen.

Vicky's eyes were shining. 'Tina, I want you to meet my husband Neil.'

Tina saw a handsome man – a smasher, she would have described him as. Vicky had done well for herself.

Neil extended his hand and they shook. 'I'm pleased to meet you,' he said.

'And this is Martha, our daughter,' Vicky went on.

Tina squatted and gazed at Martha. 'You're going to be a beauty when you grow up.' She smiled.

Martha was instantly won over. 'Hello,' she murmured and glanced at the floor.

'You're not bashful are you?' Tina teased.

Martha grasped hold of Vicky's skirt and hid her face in it.

'I've got something for you,' Tina said and from a paper poke produced several bars of chocolate.

'You shouldn't have. That must be your ration for the entire month!' Vicky exclaimed.

'The pleasure's mine to give it. And anyway, sweeties are the last thing I need,' Tina replied, and prodded her side, which wobbled.

'I've got something else for us,' Tina went on, and delved into the paper poke to pull out a small bottle. 'Fowler's Wee Heavy, do you remember? I've got six of them here.'

Vicky clapped her hands in glee. 'Remember! That was my first Saturday night in –' She came up short. Duncliffe and Duke Street were never mentioned in front of Martha. 'I remember all right, but we'll talk about these days later, when Martha's gone to bed.'

Tina got the message. 'Clear as crystal.'

Neil decided he liked Tina. There was something very winning about her.

'But now I want to hear about you and what you've been up to?' Vicky demanded.

Tina and Neil sat, Neil with Martha on his knee, while Vicky went about putting out the meal.

'Well, when I left that place down the coast, I went home and soon got a start. Time went by, with nothing much happening at all. Then one day my da announced he'd got a better job with a Coventry firm. So how did we all feel about flitting down to England?

'I must admit, I wasn't all that keen to begin with. Then I thought, why not? A clean break might be just the very thing, and so down to England we all went.

'We settled in right nicely, and got on well enough with

our neighbours. Though I must say at the beginning we had
trouble with the accent, for they don't half talk funny . . .'

'I wonder what they thought about your accent?' Vicky
interjected with a smile.

'Me? What accent?' Tina replied, straight-faced, and they
all laughed, for she was broadest Glasgow.

Tina went on. 'Then the war happened, and my da got
his papers. He went into the army and fought in D-day. He
was wounded in the subsequent advance through France –
nothing all that serious, but serious enough to have him
sent back to Blighty. He never saw active duty again after
that.

'Meanwhile, fairly early on in the war, as you'll know,
Coventry took an awful plastering from the Luftwaffe, and
Ma and I had our house blown up around our ears. We were
extremely lucky to walk away from that. As for the city,
the devastation was dreadful. Whole areas flattened flat as
a pancake.'

'I saw it on the newsreel and thought about you at the
time,' Vicky said, laying out plates of steaming vegetable
stew. Many foods, clothes, sweets and even bread were
rationed. Meat was at a premium.

They sat round the table and Neil opened three bottles
of Fowler's Wee Heavy. He had a half-bottle of whisky for
the occasion, which he would bring out when the Wee
Heavys were finished.

Vicky continued. 'After Ma and I were bombed out, we
managed to find a new place in Burton Green, a small
village on the outskirts of Coventry, and while there I
worked as a land-girl.

'When Da came out the army he found that his old works
had gone, a casualty of the bombing, and so we decided to
return to Glasgow, which we'd all missed like billy-o. When
we got here we went round various factors and ended up in
a really nice tenement in St Vincent Crescent, which is
behind and down from Argyle Street. We're very happy
there.'

'I know St Vincent Crescent. It's overlooking the river,'
Neil said.

'Aye, that's right. We're on the top landing, so from our front window you can watch the ships coming and going, it can be a terrific sight.'

'And what about work, what are you doing?' Vicky asked.

'Have you heard of Tom Allen, the MP for Glasgow Kelvinhaugh, and Sandy Millar, the MP for Glasgow Bridgeton?'

'Of course, they're both well kent. Particularly Tom Allen. I've never heard him myself, but they say he's a tremendous speaker,' Vicky answered.

'Well, they share me as their Glasgow secretary, and I have an office in the Kelvinhaugh constituency's Labour Hall. I also help out with typing and clerical work for the Labour Halls in both constituencies. So Tom and Sandy each pay a third of my wages, the Labour Halls a sixth each.'

Vicky was fascinated. 'And do you like it?'

'It's fantastic. What I do is varied and exciting, and not only that but important. Up until I joined them, I wasn't much of a political animal, but I am now. I fairly live and breathe Labour politics.'

'Wasn't Tom Allen one of the original Red Clydesiders?' Vicky asked.

'He was indeed, and was locked up on several occasions because of it, once in a dungeon in Edinburgh Castle, would you believe. He and James Maxton, despite their political differences, were thick as thieves.' James Maxton had died the previous month, on 23 July, to be precise.

'A union man before he became an MP, and brilliant at it,' Neil added.

'I'd do anything for him. He's that sort of person.' Tina smiled.

They chatted on about Tina till the end of the meal, when it was time for Martha to go to bed. Neil volunteered to take Martha through and get her ready, and while he was doing this Vicky and Tina washed, dried and put away the dishes.

Neil poured whiskies as Vicky was giving Martha a goodnight kiss and tucking her in. When Vicky returned to the kitchen they settled round the fireplace.

'Now I've given you all my guff, I want to hear about you,' Tina prompted.

'First of all I want to know why you never tried to get in touch with me?' Vicky asked. She had inquired of Mary about that when she had returned from sea, and Mary had said Tina had neither written nor chapped the door in her absence.

'The answer to that is dead simple. You were due to be released in March '36. At the end of March I went to look for your address and couldn't find it. I'd lost the bloody thing. So all I could do was wait for you to contact me, which you didn't. Or at least, according to you, not until after we'd flitted to Coventry. So why did you wait so long?'

Vicky gave a pained smile. 'I wasn't released in March of '36, Ganch's report on me was a bad one and I was made to serve my full sentence. I served the remainder in Duke Street prison.

'Oh, that bitch, that dirty rotten lesbian bitch!' Tina swore, eyes blazing anger.

'It was her final revenge for me refusing her and gouging her face as I did,' Vicky said softly.

This was all new to Neil. Vicky had never spoken to him about Duncliffe. 'Refused her what?' he asked.

Vicky told the story, all of it, including the horrors of the Black Room. When she was finished, a silence fell between them.

'Jesus H!' Neil said after a while.

Vicky wiped away a tear that had seeped onto her left cheek. She then went on to tell Tina about her fleeing Glasgow after being released from Duke Street, and the time she had spent aboard the *Atlantic Star* as assistant to the purser.

Tina left only in order to catch the last tram. On the outside landing she and Vicky hugged one another tight.

'Telephone me at the Labour Hall in a couple of days' time. We'll arrange to meet again,' Tina said, having already given Vicky her home address, work address and work telephone number.

'I'd like that,' Vicky whispered.

They squeezed one another again, then Tina took her leave. Neil walked her to the tramstop.

When Neil returned, he found Vicky in bed, staring at the ceiling.

'I knew Duncliffe couldn't have been a bed of roses, but I never dreamed it was as diabolical as that. The Japs had a torture similar to your Black Room. It sent more than one poor bugger completely round the twist,' he said, starting to get stripped.

A shudder ran through Vicky.

'There are nights when you cry out in your sleep, a cry that never fails to waken me and cover me from head to toe in cold goosebumps. Is that you having nightmares about the Black Room?' he asked softly.

'It happens every so often. I'm back there in the blackness, the entire world crushing in on me. Other times I'm reliving the hallucinations I had, some pleasant, some unspeakably horrible. But the most awful of all is the one where I suddenly come to believe that I'm locked away for ever, that I'm never ever going to be let out. That must be the cry that wakens you.'

He was in his pyjamas now and joined her in bed. He gently stroked her forehead, trying to ease away the pain that was showing there.

'I'll have nightmares about the Black Room till my dying day. I'll never forget that place, or the morning runs, or Miss Ganch's riding crop, or dozens of other things. They're all there, for ever branded into my memory, till whenever that memory ceases to function,' she said in a whisper.

He moved his fingertips to her temples, massaging them in circular motions. 'I enjoyed meeting your friend. I hope she comes here often.'

'Good, and I hope she will too.'

'You won't ever tell her about me, will you? I don't want anyone else to know,' he said, referring to his impotence.

273

'I won't. You have my word on that.'

'Thank you,' he whispered, and kissed her neck.

He gathered her to him, and his hands began to move. She closed her eyes and remained passive. That was how he liked her to be.

A little later she gasped. He had learned well what she had taught him. He had become so skilful that it was almost as good as the real thing.

Almost.

The next Friday night Neil babysat while Vicky and Tina went to a picture house in the town. After that the two women continued seeing one another regularly. Sometimes Tina came to the house, other times they went to a café or the flicks. Occasionally Mary and George would mind Martha and Neil would go with them. On a night in early October Tina suggested the dance.

'It's a dance I'm organising at the Kelvinhaugh Labour Hall where I work. I've got a good band lined up, and at the end Tom Allen will be speaking.'

'Tom Allen! That sounds marvellous,' Vicky exclaimed.

'I'll arrange it so that you meet him if you like.'

'That would be rare,' Vicky enthused.

'I'll pay for the tickets now,' Neil said, as keen as Vicky to hear and meet the great man.

Vicky and Neil were thoroughly enjoying themselves. They had been on the floor quite a lot of the time, but at the present were taking a break in order to catch their wind.

They watched Tina swirl by in the arms of a man she had been dancing with most of the night. Tina had confided to them earlier that she thought the man was going to ask if he could lumber her home.

Vicky nudged Neil. 'Over there,' she said and nodded.

It was Tom Allen. They both recognised him from pictures in the newspapers. He was powerfully built and short in stature. His face was rough-hewn, filled with strength and resolve. Even at that distance Vicky could sense his natural charisma. She judged him to be in his late fifties.

The band played several more numbers, then laid down their instruments and left the rostrum. An excited hum of anticipation filled the hall. Tina ran up the rostrum's side stairs and Tom Allen followed her. On reaching the centre of the rostrum she held her hands aloft for silence, and then thanked everyone for coming along.

'And now, the moment you've all been waiting for. Mr Tom Allen, your MP!' she announced and led off the applause, which became a roar of clapping, whistling and stamping feet.

Tom Allen gave his audience a friendly smile and waited till the applause began to die. Then he started to speak. He wove a spell of words that Vicky found sheer magic. His theme was the chronic housing conditions found not only in Kelvinhaugh but in many parts of working-class Glasgow.

He spoke of stairhead toilets that were nothing short of abominations, of overcrowding that forced entire families of five and six to share the same inset bed in a single end, leaking roofs, running walls, rats, mice and other vermin, and of the ill health and disease that were the direct result of such a hellish environment. The old slums must be bulldozed, he argued, razed to the ground, and clean, modern units built in their stead, houses that would allow their occupants to live in dignity as human beings, and not like pigs in a sty.

When Allen finished, the applause was rapturous, and even louder than before. This time Vicky was one of those stamping her feet. He came down from the rostrum to be instantly mobbed by admirers. His back was thumped again and again as he shook hand after hand.

'Fabulous,' Vicky said to Neil, who nodded his agreement.

The band returned to the rostrum. 'Take your partners for the last waltz please!' their leader cried out, and the band struck up.

A few minutes later Tina somehow managed to disentangle Tom Allen and bring him over to where Vicky and Neil were standing.

'Tom, I'd like you to meet Mr and Mrs Seton,' Tina said.

Allen shook hands with Vicky first. 'A pleasure to meet you. Are you newly moved into the area?'

'We live in Townhead. We're here because we're friendly with Tina, and because we wanted to hear you speak. If I may say, that was one of the best speeches I've ever heard,' Vicky replied.

Tom Allen could see that she meant what she said, that it wasn't flannel. 'Thank you.' He smiled.

He shook Neil by the hand, then turned his attention back to Vicky. 'A pity you aren't local. We're always on the lookout for helpers. We only ask a couple of hours a week, but what a contribution it makes to the cause. Isn't that so, Tina?'

'They're invaluable,' Tina agreed.

'Would those couple of hours be during the day or in the evening?' Vicky queried.

'Whenever they're most convenient to the person involved,' Tom Allen replied.

Neil read Vicky's thoughts in her face; he approved of them. When she glanced at him, he nodded.

'I'd like to help, even though I'm not local. I can manage during the day while my little girl's at school.'

Tom Allen beamed.

'That's fantastic. You can be with me in my office,' Tina said to Vicky. Then to Tom Allen: 'She's a shorthand typist, same as me. We trained together.'

'Better still,' Allen replied, his beam widening.

'I'm looking forward to it,' Vicky said.

Allen patted her on a shoulder. 'Welcome aboard, Mrs Seton.'

'Oh, please, you must call me Vicky. And this is Neil.'

'All right, Vicky and Neil it is, and I'm Tom. But tell me, Neil, what do you do?'

'I'm a solicitor with MacDonald, Lindsay and Hogg.'

'Indeed! A much respected firm, and expensive. I know a dozen people needing legal advice, but none of them can afford to pay for it, far less the prices MacDonald, Lindsay and Hogg charge.'

'They're certainly not cheap, there's no argument about

that. But these people you're talking about, tell me about them. I'm interested.'

'They're poor people, Neil, unable to work because of old age, sickness, that sort of thing.'

Neil cleared his throat. 'I'd be happy to give them free advice. In fact, assisting folk like that has always been my aim, and why I became a solicitor in the first place. How about if I held a surgery once a week? Right here in the Labour Hall, say. Or, if the people were unable to get here on account of infirmity or sickness, I could go to them.'

'I think that's a splendid idea!' Vicky exclaimed.

'If you give me the names and addresses of these people, I'll arrange everything,' Tina said to Tom.

'And this wouldn't be just a one-off thing. You'd do it for some while to come?' Tom asked Neil hopefully.

'I don't see why not,' Neil replied.

Tom Allen grasped Neil by the hand a second time, and vigorously pumped the hand up and down. 'You're a gentleman, lad, a real gentleman. I'm in your debt.'

Neil flushed with pleasure. How marvellous to be held in such high esteem by a man of Tom Allen's eminence!

'He's not only a solicitor, but a damn good one too,' Vicky said proudly.

Neil flushed again, this time with embarrassment.

'I'm going to really enjoy doing this,' Neil said after Tom Allen had moved on.

Vicky kissed him on the cheek.

Tina caught sight of the chap she had danced with so much. He was hovering, trying to catch her eye, which he had now succeeded in doing. It was clear what the chap wanted, so she quickly excused herself. Her lumber was on.

On the tram returning to Townhead Vicky snuggled up to Neil. Right then she felt closer to him than she had ever felt. She still didn't love him, and didn't imagine that she ever would. But she had a great deal of affection for him, and he was an excellent husband.

'Happy?' he asked.

'Hmmh!' she mumbled.

'I'm glad we went tonight. Look what came of it.'

'Do you think the city will ever get those new houses Tom was talking about?'

His eyes glittered. 'Some day. You wait and see. Some day it has to come. And I'll tell you this, if there's any way I can help bring it about, I will.'

She glanced round, confirmed they were alone on the top deck and kissed him full on the mouth. 'You can be smashing at times.'

'You can be smashing at times yourself,' he replied.

They went back to snuggling, she thinking how tremendous it was going to be helping Tina a couple of hours a week, he dreaming about the new houses that would replace the old, squalid tenements.

The electric atmosphere in the room was generated by the burly man sitting opposite Ken Blacklaws: Gordon Tucker, known the length and breadth of Clydeside as The Rock.

The room was The Rock's office, the office of the president of the Glasgow Wharf Workers' Association, which would merge with the Clyde Dockworkers' Union when The Rock and Ken signed the papers now in front of them.

The Clyde Dockworkers' Union had come into being two years previously on the merger of Ken's old union, the Honourable Society of Dock Workers, with the West of Scotland Union of Dockers. Ken was its president. When Ken had stepped into Jack Fyfer's shoes there had been four dockworkers' unions. When these papers were signed and witnessed, there would be only two.

Ken was flanked by two lawyers, one on either side, as was The Rock. Behind The Rock stood the four men who comprised his union executive. Unknown to The Rock, two of these men were in Ken's pocket, thanks to indiscretions on their part and Ken's subsequent blackmail of them.

Ken had set up both of them. He had explicit photographs of Ross Moir having sex with a prostitute which would go to Ross's wife should Ross not do as he was told. And Ross loved his wife.

As for Keith Kirkland, Ken held a gambling note of Keith's to the value of £26,500. Keith was not aware that the roulette table had been rigged, the croupier under orders to take him to the cleaners. The gambling club had been paid handsomely by Ken for their troubles, on top of which he had bought the note from them.

Ken's plan had been to get a hold on all four of the union executive and make them force The Rock into agreeing to a merger. Under this combined assault, in accordance with the union's rulebook, The Rock would have had to give way, or resign, which would have had the same result.

This had been the state of affairs, with Ken trying to devise a way of compromising Russell Hadwin, one of the two executives not yet under his control, when the situation took on a new dimension.

The Rock was a widower who lived alone, his wife having died of cancer halfway through the war. Ken got word that his only son, Donny, who had emigrated to New Zealand twelve years earlier, was bringing himself and his family home to Glasgow for a visit. The Rock was ecstatic. Though he had never met them, Elizabeth and Jane, his five-year-old granddaughters, were the apple of his eye. Already besotted by the twins, he had really gone ga-ga over them in the flesh.

Realising how he could exploit the Tucker twins, Ken had abandoned his original intention in favour of short, sharp and devastatingly effective action – action that would give him the Glasgow Wharf Workers' Association on a plate within days rather than long-drawn-out months. The quick thrust of the poniard as opposed to the battering of the claymore: far more efficient and time-saving.

Donny Tucker and family had been enjoying a marvellous holiday – until the previous afternoon, when the professional criminals Ken had imported from London struck.

Donny had been knocked senseless to the ground, Yootha his wife thrust aside and the two five-year-olds bundled into the rear of a car. The car, containing kidnappers and kidnapped, roared away.

The Rock had ranted and raved, almost frothing at the

mouth, but wisely had done what Ken had said and refrained from contacting the police. Ken had told him that, if he did, his granddaughters would never be seen alive again.

Between the conception of the kidnap and its execution, Ken had ordered the necessary papers for the merger to be drawn up, the same papers now before him and The Rock. When they were signed and witnessed, Elizabeth and Jane would be released. All Ken had to do was make a phone call.

Ken looked directly into The Rock's eyes, which were blazing with hate and loathing. 'Shall we get on with it then, Mr Tucker?' He smiled.

The Rock lifted the pen beside his set of papers, paused for the briefest of seconds, then hastily began scribbling his signature. He signed paper after paper, and each paper as it was signed was witnessed by his two lawyers, passed to Ken, who countersigned, and then his signature was witnessed by his two lawyers.

In less than a minute it was over. The Glasgow Wharf Workers' Association had merged with the Clyde Dockworkers' Union; the new union was to retain the name of the latter.

The Rock threw his pen back onto the table and lurched to his feet. 'You'd better keep your side of the bargain,' he said huskily, referring to the release of his grandchildren.

'There's no advantage to me not to,' Ken replied levelly.

'The phone call . . .'

'. . . will be made directly you're gone,' Ken interrupted swiftly. No one in the room, other than himself and The Rock, knew about the abduction.

The Rock's chest heaved. He glanced one last time round the office that contained so many memories. He knew he would never enter it again.

'Enjoy your retirement,' said Ken.

The Rock turned and strode from the room, his lawyers hastening after him.

Ken stared at the four members of what had been the Glasgow Wharf Workers' Association executive. 'I've decided that Moir and Kirkland will be part of the new organisation. I'm afraid I can't accommodate you other two. I'm sorry.'

Russell Hadwin went white. Bob Leckie, the fourth member, slumped where he stood.

'You'd better go and clear out your desks.'

Hadwin and Leckie did not even bother arguing; they knew enough of Ken to be sure that he wouldn't change his mind.

Hadwin and Leckie trooped out of the office, leaving Moir and Kirkland.

'I want to be alone,' Ken told them. They fled, Kirkland closing the door behind him.

Ken grinned, then walked round the desk to sit in what had been The Rock's chair. Tilting the chair back, he put his feet on the desk and clasped his hands behind his head.

Only the Union of Longshoremen remained. Once he had engineered its merger with the Clyde Dockworkers', he would control all of Clydeside. Oh, what a beautiful thought that was! A Clydeside monopoly, no competition; it would virtually be a licence to coin money.

But his ambition didn't stop there, no sir. Once he controlled Clydeside, he intended picking off the other Scottish dock unions till in the end there was one huge union: a national union, the Scottish Union of Dockworkers, with him at its head. After Glasgow he would start in on Leith, then Dundee, followed by Aberdeen. When those major ports had fallen to him, the tiddlers that were left would go down like ninepins.

President of a national union: the thought of the power he would have made his mouth water. Power and money, and everything they could bring. Beautiful women, expensive cars, a mansion, virtually anything he desired could be his. He'd just have to snap his fingers and it would be there. He'd just have to utter and people would jump and scurry around like frightened rabbits, the way Moir and Kirkland had done a minute earlier.

The Scottish Union of Dockworkers *would* come into existence, and he would be its president. Nothing, but nothing, was going to stop that happening. He would bring it about by whatever means were necessary, fair or foul.

Swinging his feet from the desk, he leaned forward and flicked the intercom switch which connected him to the woman who'd been The Rock's private secretary. He didn't know her name.

'Yes, sir?'

'I want a letter sent off to every member of staff, with the exception of Mr Moir and Mr Kirkland, giving them a fortnight's notice as from this Friday. When you've done that, have this building put up for sale.'

There was a stunned silence.

'Have you got that?'

'Yes, sir. Fortnight's notice and the building up for sale,' the woman quavered in reply.

'Right,' said Ken, and flicked the intercom switch down again.

Then he picked up the telephone and made the call ordering the release of Elizabeth and Jane. He had no fear of The Rock going to the police once they were released, for he had told The Rock that, if he did, sooner or later, in Scotland or New Zealand, the twins were dead.

'Congratulations!' Vicky squealed, and fell upon Tina, hugging her tight. Tina had come over to Parr Street to tell Vicky and Neil that she had become engaged to Sammy Walker, the chap she had met at the dance in the Kelvinhaugh Labour Hall. Sammy was an electrician.

'Let me have another look,' Vicky said, releasing Tina and grabbing hold of her friend's left hand.

'I've got a wee drop of whisky in, this calls for a toast,' Neil said and crossed to the sideboard to fetch the bottle and glasses.

'It's a smashing ring!' Vicky enthused. In fact it was a very ordinary engagement ring, similar to thousands of others to be found on the left hands of working-class women in the city. Not too big, not too small, not too expensive, but not too cheap either. In other words, just right for a working man's pocket.

'The wedding's next month. You're both invited of

course. And, Vicky, I was wondering if you'd be matron of honour?'

'I'd love to be.'

'And you, Neil. Would you be an usher?'

'I'd be honoured.'

'That's settled then,' Tina said, accepting the glass Neil handed her.

'To a long and happy married life!' Neil toasted.

'Aye, lang may your lum reek,' Vicky added.

'Only four months you've been going out together. It didn't take the pair of you long to make up your minds,' Vicky said. Tina had met Sammy the previous October; it was now late February, 1947.

'It was a click right-off. I think we both knew within a few weeks that we were right for each other. But I didn't say, not even to you. Just in case.'

'I understand. It's always best not to tempt fate,' Vicky replied. She was really chuffed at Tina's news.

'Sammy's decided we'll go doon ra watter for our honeymoon, either Rothesay or Millport,' Tina said, meaning down the River Clyde.

'It'll be gey cold there in March, but I don't suppose that will be bothering you two any,' Vicky teased.

It was Neil who glanced away. His embarrassment was combined with a bitter resentment about his own condition. Hardly a day went by when he didn't curse his impotence, and Ken Blacklaws for making him that way.

Tina gave a lecherous leer. 'I don't suppose it will.' She giggled.

'What about a house for the pair of you?' Vicky asked.

'I'd like to get one in St Vincent Terrace because I like it so much there. Sammy's going to call on the factor my da rents his house from.'

Neil went over and poked the fire. Wind was howling outside. He paused to listen to the sound of a broken chimney top birling away good-o.

'There's just one problem about the honeymoon. I'm going to need someone to fill in for me at work, and I thought you might do it? Helping me as you have on a

Wednesday these past months makes you the obvious choice,' Tina said.

Vicky glanced at Neil. 'It's up to you, pet,' he told her.

'I'd like fine to do it but I'll have to speak to my mum first. It would mean her taking Martha to school and looking after her from when school came out till I got home.' Vicky sipped her whisky and thought about that. She went on, 'Tell you what, you stay here and I'll nip over the road and have a word with Mum now.'

'Terrific!' Tina smiled.

Ten minutes later Vicky was back to say that Mary had agreed. Vicky would do Tina's job while Tina was on honeymoon.

Vicky poured out a cuppa for herself, weak tea without milk or sugar. Many Glasgow folk drank their tea that way, a result of the rationing. It was Friday afternoon, and in a couple of hours she would have finished her first week in Tina's job – a week she had thoroughly enjoyed. It had been marvellous to return to full-time work. She found this job extremely interesting and rewarding. When she was at it, the hours just flew by.

Only the previous night Neil had remarked at the difference in her. She had a whole new zest and zing, a sparkle that had been missing over the past few years. There was no doubt that her relationship with Martha had improved now that her life had expanded from the narrow confines of house-house and wean-wean – as indeed had her relationship with Neil. The outside interest and stimulation made a world of difference.

She decided that in the near future, some time after Tina's return from honeymoon, she would have a long chat with Mary about the possibility of her looking after Martha on a long-term basis so that she could have a full-time job of her own. Neil wouldn't object, she was sure of that. In fact, pound to a penny he would be all for it. Thankfully, he wasn't one of those husbands who thought it wrong for a woman to have aspirations other than slaving at the kitchen sink all day. Humming happily, she resumed typing, her fingers flying over the keys.

Vicky had just returned to the kitchen from putting Martha to bed and reading *Goldilocks and the Three Bears* yet again – Martha absolutely adored the story of Goldilocks and would have listened to it twenty-four hours a day given the chance – when there was a knock on the outside door.

Neil glanced up from the law book he'd been engrossed in. 'I wonder who that is?' he said, frowning.

'Probably Mary,' Vicky replied over her shoulder, making for the door.

'It's me. I've come visiting,' smiled Tom Allen and held up a large brown-paper poke which chinked.

'This is an unexpected pleasure. Come away in,' said Vicky, wishing she had something nicer on than the old dress she slopped around the house in, and ushered Tom Allen through.

Neil jumped to his feet when he saw who their caller was.

'I hope I'm not interrupting?' Tom inquired politely.

'Not in the least,' Neil reassured him.

Tom handed Vicky the poke. 'Some screwtops. I thought we might wet our thrapples while we talked.'

The two men sat on either side of the fire and Vicky opened several of the screwtops and poured them all beer.

'Well, Tom, what brings you to Townhead?' Neil queried when the three of them had a glass in their hands and Vicky had sat down.

'You do. I want to have a chat with you.'

There was an undercurrent in his tone that caused Neil to glance quickly at Vicky. 'Is there some sort of legal problem you want me to help out with?' he asked.

'No. Although your helping my constituents in that department has got to do with why I'm here tonight. Did you know you're building something of a reputation for yourself in Glasgow Kelvinhaugh? You're very highly spoken of, and spoken about more and more.'

A tinge of redness crept into Neil's face. 'That's kind of you to say so,' he mumbled.

'And I personally like you a great deal. Which is what made me think of what Mr Attlee said to me only recently in the House of Commons.'

'And what was that?' Neil asked, intrigued.

'The Prime Minister believes that the Labour Party has now reached a point in its existence where, if it wishes to survive as a major party, it has to broaden its base of appeal.

'You see, the plain fact is that, with mechanisation, automation and the great technological advances that have taken place during the last decade, the structure of society in Britain is rapidly changing. To put it bluntly, the working class is already contracting, whereas the middle class is expanding, the latter at the expense of the working class. To avoid losing these votes to the Liberals, the Labour Party must alter its image.

'The old-fashioned street corner ranters and ravers, such as I am, are yesterday's Labour Party. The men of tomorrow will have working-class roots but will have moved on in life, as you have done Neil. Lawyers, journalists, teachers, doctors and dons, those are the sort of people who'll be leading the party before long. That is Mr Attlee's belief, and mine also.'

Neil nodded. 'I couldn't agree more. The party must broaden or eventually wither, no doubt about it. But an awful lot of folk are refusing to admit that the signs exist, far less accept them.'

'You've hit the nail on the head, particularly where Glasgow and other big industrial cities are concerned. Their thinking has become entrenched, and because of this not nearly enough new blood is brought along or even actively encouraged to be party members.

'That's why I've come to see you this evening. How do you feel about speaking on the same platform as me a week on Friday?'

Neil sat back in his chair, aghast at Tom Allen's suggestion. 'But I've never spoken publicly in my life!' he croaked.

'That doesn't mean you can't do it. I think you can, and believe you should. From the number of political conversations I've had with you I'm convinced you have a tremendous amount to contribute. And you're a professional man, born and bred working class but now in one of Glasgow's top firms of solicitors – exactly the sort of person I've just been going on about.'

Neil swallowed what remained of his beer and looked to Vicky for a refill. 'It's just so . . . unexpected, that's all. I've never even considered speaking in public.'

'Vicky, what's your opinion?' Tom asked her, for he had come to respect her judgement while she'd been filling in for Tina.

Vicky gave Neil his refill, then topped up Tom Allen's glass. 'I agree with you that Neil has a tremendous amount to contribute, and think he should do so. As for his never having spoken in public before, I'm certain he'll enjoy it once he's up there and spouting. There's nothing he likes more than spouting his views,' she told Tom.

Neil barked out a laugh. 'Enjoy! Are you mad, woman! I'd be scared stiff, absolutely petrified.'

'To begin with maybe, but you'd soon get used to it,' she countered.

'And if I didn't?'

'Then never speak in public again. No harm will have been done.'

'Except an acute case of embarrassment.'

She shrugged. 'Embarrassment won't kill you. Some of the conditions in this city do, and those are the conditions you feel strongly about.'

A gleam came into Neil's eyes. She was dead right of course. This was a golden opportunity to speak out about many of the things that so concerned him, various conditions in the city which were appalling in the extreme and crying out for something to be done about them. And on a national level he could add his voice to those already clamouring for the government to push ahead with its nationalisation plans. The coal industry had been taken into public ownership on the first of January that year, but what about electricity, gas and the railways? There must be no backsliding when it came to those.

'You're not the man I imagine you to be if you back down,' Tom Allen said bluntly and even a little brutally.

'You really do believe I can pull it off?' Neil asked Vicky. She nodded. 'I do.'

Neil made up his mind. 'Right then, I'll spout a week on Friday,' he said, and they all laughed.

Tom Allen came over and shook him by the hand.

'So what's the verdict?' Neil demanded eagerly, having just read to Vicky for the first time the speech he'd been writing.

She was disappointed, but didn't want him to know. 'It was all right.' She smiled.

His face fell. 'Only all right?'

'It was very good.'

He gazed deep into her eyes, then glanced away. Crossing to the kitchen table, he threw down his speech onto it.

'No, it wasn't, it was lousy,' he said miserably.

'It was nothing of the sort. It had many fine points. It was, however – how can I put it? Somewhat constipated and pedestrian.'

He flung himself into a chair. 'Constipated and pedestrian – oh, charming!'

'It needs additional work and polishing. And you need to relax. You're awfully tense, which is badly affecting your delivery. Try and put the speech across the way you put your ideas and views across to me at home.'

'Constipated, pedestrian – and now stilted! It gets better and better.'

'That's quite the wrong attitude to take. You should be positive. And there's no need to be so cross with me. I'm only trying to help.'

He made a disbelieving harumphing sound and stared blackly into the fire.

'I'll put the kettle on,' she said, and rose.

'Not for me.'

She sat down again.

'But don't let me stop you if you want a cuppa,' he said airily.

She silenty counted up to ten. 'Would you have preferred if I'd lied and told you it was bloody brilliant?'

'I don't think it's as bad as you're making out.'

'You said yourself it was lousy.'

He glared at her. 'I didn't mean that literally.'

'I should hope not, otherwise you'd have meant it was crawling with lice.'

'Don't be so damned pedantic!' he said, voice rising.

'That's exactly what you're being in your speech, pedantic,' she retorted.

He clenched his fists. 'Maybe I should get in touch with Tom Allen and tell him I won't be able to do it,' he said huffily.

'Don't be pathetic. The speech itself needs more work on it, that's all.'

'I don't know,' he mumbled, and poked the fire with the First World War bayonet they kept for that purpose.

'Do you want me to have a look at it for you?'

'No,' he replied emphatically.

'Oh, grow up!' she exploded, and strode from the room. He was being so unreasonable!

When she returned to the kitchen a little later, he was still staring into the fire but the speech had gone from the table. Nor would he discuss it further when she tried to broach the subject again. Silly bugger! she thought to herself.

Vicky and Tina were leaving the pictures when it happened. Tina suddenly stumbled and bent over groaning. 'Awful pain in my stomach,' she gasped. Tina tried in vain to straighten. 'It feels like I'm bleeding down there,' she whispered to Vicky.

'Is it your time of the month?'

'No,' came back the anguished reply.

'I'd better get you into the manager's office,' Vicky said. The pair of them had staggered only a couple of steps when out of the corner of her eye Vicky saw a taxi loom into view.

A couple flagged the taxi down first but quickly relinquished their right to it when Vicky explained that her friend had had an attack of some sort and she needed to take her to the hospital.

Providentially the journey was short. When they arrived, the driver ran to summon assistance while Vicky did her best to comfort the distraught Tina, who was still groaning. Two uniformed men appeared with a stretcher on a trolley and gently lifted Tina onto it. They wheeled her into the hospital, where she was immediately wheeled off to see a doctor.

Vicky gave Tina's details. Just over fifteen minutes later a young doctor came to inform her that Tina was being admitted.

'What's wrong with her?'

'She's on the verge of losing the baby,' the doctor replied.

Vicky looked blank. 'I didn't know she was pregnant!'

'Neither did Mrs Walker, it seems, but she is.'

She must be only just pregnant, Vicky thought. Otherwise she would have known. Two months gone at the most, with one missing period, or more likely a lighter period than usual which Tina hadn't twigged had been caused by pregnancy. If Tina was two months gone, she must have been sleeping with Sammy before the wedding. But that was none of her business.

'Is there anything I can do?'

'You can inform the husband.'

'I'll do that right away. How is Tina?'

'In pain. We don't want to give her anything for it until we know exactly what's what.'

'How about the bleeding? Has that stopped?'

'It has. Let's just hope it remains stopped. If it does, she has a chance of holding onto the baby.'

Please God it would! Vicky silently prayed.

'Right then, I'll be on my way. I'll take a taxi over to St Vincent Crescent, where she lives. The sooner her husband gets here the better.'

'Tell him to bring some personal things, nighties and such. She'll need those whatever happens,' the doctor advised.

Vicky thanked the doctor, then ran out into the night searching for a taxi. Her luck was in; she found one almost immediately.

'So that's it. I'm going to be here for quite some time if I'm to hold onto the little blighter. It's a case of feet up and stay that way.'

Vicky took hold of one of Tina's hands and squeezed it. 'You'll enjoy that, you always were a lazy bitch,' she teased.

Tina grinned. 'It's going to be dead boring in here, but if I win through and have the baby it'll be worth it. Sammy's besotted by the idea of having children. It would break his heart for us to lose this one.'

'Then you'll just have to lie there with your legs crossed,' Vicky replied, and they both laughed.

'But seriously, what about my job?' Tina went on.

'Don't you worry about that. I had already spoken to my mother about taking a full-time job, and she'd agreed to help, so I'll step in, if that's all right with you?'

'I was hoping you'd say that. It certainly takes a load off my mind.'

'Good. Worry is the last thing you need. Peace and tranquillity, that's the ticket, until the big event takes place.'

The next morning Vicky reported to the Kelvinhaugh Labour Hall, thoroughly delighted to be back doing the job she had come to enjoy so much.

Tom Allen was so pleased to see her that he actually made the eleven o'clock tea for the pair of them.

Vicky listened to the chime of church bells in the distance: midnight. When they stopped, it would be Friday morning. The meeting at which Neil was due to speak would start at half past seven that evening.

She put a thumb in her mouth and gnawed the nail.

291

Earlier, when Neil had thought her busy with Martha, she had overheard him rehearsing his speech. He had come over far more relaxed than previously, but the speech itself, though altered, was only fractionally less stodgy. The content was good, better than it had been, but the prose let it down.

'Neil?' she whispered very quietly. There was no reply. He was sleeping soundly.

She slipped from bed and put on her dressing gown and mules. Picking up his briefcase – he always left it in the same place beside his clothes, so she was able to lay a hand on it without switching on the light – she padded from the bedroom.

It was cold in the kitchen. Raking the remains of the fire, she uncovered some cherry-hot cinders, over which she laid some kindling, and a shovelful of coal on top of that. The crackling kindling told her that the newly set fire would soon take. She made herself a cup of coffee, then settled down at the table with his speech, which she had taken from his briefcase. Slowly she began reading it through.

Highs and lows, light and shade – that's what it lacked, she decided. And wit; there was nothing Glasgow folk loved and appreciated more than wit. She sipped her coffee, and re-read the opening paragraph. If he rephrased that, and maybe inserted a joke there . . . and if he simplified those three sentences, condensing them, and replaced the high-falutin words with ordinary workaday ones, the paragraph would not only come alive, it would be far easier to deliver.

She went over to the sideboard and took out pen and paper from the left-hand drawer. Sitting again at the table, she started to write.

She told Neil what she had done over breakfast, hoping that Martha's presence would stop him blowing his top. It did, but only just.

'All I ask is that you read my version and compare it with what you wrote. It's still the same speech. I haven't altered one jot of content, but I have, I hope, injected some life and excitement into it. The two speeches are in your briefcase. It's up to you which you use tonight.'

Neil, quivering with rage, wiped marg onto his toast, then spread it with some Victoria plum jam that Mary had made with a quantity of black-market sugar she'd come by.

'Up to you,' Vicky repeated.

Neil did not reply.

Vicky washed up, then got Martha ready to take over to Mary's. She always left before Neil. He had a later start at work than her.

'Bye, bye. See you at teatime then,' she called out to Neil after Martha had given him her usual parting kiss. She normally kissed him as well, but hadn't attempted to do so that morning because of his reaction to what she'd done.

There was no reply from behind the raised newspaper.

Vicky was about to slam the outside door, then stopped herself. She wouldn't give him the satisfaction of that.

The Cooperative Hall was packed with Cooperative workers and their families. It was a grand turnout, but then Tom Allen was a popular speaker.

There were three people on the platform: Tom Allen, Neil and a Cooperative official by the name of Beath.

Vicky was in the sixth row from the platform, sitting to one side. She had not wanted to be directly in front of Neil in case that put him off.

After tea, they had returned Martha to Mary, then come on to the hall. He had made no comment about her version of his speech, and she, although dying of curiosity, had not asked.

Mr Beath, a man so incredibly ordinary-looking that he seemed almost invisible, rose to appeal for quiet. He then made a short speech of welcome to those in attendance and to Tom Allen.

'And now I'd like you to give a generous hand to a new

speaker to us, but one whom Mr Allen assures me we're going to hear a great deal from and about in the future: Mr Neil Seton!' Mr Beath announced and led the politely enthusiastic clapping.

Neil stood up and approached the microphone.

Vicky, extremely nervous for him, closed her eyes and crossed her fingers.

It was her version of his speech! He hadn't allowed his wounded pride and feelings of masculine superiority to get the better of him after all!

She opened her eyes to see him standing quite relaxed, at ease with himself and audience. There wasn't even a trace of nerves! She knew then, without the shadow of a doubt, that the evening was going to be a success for him.

'You did fine, lad, just fine. But then I never doubted you would,' said Tom Allen, playfully punching Neil on the arm. The meeting was over, the people starting to disperse.

'I enjoyed it, just as Vicky predicted I would,' Neil replied, glancing sideways at Vicky and smiling at her.

'I have another meeting to address in Parkhead next week. How would you feel about speaking there?' Tom asked.

'I'd love to.'

'Consider it a date then,' Tom said, then turned to a knot of folk waiting to talk to him.

'You were terrific. I was real proud of you,' Vicky told Neil.

'I'd have gone down like a lead balloon if you hadn't rewritten my speech,' he confessed.

'The ideas were all yours. I just polished up your prose, that's all,' she protested.

'If I was successful tonight, it was because of you.'

She slipped an arm round one of his. 'Then let's agree to say that what was accomplished was accomplished together, as a team, the way a good marriage should be.'

He kissed her on the cheek. 'I love you,' he whispered.

'I know.' She smiled.
'Together,' he nodded.
'Together,' she echoed and kissed his cheek.

Ten

Vicky carried a bag of fruit, Neil several books about the Labour Party which he had found in a secondhand bookshop. It was June 1948 and they were in the Western Infirmary, en route to visit Tom Allen, who had suffered a heart attack three days previously.

That morning Mrs Allen had rung Vicky at her office in the Kelvinhaugh Labour Hall – since Tom's heart attack Vicky had been round to see Mrs Allen in her home, and had also rung twice inquiring about Tom's condition – to say that Tom was feeling a bit better and wanted urgently to speak to Neil.

The previous November Tina had given birth to a little boy, Ronald, and then decided, under strong pressure from Sammy, that she would not return to work. Consequently Vicky now had Tina's former job permanently.

Vicky and Neil found Tom's ward without difficulty but had to wait outside in the corridor for a few minutes for visiting time to begin. Then the handbell was rung and they went inside.

They found Tom at the top end of the ward. Vicky thought he looked absolutely dreadful. His face was dirty grey, his cheeks sunken. His hair hung limp and lifeless, while the whites of his eyes had a definite yellowy tinge. He smiled weakly and offered up his right hand, which Vicky grasped. Then Neil did the same.

Vicky sat on a wooden chair; Neil made do with the edge of the bed. They chatted for a wee while, then Tom dropped his bombshell.

'I'm going to have to stand down as MP for Glasgow Kelvinhaugh. The specialist has told me that, if I take it easy, I've probably got between five and ten years left. If I continue working, he doubts I'll be around for the Christmas after next.'

'Oh, Tom!' Vicky exclaimed softly, knowing how much politics and the Labour Party meant to him.

He gave them another weak smile. 'Mustn't grumble, I suppose. I've had a good run for my money, a damn good run. But that run's over now, and I've got to accept the fact.' He paused to catch his breath, then went on. 'Mind you, the attack wasn't totally unexpected. There's a history of heart attacks in my family. And I did have a warning a few years back. I should have paid it heed and slowed down then, retired even, but I didn't, and have now paid the penalty, though fortunately not the ultimate one.'

'I'm sorry,' said Neil.

'Well, look at it this way. One man's loss is another's gain. I want you to be the Labour Party candidate in the by-election.'

Neil's jaw dropped. 'You what!'

'You heard. I want you to be the Labour Party candidate in the by-election,' Tom repeated.

Neil shot a glance at Vicky.

'Why Neil?' Vicky asked.

'Let me explain. This isn't a sudden notion on my part. It's been in my mind that Neil would be my eventual successor ever since that first time he spoke at the Cooperative Hall, and if I had any lingering doubts these were dispelled when he spoke in the St Andrew's Halls alongside Stafford Cripps and myself. That performance was outstanding, and I knew then that I wanted Neil to replace me when the time came.' He went on ruefully, 'Though, to tell the truth, I hadn't expected that succession to be quite so soon . . . So what do you say, Neil. Will you do it?'

Neil bit his lip and glanced again at Vicky. 'You make my selection sound a certainty. What if the selection board reject me?' he asked, turning back to Tom.

Tom's lips twisted into a thin, cynical grin. 'That lot will do exactly as I tell them. If I say you're to be my successor, then my successor you'll be. You have my word on that.'

'Vicky?'

'All your life you've wanted to help the deprived and underprivileged. This is a chance to help them on a far grander scale than you could if you remained a solicitor. It will give you power and influence not only to have things changed on a local level but on a national one as well. If you're foolish enough to let this chance slip by, you'll regret it all the days of your life,' she told him.

'And you'll back me?'

'To the hilt.'

'I'm your man then,' Neil said to Tom Allen.

'I'll write out my resignation later on today, or have a nurse write it out for me, and I'll sign it. I'll have the selection board here in the next day or two and tell them what I've decided, and some time after that they'll be in touch with you. They'll have to appear to go through the proper procedures, of course, but when the candidate is finally chosen from the shortlist you'll be it, I promise you,' Tom replied.

All the way back to Parr Street Neil and Vicky talked excitedly about the forthcoming by-election and discussed in broad terms the many speeches Neil would have to make.

'Checkmate,' said Ken, voice swollen with emotion. It was the first time he had ever beaten Dov Berkoff, the South of Scotland chess champion.

The old Jew's eyes twinkled. It was rare for him to be beaten – an experience he enjoyed nonetheless, for it kept his interest in the game alive.

Berkoff brought his gaze to bear on Ken. 'You have developed an excellent endgame, a ruthless one even. That is most unusual for a British player.'

'Thank you,' Ken replied softly. A compliment from Berkoff was a compliment indeed.

Ken had joined the Nether Pollok Chess Club a little over two years previously. The top players in the city and that part of the country all belonged to it, and the best of them was the man now facing him; Dov Berkoff, a Russian Jew who had come to Glasgow shortly after the Red Revolution. Berkoff was a tailor by trade, chess master by calling.

'I knew you would beat me one day. I have seen it coming for some while now.' Berkoff waved a brown-spotted hand at the board between them. 'Your Zugzwang was particularly good.'

Zugzwang was from the German, *Zug* meaning move, *zwang* to force.

'I still have a great deal to learn, which I do every time I have the honour of playing you,' Ken replied.

'You learn quickly, far more quickly than most. And you have a natural aptitude for the game. You would have made a fine general.'

Ken laughed. The old Jew was closer to the mark than he realised. For, looking at it from his point of view, wasn't he a general already? A general with his own private army and war to fight and win.

'Do you know who your game reminds me of?' Berkoff said, and lit a cigarette. He was a chain smoker – except when involved in the process of playing.

Ken thought Berkoff was going to name another Scottish player but he was wrong.

'Alekhine, often called "the fighter",' Berkoff stated, and took a deep drag on his cigarette.

Ken flushed with pleasure. Alekhine was one of the greats, who had died a few years previously.

Berkoff went on, 'The strength of your game is the same as his – your ability to create and prepare a position long before you have conceived the form your winning combination or mating attack will take.

'And you have the same aggressiveness in your play. Oh yes, very much so. Like him, you don't just want to beat your opponent, but to annihilate the unfortunate.'

Ken could not deny it. He did prefer winning, as he would have put it, decisively.

'Now, as you've finally succeeded in beating me, I will first of all allow you to buy me a drink, then I shall hope to exact my revenge.'

'Wait!' Ken said, as Berkoff reached out to begin resetting the board. 'I'll order the drinks now, but before we start again there were several moves you made on which I'd like you to explain your thinking.'

Berkoff nodded. 'My pleasure.'

Ken beckoned to a steward and placed their order. Then he asked his first question of the old Jew, listening with brow furrowed in concentration as Berkoff replied.

Vicky glanced anxiously at the clock. She had thought Neil would have been home by now. He had gone to the Kelvinhaugh Labour Hall where, that night, the selection board was choosing the candidate from the shortlist. What if something had gone wrong? What if he hadn't got it? What if Tom Allen didn't have the sway over the board he thought he had?

Sitting here worrying like this was no good, she told herself. She must do something to help take her mind off things. She would polish the brasses, she decided. She always found that soothing. She started on the brass pole slung underneath the mantelpiece, and soon had it gleaming.

Yet another glance at the clock told her that a further twenty minutes had passed. Something must have gone wrong. Where was he! Going down on her knees, she attacked the fender. As she polished, she found herself listening to the tick-tick-ticking of the clock.

After the fender came the brass shellcase that stood on the hearth. The shell itself had been fired at Ypres – so the man who'd sold it to her father had told him when George had bought it as a present for her and Neil. She was just finishing the shellcase, and thinking that she would put the kettle on again, when she heard the sound of Neil's key in the outside door.

Instantly she was on her feet, wiping her hands on her pinny; then, using a clean area of her pinny, she cleaned away sweat that had gathered on her forehead and temples.

Neil came into the kitchen with a face so long that he was nearly tripping over it. With shoulders drooping he stopped and stared at her. Neither spoke. Then suddenly his gloom vanished and he gave a whoop!

'Oh, you beast for doing that to me!' she exclaimed, and ran at him, intending to pummel his chest.

Before she could do so, he grabbed her and held her fast. Then, lifting her right off her feet, he whirled her round and round, as she screeched with a combination of alarm and excitement.

Finally he set her down again and kissed her.

'Neil Seton MP: it has a ring about it, don't you think?' he said when the kiss was over.

'I think it sounds quite beautiful.'

They went over to the seats by the fireplace and there he told her all that had happened at his interview. Vicky eagerly drank in every word.

Vicky woke as dawn was breaking to discover she was alone in the bedroom. She lay for a while, thinking that Neil must have gone to the bathroom and would soon return, but when he didn't she got out of bed and put on her dressing gown and mules.

He was in the kitchen, huddled in darkness in his seat by the fireplace. He blinked when she switched on the light. His face was drawn, and there was a look of anguish in his eyes – anguish and terrible despair.

She went and knelt beside him. 'What is it, Neil?'

He ran a hand through her hair and grasped a fistful of curls, but not tightly enough to hurt her.

'Years pass, but the urge, the desire, never diminishes. I want you so badly I could scream with it. The mind wants but the body can't deliver. I'm just dead there, stone dead. Can you have any idea what that's like? To know, to have to live with the fact, that never ever in my life will I be able to do it?'

He took his head in his hands and his body shook.

She put an arm round his shoulders and tried to draw him close, intending to cuddle him. But he wouldn't let her. He shrugged himself free.

'If you don't mind I'd rather be alone right now. Please?' he said in a voice that was strangely grating.

With a lump in her throat and tears stinging her eyes, she left him and went back to bed.

Neil had spoken better than he had ever done before. His speech, which the pair of them had laboured at, had been an absolute cracker. It received a standing ovation from nearly the entire gathering.

This Tuesday night was the first time that all three candidates of the major parties had spoken under the same roof. The Tory and Unionist had spoken first, the Liberal second, and Neil last. His speech had been in a different class from his rivals'.

Both Vicky and Neil had wished that Tom Allen could have been there, but that had been impossible. He was home now, but bedbound. It would be weeks yet before he would be allowed out and about.

Tina had come though, having told Sammy that he had to babysit for wee Ronald. She had had Vicky in fits describing Sammy's horrified reaction.

'But I'm a man. Men don't look after weans!' he'd protested.

'Well, this man is going to have to, and that's all there is to it,' she'd informed him.

She had left him staring at the baby as though it was a bomb which might explode at any moment . . .

'Absolutely first rate!' said Mr Black, one of the Labour Party's selection board, coming up to Vicky and shaking her by the hand.

'Yes, it did go down very well, didn't it,' she answered with a smile.

'A right treat, hen, a right treat. By the way, have you met the wife?'

Vicky shook hands with Mrs Black and was again congratulated on Neil's speech. She glanced over to where Neil stood surrounded by admirers and well-wishers. He was deep in conversation. She was about to return her attention to the Blacks when she suddenly became aware of a woman studying her, a woman whose face was vaguely familiar. Their eyes locked for a brief second, then the woman broke contact and addressed herself to the Liberal candidate, a tall man called Brian Brown, who bent to listen. Vicky could see that the woman was speaking quickly and intensely.

'I understand Neil is speaking tomorrow night.' Mrs Black broke into Vicky's reverie.

She resumed her conversation with the Blacks, and before long had forgotten all about that vaguely familiar face across the hall.

The following afternoon Vicky was in the middle of typing a letter at work when, in a flash, the recognition came to her.

'Oh, my God!' she exclaimed, her hands dropping away from the typewriter.

Muriel Mitchell: the bitch who had nicked a new sweater from her, leaving an old threadbare one in its place, during her first days at Duncliffe. Muriel had been Miss Ganch's 'special friend' at the time.

So what had Muriel been saying to Brian Brown? Had she told him that she, the Labour candidate's wife, was a convicted thief and had served time in borstal and prison because of it? She went ice cold at the thought. She had to speak to Neil right away. Picking up the telephone, she hurriedly dialled the number of MacDonald, Lindsay and Hogg.

They met halfway between his place of work and hers. Already waiting impatiently when she arrived, he grasped her by the elbow.

'Now what is it that's so bloody important you had to see me so urgently?' he demanded, for it had not been easy for him to skive off from the office.

In a rush of words she told him.

When she was finished, he took a deep breath and swore. 'Are you one hundred per cent certain it was her?'

'Oh yes. I'm not mistaken. The hairstyle was different, and she's a lot older and thinner than she used to be, but it was Muriel Mitchell all right.'

'But Tina was also there last night. Why didn't she recognise her?'

Vicky shrugged. 'Maybe she didn't see Muriel. There was a large number present, after all.'

'And you say she was chummy with Brian Brown?'

'It appeared to me she was. There was something about the way she was speaking with him, a relaxed manner if you like, which suggested they were at least acquaintances, if indeed not friends.'

Neil's features creased into a scowl, while his eyes took on a worried, brooding look. 'Brown may come over as a bit of a softie and goody-goody, but nothing could be further from the truth. Underneath that carefully cultivated act he's as ruthless as they come and hard as tempered steel. If this Muriel has handed him a weapon he can use against me, then use it he will, without a moment's hesitation. He'll do his damnedest to discredit and destroy my candidacy.'

'We must go to Tom Allen for advice right away,' Vicky urged.

Neil thought about that and nodded.

'Hell's bells!' he cursed as they made for the tramstop.

Tom Allen, sitting up in bed, listened to their tale from behind hooded eyelids. He tried not to show it but he was shocked at the revelation that Vicky had been in borstal and prison. He never would have believed it if he hadn't heard it from the horse's mouth.

'You should have told me about Vicky's past before you agreed to be candidate,' he said angrily when they finished.

Neil blushed. 'I know. That was quite negligent on my part,' he admitted.

Vicky chipped in. 'The fault's mine. I should have made sure you were told. But I suppose like many skeletons in the cupboard you wish so hard they weren't there that you end up half believing that to be true.'

Neil shook his head. 'I should have said. It was stupid of me not to. I mean, most of Townhead knows about Vicky, so it was bound to come out some time. I suppose the idea of being an MP appealed so much that I played the ostrich.'

'We both did,' Vicky said.

There was a pause. 'Is there any way of salvaging this, or is that it for me?' Neil asked anxiously.

Tom stroked his chin. 'Muriel Mitchell or not, it's best this thing comes out now. If only we could somehow twist it to our advantage,' he mused.

'Would it help to know that, although I confessed to the thefts, in reality I was innocent of them. I was covering up for someone else,' Vicky said.

'Why on earth would you do that?' Tom queried.

Vicky glanced at Neil, then back at Tom. 'I was covering up for the man I loved at the time.'

'It's true. I know that for fact,' Neil added.

'There's no way you can prove this I suppose?' Tom said to Vicky.

She shook her head.

'Pity,' Tom muttered, and chewed a nail.

'Is that any help?' Neil asked.

'Possibly. I have to think it through first before I can say. But now I want you to tell me all about these thefts, and this boyfriend you were covering up for – in fact, the whole thing.'

And so Vicky did – everything, with one exception. She did not tell him that Neil had been made impotent as a result of the kicking Ken had given him.

Jim O'Donovan, a small, broad-shouldered man in his early fifties, was the general secretary of the Union of Longshoremen, which owned the ninth floor of a Jamaica Street building. He and the four members of his executive were gathered there in his office that Friday afternoon, as they were every Friday afternoon, to discuss and thrash through union business. He glanced at his watch. They had been talking solidly, without breaking for dinner, since mid-morning, and he was whacked. Thank God they were almost finished.

'What about Blacklaws? Have you heard any more from him?' Ritchie Allness asked.

Jim picked up a piece of paper he'd been doodling on and

noisily screwed it into a ball. 'Not a dickie bird since a fortnight ago when he sent us his latest offer for a merger – an offer we all agreed he could stick up his arse.'

'Do you think he's finally got the message that we've no intention of merging?' asked Bob Wyllie.

Jim had been clipping the end of his cigar. He now put the cigar in his mouth and lit it. 'To be frank, I doubt it. He's one of those bastards who thinks that, if he keeps coming at you, you'll eventually give in. But, no matter what offers, deals, inducements or whatever he comes up with, our answer is always going to be the same: our union stays independent, we remain in charge of it, and he can go fly a kite.'

A growl of approval ran round the room.

'We just have to remain solid and see that he doesn't get a hold on any of us as individuals. For, as we all know, it's been rumoured he's previously managed that amongst the upper echelons of other unions, unions he subsequently took over,' Jim went on.

Robbie Campbell thought of the mouthwatering temptation that had only recently been put his way. But he'd put two and two together, got Blacklaws as the answer and run a mile in the opposite direction. 'None of us can be too careful. That one's cunning and devious as a fox,' he said.

'And sly as one,' Tom Spicer added, which caused Ritchie Allness to nod in agreement.

'Anyway, enough about business and Blacklaws. We'll away over the road and have a bevy. I'm so dry I could spit cotton wool,' Jim said.

The five men in the office rose from their seats.

'As you've just become a grandfather for the first time, Bob, the first round is on you. Pints and large whiskies to wet the wean's head,'' Jim said teasingly.

'Aye, all right then. I suppose I should,' Bob Wyllie replied reluctantly.

Jim chuckled. If Bob had a fault, he thought, it was that he hated parting with money. Bob would not have agreed with that at all. He wouldn't have described himself as mean, but as someone who was 'careful' with his bawbees.

Bob was an Aberdonian, though long resettled in Glasgow.

The five men were laughing and joking as they left Jim's office, bound for Carmichael's pub across the road, where, traditionally, they went every Friday after their weekly meetings. They walked down the corridor to the lift, to find the lift doors open and a workman tinkering inside.

'You fellows have timed it spot on. I've just finished,' the man said. Chucking a screwdriver into a bag of tools, he picked up the bag and got out of the lift, leaving it free for them.

'Thank goodness for that,' said the portly Ritchie Allness, thinking of the stairs to the ground floor. He loathed exercise of any kind.

Jim O'Donovan, exuding clouds of cigar smoke, pressed the button to descend.

'Sounded English, that workman chap,' Robbie Campbell commented to Bob Wyllie.

Tom Spicer, renowned for his dirty jokes, started to tell one about a cannibal and a missionary's wife with ginormous breasts, when the lift suddenly stopped dead.

'Christ, I hope it hasn't broken down again,' muttered Ritchie Allness, thinking again of the stairs.

Jim repeatedly pressed the descend button.

There was a creak, followed by the sound of a snap, and one side of the lift floor fell, to end up tilting downwards at about a twenty-degree angle. Bob Wyllie yelled as they were all thrown sideways.

'What the hell's going on!' Jim O'Donovan swore, groping for the cigar that had tumbled from his mouth. Robbie and Ritchie were still on their feet, the other three on their hands and knees.

Twang!

Someone screamed, but Jim O'Donovan didn't know who.

'Oh, Jean!' Jim whispered, thinking of his wife, as the lift plummeted downwards.

Then it smashed into the concrete bottom of the lift-shaft.

•

'Brown's over there. Do you see Muriel?' Neil muttered to Vicky and nodded in Brian Brown's direction.

Vicky glanced over and, sure enough, there was Muriel Mitchell in Brown's company.

'That's her in the blue dress and matching coloured hat,' she replied.

It was Friday night, and they were on the grassy area behind the museum and art gallery, where the second meeting featuring the candidates from the three major parties was due to take place. The museum and art gallery were situated in the north part of the Glasgow Kelvinhaugh constituency.

Vicky watched Muriel gazing about her, as if searching for someone. As before, their eyes met and locked. Muriel smiled, a vicious, razored smile that left Vicky in no doubt about two things: Muriel had told Brian Brown about her and, just as Tom Allen had said he would, Brown was going to denounce her that evening. Because the press attended these meetings in force, Brown would get maximum impact and coverage by choosing that occasion.

'How do you feel?' Neil asked Vicky.

'Sick as a pig with nerves.' She was not exaggerating.

'You can still back down, you know. You don't have to go through with it.'

She fixed him with a level stare. For some illogical reason, she could have slapped him for saying that. 'If I don't do as we planned, Brown will damn me and lose you God alone knows how many thousands of votes – if indeed you're not forced to resign your candidacy before polling day. This way there's the possibility we can defuse the situation and still get you elected,' she replied.

Twist the situation to your own advantage, was how Tom Allen had put it. Aye well, maybe. But Neil wasn't at all sure that this would work.

A camera flashed as a press photographer took a picture of Neil and Vicky. 'And another. How about a smile this time please, Mrs Seton?'

Vicky duly obliged, though the smile was so false that she felt it would crack her face.

Dickie Fleet, Neil's agent, came bustling up. His profuse perspiration had nothing to do with the August heat. 'It's fixed. The Tory and Unionist will speak first, then you, then Brown,' he said to Neil.

Neil grunted his satisfaction. It was imperative that he spoke before Brown. 'Good work.'

'The only problem was getting the Tory to agree to speak first. Brown was as keen to come after you as you were to go before him,' Dickie said.

'Give them laldy!' A Labour supporter cried out to Neil, who waved back that he'd heard.

'It's going to be a big turnout,' Dickie said, gesturing to the rear of the art gallery from where streams of people were continuing to appear.

So many people! Vicky thought. Her palms were oozing sweat, making the covers of the bible she was carrying glisten wet. She thought of the Black Room. What she had to do now would be a dawdle compared to what she'd endured in that hellhole.

The crackle of microphones filled the air. A man on the speakers' platform was making final adjustments.

'My seat in the front row has been reserved?' Vicky asked Dickie.

'Directly facing one end of the table. When Neil calls you, all you have to do is go up onto the platform and round the table.'

'Let's get to the platform,' Neil said, and the three of them moved in that direction, stopping, and being stopped, every few yards to talk to supporters and well-wishers. Vicky wondered cynically if the same people would still be wishing Neil luck after he and she had said their pieces.

Vicky became aware of swarms of midgies darting hither and yon, and even above the chatter she could hear the steady drone of flies. She blinked when several searchlights, relics of the war, sliced the gathering evening gloom. The searchlights began weaving patterns in the sky. More lights came on, round the platform itself. A cheer went up for the Tory and Unionist candidate, Alexander McGhie, a stockbroker on the Glasgow Exchange.

Finally the speakers were called onto the platform, and Vicky took her seat, Dickie Fleet sitting beside her. Then Alexander McGhie was introduced and the meeting began.

Vicky's insides were jumping and she had gone terribly dry. She stared enviously at the water jug and glass standing before each candidate. She felt that she could have drunk all three stone dry.

McGhie spoke well – from the Tory point of view, that is. He attacked the government's policy of nationalisation and the programme of 'austerity' instigated by Sir Stafford Cripps who held the combined post of Chancellor and Minister for Economic Affairs. Cripps had introduced heavy taxation on internal consumption and restrictions on overseas purchases and foreign travel to alleviate the country's foreign exchange crisis which had occurred the previous year.

McGhie received an enthusiastic hand from the small band of Tories present. Then it was Neil's turn. He glanced sideways at Vicky, who had gone white as a sheet.

'I had a speech prepared for this evening, a speech I've left at home. This is because last night my wife, whom many of you Labour supporters will know from her work at the Labour Hall, reminded me of what had happened to her a few years back, just before the war, and which, though serious it had been, even horrendous for her, I had so pushed to the back of my mind that I had more or less forgotten about it . . .'

Brian Brown suddenly sat up straight to stare with new interest at Neil. In the audience, six rows behind, and hidden from Vicky, Muriel Mitchell pursed her mouth and she stared at Neil through slitted eyes. Like Brown, she had guessed the drift of what was coming.

Neil went on, 'Vicky and I both come from Townhead, born and bred there, and the people of Townhead know about her past, though it's rarely if ever mentioned nowadays. Vicky says, and she's quite right, that the folk of Kelvinhaugh constituency should also know about that past, and you should know before voting takes place, not afterwards. And so, tonight, you're going to be told. But not by me – by my wife Vicky herself.'

Neil did not ask the permission of the two other candidates in case either refused. Instead he gestured to Vicky. 'Could you come up here please, Vicky?'

A buzz of puzzlement and general 'what's this all about?' ran through the audience. The press section were suddenly very animated and, as Vicky ascended the platform, at least a dozen camera bulbs popped.

She had been a bundle of nerves while waiting for this moment, but now a transformation came over her. Her apprehension and fear completely vanished, to be replaced by total calm and serenity. She feared no one, she was afraid of nothing. When she realised that her palms had stopped leaking, she gave a small, soft smile. Raising her bible, she held it just under her breasts.

In the front row Dickie Fleet put a hand over his face and closed his eyes. As far as he was concerned, the by-election was about to go down the plughole.

When Vicky spoke her voice was strong, vibrant and charismatically compelling.

'Thirteen years ago this month I was tried and convicted of theft. My sentence was three years, part of which I spent in Duncliffe borstal down the coast, the remainder in Duke Street prison.'

Pandemonium broke out. Camera bulbs started popping again. Alexander McGhie was so taken aback that he nearly fell off his seat. Brian Brown somehow managed to look both furious and pleased at the same time.

Despite the heat of the evening, Neil was icy from head to toe. He sat expressionless. There seemed to be a great gaping hole where his brain and mind had been.

Vicky held up a hand for silence and went on, 'I confessed to the thefts I was convicted of, but until tonight only a handful of people knew that I lied, that I wasn't the thief.'

Brian Brown spluttered in disbelief.

'And why would I do such a thing, you ask. The answer is, and I swear it on this bible I'm carrying' – she held the bible aloft for all to see – 'that I was in love with the man doing the thieving, and lied to protect him because of that love, and because I mistakenly thought I might not be prosecuted, whereas he was bound to be.'

She paused for breath, fixing her audience with an unwavering stare.

'Only I was wrong. I *was* prosecuted and, as I've already said, sentenced to three years. And the chap I lied to protect? He ditched me during my time in borstal and married another.'

Still holding the bible aloft, she continued, 'I cannot prove what I have just told you, but may I stand damned in the sight of God for ever if it is not the Gospel truth. It is now up to you whether or not you believe me, and whether it will affect those amongst you, and those not here this evening, who intended voting for my husband. I sincerely hope it doesn't, for he's the man Kelvinhaugh needs, the right man for this constituency . . . Thank you.'

She lowered the hand holding aloft the bible and turned to Neil, who had been standing a little behind her. He took her into his arms and hugged her tight.

There was no reaction whatever from the audience. Vicky was surrounded by eerie silence as she returned to her seat.

A sixth sense warned Brian Brown not to attack Vicky over what she claimed was the truth of her past. Instead he ignored what she had said and made an impromptu speech attacking the Labour government as a whole and throwing in what he saw as some very cutting remarks and jibes about the Tory Party.

Not once did he mention either Neil or Vicky.

Tom Allen sipped a well-watered whisky. Vicky and Neil had gone directly to his house after the meeting and described in detail all that had taken place.

'No reaction at all?' Tom queried.

'None,' Vicky confirmed.

He lifted an eyebrow and shook his head. 'Well well,' he mused.

'So now it's just a case of sit back and wait to see what happens,' Neil said, biting a fingernail.

'That's it,' Tom agreed.

'It'll be all over the morning papers. I think every daily in Glasgow must have had a reporter and photographer there,' Vicky said.

Neil bit a thumbnail right down to the quick. What had possessed him to allow himself to be talked into standing as a candidate in the first place! Stupid stupid stupid! And now this, this unholy mess. An ostrich, that's what he'd been, a bloody ostrich! But what a golden opportunity to dangle before him – the temptation had just been too great.

Vicky was thinking how much she now regretted taking the blame for Ken Blacklaws. If there was one thing in her life that, by some miracle, she could have undone, it was that. But she had been young and in love, oh so desperately in love.

Tom Allen sipped more whisky. 'No reaction at all,' he repeated to himself in a bemused tone and shook his head.

The next morning Ken was humming when he appeared for breakfast. He always had a special breakfast on Saturdays and Sundays: fried egg, bacon, mushrooms, black pudding and fried bread. He referred to it as 'the works'.

'You're in a good humour today,' Lyn commented, thinking what a pleasant change it was to see him so bright and breezy. He had been terribly tense of late, given to dark moods and snapping at all and sundry.

Ken kissed her on the cheek, then ruffled Kenny's hair. At eight years old Kenny was a fine-looking, sturdy lad. Pity about the kid having to wear specs. Kenny's eyesight was even worse than his own.

'Slept like a log, first time in ages.' Ken beamed and sat at the table. Lyn rang the handbell to tell Craig, the butler, that Ken was down, then poured him some coffee while he shook out his napkin.

'Will you play a bit of footer with me today, Dad, please?' Kenny demanded eagerly. He was football and Rangers daft.

'Aye, sure I will. Wait till my breakfast has settled, then we'll have a wee game of kickabout out on the lawn.'

Ken and Lyn's house had once been Jack and Wendy Fyfer's. It had come to them on Wendy's death several years previously. Ken thoroughly enjoyed living in Balfron; though, like Jack before him, and despite the fact he had a chauffeur permanently at his disposal, he found the travelling something of a bind. Ken never drove any more. Shugs, a registered dockie, did that for him. Shugs had a reputation for being handy with his fists and feet when necessary.

There was a stack of papers beside Ken's sideplate. He picked up the top one and found what he was looking for on page two. His mood changed instantly when he read that Jim O'Donovan had survived what was described as a terrible accident. O'Donovan had two broken legs, a broken arm, broken collarbone and concussion. Amazingly he had no internal injuries. A few months and he'd be back at his desk, O'Donovan himself predicted. Ritchie Allness, on the critical list but expected to pull through, had also survived. Bob Wyllie, Robbie Campbell and Tom Spicer had all been killed.

Ken, face a thundercloud, tossed the paper aside and glared into his coffee cup. The team he had brought up from London had failed him. They had sworn that no one could survive that drop.

Rage seethed in Ken. He had thought that, at long last, Clydeside was his. For, with O'Donovan and the others dead, it would be a simple matter for him to bring about the merger of the Union of Longshoremen with the Clyde Dockworkers' Union, to give the Clyde Dockworkers' Union a monopoly on Clydeside.

Craig entered with Ken's breakfast. 'The egg was freshly laid this morning, sir,' he said. The plate was piled high with 'the works'. There might be food rationing in Britain but that didn't apply to Ken's household. He had long since arranged it otherwise.

Ken glowered at his breakfast. He had been looking forward to it since getting up; now he'd lost his appetite. God damn those English incompetents!

He pushed his plate away. 'Apologise to cook. Bit of a dicky tummy. I'll settle for the coffee,' he growled.

'What is it?' Lyn asked after Craig, and Ken's breakfast, had gone.

'Nothing,' he replied, lighting a cigarette.

If he wasn't going to tell her, then she wasn't going to persist; she knew better than that.

'If you're not having any breakfast, can we play right away?' Kenny demanded.

'Eh?' Ken answered, lost in thought.

'If I run up and get my ball, can we play footer right away?'

The last thing he wanted to do now was play football. He would get onto London right away. He hadn't paid the second half of the team's fee yet, nor would he until the bastards had rectified their mistake. He didn't care about Allness, but he wanted O'Donovan dead, as soon as possible.

'Can we?' Kenny asked again.

'You did promise,' Lyn softly reminded Ken.

It was on the tip of Ken's tongue to snap back that he wasn't in the mood any more, then he relented. What the hell! Half an hour and the kid's day, if not week, would be made. Kenny was his son, after all, and he did play with him so rarely.

'Get the ball,' he told Kenny.

Kenny whooped and ran from the room.

'Thank you.' Lyn smiled.

Ken was about to reply when his eye was caught by a picture in the paper he had tossed aside.

Picking up the paper again, he stared at the picture. Mrs Neil Seton, the caption proclaimed. The story was a long one, twice the size of the 'horrible accident'.

Slowly he began to read.

Later that morning Vicky was about to turn into her close, having done the weekend shopping at the Coop, when a monstrous car drew up at the kerb and a window hissed down.

'Hello, Vicky,' Ken Blacklaws said.

She stared at him, surprised at the little jolt that went

through her to see him again. 'What brings you to Parr Street?' she asked.

'I was coming up to chap your door. I want to speak to you,' he replied.

'Get knotted,' she said, and entered the close.

She had taken only a few steps when the man who had been driving the car ran round in front of her, blocking her way.

'The boss says he wants to talk to you.'

Then Ken was there. 'That's all right, Shugs. Get back in the car.'

'You've got fat,' she told him, a hint of relish in her voice.

He patted his stomach. 'Always did have a tendency that way,' he admitted.

'Pigs do.' She smiled.

He winced. 'I know I've treated you badly. I deserved that.'

'And you've got bald, I see.'

'Not bald, *balding*. I have a bit to go yet before I'm bald,' he replied testily.

She noted that he had shaved off his moustache. 'Well, I don't want to speak to you,' she said, and made for the stairs.

'It could harm Neil if you don't.'

She stopped and twisted to face Ken. 'In what way?'

'Let's go for a spin in the car while we chat,' he said, relieving her of her heavy shopping bag.

The upholstery was leather and smelled absolutely delicious, Vicky thought, as she sank into it.

'So what do you think of my Caddy?' Ken asked proudly.

'Your what?'

'Cadillac. It's an American car.'

Vicky had seen Yankee cars before, in South America. There they had seemed to fit. Here they screamed ostentation. Or, to put it another way, were dead vulgar. 'You always were a flash bugger.'

'The only Caddy in all of Scotland,' he said, still trying to impress.

'I'm not surprised,' she replied ambiguously.

Ken scowled and lit a cigarette. He now smoked Lucky Strikes, also American.

'Imagine you marrying Neil after all! Tell me, is he still troubled with spots?' Ken laughed unkindly.

Vicky's right hand curled into a talon. What a pompous, insensitive bastard! For two peas she would have raked his face the way she'd raked Miss Ganch's.

Coldly she replied, 'Neil isn't spotty any more. In fact he was the ugly duckling who turned into a swan. He's very handsome now, and . . .' Her eyes fastened on Ken's waist-line. 'He *kept* his figure.'

Why did she have to keep going on about his increased weight! Ken was as irritated as she had intended him to be. He hated being reminded that he had put on so much beef or that his hair was thinning.

'Are you still married to Lyn?'

He nodded.

'I feel sorry for her.'

She had the satisfaction of seeing his face colour.

'Now what's all this about harming Neil?' she demanded.

'I read the story in the morning papers.'

She should have guessed. 'And?'

'I was pleased, and relieved, that you didn't mention my name.'

'There was no need.'

'What happens if you're pressed to put a name to the boyfriend you took the blame for and who let you down?'

'Why should I be pressed?' she asked.

'It's a good story. The newspapers might well want to follow it up.'

She shrugged. 'If it'll help Neil's candidacy to name you, then I will. For I don't owe you anything, Ken, nothing at all.'

Ken leaned forward and pressed a concealed button at the back of the driver's seat. A panel slid open to reveal a miniature bar.

'Would you like a drink?' he asked.

'No, thank you.'

He poured himself a stiff whisky. He had tried to switch to rye and bourbon, but both had made him feel queasy and given him unbelievable hangovers.

In a voice devoid of all emotion, he said, 'If you do name me as the boyfriend, then I will release my version of what happened, which will be quite different to yours.

'I will insist you were the thief. I will say Neil mistakenly believed I was and, being besotted by you, made the phone call to Copland and Lye thinking it would result in my arrest and imprisonment, leaving the way clear for him to take over with you where I had been forced to leave off. Only, as it transpired, you, the real thief, were arrested and put away, while I, the innocent party, went free.

'You'll continue to be branded a thief, while Neil will be seen as someone who tried to hand his best pal over to the police. And we both know what the majority of Glaswegians think of people who do that sort of thing, don't we? Any chance Neil had left of winning this by-election would go right out the window.'

'You really are a first-class shit,' she said.

'Self-preservation. That's what this is all about, Vicky, self-preservation.'

Ken was right. Glaswegians loathed people who cliped, particularly when it involved the police. Even the fact Neil had done it for love wouldn't save him; his political career would be well and truly over before it had even begun.

Vicky felt tears edging into her eyes. She turned away from Ken so that he wouldn't see them.

'I've read about *you* from time to time. You've done well for yourself,' she said, voice rock steady.

'I always intended to get on, and have,' he boasted.

'No matter who you've had to stand on to get there.'

He didn't reply, knowing that she was referring mainly to herself.

'Have you any family?' he asked.

Panic flared in her. 'Why do you say that?' she replied sharply. Did he know something? Had he guessed?

'No reason other than curiosity.'

Her panic subsided. She believed him. Curiosity *was* the reason behind the question, nothing else.

'A girl called Martha. She's an adorable wee thing. And what about you and Lyn? Any additions to Kenny?'

He shook his head. He had insisted that Lyn have the operation which rendered her incapable of getting pregnant again. He couldn't have faced a second time what he'd gone through following Kenny's birth. It was only in the last few years that their sex life had regained a semblance of normality.

'We decided not to have any more. Kenny's eight now, shooting up like a weed.'

Vicky was about to say how old Martha was, then changed her mind when she realised it might, just might, give Ken cause to wonder.

'You can take me back to Parr Street now,' she said.

'So I can rest assured I'll never be named as the boyfriend you took the blame for and who let you down?'

'You can rest assured.'

The Cadillac stopped outside her close. She got out, and Ken handed her her shopping bag.

'It's been a pleasure seeing and talking to you again.' He smiled.

Vicky did not reply. She simply walked off into the close, leaving him staring after her.

The following Monday evening Neil came home from work looking pale and shocked. Vicky, back before him as she always was, had already given Martha tea and changed her into her pyjamas.

'What's wrong, love?' Vicky asked when she saw Neil's face.

He dropped his briefcase by the side of the fireplace and flopped into a chair. 'I've had the bullet from MacDonald, Lindsay and Hogg.'

Vicky bit her lip. 'Because of the press coverage about me?'

'Michael Lindsay argued on my behalf, but not very forcibly, I'm afraid. It was bad enough that I was standing as a Labour MP, but to have it revealed that my wife had done time, whether innocent or not – well, that was just too much! "Not consistent with the company image, don't you know",' Neil said, imitating old man Hogg's fruity upper-class tones.

'You were going to leave them anyway.'

'That was when I believed I was going to be elected. Now, who knows whether I'll be or not.'

'Then you'll just have to set up on your own, as you originally intended before the idea of you running for Parliament came up.'

He gave her a sickly grin. 'Two things against that, Vicky. Number one, I'm not really experienced enough yet. And number two, though I want to help the poor and underprivileged, on a practical level I'll need paying clients to make the business viable. If the voters turn against me, you can be sure potential paying clients will stay away for the same reasons.'

'Damn!' Vicky swore.

Martha, eyes wide, suddenly started to wail.

Vicky clutched Martha to her and began rocking the wee girl back and forth.

'At least I don't have to speak tonight, it would have been a right sod to do so in the circumstances,' Neil said.

'I don't want Mummy and Daddy to be unhappy,' Martha blubbered.

Vicky somehow forced a smile onto her face. 'There there, pet, it's just a little upset, that's all, nothing Mummy and Daddy can't cope with. So let's stop this crying, eh?' With that, Vicky kissed Martha on both wet cheeks and equally wet mouth.

'Come over here. Let's you and I have a big cuddle,' Neil said and held out his arms.

Neil lifted Martha onto his lap, where she noisily sucked her thumb while he hugged her tight.

'As Mummy says, it's just a little upset, nothing to warrant tears,' he murmured, consoling her, thinking to himself how marvellous children were.

After a while, Neil said, 'I'll take you through and read you a story. Which one would you like?'

'Goldilocks,' Martha replied instantly.

Vicky laughed. 'What else! Give her the choice and it's always Goldilocks.'

Once Martha was tucked in, and with Vicky cooking the adult tea ben the kitchen, Neil proceeded to spoil Martha by reading the story three times.

How Martha loved that! The third time, having long known it off by heart, she recited it with him, word for word.

Several hours later Vicky and Neil were sitting across from one another by the fireplace, she darning a pair of his socks, he sunk in gloomy thought, when there was a rat-tat-tat on the outside door.

Neil answered the knock and returned to the kitchen with Jock McLean, their local MP, who lived only a couple of streets away. They both knew him well.

Vicky put down her darning and jumped to her feet. 'Come away in, Jock. I'll stick the kettle on,' she said, and strode over to the stove.

'Were you really innocent of that Copland and Lye business?' Jock asked gruffly. Jock was a man who prided himself in always coming right to the point.

Vicky looked him straight in the eye. 'I was.'

Jock held her gaze for several seconds, then gave a slight nod of his head. 'Aye, well that settles that then,' he said and, sitting, produced a battered briar. 'Do you mind if I stink your house out?'

Vicky laughed. 'Go ahead. We both enjoy the smell of pipe smoke.'

'It would be Ken Blacklaws you were covering for then? I recall that you and he were going out together at the time, and he also worked at Copland and Lye,' Jock said.

Vicky glanced at Neil, then brought her attention back to Jock. 'I don't see any point in raking over those old coals. I have no intention of saying who the man was, not now or ever. It's unnecessary, and could only cause distress to the family the man now has.'

'Everyone round here will know who it was, of course, but no one will say to any outsider. The way they'll see it is: if Blacklaws is to be named, you're the one should do the naming. After doing a stretch in borstal and prison for him, that's your right.'

'Then he won't be named,' Vicky said firmly, and started putting some teacakes and slices of home-made cake onto plates. The cake was a walnut one, a gift from Mary.

Jock addressed himself to Neil. 'Now, how about the by-election in Kelvinhaugh. Do you think you can still win?'

Neil shrugged. 'You tell me. It isn't clear at all yet how Vicky's confession is going to affect the voting.'

'I spoke to Tom Allen earlier in the week. He confided in me why Vicky did as she did. I agreed with him. In the circumstances, it was the only thing to do.'

'Then Tom must have told you that Vicky was really innocent?'

A thin smile stretched Jock's mouth. 'He did, but I wanted to hear her tell me that was so herself. I wanted to be absolutely certain.'

Neil was baffled. 'I don't wish to sound rude, but why should that be so important to you?'

'Tom tells me you'll make a first-class MP, given the chance. He says you've got tremendous talent and commitment. Personally I've only heard you speak once, but was most impressed. Aye, most impressed. And others, whose opinion in these matters I hold in high regard, have nothing but praise for you.'

'Well, thank you,' Neil replied, a trifle embarrassed.

'Which brings me to the purpose of my visit. After visiting Tom, I had consultations with the local powers that be, and it's been agreed, unanimously I might add, that, should you fail to be elected in the Kelvinhaugh constituency, we'd like you to stand for the Townhead seat come the next general election.'

Vicky gasped with delight and spilled some of the tea she was pouring.

'But what about you? You've been MP here for twenty-odd years?' Neil spluttered in reply.

'I'm well over sixty, Neil, and I've fought a hard battle all my life. First as a shop steward, then in local government, and as a Member of Parliament after that. It's high time I called it a day and retired, which is precisely what I'm going to do come the next general election.'

Neil was flabbergasted, quite stunned by this turn of events.

'So do you agree?'

'Agree? Of course I agree!' Neil exclaimed.

Vicky had a sudden thought, seeing how Neil could use this to current advantage. 'Would you, Jock, or the Townhead Labour Party mind if Neil told the newspapers about your offer?'

'You mean as a help to him in the by-election?' Jock replied shrewdly, not one to miss a trick.

'Exactly.'

Jock took a pull on his pipe. 'I don't think we'd have any objections. No. Go ahead, give it to the papers if you want. I'll happily corroborate the story if any of them want to get in touch with me.'

Then Vicky had another thought, a real bobby dazzler. Neil wouldn't like it, but she'd get round him.

Vicky arranged the press conference for the following afternoon. Neil took the afternoon off work, without a murmur of objection or protest from MacDonald, Lindsay and Hogg. As he said to Vicky, having already sacked him, the worst they could do now was dock him half a day's pay, which he was entirely agreeable to.

In preparation Vicky moved the kitchen table to one side and covered it with a snow-white linen cloth. Tom Allen had told her to lay on plenty of alcohol, and this she did with the help of the Kelvinhaugh Labour Club. There was enough whisky, gin and beer to sink a battleship, plus oodles of crisps, sausage rolls and fancy cakes.

But the most important item of all was Neil's Victoria Cross, which she displayed on the mantelpiece, its crimson ribbon showing up vividly and magnificently against the black satin interior of its presentation box.

'Now don't forget, when you talk to the journalists, you stand beside the medal so that they can't fail to see it. Not in front of it, beside it. And should they ask, it wasn't put on show especially, but is always kept there,' Vicky instructed Neil.

He pulled a face. 'I still hate the idea of it, Vicky. It's cheap and tricksie.'

'There's nothing cheap about a medal won for Conspicuous Bravery, the highest award a British serviceman can be given. You won it, and there's no harm in people being reminded that you did.'

Neil thought back to what had been tormenting him when he had stood up that day in December 1940 and all by himself walked into the murderous hail of machine-gun fire, while all around him the rest of his section lay dead or wounded.

Brave? Not him. The forces that had driven him to do what he'd done were fear, frustration, anger and self-pity. He had wanted to die and, because he had, death had perversely passed him by. There had been nothing conspicuously brave about his action. He was a fraud, a sham and, worst of all, in the final analysis, probably a coward.

'It just doesn't seem right,' he mumbled.

'Nonsense. Now pour us both a dram to get us in the mood for the invading hordes.' She smiled.

The press conference had been called for three o'clock. The first arrivals turned up at ten to. After that they came in quick succession.

As Tom Allen had told her to do, Vicky plied the booze and kept on plying it. A glass was no sooner empty than she refilled it. Tom had warned her that there was nothing nastier than a journalist who thought you were being tight-fisted with the bevy, and nasty journalists wrote nasty copy.

Finally Vicky judged it time to call the gathering to order. Neil took up a position in front of the fireplace, beside the VC. From there he told the gathering about Jock McLean's intention to retire at the next general election, and how Jock and the Townhead Labour Party had asked him to be their candidate then should he fail in his bid to win Glasgow Kelvinhaugh.

Pencils flew and flashbulbs popped. Questions were asked. Vicky eased herself round the room, refilling glasses as she went.

As she and Neil had expected, questions were asked about her conviction for theft and subsequent borstal and prison sentence. Vicky answered all these questions openly and truthfully. The only one she baulked at was the name of the man she alleged – in the journalists' words – she had taken the blame for.

She refused point blank to name Ken, giving the same reason she had given Jock McLean; that he now had a family and she had no wish to cause them any distress.

'Excuse me, Mr Seton, but what's that medal on the mantelpiece?' the journalist from the *Daily Record* asked.

Neil blushed. 'It's the Victoria Cross.'

An excited buzz ran round the room.

'Who does it belong to?' the same journalist went on.

Vicky piped up, knowing that Neil wouldn't blow his own trumpet. 'It belongs to my husband, and was presented to him by the King himself. He won it in Egypt, at Sidi Barrani.'

There was a new interest in the gathering. If no one asked what Neil had done to win the medal, Vicky intended volunteering the information.

'Here, I think I remember writing about that. Didn't you capture a whole bunch of Eyeties?' the man from the *Mail* queried.

'A number, yes,' Neil answered, still blushing, and swallowed a dollop of whisky.

Repeating almost word for word the article she had first read almost eight years previously, and which she still had in a bedroom drawer, Vicky said, 'Neil singlehand-edly attacked a machine-gun post, bayoneting seven men to reach the post, and shooting dead the two Italians manning it. Then, not bothering to wait for help, he made his way along a trench for a couple of hundred yards, attacked a dugout and forced thirty-seven enemy soldiers to surrender.'

The journalist from the *Express* whistled.

'By doing this, Neil turned the tide of the battle in favour of the British by allowing them to break through what until then had been an impenetrable wall of bullets. The British then went on to take their objective, the town of Sidi Barrani. General Wavell personally promoted Neil to the rank of captain after the battle was over.'

'So you were a war hero,' the man from the *Daily Record* said to Neil, who went a deep shade of crimson.

'That's maybe putting it a bit strong,' Neil mumbled.

'Everybody knows you have to do something very very special to win the Victoria Cross,' the *Guardian* chap said, admiration and awe in his voice.

'Would you give us a picture of you holding it up?' a photographer asked.

Neil shook his head. 'No, that I won't do. Sorry,' he said firmly.

'It would look terrific on page one,' the photographer cajoled.

'No,' Neil replied emphatically.

Vicky was about to intervene to try and make Neil do as the photographer wanted, then thought better of it. Perhaps Neil's instincts were right in this instance. It could be counterproductive if he was seen to come across as boasting about or capitalising on his vc.

She went back to refilling glasses.

Next morning, with the newspapers spread before her, Vicky rang Neil from her office in the Kelvinhaugh Labour Club.

'What do you think, eh? Haven't you got tremendous coverage?'

'There's certainly a lot of it,' he admitted.

'THE VC HERO OF SIDI BARRANI FOR TOWNHEAD IF HE FAILS AT KELVINHAUGH,' Vicky said, reading out one headline.

'There's a nice picture of us in the *Express*,' he told her.

She had already seen the picture but now had another look. It *was* a good picture, particularly of Neil. He came over as handsome, intelligent, relaxed and with a sense of humour. All in all, a winner. She didn't come over so badly either. They made a striking couple.

They talked about the various stories and photographs for several minutes. Then she said, 'Don't forget we're "on the knock" tonight.'

'I won't forget. I should get to your office about half past six.'

'There'll now be ten of us, and we've a thousand leaflets to distribute.'

He blew her a kiss down the phone. 'I love you rotten,' he whispered.

She returned the kiss. 'Till later, vc hero,' she replied, and laughing, hung up.

Vicky chapped her umpteenth door that night and waited. There was a strong smell of boiled cabbage in the close, that and whitewash, and the all-pervading odour from the half-landing wcs.

The door opened a crack and a suspicious eye peered out. 'Who is it?' an old female voice demanded.

'I'm here on behalf of the Labour Party candidate. Can I give you a leaflet?'

The door opened wider to reveal an ancient stooped crone with a tramlined parchment face. The pale blue eyes were lively and deep with intelligence. The crone might be ancient, but she most certainly wasn't senile. As the saying went, she still had all her marbles.

'Is that Seton you're talking about? Him that won the vc?'

'That's him.'

'See us a leaflet then.'

Vicky placed a leaflet in a gnarled and withered hand.

'He'll never replace Tom Allen, mind. Yon man's a gem,' the crone said.

327

'My husband also thinks very highly of Tom Allen. Mr Allen is an inspiration to him,' Vicky replied.

The blue eyes wrinkled. 'Your husband, eh? So you'll be the one cried Vicky Seton. I read about you. It was very interesting.'

Vicky had earlier decided not to disguise who she was when 'on the knock'. If people wanted to ask her questions, she was prepared to answer them, most of them.

'Is there anything about my husband you'd like to know? Or do you have any special problems or complaints you want looking into?'

The crone shook her head.

'Then can I ask you if my husband can count on your support?'

'You mean my vote?'

'That's right,' Vicky smiled.

'Aye, of course he can. Tom Allen personally recommends him, and that's good enough for me.'

'Thank you,' Vicky replied, and ticked off the house in the tally book she was keeping. 'And the rest of your household?'

'There's nobody else, only me. They all kicked the bucket years ago.'

'I'm sorry,' Vicky said.

'No' me. I prefer being on my own. My husband was a drunken slob, my two sons out the same mould. It was a relief to get rid of the buggers.' The pale blue eyes twinkled. 'Do you mind if I ask you something?'

'No. Go ahead.'

'Did you really do it for love?'

'You mean take the blame for those thefts?'

The crone nodded.

'Yes,' Vicky whispered.

The crone let out a long breathy sigh. 'That's ever so romantic,' she said wistfully.

With a faraway, dreamy expression on her face, the old woman started to shut the door. 'Goodnight then, hen.'

'Goodnight,' Vicky replied, a second before the door snicked shut.

Returning to the street, Vicky found Neil waiting for her. 'How's it going?' he asked.

'The feeling is good, very good.'

'Same for me and the others "on the knock" I've spoken to. I think, I really do think, I'm going to pull it off.'

Vicky held up a hand and crossed two fingers.

She went into the next close along, Neil the close after that.

Ken Blacklaws was checking through a new revised union contract form – the revisions made by him in the union's favour – when the door to his office flew open and Ina Finlayson burst in. A statuesque blonde, she was twenty-two years old and had a knockout figure. She had been Ken's secretary for the past nineteen months, his lover for fifteen of them.

'There's been a gas explosion at Camphill private nursing home, where Jim O'Donovan was being treated. He and fifteen others have been killed, and there are lots of casualties,' Ina said in a rush of words.

O'Donovan dead! Elation surged through Ken, but he strove to keep it from his face.

He placed the contract form on his desk. 'How did you hear this?' he asked quietly.

'Betty-in-records' boyfriend has just rung to say he won't be able to meet her early evening as they'd arranged. He's one of the firemen who've been called out to the explosion. He says it's likely he and his mates will be there for half the night.'

'And he mentioned O'Donovan specifically?'

'He did, thinking it would be of interest to Betty, she working for a dock union. According to Alan, the centre of the explosion was in the basement directly under Mr O'Donovan's room. Mr O'Donovan was blown to bits. Isn't that dreadful?'

'Dreadful,' Ken agreed, trying to sound as though he meant it.

So, the London team had succeeded in their second attempt. He would put a cheque for the balance of their fee in the post just as soon as O'Donovan's death had been officially confirmed.

He would move quickly. Within weeks, a couple of months at the most, the Union of Longshoremen would have merged with the Clyde Dockworkers' Union, leaving the Clyde Dockworkers' Union the last dock union on Clydeside. And with that he'd have achieved the Clydeside monopoly he'd schemed so long and hard to bring about.

His next target would be the Port of Leith on the east coast, and Dundee after that. One by one they would fall to him, till in the end there was only one union left, a national union, with him at its helm. The thought of that made his blood race and his ears pound.

'Choose a suitable condolence card for the wife – Jane, I think her name is, or it could be Jean. Better check on that. Anyway, choose a suitable card which I'll sign and you send directly O'Donovan's death is confirmed. And arrange a wreath or floral tribute for the funeral. The best the shop can provide.' Ken paused. 'By the way, did Betty's Alan say what caused the explosion?'

'They're not certain yet, but the theory is the main gas pipe coming into the Home cracked. A large amount of gas then swiftly built up, which was probably ignited by an electrical spark.'

Ken shook his head as if in sympathy. 'You never know, do you? You just never know.'

'How terribly unlucky for him after surviving that appalling lift accident.'

'Terribly unlucky,' Ken agreed.

'When the evening papers go on the streets, I'll pop out and buy copies. They should be carrying the story.'

'Excellent idea,' he said.

She started to turn away.

'Oh, Ina?'

She turned back again.

'I've had some really good news today and thought we might go out this evening for a celebratory meal? We could go on to your flat for an hour or two afterwards.'

Her face lit up. 'I've nothing planned, so that would be terrific.'

'Pick a restaurant, one you fancy, and then go ahead and book a table.'

'How about Ferrari's? I've always fancied going there.'

Ken went ice cold inside. Pictures jumped into his mind of the last time he'd been there, with Vicky. He had bumped into the gorilla whose house he'd twice burgled. If it hadn't been for Vicky crowning the sod with an ashtray, he would have ended up in the nick that night, to be sent down for God knows how long. He had never been back to Ferrari's since, nor did he ever intend to. As far as he was concerned, Ferrari's was a bad-luck place.

He shook his head. 'Any restaurant but that one. I don't like it.'

Ina had been Ken's secretary, and lover, long enough to know that when he used that tone of voice there was no arguing with him. 'How about Sans Souci then?' she suggested.

'Fabulous.'

'Do you wish to pick me up later? Or would you prefer to come home with me after work and wait while I bath and change?'

Before the meal and after: that would be very nice indeed, he thought. Her flat was owned and maintained by the union: it didn't cost her a penny to stay there.

'I'll be in the mood for a bath then myself.' He smiled.

She matched his smile, knowing full well what that meant. They would bathe together and make love in the bath.

Still smiling, Ina left Ken's office.

Ken took a deep breath. O'Donovan dead! He could have shouted for joy.

The union was going to need new premises, he decided, something far larger and grander than they now had. He would begin making inquiries directly after the merger.

Picking up the phone, he dialled Balfron and told Lyn about the gas explosion and Jim O'Donovan. He then explained his plans for the merger, using that as his excuse for having to work late. It was doubtful that he would be home before the wee hours, he said. She shouldn't bother to wait up.

Ritchie Allness, now off the critical list, and the only remaining member of the UOL upper echelons, was the key to the merger. For appearances' sake, he'd wait until after O'Donovan's funeral before paying Allness a visit. He would take Sawyers, his tame KC with him. And Paddy Troy, a Dublin-born dockie of terrifying strength, who was now his shadow and general right hand. Between the three of them, they would persuade Allness to see things their way.

Vicky felt sick with a combination of fatigue and nerves. It was a quarter to one in the morning. She had been on the go for over twenty hours. The polls were long since closed, counting nearing an end. The declaration would take place at any minute.

Neil sat worrying a nail. He was white as a sheet and – Vicky wasn't sure whether or not it was her imagination – every so often he seemed to twitch.

The three candidates and respective entourages were in a room off the hall where the counting was proceeding. Brian Brown, the Liberal candidate, was deep in conversation with his wife Fiona, a mousy thing with about as much personality as a limp teatowel. There was no sign of Muriel Mitchell, nor had there been all night. Vicky had been keeping an eye out for her.

Alexander McGhie, the Tory and Unionist candidate, his wife Charlotte, and a gaggle of his party workers, stood grouped in a corner. Their mood was buoyant, though everyone knew McGhie hadn't a hope of winning. If Neil lost, it would be to Brown.

Dickie Fleet lit yet another cigarette. The fingers of his right hand, which he used to hold his cigarettes, were stained saffron. 'This is murder,' he complained, thinking that, with Tom Allen, the result had always been a foregone conclusion; whereas, with Neil, who knew what was going to happen!

'I was sure up until this morning and then, suddenly, I wasn't so sure any more. The confidence seemed to drain out of me,' Neil confided quietly to Vicky.

She took one of his hands and squeezed it reassuringly. 'Not long now.'

'Jailbird.'

The word stood out clearly and distinctly above the hum of conversation. Vicky didn't know who had spoken it, but it had definitely come from the Brown contingent.

Neil started to rise, but she pulled him back down again. 'Leave it, it isn't worth it,' she told him.

Neil glared at the Brown lot. 'Ignorant bunch of sods,' he muttered angrily.

Alexander McGhie had also been angered by what had occurred. He crossed to where Vicky and Neil were sitting and produced a silver flask from an inside pocket. 'I'd be honoured if you'd take a drink with me, Mr and Mrs Seton. I want you to know that, despite our political differences, I think highly of the pair of you,' he said, not particularly loudly, but loud enough for everyone in the room to hear.

Neil stood, as did Vicky. 'We'd be pleased to have a dram with you, Mr McGhie,' Neil replied.

McGhie filled the top of his flask and handed it to Vicky. She drank it off, and gave it back.

When Neil had drunk his tot, Vicky said, 'You're a gentleman, Mr McGhie. Head and shoulders above some I can think of.'

The returning officer entered the room. 'I can declare now,' he announced.

Throat dry, and with what seemed like a dozen or more butterflies fluttering around inside her tummy, Vicky went side by side with Neil out into the hall, where counters and supporters milled. The three candidates and their wives mounted the rostrum at the head of the hall.

The returning officer asked for silence and launched into

a short speech. Then he said, 'I shall now announce the results.'

Vicky glanced at Neil. His eyes had gone glazed and, almost impossible to believe, he was even whiter than before.

The results were to be announced in alphabetical order. The returning officer cleared his throat and Vicky took a deep breath. A cold and clammy hand crept into hers.

'Brown, Brian Robert Scott: ten thousand, four hundred and seventy-two.'

The Liberal supporters erupted; they obviously thought that good enough to send their man to the Palace of Westminster. Brown acknowledged the applause by punching the air.

'McGhie, Alexander Ogilvie Maitland: six thousand, three hundred and seventy-four.'

Vicky's hopes were rekindled. That was a rotten result for the Tory, well below what she'd expected him to get. It meant that Neil still had a chance.

Brian Brown was no longer jubilant. He shifted nervously from foot to foot.

Neil stood rigidly still, staring out over the crowd, seeing nothing. His brain and senses had gone completely numb. He might have been a statue carved from stone.

'Seton, Neil Malcolm: twelve thousand and eighty-eight. Mr Neil Malcolm Seton is duly elected as the Member of Parliament for Glasgow Kelvinhaugh.'

Vicky shrieked with delight. They had done it, they had bloody well done it. Neil was an MP!

Neil pulled her into his arms. She could feel his heart thudding nineteen to the dozen. Tears dribbled down her cheeks, but that didn't worry her. They were tears of happiness and joy.

After a few seconds she pushed Neil away from her, and straightened his tie, which had become skewwiff. 'I think the Honourable Member is expected to make a speech.'

He smiled at her, and ran a thumb across one of her wet

cheeks. Then, squaring his shoulders, he stepped forward to the microphone.

I am so proud of him, Vicky thought to herself. So proud.

Eleven

'My God, it was a close-run thing. Only an overall Commons majority of six. Not a lot of room there for manoeuvre,' Tom Allen said from the back seat of Neil's car.

It was 25 February 1950, two days after the general election which had returned Neil as Member for Glasgow Kelvinhaugh. He had increased his personal majority over the Liberals, and Brian Brown again, by three thousand and twenty-nine, a personal triumph.

'But it *is* an overall majority, thereby allowing the government to remain in power, that's the main thing,' Vicky retorted. She was sitting beside Neil, who was driving.

'An overall majority *just*,' Neil said.

Vicky and Neil had picked up Tom from his home and were taking him to the site in Glasgow's south side where building had just started under the great new housing scheme. Tom had never really recovered from his heart attack and now rarely left the house. This outing, at his suggestion, was one of the exceptions.

The car was a wee Singer that Neil had bought the previous year. He found it tremendously helpful in getting round his constituency and Glasgow in general. It would allow him to get more done in the day, was the argument he had used to persuade himself to buy it, and so it had proved. Now both he and Vicky had licences.

Neil went on, 'It's a worrying situation right enough, with the PM not in the best of health, and Bevin and Cripps in the same boat.'

'Aye, it's very dicey,' Tom Allen agreed.

This part of Glasgow was new to Vicky. Once they were clear of the Gorbals, conditions had rapidly improved; there

336

was a lot more space than in Townhead and the streets were noticeably cleaner.

'Do you think you'll be able to stay in power long enough to get iron and steel nationalised?' Tom queried. It was always a treat for him to see Neil and have a good old chunter about politics.

Neil shrugged. 'I certainly hope so, but with such a slender majority, and with some of the bigwigs poorly, who can tell?'

'He's going to be a bigwig himself one day, you mark my words,' Vicky said over her shoulder to Tom.

'I've no doubt about that,' Tom replied. He knew from correspondence with old friends in the House that Neil was marked for higher things. He was potential ministerial material; no less a personage than Attlee had said so.

They made their way up through Croftfoot, arriving eventually at a street bordering what had been Campbell's Farm, the site of the new housing scheme. Neil parked the car on the verge of the road, then helped Tom get out. The three of them stood staring over the rich farmland now being dug up by earth excavators.

Vicky looked at a vast pile of drainage pipes and, adjacent to that, an enormous stack of water tanks. Besides the excavators there were dozens of tractors and lorries going this way and that.

Tom Allen's eyes shone with pride and pleasure. 'This is the beginning of the realisation of a dream. When those houses are finished, a working-class family will be able to live here in comfort and, above all, dignity.'

'Above all, hygienically,' Vicky chipped in, causing Neil to smile at her practicality.

Tom gave a small mock-bow. 'I stand corrected.' He went on enthusiastically, 'Inside toilets, running hot and cold water, electricity in every room, lots of glass to let in the light and green grass front and back: a veritable paradise.'

'And smell that air, fresh as can be. It'll do the children who come to live here a power of good,' Vicky said.

'It's taken the Corporation long enough to get round to it, but now, at long last, the scheme's under way. And the great thing is there isn't going to be just one scheme, but many,' Tom breathed.

'A whole new Glasgow, a far better Glasgow than the dirt-encrusted, vermin-infested slums existing today,' Vicky said, and gave a soft smile; it *was* a dream come true.

Tom gazed out over the acres rolling off into the far distance, visualising in his mind's eyes the rank upon rank of houses that were going to be built there, and was gratified to think that he had played no small part in bringing all this about. For years he had carried the banner for new housing, a banner Neil had picked up when he had been forced to drop it.

'I can't tell you how glad I am I was able to come out here and see the beginning of the birth before – well, before I go,' Tom said in a quiet, emotionally charged voice.

'Och, don't haver. Take life easy and you've got years left in you,' Vicky admonished.

A secretive smile crept onto Tom's face, as though he were enjoying some private joke. 'When the folks are settled in the new schemes, the old slums must be razed to the ground, wiped from the face of the earth. It must be as though they'd never existed. Promise me you'll see that happens,' he said to Neil.

Neil shared his wish: the slums were an abomination, a running sore that had to be cauterised to extinction. If they remained standing, they would be refilled with newcomers to the city, and that must never happen. 'I promise. If it can be done, I'll do it,' he answered.

Tom grunted. That was good enough for him. Neil would find a way.

He turned to gaze one last time over the fields of tomorrow. If there was a climax to his life's work, all that he'd striven for, it was here and now. 'Let's go back,' he said quietly.

Less than a month later Tom Allen was dead.

Early the following morning Vicky was wakened by Neil tossing and turning beside her. She touched him and her

338

brow knitted in concern. His skin was feverishly hot and slick with sweat.

She switched on the bedside light. 'Neil? Neil, are you all right?'

He groaned, then coughed. A wet rattly cough that sounded ominous.

'Neil?' This time she shook him.

His eyes slowly blinked open. 'Feel . . . terrible,' he mumbled, and coughed again.

This was a case for the doctor, Vicky decided.

Getting out of bed, she put on her dressing gown and mules, then got a towel, with which she wiped his face. She had hardly started on his chest when his face was awash again.

'Thirsty,' he croaked.

She gave him some water to drink, then went through to rouse Martha. 'Your daddy's ill, so I want you to get dressed and run over the road and get grandpa. Understand?'

Eyes large, Martha nodded.

Vicky hurriedly helped Martha into her clothes, then saw her out the door. Returning to their bedroom, she began setting a fire, which she soon had lit. With a temperature like Neil had, it couldn't be good for him, even though well covered with bedclothes, to be in an icy-cold room.

Martha arrived back with not only George but Mary. In a few terse sentences Vicky explained the situation.

'So could you go to the public phone box for me and telephone the doctor?' she asked George.

'On my way,' George replied and disappeared from the room.

Mary went over to Neil and had a good look at him. His upper lip was beaded with pearls of sweat, the whites of his eyes had gone dull and yellowy. He told her that his pyjamas were soaked through.

'You air a clean pair of pyjamas in front of that fire while I put the kettle on. We'll sponge him down and dry him, then slip him into the clean pyjamas. At the very least that'll make him feel a bit better,' Mary said.

Vicky crossed to the chest of drawers where Neil's clean

339

pyjamas were kept, and was about to come away from there again when Mary caught her eye in the mirror hanging above the drawers. She made a sideways motion of her head, signalling that she wanted to speak to Vicky in the kitchen.

Vicky laid the clean pyjamas on the bed. 'I'll get that big Turkish towel from the kitchen press,' she said to Neil and followed Mary out of the bedroom. Martha, now alone with her dad, did her best to comfort him.

'It could be pleurisy or pneumonia,' Mary said in a quiet voice, once she and Vicky were in the kitchen.

'Exactly what I thought, which is why I was so quick to send for the doctor.'

The two women stared at one another, each well aware how dangerous, indeed potentially fatal, pleurisy and pneumonia could be.

'He's got a very strong constitution, and there are many new drugs out nowadays,' Vicky said.

'I'll put the kettle on,' Mary replied.

Vicky bit her lip, then took the Turkish towel from the bottom of the press and hurried back to Neil.

The clean pyjamas had been nicely warmed by the time Mary appeared with a basin of hot water and a couple of flannels. As Neil was to be stripped, Vicky sent Martha from the room. It was an indication of how ill Neil was that he didn't protest about Mary helping Vicky to take off his sodden pyjamas, sponge him down and dry him. In the middle of this, George returned to say the doctor wouldn't be long. Roughly ten minutes later a chap on the front door announced his arrival.

Vicky remained with Dr Sharp while he made his examination; the others closeted themselves in the kitchen. Vicky hovered anxiously while he took Neil's temperature.

'Flu, a very bad dose of it,' Dr Sharp pronounced.

Vicky gave a sigh of relief. 'My mother and I feared he might have pleurisy or pneumonia.'

'Aye, well in this case the symptoms, to the layman that is, would appear similar. But it's flu, no doubt about it.'

Vicky smoothed Neil's bedclothes. 'So what do we do?'

'The most important thing is that he stays in bed. Do you have a po'?'

Vicky nodded.

'He's to use that. I'll give him some tablets now, then I'll write out a prescription which you've to get from the chemist as soon as it opens. I'll come back this evening round about six o'clock to see if there's any improvement.'

Neil, who had been listening to this, attempted in vain to struggle onto an elbow. 'Can't stay in bed, have an important engagement to attend, and speech to make, tonight,' he gasped.

'You can forget all about that. You're going to remain in bed for the rest of the week, *at least*,' Dr Sharp replied sternly.

'It's an awfully important engagement and speech for me,' Neil persisted.

'Don't be bloody stupid. You're in no fit condition to go anywhere and speak,' Vicky said firmly.

Neil coughed, the same wet rattly sound as before.

Dr Sharp took a box of tablets from his bag and handed Neil two. Vicky held a glass of water to his lips and he washed them down.

'I want to remind you that, even with modern medical advances, people can still die of flu. I strongly advise you not to forget that,' the doctor said to Neil.

Tears brought on by his fever burst from Neil's eyes. When he started to splutter, Vicky quickly found him a handkerchief.

'You did the right thing in putting the fire on. Keep it on twenty-four hours a day for now,' Dr Sharp told Vicky.

'And sponging and changing him?'

'Use your own judgement about that. Hopefully the tablets will begin to reduce his temperature by this evening, and when that's nearer normal sponging and changing won't be quite so necessary.'

'I understand,' Vicky replied.

The doctor wrote out Neil's prescription, then took his leave. He paused at the front door to remind Vicky yet

341

again that it was imperative Neil stay in his bed; she mustn't be swayed by him pleading or any argument he might come up with. Vicky assured him that Neil would be staying put, even if she had to tie him down.

When the doctor had gone, Vicky went into the kitchen to announce the verdict. George and Mary were just as relieved as she had been – though, as Mary pointed out, corroborating what the doctor had said, flu might not now be in the same category as pleurisy or pneumonia, but nor was it to be lightly dismissed.

George and Mary left after it had been arranged that Mary would come back over at eight o'clock so that Vicky could take Martha to school and go from there to the chemist's to get Neil's tablets.

Vicky then had a little chat with Martha, telling her that she had been a big help, and not to worry about her daddy, he would soon be well again. As they talked, Vicky helped Martha change back into her nightie. Within minutes of crawling underneath the covers of her bed, Martha was once more fast asleep.

Returning to their bedroom, Vicky banked up the fire, then went over to sit with Neil.

'Thanks to those tablets the doctor gave me, I'm feeling a lot better. Things aren't so hazy,' Neil said.

'Could you manage a cup of tea?'

'In a minute or two maybe. With only an overall majority of six, Vicky . . .'

She placed a finger across his lips. 'For the meantime it's going to have to be an overall majority of five, and that's all there is to it. You'll catch the train for London when you're over this, and not before. Is that clear?'

He pulled a face. 'You can be a gey stubborn woman, Vicky.'

'I've told the doctor I'll tie you down if needs be and, so help me, I will.'

Picking up the Turkish towel, she wiped down his face, neck and the top of his chest. As she did this, he regarded her with an expression of deep frustration.

'The speech is such a good one too, and it's a tremendous

342

honour to be asked to speak on the same platform as McIntyre,' he said when she was refolding the towel.

Hector McIntyre was the Secretary of State for Scotland. That night he would be present at the famous Kelvin Hall, where a Labour victory rally was to be held.

Also, Jock McLean was to give his farewell speech there. True to what he had told Vicky and Neil eighteen months previously, Jock had not run again for the Townhead seat at the general election, that having been successfully fought on behalf of the Labour Party by a chap called Jimmy Downie.

'It's a shame, right enough,' Vicky replied. A crowd of about ten thousand was expected.

'There's no way I can cajole you into letting me go?'

Smiling, she shook her head.

'Bugger!' he swore, and coughed.

'I'll get you that tea now,' she said, and left him.

When she returned with two steaming cups, she found him looking thoughtful. 'I've had an idea,' he said.

'Oh aye?'

'If I can't deliver the speech, why don't you?'

She stared at him, aghast. 'Me!'

'Why not?'

'Because . . . Well, because I've never spoken in public before – with the exception of when I made my confession, that is.'

'You did that all right. In fact, you were damned good.'

'Maybe so, but that was a special circumstance.'

'Special circumstance or not, you spoke damned well, which shows you have that capability. What you can do once you can do again, particularly when you have the material to back you, as you have in this speech.'

Vicky did not know what to think. The thought of delivering Neil's speech scared her stiff. Then she had been scared stiff prior to speaking at the museum and art gallery, but once she had started to speak, her nervousness and fear had vanished.

Neil went on, 'It's not as if you don't know the speech. You've been over it a dozen times with me, and even wrote

343

large chunks of it yourself. So, come on, what do you say?'

'They might not want me to speak in your place.'

'You'll merely be delivering my speech because of my illness. No one is going to object to that.'

She sipped her tea, her mind racing. 'And you definitely think I'd be all right?'

'Vicky, the last thing I'd do would be put you in a situation where you're likely to make a fool of yourself. On the contrary, you'll be first class. I know it.'

She hurriedly thought over her wardrobe. What could she wear?

'I'm sure Mary won't mind looking after you and Martha,' she said hesitantly, not yet entirely convinced.

Neil opened his mouth to reply, but instead broke into a prolonged bout of coughing, during which he brought up a great deal of horrible slimy phlegm. At the end of the coughing, he was so exhausted that he closed his eyes and almost instantly fell asleep.

Vicky went to Neil's briefcase, where she knew his speech, typewritten by herself, to be.

Neil would sleep for a while, she decided. Probably an hour or two. She went through to the kitchen and there began quietly reading the speech aloud.

They had expected ten thousand; they got twelve, with many more turned away at the doors. Inside the Kelvin Hall the Labour supporters were packed like sardines. The atmosphere was euphoric, carnival almost. VICTORY 1950, huge banners in red and yellow proclaimed. Behind the speakers' platform hung a huge picture of Clement Attlee, Labour leader and Prime Minister.

Vicky regretted having agreed to speak in Neil's place. One glance at that enormous crowd had been enough to make her want to bolt, to get out of there and as far away as possible.

Dickie Fleet entered the ante-room where the speakers and various others connected with the event were congregating. He crossed over to Vicky. 'How are you feeling?'

'Terrible.'

'Just try and . . .'

She held up a hand to silence him. 'Please, Dickie. I appreciate you're doing it with the best of intentions, but right now the last thing I need is advice.'

'Suit yourself,' Dickie replied, looking none too pleased, and slouched off again.

She knew that she had upset him, which she hadn't wanted to do at all. It was just that she was in such a state!

A smiling Jock McLean came over. 'I feel like a horse about to have its last race before being taken to the knacker's yard and melted down into glue,' he said.

His joke helped ease the tension for her, and she laughed. She had a mental picture of Jock in a large pot or cauldron being boiled down, the top half of him as he stood before her, the bottom half a gooey mess.

'It's time to go and face them,' Jock went on, still smiling.

Her laughter died. The dreaded moment had arrived. 'Let's get it over with then,' she replied, and stood up.

Clutching the speech in her right hand, she walked alongside Jock, making for the door that led to the platform from where they would speak. Hector McIntyre was in the lead.

There were six speakers in all. McIntyre, Jock McLean, Leonard Carter, MP for Renfrewshire North, Danny Rose, an official with the Boilermakers' Union, Peter Strathern, representing the Corporation, and Vicky. She was scheduled to speak third, after Leonard Carter and Peter Strathern.

She sat beside Jock McLean, laid her speech in front of her, then looked out over the gathering. Her heart leaped into her mouth; there were so many of them! And all of them seemed to be staring directly, and critically, at her.

Jock leaned close to Vicky. 'This is a victory rally. All of these here will be members of the faithful, come to celebrate and generally have a good time. They'll be on your side, and very sympathetic because they know you're filling in for Neil on account of his illness. You've nothing to fear, lassie, I promise you,' he whispered.

She could have given him a big smacker for putting it all into perspective. 'Thank you,' she whispered back.

Leonard Carter, a portly jovial man in his late fifties, got up and led off. Within seconds he had the audience roaring and clapping in appreciation.

Peter Strathern was a dry stick of a man with a biting, incisive wit. Most of his speech consisted of tearing into the Tory Party, which he did extremely effectively. Four times he called Winston Churchill a warmonger, and four times got a round of applause for it. He wound up by extolling the government for recognising the Communist government of China, which it had done the previous month.

Then it was Vicky's turn.

As she rose, she underwent the same transformation as had occurred behind the museum and art gallery. Her nervousness completely vanished, replaced by total calm and serenity. When she spoke, her voice was strong, vibrant and compelling, the voice of a natural orator. She soon had her audience spellbound, hanging on her every word.

'. . . There is a continuing need to nationalise, to give the nation's wealth back to its rightful owners, the people. This will lead to greater efficiency, pride in job, and greater sense of work responsibility. The time of the bloated, parasitical capitalist is over. This is the beginning of the time of the people, the ordinary working keelie and his family . . .'

The audience lapped it up, and cheered her to the echo when, finally, she sat down again.

'Marvellous. Best female speaker I've ever heard,' Jock McLean whispered.

She had enjoyed that! she thought in wonder. She had thoroughly *enjoyed* that. In fact, she only wished it could have gone on for longer. She saw Hector McIntyre looking at her with a surprised, yet appreciative, expression. He smiled and nodded acknowledgement of her success. She flushed with pride and a tremendous sense of gratification.

She had to force herself to concentrate on the next speaker, Danny Rose of the Boilermakers' Union.

346

Tina squealed with delight and threw her arms round Vicky. 'You were absolutely amazing, absolutely! Wasn't she, Sammy?'

'T'rific,' Sammy agreed.

'I was helped a lot by having a good speech to deliver,' Vicky said modestly.

'Speech be blowed. It was you yourself that was magic. I couldn't take my eyes off you, and neither could anyone else. You had us all, each and every one, in the palm of your hand.'

'. . . Palm of your hand,' Sammy echoed.

'You were outstanding,' the man with Tina and Sammy said.

'Vicky, I'd like you to meet Chris Walker, Sammy's brother. Be careful what you say in front of him. He's a policeman.'

Vicky shook Chris's extended hand. He seemed a personable chap – a few years older than herself, she judged, which would make him about thirty-five.

A pipe band that had been playing earlier started up again. Vicky saw Jock McLean wave to her, and waved back. He was talking to Hector McIntyre.

'Listen. What do you say we get out of here and find a pub?' Tina suggested.

'I'd love to but, as you know, Neil's at home with the flu. I really should get back right away.'

'Och, after the triumph you've just had, a wee celebration is in order. Come on, don't be miserable, Neil won't mind. I'm sure if you could ask him he'd tell you to go right ahead. And we won't stay long, I promise,' Tina argued.

Vicky knew Tina was right, that Neil wouldn't object to her having a dram with her old pal and Sammy. And she could certainly use a whisky, if not two.

'Only ten or fifteen minutes then,' she said.

Sammy and Chris went first, carving a passage through the crowd towards the nearest exit. Vicky and Tina followed close behind the two men, Tina with an arm hooked round one of Vicky's. As they progressed towards the exit, Vicky was tapped again and again on the shoulder and told how good her speech had been.

As the pubs round the Kelvin Hall were bound to be choc-a-bloc from the people who had attended the rally, Vicky had everyone pile into the Singer and drove them to the Byres Road, where the pubs would be quieter.

Once inside the pub they'd selected, Sammy made a beeline for the bar, while Tina excused herself to go to the ladies' room.

Vicky and Chris sat down. When Chris glanced at her, his look was of admiration tinged with awe.

'I didn't know Sammy had a brother. Neither he or Tina have ever mentioned it,' she said.

'Probably because I was in Hong Kong for twelve years. I only came back to Glasgow in November,' he explained.

'Were you in the police out there?'

'I was a superintendent when I resigned. I originally started with the Glasgow police, who've taken me on again, but at a reduced rank to what I was in HK. I'm a sergeant now.'

'Why did you come back? Homesick?'

Chris looked over at Sammy, who was still waiting to be served. There was still no sign of Tina.

'My wife and little boy died in a street accident. They were crushed when a lorry shed its load of steel girders. I couldn't stomach staying on in HK after that, so I came home,' he said, voice tight and an expression of indescribable sadness on his face.

'I am sorry,' Vicky whispered.

'She was a lot younger than me, only twenty-four. The lad was three and a half.'

'What was her name?'

'Wei Wei, my boy's name was Keng Meng.'

He saw Vicky's look of surprise. 'Yes, she was Chinese, and we gave our son a Chinese name because that was what she wanted.'

Chris offered Vicky a cigarette, which she refused, explaining she didn't smoke. He lit up.

348

'Would you like to see a picture of them? If it wouldn't bore you, that is?'

'I'd like to very much, and it won't bore me, I assure you,' she replied.

He produced a picture from his wallet and handed it to her. Wei Wei was petite with long black lustrous hair that had a brace of bone combs in it. She was very beautiful in a delicate, sculptured way. Keng Meng was plump and smiling, with black spiky hair. The only non-Oriental feature about him was his eyes; they were western and just like Chris's.

'It must have been dreadful for you to lose them, and in such a horrible way,' Vicky said sympathetically, returning the picture.

Chris shrugged, but did not reply. For the moment he did not trust himself to speak.

He was putting the picture away when Tina reappeared. With that, the subject was changed and the conversation brightened. Before long the four of them were laughing and joking – having, as the Glasgow saying went, a 'rer old ter' together.

It was during March that Tom Allen passed away in his sleep, and several days later he was cremated at Craigton crematorium. Neil came north for the ceremony, as did Hugh Gaitskell, representing Mr Attlee. The opposition had allowed Neil and Gaitskell to be paired for the visit. Tom had been well liked and respected on both sides of the House.

When the ceremony was over, Vicky and Neil had a few words with the widow, who was distraught with grief. Hugh Gaitskell also spoke to her, giving her a personal message of condolence from the Prime Minister.

While Vicky and Neil were talking to another mourner, Gaitskell came over. Neil introduced Gaitskell to Vicky and the mourner, then Gaitskell asked Neil if they could have a chat outside.

'Private?' queried Neil, meaning should he include Vicky or not? Gaitskell shook his head.

349

Outside, a flurry of snow was blowing and the wind was sharp as a razor's edge. Vicky shivered when a gust swirled up her dress.

'Missed you on the train up, Neil. What train are you taking back?' Gaitskell asked.

'I thought I'd catch the late sleeper, that gives me a chance to do a little constituency work,' Neil replied. What he didn't say was it also gave him a few extra hours to be with Vicky, whom he was missing like mad in London.

Gaitskell nodded his understanding. 'This tiny majority is playing havoc with constituency work. Those outside the Home Counties are finding it nigh on impossible to get any in at all, so you're right to maximise the chance when you have it. I shall be returning on the three o'clock and will be lunching at the Central Station hotel before that. I would like you and Mrs Seton to join me. I have something to discuss with you that you might consider to be in your interest.'

Neil glanced quickly at Vicky, then brought his attention back to Gaitskell. 'What time would you like us to be there?'

'One thirty in the restaurant?'

'One thirty it is,' Neil agreed.

'Cheerio for now then,' Gaitskell said, and left them, heading for the car and driver that had been laid on for him.

Neil turned to Vicky, and raised an eyebrow. 'In my interest?' he echoed.

Vicky stared thoughtfully after the rapidly receding car. She was just as intrigued as Neil.

The wine, Chateau Lascombes, was the best Vicky had ever tasted. It was like smooth, warm, red velvet.

'Tom Allen was a great man, and in his day a tremendous influence within the Labour Party. That's why I was honoured when the PM asked me to represent him at the funeral,' Hugh Gaitskell said.

'I've always had an interest in politics, but it was Tom who activated me. It was his idea I run for his seat when he stood down,' Neil explained.

350

'We thought the world of him. I still can't believe he's gone,' Vicky said.

The waiter appeared with their main course, which was then duly served up. Vicky was having veal and spaghetti, her first experience of a dish which she had only read about. Used to simple Glasgow cooking, it seemed quite exotic to her.

Gaitskell waited till the waiter had left them, then said, 'I have some news.'

Vicky tried to keep excitement from her face. Neil, without realising it, leaned fractionally forward.

'I've been offered the post of Minister of State for Economic Affairs. When I see the PM tomorrow, I shall be telling him I accept.'

'Congratulations!' Neil exclaimed, genuinely pleased. He was a great admirer of Gaitskell, a rising star if ever there was one, though somewhat left of him in his beliefs.

'Congratulations also,' Vicky smiled, thinking there had to be more to this than that news. Gaitskell hadn't invited them out to lunch just to tell Neil, a backbencher, that he was going to be Minister of State for Economic Affairs.

'Val Tester, my PPS, is excellent, but with my new responsibilities he's going to need help. I've had my eye on you for some time, Neil, and was wondering if you'd be interested in the job?' Gaitskell went on.

Neil, a tinge of red staining his neck, slowly laid down his knife and fork. What little appetite he'd had had just vanished. 'You're asking me to be your second PPS?' To become a Personal Private Secretary was often a stepping stone to higher things.

'I am.'

Neil swallowed. 'Then of course I accept, and am delighted to do so.'

'Marvellous. See Val tomorrow and he'll brief you on your new duties. I'm very pleased to have you on the team,' Gaitskell said and raised his glass in salute.

PPS to Hugh Gaitskell, a man being more and more spoken of within Labour circles as a future Prime Minister! Now Neil really was on his way, Vicky thought jubilantly.

•

351

'Neil, how are you love?' Vicky was ringing Neil at his office in the House of Commons from her own office in the Kelvinhaugh Labour Hall.

'Whacked out. We were sitting till two a.m., and then went back hard at it first thing today. None of us dares miss an important division in case the government suffers a premature defeat, and this pressure is beginning to tell, particularly amongst the older Members. Then there's the bill for the nationalisation of iron and steel on the stocks. We're having to absorb a tremendous amount of flak and pressure over that. The Tories are dead set against the bill going through, but go through it will – we're all determined about that!'

'Two a.m! No wonder I didn't get a reply when I rang you at the flat last night. I tried several times, then finally gave up just after eleven,' Vicky said. Neil shared a flat with three other Labour MPs in Petty France, a short walk from the House of Commons.

He sounded dead beat, she thought. But that was hardly surprising with so many late and all-night sittings to contend with. The last time he had managed to come north, in a lightning twenty-four-hour visit, she'd discovered that he had lost nearly a stone in weight and looked quite haggard.

'I'm ringing to tell you I've received an invitation to speak at the Hamilton Miners' annual gala,' she said.

'You mean, speak on my behalf?' he queried. She had now done that on a number of occasions since the Kelvin Hall, acting as substitute because of his general unavailability to speak personally.

She laughed. 'That's the thing. The invitation is for me, not you. I've been asked to speak in my own right. I wanted to know what you thought before I answered the invitation.'

'I don't see why you shouldn't speak, if you want to, that is.'

'I do, very much so. But I didn't want you getting jealous or taking the hump.'

This time it was Neil who laughed. 'You should know me

better than that. If you want to speak, go ahead, and with my blessing.'

He was a real sweetie, she thought. There were many husbands wouldn't have liked her striking out on her own. Glasgow men in particular could be very possessive and restrictive where their wives were concerned. But not Neil. He was bigger, and more understanding than that.

'Any chance of you getting up here soon?' she asked.

'Not a hope. Johnny Gaskin, Houghton-Le-Spring, was taken into hospital this morning with appendicitis, which means our majority is down to four, because another Labour Member is also in hospital with meningitis. It has to be virtually life or death for any of us to get away at the present moment.'

'Your summer break isn't all that far away. We'll just have to look forward to that,' she said.

'I love you, Vicky,' he whispered.

She blew him a kiss down the receiver. 'Speak to you soon, darling,' she replied, and hung up.

She studied the invitation from the Hamilton Miners that lay in front of her. She was thrilled at the prospect of speaking as herself and not on behalf of Neil. She would get working on her speech that night, she decided. It would be the first speech she had ever written totally on her own, and she was looking forward to it.

She had just typed out and signed her acceptance when there was a tap on the door.

'Come in!' she called out.

Chris Walker entered. It was the first time she'd seen him since the night they'd met.

'Why, hello. How are you?' she greeted him. He was wearing fawn trousers and a matching windcheater, which she guessed from their cut and quality had come from Hong Kong.

'I'm fine,' he replied, and gazed around. 'So this is where you hide away.'

She indicated a chair. 'Take a pew. And to what do I owe the honour?'

He had a very easy physical way about him, she thought, as he sat. He moved effortlessly, like a cat.

'Tina tells me you're always on the lookout for helpers, and I was wondering if you'd have me?'

'But how about your job? I thought policemen work all sorts of long hours.'

'Well, for a start, it's shift work, which means I often have free mornings, afternoons and even entire days. And, as I don't seem to require a great deal of sleep, I end up having time on my hands, time I'd like to fill doing something constructive,' he answered.

Time other men his age devoted to their families, she told herself grimly. His story of losing his wife and boy had touched her deeply. She had thought about it, and him, more than once.

'Right then. Are you free now?' she asked.

He nodded.

'Then get that windcheater off. I've a whole stack of envelopes for you to address.'

During their coffee break, he regaled her with tales of Hong Kong. She found him a natural storyteller, fascinating to listen to.

Ken lay staring at Ina Finlayson's gently rising and falling naked breasts. He found them wondrously beautiful, erotic works of art.

He and Ina were lying on her bed, having just made love. Her eyes were closed and there was a small smile of contentment and satisfaction playing round her lips.

Reaching out, he laid a hand on the breast nearest him. It was so smooth, warm and perfect. He never tired of touching and caressing her breasts, enjoying that almost as much as the act of sex itself. He flicked a nipple and flicked it again. It deepened in colour and stiffened slightly. He rolled it between thumb and forefinger.

Ina opened her eyes. 'Again?' she queried throatily.

'Not yet,' he whispered in reply, and kissed the nipple he had been manipulating.

'Hmmh!' Ina murmured, and a shudder ran through her, causing her buttocks to wriggle.

'I'll get us a drink,' Ken said and, rising from the bed, crossed to the occasional table on which stood the bottle and glasses. He poured himself a hefty one, Ina only a dribble, which he topped up well with lemonade.

Returning to the bed, he gave her hers, then went over to the window and stared out. She regarded him through slitted eyes. His mood had suddenly changed.

'What's wrong?'

He shrugged.

Laying her glass by the side of the bed, she padded over to him. She squashed her breasts against his back, knowing he loved that, and placed her hands on his hips.

'Is it me? Have I done something, or not done something?'

'It isn't you, Ina. It's those damned new premises I want for the union, and which I can't find. It depresses me every time I think about it.'

She remembered then that she had made an appointment for him to see a building earlier on that afternoon, a building that had only come on the market at the beginning of the week.

'No luck at the Broomielaw then?' she asked.

'Awful. The place was awful. Besides needing gutting from top to bottom, it was the ugliest building I've seen in a long time.'

Ken took a pull of his whisky. 'As you know, I've looked at everything that's been on the market since I decided the union needed new premises, and there just hasn't been anything suitable. It's either too big or too small or too ugly, or something else is wrong with it,' he said miserably.

'Sooner or later the right place is bound to come up,' she replied, trying to console him.

He snorted his impatience and exasperation. Beyond the window, the hundreds of thousands of white and yellow lights reminded him of those he had recently seen in a magazine photograph, lights that had formed the backdrop to a spectacular building.

'There's a building in Chicago designed by a chap called

355

Frank Lloyd-Wright which is so stunning to look at it actually took my breath away. The outside is made entirely of glass and steel, and with night lights playing on it the whole thing gleams like a highly polished, sparkly diamond.'

He paused, then went on. 'Now that's what I would give my eye teeth to have for my future national union headquarters. A building that would be the best, the most modern, in all Scotland.'

Ina thought of central Glasgow, old and antiquated, a place of mausoleums. 'If you want a building like that, you're going to have to have it built yourself,' she said.

He stared at her in astonishment. 'Why didn't I think of that! Of course, that's the answer,' he exclaimed.

'Could you . . . I mean, could the CDU as it stands afford that?' she asked.

'Oh aye, no bother. You'd be surprised at the financial depth the CDU has behind it. From Picassos to Argentinian beef, our money is well invested, and growing with the vigour of an adolescent all the time.'

Then Ken had an idea that was an extension of hers. 'I know what I'll do, I'll buy that monstrosity in the Broomielaw and have it torn down. The site is ideal for my new building.'

He took another pull at his drink, excitement and pleasure racing through him. Turning, he took her head in his free hand and kissed her lightly on the mouth. 'Not only gorgeous, but a genius with it.' He smiled.

She felt him stir against her thigh. 'Again?' she asked, repeating her earlier query.

He placed his glass on the window ledge and swung her up into his arms.

'Again,' he confirmed, and crossed to the bed.

Later he would telephone Sawyers, his lawyer, and give him instructions to find out the best architects in Glasgow and to set up an appointment for him to see their top man. After he'd spoken to Sawyers, he would draw a rough sketch of what he had in mind. Dammit to hell, he was so excited!

Ina gave a small groan of appreciation as he sank into her.

•

Vicky glanced up from her typewriter and over at Chris, who was engrossed at an adjacent desk. He had been helping for six weeks now, and a more willing or industrious helper she could not have hoped for – nor one who made her laugh so much; he had a tremendous sense of humour. She suddenly realised that she knew nothing about him other than that he was Sammy's brother, that he'd lived in Hong Kong and had lost his wife and boy.

'Chris?'

He stopped writing and looked at her.

'You've never said. Where do you stay?'

He sat back in his chair. 'I've got police accommodation just off the Dumbarton Road.'

'What sort of accommodation, a house?'

A rueful smile twisted his mouth. 'Aye, a section house, which isn't the sort of house you mean. It consists of individual bedrooms plus communal areas. There's also a canteen where we eat.'

'Like a barracks?'

His mouth twisted even more. 'If there's a difference, I couldn't say what it is.'

'And what about the food?'

'I've tasted worse. It's not exactly home cooking, but it keeps you going and your strength up.'

'The whole thing comes across as being pretty grim,' she said.

'Och, the section house leaves a lot to be desired, but it's not that bad. It is convenient for someone on his own.' He tried to inject a cheery note into his voice, which didn't sound at all convincing. 'I'm the daddy, being the eldest and only sergeant there. The rest are all young constables, a good bunch, but I don't mix too much with them because of the age and rank difference.'

She could just imagine how lonely it must be for him in this section house, and her heart went out to him.

'Do you go to Tina and Sammy's quite a lot?' she asked.

'They've got their own life to lead so, although I'm always made welcome, I try not to intrude too often. I'm sure you understand?'

She did not inquire about his parents, knowing from a conversation she had once had with Sammy that they were both dead. Nor were there any other brothers or sisters.

'I was wondering, would you like to come over to my place for tea one night?' she said.

He hesitated. Was this invitation out of pity for him? If so, he wouldn't accept.

'I'm not that great a cook, but I'm sure I can manage something better than your canteen,' she went on.

He gave a dry laugh, but still did not answer.

Vicky guessed why he was holding back. She could see it in his face and eyes. 'It would be company for Martha and myself. Neil being away so much, we get quite lonely at times,' she said, which wasn't true at all. With Mary, George and various neighbours in and out the house like a fiddler's elbow, they were never that. But she wanted him to think he was doing her a favour, rather than the other way round.

'How about Saturday evening?' she suggested.

'That's out. I'm on late duty.'

'Friday then?'

'You're on,' he said.

She wrote out her address. 'About seven?'

'I'll be there,' he grinned.

She returned to her typing, pleased he was coming. In fact, she was more than pleased; she was really looking forward to it.

That Friday, a little after three in the afternoon, Ken left his architects' offices with a rolled-up set of preliminary sketches under his arm.

The architects Sawyers had recommended had jumped at the chance of designing a new building for him, seeing it as a very prestigious contract and, because this ultra-modern building was to be erected in the central city area, one of the most important ever to come their way. They had said that they understood perfectly what he was after, and the preliminary sketches now under his arm, which he'd given the go-ahead to be expanded into proper drawings, proved them right.

The other good news was that the monstrosity in the Broomielaw had become CDU property that morning. The demolition would be starting first thing Monday.

A satisfactory set of sketches, procurement of the ideal site: this called for a celebration, he decided. He would pick up Ina and together they'd paint the town red. Red! They'd paint it bloody tartan, the way he felt!

Ken was not the only one to decide on a celebration that Friday. George Devine had won five pounds seventeen and six on the dogs, having placed his bet with the bookie's runner who came round the tram depot every day the dogs and horses were running. Bonnie Mary, his dog had been called, and, although it was a rank outsider, he'd chosen it because of the name. And by God, rank outsider or not, the beauty had won, beating the favourite by a head at the last moment.

George finished his pint and gazed about. There had been a few other tram depot staff in but, despite its being pay day, they had now left. He glanced up at the wall clock and saw that it was time he was heading for home himself. In fact it was well past time he was heading for home.

Och, Mary wouldn't mind him being late, he thought. It was a rare enough occurrence, just as it was a gey rare occurrence for him to have one of his occasional flutters come up, and so handsomely at that.

Raising a hand, he signalled to a bartender. 'Another pint and large whisky,' he said, his fifth such since coming into the pub.

Ken and Ina were in the back of Ken's Cadillac, having just left the private club where they had been drinking since the latter part of the afternoon. Shugs was driving, Paddy Troy beside him. They were en route to Ina's flat, where Ken intended spending an hour or two before being driven back to Balfron.

Ken pressed the concealed button at the back of the driver's seat and the panel slid open to reveal the miniature bar. 'Another g and t?' he asked.

Ina shook her head.

He contemplated the whisky decanter, wondering whether he really wanted one or not. He switched his gaze to the mixers. His throat was so parched that he would have had one of those if they'd been cold instead of warm. And then he had it. What he needed to wash away the desert in his throat was a dirty big pint of thirst-quenching heavy.

'Pull up outside the first boozer you come to,' he instructed Shugs.

He explained to Ina why he wanted to stop at a pub, and she agreed that a beer was the very dab. She was dry too.

George was well away with the fairies and thoroughly enjoying himself. He would take a taxi home, he thought. And he'd pick up a bunch of flowers on the way. He would get the cabbie to go via the main entrance to Union Street station; a flowerseller had a pitch on the pavement there.

Five pounds seventeen and six! he thought jubilantly, and congratulated himself for the umpteenth time. Besides the flowers, he'd slip Mary a couple of nicker to buy herself a wee something. She'd like that. And he'd take home a carry-out as well, some screwtops and a half-bottle.

A last one for the road, he thought, and raised a hand to signal a barman. He suddenly found himself swaying and had to grab hold of the bar to stop himself from pitching over. Enough, he thought. He'd had enough for now. He'd leave it till he got home and could get stuck into the carry-out. He burped, and beer and whisky fumes filled his mouth, mixed with the sour taste of vomit. He'd go out into the street and wait there for a passing cab. Being a Friday night, it shouldn't be too long before one happened along – he hoped.

The fresh air hit him like a slap in the face. His stomach heaved and the taste of vomit was back in his mouth. Then it wasn't just the taste of vomit but the actual stuff itself. He noticed an alley leading off. Best be sick there, he told himself, less embarrassing.

It was only a few gobfuls of vomit, not the gush he'd expected. As he was wiping his lips with his hanky, a big foreign car drew alongside the street kerb and parked in a spot visible from where he was standing.

He ran a hand through his hair, then over his eyes. Bile churned in his gut. Was he going to throw up again? George leaned against a wall, and in that position heard two voices talking, a woman's and a man's. The man's was strangely familiar.

'Oh, Ken, that was ever so funny,' the female said, and laughed.

George twisted round and peered at the chap the woman had been addressing. The chap was plump and balding and wore glasses. He did know him, he was sure of it.

'Do you want me to come in with you or remain here?' a second man asked the first, this one speaking with a pronounced southern Irish accent.

George could now see there were three men, including a driver, who was still behind the wheel of the big foreign car.

'Come in with us. You never know,' the chap with glasses replied to the Mick.

Then George had it. The years flew back and he saw that face as it had used to be: slimmer, with more hair on top, and glasses that had been nowhere as fancy as those Blacklaws now wore.

Ken Blacklaws: the stinking rat who had let Vicky take the blame for his thieving, then abandoned her while she was still in borstal to go off with another – maybe even this blonde piece he was now staring at.

Anger blossomed in George. Fuelled by alcohol, the anger was almost instantly transformed into blind raging hatred. Heedless of his churning stomach, stumbling and lurching, George went after Ken.

'You, Blacklaws!' he yelled.

Paddy Troy whirled round. Ken and Ina turned more slowly, Ken frowning.

George came to a halt several feet away from Ken and glared at him. 'Remember me?' he demanded in a harsh voice.

'Mr Devine from Parr Street. How are you?' Ken smiled.

'For years I've been hoping to bump into you again. I'm claiming you, son,' George snarled, and launched himself at Ken, to grab him by the jacket lapels.

A split second after George moved, Paddy Troy did likewise. Paddy hit George twice, very hard, in the kidneys. The breath whoofed out of George. Groaning, he released Ken and doubled over. Paddy grabbed hold of George and threw him backwards away from Ken and Ina.

Arms flailing, George smashed into the side of the Cadillac. He went over the fin nearest the pavement, from where he fell head-first to the ground. He landed awkwardly, to lie in an untidy tangle of limbs.

'What was that all about?' Ina asked. She had been rooted to the spot with surprise while the brief rumpus had taken place.

Ken ignored her question and took a deep breath. He had found that quite distressing. Stupid drunken old fart! he thought, for it had been obvious that George was guttered.

'You all right?' Paddy Troy demanded.

Ken nodded.

Shugs, worried about damage to his beloved Caddy, had come out the car like a shot when George had hit it and was now hurriedly inspecting that side panel and fin. He sighed with relief to find there was neither mark nor dent. He was about to walk round George when something about the way he was lying stopped him. The angle of George's head was wrong, unnatural. Kneeling beside George, he turned him over. George's eyes were open and glazed, his expression one of total amazement.

'Shit!' Shugs muttered and placed an ear against George's chest to confirm what he already knew to be so.

'Boss, this man's dead,' Shugs said quietly to Ken.

'Eh!' Ken exclaimed, completely taken aback.

Shugs looked at the disbelieving Paddy Troy. 'He must have broken his neck when he hit the deck,' Shugs said.

Panic surged through Ken, but he quickly brought it under control. Mind racing, he gazed about. They were alone on the pavement. Two young boys had appeared on the other side of the street, but they seemed interested in

362

the car more than anything else. He was almost certain they hadn't been there when the rumpus had taken place. A tram clanked by but it was nearly empty. Only one woman on it stared curiously at them.

Paddy Troy had knelt beside Shugs. There was no mistake. George was dead as mutton.

Ken made a decision. He must not be associated with George's death. No matter that it had been a genuine accident. He could just imagine what the police would think. He had been known to George; therefore there had to be a reason for George attacking him – an assumption which would be entirely correct.

Then it would emerge – and how the newspapers would love it! – that he was the boyfriend who had let Vicky down, and whom she had taken the blame for. He would then have to counter with his version of events and, although certain he could wriggle out of her accusations, vindicate himself, it would all be messy messy messy! The last thing he wanted was the public eye focused on him and his union. The last thing!

No. There was only one thing he could do, and that was dissociate himself from this, and fast. Brain working at lightning speed, he began speaking very quickly, the words machine-gunning from his mouth.

Half a minute later Ken and Shugs were en route up the alley and Paddy Troy was heading for the pub to ask if he could use their phone to report an accident to the police.

It had been a huge stroke of luck that, apart from the two young lads and the tram that had gone by, the street had been deserted, Ken thought to himself as he strode along.

As for him and Shugs? They had been a couple of passers-by who had paused briefly, having seen nothing of the incident, then continued on their way, refusing to get involved. So Paddy and Ina would tell the police as their presence was bound to be mentioned when the two young lads were questioned. It would also square with the woman on the tram's testimony, should she either be located or come forward of her own volition.

Ken and Shugs emerged from the alley at its far entrance, where they split up. Going in opposite directions, they both disappeared into the night.

Chris Walker arrived with a bottle of Chinese wine which he presented to Vicky at the door.

'How lovely, and unusual. Thank you,' she said, ushering him through to the kitchen, where Martha was waiting.

Martha solemnly shook hands with Chris. 'Pleased to meet you,' she said, very formally.

'And I'm pleased to meet you,' Chris replied.

Vicky told Chris to sit. Then, getting out a corkscrew, proceeded to open the bottle of wine he'd brought. Chris offered to do it for her, but she replied that she was quite capable.

'I can mend fuses and change plugs too,' she added, which made him laugh.

While she was fetching glasses from the sideboard, he had a quick shufti round. He liked the room, he decided. Like Vicky herself, it was warm and friendly.

'How on earth did you manage to find Chinese wine in Glasgow?' Vicky asked.

He tapped his nose.

'Oh well, stick then,' she retorted, making him laugh again.

'There's a Chinese importer lives in my manor. When he found out I'd developed a taste for Chinese wine while living in Hong Kong, he arranged for me to buy some through his firm whenever I want to. I buy a case at a time.'

She handed him a brimming glass and raised hers in salute. 'Slainthe!'

'Slainthe!' he responded.

It was awful, sweet and nasty, she thought. She wouldn't be able to stomach much of this.

'What do you think?' he asked eagerly.

'It's absolutely delicious,' she lied, not wanting to hurt his feelings.

He beamed at her. 'I always get this particular label, it was Wei Wei's favourite. I'm pleased you like it also.'

Vicky had gone to town on the meal, for points rationing had ended the previous month after being in force for eight years. It was still difficult to believe that you could go into the butcher's or grocer's and purchase whatever you wanted, in whatever quantity you desired.

She served up plump gigot chops, two each for Chris and her, one for Martha, cauliflower drenched in cheese sauce, diced baby carrots smothered in butter, and haricot beans. For sweet it was a milky rice pudding she'd made from an Australian recipe, and prunes. It was a veritable feast compared to what had been available during the war years and after.

All through the meal Chris kept up a steady banter. One of his jokes convulsed Vicky so much that she had to be thumped on the back to stop her choking. Chris and Martha both thumped. He was so easy, Vicky thought. And, like this, so full of joy. Yes, that was the right word, joy. He fairly bubbled with it.

When the meal was finished, Chris said that he would help wash and dry, but Vicky wouldn't hear of that. Martha then piped up to ask coyly if he would read her a story.

Vicky had just begun drying, and Chris was nearing the end of the story – thankfully, Goldilocks was now long in the past – when there was a knock on the outside door.

'Probably my mother,' Vicky said to Chris.

But it was a uniformed constable. Immediately Vicky presumed that he had come for Chris on police business.

'He's in the kitchen. Follow me,' Vicky said and returned to the kitchen, leaving a perplexed constable staring after her.

'I said, he's in here!' Vicky called out. Then to Chris, 'It's one of your lot, looking for you.'

A puzzled Chris rose from his seat. He hadn't mentioned to anyone either at the station or section house where he was going that night. How the dickens had they known where to find him!

The constable, holding his hat, entered the kitchen.

'I'm Sergeant Walker. Mrs Seton says you're looking for me,' Chris said to the constable.

'Sorry, sergeant, there's been a misunderstanding. It's Mrs Seton herself I've come to see,' the constable replied.

Vicky became uneasy. 'Yes?' she asked, frowning.

'I've just been over to your mother's, where I've left a female colleague. It was Mrs Devine who requested I call on you. I'm afraid I bring bad news. There was a street accident, and your father was killed,' the constable said.

Vicky, totally stricken, stared in horror at the constable. 'Killed?' she echoed.

'I'm sorry.'

'How?' she choked.

The constable glanced at Chris, then back at Vicky. 'He died as the result of a broken neck.'

As if she'd been physically hit, Vicky staggered where she stood. She clasped a bewildered Martha tightly to her.

'Oh, Dad!' Vicky whispered, tears sparkling in her eyes, and slipping down her face.

Chris took charge of the situation.

'Death was due to misadventure. The defendant is hereby dismissed,' Lord Smellie-Cameron pronounced.

Vicky bowed her head. It was the verdict she, and everyone else, had expected. Drink, or the excess of it, the curse of the Glasgow working man, she thought bitterly. It had been rare for George to get belligerently drunk, but not unknown. Jekyll had become Hyde, and he'd died as a result.

She glanced over to where the defendant Patrick Troy was being congratulated by his girlfriend, Ina Finlayson. The story was that George, lurching drunk, had bumped into Ina. Troy had told him to mind where he was going. George had thrown a punch at Troy, who, defending himself, had pushed George away. George had then fallen over the rear of Troy's car and broken his neck on impact with the pavement. Such a silly way to die, but fatal nonetheless. She bore no enmity towards Troy. How could she? The fault had been George's.

'You go on out to the car. I'll secure release of the body, and ring the undertaker's to confirm he can now come and collect it,' Chris Walker said softly. He was sitting beside Vicky.

It was six weeks since George's death, but his body had been impounded until the trial was over.

'Thank you,' Vicky replied and, standing up, made her way from the High Court to the Singer.

Anticipating the verdict, Chris had suggested that they have the funeral that coming Saturday, so Neil could manage up from London for it.

She thought of Chris. How marvellous he had been in Neil's absence. He had taken over and organised everything. Neither she nor Mary had had to do anything.

She would never forget this help and support he'd given them. Never.

Twelve

One bitter cold day in October Vicky's office telephone rang. It was Neil. She had been expecting the call.

'Wait a mo',' she said and glanced over to where two helpers were sorting through piles of jumble donated for the Kelvinhaugh Labour Hall's forthcoming jumble sale. Edna Galloway and Mr Porteous were both old-age pensioners.

'Do you think you could go for an early teabreak? It's my husband in London ringing. We've something personal to discuss,' Vicky said.

'We'll away over to the café across the road then. They've some fresh custard creams in,' replied Edna and giggled. She was a great giggler.

'All right, love,' Vicky said to Neil once the two were out of the room.

'It's happened. Sir Stafford Cripps has resigned. It'll be announced in about an hour that Gaitskell is to be the new Chancellor.'

Vicky knew from previous telephone conversations with Neil that Cripps's resignation, in consequence of continuing and worsening ill health, had been expected daily. What neither Neil nor anyone else, with the possible exception of the PM, had known before now was who the new Chancellor would be. Gaitskell had been heavily tipped, but there had been several other strong contenders. Chancellor at forty-four! There would be no stopping Gaitskell now, Vicky thought.

'And what about you?' she asked excitedly.

'Gaitskell has already spoken to me. I'm to soldier on as one of his PPSS,' Neil replied, disappointment in his voice, for he had been hoping for promotion.

Prior to the phone call, Vicky had already worked out

368

something comforting and consoling to say to him should the hoped-for promotion fail to materialise.

'Well, you know this government can't continue on for much longer with its slender majority. Again and again you've told me yourself that its demise is only a matter of time, and a short time at that. And when the next general election takes place Labour are bound to be returned with a far larger majority. That's when Mr Attlee will make big changes, and when your opportunity will come. If you stop and think about it coldly and rationally, you know I'm right,' she said.

'I suppose that's so.'

'You know it is. So don't start getting depressed. Your opportunity is just round the corner, perhaps only a few months away.'

She *was* right. It was daft of him to be downhearted. The election, and the new Labour government which would be formed afterwards, would sort things out for him.

'You've cheered me up, so thanks. But I'm going to have to run now. There's a division in just a few minutes, and it would be worth my life, and prospects, to miss that,' he replied.

'Remember to keep eating properly. I don't want you getting thin again,' she said. It had taken her the entire summer recess, and lots of mince and tats, to put weight back on him.

'Don't worry. I've learned my lesson. I'm taking care of myself,' he reassured her. 'Now I really must dash.'

She blew a kiss into the receiver. 'Ring again soon,' she said and hung up.

She stared thoughtfully at the telephone. She was not surprised that he had not been promoted. If she had been PM she would have done just as Mr Attlee was doing; rock the boat as little as possible, to minimise the chances of it sinking. If she was surprised it was that Neil hadn't also realised the importance of that. Then again, removed from the hustle and bustle of the House, perhaps she could be more objective about this than him, especially as his objectivity would have been clouded by personal ambition.

369

She realised that she needed to go to the ladies' room. Then she'd away over to the café and join Edna and Mr Porteous; she liked the sound of those fresh custard creams. But she never made it to the café. On entering the toilet, she heard someone crying. It was Mrs Malarkey, the cleaner.

'Oh, I'm sorry, Mrs Seton. Whatever must you think of me?' Mrs Malarkey said when she looked up and saw Vicky staring at her. She wiped her face with her sleeve and reached for her mop.

Vicky took Mrs Malarkey, a woman in her late forties, by the elbow. 'What's wrong? Can I help?' she asked gently.

Mrs Malarkey shook her head, then burst into a fresh bout of tears.

'There there,' said Vicky and fumbled for her hanky, only to discover that she'd left it behind in the office.

'Now what *is* all this about?' Vicky persisted.

There was no reply.

'Are you in some sort of trouble? Is that it?'

Mrs Malarkey took off her pinny, scrunched it up and used it to dab at her tear-streaked face.

Vicky stared at Mrs Malarkey in consternation. She was genuinely fond of the woman, a right good soul, and most upset to see her this way.

She saw that her eyes were haunted with worry, while the crows' feet round her eyes had deepened considerably so that they now showed up starkly against her greyish pallor.

'Have you got a fag for yourself? If not I'll run and get you some,' Vicky suggested.

'My handbag's in the cleaning cupboard. I've got a five packet of Pasha in it,' Mrs Malarkey choked.

'I'll get them for you. I'll only be a minute,' Vicky replied, and hurried from the toilet.

She was soon back with the cigarettes and a box of matches. In the meantime Mrs Malarkey had managed to pull herself together a bit. She had stopped crying, but her chest was heaving, and her hands shaking. They shook like billy-o as she lit up.

Mrs Malarkey took a deep draw on her cigarette, then

slowly exhaled. 'That's better,' she muttered, and pushed a stray wisp of straggly hair away from her face. 'I'm sorry I broke down like that. It must have been embarrassing for you.'

'Och, don't be silly. But I still want to know what your problem is. I can't have one of the Hall's employees in such a state. Apart from the fact I want to know as your friend, I have to know because of my position here. Has it to do with your work? Has someone upset you?'

Mrs Malarkey gave a quick shake of the head. 'It's nothing to do with this place. It's . . . something at home.' She took another draw on her cigarette. 'I shouldn't really be smoking when we can't afford it,' she said, as though telling herself off.

Vicky recalled how George had been forced to stop after Agnew's had closed down, and what a trial that had been for him.

'Are you saying you're short of money? Have you got yourself into debt?'

Mrs Malarkey's expression crumpled into one of total wretchedness. 'We're not in debt yet, I've been able to avoid that by paying the rent and penny in the slot out of my wages. We only had a few pounds put by, living week to week as we do, like, and Mr Malarkey was never one to save when he could spend, and that soon went on food . . .' She trailed off, biting her lip.

'Are you saying Mr Malarkey has lost his job?'

'Not . . . not yet. But he will, this Friday.'

Vicky was baffled. Mrs Malarkey wasn't making sense. 'If Mr Malarkey is still in work, why are you having to use your wages to pay the rent?'

'He's in work, but not in work. He's not earning,' Mrs Malarkey mumbled.

Vicky was further confused. 'How can he be in work but not earning?' she persevered.

'I can't say. He told me not to tell anyone.'

Vicky took a deep breath. This was like trying to solve a puzzle where you were denied half the clues. 'Is Mr Malarkey at work now?' she asked.

'No, he's at home.'

'Right then. You're going to take me to him and he can explain all this to me himself.'

'I can't do that!' Mrs Malarkey exclaimed in alarm.

'Yes, you can, and will. I intend to get the pair of you out, if I possibly can, of whatever mess it is you've got yourselves into.' Vicky paused, then switched to a brighter tone. 'Now, if you've gone through your savings, when did you last have a square meal? And the truth mind!'

Mrs Malarkey dropped her gaze. 'Twelve days ago. We've been living off bread and dripping since,' she said quietly.

'Twelve days ago!'

When Mrs Malarkey glanced up again, her expression tore at Vicky's heartstrings. 'The rent was more important than food, you see. If we hadn't paid that, then the factor would soon have had us out in the street. He's a terrible hard man our factor. Fall behind and before you know where you are you're evicted.'

'But what about the neighbours. Haven't they helped?'

'They don't know we haven't been eating properly. We've kept that to ourselves. Mr Malarkey is an awfy proud man, you must understand, no' the sort to go cap in hand to anyone.'

'And that includes relatives I suppose?' Vicky said drily.

'Aye,' Mrs Malarkey whispered.

Vicky hadn't made any inquiries about children because she knew that the couple were childless. 'We'll get your coat, then mine,' Vicky said, steering Mrs Malarkey towards the door.

Vicky's curiosity was well aroused. In work but not in work, and not earning. It was a real teaser.

En route to the Malarkeys' she stopped off at the chippie and bought fish suppers for them. Mrs Malarkey tried to stop her, but she was insistent. Mrs Malarkey devoured hers in the street with a ferocity Vicky hadn't seen since the bad old days of the Depression.

·

'I won't take charity!' Mr Malarkey thundered, glowering at Vicky and the fish supper she was holding out to him.

Vicky was shocked by Mr Malarkey's appearance. Both his eyes had been blacked – each now a riot of colour, thanks to the healing process which was under way – and his nose was broken. Swathes of bandages were visible beneath his open shirt neck.

'It's not charity. It's . . . well, I've been starving hungry myself and know what it's like,' Vicky replied gently.

Mr Malarkey softened a little on hearing that.

'Oh, come on man, get stuck in. If you feel you have to, then you can pay me back some time,' Vicky urged.

Still Mr Malarkey hesitated, clinging to his pride.

'I'll put it on a plate for you,' Mrs Malarkey said to her husband, and took the succulent-smelling newspaper-wrapped bundle from Vicky.

Mr Malarkey stared at the steaming meal that his wife placed on his lap. Slowly, and with tremendous dignity, in complete contrast to the way Mrs Malarkey had wolfed hers down, he began to eat.

When he was finished, Mrs Malarkey offered him one of the two remaining cigarettes in her packet. 'There's nothing like a good bit of cod,' he said gruffly, and lit up.

'I found Mrs Malarkey in the Hall toilet. She was in floods of tears,' Vicky said to him.

Mr Malarkey looked at his wife, his expression grim.

'She won't tell me why you're apparently employed, yet not at work, and not earning. Are you in difficulty with your work because of an accident? Don't think me rude, but you look in a right old state,' Vicky said.

Mr Malarkey gave a wry, bitter, laugh. The laugh changed to a grimace of pain, causing him to clutch at his chest.

'Cracked ribs?' Vicky queried.

'Broken. Four of them,' he replied.

'How did that happen?'

Mr Malarkey glanced again at his wife, but did not reply.

The silence in the room lengthened and lengthened. 'I've heard Mrs Malarkey speak about you many times. I'd have never believed you to be a coward,' Vicky said eventually.

'I'm no' that!'

'You're *scared* to tell me what this is all about, aren't you? What's that if not being cowardly?'

Mr Malarkey opened his mouth. Unable to think of a suitable reply he snapped it shut again. He stared hard into the empty grate.

'I could arrange a loan for you until you start earning again,' Vicky suggested.

'Lex?' Mrs Malarkey said, hope creeping into her face.

Mr Malarkey turned to Vicky. 'I've already tried to get a loan, but nobody would gie me one. They all wanted what they cry collateral, which I don't have.'

'Being an MP's wife has its advantages; there are ways and means.' Vicky smiled.

Mr Malarkey studied her. 'I need two hundred pounds,' he stated bluntly.

'Two hundred pounds!' Vicky exclaimed, shocked a second time since entering the Malarkey home. No wonder he had been asked for collateral.

'Two hundred pounds, by Friday. After that it's too late. After that I'm out of work with no hope whatever of finding another job, for at fifty-three I'm too damned old for anyone else to take me on.' Mr Malarkey's voice was tight and crackling with emotion.

Vicky looked straight into his tortured eyes. 'You tell me your story from beginning to end and then I'll tell you whether or not I can get you a loan of this two hundred pounds you appear to so desperately need.'

'Lex. Please?' Mrs Malarkey said.

Several seconds ticked by. The woman started to cry again, the hot tears spilling down her cheeks.

'If I do tell you what this is all about, will it be in the strictest confidence? For if it gets out that I've yapped, I'll pay for it,' Mr Malarkey said to Vicky.

'You have my word.'

He ground out the remains of his cigarette in an ashtray on the hearth. 'I'm a dockie, Mrs Seton, have been man and boy. It's all I know. Well, over the past few years, I've been getting more and more disturbed by the way my union keeps putting in higher and higher demands to the employers. I mean, it's getting ridiculous. Loading and unloading fees have gone right through the roof. And although it's marvellous to earn a bloody good wage, the whole thing could be in the long run, as I see it, a case of cutting off your nose to spite your face.'

A dockie! Vicky hadn't known that. For some reason she had thought him to be a labourer. She listened intently as Mr Malarkey continued.

'I've said my piece at a number of union meetings, explained how I was worried that, if we continued to make such high demands, it could get to the stage where the employers would say, sod you!, and move their business to another port where they'd get a far better deal. And if that happened, Clydeside dockies would go from being excellently paid, to on the 'Broo, unemployed.

'Although some of the men were interested, the shop stewards and other officials weren't. Then at the meeting before last I was told not to bring the subject up again, to put a sock in it.

'Well, I didn't. I did argue the point yet again at the last meeting – and paid the penalty for not heeding their warning.

'I was walking home with several pals, like, when suddenly Paddy Troy and some shop stewards appeared beside us . . .'

'Who?' Vicky broke in, frowning.

'Paddy Troy. He's a right brute of an Irishman who's Blacklaws's bodyguard. Blacklaws is the president of the union,' Mr Malarkey explained.

Paddy Troy . . . Patrick Troy? A Patrick Troy had been involved in her father's death. Troy, like Malarkey, was an uncommon name in Glasgow, even though the city did boast a large population of Irish and Irish descent. As Irish Patricks were often called Paddy, could it be that they were one and the same man? A man who worked for Ken? She went cold at that thought.

'Go on, please,' she said to Mr Malarkey, feeling both

electrified and confused at the possibilities opened up by this new dimension.

Mr Malarkey shrugged. 'I'd heard whispers, rumours, but I'd always taken them with a pinch of salt. That night I learned otherwise.

'My pals were told to hop it. Troy and the shop stewards wanted a confidential word with me. Reluctantly my pals went, for you don't argue with Troy. When they were gone, Troy told me I was a trouble-maker and that the union had no time for those. He then, all by himself, proceeded to beat the living daylights out of me. When he'd finished he bent over me – I think he'd left me conscious deliberately – and said that, if I ever mentioned this to anybody, he'd look me up again and break both my legs in several places.'

Mr Malarkey paused for breath.

'That's not the worst of it, not by a long chalk,' his wife said shrilly.

Mr Malarkey continued, 'I got myself home here, and the doctor had been sent for but not yet arrived, when there was a knock on the door. It was my own shop steward with a hand-delivered letter from the union. The letter said I had been fined two hundred pounds for dangerous work practices – a completely trumped-up charge, I assure you – which had to be paid four weeks from that Friday. In the meantime I was temporarily suspended from work, and if the fine wasn't paid by the expiry date I'd lose my union membership, and with that of course my job, as the docks are a closed shop.'

Vicky was appalled by the terrible tale. The two hundred pounds' fine was clearly a device to get rid of Mr Malarkey, for what ordinary working man, even a well-paid one, could lay his hands on that sum in such a relatively short time?

'Does this sort of thing go on a lot in the union?' Vicky asked.

'Well, let me put it this way. I knew the union was rotten, but I never dreamed it was so rotten. These are out and out Nazi tactics,' Mr Malarkey replied.

He was dead right, Vicky thought. Ken must know this

was going on in his union, and it had to be going on with his blessing. What had he become!

'It's the ones coming after us that I worry about most. If the Clydeside docks do eventually close because of greed, what happens to them? Families who for generations have worked these docks will have to go elsewhere, if their menfolk are lucky enough to find employment, that is. As for the area itself, if people move out in large numbers, and those that are left are idle, it won't take long for the place to run down, become a partially inhabited ghost town . . . But the shop stewards and other union officials I've been telling you about won't have that; they think the goose will go on laying bigger and bigger golden eggs for ever.'

Today was Wednesday. Forty-eight hours in which to raise the money, Vicky thought.

'You'll have your two hundred pounds, I promise you,' she said.

'Oh, lass!' exclaimed Mrs Malarkey softly, and bit into a thumb.

Mr Malarkey had gone very still. He stared at Vicky, his gaze penetrating. 'You really mean that?'

'I really mean that. I'll have it here on time, you can rely on it,' she answered levelly.

Mr Malarkey bowed his head, not wanting Vicky to see the look on his face. 'Thank you, Mrs Seton.'

'Now tell me all you know about this Paddy Troy. I have personal reasons for asking,' she said.

Before Vicky left it was agreed that, on resuming work, Mr Malarkey would repay the loan which Vicky would arrange on a weekly basis. He gave her his unsolicited word of honour that he would never default by so much as a single week.

Vicky was so dog tired that she had asked Chris to drive. They were returning from Camlachie, where she had given a speech to the local Women's Guild. The speech had gone down well and had been enthusiastically applauded. Within a few minutes of standing up she'd had them eating out the palm of her hand.

She brought her mind back to the story Mr Malarkey had told her the previous day. She had been waiting for the right moment to speak to Chris about it.

'Will you do me a favour?' she asked.

Chris changed gear. 'If I can,' he replied, and gave her a quick sideways smile.

He was a godsend, she thought. More and more he was acting as a sort of personal manager to her: taking her here and there, organising this and that, generally making life easier for her.

'What I'm about to tell you was told to me in strictest confidence, so that strict confidence now applies to you. This stays between the pair of us, all right?'

Chris nodded.

She repeated Mr Malarkey's story while Chris listened in brooding silence.

'So what I'd like you to do is find out if this Paddy Troy and our Patrick Troy are one and the same. And if they are, I'd like you to discover his police history. For, if they are the same man, that just might put a different complexion on what supposedly happened to my dad.'

'You think he might have lied in court?' Chris asked.

'Well, you see, there's more to it than I've so far explained. Paddy Troy's boss, whom he's bodyguard to, according to Mr Malarkey, is an old friend of mine and Neil's . . . Did you know I'd been in borstal and prison?'

Chris gave Vicky another sideways glance, but this time he was not smiling. 'Tina mentioned once that you and she had been in borstal together. That was all though, she didn't elaborate.'

'Didn't that make you curious?' she asked, curious herself that he apparently hadn't been so.

'If Tina had wanted to tell me about her being in borstal, the full facts and details, that is, she would have done. She never has, nor has Sammy. So as far as I'm concerned, that remains their business and it would be rude of me to probe. Same applies to you. If you want to tell me the whys and wherefores, fine. But I'd never ask.'

She understood now. To take such a line was not only

thoughtful and considerate, it showed sensitivity, a quality she already associated with him.

'I was convicted of theft and sent down for three years. But I wasn't the thief. I was covering for the real thief, whom I was in love with at the time. He was my boyfriend, Ken Blacklaws, who's now president of the Clyde Dockworkers' Union, and Paddy Troy's boss.'

Digesting that, Chris took a handful of seconds before replying. 'You must have loved him very much to do that?'

'I was head over heels. The sun rose and set on him.'

'And now?'

'Now I'm a happily married woman,' she answered.

He let it go at that. 'So what you're wondering is: if Paddy and Patrick Troy are one and the same, was this Blacklaws somehow involved? I take it your dad wouldn't have known Troy, or the Finlayson female?'

'That's exactly what's going through my mind. For if Paddy and Patrick are the same person, the whole thing becomes far too coincidental don't you agree?'

'I do,' Chris replied grimly.

Vicky was suddenly aware of Chris's maleness and potency. She had been vaguely aware of it on previous occasions, but nowhere near as strongly as she was now. She experienced a slithering sensation in her stomach, while her muscles there began to quiver. There was a warmness and a tingle where there hadn't been for years. She looked at Chris. He was an attractive man, very attractive. A shiver ran down her spine.

'Are you cold?'

'No, just someone walking over my grave, that's all.'

His eyes flicked sideways, then returned to the road again. 'You asked me to do something for you. Now will you do something for me?'

'Of course.'

'I think you're overdoing it, doing far too much. You've got your full-time job as Neil and Sandy Millar's secretary, plus the work you do for the Kelvinhaugh Labour Hall and Bridgeton Labour Hall. And, with Neil away nearly all the time, you've been taking his surgeries and fulfilling his speaking engagements, on top of which there are your own speaking engagements, whose number are far greater than those you do for Neil. As if all this wasn't enough, you have a home and daughter to look after. My own opinion is that you should ease off somewhere before you collapse from total exhaustion or, worse still, have a nervous breakdown.'

She was touched by his concern and amused by the rather schoolmasterish way in which he had delivered his wigging. She could just imagine him talking to erring constables like that.

'It's not quite as bad as you think, Chris. I hardly do a hand's turn round the house any more. My mother Mary does virtually everything for me, shopping, cleaning, etc. Nor do I mind her doing it, for with my father gone it helps fill the time for her. It's the same with her looking after Martha, which she does so often; it's another filler for her, and one which she loves, as she absolutely dotes on Martha, and Martha on her.'

'Be that as it may, you're still doing far too much. Why don't you cut back on the speaking engagements a bit? That would be a help.'

She had an almost overwhelming desire to reach out and touch him. His personal odour was heavy and pungent in her nostrils and made that tingle even stronger.

'I'll see,' she replied, having no intention of cutting back at all. She decided to change the subject. 'I want to call in at the Malarkeys' before I go home. I have his money on me.'

Chris reacted in alarm. 'You mean you've been carrying that amount on you all evening!'

She had to laugh at his outraged expression. 'It was perfectly safe.' Then teasingly, and tauntingly, 'After all, I had a big strong polisman to guard me.'

Chris coloured in the darkness.

Vicky laughed again. It was a good-humoured laugh, but there was a trace of mockery in it. Or perhaps it wasn't mockery. Perhaps it was something else.

As the Singer continued to sigh through the night, Vicky fell asleep to dream about her and Chris, about what Chris could do which Neil couldn't.

•

The skeleton of the new building was now complete. Ken stood on one of its topmost girders staring out over the Broomielaw and Glasgow's south side, the latter a legion of tenements belching black smoke into a grey, lowering sky.

It was a terrific feeling being so high up and in such precarious surroundings, Ken thought. The ground and river below seemed a terrifying distance away. Another eight to ten months and the building would be ready for the CDU to move in. What a red-letter day that would be!

Ken had had Ina choose the carpets, furniture and decorations. For his own office he had indulged himself by buying two American pictures of Western scenes in the nineteenth century, one by an artist called Lou Megaree, the other by E. Irving Couse. The subject of the former was of a group of cowboys, of the latter several plains Indians stalking game.

A gust of wind caused him to clutch at the upright girder at the junction where he was standing.

'All right?' inquired the foreman who had brought him up.

Nodding, he gazed out over Clydeside, seeing all the way down to Yorkhill Quay where the river bent and was lost to view. His kingdom, *his*!

His thoughts turned to the port of Leith, making him frown, and a thundercloud settle on his face. Of the two dock unions there had been in Leith, the larger had now fallen and was merged with the CDU. The smaller was being far more resistant, and that resistance was now proving damned annoying. There was nothing else for it; he would have to dispatch Paddy through there. If the union had a weakness, it was its limited financial reserves. That was the Achilles heel he'd work on, through Paddy Troy.

First of all there must be a series of disruptions, all designed to slow down work and invoke the time-penalty clauses inbuilt in the contracts that union still worked under. (Honest to God, if nothing else, that showed how much they needed him and the CDU. Still accepting time-penalty clauses, it was unbelievable! Not to mention downright stupid.)

These disruptions would consist of 'accidents', both to personnel and machinery, acts of sabotage such as fires, and of course the old favourite, strikes, which Paddy Troy would organise within the union ranks by employing 'friendly persuasion'. As the disruptions got under way, he would think of other means and ploys to bleed the union of its cash until, in the end, the union would be forced either to merge or expire.

Vicky was on the point of finishing Neil's bi-weekly surgery when Chris turned up. 'Let's go for a drink, I've got some information for you,' he said to her when the last constituent had left.

They found a quiet pub and settled themselves with their drinks in a secluded corner.

'Your Patrick Troy and Blacklaws's Paddy Troy are the same man,' Chris announced.

It was as if a sharp knife had been thrust into Vicky's chest and twisted. 'I see,' she said quietly. The words came out as a hiss.

'I ran a check on him and drew a blank. Although he was in our records because of your father's death, he has no "previous" in this country. So I asked our Irish colleagues what they knew of him, and that turned out to be quite a history. They've done him for larceny, assault, assault causing GBH, and finally, but not least, several times for procuring. In Dublin he's known as what we would call a hard man, a dyed-in-the-wool villain.'

Vicky's eyes narrowed to slits. 'Ken had to be somehow involved in my father's death. It just doesn't make sense otherwise.'

'I also spoke to the officers who attended the scene of your father's death. According to them, there was absolutely nothing to arouse their suspicions that Troy was telling anything other than the truth. The drawback was of course there were no witnesses, but then you know that from the trial.'

'So basically it boils down to us taking Troy and the Finlayson woman's word that what they say happened actually did.'

Chris nodded. 'Just as it was at the trial.'

'But then we didn't know that Troy worked for Ken, or that he was a villain.'

Vicky brooded on this information for a few moments. As far as she was concerned the whole thing stank to high heaven. 'And the police officers who attended the scene of my father's death say that, in the circumstances, there was nothing unusual? Nothing at all?'

Chris shook his head. 'Nothing other than the car Troy was driving, which they all remembered. A huge American job, the size of a tank, one of them described it as.'

The knifelike pain was back, stabbing and twisting in Vicky's chest. 'Was it a Cadillac by any chance?' she asked slowly.

Chris's whisky stopped halfway to his mouth. 'Yes, it was. Why, is that significant?'

'Just that Ken owns a Cadillac – the only one in Scotland, he once boasted to me.'

Seconds ticked by during which Vicky and Chris thought about that.

'But Troy works for Blacklaws, so there are all sorts of reasons why he might have been driving it at the time,' Chris said.

'Maybe so. But in court, by assumption I now realise, we were led to believe that the car belonged to Troy. Ken's name was never mentioned, neither as car owner, or Troy's employer.'

'I can certainly find out who the car *does* belong to; that'll be a matter of record,' Chris suggested.

'You're thinking Ken might have sold or even given the Cadillac to Troy?'

Chris shrugged. 'It's possible.'

More seconds ticked by. 'If Ken is still the owner, then he was there that day, and Troy is covering for him, just as I covered for him all those years ago,' Vicky said.

They stared hard at one another, each trying to imagine what had really happened on that fateful day.

*

Chris rang Vicky at her office next morning just after coffee break. 'The Cadillac doesn't belong personally to Blacklaws, or to Troy; it belongs to the Clyde Dockworkers' Union. Therefore, technically, it can be argued that the car belongs to both of them, just as it belongs to every member of the union. I also checked the insurance policy, but that was no use, as the union have a blanket policy covering all their cars, of which there are a number. Troy is a named driver on that policy, as is Blacklaws, and others,' Chris told her.

They chatted for a few minutes, then said goodbye.

Vicky stared thoughtfully at the phone. It didn't matter that Troy was off the hook over the ownership of the car; she knew damned well that he had lied in court.

An ashen Ina Finlayson knocked, and entered Ken's office. 'It's Mrs Seton, the daughter of that Devine man who died, here to see you,' she blurted out. She hadn't been aware that Ken and Vicky knew one another. Ken had kept stum about that.

A heavy lunch had made Ken feel drowsy. When he heard of Vicky's arrival, the drowsiness abruptly left him. 'You'd better let her in.'

'Why can she be here?' Ina whispered, as though Vicky might have been able to overhear, although there were two doors and a passageway separating her from them.

'Maybe she's paying us a visit for old times' sake. She used to work here once.' Ken smiled.

Ina gave him a strange look and waited for him to elaborate. When he didn't, she left the room to fetch Vicky.

Ken stood in front of his desk and straightened his tie. It might have nothing whatever to do with George Devine's death, he told himself. Then he realised that Vicky now knew Ina was a CDU employee – and Ina had been in court as Paddy Troy's supposed girlfriend, and she had been there when George died.

'Fuck!' he swore.

He was smiling again when Ina ushered Vicky in. 'It's good to see you again,' he said, approaching Vicky with an extended hand.

Vicky ignored the hand. 'So Miss Finlayson is your secretary. How extremely interesting.'

Ken flinched.

'And Troy works for you as well.'

Ken regained his composure. 'Right on both counts,' he replied casually, and headed for the drinks cabinet. 'Dram?' he asked.

'No, thank you,' she replied coldly.

He poured himself a hefty one, noting as he did so that his palms were sweating.

'A very pretty female Miss Finlayson. I never really took that in while we were in court. But I can see now she is; quite a stunner in fact.'

'I suppose she is,' Ken replied vaguely, and added some bottled spring water to his whisky.

Vicky glanced over at the door beyond which was the small apartment where she and Ken had so often made love. Martha had been conceived in there. Their daughter, whom Ken didn't know was his, nor would he ever know.

'What do you think of this?' Ken said, going over to a table adjacent to his desk and indicating a scale model of his new building.

'I'm having it built down at the Broomielaw. It's the new union premises to replace this dump. Something eh?' His voice oozed pride.

'How often has Miss Finlayson been through there?' Vicky asked, pointing at the apartment door. There was a flicker in Ken's eyes, which was quickly gone. But it was enough; it told her that she was right.

'Miss Finlayson is Paddy Troy's girl,' Ken answered levelly.

'Come off it! Are you seriously asking me to believe that you could have such a gorgeous female as a secretary and not have her as your mistress, that you'd let one of your minions have the privilege? No, no. She's yours, not Troy's.'

Ken sipped his dram, studying Vicky over the rim of his glass.

'What's all this in aid of? Why are you here?' he demanded, a vein of harshness creeping into his voice.

Vicky went over to stare at the model. It was an attractive building, she thought, vibrant, somehow full of energy.

'Do you know what I think really happened the day my father died?' she said softly.

Ken gave no response.

'I accept he could have been lurching drunk – the post mortem proved he had an extremely high level of alcohol in his blood when he died. But if that's true, it's about the only truth in Troy and Miss Finlayson's story.'

Ken, lips thinned, stayed silent.

Vicky turned to fix him with her gaze. Holding his eyes, she continued, 'My father came out that pub and bumped into you, you with *your* ladyfriend, I now realise. I've no idea why you were in that area, probably on union business, but it doesn't really matter. All that does matter is that you were there.

'My father recognised you, approached you and, from a combination of alcohol and emotion, began abusing you. A fight then developed, during which either Troy or yourself killed my father.'

She paused, noting that he had gone pale just as the Finlayson female had done a few minutes earlier when they had come face to face. 'Never slow off the mark, you realised there weren't any witnesses, quickly concocted the story Troy and Miss Finlayson gave to the police, and fled, leaving Troy and Miss Finlayson to report as an accident what in reality had been murder.'

There was now a jagged bitterness in her voice and a shrill note of potential hysteria.

'So which one of you killed my dad, you or your hired thug?' she demanded.

Ken was much more shaken by her accusation than he appeared. 'Neither Paddy nor I killed him. Nor Shugs my chauffeur, who was also present,' he replied, having decided that the best thing he could do now was tell her the truth in the hope that that would calm things down again and stop her going to the police. Then a horrible thought hit him. 'You haven't already been to the police with this, have you?' he queried, his composure slipping.

'And if I have?'

He ran a hand over his damp forehead. The small of his back had also begun to sweat. 'It's as I say, I swear. We didn't kill him. He broke his neck, just as Paddy Troy described in court.'

In her mind Vicky was seeing her father, remembering him from all sorts of occasions during her childhood, and later. 'Liar!' she spat.

'I ran because I had to. I knew your dad. Once the police had established that, which they were bound to have done, they would have suspected that he had a motive for attacking me as he did . . . When I say I had to run, let me rephrase that. It was prudent of me to do so, for your and Neil's sake as well as my own.'

'How do you make that out?'

'Do you remember that day I took you for a run in my Caddy? I explained to you then what I would do if you named me as a thief, and it's what I'll do still if you have gone to the police now. Any shit you throw will boomerang back to you and Neil, I promise.

'As for me? I can well do without any such publicity, even when I will be vindicated.'

Ken stared at Vicky. Now he'd had time to think it through, he was certain that she hadn't been to the police yet. She wouldn't be here like this if she had; the police would have been with her or – more probably, here without her – if she had.

'Now this is what actually happened that day,' he said, and related in detail all that had occurred.

Vicky listed in stony silence. When he finished, she crossed to the window and stared out. She believed him. His account of the tragic affair had the distinctive ring of truth about it.

She thought of Ken and all the misery and pain he'd brought into her life: Duncliffe, Miss Ganch, the Black Room, Duke Street prison, and now, because of her past association with him, the death of her father. On the one hand, it was true to say that he hadn't killed George, that George had died as the result of an accident. But, on the other, was it not also fair to say that he had killed George by what he'd done to her, just as surely as if he'd broken George's neck himself? If Ken hadn't treated her the way he had, George would never have gone for him, and George would still be alive. So the fault was his, if not by direct action, then by past deed.

It is said that there is a fine dividing line between love and hate. Having reached the conclusion she had, Vicky passed over that divide. The great love and passion she'd once felt for Ken was now transformed into a hatred of equal intensity.

'You haven't been to the police yet have you?' Ken said.

'No,' she answered, her voice cold and distant.

He came to her and would have touched her, but she shrank away from him. 'It's best to let sleeping dogs lie, Vicky, for all concerned.'

'I'll have that drink now,' she replied.

She watched him as he poured the whisky and added spring water.

'I really am sorry for what happened,' he said, handing her the dram.

She threw the whisky and water straight into his face.

Eyes brimming with tears, she marched from his office, past a startled Ina Finlayson, and on out of the building.

Thirteen

One night during the following April, 1951, Vicky had said goodnight to Martha and was filling the kettle with the intention of making herself a cup of coffee, when the phone rang. They had had the phone, the only one in Parr Street, installed nearly a year now. It was Neil telephoning from his flat in Petty France.

'Have you heard the news?' he asked.

'What news?'

'Bevan, Harold Wilson and John Freeman have all resigned because Gaitskell put charges upon the supply of spectacles and dentures in his budget.'

Aneurin Bevan was Minister of Labour, Harold Wilson President of the Board of Trade, and John Freeman Parliamentary Secretary to the Ministry of Supply.

'That's a big loss to the government,' Vicky replied, thinking that Bevan was a particular loss. She was a great admirer of his.

As for the spectacles and dentures charges, Vicky knew that it was the heavy costs of the rearmament programme necessitated by the Korean War which had forced Gaitskell to levy them. Or, to put it another way, depending upon your point of view, the war was his excuse for doing so.

'There's something else,' Neil went on. He paused, then added, 'I agree with the stance these men have taken, and because of that have resigned my post as Gaitskell's PPS.'

Vicky was immediately alarmed. 'I'm not certain that was the right step to take,' she said slowly.

'I am. A man has to stand by his beliefs and principles. He isn't a man if he doesn't.'

Vicky sighed. 'It's all very well for established, and major figures within the party to make these gestures, but you're neither yet. So don't you think it was somewhat precipitate of you?'

'No, I don't. If anything, it could be the making of me.'

'What you mean is, it sets you clearly within the left's camp.'

'But I *am* of the left,' he replied tartly.

'Maybe so, but that doesn't mean you have to let yourself be so clearly identified with them. For, you mustn't forget, the moderates are the majority within the party.'

On the other end of the telephone Neil was scowling. There were times when Vicky's arguments irritated him, and this was one of them. As far as he was concerned, the issue was clear cut and, by his lights, he had done the right thing.

'Well, I tendered my resignation and Gaitskell accepted it. Even if I wanted to, which I don't, I can't undo that now,' he said.

'You might have talked it over with me first,' she chided.

'I don't have to ask your permission. I wear the trousers in our family,' he retorted. Then, realising what he had said, and his own sexual inadequacies, his face flamed scarlet. 'You know what I mean,' he added lamely.

It was a political error on his part, Vicky was convinced of that. A luxury which a man of ambition who was still in a lowly position couldn't afford. 'I didn't say you had to ask my permission. I just said you might have talked it over with me first.'

There was silence between them. The line crackled with static.

'You think I've made a mistake, don't you?' he said quietly.

'Yes, I do.'

They spoke no further on the subject.

'The results for Bury St Edmunds are . . .' the announcer intoned.

Vicky, Neil, Chris Walker and Mona Bryce, Chris's girlfriend, leaned closer to the wireless set. It was the early morning of 26 October 1951, the day after the general election.

Neil had been re-elected as Member for Glasgow Kelvinhaugh a little before one a.m., again with an increased majority, mainly at the expense of the Liberals. There had been drinks at the Labour Hall after his re-election had been confirmed, then it had been back to Parr Street to await the rest of the results.

So far, those results had not been good for the Labour Party; vital seats had been slipping away to the Conservatives. But all was not yet lost, not by a long chalk.

'W. T. Aitken, Conservative: twenty-four thousand, six hundred and seventy-nine. N. Stanley, Labour: twenty thousand, six hundred and ninety. There is no Liberal candidate . . .'

The rest of what the announcer had to say was drowned out by groans and a loud expletive from Mona Bryce.

'Another Tory win,' Neil said despondently.

'But the last two were Labour,' Chris reminded him.

'True, except that they were safe seats. It would have been unthinkable for us to have lost either.'

Mona yawned and glanced at her watch. It was 3.52 a.m., and there were still quite a number of results to come through. 'I could murder a cup of tea,' she said.

It annoyed Vicky that Mona had felt that she had to ask. She had been just about to stick the kettle on anyway.

'Perhaps you'd care to make a pot if I show you where everything is?' she smiled at Mona. She didn't care for Mona, thinking her a bumptious little bitch. She could not think what Chris saw in her.

'Certainly,' Mona replied, returning Vicky's smile, and rose to smooth down the shantung-silk dress she was wearing. She had a beautiful figure and was well aware of the fact. She always tried to show it off to best advantage.

It might be a beautiful figure, Vicky thought, but the face left a lot to be desired. It was the sort of face that would have gone down well with a bag of chips.

Mona, still smiling, contrived to touch Chris's shoulder as she passed him. She was always touching him, Vicky thought. In fact she couldn't keep her hands off him. Not for the first time she wondered if Chris and Mona were sleeping together; it always made her angry to think they might be. Not that it was any of her business.

'And now the results for Aberdeen East . . .' the announcer said.

Vicky stopped and turned, as did Mona. In unison, Neil and Chris leaned closer to the set.

'Ronald Arthur Abercrombie Hughes, Conservative: twenty thousand eight hundred and twenty. Hector McQuarrie, Labour: twenty thousand and thirty nine. Philip Alan Watson, Liberal: four thousand nine hundred and sixty-three. Thomas Troon Gallacher, Independent: one thousand five hundred and forty-four. Ronald Arthur Abercrombie Hughes is therefore . . .'

'Buggeration!' Neil exclaimed, and smashed a fist into an open palm. It was another Tory win, and *gain*.

Neil glanced over at Vicky and their eyes locked. 'If we do hang on, it's not going to be with the larger mandate that's so essential,' he said.

For the first time Vicky started to consider the dismaying prospect of Labour losing the election. 'I've got some Battenberg; we'll have that with the tea,' she told Mona, and led Mona over to the cupboard where the cake and caddy were kept.

Neil sat staring gloomily into the fireplace where, in complete contrast to his mood and expression, a cheery fire was blazing. He and Vicky had recently returned from a restaurant where he'd taken her for a celebratory meal. It was 24 March 1953, Vicky's thirty-fourth birthday. Neil had managed to get paired and come north to spend a few days with her. He had arrived in late that afternoon.

Since the October 1951 election, which the Conservatives had won with an overall majority of seventeen, it had been possible for him to come home more often than previously. Not that there was a tremendous amount for him to do when he did get up; Vicky had the constituency business well under control. The only important thing he had to do was put his face about and shake a number of hands. The rest had become Vicky's domain.

Vicky came into the kitchen, having been through to their bedroom to change. She was wearing a cotton, floral, Japanese wrap that was his birthday present to her. The label on the inside said it came from Harrod's.

'All right, you can forget it's my birthday now. Out with whatever's been bothering you since you arrived,' she said.

Neil roused himself and sniffed. 'Since we went into opposition, I feel I've become bogged down, that I'm failing to make headway. If only . . . Well, if only I could find some way of distinguishing myself, of making myself stand out from the herd, most of whom are also trying to make a name for themselves, their eyes fixed firmly on the next Labour government, which surely must be formed after the next election.'

'What about your articles for the *New Statesman*? Aren't they helping?'

'I thought that appearing in print alongside such luminaries as Foot, Driberg, Crossman, etc., would do the trick. But, sadly, it hasn't. It's a firecracker where I need a stick of dynamite.'

Vicky laughed. 'Well put. A stick of dynamite indeed!' She refrained from saying that his position would have been a lot better if he'd remained as Gaitskell's PPS. It would only have annoyed him for her to have done so.

Neil made a fist and shook it in front of him. 'There's so much I could do in, and for, Glasgow if only I had access to power. Power to use and trade,' he declared.

'The housing schemes are going ahead.'

'They're a start, but only that.' He gave a weary sigh and sank back into his chair.

'You look dead beat,' she said sympathetically.

'I've had a lot on of late, and that train journey always takes it out of me. Especially when the train's jam-packed, as it was this time.'

She went over to kneel beside him. 'Away through and get your head down. I'll be in shortly.'

'Do you want me to . . .'

393

She shook her head, knowing that he was referring to the one-sided lovemaking they indulged in. 'No. Tomorrow night maybe,' she whispered.

He caressed her cheek. 'I don't know what I'd do without you and Martha. The pair of you are the sun and moon to me.'

'She loves you too. And is very proud of you and your work.'

'And what about you, Vicky?'

'I'm proud of you too.'

He smiled inwardly. She had answered only half of his question. She had never told him she loved him, never had, not once. But still he was content. He might not have her love, but he did have her, and that was the next best thing. Taking her face in his hands, he bent down and kissed her, lingering over the kiss, savouring the sweetness of her mouth and her delicious smell.

'Now, away ben, I won't be long,' she said, rising to her feet and drawing him to his. 'Start on my side, warm it up for me.' She smiled.

He pecked her on the cheek.

When he was gone, she sat where he'd been sitting and gazed into the fire's flickering, dancing depths. If only Neil *could* find a way of distinguishing himself from the other Labour backbench hopefuls! she thought. Something that would draw attention, praise and respect. He was right about the stick of dynamite.

Lost in thought, Vicky remained transfixed by the fire.

As the mantelpiece clock chimed midnight the idea came to her. It made her go cold all over and imagine that she could see her father's face in the glowing embers of the now dying fire.

Next morning during breakfast Vicky bided her patience while Neil chatted to Martha about her forthcoming qualifying exam, or 'quali' as it was generally called. The results of this exam would determine whether she went to junior or secondary school, and in the case of the latter which grade of class she would be assigned to. They were all hoping that she would achieve an S1 pass, the highest. That would put her into senior secondary and class 1A, the top class.

Vicky waited till Neil returned to the kitchen from seeing Martha off to school at the outside door, as he always did when at home, then said. 'I think I might have the answer, that stick of dynamite you were talking about last night.'

Neil, about to pick up the newspaper, stopped, turned to her and raised an eyebrow.

'Do you remember that business with the Malarkeys, and the loan I raised for Mr Malarkey to enable him pay off his union fine?'

'I mind it fine.'

'And that Chris Walker helped me establish that Patrick Troy and Paddy Troy were one and the same – Troy being Ken Blacklaws's bodyguard, who'd given poor Mr Malarkey such a beating?'

'Aye,' said Neil, nodding. Vicky had written to him about that, spoken about it on the telephone and, as he recalled, brought it up again the next time he'd come home.

'Well, I believe Ken could be your stick of dynamite.'

Neil frowned. 'I don't understand?'

'What I've never told you is, because of Troy's involvement in my father's death, and also, I suppose, because I was curious about Ken and the sort of person it appeared he'd become, I made several inquiries into CDU matters. Oh, nothing extensive, but enough to be a real eye-opener. The union is rotten through and through and, as Mr Malarkey claimed, employing Nazi tactics to achieve its ends. And when I say union I mean Ken, for he is the union.'

'I still don't understand what you're driving at? How could Ken be my stick of dynamite?'

'We know for fact that the union uses intimidation and violence, Mr Malarkey proved that. I also heard of sabotage, arson, blackmail, and murder even.'

Neil gazed at her in amazement. 'Are you serious?'

'The people I talked to were. Couldn't have been more so.'

Neil's brow clouded in thought. 'Ken certainly has

395

become very powerful over the past few years. That union of his just keeps on growing and growing, and at a remarkable pace too.'

'I'm suggesting that we have Ken and his union investigated properly – we'll get Chris Walker to help us there; and then, when we have enough to hang Ken and his union, bring a case against them and smash them,' Vicky said.

Neil blanched. 'Are you mad! I'm a Labour MP. Labour MPs don't go round trying to smash unions. Without unions the party couldn't financially exist. We're dependent on them.'

Vicky gave a razored smile. 'That weakness is also your strength. A union like the CDU can only harm and dishonour the entire trade union movement. Smash the present Nazi hierarchy of the CDU, give it back to its members, and you would be a Labour hero, a champion of the people, and bound to be offered a position, and who's to say not a senior one, in the next Labour government.'

Neil's eyes gleamed. 'Labour hero, eh?'

'And champion of the people. A man who found corruption on his own doorstep and wasn't afraid to purge that corruption. To scour the evil clean, and banish it from the shores of Clydeside.'

Neil's mind flew back to that night in the downstairs dunny when Ken had claimed him, giving him the kicking that had rendered him impotent. How he hated Ken for that. Ken had deprived him of so much; now here was a chance to pay him back a little, and do himself a lot of good at the same time.

'Murder even?' he queried.

'So the rumours and stories say.'

'What about proof?'

'That's what we'll have to get: witnesses and proof for all that we eventually come to accuse Ken and his union of in court.'

Neil licked his lips. 'It could be dangerous?'

'So can crossing the street. Last night you said there was so much you could do for Glasgow if you only had access to power. Well, this could give you that access. And, if we pull it off, is almost surely likely to.'

A senior position in the next Labour government, he thought excitedly. 'Who knows, maybe the PM might even make me . . .' Neil took a deep breath, then exhaled slowly. 'Secretary of State for Scotland?' Oh, that would be a dream come true indeed!

'Why not?' Vicky smiled in reply.

'If there's a post in a Labour government I covet, it's that one,' he admitted.

'There would be a certain irony, not to mention justice, should you achieve that ambition at Ken's expense,' she replied.

'Yes . . . exactly,' he breathed. Then he was frowning again. 'The only trouble is that all this is going to take a great deal of hard work, work that has to be done on the spot, and my time in Glasgow and Scotland is limited, as you know.'

'Leave all that to me, and Chris Walker, I hope.'

'How is Chris? You haven't mentioned him much of late.'

'He hasn't been in touch, or around the Labour Hall for a while.' Her brow creased as she totted up the weeks. 'In fact, it's nearly four months since I last saw him.'

'Perhaps something's wrong. He might have been ill, say? You should have contacted him.'

'I did ring the section house several times and leave messages but he never replied to any of them.' She turned away from Neil so that he couldn't see her face. 'He's probably been busy with that Mona Bryce. The pair of them out gallivanting together during most of his spare time.'

'In which case he might not want to help you?' Neil said.

'If not, he can at least give me some advice on how to go about things. I'm sure he won't refuse me that.'

'I'm sure not.'

She would try and contact Chris directly after she had done the dishes, Vicky decided. She would telephone his section house, and if he wasn't there try him at his station.

•

The street was just off Anniesland Cross. The close bearing the number she'd been given had a metal gate at its mouth and smelled of fresh whitewash inside. It was a good close, proclaiming that the folk who lived in and up it were respectable people who took a pride in where they lived.

Going up the stairs, Vicky had a peep in the first stairhead toilet she came to. It was neat and clean, well looked after. She found Chris's name on the middle door of the third landing. She tugged the brass handle pull and the bell gave a series of dull clangs.

'Hello, stranger.' Vicky smiled to Chris when he opened the door.

Surprise and pleasure flashed across his face. 'Hello, yourself. It's good to see you.'

They stared at one another.

'I was hoping you might offer me a cup of tea?' she suggested, breaking the pregnant silence that had fallen between them.

'Oh, aye, sure. Come away in,' he said, and stood aside to let her pass. 'How did you find me?'

'The section house told me you'd moved out, so I went to your station and got your address from them. That and the information it was your day off.'

She saw a kitchen and another room. Through an open doorway she glimpsed an unmade bed, then Chris was ushering her into the kitchen. It sparkled like a new pin, everything tidy and in its place. The linoleum had been polished so hard that the effect was positively dazzling. Mona? Vicky wondered. She gazed about, looking for female signs.

'It's very nice. Did you decorate it yourself?'

'I did,' he answered, chuffed that she liked his taste.

'I know the station shouldn't have given me your address, but I wangled it out of them by telling a wee lie or two. Of course, being an MP's wife they never dreamed I was lying. I hope you don't mind?' she said, and smiled sweetly.

'No. I really should have notified you of my change of address,' he replied somewhat lamely.

No tang of perfume or smell of powder other than her

own. No female garments, or female accoutrements that she could see. Yet the place smacked of a female hand.

'I have tried to reach you on the phone several times and did leave messages,' she said, and stared at him, waiting for an explanation.

He shrugged. 'I've been doing an awful lot of night shifts, sleeping all day and working all night. I just haven't had the time recently to come round and help,' he lied.

And Vicky knew it was a lie. There was that in his voice told her so.

'How's Mona?' she asked.

'We, eh . . . broke up six weeks ago. It didn't work out, I'm afraid.'

'I'm sorry to hear that,' she lied.

He shrugged again. 'Just one of those things. Not the right woman for me.'

And who do you think is? Vicky nearly found herself saying, but bit it back. 'I'm sure you'll find another right woman for yourself one day,' she said instead.

'I'll make that tea then.'

Vicky watched him as he filled an electric kettle and switched it on.

'I must say you're an excellent housekeeper,' she said.

He laughed. 'Not a bit of it. There's a wifey in the next close comes in and does for me. The place would be a shambles if it wasn't for her.'

Though it was really none of her business, Vicky was pleased that it wasn't a girlfriend who'd replaced Mona.

Chris put Penguin and Blue Riband biscuits on a plate. 'Mrs Bone, that's the wifey, also does my shopping. That's useful as well.'

'And what about cooking?'

'Och, I can scrape by at that. Stews, casseroles, chops and suchlike. Occasionally I do a Chinese dish. Quite a few of those are fairly simple.'

They chatted till the tea was ready and poured. Vicky accepted her cup, but refused the biscuits.

'I've come here to ask your help, on a personal matter,' she announced.

Instantly a change came over Chris. Gone was the easy-going civilian; he was now all policeman. 'Are you in some sort of trouble?'

She shook her head. 'Remember the story I told you about Mr Malarkey?'

'Aye.'

He listened intently while she spoke about what she intended to do and her and Neil's reasons for doing so. She didn't mention Neil's impotence or how that had come about.

When she finished, Chris took her cup from her and refilled it. He could understand the political reasons behind it; it was Vicky's personal motivation that made him uneasy.

'Vengeance is a bad thing, Vicky, often just as damaging to the person who wreaks it as to the person it is wreaked upon,' he said slowly.

'My dad would be *still alive* if it wasn't for Ken Blacklaws!' She paused, then continued, 'And there's something he did to Neil which I can't tell you about other than it was terrible, and Neil has suffered agonies because of it. Now his exposure and downfall can, and will if I have anything to with it, be the making of Neil's career.'

Chris sipped his tea. 'And you want me to help bring all this about, is that it?'

'Will you?' she replied quietly, voice brittle with intensity.

He thought how marvellous it was to see her again, to be in her presence. He had missed her dreadfully. 'Tell me about those inquiries you made yourself, and who you spoke to and what they said.'

When she left his house an hour later, a plan of campaign had been mapped out between them.

Ken's intercom, a relatively new toy, buzzed. He depressed the lever that allowed him to talk to his secretary, and she to him. 'Yes, Ina?'

'There's a Mr Heggie here insisting to see you personally. He's a union member, and says it's important.'

'Send him in,' Ken replied and let go the lever.

400

Heggie was a small, wiry man of about thirty. He was wearing his Sunday suit and a neat collar and tie.

Ken stood and shook Heggie by the hand. These little courtesies were always winners. 'Not working today?' he asked.

'I didn't go in because I wanted to come and speak to you,' Heggie answered.

Ken gestured Heggie to a chair, then sat himself. 'So what's your problem?'

Heggie shook his head. 'It's not a problem, at least not for me, that is. It's more what you might call a matter of information, information I think you might be interested in.'

Ken studied Heggie. The eyes were bright and had depth. They also had a certain animal craftiness about them. 'I'm listening,' he said.

'I won't beat about the bush. I'm after something you're capable of giving me. If my information is as important as I think it might be, will we have a trade?'

Ken smiled. 'Depends on the information and what you want.' He liked the man's directness and lack of apology.

'I want to be a gaffer,' Heggie stated.

Ken nodded. 'Now I know what you want. What's the information?'

'There's a copper called Walker whom I had a run-in with some time back, a sergeant at Tobago Street, and a real hard-nosed bastard. Well, suddenly I start noticing him round the docks, always chaffing to dockies in corners and out-of-the-way spots, and somehow being furtive like.

'Then, just yesterday, he saw me, only instead of facing me down as coppers would normally do in that sort of situation, he backed off and did a disappearing act.

'After he'd gone, I tried to have a word with the bloke he'd been talking to. Honest to God, I thought the bloke was going to shit himself when I asked him what he and Walker had been speaking about. He said Walker had only stopped him to inquire the time, and with that scarpered, walking away from me so fast it was almost a run.'

Ken tapped a pencil on his desk. 'Is this Walker CID?'

401

'No, he's not. And that's another point. On each occasion I've seen him sniffing round the docks he's been in plain clothes.'

'He might have been transferred to CID,' Ken mused.

'Uniformed copper or CID, whichever, he's up to something and I thought you would be interested in that,' Heggie replied.

Ken swivelled round his chair so he could gaze out of the window. It was a marvellous view of the Clyde and southside. He could not have been more pleased with his new building; it was a jewel among dross, a stotter.

Heggie was right. He was interested to learn about this. If the police were poking their noses into the docks, he wanted to know what they were after.

'Well?' Heggie demanded anxiously.

'You did the right thing in coming to me,' Ken replied, swivelling his chair back again.

'And the job as gaffer?'

'Let's just wait until we find out what this is all about first. For the moment, go and sit outside again, will you?' Ken answered.

Heggie left the office. As the door clicked shut, Ken depressed the intercom lever.

'Find Paddy Troy and send him to me,' he instructed Ina.

Paddy Troy appeared a few minutes later and Ken related what Heggie had told him.

'So what do you want me to do?' Paddy asked.

'Take Heggie to Tobago Street nick. He may be able to do it today, or you may have to go back tomorrow or the next day even, but hang around there until Walker appears and he can identify him to you. From there on in I want Walker watched round the clock – you'll need a team for that which you can organise yourself – until we know what he, and anyone else he might be working with, are up to.'

'I understand.'

'On no account are you or any of the others to lay so much as a finger on him. He's a policeman, don't forget. If you rough up one of their lot, it's just like pulling the pin out of a hand grenade. Before you know where you are, there's a very loud and damaging explosion.'

Paddy Troy grinned. 'I won't so much as breathe on him,' he said. This was a private joke between him and Ken, who the previous week had chided him for smelly breath.

He would soon find out what this was all about, Ken thought after Paddy Troy had gone. Probably, from his and the union point of view, nothing to worry about. But better to be safe than sorry. His thoughts then turned to Aberdeen, the last bastion that would soon be falling to him. When that happened, and his union reigned supreme in Scotland, he would change its name to the Scottish Union of Dockworkers.

'Scottish Union of Dockworkers,' he said, speaking the name aloud, lovingly.

Weeks, that's all it was now. A matter of weeks and all his long schemes and plans would come to fruition.

Three days later, mid-afternoon, Ken's office telephone rang.

'You'll never guess who Walker has met up with,' Paddy Troy said.

'Who?'

'Remember Mrs Seton, the MP's wife whose father broke his neck?'

Alarm bells went off in Ken's head. Walker and Vicky! 'Is he still with her?'

'They're in a teashop in Rottenrow. Walker met up with Mrs Seton, then the two of them went to a school in Townhead, where they picked up a lassie, and from there they drove to this teashop which they've just gone into. I'm in a phone box across the way.'

A lassie from a school in Townhead; that would be Vicky's daughter. What was her name again? Vicky had told him, if only he could mind. Martha, that was it. And Vicky and Walker had taken her to a teashop; that could only mean that Vicky and Walker were friends. He didn't like the sound of that, not one little bit. He decided that he wanted to have a look at this Walker himself.

403

'Where exactly in Rottenrow are you?'

Paddy told him.

'I'm coming there to join you. But should they leave before I get there, go with them, otherwise I'll see you shortly,' Ken said, and hung up.

Vicky friendly with a bluebottle who was nosing round the docks. He didn't like the sound of that at all!

Martha laid her third cake, this one a meringue, on her plate. It was a scrumptious-looking meringue, thick in the middle with cream. 'It's just as well I don't get the opportunity to do this very often or I'd be fat as a pig,' she said.

Chris laughed.

'Let's just hope it's going to be an S1 pass,' Vicky replied, for Martha had sat her 'quali' that day, and this was the treat she had promised her for afterwards.

'It wasn't that difficult, but difficult enough.'

'Did you get stuck on anything?' Vicky asked anxiously.

'My old bogey spelling was hard, at least for me.' To Chris she explained, 'Spelling's given orally, you see. The teacher calls out the word and you write it down.' Bringing her attention back to Vicky, she went on, 'The first word was "leopard", which stumped me. Then I got it later on.'

'How did you spell it then?' Vicky queried.

'L-e-p-p-a-r-d,' Martha replied, straight-faced.

'Oh!' Vicky exclaimed, and bit her lower lip.

'Got you! I spelled it l-e-o-p-a-r-d.' Martha laughed, and sank her teeth into the meringue.

'Minx!' Vicky said, wagging an admonishing finger at her. To Chris she added, 'She really had me believing that.'

Chris, thoroughly enjoying himself, indicated to a passing waitress that they wanted a fresh pot of tea.

Ken had Shugs drop him off round the corner from where Paddy Troy had said his Zephyr was parked. He told Shugs to wait for a few minutes and if he didn't return in that time to drive back to the Broomielaw. He then walked away from the shining black Lincoln Continental that had replaced the Cadillac and turned into Rottenrow.

The Zephyr was still there, with Paddy Troy slumped in the driver's seat. Opening the passenger door, Ken slid in beside him.

'Just in time. They're about to leave. That's Walker at the cash desk,' Paddy said.

Chris Walker was plainly visible through the teashop's plateglass front window. Ken saw a man roughly his own age whose face had a pleasant but determined stamp about it. The door to the teashop tinged open, and Vicky and the lassie came out to stand on the pavement, waiting for Walker.

It was nearly three years since he had last seen Vicky, and she had aged, but not drastically so. Her face was thinner and more taut somehow. The figure was still trim, the hair that cap of curls he remembered so well. If he'd been closer, he would have seen that the curls were now streaked with grey.

He turned his attention to the lassie. She had chestnut-coloured hair cut at neck length, a rather podgy adolescent figure and glasses. The face . . . the face held him. Had he seen Martha before? No, of course he hadn't, he was certain of that. And yet her face was strangely familiar.

Chris joined Vicky and Martha, and the three of them exchanged a few words.

Powerfully built, and intelligent, very much so. Intelligent, determined and exuding authority – that was how Ken would have described Chris Walker. He knew from long experience of dealing with men that this was one to be reckoned with.

Then the threesome were making off up the street, Martha between the two adults.

'Their car's about a hundred yards up on the opposite side,' Paddy said, switching on the Zephyr's engine.

'I've seen all I wanted to. Drop me off at the first set of lights you have to stop at.'

As the Singer joined the traffic, Paddy did a quick U-turn and set off in pursuit, eventually tucking the Zephyr into a position several cars behind the Singer.

'Has Walker been down at the docks today?' Ken asked,

knowing from the reports given him by Paddy and his team that Walker hadn't been near the docks since being put under surveillance. The last report had been that morning from Chic Henderson, whom Paddy had taken over from.

'Nope.'

'Well, maintain the round-the-clock watch all the same. It's even more important now we've discovered he knows Mrs Seton.'

For the rest of that day Ken was plagued with the memory of Martha Seton's face and the feeling of déjà vu he'd experienced when looking at it.

The pub was in Maryhill, an area as rough as any to be found in Glasgow. The very air was menacing.

The outside of the pub was covered with graffiti and the yellow-tiled façade beneath the graffiti was chipped and scarred in a thousand places. Both front windows were protected by thick iron bars.

'Very salubrious,' Vicky said sarcastically as they went inside.

Chris gave a dry chuckle. He didn't mind places like this. In fact, perversely, he rather enjoyed them.

The pub was busy, the three barmen working flat out. A brace of females smiled brazenly at Chris. Then, realising that he was with a woman, dropped the smiles and went back to their drinks.

Vicky glanced about. The man they'd come to meet had not given them a physical description of himself. He had said that he would know who they were when they came in and make contact. Chris was about to pay for the drinks he'd ordered when a man standing beside him suddenly turned and said, 'You'd better get another pint in if we're to talk.' Chris did as he was bid.

The man led them through the throng to the rear, where, miraculously there was a free table. He told them to sit.

'The name's Norrie Telfer,' he said, and stuck out a hand to Chris, who shook it. He then greeted Vicky.

'I've heard what you're trying to do, which is why I rang. I want that bastard Blacklaws and his cronies to get their comeuppance, and I'm prepared to do my bit to help. And I *can* help in a big way,' Telfer announced.

'Are you a dockie?' Chris asked.

Telfer shook his head. 'But my brother Andy is – or was, rather. He lives in Leith, having married a lass from there. He has three children, and no legs now,' Telfer replied grimly.

'Accident?' Chris queried.

Telfer, eyes flashing with anger, supped from his pint. 'That's what it was called, but Andy and I have another name for it. I presume you know of Paddy Troy?'

Chris nodded.

'Just before the CDU took over Andy's union, the old Leith Dock Workers' Union, Troy put in an appearance, and from that moment all hell broke loose. There was a spate of so-called "accidents", one of which was when a conveyor belt Andy was working on suddenly went berserk; part of the belt snapped and neatly severed Andy's legs just below their knees. Troy had been noticed hanging round the belt's motor only minutes before it went daft.'

Telfer paused, then continued. 'And my brother wasn't the only one to suffer. Quite a few of his pals also came to grief, one of them actually drowning in another so-called "accident".'

'So how can you help us bring Blacklaws and his thugs to book?' Vicky asked.

Telfer lit a cigarette, then had another pull at his pint. 'Did you know Blacklaws owns a yacht?' he said quietly.

Vicky looked at Chris. This was new. She shook her head.

'Or that he owns a villa over in Spain, at a place called Marbella?'

Vicky shook her head a second time.

'I was at sea for a number of years, working as a steward. The last job I had was on the *Seven Seas*, Blacklaws's yacht. A yacht he paid for out of union funds, but which is registered in his name.'

Excitement gripped Vicky. 'Are you sure about that?'

407

'Oh, aye, just as I'm sure the villa was paid for the same way, and that it is also in Blacklaws's own name.'

'This is it, what we're looking for,' Vicky said to Chris.

'Embezzlement of funds, that should put Blacklaws away for quite some while,' Chris answered softly.

Vicky made a tight fist and shook it in triumph. Until now there had been nothing they could use personally against Ken. This was the breakthrough she'd been praying for.

'How do you know the yacht and villa are in Blacklaws's name, and that he paid for them out of union funds?' Chris queried.

'The *Seven Seas* might seem a fair-sized yacht but, relatively speaking, it's actually quite small inside. A person in the position I held was bound to hear many things he shouldn't. What I've told you about the yacht and villa were two of the things I inadvertently overheard,' Telfer replied.

'How do we prove this though?' Vicky asked Chris.

'There are ways and means. You leave all that to me. In the meantime though we should tell Kingsland about this development when we meet with him tomorrow morning,' Chris said. Sir Oliver Kingsland would be acting for them when they brought their case against the CDU.

Chris rose. 'I'll get another round in,' he said and headed for the bar.

At the bar, and partially screened by a pillar, Jim Robertson, a member of Paddy Troy's team, had been watching Telfer, Vicky and Chris. He had already placed Telfer as an ex-steward on the *Seven Seas*, Telfer having served him a number of times on the one occasion he'd sailed with the boss and others to Spain on the yacht.

Seeing Chris approaching, Robertson left the spot where he was standing and slipped outside.

Vicky parked the Singer outside Chris's close. She was still filled with excitement and elation after their meeting with Telfer.

'I'll pick you up at nine tomorrow morning, and we'll go

straight to the central station,' Vicky said. Neil was coming from London; they'd collect him, then the three of them would go to see Sir Oliver Kingsland.

Chris glanced at his watch. 'It's early yet. Do you fancy coming up for a nightcap before going home?'

'There's nothing I'd like more,' she replied, knowing that it was going to be hours before she calmed down sufficiently even to consider going to bed.

As they went up the stairs, they both fell silent. His hand brushed against her when he reached for his key, causing a sudden ripple of gooseflesh across her back.

Chris clicked on the lights and opened a window, for it was a hot and sultry June night. He then closed the curtains. He turned to her and smiled. The smile turned rigid as electricity flashed between them.

'Just a small dram, as I'm driving,' Vicky croaked, her throat feeling constricted.

His hand trembled a little as he poured their whiskies. She asked for water with hers. He gave her lemonade. Neither noticed.

They spoke, but their conversation was unnatural, stilted. She refrained from looking him directly in the eyes in case he read what was in her own.

She finished her drink, not having tasted any of it. 'I'd better go now,' she mumbled.

She didn't know how it happened, but she was in his arms, their mouths joined, his tongue darting and flicking against her tongue. One of his hands dropped to her bottom, to cup and caress it. His other hand sought out a breast. Her heart was thumping, and she was filled with a roaring liquid fire. Laying her head on his shoulder, she moaned.

'I've been in love with you right from the beginning, you must have known,' he whispered.

How she wanted him! Wanted what Neil had never been able to give her: joining and total satisfaction – not just the partial satisfaction that had been her lot since marrying Neil. Then, with a shock, she realised that it wasn't merely the sex she craved but Chris himself. She *loved* him, the first man she'd fallen in love with since Ken.

409

But why hadn't she realised that before now? Maybe she had subconsciously, but been afraid, unwilling, to admit it to herself. And the reason? Because she was a married woman with a husband who not only loved her but worshipped the very ground she walked on. A husband who needed her and was dependent on her. A husband whom she would destroy if she ever left him.

'Oh, Vicky!' Chris whispered and sought out her lips again.

She could feel his manhood against her thigh. How she longed, ached, to touch it, to have it inside her.

She forced Chris from her and took several steps backwards. 'No,' she stated emphatically.

He gazed at her, stricken.

'It's not that I don't . . . feel for you, Chris. I do, a great deal. But I have Neil to think about. I can't let him down. I won't cheat on him, nor will I leave him.'

Chris could see she meant what she said, that no amount of argument on his part would change her mind. He bowed his head.

'I think I've known that all along, why I never made a move before now. And I didn't mean this to happen either; it just sort of did.'

He looked up at her. 'Do you forgive me?'

'There's nothing to forgive. If things were different, if I wasn't married, then I'd jump at the chance to be yours. But things are the way they are, and that's that.'

He ran a hand through his hair. 'I don't seem to be very lucky in love.'

'No.'

'I stopped seeing you, coming round to the Labour Hall to help, because of what I feel for you. I tried to make the break and then you came back into my life.'

'I'm sorry,' she said softly.

'To tell the truth, I don't know what's worse. Not seeing you at all, or seeing you and not being able to do anything about my feelings.'

'The devil and the deep blue sea.' She smiled.

He nodded.

'Can we just be good friends? I appreciate it'll be difficult, for both of us. But if it's possible, I don't want to lose you again.'

He stared at the floor, as if studying it.

'Should you meet someone else, I'd understand. But I don't want to lose your friendship.'

He glanced up again, having forced a smile onto his face to match hers. 'All right, friends it is. Now and always,' he replied.

She held out her glass. 'I've changed my mind. I'll have another drink before I leave. And blow the driving, make it a biggy.'

On leaving Chris's, she drove till she came to some waste ground, where she pulled the car off the road. She slumped over the wheel.

'Oh, Chris!' she sobbed, filled with agony, despair and thwarted love.

But she could not let Neil down.

Ken woke with a start and sat bolt upright in bed. Now he knew where he'd seen Martha Seton's face before. It was a younger, female version of his own! No wonder it had taken him so long to place it, for who, straight off anyway, recognises himself! It had been like looking into a mirror, the image gazing back distorted by time and a change of gender.

Could he possibly be wrong? No, he wasn't. That face was out of the same mould as his own. There was no doubt whatever about it.

Martha Seton was *his* daughter.

Ken laid down the phone. It was later on that morning and Jim Robertson had just delivered his report.

A copper nosing round the docks, a copper who turned out to know Vicky, and now the pair of them having a comfy little chat with a steward who had worked on the *Seven Seas*. The whole thing was beginning to stink to high heaven.

Picking up the telephone again, he dialled Paddy Troy's

number. When Paddy answered, he said, 'Now listen carefully, Paddy. This is what I want you to do . . .'

Chic Henderson rang through his report on Chris that
afternoon. Ken listened intently. When it was over, he
cradled the telephone and went to his window to gaze out
over the Clyde and the southside.

Sir Oliver. Kingsland was a legend, the most famous
and successful prosecuting counsel, Judge Advocate, in all
Scotland. The man was number one in his field. If he'd ever
lost a case, Ken had certainly never heard of it.

Of course it could still be that all this had nothing
whatever to do with him and the CDU. But he would know
for certain, one way or the other, before long. Paddy Troy
would make sure of that.

Norrie Telfer was getting ready for the evening shift at the
posh West End hotel bar where he worked when there was
a knock on the outside door.

'I'll get it,' said Agnes, his common-law wife. Drawing
her pink candlewick dressing gown around herself – she and
Norrie had just made love, as they often did in the afternoon,
Norrie having a liking for it at that time – she left Norrie
whistling tunelessly while knotting his black bow tie.

'Some friends to see you,' Agnes announced, returning
with three men.

Norrie's whistling died when he saw that one of the three
was Paddy Troy.

'I've come to have a word, Telfer,' Paddy said with a
chilling smile.

Norrie Telfer was stock still, as though rooted to the spot,
his expression one of stark terror.

'Aren't they friends then?' Agnes queried, forehead creasing into a deep frown.

Paddy Troy unzipped the leather message bag he was
carrying and took out a dockie's hook. Two feet long and
an inch in diameter, it curved into a needle-sharp point.
Dockies used these steel hooks to shift and manipulate
cargo.

'Oh, my God!' Norrie croaked.

Agnes opened her mouth to scream, but before she could make a noise she was backhanded across the face and sent sprawling. Her attacker was one of Paddy Troy's two companions.

'Not a squeak or you'll get this after Telfer,' Paddy said and waggled the hook at her.

With three of them between him and the door, Norrie Telfer knew that he hadn't a hope of escape. There was the window, but they were on the fourth floor.

Paddy Troy advanced on Telfer, who retreated until he could go no further, eyes bulging, back pressed hard against a wall. Paddy slipped the hook between Telfer's legs, bringing its tip up and forward till it was lodged behind his scrotum.

'Now I want to hear all about your conversation with Walker and Mrs Seton,' Paddy Troy said.

Shugs turned the Lincoln into Parr Street and pulled up behind Jim Robertson's car. Ken was about to get out when Martha emerged from her close to walk past the Lincoln. He waited in the Lincoln till she was out of sight, then got out, allowing Jim to assist him.

'Are they both still in?' he asked Jim, who nodded.

Ken glanced up at Neil and Vicky's window. He had taken Paddy Troy's team off Walker to follow them. He had wanted to speak to them as soon as they were home together. It was a bonus that the lassie had gone out.

He looked along at his old close. So many memories, so long ago. It seemed a different lifetime.

Taking a cigar from the case he always carried with him, he lit it with a silver-coloured Ronson which had the initials K. B. engraved on one side in fancy script. Old now, and with several bashes in it, but still in good working order, it was the lighter Vicky had given him for his seventeenth birthday, nineteen years before. He'd had other lighters since, but had always gone back to the Ronson because he liked it, and for sentimental reasons.

He instructed Jim Robertson and Shugs to wait. Then,

413

entering Neil and Vicky's close, he began to mount the stairs.

Vicky was washing up – they'd just had tea – when there was a chap on the front door.

'Will you get it? My hands are wet. It's probably Martha back for something she's forgotten,' Vicky said to Neil, who was leafing through a batch of parliamentary papers that he'd brought north with him.

Ken stood on the landing thinking that Parr Street hadn't improved any; it was still as mean and squalid as ever. It amazed him that Neil and Vicky continued to stay in it. Then again, knowing Neil, maybe he wasn't so amazed.

Vicky was scraping at a Pyrex dish that had a hard crust rim on its inside when Neil returned to the kitchen. She looked up and, when she saw who was with him, the knife she was using froze in mid-action.

'I'm sure you can guess why I'm here,' Ken said.

Vicky laid the dish and knife aside and dried her hands on a teatowel. 'You always did have a brass-neck cheek,' she replied.

Ken had a puff of his cigar. 'I could bring up the business of Copland and Lye, and tell how it was Neil who cliped on his best pal. That would sink him,' he said to Vicky.

'We'd deny that accusation, say it was a crude attempt on your part to discredit Neil. Crude and completely unfounded. There would be no question of people believing you, not after what's going to come out about you and your union during the case. So this time, that club won't work.'

Ken had another puff of his cigar. The atmosphere in the room was electric. It reminded him of a card game he'd once played when the stakes had been exceptionally high.

'You've got me then,' he said, as though conceding defeat.

'That's right,' Vicky replied, flushing with triumph.

Casually, Ken strolled over to the mantelpiece. Standing on it was a silver-framed photograph of Martha, which he had noticed on coming into the room.

Staring at the photograph, he said over his shoulder to Vicky, 'I won't ask why. I've given you reasons enough over the years to want to destroy me.'

He turned his head sideways to look at Neil. 'As for you getting in on the act, is it purely being supportive of her? Or is there a political motivation?'

Neil's lips thinned.

'Well, it's one or the other, no matter which.' Ken smiled and brought his attention back to Martha's photograph.

Ken picked up the photograph and turned again to Neil. 'By the way, did Vicky ever tell you Martha is my daughter?' he asked lazily.

Neil's mouth fell open.

'That's a lie!' Vicky said, taken so completely by surprise that there was no conviction in her voice.

Ken went over to Neil and held the photograph up in front of Neil's face. Neil's expression told him that he hadn't known until that moment.

'So Vicky *didn't* tell you. Well, well, well. Mind you, I'm surprised you never noticed the resemblance. It really is quite startling. Two peas in a pod, that's us.'

Vicky dashed across and snatched the photograph from Ken's grasp.

'She's even more like me than Kenny is.' Ken smiled.

Vicky hit him as hard as she could, the flat of her hand cracking against his cheek. He reeled back but never stopped smiling.

Neil was in a daze. Martha, Ken's daughter! Ken was right: the resemblance *was* startling. Why had he never seen that before now?

Ken took another puff of his cigar, thinking that the look on Neil's face was priceless. He noted that there were tears in Vicky's eyes.

'I'm not sure how to play this yet. On the one hand I can say she hoisted another man's child on you, *mine*. Or on the other I can say she cuckolded you with me, and passed off my child as yours.'

Ken paused for emphasis, then went on, 'Whatever way, coming as it will during the trial the newspapers will have a field day. From John o' Groats to Land's End you'll be a laughing stock. And your public career? That'll be finished. For how would you ever again be able to face your colleagues, opponents or an audience knowing what was going through their minds?'

Ken paused to let that sink in, then continued, 'So, the pair of you have it within your power to drag me down, but if I go so do you, Neil, all the way. I want that clearly understood.'

Ken threw his cigar into the empty grate and walked to the door. There he stopped and turned.

Neil stood in a slumped position, a man devastated. Vicky was clutching Martha's picture to her bosom while hot tears spilled down her face.

'The choice is up to you,' Ken stated. Then he smiled again and left the house.

Neil stared out of the train window, seeing nothing of the passing scenery. He was writhing inside, grappling with a combination of humiliation, hurt and profound sense of loss.

Ken Blacklaws. The name burned in his brain, writ there in letters of searing fire. All his life he had played second fiddle to Ken, been second best. Ken the high and mighty, the perpetual winner, and spoiler. It was Ken who'd robbed him of his manhood, kicking it out of him that night in the back-close dunny, robbed him of the ability to make love properly to the woman he loved – a woman whom, he'd now learned, Ken had cast aside not only once but twice. A woman who had never loved him, but had loved Ken.

How Ken must have laughed to learn that he'd married Vicky and accepted Ken's child as his own. He must have laughed himself sick! Ken had not only made it impossible for him to father a child, but had stolen back the one he'd fallen heir to, and whom he loved next only to Vicky herself.

As for Vicky, how could she have let him marry her without telling him the child she was carrying was Ken's? How could she do that!

Self-pity welled in Neil. What had he ever done to deserve all that had happened to him! What had he ever done to deserve Ken Blacklaws!

Last night, in bed – if only he could have taken Vicky,

416

everything might still have been salvaged between them and he might not have felt as he now did; a fool, second-rate, used and useless.

Black, black despair rose up to engulf him, and in that pit of despair a face, beckoning. The face of his father.

Vicky was on the telephone when Dickie Fleet, Neil's agent, appeared in her office. She waved him to a chair but he remained standing.

She hung up and laughed. 'What's wrong with you, Dickie? You look like you've lost a pound and found sixpence.'

He twisted the flat cap, or hooker doon, he was holding. 'I'm afraid I've got some terrible news about Neil . . .'

After a while, Dickie took her home.

She had expected the ashes to be similar to the ashes from the fireplace, but they weren't at all. They were pure white and in crystalline lumps that were jagged at the edges. She scattered them over the grave where his mum and dad were buried, certain that that was what he would have wanted.

She had gone south for the cremation and brought the ashes back with her. Originally she had intended to bring back the body, but on learning how drawn out and complex a business it was to take a corpse from England into Scotland she had opted instead for cremation.

A ticket inspector had forced the toilet door at Crewe to discover Neil hanging from a metal fixture on the roof. Neil had torn the towel into strips and used that.

Everyone, and most of all Chris, had been marvellous. The story she had given the newspapers, which they had accepted without question, was that Neil had been working so hard that he had suffered a nervous breakdown and killed himself as a result.

She turned to where Martha and Chris were standing by the graveside, Martha holding a floral display. Others had wanted to come, but she had refused them all, with the exception of Chris. He helped Martha forward to lay the flowers on the grave.

417

Vicky closed her eyes and offered up a silent prayer for Neil's soul.

'He was so young still,' Martha said, clinging onto Chris.

'Yes,' he agreed, grim-faced.

As they were leaving the cemetery, Vicky asked Chris if he would first of all drop Martha off at Parr Street, then drive her into town. She intended speaking to Sir Oliver Kingsland.

Neil's death had placed him beyond further pain, hurt and humiliation. It was a death that had to be paid for, and Ken Blacklaws was going to do the paying.

As God was her judge, she swore it.

Three nights later Dickie Fleet came to see Vicky. 'The selection board have discussed it and their decision was unanimous. There's no one more fit, or better qualified in their book, to replace Neil as MP for Glasgow Kelvinhaugh than you. Will you stand for us in the by-election?' he asked.

Vicky took a deep breath, then exhaled slowly. 'I have Martha to consider. If I was elected, it would mean being in London a great deal. That wouldn't be fair on her.'

Dickie turned to Martha. 'What do you say, lass?'

'I say, if it's what Mummy wants, then it's what she should do. Granny and I would manage when she wasn't here, and although I'd miss her, I'd understand she was doing something worthwhile.'

Martha went over to Vicky and took her by the hand. 'I think you should continue Daddy's work. Do all the things for Glasgow that he wanted to.'

Vicky pulled Martha down and kissed her on the cheek. 'I knew you were grown up but, until now, hadn't realised how much. Thank you, darling.'

She looked at Dickie Fleet. 'I'll run,' she announced.

Postscript

Chris met her off the Euston train. It was almost seven months to the day since Ken had been arrested, to be held without bail.

'Well?' Vicky demanded, knowing that Ken was due to have been sentenced that afternoon.

'Life, for being an accessory before the fact,' Chris replied.

Vicky let out a soft sigh of satisfaction. The original charges of embezzlement against Ken had proved to be only the start. Once the can had successfully been opened, the worms had come pouring out.

'And Troy?'

'The death penalty for the murder of John Elder.' Elder had been a Leith dockie, and friend to Norrie Telfer's brother. He had been murdered by drowning – a crime to which, as it had transpired, there had been witnesses.

Tears blossomed in Vicky's eyes. Tears for Neil, tears for her dad. And tears for herself.

'I said I'd give you my answer when this was all over, and now I will. I'd be honoured, and very happy, to marry you,' she told Chris.

He didn't give a damn who might see them. He kissed her passionately but gently, a kiss full of love.

When it was over, she wiped her eyes with a hanky and blew her nose.

Linking arms, they made their way along the platform.